Do Not Disturb

Also by Tilly Bagshawe

Fame
Flawless
Scandalous
Adored
Showdown
Sidney Sheldon's Mistress of the Game
Sidney Sheldon's Angel of the Dark
Sidney Sheldon's After the Darkness

Do Not Disturb

TILLY BAGSHAWE

Montlake
Romance

First published in 2008.
Copyright © 2013 Tilly Bagshawe
All rights reserved.
Printed in the United States of America.

Published by Montlake Romance
PO Box 400818
Las Vegas, NV 89140

ISBN-13: 9781612186955
ISBN-10: 1612186955
Library of Congress Control Number: 2012943131

To my parents, Nick and Daphne Bagshawe.

Whenever I count my blessings, you're first on the list.

PART ONE

CHAPTER ONE

"OVER MY DEAD BODY! D'YOU HEAR ME? YOU'LL TAKE PALMERS over my dead body, you scheming, greedy little—"

A fit of wheezing stopped Trey Palmer from finishing his sentence. But Honor, his eldest daughter, had already gotten the gist. Alzheimer's may have cruelly eaten away at his mental faculties and old age ravaged his once-enviable physique, but his bitterness was as razor sharp as ever.

"Mr. Palmer, please, don't upset yourself," said the lawyer. Sam Brannagan had sat through more family disputes than he could remember, many of them in this very room. With its dark oak-paneled walls and reassuringly expensive soft furnishings it was all very old-school Bostonian—an appropriate setting for internecine warfare if ever there was one.

Watching the old man grapple with his oxygen mask while he glared at his hapless daughter, however, Sam didn't think he'd ever seen quite as much open hatred as he'd witnessed today. Looking around the room at the eager, greedy faces turned toward him, he felt intensely depressed.

Honor Palmer, who had convened today's meeting, was the only decent one among them. But even she was not exactly warm and cuddly. With her spiky, boyish hair, aquiline features, and tiny, taut athlete's body, the newly minted Harvard Law graduate looked beautiful but forbidding. Everything about her, from her four-inch Louboutins and starkly formal black Prada pantsuit to her low, authoritative voice and impressive grasp of the complex legal issues being discussed, betrayed a steeliness unusual in one so young. Especially a woman.

As for the rest of them—crowded into his office, huddled around the old man like sharks circling a wounded seal—they made his stomach churn.

There was Tina, Honor's younger sister, looking bored in the corner, glancing pointedly at her Chopard diamond watch. Also beautiful, but in a polar opposite way from her sister: blonde, blowsy, and buxom were the three words that most readily sprang to mind. Tina looked like she'd picked up her wardrobe from Hookers-R-Us. Even at an important legal meeting like this, Boston's answer to Paris Hilton had shown up in a frayed denim skirt that barely covered her crotch and a pink man's shirt tied beneath her breasts to reveal a mind-boggling expanse of cleavage. From the look of distaste on her face as she listened to her father's phlegmy spluttering, it was clear she had no sympathy for him; nor did she seem remotely interested in her sister's attempts to save them all from financial ruin.

Even more see-through were the Fosters. Jacob, a distant cousin from Omaha, and his wife, had heard in the press about Trey's Alzheimer's and the threat to his empire and crawled out of the woodwork to see what they could scavenge. Both wore ostentatious crosses and proclaimed themselves loudly to be born-again Christians, but every reference to Trey's frozen bank accounts had them salivating like starving puppies. They'd spent most of today's meeting glowering disapprovingly at Lise, Trey's bimbo wifelette, whom they wrongly considered to be their key rival for the family inheritance.

Lise might give Lil' Kim a run for her money in the slutty dressing stakes, but unlike the Fosters, she did at least have the advantage of being recognized by her husband. It was clear to Sam that neither Trey nor his daughters had ever set eyes on Cousin Jacob before in their lives.

On reflection, perhaps it was hardly surprising that they'd all shown up today. There was, after all, a lot at stake. The Palmers were one of the wealthiest, most prominent families in Boston and had been for three generations. Already rich when he emigrated from England, Trey's great-grandfather had multiplied the family fortune fivefold, becoming one of the first great American hoteliers. His first hotel, the Cranley on Boston's exclusive Newbury Street, made so much money that within a decade he'd opened two more: the King James Hotel in Manhattan and the now-legendary Palmers in East Hampton. By the time Trey's father, Tertius Palmer, came into his inheritance, the family's net worth was conservatively estimated at over ten million dollars. And that was in the fifties. Heaven only knew what it translated to in today's money.

Like his father and grandfather before him, Tertius had been a naturally shrewd businessman. But whereas they had been expansionists, Tertius was a consolidator. Cashing in on the postwar real estate boom, he sold the original two hotels for an outrageous profit, which he went on to invest very successfully in the equity markets. Having hired a raft of stockbrokers to manage his portfolio, he was free to focus his own energies exclusively on the one hotel he hadn't sold: Palmers. By the time of his death—the year before Honor was born—Palmers was widely considered to be the most exclusive, most desirable hotel in the world.

Honor and Tina grew up surrounded by reminders of its illustrious history. The hotel itself was like a second home to them. As little girls they could hardly contain themselves with excitement when, every summer, their mother, Laura, would help them pack their cases and they'd set off for three joyously long months of fun in East Hampton.

But when their mom died—Laura Palmer was killed in a car accident when her daughters were aged ten and eight, respectively—everything changed. Trey, unable to admit his grief for fear it might overwhelm him, had cut himself off emotionally from everything that reminded him of his wife and their former life together. This included not only his children, who needed him more than ever, but also Palmers. The hotel that had been the jewel in the Palmer family crown for half a century rapidly lost its premier status as Trey started spending less and less time there.

Now, some thirteen years later, it had become little more than another dime-a-dozen "luxury" hotel, perhaps even a little shabbier than most of its rivals. If it hadn't been for the Palmer fortune propping it up, and for its still-legendary name, it would doubtless have closed years ago.

Honor took a deep breath to calm herself and gazed out the window. She knew that what she was doing was right. Taking control of her dad's assets was the only way to save Palmers and what little was left of her once-immense inheritance. But she still couldn't look Trey in the eye. Even after all these years, his dislike and distrust of her still hurt her very deeply.

Ironically, Brannagan's offices were on Newbury Street, almost directly opposite what had once been the Cranley hotel and was now a souped-up shopping mall. It was June, the schools had just got out for summer, and the place was busy. Students in shorts and varsity T-shirts stood around in groups laughing, sipping their Frappuccinos in the courtyard café out front, while wealthy women hurried past them into the designer stores, no doubt looking for bargains in the summer sales.

They all seemed to be having so much fun. For a fleeting moment, Honor wished she were down there too, frittering away her trust fund like she didn't have a care in the world. That was how Tina lived her life, after all, along with most of the other vacuous Boston rich kids they'd grown up with. So why not her?

But her stepmother's whining, wheedling voice soon dragged her back to reality.

"It's outrageous, Mr. Brannagan," Lise was saying, doing her best to look hard done by, which wasn't easy given the twenty-odd carats of diamonds scattered generously about her person. "Just because my baby is sick," she placed a skinny, red-taloned hand on Trey's wizened leg, "these vultures are trying to move in and take advantage."

"Oh, please," said Honor witheringly. Her voice was low and husky, making her seem even more masculine. "Dad's nobody's 'baby.' And if anyone's the vulture here, it's you."

Though officially her stepmother, Lise was actually only a couple of years Honor's senior. A former flight attendant with inflated Angelina Jolie lips and hair extensions that must weigh more than she did, she was the fourth bimbo Trey had married in the last twelve years, in the vain hope that one of them might bear him his longed-for son.

Ever since Honor and Tina's mom died, Trey had been obsessed with fathering a boy to take over Palmers and carry on the family name. Honor, who loved her father deeply and wanted desperately to please him, had spent most of her teenage years trying everything she could think of to become the son he wanted. Not content with excelling at both academic work and overtly male sports like baseball and shooting, she started cutting her hair short and wearing boyish clothes in an attempt to make him happy. She even began starving herself: anything to stave off the arrival of puberty and the breasts she dreaded as unwanted, but irrefutable, symbols of her femininity.

But nothing was ever enough for Trey.

Unwilling to accept it was *he* who had the fertility problems, he'd refused to give up hope, foisting a series of ridiculously young stepmothers on his daughters. When each one failed to get pregnant, he simply divorced her in favor of a newer, younger model. But not before he'd been forced to pay out a small fortune in alimony.

After a while, Honor had become immune to these women. Lise was no better or worse than the others. But at twenty-seven, she sure wasn't with an elderly cripple like Trey because she loved him. To pretend she was was laughable.

"Dad's been declared incapable of managing his own affairs," Honor continued matter-of-factly. "That gives Mr. Brannagan, as his trustee, automatic power of attorney. The decision to put me in control of Palmers, and the rest of the family assets, was his and his alone. Right, Sam?"

The lawyer shifted uncomfortably in his seat. Was it just him, or was it getting awfully hot in here?

"So you're saying it means nothing that cousin Trey made it abundantly clear during his lifetime that he wanted Palmers to pass down the male line?" spluttered the Omaha cousin, sensing his hoped-for payday slipping through his fingers.

"It's still his lifetime, Mr. Foster," said Honor scathingly. "He's not dead yet."

"I've told you," the cousin snapped back, "it's Jacob."

"Sorry," said Honor, with heavy sarcasm. "I'm afraid I was raised never to use first names with people I don't know from Adam."

"Who's not dead?" Trey looked around him, bewildered. "And who's Adam?"

Despite everything, it broke Honor's heart to see him so lost and confused. If the doctors were right, he might not remember who she was in a few months' time. Alzheimer's was a bitch of a disease.

"It's nothing for you to worry about, Mr. Palmer," the lawyer interjected kindly. "I can assure you that your daughter is acting in your best interests. She's very well qualified to take over the running of the business."

Trey gave a short, derisory laugh. "Well qualified? She's a woman, Mr. Brannagan," he sneered. "Evidently she's every bit as sly and conniving as the rest of her sex. But that hardly equips her to run the greatest hotel in the world."

"But a dick and a pair of balls would equip her perfectly, right?" chimed in Tina. "You're so pathetic."

It was the first time she'd spoken since the meeting began, and everyone turned to look at her. Cousin Jacob's wife looked like she might be about to spontaneously combust with disapproval at the coarseness of her language. "Don't get me wrong," Tina continued, smiling at Brannagan. "I really don't give a rat's ass what happens to Palmers. But if Honor wants to play the great white hope, I say we should let her. As long as I get my trust fund *and* my allowance, I'm easy."

"Yes, we all know how easy you are," said Honor furiously. It was bitchy, but she couldn't help it. Tina's devil-may-care wantonness had always provoked a mixture of revulsion and envy in Honor.

She certainly didn't need it in her face today. "And for your information, I'm not 'playing' at anything. I'm only doing this because Dad's so ill."

"Please," said Tina, reaching down her bra to rearrange her breasts without a hint of embarrassment. "That's bullshit and you know it. You've wanted to run Palmers since the day you were born."

Honor was silent. It was true: she had always wanted Palmers. But not like this.

From her earliest childhood, Honor Palmer knew she was different.

It wasn't just the envious way her little friends looked at her when the chauffeur would drop her and Tina off at elementary school in the Bentley T-type. Or the photographers who frightened her by swarming around her mother and father whenever they went out to dinners or charity events. It was more than that. It was an awareness, reached very early, that the Palmer name she bore was not just a privilege but an immense responsibility.

She had never known her grandfather, and yet Tertius Palmer's presence seemed to be everywhere when she was growing up. His portrait hung in the entrance hall of the family's grand Boston townhouse. His books were on the shelves in the library. His heavy mahogany desk still dominated Honor's father's study. Even the gardens where she and Tina used to play, with their formal maze and the willow walk along the banks of the Charles, had been designed and planted by Tertius.

Nowhere, however, was his spirit more alive than at Palmers. In the early days, before her mother died, Honor would spend every summer at the grand old Hamptons hotel listening to stories of her grandfather and the wild and wonderful times he'd had there. To her child's eyes, Palmers was a wonderland. When she and Tina played mermaids in the pool or had tricycle races along the endless polished parquet corridors, it was as if the outside world didn't exist.

The hotel guests, many of whom were elderly and had been coming for years, were remarkably tolerant of Trey's two boisterous little girls. Those who remembered Tertius were happy to pull Honor aside and tell her tall tales about the New Year's Eve party when her grandfather had danced with an Italian princess or the day he'd landed a biplane on the hotel's croquet lawn.

Honor lapped up the romance of it all like a bear with a pot of honey. She wasn't the most attractive child—with her short hair, wire-rimmed glasses, and skinny, matchstick legs, strangers often mistook her for a boy, and a nerdy boy at that. But at Palmers, she always felt like a princess. She was the chosen one, born to inherit and preserve all the excitement and magic that surrounded her. Because for Honor, above all, that's what Palmers *really* meant—magic.

Tina saw things differently, even back then. Two years younger than her sister, Cristina Maud Palmer was as blonde, blue-eyed, and chubby-cheeked as a Botticelli cherub, with a line in cuteness that would have put Shirley Temple out of business had she been born a generation earlier. Adults universally pronounced her "adorable." And she was, if pink hair ribbons, a frilly dress, and an ability to sing, "How much is that doggie in the window?" were all you looked for in a child. But underneath the butter-wouldn't-melt exterior, a frighteningly detached, self-centered little person was forming.

Having learned early how to bend adults to her will, Tina pursued her own pleasure with all the ruthless determination of a general before battle. "Pleasure" for Tina meant, very simply, the accumulation of things: toys, clothes, money, a puppy. Whatever the flavor of the month was, Tina Palmer would twirl and simper and cajole until it was hers.

Like Honor, she understood from an early age that her family was rich and important. But as far as Tina was concerned, that simply meant that she would grow up to have even more stuff, and live in even more luxury, than she did now. Palmers was nothing more or less than another sign of that wealth. She had never understood Honor's sentimental obsession with the place and its history. As a child she longed for people to stop blathering on about her boring, old, dead grandfather and bring her another ice cream. Preferably with hot fudge sauce and a cherry on top.

Despite their differences, Honor and Tina had tolerated each other well enough in those early years. It was their mother's accident that changed things between them. Honor still remembered the awful day as though it were yesterday. She'd been up in her room in Boston, playing an imagination game with her dolls, and had jumped out of her skin when Rita, the nanny, burst in. She was supposed to have grown out of the dolls and passed them on to Tina. But all Tina ever wanted to do was dress them up, and Honor felt sorry for them, discarded in her sister's toy box, never getting to go on any fun adventures anymore. Her first thought was that Rita was mad she'd taken them back. She remembered feeling almost relieved to be told it was only her father wanting to see her downstairs.

Needless to say the relief was short-lived. The first thing she saw when she walked into Trey's study was Tina sobbing hysterically on the couch. Honor remembered being shocked, because these clearly weren't her sister's usual crocodile tears. Something was very wrong.

Trey was making no move to comfort her. He just stood there, as gray and still as a granite statue in the middle of the room. "Honor, there's been an accident."

That was all he said at first. He wasn't crying. In all the weeks and months and years that followed, in fact, Honor never once saw him cry for the wife she knew he'd loved more than anything. But still, he seemed to be having difficulty getting his words out. "Mommy's dead. She's not coming back."

Clearly her father was not a subscriber to the "break it to them gently" school of parenting. As an adult, Honor often wondered how many thousands of dollars in therapy that moment alone would have cost her had she grown up to be the navel-gazing type. Thankfully, she hadn't. Because as awful as her mother's death was, far, far worse was to come.

Tammy. That was the name of their first stepmother. And what a fucking nightmare she was. Unlike the later models, she came from a respected Boston family, but her upbringing didn't seem to have prevented her from growing up into a class-A bitch. It was a year almost to the day since their mom's death and Trey brought Tammy home like a trophy, beaming with a pride and happiness that Honor couldn't fathom.

"Honor, Tina, this is Tammy," he said, kissing the strange woman on the lips. Honor, who was eleven at the time, thought she looked like a taller Snow White, with short black hair and porcelain-pale skin. But she wasn't kind and smiley like Mommy. "She's going to be living with us from now on," Trey continued. "And we hope that pretty soon she's going to give you girls a little brother."

We? Who was this *we?* Honor didn't hope for any such thing.

It was the first time she'd heard her father express a desire for a son. Over the next decade, that desire was to bloom into a full-grown obsession.

"Why?" Tina had asked, twirling her ringlets skeptically in the corner.

"Your daddy needs a boy so he can take over Palmers one day, honey," simpered Tammy. "And take care of you girls, too. That's what brothers do."

"Daddy doesn't need a *boy*!" yelled Honor, pulling herself up to her full four foot nine, her jaw jutting in defiance. "*I'm* going to take over Palmers when I grow up. What do you know about it, anyway?"

"Honor." Her father's voice was stern. "Don't you dare speak to Tammy like that. Apologize at once."

Honor had apologized. Not because she was remotely sorry. But because she couldn't bear for her father to be angry with her.

That night, she'd tried to talk to Tina about it. "We have to do something to get rid of her," she'd whispered, once the sound of their nanny's footsteps had finally died away.

"Like what?" Tina had her Winnie the Pooh flashlight on under the covers and was brushing her hair, admiring its shiny blondeness in the mirror with quiet satisfaction. Though only nine, she was already taller than Honor and much more physically developed, with tiny, nascent breasts of which she was inordinately proud. "It's not up to us."

"For goodness' sake," hissed Honor, exasperated. "Don't you understand how serious this is? She's horrible. She's a witch. And if she does have a baby boy, Daddy won't want us anymore."

"I don't think he wants us now," shrugged Tina, not missing a beat.

"Of course he wants us!" said Honor hotly, although deep down she knew that the tears were pricking her eyes because her sister was right. Since their mom's death, Trey had been distant to the point of neglect.

"It's Tammy that's the problem. You know she's going to try and act like she's our mom. *And* I bet she'll try to take Palmers away. Her and her new baby."

Sighing, Tina reluctantly switched off the flashlight and slipped the mirror under her bed. "I wish you'd stop talking about Palmers. It's only a stupid hotel." Honor was so flabbergasted by this she was temporarily speechless.

"And if she does try to act like our mom, we'll just ignore her. It's really not a big deal. Anyway, I'm tired. Let's go to sleep."

Seething with frustration, Honor pulled her bedspread up to her shoulders and turned her head to the wall. There was no point pushing it any further. Clearly Tina had no understanding whatsoever of the dangers they were facing. As usual it would be up to her, Honor, to do something.

If a son was what their father wanted—and clearly it was—then that was what she'd have to become.

———————   ———————

"Miss Palmer?"

Honor looked up with a start at the sound of Sam Brannagan's voice. For a moment she'd forgotten where she was.

"Shall we continue?"

"Yes, yes of course," she said, smoothing the crease in her black pants as she got to her feet. This was no time for melancholy reflection. She needed to be in control.

"The fact is that, while I appreciate all of you coming, there's really nothing left to discuss. The trustees have appointed me to manage Dad's affairs, including Palmers, and that's what I'm going to do. I had hoped," she looked plaintively at Trey, "to make you understand why I'm doing this, Daddy. Believe me, if there were any other way—"

"I'll change my will!" Trey shouted, the effort plunging him back into another bout of coughing. Jacob Foster made a great show of passing him his oxygen mask, but the old man pushed him angrily away.

"You're a viper, Honor. A snake in my house!"

"Mrs. Palmer." Seeing Honor struggling to suppress her emotions, the lawyer addressed himself calmly to Lise. "For your husband's sake, I think you'd better take him home now. And that goes for the rest of you, too. All interested parties will be receiving copies of the documentation in due course. But this meeting is over."

Slipping on her oversize Gucci sunglasses, Tina was the first to head for the door, without so much as a backward glance at Trey. "Honor, call me," she said brusquely. "I wanna know when that money will hit my account."

"This isn't over, you know," said Jacob furiously, yanking his dumpy wife up out of her seat. "Not by a long shot. You'll be hearing from us again, Mr. Brannagan." Honor said nothing as they filed out of the room, but her heart was pounding. Harvard may have taught her how to deal with confrontation and take control of a hostile meeting, but it hadn't taught her not to feel sick to her stomach each time, especially when her adversary was her own father, whose mind had been taken over by dark, inexplicable shadows that made him distrust everything and everyone around him. He couldn't even trust his own senses anymore, the poor bastard.

Lise was the last to go, leading the doddering Trey by the hand. Honor winced to see him so frail. She could only pray that, behind closed doors, his child-wife treated him with more kindness and compassion than she'd shown today. Somehow, she doubted it.

"I'll make you proud, Dad," she heard herself calling after him, ashamed to hear her voice breaking with emotion. Why did she still need his approval so badly? "I'll make Palmers great again. You'll see."

Turning to look at her as the elevator doors opened, Trey shook his head bitterly. He knew his periods of lucidity were getting rarer and rarer. But to be outwitted by his own daughter was more than his pride could bear.

"I hope God forgives you for this, Honor," he muttered darkly. "Because I never will."

And stepping into the elevator with the rest of his so-called family, he was gone.

CHAPTER TWO

*L*UCAS, STOP—WE CAN'T! MY HUSBAND MIGHT COME ANY minute."

Lucas Ruiz unzipped his jeans and pushed Mrs. Leon back against the living room wall, hitching up her skirt as he did so.

"Fuck your husband," he growled. "*I'm* going to come any minute. And I intend to be inside you when I do."

They were in the living room of the Leons' luxury villa in Ibiza. To Lucas's left, double-height glass doors gave way to one of the most stunning panoramas on the island. Manicured gardens ran down the hillside, merging into olive groves that in turn blurred into the still, sparkling blue of the Mediterranean.

But Lucas was focused on a different view.

At forty-four, Carla Leon was twenty years his senior, but she still had a body designed for fucking. Her tits were round and high and seemed to be straining now at the silk and lace of her bra as if willing him to release them. Her legs were long but shapely, not like the twiggy twentysomething models at Pacha who seemed to think it sexy to starve themselves skeletal. Boy, did he hate that look. And even after three children her stomach was flat and toned, a testament to the long hours she spent each week in the gym.

Lucas was impressed. He liked a woman who took care of herself.

"Oh, God," Carla moaned, closing her eyes and squeezing her muscles tightly around his dick as he powered into her, despite her earlier protests. "That's so good."

"Shhh," he said, slipping a rough, warm hand over her mouth. "Your husband, remember? Besides, I've hardly started."

It was by no means the first time that he'd "visited" Mrs. Leon. They'd first met five years ago, when he was still in his teens, and she and her husband were vacationing in Ibiza for the first time. Back then he was stuck working for that asshole Miguel, washing sheets and scrubbing toilets at the dreadful Hotel Britannia in San Antonio, the scummiest part of the island.

Even then, he already knew he was going to get out one day. One thing Lucas Ruiz had never been lacking was ambition. Nevertheless, it was Carla Leon who'd bought him his ticket to a new life, funding him through hotel management school in Switzerland.

This was the summer after his graduation, and he'd come back to see her to express his gratitude the best way he knew how.

Staggering across the room with Carla's long legs wrapped around his waist, he laid her down on the pool table.

"Careful! Don't break it!" she gasped, arching her back and throwing her arms back behind her head so she could grip the corner pockets. Ignoring her, Lucas climbed on top of her, increasing the pace of his thrusts as he ripped at the lace of her bra with his teeth.

"You are so fucking sexy," he breathed, his long black hair tickling her shoulders and neck now as he whispered in her ear. "I'm gonna make you come so hard you won't walk for a week."

"Carla!" Pepe Leon's gruff, booming voice echoed through the house like the voice of God. "*Donde estas tú?*"

"Lucas!" Carla's eyes widened with panic. "For God's sake, get out of here. Pepe's back."

"I'm not going anywhere," he said, his eyes lighting up like a mischievous schoolboy's. "Not until you come for me, my lady."

"Lucas!" she hissed. But at the same time she felt his hands slipping downward beneath her bottom and his fingers probing her everywhere, rubbing and stroking as he pushed his huge cock deeper still inside her.

This was the sort of fuck that was worth losing your marriage for. Gripping him tightly around the neck like a drowning woman grasping for a buoy, her body exploded into shuddering orgasm. Moments later Lucas also came, biting down hard on his forearm to muffle the sound of his own delight.

"What are you waiting for?" he whispered, grinning, once he'd finished. Leaping off the table, he started pulling up his jeans with lightning speed. "Don't you know your husband's home?"

Before Carla could catch her breath, he'd pulled open the French doors, blown her a kiss, and sprinted off down the hillside like Carl Lewis.

She only just had time to do up her blouse and jump off the table herself before Pepe walked in.

"There you are, darling," he said, kissing her on the cheek with the routine, absentminded affection of the long married. "Did you have a good morning?"

"I did, thank you," she said, glancing briefly out the window. Thankfully, Lucas was nowhere to be seen. "I had a very enjoyable morning. Very enjoyable indeed."

Lucas's birth had been a difficult one.

His mother, Ines, at only sixteen and unmarried, had been left to cope with her delivery alone. Too frightened to go to a hospital, she endured a long and terrifying labor in a remote olive grove close to the ramshackle farmworkers' cottage where she and Lucas's father, Antonio, were living.

Antonio had promised to be there for the birth. But of course when the time came he was too high on heroin to see straight, never mind deliver a baby. This was the seventies, at the dawn of the tourist explosion on Ibiza, and drug culture had descended on the once-unspoiled island like a plague, bringing misery and destruction in its wake.

Lucas's father was only one of its many early victims. By the boy's first birthday he had disappeared from the scene completely. Ines presumed him dead, overdosed in a doorway somewhere, but she never knew for sure. In any case, within a year she was married, under intense pressure from her family, to a reclusive local farmer named Jose Ruiz.

Twice her age and a heavy drinker, Ruiz was not much of a husband. Nor did he have any interest in his young wife's brooding, withdrawn two-year-old son. The marriage was miserable from the start, but Ines nevertheless went on to produce three more sons in as many years. Lucas's earliest memories were of fighting with his brothers—for some reason they were always fighting—in the filthy two-room shack up in the hills that the Ruiz family called home.

They weren't happy memories. But as the years rolled by, they were to get worse. Jose's drinking spiraled into full-blown alcoholism, and shortly afterward the beatings began. One day, an eight-year-old Lucas arrived home from school to find his stepfather passed out on the kitchen floor and his mother hunched over the dishes, crying and trying to hide her split lip and swollen eye.

"Mama!" Running over to her, he wrapped his arms around her waist, as fiercely protective as a little terrier. "What happened? Did he hurt you, Mama?"

But Ines just shook her head angrily. "Do your homework, Lucas," she said, without looking up. "Everything's fine now. Off you go."

It was the moment that crystallized the boy's dislike of his stepfather into hatred. And it was also the first time he fully realized what it meant to be powerless. Those two feelings—hatred and powerlessness—became the driving forces of Lucas's adolescent years.

When Jose hit him there was physical pain, but Lucas rapidly learned to cope with that. It was the emotional torture of seeing his mother and little brothers being hurt that kept him awake at night, sobbing tears of frustration and rage. He knew what he had to do, of course: grow. Once he was big and strong enough to take on his stepfather physically, *then* he would know freedom. Then, and only then, he would know revenge.

He first started lifting weights at the age of ten. Not dumbbells, just any of the heavy detritus left strewn around the farm—tractor wheels, old crates of grain, rusting parts of long-abandoned harvesters. Though he was still short for his age, he rapidly saw a change in his build from wiry and athletic to stocky and strong. It was the first time any action of his had actually achieved something tangible. Before long he was hooked.

His longed-for day of reckoning didn't arrive for another five years, however. After a sudden growth spurt right after his fifteenth birthday, Lucas was finally able to look in the mirror and see a grown man staring back at him. Six feet tall, with an almost comically overdeveloped upper body, he was the sort of boy that anyone would think twice about picking a fight with. But it was the look in his eyes that really put the fear of God into would-be opponents. Underneath that wild, jet-black mop of Jim Morrison hair, two darkly narrowed slits of liquid rage glinted murderously. All he needed now was an opportunity.

The next time Jose raised his fist to his wife, Lucas didn't just hit him. He beat him into bloody unconsciousness on the kitchen floor. Turning to his mother, flushed with triumph, he was horrified to find himself being screamed at.

"Lucas!" she yelled, tearing her hair, while his younger brothers looked on in awe. "What have you done? You could have killed him!"

"And why shouldn't I kill him, Mama?" Lucas looked baffled. "After the way he treats you. The way he treats all of us."

"He feeds us, Lucas," said Ines, shaking her head. "He clothes us. He puts a roof over our heads."

"Barely," spat Lucas, pulling at the peeling paper on the wall in disgust.

"Who's going to take care of us if your father can't work?"

"He's not my father," said Lucas indignantly. He couldn't believe that they were having this conversation. Didn't his mother want to escape? Didn't she want to be free of him? "And I can take care of us, Mama. I'll get work in town, in the hotels. I won't even drink away three-quarters of my wages. How's that?"

"You don't understand!" said Ines. Wetting a tea towel, she sank down to her knees and began mopping away the worst of the blood from Jose's face. "You're still a child. You don't understand anything."

She was right about that. He didn't understand.

Within twenty minutes, he'd thrown his few paltry possessions into a bag and was on the point of storming out. Jose remained motionless on the floor, although occasional soft moans indicated he was still alive—sad fact though that was.

"Mama," said Lucas, hesitating at the last moment. "Please. Come with me. Bring the boys. What do you have to stay for, for Christ's sake?"

He felt betrayed, bewildered, hurt beyond belief by her behavior. But he still loved her, and his brothers. If there was any chance at all to rescue them...

"*Querido*," she whispered. There were tears in her eyes. "I can't." It was the last time Lucas was to see her for four years.

The first twelve months were the worst. Lucas was used to poverty, but he wasn't used to having to sleep on the beach or in shop doorways. His first few jobs were all in the kitchens of cheap tourist cafés. The pay was third world, but the food was free, and a couple of the places even let him sleep on the floor behind the counter during the winter months.

The problem was that Lucas could never hold down a job for more than a few weeks. As soon as anyone crossed him—a temperamental cook, a demanding boss, or a dissatisfied customer—he flew completely off the handle, settling disputes the only way he knew how: with his fists. Having worked so hard for it, it came as a shock to him to discover that his physical strength did not automatically translate to power and control. That sometimes it could lead him into situations beyond his control—situations that harmed him.

At sixteen, waking up cold and aching from yet another long night on the beach surrounded by junkies and hobos, he decided that his days of drifting were over. He needed a steady job, one that provided meals and accommodation as well as a wage. By the end of that week he'd found one.

The kindest thing you could say about the Britannia Hotel in San Antonio was that it was a shit hole. Managed by a fat, ignorant sadist named Miguel Munoz, the place smelled constantly of disinfectant—it was that or vomit and operated against a constant background white noise of electronic slot machines, arguing couples, and screaming children.

Lucas worked in the laundry room, which in some ways was a blessing, as it kept him away from the obnoxious British and American guests, whom he soon came to loathe with a passion. But the work was tough and often revolting, with sheets regularly covered in vomit or worse. It made Lucas seethe that these rich foreigners— rich by his standards, anyway—flocked to his beautiful island in droves, but when they got here, all they wanted to do was drink themselves into oblivion.

None of them made even the most cursory attempt to speak Spanish. They couldn't even be bothered to sample the cuisine, eschewing the delicious local tapas and fresh traditional dishes in favor of spaghetti Bolognese or the ubiquitous "chicken 'n' chips."

But his time at the Britannia wasn't wasted. The hotel, like the rest of the dives in San Antonio, opened his eyes to a world of possibilities. If a fat slob like Miguel was making money hand over fist offering a service as atrocious as this—and he was, as he liked to remind his impoverished staff constantly—how much more money must there be in a decent, professionally run hotel?

Lucas had no intention of spending the rest of his life removing used condoms from other people's filthy bedding. He was going to get out of Ibiza. And he was going to get rich in the hotel business.

The first thing he needed, he rapidly realized, was an education. School had never felt like much of a priority during his hand-to-mouth childhood, and the gaps in his basic learning were huge as a result. Undaunted, he enrolled himself in night school, and though he was often so tired after a day's work that he fell asleep in class, he nevertheless managed to complete his high school diploma within a year.

"I don't know what you're so happy about," Miguel had taunted him the day he heard his results. "What do you expect to do with that? Run Goldman Sachs?"

But for once, Lucas didn't rise to the insult. Instead he quietly continued with his studies, focusing on the subjects that he knew would provide a passport to the better life he craved. To his own amazement and delight, he turned out to have a marked aptitude for languages. He'd already picked up a lot of English by osmosis from the tourists at the Britannia, and he rapidly added German, French, and Italian to his repertoire. Not since he first started weight training as a kid had he experienced such a sense of achievement in such a short space of time. Slowly, like an early spring flower struggling up through the frost toward the sunlight, his confidence began to grow.

And languages were not his only talent. At school he'd been so withdrawn and moody he'd barely noticed the lingering looks he got from girls in his class. But by seventeen he was well aware of the effect he had on the opposite sex, and the power it gave him.

Lucas's attitude toward women was complicated. Having grown up watching his mother suffer, he felt protective toward most of the girls he slept with. His natural instinct was to like them. But his mother's example had taught him other things too: namely that women were weak and not necessarily deserving of respect. These two conflicting beliefs, combined with his naturally awesome libido, made Lucas that rarest and yet, to many women, most desirable of males: a benevolent chauvinist pig, the sexual equivalent of a benign dictator.

Older women in particular found his combination of Latin good looks and macho sexual dynamism irresistible. Lucas made them feel beautiful, because that was truly how he saw them. But he refused to be controlled or tied down in any way.

Getting one of his wealthy, older lovers to fund his education was never something he consciously planned. And yet, when it happened, he felt quite happy to accept it as no more than his due.

As the months and years passed at the Britannia, his fantasy of one day owning his own hotel became more detailed and fully formed. His hotel would be the polar opposite of the Britannia: simple lines, an aura not just of luxury but of peace. In his mind he'd planned everything, right down to the linens and the table settings. It even had a name.

Luxe.

Not "The Luxe" or "Hotel Luxe." Just the one word: four letters to symbolize Lucas's vision. His little piece of heaven on earth.

He was describing the place to Carla Leon one Sunday afternoon five summers ago, after making love. The latest in his seemingly never-ending stream of Mrs. Robinsons, Lucas liked

Mrs. Leon because she was adventurous and funny, and because she seemed to know so much about the educated, wider world that he yearned to be a part of. "It sounds incredible, my darling," she murmured, lying back against the mossy ground of the secluded woodland where he'd taken her. "But you mustn't underestimate what you're going to need to make it happen."

"You're talking about money?" said Lucas, sitting up and gazing moodily ahead of him. Why did everything always come down to that in the end?

"Not just money," said Carla. "The hotel trade is highly competitive. You need an education."

"I'm getting one," said Lucas proudly. "I've told you that."

Sitting up herself, gloriously naked, Carla leaned forward and began to stroke his bare back. Sometimes his strength frightened her. His muscles were so taut and bulging they looked like they might be about to erupt through his skin.

"It won't be enough," she said gently. "You need relevant qualifications. An MBA. The place you should really aim for is in Switzerland. The Ecole Hôtelière in Lausanne. EHL. That's where all the top hoteliers train. Have you heard of it?"

"Of course," said Lucas, who hadn't but was too arrogant to admit it.

By the end of the week, he knew all there was to know about the school—courses, entry requirements, fees, foreign student visas. Carla was right. Lausanne was exactly where he needed to be. But getting there was going to be a daunting task.

The night she left with her husband for Madrid, Carla made Lucas a promise: "This time next year, if you've succeeded in passing all the international exams you need for entry, I'll fund your application."

He neither thanked her nor questioned her. He simply trusted in her word and set about studying like he never had before, slaving over his books and sleeping with a copy of the EHL prospectus under his pillow, like a holy text. When at last he earned his qualifications, with a month to spare before his year was up, he called her.

They hadn't spoken since she'd left the previous summer. But Carla didn't sound remotely surprised to hear from him.

"Send me the application form, Lucas darling," she told him. "All you have to do is sign it. I'll take care of the rest."

And so she had.

———

Lucas adored Lausanne. His courses were hard work, but nothing compared to the hell of the Britannia, and his ambition and drive carried him through the four years like adrenaline spurring on a marathon runner.

Most of his classmates were from wealthy or, middle-class families, but to his surprise, Lucas found it easy to fit in. Social life at the EHL revolved around frat-house parties and weekend ski trips, both of which he took in his stride. And of course, it didn't hurt that he was far and away the best-looking guy on campus.

"Are you sure you haven't skied before?" Daniel, a buddy from his macroeconomics class, quizzed him suspiciously on their first trip to the mountains. "You sure don't look like a beginner to me."

They were in Murren, a tiny, car-free hamlet burrowed into a mountainside in the Jungfrau valley. Home of the famous Downhill Club in the 1920s, it remained popular with British skiers looking for natural Alpine beauty, but without the ritz and pretension of the big resorts like St. Moritz or Courchevel, and was also favored by the local Swiss. Lucas, who didn't know such storybook Hansel and Gretel villages still existed, was utterly charmed.

"What can I say?" He grinned. Having just completed a tricky black-diamond run, he was feeling more than a little pleased with himself. "I guess I'm a natural."

"Right. A natural asshole," the girl taking her skis off next to him muttered sourly, trudging up the hill to the restaurant to join the others.

Lucas had won over 99 percent of his female classmates at Lausanne with his combination of humor, confidence, and insanely good looks. But Petra Kamalski remained immune to his charms. The only serious challenger to his crown as EHL's top-performing student, she was just as beautiful as Lucas, although in a polar opposite way. In fact, with Petra, "polar" was definitely the operative word: tall, reed-thin and as pale as the Snow Queen, she had cheekbones that could cut glass and the sort of ice-blue Russian eyes that both mesmerized and terrified at the same time. Her long blue-black hair was always worn up in a high, tight chignon and her body, though clearly perfect, was hidden at all times beneath polo-neck sweaters and long governess-style skirts.

"What's her fucking problem?" Lucas asked Daniel, glaring after Petra as she strode up the hill in her ultraexpensive, fur-lined Prada ski suit.

"Don't take it personally," said Daniel, slapping him on the back. "That's just Petra. She hates anything with a penis." Although this was true, Petra's dislike of Lucas clearly ran deeper than generic animosity toward the opposite sex. In lectures, she was constantly trying to trip him up, picking holes in all his arguments and doing her utmost to embarrass him in front of the professors. She'd even gone so far as to accuse him of pla-giarizing one of her papers last semester—a serious allegation that, had she proved it, would have gotten Lucas kicked out. As it was, the authorities had ruled "insufficient evidence," hardly the ringing endorsement of his honesty that Lucas had been hoping for. How come *Petra* had never been reprimanded for bringing the case maliciously and stirring up trouble?

The answer to that one was simple. Petra's uncle was the oligarch Oleg Kamalski, a man rich enough to buy the whole of Lausanne, if not Switzerland, with his loose change. Old Oleg was not a man that anyone wanted to alienate—least of all an institution second only to Harvard Business School in squeezing cash out of its successful alumni.

For the rest of the ski trip, Lucas did his best to keep out of Petra's way. But it was hard. Not only were they sharing a chalet along with nine other classmates, but Murren was so minuscule it made Ibiza look like New York City, making it even harder to escape.

When the day of their departure finally dawned, Lucas wasn't sorry. He'd come back to Murren another time on his own, or at least without Petra, when he'd be able to relax. Checking out of the chalet with only ten minutes to go before the train for Lauterbrunnen was due to leave, he suddenly discovered that his briefcase was missing.

"I don't understand it," he said, spinning around in frustration. "It's been under my bed the whole trip. Where can it possibly be?" Then, noticing Petra standing smugly in the lobby with the others, firmly clasping her own matching Chanel luggage, it dawned on him. "You moved it, didn't you? What the hell have you done with it, you shit-stirring bitch?"

"My, my, we *are* paranoid," she smirked. "It's no good blaming others for your own disorganized habits. I don't know why you brought work up here with you anyway. I'm going to trounce you in management theory no matter how hard you cram."

Lucas, who had never hit a woman, contemplated breaking his streak. But he knew that if he laid one finger on Petra he would get kicked out. And he wasn't about to risk that for anything.

There was nothing to do but to stay behind and hunt. After three long hours, he found the case stuffed behind a pile of ski boots in the garage—damn that stupid woman. But by then it was too late to get a connection to Lausanne. He'd have to stay in the village another night—yet more wasted time and expense— and catch a train first thing in the morning.

With nothing else to do, he trudged up the snowy hill to the Regina Hotel and settled in for a long night at the bar. His plan was to stare into his whiskey glass until a strategy for wiping Petra Kamalski off the face of the earth appeared before him. But after about fifteen minutes he found himself joined by a big blond Englishman about his own age who looked even more depressed than he did.

"Would you do me a huge favor?" the man asked, looking nervously about him. His accent was pure cockney, straight out of Mary Poppins, and deep enough to be menacing had it not been for his gentle-giant aura. "Would you pretend you know me?"

Even sitting on a bar stool, Lucas could see he was huge, at least six foot six and broader than a WWE wrestler. But his kind, slightly drooping eyes, freckles, and mop of surfer-blond hair were all more overgrown Labrador than killer Doberman. He was handsome, in an Iowa-farm-boy-meets-London-barrow-boy sort of a way. And right now he had a desperate, pleading look in his eye that not even a hardened cynic like Lucas could ignore.

"Sure," he said, smiling. "Why?"

Before the man could explain, three of the dullest-looking businessmen you could imagine—gray suits, center-parted hair, matching blue ties done up to strangulation point—walked into the bar and headed in his direction. Flinging his arms around Lucas in a bear hug, the stranger started loudly proclaiming his surprise and delight to see him.

"After all this time! Amazing!" he gushed enthusiastically. "Fancy seeing you in Murren, of all places!"

The three Swiss stooges held back and hovered, looking baffled.

"This is Jimmy," the man explained to them, gesturing toward a mutely smiling Lucas. "We used to knock about together as boys. Haven't seen each other in…oooh, how long has it been now, Jim?"

"Longer than I can remember," said Lucas, who was rather enjoying himself.

The blond turned back to his companions. "Look, d'you mind if we catch up for a bit? You guys go on to the fondue restaurant, and I'll, er…I'll join you a bit later, yeah?"

"But…but…" the first suit stammered, "we booked the table for four. Without you, we will be three."

Jesus, thought Lucas. They couldn't have been any more Swiss if they'd been full of holes and gone "cuckoo" on the hour.

"They'll understand at the restaurant. They know me there," said the blond, reassuringly. "Honestly, you lot go ahead and have a good time on me, all right? I'll catch up with you later."

After more persuading in a similar vein they finally waddled off, like three penguins skidding back out onto the polar ice. Only then did the blond breathe a sigh of relief and introduce himself.

"Thanks," he said, pumping Lucas's hand like the arm of a slot machine. "I'm Ben. Really, thanks so much. I swear to God, if I had to spend one more hour with those guys I'd have flung meself off the north face of the Eiger."

"They did seem a little tightly wound," conceded Lucas with a chuckle. "I'm Lucas."

"An honor and a joy to meet you, Lucas." Ben grinned. "Let me buy you a drink."

Ben Slater, it turned out, ran a hedge fund in London and was in Switzerland wooing possible institutional investors. The three stooges were all senior management from UBS, men almost exactly as powerful as they were dull.

"I know I ought to be over there with them, dunking my bread in the cheese and talking bond yield curves," said Ben with a sigh. "But I really can't face it. That fondue cheese is fucking disgusting anyway."

Lucas laughed. "I agree. Here's to ditching them."

In the end, they got along so well that they both decided to stay on for a few more days and this time actually enjoy the skiing. The staff at the Regina knew Ben well and were happy to move him into a larger two-bedroom suite so that he could share with Lucas. Better yet, he insisted on footing the bill for them both—"Honestly, mate, my fund is paying. It's a corporate expense; you don't owe me a penny"—and had been so persuasive that even the notoriously proud Lucas felt comfortable accepting.

Neither Ben nor Lucas was naturally a big talker. But over the course of numerous long slope-side lunches and evenings propping up the bar, they came to share pieces of their respective life stories and discovered themselves to be somewhat kindred spirits. Ben had grown up in a happy family, unlike Lucas. But he had also been very poor and had to work against the odds to shake off his background and achieve the professional success that he had. And there was something so impossibly good-hearted about him, so jovial and warm and open, one couldn't fail to be drawn to him. Having always hated Englishmen, and especially cockneys since his string of bad experiences at the Britannia, Lucas was shocked to discover that the country could also occasionally turn out some genuinely charming people. Ben was the archetypal diamond in the rough, and from day one Lucas adored him.

For his part, Ben didn't think he'd ever met someone with as much energy and ambition and lust for life as Lucas. After the mind-numbing tedium of his business trip, being in Lucas's company was like being jolted back to life with a cattle prod—only funnier. They laughed all the time, about Petra and Ben's hopeless love life and the fat Swiss matrons in their bright-pink jumpsuits, wiggling their hippo-like rear ends down the bunny slopes. By the time Lucas finally returned to Lausanne and Ben boarded his private jet back to London, both of them nursing hangovers worthy of a mention in the Guinness Book of World Records, a lasting friendship had been forged. For a loner like Lucas, this was a seismic event in his life and, though they didn't see much of each other for the next few years, he never lost the feeling that in Ben he had gained a new brother.

———————   ———————

Those carefree days in Murren with Ben felt like light-years ago now. Jumping onto the bus for Ibiza Town, Lucas sank gratefully into a vacant seat and began to get his breath back. He flattered himself that he was still fit, but there was no doubt that the adrenaline involved in putting distance between himself and a potentially murderous, cuckolded husband took a lot more out of him than an hour on the treadmill.

Still, Carla was definitely worth it. She always had been. And a summer of exciting extramarital sex was the very least he owed her after everything she'd done for him.

As the rickety blue bus wound its way down into town, he could see the tan-tiled roof of the guesthouse where he was staying. It wasn't the Ritz, but it was clean and the service was friendly. Certainly it was a world away from the dreaded Britannia.

He'd already come a long way. He knew he ought to feel happy, coming back home triumphant after graduating top in his MBA class. But in fact he felt more anxious than he had in Lausanne before his finals. Part of it was nervousness about his upcoming interviews in London. He was applying for jobs at a number of hotels there, but the one he really wanted—a junior management position at the world-famous Tischen Cadogan in Chelsea—was going to be very hotly contested. Candidates with a lot more experience than he had were sure to be applying. And yet he knew, he just knew, that he could do a better job than any of them, if only he were given the chance.

But it wasn't just work that was bothering him. Yesterday he'd been to see his mother.

It was only the second time Lucas had been back since the day he'd stormed out at fifteen. The first time was after he got accepted at EHL four years ago, and that had been so uncomfortable he'd been in no hurry to repeat the experience. He and his stepfather had hovered in the same room, barely acknowledging each other's presence, as awkward and stilted as teenage lovers at their first dance. Their mutual loathing hung in the air like the stench of rotting meat, but the only way to break the tension would have been through violence, a step neither man wanted to take.

It wasn't that Lucas didn't miss his mom and brothers, or that he'd stopped loving them. Far from it. But the pain of watching Ines wasting her life and continuing to take abuse from that monster Jose was more than he could bear. Instead he'd salved his conscience by writing and sending money. Even back in the Britannia days, when he could barely afford a stamp, he made sure to save something each week for his mother. Inevitably, though, the distance between them took its toll.

He hadn't realized quite how irrevocably his life had diverged from the rest of his family's until yesterday. Thankfully this time his stepfather was not around when Lucas turned up at the house. But that was all there was to be thankful for.

The house itself was even more dirty and dilapidated than he remembered it.

"Jesus, Mama," he said, looking around him in horror at the grimy windows, crumbling woodwork, and broken furniture. "What did you do with the money I sent you last month?"

Ines shrugged. "Your father took it. He had to pay some bills."

Had to buy some more whiskey, you mean, thought Lucas bitterly. The lines around his mother's mouth and etched-in deep grooves along her forehead spoke of a lifetime of hardship—hardship that could have been avoided, if only she'd had the courage to come with him, to break away. She was only forty, but she looked twenty years older at least and so fucking defeated it made him want to scream.

"And what about Paco? He's earning, isn't he? Or Domingo. Why aren't they contributing?"

The two older boys were eighteen and twenty now and still lived at home. It was a disgrace that they'd let the place sink into such squalor.

Ines gave a short, bitter laugh. "Your brothers? Since when do they help me? Paco's girlfriend is pregnant, nearly six months now. All his money goes to her."

Lucas shook his head. Fucking idiot kid. How hard was it to use a condom?

"And Domingo, he's just like his father. Drinking." She picked up an empty beer bottle from the table and threw it onto the overflowing trash.

Sighing, Lucas rolled up his sleeves and set about tidying the place up. He'd wanted so badly to talk to his mom—really talk—about his life in Switzerland and London and his plans for the future. But he realized now how futile that would be. There was nothing about his world or his friends that Ines would understand. Nothing at all. The education that had liberated him had also driven a wedge between the two of them that made communication impossible. He may as well have been talking Urdu.

By the time he left, the house was at least clean, and the flowers he'd brought his mother added a tiny touch of color and joy to the otherwise cheerless kitchen. That had made her smile, as had the rolled-up wad of bills he'd pressed into her hand despite her protests and made her promise to hide from Jose.

Even so, when they said their good-byes, Lucas drove straight down to the first dive bar he could find and drank until he could hardly stand. He didn't think he'd ever felt so depressed in his life.

"Ibiza Town!" The bus driver's voice jolted him back into the present.

"Everybody off, please."

Wearily, Lucas got to his feet and staggered down the steps into the harbor. It was after two now, and the early afternoon sun beat down on his head remorselessly, reawakening the hangover that his tryst with Carla had made him temporarily forget.

He'd go back to the guesthouse and sleep. And then tomorrow he'd look into booking himself onto an earlier flight to London. Summer in Ibiza had seemed like a great idea when he was back in Lausanne. But now that he'd done his duty by the lovely Mrs. Leon, he realized there was nothing left here for him to stay for.

The Tischen Cadogan. That was the future.

And as far as Lucas Ruiz was concerned, the future was all that mattered.

CHAPTER THREE

$\mathcal{A}$FTER AN UNPLEASANTLY HUMID AND MUGGY START TO the summer, July brought a welcome still, dry heat into Boston that was already starting to turn the city's leaves a glorious pale gold. Like most college towns, Boston sank into a weird sort of suspended animation during the summer. The sedate flow of the Charles was no longer disturbed by rowdy rowing squads every morning, and America's gilded youth with their armfuls of books suddenly vanished into the ether, replaced by flocks of summer tourists who crawled all over Newbury Street with their cameras and fanny packs like so many heat-exhausted ants.

With the students gone, city gossip shifted from academic backstabbing and faculty affairs to the comings and goings of the great old Boston families. Gossip, Honor had often thought, was Boston's lifeblood, and this past summer it had been her family's turn to provide the civic entertainment. Everyone who was anyone in Boston society had an opinion about Trey Palmer losing control of the family assets to his headstrong elder daughter. Most of them, Honor was all too uncomfortably aware, seemed to have decided that she was the villain of the piece.

"Do you still prefer to wait, Miss Palmer, or would you like to order an appetizer now?"

The waiter hovered awkwardly by Honor's table, waiting for a response. He looked barely old enough to have left high school and seemed to suffer agonies of embarrassment every time she looked him in the eye. Beautiful women clearly made him nervous, poor kid.

"I guess I'll order," she sighed, glancing again at the understated antique man's watch on her wrist. "Fucking Tina," she added under her breath.

She ought to have gotten used to her sister's lateness by now, but somehow it still pissed her off every time. How come she, with a vast business empire to run and a schedule so rammed with work it made the president's look lightweight, could manage to show up to lunch on time; but Tina, who appeared to do nothing but paint her nails all day and get her picture taken, was incapable of getting her shit together?

What made it worse was that they were meeting today at Tina's request. She was demanding an astronomical raise in her monthly allowance from the trust, which Honor had flatly refused to authorize. But Tina wasn't about to take no for an answer.

A commotion out on the restaurant terrace made Honor look up. A small gaggle of kids, college boys by the look of them, had pushed their way through the tables and were fighting with each other trying to get pictures on their cell phones, much to the annoyance of the alfresco diners.

"Step back now, please." A booming male voice rang out through the melee. "No pictures. Let Miss Palmer through."

Honor put her head in her hands. Why did her sister always, always have to make a scene?

Dressed utterly inappropriately for the formal restaurant in a tiny pair of white shorts and pink tank top, Tina was strutting through the throng, accompanied by a suited black man not much smaller than a rhino.

"Hi," she said breathlessly, reaching Honor's table at last but sitting down only once she was sure that all eyes in the room were on her.

"Sorry about that. Ever since I hooked up with Danny I can't seem to go anywhere without, you know," she waved regally at the gaggle of boys outside, "all this shit."

"Is Godzilla staying for lunch?" Honor asked frostily, nodding at the black giant who stood looming over them, arms folded, like a sentinel. "Because if so, you can eat on your own."

"He's my security," Tina pouted. "I need him."

Seeing Honor pushing her chair back to leave, she reluctantly relented.

"Oh, all right then. Mike," she turned to the heavy, "you'd better go wait in the car. I won't be long."

Once he'd gone and the furor in the restaurant had finally died down, Honor let her have it: "What the hell do you think you're doing?" she hissed.

"What do you mean?" Tina feigned innocence. It wasn't a look that suited her.

"Turning up here looking like Christina fucking Aguilera," said Honor. "Courting publicity like some cheap starlet. You promised me you'd cut it out, at least until I make some progress with Palmers. You know how conservative our clientele are—what's left of them," she added ruefully. "Everything this family does reflects on the business."

"Blah, blah, blah," said Tina, looking bored. "Change the record, would you? Martini," she added, barking at the waiter without looking up.

"And you're late," said Honor. Her green cat's eyes were flashing with irritation, and her knuckles were white from where she'd been clenching her napkin so tightly. But other than that she betrayed no outward sign of her fraying patience. Unlike Tina, she had always preferred to keep her inner feelings private. Even at school, kids used to tease her that the "C" of her initials—actually "Constance" in Honor C. Palmer—stood for "Control."

"I'm late because people kept stopping me for pictures," said Tina. "And I'm not courting publicity, thank you very much. I can't help it if people find my life exciting or think I'm a sex symbol or whatever, can I? That's the way life is when you're a famous actress."

Honor bit her lip. The arrogance was breathtaking.

"Tina, you've done two commercials. That doesn't make you a famous actress."

"It makes me an actress," Tina shot back. "And dating Danny's made me famous. Whether you like it or not."

Ah, yes. Danny.

Danny Carlucci, officially a local real estate entrepreneur, was in fact a well-known mafioso, tapped by those in the know as the likely future boss of Massachusetts. He was pushing sixty, heavily overweight, and already had a wife, two grown sons, and a legion of grandchildren. He was also Tina Palmer's latest lover.

"We need to talk about that, too," Honor whispered. "It's got to stop."

Tina's martini arrived at the same time as Honor's sparkling water. Taking their drinks, they both ordered salads—Tina was on a diet and Honor seemed to have suddenly lost her appetite. It was a few minutes before either of them spoke again.

"I'm open to it. Breaking it off with Danny, I mean," said Tina, taking the olive out of her drink and pulling it in and out of her mouth slowly, like a porn star.

"Really?" Honor was surprised. She hadn't expected her to give in so easily.

"Sure," said Tina. "If I can afford to, that is. Danny pays for a lot of my shit right now. And he's been talking about setting me up in my own place in LA. I really need to be there now, for my work." Oh, so *that* was the deal. Blackmail. She'd drop the mobster if Honor upped her cash. It was such vintage Tina, it actually made her smile.

"How much?"

Tina looked blank.

"How much for you to drop Danny and move to the West Coast?" Honor clarified.

"Well, LA's not cheap," said Tina, downing the last of her cocktail and immediately scanning the room for the waiter to order another. "And I'd have to live in Holmby Hills, obviously."

"Oh, obviously," said Honor, rolling her eyes. Holmby was by far the most expensive neighborhood in the city, outpricing homes in next-door Beverly Hills by almost three to one. "So. How much?"

"Forty-five a month," said Tina.

Honor choked on her water. "Forty-five thousand? Dollars?" she spluttered. "A month? Jesus, Tina. Do you understand the financial hole Dad's gotten us into? Palmers is losing money every day. Every fucking day."

"Fine." Tina shrugged as her salad arrived and started attacking it with gusto. "So I'll stick with Danny. He can pay. Or I'll move to New York. See what turns up there. I am willing to compromise, you know, Honor. I don't know why you always make me out to be this, like, unreasonable bitch."

A move to New York was Honor's absolute worst nightmare, and Tina knew it. It was bad enough having her sister all over the gossip columns in Boston. But at least Boston was insular, a tiny social world unto itself. Once Tina started flashing her underwear and flaunting her underworld sugar daddies on the New York club scene, it was only a matter of time before the bad press went national.

Honor was flying out to the Hamptons herself next week, and when she did she wanted Tina to be as far away as possible. For the last month she'd been holed up with the accountants in Boston, poring over Palmers' depressing P and L and trying to figure out a plan of action. But the time had come to see the hotel's problems for herself. She was dreading it.

"Fine," she said, waving at the waiter for the check, although she hadn't touched her own food. "You win. I'll sign off on forty-five thousand."

"Good." Tina positively beamed with triumph.

"But I want you on a plane to LA by the end of the week. And the very first whisper I hear about you and that slimeball Carlucci…" Pushing back her chair, she got to her feet. "The money stops like *that*." She snapped her fingers for emphasis. "Are we clear?"

"Sure," said Tina. Having gotten what she wanted, she was more than willing to be accommodating. "I'll get the check here, don't worry. And hey, good luck with the hotel next week, OK?"

"I don't need luck, Tina," said Honor drily. "At this point I need a miracle."

Slipping on her sunglasses, she strode out of the restaurant.

———————   ———————

Sitting in the back of a blacked-out limo five days later, Honor tried again to focus on the papers in front of her. On the top was a spreadsheet of all the Palmers staff and their monthly wages. Normally she was brilliant with figures, but today for some reason the numbers swirled around her head like the pink elephants in *Dumbo*, and she couldn't concentrate.

Giving up, she gazed out the window instead. They were almost at Southampton now, and she could still feel a faint echo of her childhood excitement as the familiar landmarks rolled past: The Boxfarm Inn; the roadside cherry stall that had been there since Honor was a tiny kid and looked completely unchanged; the hollow tree where she and Tina used to play hide-and-seek.

Honor hadn't been back here in almost seven years, not since she first started college, and already she was regretting her long absence. Despite everything, the Hamptons still felt like home.

Not that today was likely to be much of a homecoming. Though she feigned indifference, the spiteful whispers about her "conning" Trey out of Palmers and "stealing" her inheritance had left her deeply wounded and insecure about the reception she'd receive. She was also acutely aware that most of the industry shared her father's view that she was far too young and inexperienced to turn around the failing hotel. They'd written both her and Palmers off, and beneath all the spiky bravado, Honor worried herself sick that they might be right.

She'd deliberately decided to show up unexpected a day early so that Whit Hammond, Palmers' dilettante manager for the past decade, wouldn't have a chance to get too prepared. However bad things had gotten at the hotel, she needed to see the reality, not the edited, Sunday-best version.

As always when there was a confrontation looming, she'd been horribly stressed the night before. Twitching with nerves and frustration in her lonely king-size bed, she'd tried to masturbate but was so tightly wound she found she couldn't come. Thanks to her short hair and deliberately masculine dress sense, most people assumed she was either a lesbian or just not interested in sex. In fact her boyish look, like her punchy, aggressive personality, was only a disguise, armor she'd donned in her teens to protect her from her father's rejection and never quite learned how to take off. She yearned to be loved and desired, but sex was a game she simply didn't know how to play. The few lovers she'd had had all tended to be older men, fairly obvious father figures, but they never lasted for long. Her longest relationship, of eight months, had been with one of her professors at Harvard, a kind, bookish divorcée in his early fifties. Drawn by her fierce beauty and intelligence, he had done his best to coax her out of her shell as a lover, constantly assuring her of her beauty and gently offering his love. But Honor's insecurities were so huge—deep down she loathed the athletic boy's body she went to such lengths to maintain, and she had about as much sexual confidence as a pimply teenager on a first date—that in the end he, too, gave up.

Sexual frustration added to the tension that snaked its way around her heart now, in the back of the limo, at the prospect of returning to Palmers. She was coming back not just as Trey's daughter and Tertius's granddaughter, but as the boss. It was a strange and, at times, terrifying feeling.

Thankfully, by the time the car swung into the grand graveled forecourt, she'd pulled herself together sufficiently to make a suitably confident entrance. The hotel's timeless, half-timbered elegance was just as she remembered it. Originally built as a wealthy merchant's summer home in the late eighteenth century, Palmers had always exuded a sort of genteel restfulness, with its wraparound wooden porches and forests of trailing wisteria clinging to the ancient walls like barnacles. Most of the older homes in East Hampton were made of gray, weathered wood. But Palmers stood resplendently white, a single iridescent flake of snow amid the verdant green of her gardens.

To Honor, that pristine whiteness had always been a large part of the hotel's magic. But today she could see that the paint was not only fading but actually peeling away in places. Even worse, nickel-sized pieces of facade had begun breaking off in chunks and had been left lying scattered on the steps and front lawn like giant crumbs from a wedding cake. As for the gardens themselves, Tertius would be spinning in his grave to see how overgrown and neglected they'd become, with dead leaves blowing everywhere and weeds left to multiply unfettered amid his beloved English rose garden.

The place was a disgrace.

Striding grimly up the steps into the lobby, Honor threw the receptionist into a spin by demanding that the manager appear immediately.

"I'm afraid Mr. Hammond is, er, unavailable just now, Miss Palmer," stammered the hapless girl. "We weren't expecting you until tomorrow."

"So I see," said Honor, snapping the dead head off one of the wilted roses in the vase by the door and staring pointedly at the overflowing wastepaper basket in the corner of the lobby. "Where is he?"

"Well, I..." The girl trailed off, blushing the color of an overripe beet. If she looked any more awkward she'd probably burst into flames. "I'm not a hundred percent sure he'd want me to say."

Honor's lips tightened. Resting both hands on the desk, she leaned forward ominously. "What's your name?"

The girl swallowed. She was older than Honor and a good foot taller, but she didn't think she'd ever felt quite so intimidated in her life. It was the deep, gravelly voice that did it.

"Betty," she mumbled. "Betty Miller."

"OK, Betty," said Honor. "I'm going to ask you one more time. And either you tell me where Mr. Hammond is, or I fire you. Do you understand?"

The girl nodded miserably.

"So." Removing her sunglasses, Honor smiled patiently. "Where is he?"

"He's at the golf club," whispered Betty. "He's been there all morning."

Guests who heard the screams and yells coming out of the manager's office a few hours later were sure that some of them must have warranted a reading on the Richter scale.

"But, Miss Palmer, you're being completely unreasonable!" Whit Hammond could be heard shouting himself hoarse. "I was entertaining guests. That's a legitimate part of my job. Perhaps if you knew a little more about the hotel business, or were willing to listen to wiser heads—"

But Honor hadn't let him get any further.

"Don't patronize me, you lazy son of a bitch," she roared. "I know enough about the hotel business to realize you've been ripping my family off for the last God knows how many years." Leaning across the desk—this morning it had been his desk, but now it was most definitely hers—she brandished the rolled-up spreadsheets like a sword.

"Those numbers don't tell the whole story," he spluttered lamely. "It's a lot more complicated than that."

Honor felt her upper lip curling with disdain. Whit personified everything that was wrong with Palmers: overweight, stubbornly complacent, his florid cheeks crisscrossed with broken veins that spoke of a lifestyle of high living and neglecting his duties.

"You're right," she said. "The numbers are only half the story. The other half is shoddy housekeeping, poorly trained staff, a kitchen that would have us closed down in a heartbeat if anyone from Safety and Health saw it. This was the greatest hotel in America once, Mr. Hammond."

"With respect, my dear," he simpered, "that was a long time ago. Things have moved on."

"Yeah," said Honor. "They have. And now they're moving on again. You no longer have a job here. And I am *not* your *dear*."

The decibel level had shot up still further at this point, with plenty of *you can't do this*es and *you'll be hearing from my lawyer*s thrown in for good measure. But within an hour the manager who only yesterday had been considered part of the furniture at Palmers, with a job for life, had packed his things into a couple of boxes and driven out of town like a spluttering, paunchy Jesse James.

By the end of the day, some twenty-five other staff had followed in his wake, fired with equal firmness and finality by a righteously indignant Honor. And there would be more to come. The era of the freeloader was well and truly over at Palmers, and anyone who didn't like it could lump it.

It was after eight in the evening by the time Honor finally emerged from Whit's ex-office. She was exhausted—she hadn't even had a chance to take her case up to her suite and unpack, never mind eat or take a shower. Right now, though, the number one thing she needed was a drink. Heading for the hotel bar through the lobby and the library with its roaring open fires and thickly comforting red velvet upholstery, she couldn't help but notice the way that staff scurried out of her way like terrified rats. Even the guests looked distinctly ill at ease. By the time she clambered up onto a bar stool and ordered her Scotch on the rocks she was starting to feel about as popular as Lady Macbeth.

"Tell me," she turned to the middle-aged man sitting next to her, "can you see the blood on my hands? Or am I imagining things?"

"I'm sorry?" He looked perplexed, and she instantly regretted being so obtuse. Partly because he was probably a guest and the last thing she could afford to do right now was alienate another paying customer, and partly because he was, she now realized, distinctly attractive, in a gravelly, distinguished, older-man sort of a way.

He was wearing a slightly threadbare tweed jacket and corduroy pants, giving him the air of a somewhat countrified Cary Grant. Until Honor had accosted him, he'd been reading Stephen Hawking's *A Brief History of Time*, which for some reason she found both surprising and endearing. Somehow it wasn't what you expected in East Hampton, or at least not in the Palmers' bar.

"Never mind," she said. "I'm afraid I'm talking gibberish. It's been a long day."

"Well." Putting his book to one side, the man smiled, revealing a row of slightly crooked teeth. Even those seemed to suit him. Perfect dentistry would have clashed with the whole academic Indiana Jones vibe he had going on. He reminded her a bit of her Harvard professor, although perhaps not quite as gentle.

"Why don't you let me buy you that drink, and you can tell me about it."

Honor waved her hand in protest, but he wasn't having any of it.

"A woman shouldn't drink alone," he insisted. "Especially not whiskey."

In another place, with another man, Honor would have taken umbrage at this sort of sexist pronouncement. As it was, she merely smiled and offered him her hand. She hadn't the stomach for another battle this evening. "Well, in that case, I'll accept the offer, thank you," she said. "I'm Honor Palmer."

For some reason this nugget of information seemed to throw him off stride. For a moment he didn't say anything at all. When he did speak again, it was hardly the most articulate of responses. "Honor Palmer. Good God." He kept shaking his head, mumbling to himself like a lunatic. "Honor Palmer. After all these years."

"Er, have we met?" Now it was Honor's turn to look baffled. Just her luck that the only attractive man in the hotel should be a nut job. It was turning out to be that kind of day.

"We have, yes," said the man. He was smiling again now. "But I don't expect you to remember. You must have been, oh, about eight at the time. Sitting on your mother's knee in the garden just out there. I'm Devon Carter," he added belatedly.

Carter. Honor turned the word over and over in her mind, like an interesting pebble, searching for some clue to its meaning. Devon Carter. It did ring a bell. But she couldn't quite place it.

"My family's from Boston too, originally," he explained. "We've been coming out here in the summers for over a century, just like the Palmers—although sadly we never did quite as well in the Hamptons as your family. My father and your grandfather were good friends."

Honor snapped her fingers. "Evelyn. Your dad was Evelyn Carter, right?"

Devon nodded. "Exactly. Apparently our great-grandfathers used to play poker together back in Boston. My dad used to say that old man Palmer died owing his grandpa a fortune. But maybe that's apocryphal."

Honor laughed. "Well, if you've come looking for your money, Mr. Carter, I'm afraid you've come to the wrong place. Between my sister and this place," she looked around her at the distinctly down-at-heel, half-empty bar, "I'm pretty much cleaned out right now."

"It's Devon," he said, looking her directly in the eye in a way she found both flattering and disconcerting. "And it isn't your money that interests me, Honor."

Honor blushed. He was flirting with her! Men never flirted with her. At long last she felt herself letting go of some of her pent-up tension and starting to relax. It was nice. He was nice. At least, he seemed to be.

"Are you propositioning me?" she asked bluntly. She never had learned how to do the coy, eyelash-fluttering thing.

Devon grinned. He was looking less teacher and more naughty schoolboy by the second. "If I am, then I'm afraid I shouldn't be," he said. "I'm probably old enough to be your father. And besides," he stared deeply into the amber liquid in his own glass, "I'm married." Honor couldn't help but notice that he said this last with all the enthusiasm of a man admitting to advanced-stage syphilis.

"You don't sound too happy about it," she observed.

Devon shrugged. "It is what it is."

It was as if she'd inadvertently popped a balloon. All at once his mood had shifted from playful to serious. The next thing she knew he was looking at his watch and gathering up his coat, preparing to leave.

"Please, don't leave on my account," she blurted, unable to keep the disappointment out of her voice. "I was only kidding about the proposition thing."

"Look, sorry," he said, pulling out a twenty-dollar bill and leaving it on the bar beside the pretzels. "It's not you. I have to get home, that's all. But it was a pleasure meeting you again, Honor. Really. Maybe next time you're in town we can catch up properly."

"I'd like that," she said. "Actually, I'll be staying in town for a while, if you—"

But he'd already gone, hurtling out the door like he had a fire to get to.

She seemed to be having this effect on people a lot today.

"What do you know about that guy?" she asked Enrique, the barman, after he'd gone.

Now in his sixties, Enrique had been running the bar at Palmers since before Honor was born. As one of the few staff who knew for sure his job was safe, he was more than happy to stop and chew the fat with her.

"Devon Carter? He's Mr. East Hampton," he said, "or at least, he is for the summers. Comes out here every year with his family, sometimes for Easter too. He's on the planning committee, secretary of the Golf Club, part-time deacon over at St. Mark's…"

"Jeez, OK, OK," said Honor, frowning. "I get the picture. He's Ned Flanders."

"Not quite so God Squad," chuckled Enrique, surprising Honor by getting the *Simpsons* reference. Somehow he didn't seem the type. "But he's big on family values, yeah. Definitely not for you, my dear."

"For me? Oh, don't be so silly," said Honor, blushing again. "Although, for what it's worth, I'll have you know I'm *huge* on family values. And I bet you my family's *much* more valuable than Devon—deacon-of-St.-Mark's—Carter's."

Enrique smiled and poured her another drink.

"It's good to have you back, Miss Palmer."

"Thanks," said Honor with a sigh. "But I'm afraid you're the only person around here who thinks so."

CHAPTER FOUR

*L*UCAS TRIED TO TUNE OUT THE DRUNKEN RAMBLINGS OF the stinking tramp sitting next to him on the tube as he reread the article in yesterday's *Evening Standard*.

"What saddens me most," says bubbly Heidi, her eyes brimming with tears, "is that Carina's the innocent victim here. She's a four-year-old child that desperately needs help. How can her own father let her down like this?"

The paper had devoted two full pages to the interview and pictures of "bubbly Heidi," explaining that she was now a trainee nursery school teacher—although looking at her brassy hair and short black skirt it came as no surprise to Lucas to learn that her previous occupation was "exotic dancer." It was in this incarnation that she'd met and become involved with the millionaire hotelier and hedge fund guru, Anton Tisch. The same Anton Tisch whose office Lucas was currently on his way to, for the third time in as many days.

"He makes himself out to be this kind, charitable man, like some sort of saint," Heidi goes on damningly, "yet he won't even provide basic medical care for his own kid. It's disgusting."

If the story was accurate, Lucas was inclined to agree. Apparently, having fathered a daughter by this cretinous-looking young woman, Tisch had only agreed to pay basic maintenance for the child when forced to do so by court order. This, despite having, conservatively, nine hundred million–odd dollars in the bank. Like so many of the Eastern European and Russian superrich who'd washed up in London in recent years, the original source of Tisch's vast wealth remained an open question. Certainly he was known to have close links with Ilham Aliyev, president of Azerbaijan and ultimate controller of the Baku-Ceyhan pipeline responsible for piping a million gallons of oil a day into Western markets. Though no longer in the energy business—his passport described him as a fund manager and investor—Tisch's money still reeked of Caspian crude.

When doctors had diagnosed his illegitimate daughter with severe autism a year ago, Heidi had gone back to her erstwhile lover asking for more money to pay for a nurse and to help fund a place for the little girl at a special school. But Tisch had told her to take a running jump. Unable to raise the legal fees to fight him a second time, Heidi had sold her story to the tabloids instead.

Of course, it might not be true. To be honest, Lucas wanted to believe it wasn't; not least because it was depressing to learn that the man he hoped would soon be his employer was tighter than a mosquito's asshole and had about as much compassion as a Nazi concentration camp commandant. But something about bubbly Heidi's face told him she was telling the truth. She might be a tart, but she didn't look like a liar.

"Embankment. This is Embankment." The oddly soothing automated woman's voice rang out through the speakers. "Next stop, Westminster. Change here for Charing Cross and other mainline stations."

Only one more stop, thank God. There were lots of things Lucas hated about London: the weather, the prices, the way strangers kept calling him "mate." But he reserved an especially vehement dislike for the filthy, overcrowded underground system. Normally he'd have walked the four-odd miles from the Cadogan, where he was staying, to Tisch's office overlooking the

Thames. But despite the fact that it was August, the rain today was torrential, and he couldn't afford to show up looking like a drowned rat.

He'd been to London before, to visit Ben, but never for more than a few days, and he'd spent most of those trips too drunk to know his left from his right, never mind what city he was in. But having lived here now for nearly two months, he was having serious second thoughts. Why couldn't he have set his heart on a job somewhere warm and civilized, like Madrid or Rome? With his languages and starred MBA, he could have gone just about anywhere in Western Europe. Did he really have to pick this grayest, wettest, most astronomically expensive of cities and surround himself with a nation of people he had long ago learned to loathe?

Unfortunately, the answer to that was yes. Lucas had made a decision years ago never to aim for anything less than the best. And in the world of luxury boutique hotels, the Tischen Cadogan was the best. No question.

Two weeks ago he'd moved out of the squalid apartment he'd been renting in Tooting and checked himself in to the Cadogan. His room was the cheapest the hotel had to offer and was little more than five hundred square feet, but it had still cost him every penny of his remaining savings. Literally every penny. As of tomorrow morning, he had no idea how he was going to eat.

Still, it had been worth it. In the past two weeks he'd gotten to know the hotel's inner workings every bit as intimately as Julia Brett-Sadler, the Cadogan's bossy, schoolmarmish manager. He knew about the morale problems in the kitchen and the Michelin-starred, megalomaniac chef who made his staff's lives hell. He knew about the barman who regularly slipped free drinks to girls he was sleeping with. He knew about the maître d's two-hundred-pounds-a-day coke habit.

If he was going to have any kind of a shot with Anton Tisch—a guy who wouldn't even give his own kid a break, apparently—Lucas knew he would have to be more informed and more impressive than everybody else. Of course, he first had to swing himself an appointment with the guy, something that so far was proving depressingly difficult.

Battling his way through the commuters at Westminster station, he finally emerged into the drizzle of the street. Storm clouds hung low in the sky like a thick, heavy blanket, blocking out so much light that it almost felt like night. Not even the gold-faced splendor of Big Ben or the intricately carved towers of the Palace of Westminster could lift the atmosphere of dreary depression lingering in the air. Clicking open his umbrella with a curse, Lucas made his way along the now-familiar route by the river, toward the Adelphi building where the Tischen Corporation had its offices.

"You 'ere again, mate?" The doorman seemed less than thrilled to see him. "Don't give up easy, do you?"

"No," said Lucas, pushing past him into the lobby. "I don't. I'm here to see Mr. Tisch." He smiled firmly at the Asian girl at the reception desk, who glowered back at him.

"Do you have an appointment?" she asked wearily. It was the third time she'd been through this charade this week, and the novelty was wearing thin.

"Yes," lied Lucas. "He's expecting me."

The girl gave him a look that made it clear she knew he was bullshitting, but that at this point she really didn't care.

"Sixteenth floor," she sighed, handing him a visitor's pass. "Once you're up there, you're Rita's problem."

Luckily for Lucas, Rita was much more amenable to his particular blend of Latin charm than the Thai harridan downstairs. Somewhere in the no-man's-land between middle-aged and elderly, her sensible tweed suit and Miss Moneypenny manner hid a mischievous streak that Lucas was quick to pick up on. He guessed it had been a long time since any good-looking young man had bothered to flirt with Rita. And it seemed he was right.

No sooner had he started to banter with her than the floodgates opened.

"Darling." Striding over to her desk, grinning from ear to ear, he kissed her hand while she laughingly attempted to get rid of another caller.

"Mr. Ruiz!" Switching off her headset, she pulled her hand away and tried to look stern.

"I know what you're going to say," said Lucas. "We must stop meeting like this. People are going to start talking. But you know, all you have to do is let me see him. Just for five minutes. Then I'll be out of your hair forever."

"I've told you," said the secretary, blushing like a giddy schoolgirl, "it really isn't up to me. Mr. Tisch's diary is booked up months in advance. I can't just squeeze people in willy-nilly. However charming they might be. I'd lose my job."

"Ah, lovely Rita, surely not?" said Lucas. He'd perched on the corner of her desk now, close enough for her to smell his cologne. Really, he could be most distracting when he wanted to…"No man in his right mind would let you go. Won't you at least let him know I'm here?"

"Well…" she said, her resolve already crumbling. "All right. I'll buzz him. But I can tell you right now, he won't see you. He's having rather a bad day, I'm afraid."

This turned out to be an understatement.

Inside his office, Anton reached for his open bottle of antacids and slipped another revolting, chalky pill into his mouth.

"No, I will not *calm down*, Roger," he yelled into the phone. "She's crucifying me. And that cunt of an editor's giving her a free pass to do it! There's more on the story in tomorrow's paper, apparently. When I think of how much fucking money I gave to their bloody Help a London Child appeal last year.

I mean, where's the fucking loyalty, Roger, huh? Answer me that!"

Anton Tisch was one of life's winners. Having cleaned up in Azerbaijan in the midnineties, he'd gotten out of the oil business while the getting was still good, before he found himself poisoned or shot or shipped off to Siberia like so many of the Russians who'd gotten greedy and kept their fat fingers in the pie for too long. Diversifying into other industries, he had reinvented himself as a legitimate businessman. His hedge fund, Excelsior, was now one of the largest and most profitable in Europe. His media empire stretched from Delhi to Vladivostok and incorporated everything from online search engines to cable TV stations. And his hotel chain—the mighty Tischens—was among the most prestigious and well respected in a notoriously cutthroat and fickle business.

Dividing his time between his home in Mayfair—he'd had three exquisite Georgian mansions knocked together to create one of the largest privately owned residences in London—and his estate on the banks of Lake Geneva, Anton surrounded himself with every luxury that money could buy.

Of course, as for so many of the world's wealthiest men, it was the things money *couldn't* buy that kept him awake at night. Having grown up poor in an obscure village in rural East Germany, what Tisch craved more than anything was social acceptance among the English upper classes—to become part of the famously amorphous British Establishment. But like so many wealthy foreigners before him, he was discovering the hard way that in England there were numerous doors that money alone could not unlock. Abramovich had won over the masses as Mr. Chelski when he bought and poured money into Chelsea football club. But Anton wasn't interested in being liked by lager louts and yobs. His social sights were set much higher.

His strategy—pouring funds very publicly into civic institutions and high-profile charities—was a good one. He wanted people to see him as a modern-day Carnegie: generous, philanthropic, paternalistic; in short, everything that the English aristocracy considered themselves, however misguidedly, to be. Eventually, the plan was for his good works to earn him a knighthood, the social equivalent of an access-all-areas backstage pass.

Only last month, his sources at Whitehall had been reassuring him that he was well on the way to achieving his coveted K. But that was before Heidi.

She wasn't the first girl to go to the papers with a story shredding his hard-earned reputation. A few years ago another ex, a journalist, had written a piece about Anton's sadomasochistic bedroom practices that had sent his social ambitions slithering back down the chute to square one.

He ought to have learned his lesson then. But even knowing the dangers he faced at the hands of the notoriously xenophobic British press—German-bashing still sold papers in England—his pathological dislike of women made it almost impossible for him to treat his lovers with the decency or generosity that might have kept them quiet. To Anton Tisch, women were possessions to be used and discarded. Any children he might accidentally have fathered along the way he viewed not so much as people but as collateral damage.

"You know what I was doing last night, Roger?" he bellowed at his British lawyer, pacing like a cat between his desk and the floor-to-ceiling window overlooking the river. "Cutting the ribbon on a brand-new fucking dialysis machine at Great Ormond Street, that's what. But do they report on that? Do they? Fuck no! They'd rather help that slut tell the world that I don't like children. It's libel, that's what it is. And she's not getting away with it."

Slamming the phone down petulantly, he sat back down at his desk. The fact was he'd lose if he tried to sue the paper or the girl, and he knew it. The picture Heidi painted might be one-sided, but it wasn't untrue. And even if it had been, dragging the thing out would only cause more damage to his good name. There really was nothing else to do but pay her off, and that was what was really driving him crazy: the thought that she was going to get the money she wanted after all. That she'd beaten him. She'd won.

Too restless and irritated to make another call, he idly picked up the piece of paper on the top of his in-tray. It was the CV for a man named Brent Dalgliesh, the candidate he'd decided to hire yesterday as deputy manager at the Cadogan.

With so many businesses under his control, a large part of Anton's time was taken up with delegation. The only areas he still focused on personally were his hedge fund, where he still made all the investment decisions himself, and his hotels.

Anton loved the hotel business every bit as passionately as Abramovich loved his football or Richard Branson his planes. In interviews, he often described the Tischens as his children, but few people realized quite how literally he meant it. His strategy had been simple and consistent from day one: he deliberately picked out locations with a dominant hotel already in place—Reid's in Madeira, the Post Ranch in Big Sur, Raffles in Singapore—and challenged them right on their doorsteps. Always the last word in decadence and hip, Tischen hotels set out to make the old giants look like what they were: tired behemoths, long past their sell-by dates.

The plan worked, time after time, but nowhere had he pulled it off with such spectacular success as in London, with the Cadogan. A stone's throw from both the Lanesborough and the Dorchester, Anton's gentleman's club–style hotel had outearned both of those giants in only its second year. As one journalist had put it in a piece that Anton had blown up, framed, and hung on his office wall: "With the Cadogan, the brilliant Mr. Tisch has out-Englished the English. A triumph of good taste."

Looking at Brent's CV again now, Anton felt his irritation mounting. It was a stupid name, for one thing. Made him so und like a shopping center, or a service station on the M. As for the litany of achievements that had so impressed him yesterday—a first-class degree from the LSE, seven years at the Georges V in Paris, the Young Hotelier of the Year Award—suddenly they all seemed cloyingly earnest and worthy. What kind of a resume-conscious suck-up became president of the student union, for God's sake?

It was at that moment that Rita buzzed his intercom.

"I'm sorry to disturb you, Mr. Tisch," she said meekly. "But there's a Mr. Lucas Ruiz here to see you. Again."

Anton was about to snap at her that "do not disturb" meant exactly that, when something made him think twice. This kid had been showing up like clockwork day after day, asking about the Cadogan job. He was fresh out of college and consequently ludicrously underqualified. But he'd refused to take no for an answer, a trait that Anton greatly admired. He was also, according to the CV he'd insisted on leaving with Rita, quite brilliant academically.

Fuck it. He couldn't focus on work anyway, not with this Heidi shit hanging over his head. What harm would it do to see the boy?

"OK, Rita," he said, ripping Brent's details into four neat pieces and dropping them into the trash can under the desk. "Show him in."

If Lucas was surprised to have been granted an audience, he didn't show it. Instead he burst into Anton's office, pushing his long hair out of his eyes and smiling, radiating confidence like a stadium floodlight.

"How do you do, Mr. Tisch?" he said, thrusting out his hand in greeting. "Thank you for seeing me." He was a good-looking boy and came across as much older and more self-assured than the twenty-four-year-old he claimed to be. Still, he hardly looked like a senior executive. Despite the suit and tie, there was a certain rock-star rebelliousness about him that was screaming to be let out. What with that and the flowing hair, he looked more like a drug dealer than a hotelier.

"I'm really not sure why I *am* seeing you," said Anton, honestly. Lucas scoured his face for clues as to his mood or character, anything he could use. But the great man was eerily expressionless, and much more waxy-faced than he appeared in pictures. Having never seen Botox on a man before, Lucas made a mental note never, ever to try it. Tisch reminded him of the dead Lenin—only perhaps not quite so warm and cuddly. He was tall, with obviously dyed chestnut-brown hair plastered to his head as though stuck on with glue, and was wearing what appeared to be some sort of naval uniform, a white jacket with blue stripes down the arms. Clearly he considered himself to be something of a snazzy dresser, but the overall effect was too Michael Jackson for Lucas's taste. He half expected to see fingerless leather gloves emerge from the military sleeves or a black armband whipped out of the drawer.

"The position at the Cadogan is far beyond your experience and capabilities," Anton went on. "It's a world-class hotel. What on earth makes you think I'd hand any part of it over to an amateur?"

Lucas took a deep breath. "With respect, sir, I think you already have. Julia Brett-Sadler couldn't run her own bath."

Tisch raised an eyebrow and suppressed a smile. The boy was cocky as hell. But he liked that about him.

"All right, Lucas," he said. "You've got my attention. Let's hear what you have to say."

And so Lucas told him. Calmly, dispassionately, he listed every problem, every failure he'd witnessed at the Cadogan in his the last two weeks there as a guest. For each one he put forward his own solution, explaining concisely but meticulously just how he would do a better job than the current manager. When he'd finished, he sat back in his chair, cracked his knuckles with confident finality, and waited for Anton's response.

When it came, it was not at all what he expected.

"Do you have a problem with women, Mr. Ruiz?" Tisch's tone was as casual, as if he were inquiring about the weather or the football results. Lucas looked surprised. "Not at all. I love women," he said truthfully. "But do I think they're better in the bedroom than the boardroom? Yes, sir, I do."

Anton was warming to this kid more by the minute.

"You realize that's the sort of statement that can get you into a lot of hot water these days," he said, without anger. "There's no sexual discrimination in my hotels. In fact, the Tischens have a higher proportion of women in management positions than any other major chain."

This was true. One of Anton's most successful weapons in countering the sexism claims made by ex-lovers was his excellent reputation as an equal-opportunity employer. He'd learned long ago that it paid to have prominent, educated women on hand whose job it was to make him sound decent and honorable.

Lucas shrugged. "I wouldn't have a problem working for Julia if she were doing her job properly. Or if I didn't know I could do it better. But she isn't. And I could."

Anton got to his feet. As a rule, he wasn't a man to make rash decisions. But every once in a while, he liked to act on instinct. And his instincts about the Ruiz boy were all good.

"I've heard what you said today, and I take those criticisms seriously, believe me," he said. "Nevertheless, Miss Brett-Sadler has done wonderful things with that hotel in the past two years. Things that you have yet to achieve, Mr. Ruiz. It would take a lot more than some internal politics to convince me to replace her."

Lucas looked crestfallen.

"However," Anton continued, "the undermanager position is still open. And I'll admit, I'm tempted to give you a shot at it, if only to put your spectacular arrogance to the test."

For once, Lucas was speechless. In fact, he was so frightened of jinxing things he could barely breathe. Still as a statue, he prayed for Anton to go on.

"Fuck it," said Anton, cracking a smile for the first time that day. "You're hired. I'm putting you on a three-month probation period. But if I'm not happy with your work, I'll have you out of there in three minutes, believe me. Got that?"

"Absolutely," said Lucas, springing to his feet. All he wanted now was to get the hell out of there before Tisch changed his mind. "You won't regret this, sir. I promise."

"I'd better not," said Anton. "Because if I do, Mr. Ruiz, it'll be you who suffers, not me."

Despite the implied threat, Anton had a good feeling about Lucas, which only intensified once the boy had left his office, so happy he was practically skipping to the elevator. Julia *had* been getting a bit complacent over at the Cadogan. It was about time he shook her up a bit.

He had a feeling that appointing Lucas Ruiz to be her number two might put the cat among the pigeons most satisfactorily. He may not be able to teach Heidi a lesson—yet—but Julia was about to learn that it paid never to rest on your laurels when you worked for the great Anton Tisch.

CHAPTER FIVE

"Lola!" Karis Carter could feel her throat getting hoarse as she yelled up the stairs yet again for her daughter. "Lola, get down here *right now*. We need those cases. Mo's loading the car."

It was mid-September, and the Carters were finally, belatedly, leaving their summer home in the Hamptons and flying back to Boston. If Karis had had her way they'd have gone home at the end of August, like everybody else. East Hampton was like a ghost town in September, whereas in Boston the endless round of parties and charity "dos" that were the center of Karis's existence was just beginning again. It was the best month to be there, and she'd missed it. All because of stupid, selfish Devon.

It was hard to pinpoint exactly when Devon and Karis Carter had grown apart. Certainly they'd loved each other once, back when Karis's modeling career was still thriving and Devon was an up-and-coming young lawyer, as handsome as he was brilliant. But those days were a lifetime ago now. The intervening years had brought them two children—Nicholas, now nineteen and his mother's favorite, and sixteen-year-old Lola—as well as enough money from both inheritance and Devon's work to pay for two multimillion-dollar homes and the lifestyle to go with them. But in other ways they'd been less kind. Though still a handsome woman, Karis's youthful beauty had faded to a pale shadow of what it had once been. Having built not only her career but her self-esteem around her looks, aging took a terrible toll, not just on her but on her marriage. Insecure and pathologically demanding of attention, she pushed Devon's patience, not to mention his credit cards, to the limit.

Karis wasn't the only guilty party, however. As the years passed, familiarity with his wife seemed to breed contempt in Devon. He made no attempt to feign interest in her life and was little better with his children, focusing instead on work and the numerous social committees that earned him his reputation as a pillar of the community in both Boston and East Hampton. Though he pretended to find these extracurricular commitments a burden, secretly Devon would rather die than lose the social prestige they brought him. Nevertheless, they were contributors to the disintegration of his marriage—or at least, the disintegration of every part of it that had once brought him joy. Even so, neither he nor Karis had ever seriously contemplated divorce. They both had too much to lose for that.

"Lola!" Karis was really starting to lose her temper now. It was bad enough that Devon had spent the last four weeks coming up with one excuse after another to keep them in East Hampton. Not just bad, but odd. Normally he was the first to want to get back to Boston. And now Lola was doing all she could to ensure they missed the plane, all because she had a bee in her bonnet about going back to St. Mary's

"Jeez, Mom. I'm coming!" came the exasperated cry from upstairs. Standing in the middle of her bedroom, surrounded by a sea of open suitcases stuffed beyond bursting with clothes, paintbrushes, magazines, and all the other detritus from a long teenage summer, Lola Carter was in an even worse mood than her mother. Dressed head to toe in black—going back to St. Mary's felt like her own funeral, so why not?—she looked every inch the archetypal sullen teen: skirt so short you could see her underwear when she bent down, ripped pantyhose, thick black Suzi Quatro eye makeup, and a silver skull-and-crossbones pendant the size of a fist swinging ominously against her chest. But not even the Morticia Addams getup could conceal her striking beauty. With her thick, russet-red hair that flowed down her back like a river of molten copper, her long, slender legs, and peaches-and-cream complexion, Lola looked like a taller, more willowy version of Lindsay Lohan. She'd been approached by scouts for model agencies more times than she could count. But (to her mother's private relief) the last thing Lola Carter was interested in was modeling. Her dream, what she longed for more than anything, was to be a fashion designer. And she'd do it too, one day. Whether her fucking father liked it or not.

"Whoa." Nicholas, her elder brother and the bane of Lola's existence, stuck his head around the door. Like his sister, he was a great-looking kid, all dark hair and smoldering blue gray eyes. Unlike her, he was also a card-carrying asshole.

Taking one look at Lola's nowhere-near-packed luggage and the chaos strewn around her Gothic-themed bedroom, he smiled nastily.

"You are so dead when Mom sees this. The flight leaves in, like, two hours."

"So?" said Lola, sitting down on the largest of her four bags in a hopeless attempt to get it to close. "I'll miss the flight, then. Big whoop. It's not like I actually care about going back."

"You know they're gonna send you back to St. Mary's whatever you do, right?" said Nicholas, idly picking up a comb from his sister's dressing table and running it through his thick black hair. "It's not like anywhere else will have you. And Dad'll drop dead before he lets you drop out."

This, unfortunately, was true. Having been expelled from every other decent private school in Boston, St. Mary's Academy for Girls had been Devon and Karis's last hope for their wayward daughter. A generous donation to the new science building had helped the nuns to see past Lola's "authority issues." It had also ensured that they steered her away from the art programs she was desperate to enroll in, toward the more academic subjects that her father had his heart set on. As far as Devon was concerned, Lola's future was a place at Harvard Law and that was that. He didn't want to hear any more bullshit about goddamn fashion school.

"Don't you have some place to be?" Lola asked her brother wearily. "Like downstairs blowing smoke up Mom's ass?"

"Very funny," he sneered, "but no." There were few things Nicholas enjoyed more than watching his little sister fuck up. Sometimes his job as her self-appointed tormentor was just too easy. "Unlike you, I don't have to go to college. I've already made a success of my life."

"A success? Really? How do you figure that?" said Lola scathingly. "So far, steamingpileofBS.com, or whatever it is you call it, hasn't earned you a red cent. Aw, *shit!*" With one last almighty tug, the zipper on her case finally pulled shut, only for the straining fabric to rip open immediately afterward like a burst artery.

"My God, Lola, how many times do I have to spell it out for you?" said Nicholas, annoyed. He didn't appreciate having his business acumen questioned, especially not by his little sister. "That's the new business model. It doesn't matter whether or not Enigma turns a profit in its first few years. This is the Internet. It's all about volume."

As founder and CEO of an inventions website he'd christened Enigma, Nicholas Carter saw himself as the next Steve Jobs. The fact that at almost twenty he still lived at home and that his playboy lifestyle was funded 100 percent by his besotted mother did nothing to dampen his self-belief. Or insufferable arrogance, depending on how you looked at it. "Speaking of volume..." Pushing the bedroom door open a little wider, he made a great show of cupping his hand to his ear. Devon was thundering up the stairs like a bull elephant on the charge. Seconds later he burst into the room, so mad they could practically see the steam coming out of his ears.

"What is your *problem*?" he yelled at his daughter. "You knew what time we had to leave today."

"Yeah," Lola shot back. "And *you* knew how much stuff I had to pack. What's the big deal, anyway? You guys go, and I'll catch the first flight out in the morning. I *am* almost seventeen you know, Dad. I am capable."

"Capable?" Her father gave a short, derisive laugh. "Do you think I was born yesterday? You've already missed two weeks of this semester. You aren't missing another one."

And whose fault was that? thought Lola bitterly. *You've been the one refusing to leave East Hampton on pain of death for, like, a month.*

"You're getting on that flight, young lady," said Devon, "with or without your clothes, if I have to drag you on myself. You have two minutes. Two! And I don't know what you're looking so damned smug about." He turned on Nicholas, who had been smirking quietly in the corner, enjoying the show, but who now looked distinctly put out to be included in his father's fury. "You should be downstairs helping your mother."

Elbowing past his son before he had a chance to defend himself, Devon stormed into his own bedroom and slammed the door.

He shouldn't be yelling at Nick. If anyone ought to be downstairs helping to load the car, it was him. And he shouldn't be hiding out in here, either. But he was so goddamn stressed right now, if he didn't take a time-out he was in serious danger of hitting somebody.

Devon didn't think he'd felt this bad, or this helpless, since he was a little boy and his mother had packed him off to summer camp despite his pleadings to be allowed to stay at home. He remembered pressing his face to the window of the train as it pulled away, his tears making two grimy rivers down the glass as he watched the platform and his mother's face slip into the distance and out of sight.

It was exactly the way he felt now, leaving Honor.

He was being ridiculous, of course. What the hell was he, sixteen? He'd only known the girl for a month or so, and their affair could still be counted in days. Plus he had work in Boston, commitments, a life. A big life, as it happened. So why did going back there make him feel like someone had punched through his rib cage and ripped his heart out whole?

"I'll be in Boston myself in a month," Honor had reassured him last night, after their poignant good-bye lovemaking session. "We can hook up again then."

Devon had taken her out on his boat for the afternoon, ostensibly for a business meeting, so they could be assured of privacy. So far their rendezvous had all taken place at Palmers, in Honor's private suite of rooms on the top floor. But he couldn't help feeling nervous there, and he wanted today to be perfect.

"*Hook up?*" He looked at her, aghast. "God, Honor, is that all this is to you? Just sex?"

Wriggling out from under the white linen sheet, she sat up, pushing her spiky fringe out of her eyes. "Of course not," she said, horrified. "You know it's not. Don't twist what I say."

But the problem was he didn't know it, not really. He didn't know anything with her. Looking at her smudged makeup and angular, jutting features, at once so aggressive and yet so vulnerable, he found himself fighting down the urge to pull her back on top of him and fuck her yet again until he was sure she loved him back. Karis was an attractive, desirable woman. But never, not even in the full flush of her youthful beauty, had his wife had the effect on him that Honor did.

The girl was such a mess of contradictions. It had taken every ounce of his charm and negotiating skills to get her into bed in the first place. He'd had to lie through his teeth about the state of his marriage, insisting that he and Karis were "as good as separated" before she would so much as kiss him. Part of him was surprised that such an obviously intelligent, tough young woman would fall for a line like that—but she had, hook, line, and sinker, taking him at his word without any further probing. Beneath her carefully cultivated ball-breaker image— he'd seen the way that the staff at Palmers visibly quaked when Honor walked into the lobby—she was actually astonishingly naive and trusting, at least in romantic matters. She was also very inexperienced sexually. Their first night together was so dreadfully awkward that Devon started to wonder if he'd lost his touch or misread her attraction for him. But after a few days, something seemed to shift. Years of bottled-up loneliness and need and sexual frustration began pouring out of her like water breaking through a dam. All at once the clunked noses and fumbled gropings were replaced by a raw, unleashed sexual energy that utterly took his breath away. It was like making love to a generator.

The problem was that the moment sex was over, Honor would pull away from him completely, slipping back into tough-little-rich-girl mode. This left him feeling baffled and, if he was honest, more than a little rejected. She possessed a very masculine ability to compartmentalize her emotions and switch off at will, which drove him insane with frustration and insecurity. On the flip side, as much as he hated it, it was that same combination of sexual neediness and emotional independence, even detachment, that had him hooked, running back to her again and again for more punishment like some masochistic junkie.

"It's not easy for me either, you know," said Honor, mollifying his wounded pride a little, though not enough, as she scrambled back into her clothes. "You won't be living here again until next summer. That's a whole year away."

"Nine months," said Devon. "We'll be back in June. But you shouldn't think of it like that. We both have to focus on the next time we'll see each other."

"Exactly," said Honor, "which is only a few weeks away, right? I'd make it sooner if I could, but you know I can't leave Palmers right now. I'm just beginning to come to grips with the problems here."

"Fucking Palmers," Devon grumbled, reluctantly getting out of bed himself and looking around the cabin for his underwear. Sometimes it felt like she was the one who was married, rather than him. Married to that damn hotel of hers.

"Anyway," she went on, ignoring him. "You were the one going on about East Hampton gossip and how dangerous it is, us seeing so much of each other here. You've got your *reputation* to think of, remember?"

She couldn't entirely keep the resentment out of her voice, although perversely Devon found this small hint of jealousy on her part more of a comfort than an annoyance.

Besides, it was true. He had begun to feel nervous. Apart from a few reckless one-night stands years ago, he had never been unfaithful to Karis, and he was finding the uncharted waters of betrayal difficult to navigate. Though he'd only been seeing Honor for a couple of weeks, there was no doubt in his mind that the affair was more than just a summer fling, which made things a lot more problematic. Truth be told, he'd become a somewhat vocal advocate of family values as he'd gotten older, using his deaconship at church as a platform to air his views. The slightest whisper of his relationship with Honor would be catastrophic for his reputation, both here and in Boston. He might be feeling like a love-struck teenager, but he was old enough and wise enough to know that no one liked a hypocrite. And why should they? Right now he wasn't even sure he liked himself.

"Come here." Grabbing Honor's hand, he pulled her down onto his lap, burying his face in the hollow between her shoulder and neck and breathing in the scent of her. "I know it's hard," he whispered. "Believe me, I wish we could stay on this boat forever.

Keep on sailing to where no one could find us. But we're both adults, right? We both know life isn't like that."

Standing with his back against his bedroom door now, listening to the kids fighting and Karis barking at the chauffeur outside, he realized just how trite his words must have sounded. "Life isn't like that"? What the hell was he, a fucking fortune cookie?

Life was what you made it. And right now Devon was in grave danger of making a serious mess of his.

"Karis!" Opening the sash window, he stuck his head outside. Even in September the gardens looked beautiful, a riot of scented blossoms and color. The yew hedges had been clipped and shaped with military precision and the graveled driveway raked into a neatly furrowed semicircle, giving the place an air of peaceful, ordered calm. If only he could regulate his family life and feelings so effortlessly.

"Oh, Devon, there you are." Karis looked up at him, clearly irritated.

"I thought you were going to help Mo with the cases. He's almost finished now. Where's Lola?"

"She's nowhere near ready," he said. Then, making a decision on the spur of the moment, added: "Look, why don't you go ahead with Nicholas? I'll stay here, make sure Lola gets her act together, and we'll fly out first thing in the morning."

Even behind her oversize Gucci shades he could see his wife's fury building. Not that he blamed her for that. Lola's behavior these past few weeks had been getting worse and worse. Today's stunt with the packing was the last straw.

"I thought we'd agreed," she said wearily. "No more excuses. If she isn't ready, she'll have to come as she is."

"I know," said Devon. "But there are things she needs for school, honey. Trust me, Karis, I'm not gonna give her an easy ride. But it doesn't make sense for us all to have to wait around. What's one more day?"

In the end, too drained to fight about it anymore, Karis had given in. Ten minutes later the Daimler containing her, Nicholas, and a trunk full of Louis Vuitton pulled sedately out of the driveway. And Devon made a beeline back to his daughter's room.

The Led Zeppelin was deafening the moment he opened the door. Lola, nodding her head to the music, was sprawled across the bed, smoking a cigarette like she hadn't a care in the world.

"Looks like we're both still here," she drawled, flicking ash into a used coffee cup on the bedside table as he walked in. "Whatever happened to dragging me onto the plane yourself?"

"You can cut out the lip," said Devon firmly, unplugging the stereo from the wall despite Lola's protests and pulling the cigarette out of her hand. "I'm going out, and I won't be back till late. Either you finish your packing and clean up this pigsty"—he picked up the coffee cup, frowning at the cigarette butts bobbing around in it like flotsam on a muddy pond—"or I cut off your allowance till Christmas. Period."

"Whatever," said Lola, although inside her defiance was waning. St. Mary's was bad enough, but St. Mary's without an allowance would be hell on earth. "Where are you going, anyway?"

"None of your business," said Devon.

It was hard to tell which of them felt more relief when he finally left the house a few minutes later, slamming the front door behind him and zooming off in his new BMW convertible. But one thing was for sure: wherever he was headed, he was in one hell of a hurry.

Anton Tisch buttered another piece of toast, cutting it carefully into four pieces before offering one of them to the slavering Great Dane that sat obediently at his feet.

"There you are, my Mitzi," he cooed, bending his face so close to the dog's that their noses were almost touching. "Who's my good girl?"

For the last six years, Mitzi had been Anton's constant companion, traveling back and forth from London to Geneva and reigning supreme as the undisputed queen of both his homes and his heart. Most people found his doting affection for the huge, intimidating-looking animal incongruous, even creepy. This was a man, after all, who couldn't seem to muster a shred of human sympathy for his own children, never mind business associates or social "friends," whom he routinely discarded with all the dispassionate ruthlessness of an executioner. Yet with Mitzi he was as adoring and besotted as any lover.

"The second mail delivery is here, Mr. Tisch." A butler in full livery glided up to the table and set a neatly bound package down at his elbow. Anton made a point of keeping a full household staff in Mayfair—one must keep up appearances at all times—although in Geneva, where nobody cared how he'd made his fortune just as long as he had made it, he "made do" with only a cook, driver, and valet.

"Thank you, Gavin." Idly, he began leafing through the stack of letters. "That will be all."

Annoyingly, there didn't appear to be anything from his New York lawyer. He was waiting on some documents that were supposed to have arrived by FedEx yesterday. As he was due to fly back to Switzerland later tonight, they'd be no use to him if they arrived in London tomorrow. It was all very aggravating.

Picking up his cell, he jabbed out a number.

"They're still not here," he barked into the handset, so loudly that Mitzi jumped. "What the fuck's going on?"

"Relax." Josh Schwartz, one of Anton's many lawyers, was used to his client's capricious moods. "They'll show up. I'll get copies faxed to you in Geneva in the meantime. But listen, I have good news on a different front."

"What?" Anton sounded distinctly nonchalant.

"I think I've finally dug up some dirt on Morty Sullivan."

Anton sat up, interested. Now this was good news. Mortimer Sullivan was the dreadful old fossil who chaired the planning committee in East Hampton. For some years now, Anton had had his eye on the town as a perfect spot to open a new Tischen. The once-great Palmers had long since declined into mediocrity, and with Trey Palmer apparently on his last legs, usurped by his own utterly inexperienced daughter by all accounts, its position was looking more vulnerable than ever. The problem was that the town seemed to be run like the Palmer family's private fiefdom. Whenever Anton had found a suitable building to convert or plot to build on, he'd been denied permission to fart there by Sullivan and his small-minded, sycophantic cronies. Those guys didn't want any change at all, never mind some upstart European showing up to build one of his flashy hotels in their backyard. It was the same old story, and Anton was heartily sick of it. "Tell me more," he said, licking his lips with anticipation of the juicy gossip to come. "Is it something we can use?"

"Hell, yeah." Josh was actually laughing now. As far as Anton knew, his lawyer hadn't so much as broken a smile since his ex-wife's rottweiler of a divorce attorney got shot in the balls in a freak hunting accident. This must be good. "It involves a twenty-two-year-old dancer called Danny Carlucci. I'm looking at the Polaroids right now. If this doesn't get the guy to back off, nothing will."

Handing Mitzi the last quarter of toast, Anton hung up, smiling broadly. This business in the papers with Heidi had put him in a foul mood, but at last he felt it lifting. Yesterday's *Evening Standard* would be tomorrow's fish and chips wrapping anyway. People would forget about the story soon enough. Whereas the prospect of a new Tischen in the Hamptons? Now that was something lasting, something real.

Trey Palmer's daughter might not realize it yet, but her special relationship with the East Hampton planning committee was about to come to an abrupt end. And just in time.

Waking up with a start, Honor looked at the time on the little electric clock by her bedside. It was ten fifteen.

"Fuuuck," she groaned quietly to herself. How had that happened? Admittedly she'd had a late and drunken night. She'd done a good job appearing together and in control on the boat, saying her good-byes to Devon. But as soon as she got back to Palmers she'd headed straight for her suite and the drinks cabinet and proceeded to take herself out on vodka, drinking into the small hours. The last thing she wanted was for him to realize how desperately she needed him and how much she dreaded his departure. They'd only been seeing each other a few weeks. She mustn't, mustn't, mustn't scare him off.

If Devon was confused by their blossoming relationship, Honor felt completely undone by it. Part of her lived for the brief hours they spent together. But another, larger part was gripped by a permanent, cold panic. OK, so his marriage was a sham, but he was still married, and with children too. After all the lectures she'd given Tina, what the hell was she doing, playing fast and loose with her own reputation and, by extension, Palmers'? She knew she ought to break it off, for a myriad of reasons. But she'd been so lonely for so long the thought of letting Devon go made her want to vomit. Subconsciously, she'd looked for father figures in the past. But in Devon she'd really, truly found one. He was so strong, so solid, so rocklike and reassuring. And sexually, he'd cracked her in a way that no one else ever had.

At some point during her drunken marathon last night, Honor couldn't recall exactly when, Tina had called. With her usual uncanny sense of bad timing, she'd picked this of all nights to moan about how hard her life in LA was without Danny.

"It's all right for you," she whined. "You're far too sensible ever to fall for a married man." Tina made the word "sensible" sound like the most pointed of insults. "You don't know what it's like, knowing that person is out there but that you can't have them. It's hell, Honor. *Hell.* You have no idea what I'm going through."

It took a superhuman effort of will for Honor to keep her mouth shut about Devon, but somehow she managed it. Sharing any kind of sensitive information with her sister was tantamount to posting it on Facebook. Tina had about as much discretion as a foghorn, as Honor knew to her cost.

Having finally managed to get Tina off the phone, it rang again almost immediately. This time it was Lise, bitching that she wasn't getting any help with the rapidly declining Trey.

"I'm on my own here with him twenty-four seven," she complained. "He can't even use the bathroom by himself anymore. It's disgusting." If she was looking for a sympathetic ear, she'd come to the wrong place.

"You married a guy old enough to be your father," slurred Honor. "What did you expect? Besides, he has two full-time nurses, Lise. No one's expecting you to play Florence Nightingale."

"Like hell they aren't," Lise snapped. "Those nurses are lazy as shit. And what the hell happened to you and Tina, anyway? When was the last time either of you visited him?"

This was below the belt.

"He refuses to see me," Honor mumbled, a knot of confused emotion forming in the pit of her stomach like a tumor, even through her drunkenness. "You know that. I'm trying to put things right at Palmers, for him more than anyone. I'm working nonstop here."

"Jesus, Honor, don't you get it?" Lise interrupted viciously. "Your dad doesn't care about Palmers. The man's incontinent, OK? He's a retard."

Honor hung up at that point and kicked up the alcohol consumption to a whole new level. Maybe it was losing her father that was making this thing with Devon so painfully important to her? She had in fact been back to Boston twice since taking over at Palmers, trips she could ill afford, but Trey had refused to let her onto the property. Back in East Hampton, she called three times a week, but not once had he allowed her to be put through. He'd told her in Sam Brannagan's office that he would never forgive her for taking control of his assets. So far, it looked as though he intended to be as good as his word.

Waking up this morning, Honor felt like someone had thrown the mother of all Fourth of July parties inside her cranium. Fumbling in the drawer of her bedside table for some aspirin, she crammed three into her mouth without water before throwing off her covers and staggering into the shower.

Slowly, as the warm jets of water pounded onto her aching body, she started to feel more alive. Squirting a dollop of her favorite lemongrass shower gel into her palms, she began rubbing it all over her body, working up a lather that she massaged into her hair and face as well. She wanted to wash away all traces of last night and was starting to enjoy the tingling sensation on her skin when suddenly, out of the corner of her eye, she saw the shower curtain twitch.

There wasn't even time to panic. Ripping the rubbery fabric aside, still half-blinded by soapsuds, she let out a blood-curdling shriek, launching herself on her would-be attacker with a well-placed kick to the groin.

"You fucker!" she yelled, kicking and punching and scratching blindly as adrenaline translated her fear into anger. "You piece of shit!"

"Honor!" It took a second or two for Devon's voice to penetrate the fog in her brain. "For God's sake stop, Honor. It's me."

"Devon?" Opening her eyes at last, she saw him lying beneath her on the tiled bathroom floor, half shielding his face with one arm. "What are you doing here? You should be on a plane to Boston."

"Lola wasn't ready to go," he panted. "And neither was I. I had to see you again."

Despite the searing pain in his balls from where she'd kicked him, the sight of her leaning over him naked, dripping, and still slippery with soapsuds was making him hard already. Reaching up around her neck, he pulled her beautiful, elfin face down until the tips of their noses touched, then let his hands glide down the wet runway of her back to rest on her butt.

"You scared me," she whispered, closing her eyes as she felt his fingers slipping around her hips and disappearing into the damp triangle of her pubic hair. So much for wrestling with her conscience. She could no more finish things with Devon than fly to the moon, and she knew it.

"Not half as much as you scared me." Unzipping his jeans, he freed his now rock-solid erection. "You might have warned me you had a black belt in karate."

Easing herself down onto his dick, Honor began rocking slowly back and forth, her hangover suddenly quite forgotten. Her face was pressed against his now, and she found herself doing something she never normally did: looking right into his eyes while he made love to her.

Before long, despite his best efforts at restraint, Devon felt his orgasm building.

"Oh, God," he moaned, looking almost in pain as he bit into her shoulder and came deep inside her. "Sorry. I'm sorry. I couldn't hold it. I shit, Honor, what's wrong?"

Opening his eyes, he saw tears streaming down her face. Still inside her, he sat up and wrapped both arms around her.

"Shhhh," he whispered, gently stroking her hair as her sobs became stronger and more violent. "What is it, my darling? What's the matter? Did I hurt you?"

She shook her head, wiping the tears away almost angrily with the back of her hand.

"No," she said. "You were fine. You were lovely. You are lovely. I didn't..." She was still struggling to get her breath, she'd been crying so hard, and was obviously having trouble getting the words out. "I didn't want you to see it."

"See what?" he said gently.

"How much I love you." Biting down on her trembling lower lip, she looked like a lost and frightened little girl. Devon felt a surge of love and protectiveness flood over him, tinged with the slightly less noble feeling of triumph. "How much I don't want you to go away from me. Ever."

It all came out then: the feelings she'd tried so hard to hide from him yesterday, Tina's phone call, her deep, profound unhappiness about her father and his continued refusal to see her.

"It's OK, baby." Holding her, he listened patiently while all the stress of the past months came pouring out.

"No," Honor shook her head again. "It's not. It's not OK, Devon. Palmers is a mess. I thought I could just come in here and fix everything, but I can't. It's going to take years, and the whole town's against me. They all think I ripped Dad off."

"I'm sure that's not true," said Devon, who knew that it was but didn't want to hurt her. If anything, the East Hampton gossips were even more small-minded and belligerent than their Boston counterparts.

"It is true!" Honor wailed. "And now you're leaving me, and I need you, and I don't want to need you; I don't want to need anyone."

"Shhh." He stopped her with a kiss. "I need you too. I do. And I'm not leaving you. I have to go back home, but I'm gonna get out here to see you. Regularly."

"But how?" Try as she might she couldn't seem to stop her bottom lip from wobbling again. What was she, six? "You have a job. You have a wife, a family, a whole life in Boston. And I have Palmers. I can't leave."

"I know," he said. "I know all that. But you just have to trust me. We'll find a way. I know your old man let you down and you've had to learn to deal with everything, with Palmers and your sister and all this shit on your own. But those days are gone now, Honor. You have me. You'll always have me, I promise."

He sounded so strong and so reassuring she longed to believe him.

"Now get dressed, and get on the phone," he said, pulling her up to her feet. "Whatever you have on your schedule today, cancel it."

Honor was about to protest, but he held up his hand for silence, and for some reason she found herself complying.

"Tell people you have the flu. Tell them whatever you want," he said. "But for the next six hours, you're mine and mine alone."

"OK." She smiled. "But we can't spend the whole time…you know."

"Fucking?" Devon laughed.

"I mean it," said Honor. "I really need your advice about Palmers. Legal advice. The surveyors handed in their structural report last night, and it's pretty grim reading."

"You want to spend our last hours together going over a surveyors' report?" He looked at her incredulously, then shook his head. "You love me, but you love Palmers more, right?"

Honor gave him her very best, most adoring smile. But she didn't correct him.

CHAPTER SIX

Are you sure you don't want me to stay a little longer?"

The girl loitering in the doorway of Lucas's apartment fluttered her eyelashes and gave him the full force of the pouty, wide-eyed look that had made her the hottest model in London this season.

"Because I *really* don't mind."

Lucas, wearing only a white towel tied around his waist, marveled again at her incredible body, shown off to perfection in a pair of skinny jeans and a tight white sweater, and felt his resolve fraying at the edges. They'd been screwing all afternoon, but he reckoned he had more than enough energy for a third round if she did.

But no, he shouldn't. It was the big Christmas party at the Cadogan tonight. Julia was probably already furious that he wasn't at work right now—bossy, overbearing cow that she was.

"You're sweet, Georgie," he said, rubbing a hand against his stubble and realizing belatedly that he needed a shave before tonight as well. "But maybe next time, hey? Tonight's a big night for me."

The girl shrugged and kissed him on the cheek. "Your loss, Lucasito," she said. Flicking her long blonde hair behind her, she skipped off down the stairs, calling out, "Oh, and merry Christmas!" over her shoulder as she disappeared from view.

"Thanks," sighed Lucas to himself. Walking back into the apartment, he shut the door behind him. "Merry Christmas to you too."

He'd been in London for five months now, at the Cadogan for four of them, and had already made a considerable splash on the social scene. With his Heathcliff looks and moody confidence added to the intoxicating whiff of his dangerous other-side-of-the-tracks background, he was an immediate hit with all the well-bred Chelsea heiresses, who'd taken to hanging around the hotel like groupies, hoping to get a crack at him. His job at the Cadogan gave him instant access to London's notoriously exclusive clubland, and to all outward appearances he appeared to have gained overnight acceptance among the city's bright young things. Night after night he could be seen squiring the most eligible girls to Annabel's and Tramp, and by day, in the rare hours when he wasn't working, he was a familiar figure in the West End, tearing around the streets of Soho on his Ducati motorbike like a Spanish James Dean.

But beneath the veneer of glamour, the reality was that he was still only a small step above broke. Anton paid him a fair wage at the Cadogan and partially subsidized his bachelor pad on St. James's, which was a godsend. But the crowd that Lucas moved in, a mixture of trust-fund brats, city whiz kids, and old-money aristocracy, all had disposable incomes to burn, and he was painfully aware of his own inadequate funds as he tried to keep up. Most of the men in his circle knew that he was struggling and, already jealous of his popularity with the It-girls and models that had swooned over them before Lucas showed up, responded by patronizing him socially. This, naturally, drove Lucas insane with rage, and he nursed his wounded pride like a stuck bull. If they'd openly challenged him, he'd have been able to hit back. But in typically British style, their exclusion of

Lucas was far more subtle and insidious than that. So a group of Goldman bankers would happily share a table with him at a restaurant or club, and might even invite him to drinks parties. But when it came to shooting weekends at Blenheim or boys-only ski breaks to Verbier, Lucas only ever heard about it after the fact. Not that he could have afforded to go anyway, but it would have been nice to be asked. In Lausanne, the European rich kids had accepted him without reservation. But British snobbery, he was beginning to discover, was of quite a different order. Outwardly, he pretended not to care about being snubbed. Inside, however, he was more determined than ever to beat the British bastards at their own game, and it wasn't long before he was living well beyond his means.

Despite these irritating problems, he had grudgingly come to enjoy London. Though he still bitched about the weather and the cost of living (black cabs in particular were astronomical, although he couldn't seem to break himself of the habit) he had to admit that the city was magically transformed at Christmastime. Everywhere he went, shop windows were illuminated with brightly colored displays, and the old Victorian street lamps were adorned with mini Christmas trees, simply lit in white, that gave the darkening afternoons a cozy, Dickensian glow. From his bachelor pad Lucas could see the shoppers darting to and fro between Fortnum's and the Burlington Arcade, stocking up on presents and candies and every possible variety of ribbons, bows, and rolls of shiny metallic paper to wrap them all up in. Though the promised snow had yet to materialize, the frost transformed the park every night into a gray-white wonderland, making Lucas's early-morning walk to work one of the highlights of his day.

Unfortunately, some days it was the *only* highlight. On top of the pressure of his unpaid credit card bills and ever-growing overdraft, recently his work at the Cadogan had become intensely stressful too. More often than not, the stress took human form in the formidable, sturdy shape of Julia Brett-Sadler.

Relations between Lucas and his boss had begun as strained, then deteriorated steadily over the next few months to their current status of raging, open hostility.

Julia despised Lucas. She considered her new undermanager arrogant to the point of insubordination, and she wasn't the only one. Ever since he'd fucked some moron on the editorial desk at *Tatler* and managed to get himself named as London's fifth-most-eligible bachelor, he seemed to have become even more full of himself, treating the Cadogan like his own private fiefdom—although even Julia had to admit that, most of the time, he worked like a dog. Nevertheless, she was seething with Anton for appointing him in the first place without consulting her. Lucas was so underqualified it was laughable. But instead of biding his time and trying to learn something constructive from more experienced professionals like her, he'd blundered in like a bull in a china shop, deliberately fanning the flames of Julia's anger by wearing his contempt for her and the other senior staff firmly on his sleeve.

For his part, Lucas resented Julia for routinely dismissing all his suggestions for change or improvements at the hotel. It didn't occur to him that perhaps a constant stream of criticism and invective might not be the best way to win her over to his point of view. With any other woman he'd have been able to flirt his way out of trouble. But Julia was such a battle-ax, she'd never displayed so much as a hint of sexual interest in him. Though he wouldn't admit it, even to himself, this also annoyed Lucas intensely.

Unfortunately, however, she was his boss, for now anyway, and he couldn't afford to lose this job. Which meant that, whether he liked it or not, her word was law. He had no choice but to sit back and watch as, one by one, his ideas and projects got sidelined. It was beyond depressing.

He could have run to Anton about it, of course. But that would have made him look weak and immature and he knew it.

Besides, Anton Tisch had more important things on his mind than the problems of one of his lowliest undermanagers.

No. It was up to Lucas to outsmart Julia. But so far, he'd gotten precisely nowhere.

Sighing, he loosened his towel and threw it down onto the sofa before wandering naked into the bathroom. Like the rest of the apartment, it was decorated in classic bachelor style, with lots of black granite and chrome crammed into a small but elegantly masculine space. There was no bathtub, just a huge shower and an ornate Oriental floor-to-ceiling mirror that Lucas looked in now, examining his reflection.

He was aware he was handsome—he wasn't blind—but he wasn't vain in the sense of being focused on his good looks. He merely acknowledged them as another fact of his existence, like being tall or good at languages. If anything, he had a tendency to be critical of himself physically, particularly if he felt his strength faltering as it had been recently. Since taking the Cadogan job, he hadn't had any free time to go to the gym. Mostly it was seventeen- or eighteen-hour days, squeezing the girls in in between. By the time he got home he hadn't an ounce of energy left for lifting weights.

Still, there was no time to worry about that now. The party officially kicked off in less than three hours' time. He'd better get a move on.

Over at the Cadogan, Julia was rushing around like a blue-assed fly getting everything ready, and silently cursing Lucas.

"For God's sake, Matt," she could be heard berating the poor head barman. "People don't want to drink vodka out of a penis. Whose idea was this monstrosity?"

She pointed to an ice sculpture of cupid, three feet high, through which a steady trickle of neat vodka was already flowing, exiting via the frostily shriveled appendage.

"Lucas's," said Matt, pulling out the order sheet like a shield. "One vodka ice fountain, Cupid," he read, adding somewhat rashly, "You signed off on it, Julia."

"It's obscene," she snapped. "Get it out of here. And find me another ice fountain within the next hour. Something that doesn't piss on people."

This really was the last straw. Against her better judgment, she'd allowed herself to be browbeaten into letting Lucas organize tonight's event, a vitally important evening for the hotel. From what she'd seen so far today—burlesque pole dancers, pornographic ice sculptures, some ludicrously overpriced DJ who'd cheerily told her a few minutes ago that he'd spent the past four months in Belmarsh for drug offenses—he seemed to have decided to turn the place into a brothel for the night.

Right on cue, Lucas, looking even more devastating than usual in a bespoke Ozwald Boateng suit (still unpaid for) and blue silk shirt, sauntered into the bar.

"Sorry I'm late, Julia," he said, with a casual insouciance that made her want to strangle him. "Something came up."

"Your dick, I shouldn't wonder," she shot back furiously. Lucas almost laughed but then wisely thought better of it. "What on earth were you thinking, Lucas?" Julia looked around her, gesticulating at the seminaked women writhing around on poles behind them, practicing their routine. "We're a traditional, conservative hotel. I have the leader of the Tory party and his wife coming tonight!" she added, tearing at her hair in exasperation.

"From what I hear, he's quite a fan of dancing girls," said Lucas. But one look at Julia's face told him flippancy was not going to score him any points. "Look, it's edgy, I grant you," he admitted.

"Edgy?" Julia looked apoplectic.

"Trust me," said Lucas. "It's what this place needs. People are going to love it."

"People are going to be offended!" she shouted at him. "How stupid are you? This isn't Ibiza. It's SW bloody three. We've got national press in here taking pictures, and you want to have the Dowager Duchess of Devonshire sucking vodka out of a baby's dick?"

"It'd sell some papers, that's for sure," he laughed.

But Julia was implacable. "This isn't a game," she hissed. "You'd better pray I'm wrong about how tonight goes down. Because whatever little boys' club you think you have going on with Anton, trust me, all Tisch really cares about is reputation."

This was undoubtedly true. Anton was the most rampant social climber Lucas had ever met, and he'd met a few. He wasn't even going to be at the party tonight, after receiving a last-minute invitation from the Duke of York to join him at the opera. Tisch wouldn't have missed the chance to rub shoulders with royalty for his own mother's funeral, never mind the Cadogan's Christmas drinks. "You think you can drag this hotel's name into the mud and live to tell the tale?" Julia gave a short, derisive grunt of a laugh and shook her head pityingly. "Maybe you are as dumb as you look."

Infuriatingly, Lucas couldn't think of a comeback and could only stand and watch as she stormed off.

Bitch.

"Matt, get me a whiskey, straight up," he said, taking a seat at the bar for a moment. The drink appeared, and he downed it in one gulp, shivering slightly as the amber liquid burned his throat and chest. He'd tried to act cool in front of Julia. But the truth was he was riddled with doubt himself about whether tonight's gamble would pay off. He'd been so full of confidence when he organized it all. So blindly certain that a genuinely hip, cutting-edge event aimed at younger clientele would catapult the Cadogan out of her safety zone as a classy, well-run boutique and into something truly iconic: the hotel synonymous with Cool Britannia, the place to be seen in London.

But maybe Julia was right. Maybe it did all look like a tacky, vulgar publicity stunt in the cold light of day?

She was certainly right about one thing. If it wasn't a success, his days at the Cadogan weren't just numbered. They were over. And what would he do with his growing collection of overdue bills then?

―――――――   ―――――――

By ten thirty, the bar was heaving.

Flitting from group to group, glad-handing and flashing his teeth like the Big Bad Wolf, Lucas still wasn't sure if things were actually going well. Everyone was congratulating him, naturally, but he knew better than to trust in that. These people were so fake, they'd say whatever they thought you wanted to hear to your face. Still, it was a relief that they had at least shown up.

Whatever he might privately think of the "in" crowd who hung out at the Cadogan, it was Lucas's job to court them and keep them coming back for more. There was no doubt that the movers and shakers crammed into the bar and lobby tonight were a PR man's wet dream. Actors, rock stars, politicians, artists, aristos, they were all mingling like old friends, their inhibitions broken by a free flow of cocktails that was costing the hotel a small fortune.

"Lucas, isn't it?"

Feeling a tap on his shoulder, Lucas spun around. He knew he recognized the strident, pushy little blonde from somewhere, but he couldn't quite place her. Part of the problem was that so many of these London socialites looked identical, with their expensive honey highlights, year-round St. Tropez tans, and Luella Bartley accessories. He'd seen countless women like them in Ibiza—spoiled, rude, and vacuous, not one of them had treated him with respect when he was a lowly laundry boy. But now that he could provide or deny access to the hottest venue in London, he couldn't seem to beat them off with a stick.

"Don't you remember me?" The girl cocked her head to one side like a hurt puppy and pushed her surgically inflated lips forward in a theatrical pout. "Caroline. Caroline Hambling. We met at Oscar's Halloween bash at Momo's."

"Oh, yes, of course," he said, unconvincingly. "I'm so glad you could make it. Are you enjoying the party?"

"It's OK." She shrugged in the manner of a person whose name was on the guest list at every A-list social event in town. "There aren't enough sexy boys, though. Naughty Lucas!" She wagged her finger at him flirtatiously. "You didn't want any competition, did you? Well, your wicked plan has worked, my darling. You've got my full, undivided attention." Lucas smiled thinly. He mustn't be rude to guests. But did she really think she was sexy, this girl, with her braying British accent and her pearls and her address book full of Tom, Dick, and Harrys?

Thankfully he only had to endure a few minutes of listening to what a marvelous time she'd had at the Billionaire's Club in Sardinia last summer—"Don't you think Flavio's a *hoot*?"— before he spotted a familiar burly figure fighting its way through the throng toward him.

"Fuck me," Ben panted, finally arriving at Lucas's side. "How many people did you invite, mate? 'Ave you seen that bar? It'll be bloody New Year's Eve before you get served over there."

Oddly, Lucas and Ben hadn't seen much more of each other since Lucas moved to London than they had when he was in Switzerland. Both of them were so busy at work there never seemed enough time to get the beers in. But they spoke regularly, and Ben wouldn't have missed tonight's extravaganza for anything.

"Caroline," Lucas grinned, "meet my friend Ben. Ben, Caroline."

"Hello." Ben turned to face the girl, smiling broadly. With his huge frame covered in a thick Aran sweater and his face even browner and more freckled than usual after a business trip to Asia, he looked more like a surf bum, or possibly a trawlerman, than a city highflier. "So," he asked brightly, "how d'you know Lucas then?" Caroline, who was not a fan of cockney accents, or fisherman's sweaters, gave a little shudder of distaste. "We met at a party," she said frostily. "Actually, er, I've just seen someone I need to have a word with. Will you excuse me?"

"Blimey," said Ben, frowning as she shimmied off. "That was quick. Was it something I said?"

"More likely something you didn't say," said Lucas. "Like your last name, perhaps?"

Had Caroline realized that the working-class lug with the appalling dress sense was in fact Ben Slater, founder, owner, and CEO of the most profitable hedge fund in the UK, Lucas had little doubt that her bra would have spontaneously unhooked on the spot.

"Forget it," said Ben. "If that's all she's interested in, I'm not bothered."

When they'd first met in Murren and Ben had told Lucas what he did for a living, Lucas hadn't thought much of it. It was only after he arrived in London that he began to piece together quite how successful, not to mention rich, his friend really was. You'd never know it to look at him, or even to stay in his apartment—which, though comfortable, was hardly a billionaire's lair. But his Stellar Fund was one of the top three hedge funds in Europe.

Most of the playboys and grandees who hung out at the Cadogan had their heads so far up their asses it was painful, bragging about their funds and their yachts and their mistresses like so many yapping dogs. But Ben, who could have bought out all of them and still had change for a twenty, was ultra-low-key about his wealth. Sometimes, Lucas thought, he was actually embarrassed about it. Certainly he blushed like a virgin whenever anybody complimented him on his skills as an investor or when the papers referred to him as "Fund God Slater."

In many ways—most ways—the two boys were very different. While Lucas slept around shamelessly with the apparently endless stream of models who threw themselves at him, especially since the *Tatler* thing, Ben was a hopeless romantic. He was forever bemoaning the fact that he couldn't seem to find a nice, decent girl who would see past his money and love him for himself alone.

"This place looks the bollocks, by the way," he said admiringly, changing the subject as he found his arms full of one of the writhing burlesque dancers. "Julia must be pleased with the turnout."

"You'd think so, wouldn't you?" said Lucas bitterly, shooing the girl away. "Actually she's done nothing but bitch at me all evening. Apparently the whole thing is 'vulgar and tasteless.'"

"Well, Tisch is gonna love your ass, whatever she says," said Ben. "I just spoke to a mate of mine from the *Daily Mail*, that bloke collapsed by the bar." He pointed to a slumped figure on the other side of the room.

"He says they're doing a huge write up tomorrow. Best Christmas do he's ever been to, he said, and believe me, he's been to a few."

"I don't doubt it," said Lucas. "But enough about my career prospects. You just rescued me from Caroline, the most appalling woman in London, and one good turn deserves another. Let's get you laid, my friend."

Ben laughed and held up his hand. "Uh, no, no thanks," he said. "I prefer to let these things happen naturally."

But Lucas had already dived into the crowd like a harpoon fisherman. Within a minute he was back, hand in hand with a stunning Brazilian in a yellow miniskirt so tiny it might have started life as a napkin.

"Kiki was asking to meet you." He grinned at Ben, ignoring his pleading eyes and head shake and shoving the girl forward. "She's *fascinated* by the hedge fund business. Aren't you, sweetheart?"

The girl nodded blankly and smiled at Ben. Clearly her English was not the best.

"Hello, Kiki." Ben shook her hand awkwardly, looking daggers at Lucas. Part of him envied his friend's seemingly limitless sexual confidence. But he could never treat sex as a sport the way that Lucas did. What was he supposed to say to this girl who couldn't understand a word he said and only wanted to sleep with him because Lucas had told her he was richer than the Aga Khan?

"Look, I'm sorry but I'm not staying," he said, slipping his coat back on despite Lucas's protests and the girl's disappointed pout. "I've got a big meeting in the morning. I need my beauty sleep."

Lucas sighed as he watched him go. What was the point of being rich and successful if you never used it to get women? Or to buy yourself a decent wardrobe? Tomorrow, he decided, he'd go over to Ben's apartment and burn that awful sweater.

"He leaving?" Kiki looked up at Lucas, bewildered. She might not be the sharpest knife in the drawer, but she had the little-girl-lost thing down pat. And by God she was sexy.

"Don't you worry about him, sweetheart," said Lucas. Figuring Slater's loss may as well be his gain, he slipped a warm hand under the sliver of yellow fabric that passed for a skirt. "I'll take care of you. Come on. Let's find ourselves a drink."

CHAPTER SEVEN

*T*HE NEXT MORNING, HUNGOVER, LATE FOR WORK, AND stuck in a hideous jam on the Embankment, Ben leaned on the horn of his bright-red Mini Cooper and swore at no one in particular.

"Fucking traffic!" he yelled, regretting it as the throbbing pain in his temples immediately kicked up a notch. "What's the bleeding holdup?" Normally he prided himself on being a pretty even-tempered guy. With billions of dollars of other people's money under management, he had learned early on how to deal with stress and compartmentalize his life. But this morning's meeting was important.

Success had come so quickly to Ben—he'd only founded his fund, Stellar, five years ago and never in his wildest dreams imagined it would grow as fast as it had. It would have been easy to lose perspective and start believing in his own hype. He'd seen it happen to countless others in the hedge fund business: Anton Tisch, Dan Frazer, Dante Capellini. They'd all turned into right self-important tossers. Ben remembered Capellini from his days as a trader at Lehman, not so long ago. He'd actually been a fun bloke back then. These days he swanned about with bodyguards and private jets, giving press conferences about his political beliefs like bloody Bono. It was sad, really.

He could only imagine that none of his competitors came from a family like his. If his mum, never mind his sisters, ever turned on the TV and saw him wearing wraparound sunglasses, pontificating about world peace—my God, he'd never hear the end of it!

The Slaters were Essex to the core and about as close as a family could be. Ben was the youngest and the only boy, but despite those two facts he'd never been mollycoddled as a child. He and his two sisters, Karen and Nikki, grew up in a poky little terraced house on Canvey Island. His mum and dad still lived on the island, although these days "home" was a sprawling single-story mansion that Ben had bought for them, complete with a five-car garage and an outdoor Jacuzzi they never used but were inordinately proud of nonetheless. Karen, married to a local hairdresser she'd been dating since she was fifteen, was ten miles away. And Nikki, also married with two kids, lived not much farther in Chingford where she had her own beauty salon, Faces. All three of the Slater kids went home every other Sunday for a family lunch and treated one another's houses and lives as an extension of their own.

They were all proud of Ben's success, if a little bewildered by the scale of it. But the Slater parents were every bit as impressed with Nikki's salon as they were with his multibillion-dollar fund. As a result, Ben's feet had remained firmly on the ground, and he'd never been allowed to let either the pressure or the adulation go to his head.

After fifteen infuriating minutes at a complete standstill, the cars in front of him finally started to move, and soon the highrises of Canon Street began looming into view through the chill December mist. Turning left onto King William Street, he swung the Mini at breakneck speed onto the parking ramp and down into the subterranean gloom of the Stellar Inc. garage.

"Morning, Mr. Slater." Jerry, the parking attendant, was chirpy as ever. "You're later than usual. Big night, was it?" He winked knowingly.

"I wish," said Ben, with feeling, rubbing his aching head. Annoyingly, having told Lucas he wasn't interested, he'd been plagued by erotic dreams last night about the Brazilian girl. "Are the Daiwa guys here yet?"

This morning's meeting was with some Japanese institutional investors. If there was one group of people you really did not want to be late for, it was the Japanese.

"'Fraid so," said Jerry. "They got here about fifteen minutes ago."

"Bollocks."

Not bothering to wait for the elevator, Ben bounded up the steps two at a time, picking up his morning bundle of press clippings from the front desk without breaking stride. He'd just closed the door to his office and was hastily putting on one of the silk ties he kept in his desk drawer while simultaneously hunting for some aspirin when his phone went off.

Seeing "mum" flashing insistently, he hit "busy" and stuck his head around the door of his PA's office.

"Morning, Tam. Are they in the conference room?"

"They are." Tammy, his utterly devoted secretary of the past three years and a fellow Essex native, flashed him a smile. "You look like shit, by the way."

"Thanks," said Ben. "I know."

"I gave them tea and biscuits five minutes ago," said Tammy. "But your mum's on line one and I think you'd better talk to her before you go in there. You forgot your nan's birthday, apparently." She raised a disapproving eyebrow. "She's not happy about it."

Ben groaned. That was all he needed. Jabbing the flashing red button on Tammy's phone, he reluctantly picked up the receiver.

"Hello, Mum."

Tammy giggled as he held the phone away from his ear, shielding himself from the rising maternal decibel level. When Mrs. Slater lost her rag, she really lost it.

"Yeah, I know, I'm sorry," he pleaded, once he could get a word in edgewise. "Yes, she does deserve better at ninety-one.

I'll make it up to her, honest. I'll come over there tonight, drop her off her present myself, how's that? No…yes, I do care, Mum, I'm just late for a meeting. Look, I've gotta go. I'll call you later, yeah?"

Handing Tammy the phone, he dashed off down the corridor, clutching his aching head and still struggling to straighten the knot on his tie. He looked more like a schoolboy late for class than the CEO of one of the biggest funds in Europe.

What a bloody awful start to the day.

Pushing open the double doors of the conference room, he wondered briefly whether Lucas was feeling as rough and hungover as he was. If there were any justice in this world, he ought to be.

In fact, at that precise moment, Lucas was feeling more than a little pleased with himself.

Though he, too, was late for work, he reckoned that even Julia would probably cut him a little slack today. Slicing his way through the traffic on Piccadilly on his beloved Ducati racing bike like a hot knife through butter, he allowed memories of his epic lovemaking session with the Brazilian girl to drift back to him, interspersed with flashbacks from last night's triumphant party.

His gamble had really paid off. Even the Tory leader's wife, a famously sour-faced killjoy, had weaved over to him at the end of the night to say how much she'd enjoyed herself. There was bound to be a big write-up in the *Standard*'s society pages tonight, which would hopefully start a trickle-down effect of positive press for the Cadogan. Anton couldn't fail to be impressed. Parking his bike in one of the public stands opposite the hotel—to his fury, he had been denied a parking space in the Cadogan's courtyard, where

Julia's mint-green Porsche was already glinting smugly in the sunshine—he sauntered into the lobby, grinning from ear to ear.

"What time do you call this?"

Derek, the flamingly gay head receptionist, fancied Lucas madly and liked to demonstrate his devotion through confrontational flirting. Happily, this was a game that Lucas also enjoyed playing.

"Shut it, Shirley," he said, with a wink that reduced Derek to jelly. "I think I earned my extra hour in bed."

"That's as may be," said Derek, recovering his composure. "But you'll wish you'd set your alarm clock when I tell you who you missed this morning."

"Who?" Lucas, rifling through his mail, was only half listening.

"Only Anton the Almighty," said Derek archly. Instantly Lucas looked up. "Tisch? He was here?"

Derek nodded. "Holed up with Julia for almost forty minutes," he said. "And when they came out of her office, I heard him tell her…hmm, no, I'm not sure I should tell you. I wouldn't want to ruin your morning."

"Spill it, sweetheart," said Lucas, "before I get behind that desk and beat it out of you."

Derek flushed with pleasure. But when he spoke again, he looked serious.

"Well," he said, "I heard Anton tell Julia she'd done an amazing job with the party and the whole Moulin Rouge thing. And she just said, 'Thank you,' that she'd decided it was time to revitalize our stuffy, conservative image. She never even mentioned your name."

"*Coño*," Lucas murmured under his breath. The bitch knew damn well he'd probably be late this morning and had deliberately arranged the meeting with Anton without him. How dare she take the credit for his idea and hard work? How dare she?

"Where is she?" he asked murderously.

"Still in her office, I think," said Derek. "Don't go doing anything silly now, Lucas," he added, as Lucas stormed down the corridor. But it was too late for that.

"You fucking liar!" Bursting into the manager's office like a comet of fury, he slammed the door behind him.

"Good morning, Lucas," said Julia calmly, not looking up from her PC screen. "Nice of you to join us at last."

"You told Anton the party was your idea," he yelled.

Slowly and deliberately, she right-clicked her mouse, minimizing the spreadsheet she was looking at, and sat back in her chair, looking at him.

"I did no such thing," she said. "Anton had heard good reports and came by to congratulate us. I merely thanked him and said that I was as pleased with how things had gone as he was."

"Bullshit!" Lucas exploded. "You took the credit for my party."

"It wasn't your party," said Julia acidly. "The entire hotel worked their asses off to make last night the success it was. As I remember, you couldn't even be bothered to show up until a couple of hours before kickoff. It was a team effort."

Lucas looked so furious she half expected to see steam coming out of his ears. Enjoying herself, she threw fuel on the flames by adding patronizingly: "There's no *I* in team, you know, Lucas. You'd do well to remember that if you want to succeed in the hotel business."

"Yeah, well there's an *I* in bitch," he said, throwing the last remnants of professional caution to the wind. "I'm going over to Tisch's office right now, and I'm going to tell him exactly what a lying piece of work you are. You had nothing to do with that party and you know it."

"On the contrary," said Julia. "I'm the manager. I had everything to do with it."

"You were trying to talk me out of it till the last second!" Lucas spluttered. "I'm going to make sure Anton knows it."

"Be my guest," she said, with a maddeningly nonchalant shrug. "You'll only end up looking like more of a spoiled child than you do already. Oh, and that little tirade of yours?" She glanced up to the corner above the window, where a tiny security camera was swiveling ominously. When the hell had she had that installed? "It's all on tape. I'm sure Mr. Tisch will find your professional conduct gripping viewing when I bike it over to him later. Close the door on your way out, would you please?"

Cursing both Julia and himself, for apparently playing right into her hands, he hurried out of her office, through the lobby, and back into the crisp December air, crossing the road to where his bike was parked. Just as he was reaching for his helmet, his cell rang. "Ruiz," he barked.

"Ah, Mr. Roooo-eeeez. I've pinned you down at laaaarst."

The nasal, droning voice of his bank manager felt like lead pouring into Lucas's heart. That was all he needed.

"Hello, Mr. Chorley." He tried to sound upbeat. "Listen, I know I owe you a call. But I'm right in the middle of something at the moment. Do you think I could call you back?"

"You owe us a lot more than a call, Mr. Roooo-eeez," said the manager darkly. "Are you aware of your last month's overdraft charges?"

"Er, yes, yes, I am," blustered Lucas.

"Because you're now seven thousand pounds over your authorized limit," whined the man from Natwest. "I'm afraid you've left me with no choice but to put a temporary freeze on your accounts."

Lucas's heart tightened. He hadn't realized that things had gotten quite that bad. Then again, he had so many unopened bank statements and angry overdue bills piled up on the floor of his apartment, it was starting to look like a recycling facility.

"I'm sure there's no need for that," he said, battling to keep the fear out of his voice. "I can raise seven thousand pounds pretty easily." Running a hand over the gleaming body of his beloved Ducati, he realized with a pang that he'd have to sell her. "It's more of a cash flow problem than anything else."

"I hope so, Mr. Rooo-eeez, for your sake." The voice on the other end of the line sounded unconvinced. "Nevertheless, I'm freezing your accounts until the funds arrive."

Deciding it was useless to try to negotiate further, Lucas hung up, angrily ramming his phone back into his inside jacket pocket.

"Fucking jobsworth," he muttered darkly. But he could only deal with one problem at a time. Pulling on his helmet and straddling the powerful bike—God, he'd miss her; what a tragedy she had to go—he started the engine. If he didn't get to Anton before Julia did, his standing with the boss would definitely take a serious nosedive. The hideous thought struck him that he might even lose his job. Please, God, no. Then old misery-guts Chorley really would have his nuts in a vise.

Tearing along the Embankment at breakneck speed, the roar of his engine audible from the south bank, he arrived at Tisch's offices within ten minutes. Leaving his bike illegally parked out front, he darted inside.

"I need to see Anton...Mr. Tisch," he panted. "It's urgent." His old enemy the receptionist smiled maliciously. "Tough luck," she said. "He's not here."

Lucas frowned. "Well where is he?"

At first the girl said nothing. But Lucas shot her a look so threatening, she eventually capitulated.

"He's on his way to City Airport," she pouted. "He's flying to Geneva this morning. You won't catch him," she yelled after Lucas's disappearing back as he raced outside. But the electric doors were already closing, and he didn't hear her.

When he arrived at City it took all his powers of persuasion to get security to allow him onto the airfield where Tisch's private jet was parked. But finally, after flashing his Cadogan ID, his passport, and his best, most winning smile to the girl on the desk, he was ushered through.

Anton, apparently, was already on board while the technicians made some final checks to the plane.

"Where d'you think you're going?"

The burly bodyguard at the foot of the stairs leading up into the cabin barred Lucas's way.

"My name is Lucas Ruiz. I need to talk to Mr. Tisch before he leaves. It's urgent."

"I daresay it is," said the heavy. "But I don't care if your name's Jesus fucking Christ. You're not going aboard and that's that."

"If you'd just let him know I'm here," said Lucas, nodding toward the walkie-talkie on the man's belt, "I'm sure he'll agree to see me."

"Read my lips," said the guard. "Piss. Off."

It wasn't perhaps the wisest of moves, but desperate times called for desperate measures and, catching him by surprise, Lucas landed a swift uppercut right under the man's jaw. Like most hired muscle, he was so unused to being challenged he seemed completely unprepared for it, staggering backward uselessly and giving Lucas a crucial few seconds in which to land two more punches followed by a sharp knee to the groin. Leaving the unfortunate guard writhing on the tarmac, Lucas straightened his tie, smoothed down his collar, and darted up the steps and into the cabin.

Inside, Anton was sitting on a couch in his reading glasses with a sea of papers spread out in front of him. He looked first surprised and then annoyed to see Lucas.

"What the hell?" he spluttered. "Who let you on board?"

"Your security was kind enough to let me pass," said Lucas, his voice drowning out the groans from outside. "I apologize for disturbing you, Mr. Tisch. I know you must be busy."

"I am," said Anton coolly. "Very."

Just then the pilot opened the door to the cabin. Ignoring Lucas, he addressed himself directly to his boss.

"We're ready to go, sir. Shall I close the doors?"

"Yes." Anton turned to Lucas. "If you want to talk, Mr. Ruiz, I suggest you strap yourself in."

Taking a seat, Lucas did as he was told. Looking out the window as they taxied toward the runway, he could see the security guard on his feet now, still bent double with pain, talking frantically into his walkie-talkie. *Too late now, asshole.*

Moments later they were airborne. The plane gave a series of little shudders as they climbed through the cloud cover before settling into a steady purr as they achieved altitude.

"So." Anton was the first to speak. "What's all this about? It had better be good, Lucas. I don't appreciate having my time wasted."

Lucas felt his stomach churning with nerves. All the *Mission: Impossible* stuff had kept his adrenaline pumping. But now that he was actually here, face-to-face with Anton, he had no idea how to begin. Julia's words about him looking like a spoiled child were ringing in his ears. But it was too late to turn back now.

"It's about last night," he began. And he proceeded to explain not only the battles he'd had with Julia over the Christmas party but the whole history of hostility and resentment between them, and their opposing views about the right direction for the Cadogan.

"I understand that she's the manager. And that she has more experience than I do. But I know I'm right about this," he said, winding up his long, impassioned speech. "We have to keep evolving to stay ahead of the competition. That's what last night was all about. And that was my vision. Not hers."

Anton, who'd kept his arms crossed and his head down while Lucas was talking, now looked up at him. He wasn't remotely interested in the micropolitical struggles at the Cadogan. But he was interested in Lucas. It hadn't escaped his notice what a name the boy had made for himself since coming to London, not easy for a broke outsider with no contacts, no title, and nothing but his good looks and confidence to recommend him. Anton himself had been trying for years to gain acceptance to the British establishment, but Lucas seemed to pick up friends in high places with the same ease and inevitability that other newly arrived foreigners picked up a cold. He clearly had a natural genius for PR, which was a very valuable asset in the hotel business and was being wasted at the Cadogan. Despite his poker face, Anton had in fact been delighted by the buzz generated by last night's party. Something about Lucas's direct, fiery gaze convinced him that the kid was telling the truth, that it really had been his idea all along.

That Julia had been less than honest earlier didn't surprise him. To be fair, he'd have done the same thing had he been in her shoes. She was sick to death of the battles with her undermanager, and Anton didn't blame her. Though Lucas didn't know it, she'd already been on the phone to him this morning, complaining that Lucas's insubordination had now gone beyond all appropriate professional boundaries and that she had evidence of this on tape. She wanted him fired.

If it had been anyone else, Anton wouldn't have hesitated. But Lucas's talent for self-promotion was too good to be jettisoned over some petty squabble. And no one could deny the boy had balls.

"Have you ever heard of a hotel called Palmers?" he asked him. Lucas looked bemused. This was a bit of a non sequitur.

"Palmers, in the Hamptons? Of course," he said. "It's a legend. Probably the most prestigious family-owned hotel in the world."

"Used to be," said Anton. He handed Lucas a spreadsheet from the pile in front of him. "These are last year's numbers. Take a look."

Lucas's eyes scanned down the page, his almost photographic memory taking in the relevant points on the P and L at once.

"Yeah, well. That's not good. How did you get ahold of these?" He handed the paper back.

"Never mind that," said Anton brusquely. "The point is that Palmers is on its last legs. I've decided to build my next Tischen in East Hampton, just a couple of streets away. It's going to be called the Herrick."

"Great," said Lucas, unsure what any of this had to do with him. "But listen, about the Cadogan—"

Anton held up his hand for silence.

"For Christ's sake, boy, stop whining about all that before I change my mind. Clearly that hotel isn't big enough for the two of you, and there's not a snowball's chance in hell I'm letting Julia Brett-Sadler go. You can consider yourself fired from the Cadogan, Lucas."

"But Mr. Tisch—"

"As of right now," said Anton firmly.

Gulping, Lucas ran a hand through his thick mop of curls, trying desperately not to show how crushed he was. He was far too proud to beg for his job—it wouldn't have made a difference anyway—but what the fuck was he going to tell his bank manager now?

Noticing the gesture, Anton added: "Oh yes, your hair. That'll have to go. From now on I want you clean-shaven and preppier than a Gap model at a loafer-wearers convention. Got it?"

"Not really," said Lucas. "I thought you just said I was fired."

"From the Cadogan, you are." Anton smiled. "In a few short months you've shown yourself to be completely incapable of compromise, taking direction, or working within a team. I'm not surprised Julia's sick to death of you."

Lucas's face fell.

"But you've also shown yourself to be an innovator and a risk taker," Anton went on, "with a quite masterful grasp of the media. Those are skills I can use."

Blindsided by relief, and not having the first idea what to say to this, Lucas wisely said nothing.

"What I need at the Herrick is youth, energy, and above all some real momentum in the press," said Anton. "Palmers may not be the giant it once was. But old names like that don't die out overnight, especially not in a closed, elitist society like the Hamptons. I've been reduced to blackmailing the planning committee just to get the damn project off the ground," he said bitterly. "None of the locals will rest until they've run us out of town, and we haven't even begun construction yet. I need someone out there who doesn't shy away from confrontation, but who can also be charming in the right quarters. You'll be project manager-cum-foreman for the first year at least, then take over as manager once she's up and running. What do you think? Are you up to it?"

Slowly, grindingly slowly, the full import of what Anton was saying began to sink into Lucas's brain.

"D'you mean...you want to hire me as the manager?" he stammered.

"Ah. You don't think you're ready." Sensing his hesitation like a shark smelling blood, Anton snapped shut the folder of documents with a sigh. "Well, perhaps you're right. You are less than a year out of school, after all. It's a big step."

"No, no." Lucas shot to his feet like he'd just been shocked with a cattle prod. "I'm ready. Of course I'm ready. When do you want me to start?"

"Soon," said Anton. "As you're here now, you can spend the next month in Geneva learning the ropes of the project. Then it'll take a few weeks to sort out your visa, et cetera...but I'll want you on the ground by February, latest."

Lucas grinned. Anton Tisch might be a bastard to the rest of the world, but he was rapidly turning into Lucas's own personal guardian angel.

"Palmers has been in a lot of trouble for years," he went on. "But their real weak spot right now is Honor Palmer, old man Trey's daughter. She's taken over as manager with no prior experience in the hotel trade, and the locals all hate her for pulling a fast one on her father, seizing control of his assets against his wishes."

"I'm not surprised," said Lucas. "Grasping bitch."

"What I want you to do," said Anton, "is to get that message out there nationally, and even internationally. Once people stop seeing Honor and Palmers as the underdog, they'll be a lot more accepting of us. I've done this many times now, and I can tell you, building a world-class hotel is only half the battle. You have to win over the local hearts and minds too. We don't want to be the Big Bad Corporate Wolf."

Lucas's heart was pumping nineteen to the dozen. He wasn't worried about turning the PR tide against Honor. That should be a piece of cake. But to be responsible for building and managing a Tischen hotel in such a prestigious location? A rival to the great Palmers, no less? That was more than a dream. It was a wildest, most ridiculous fantasy. And it was about to come true.

Sensing his excitement, Anton smiled and dropped the heavy bundle of paperwork in Lucas's lap.

"Merry Christmas," he said drily. "Oh, and Lucas? I'm serious about the haircut. I'm not having my hotel run by Steven bloody Tyler."

CHAPTER EIGHT

ONOR GLANCED UP AT THE OMINOUS, BRUISE-GRAY storm clouds gathering over the ocean and stepped up her pace a notch. It was a typical drab, windy January morning, and apart from her devoted boxer, Caleb, jumping excitedly at her heels, the beach was deserted. That suited Honor just fine. She preferred to be alone when she ran. It helped her to think.

Right now she had a lot to think about. Ignoring the ache in her thighs as the lactic acid streamed through her veins, she made a sharp left and began pounding her way over the bumpy dunes, trying to sort her various problems into some sort of order.

First, as always, there was Palmers. The first whisper she'd heard about a new Tischen hotel being built right on her doorstep had come via Devon, back in October. She'd been worried, of course, but had somehow convinced herself that this was a problem to be faced in the distant future, long after she'd restored Palmers to its former glory. She never imagined that things would move as fast as they had. Less than twelve weeks later and the old houses on the proposed Herrick site had already been demolished, with a forbidding chain-link fence erected around the resultant vast plot of muddy earth. Even if they only built on half that space, it would be twice the size of Palmers.

At first Honor was pissed at Devon for failing to do anything to stop the development.

"You're on the damn planning committee, aren't you?" she'd yelled at him in bed, after a particularly unsatisfactory bout of lovemaking. They saw each other so rarely these days—one snatched weekend in three, if they were lucky—that the pressure for everything to be perfect when they did meet hung over them like a death sentence. Her desire for him was as strong as ever, but the wave of sexual confidence that had swept her away in the early months was already subsiding, and all her natural insecurities were creeping back. "Can't you do something?"

"Like what?" Devon, equally frustrated by the sex, sounded exasperated. "I told you, Tisch clearly has some dirt on Mort Sullivan. The guy did a total U-turn overnight, and he's got enough influence on the other members to swing the thing his way, whatever I say or do."

"But there must be something…an appeal, maybe?" Sitting up in bed, Honor ran her fingers through her hair. Devon reached up and started stroking her back, trying to calm her.

"On what grounds? You don't want the competition? Look," he added more gently. "The planning decision's been made. Trying to fight it will be a waste of your time and money, believe me. But that doesn't mean there's nothing you can do. You can turn Palmers around, just like you planned. And you can beat Anton Tisch at his own game."

His words came back to her now as the cold wind whipped against her face. He was right, of course. It was pathetic how frightened she was of a little competition. Her grandfather Tertius had seen off more rivals than he could count in his thirty years at Palmers' helm. And here she was, after only a few months, running scared at the first whiff of a threat. Then again, in her grandfather's day, Palmers hadn't been falling apart at the seams. Among the myriad problems that the surveyors' report had thrown up last year, two were particularly serious. They needed a new roof, and the entire building would have to be rewired.

"If you only had the funds to fix one of those things, which would you fix?" Honor, ever the pragmatist, had asked the surveyor.

"I'd fix my bank account," he said grimly. "You really can't cut corners here, Miss Palmer. These are essential repairs, and they'll cost you a lot more in the long term if you don't deal with them now."

Which was all very well. But it would be at least a year, assuming she got her bookings back up to year-round capacity (and how the fuck was she going to manage that?) before she could begin to afford such a major refurb. In the end, deciding that a working roof really was a genuine essential, she'd begun only minor repairs to the wiring. She figured if she got the roof fixed by May and got enough bookings over her first summer season in June through August, in a pinch she might be able to rewire before the following summer, when the Herrick would be up and running. But she still tossed and turned in bed each night praying that she'd made the right decision. What if something really went haywire and she woke one morning to find the building being consumed by an electrical fire? At least if the roof had still leaked, it might have doused the flames. Oh God! Why did Anton bloody Tisch have to crawl out of the woodwork now?

Reaching the top of the dunes, she began the long descent back toward the shore. Caleb had run so far ahead he was little more than a speck in the distance, but there was no way he'd hear her above the breaking waves if she whistled for him now. A parting gift from Devon, the rescue dog was affectionate and loyal to a fault, but obedience had never been his forte—something else that Honor loved about him.

If it hadn't been for Caleb, she'd probably have had a nervous breakdown over Christmas. Desperately lonely without

Devon—she couldn't even call him over the holiday season; it was too risky with his family around—it felt like one thing after another had conspired to dampen her festive spirits.

First there was the situation with her father, which only seemed to get worse as the weeks passed. He was still refusing to see or talk to Honor, but she knew from the few family friends who visited that his Alzheimer's was in full, raging swing now, and he probably wouldn't know who she was even if he *did* take her calls. Devon had promised her he'd check up on the old man while he was in town, to make sure Lise wasn't abusing him. She wasn't, but the picture he painted for Honor was still pretty grim: Trey rarely acknowledged his wife at all and spent long periods each week in a state of total regression, even to the point of sucking his thumb and asking repeatedly for his mother. Honor's desperation was made worse by the fact that relations between her and her stepmother were at an all-time low.

"You know, you're very good at telling everyone else what to do," Lise had told her angrily during a Christmas Eve phone call that had deteriorated, as usual, into a slinging match. "But I'm the one that's here with him every day. You can't even be bothered to make it home for Christmas."

"It's not a question of being bothered," Honor shot back angrily. "What's the point of me being in the house if Dad won't see me? Besides, Christmas is a crazy time at the hotel. I can't just abandon ship."

In fact Palmers was depressingly empty of guests over the holiday. True, East Hampton was primarily a summer resort, but another winter like this one would finish them. The real reason she hadn't gone back to Boston for the holidays was that she couldn't bear the thought of running into Devon there with Karis and the kids. From the beginning he'd assured her repeatedly that his marriage was one of convenience, and that both he and Karis stayed in it for the children. Honor told herself she believed him, but going to Boston would mean putting that trust to the test, a thought that filled her with a lot more fear than it ought to have. But after what Devon had told her about her father, she realized that she would have to bite the bullet soon and force her way in to see Trey, whether he liked it or not. After all, as long as she didn't leave the house, she *couldn't* run into Karis Carter, could she? She had a two-day trip penciled in for the end of the month and was absolutely dreading it.

She was at the end of the beach now, in the flat, scrubby area where the sand petered out and the bracken and spiky grass began. A narrow, winding path led from here up to the road and a two-mile flat jog back to Palmers. Caleb, for once, had decided to stop and wait for his mistress, and Honor spent a few seconds patting and praising him while she caught her breath, before sinking down onto the grass for her sit-ups.

Ever since she'd turned thirteen she'd been obsessive about staying in shape and maintaining her lithe, boyish figure. At first, exercise was a weapon in the losing battle against puberty. But once she grew up and realized that not only could she not become a boy, but her father probably wouldn't love her even if she did, the focus of her workouts changed. Now they were all about control, about power. As though if she could keep her own body in check, she stood a chance at doing the same with the rest of her life. Or something.

As she jackknifed into a series of painful-looking crunches, her mind wandered to Tina, who was supposed to be joining her on her upcoming visit to their father. Although relieved her sister's relationship with the awful Danny was at an end, Tina's move to LA had not meant the end to all the gossip that Honor had hoped for. No sooner was she out of one inflammatory relationship than she had launched herself headlong into another, this time with a nineteen-year-old boy-toy model and sometime porn star who rejoiced in the name of Dick Grate. Really, you couldn't make up Tina's life if you tried. She and Dick seemed to spend an inordinate amount of time making out (or worse) in public places and had generally succeeded in establishing themselves as Hollywood's most watched It couple. Rarely did a week go by without some compromising picture or other making its way into *US Weekly* or the *National Enquirer*. It didn't help that, if anything, Dick actually looked even younger than he was—like an overgrown schoolboy out on a date with his buxom math teacher.

Tina, however, refused to see any problem with the relationship.

"You're just jealous," she said breezily when Honor tackled her about it before Christmas, insisting it was doing harm to both the family's reputation and Palmers'. "Dick's single, I'm single, so what? It's not my fault you never get laid and waste your life stuck in that mausoleum of a hotel."

To add insult to injury, she'd positively insisted on bringing the infamous Dick back to Boston with her in a few weeks as well, which meant Honor was going to have to meet him.

"You don't understand the passion we have for each other," Tina explained to a by-now nauseous Honor. "We can't be apart at all, not even for one night. Anyway, Dad's not gonna care, is he? He won't know who we are, never mind Dickie."

This was true. But it didn't make Honor feel any better.

"C'mon, boy." Bouncing back up onto her feet, she dragged Caleb by his collar up the steep path to the road. Normally she treated this last stretch of her morning run as a cooldown. But just thinking about Tina and Dickie made her so mad, she found herself sprinting faster than ever, her soles pummeling away at the tarmac as if they had some sort of personal vendetta. By the time she rounded the corner into Palmers' driveway she was dripping with sweat, and even in the chilly January air her cheeks were flushed redder than a Russian doll's.

"Miss Palmer?" The girl on reception was new and even more afraid of Honor than the rest of the staff. Her voice sounded positively querulous, and Honor found herself battling down irritation. As long as people did their jobs right, they had nothing to fear from her. She hated when they cowered like she was Saddam Hussein or something.

"What is it, Agnes?" she snapped, unclipping Caleb from his leash and shooing him out into the gardens.

"You have a visitor," mumbled the girl. "He's waiting in the parlor. I lit the fire for him."

"Well, who is it?" said Honor. "Can they wait fifteen minutes? I need to take a shower."

"Erm, I'm not sure." The girl looked properly panicked now, as if she'd just been asked to explain quantum theory or translate the Koran into Urdu. "It's Mr. Carter. He seemed...he looked...I think it might be important," she blurted.

Typical. Devon showed up to surprise her for the first time in almost a month, and she looked like something the cat had dragged in. Torn between running into his arms right away and disappearing upstairs to at least wash the sweat out of her hair, the decision was taken out of her hands when Devon appeared in the lobby. "I need to talk to you," he said stiffly. He couldn't risk showing any affection in front of Agnes. "Can we talk in private?"

"Of course," said Honor, matching his businesslike tone, although inside her heart was pounding. "Come on up to my rooms. We can talk there."

Only when the door of her suite was safely closed behind them did she reach up and put her arms around him. Kissing him softly on the mouth, before he had a chance to say anything, she breathed in the comforting man-smell of his body, a combination of aftershave, sweat, and the starch from his shirt, and felt herself relaxing like a stretched spring.

Her euphoria, however, was short-lived.

Pulling away, Devon looked her in the eye. She could tell at once that something was wrong.

"What?" she said. Oh, please, please let him not have come to finish things between them. Anything but that. "What is it?"

"Honor, I'm so sorry," he began. She felt the bile rising up in her throat. He had come to dump her! But he didn't even love Karis. Why? Why would he leave her, why now?

"Your father passed away this morning."

She stood there staring at him blankly. After what felt like an age, she eventually managed a strangled "I'm sorry?"

"It was very peaceful," said Devon. "I was with him when it happened, purely by chance. I stopped in to see him on my way to work, and Lise told me he'd taken a turn for the worse last night. The doctor was with him, but I don't think there was anything he could have done."

"Lise didn't call me," said Honor. She was still staring straight ahead, like a zombie. "No one called me."

"I asked her not to," said Devon. "My pilot brought me straight down here. I thought…I don't know. I didn't want you to hear over the phone. And I figured you could use a shoulder to cry on."

"But…I'm coming to see him," Honor whispered. "This month. I booked my flight."

With infinite tenderness, Devon pulled her to him, wrapping his arms tightly around her.

"I'm sorry, sweetheart," he said. "I really am sorry."

Trey Palmer's funeral was a circus.

A stream of black-clad bimbos, like aging ghosts of Christmases past, filed into St. Stephen's Cathedral and proceeded to argue loudly about which of them should have precedence in the seating arrangements. They were fighting for space with all the great and the good of Boston: hoteliers, captains of industry and their wives, and old family friends like the Carters, most of whom hadn't laid eyes on Trey for a good twenty years. Then there was the press, none of whom Honor could recall inviting, but who seemed nevertheless to have turned out in spectacular force to see the old man off.

"Did you ask these people to show up?" Honor hissed at Lise after one particularly insensitive photographer had shoved a lens within inches of her face.

"Of course not," Lise snapped back. Her skintight Dolce & Gabbana minidress, though black, was possibly the most unfunereal item of clothing Honor had ever seen, and the red soles of her sky-high Louboutin stilettos undoubtedly said more about her true feelings than anything else she was wearing. "Tina's the one who can't take a shit unless it's on film."

Of course. Tina. Sharing the front row with her sister, stepmother, and of course the ubiquitous Dick, she was, as usual, reveling in the attention in a bright-red pantsuit and more diamonds than a De Beers advertisement.

"I look on today as a celebration of my dad's life," Honor overheard her earnestly explaining to a reporter behind them. "He would have hated to see all this black. It's so depressing."

What was truly depressing, of course, was the hypocrisy. In private, Tina had made no effort to hide her elation that the final chunk of her trust fund would at last be made available to her. All she wanted to talk about was selling the house and how quickly they could come to a financial agreement with Lise.

Admittedly, Trey had been a pretty awful father. Even so, her sister's utter lack of compassion shocked Honor to the core. Especially when she herself was struggling with feelings of guilt for not having visited him enough and regret that his last lucid memory of her was having Palmers wrenched out of his control. She desperately wanted someone to confide in, to unburden herself to, but Devon was with his family, as usual, and as unavailable to her as if he'd been on the moon.

Looking across at him now, she felt her frustration mounting. Poring over his hymnal, looking every inch the upstanding family man, he was pointing something out to his daughter.

Karis, elegant in floor-length black, stood dutifully beside him, with their son, Nicholas, on her other side. Honor knew it was wrong to feel jealous. What right did she have to resent his family? But she couldn't help it. Despite his protestations to the contrary, looking at them now she could easily believe he and Karis were exactly what they seemed: a strong, loving unit, shored up against the hard times by twenty-five years of marriage, two children, and a whole life built together.

There were days, mostly when she was alone and exhausted at Palmers, when she thought she wanted nothing more than to marry Devon. As though being his wife would complete her, and give her the security and unconditional love she'd craved ever since her mom died. But at other times, the nagging doubts she'd harbored from the beginning of the affair grew louder and harder to ignore. Both his kids were adults now—it wasn't as if they were nine. Surely, if he really loved her, he'd find the courage to call it quits with Karis and make a commitment to her?

He often talked about their future together as if it were a fact. But whenever she pressed him on timing, or mentioned the dreaded *D* word—divorce—he became defensive and shut the conversation down.

The service dragged on for what seemed like an age. The priest read out a eulogy that bore so little resemblance to her father it almost made Honor wonder whether she'd accidentally wandered into the wrong church, and Tina read a Rudyard Kipling poem in a faux-sentimental voice that she thought made her sound like a serious actress but that made Honor want to throw up.

Afterward there was some general milling about outside, although thankfully the weather was so arctic that no one wanted to linger long. Honor shivered in her black mink coat, gracefully accepting condolences from people she barely knew and pretending not to notice the disapproving whispers and sly, condemning looks from mourners and onlookers alike. Even the priest had been distinctly chilly toward her. What was it with people in this town? You'd have thought by now they'd have found somebody else to hate. Not that it was much better in East Hampton, where to Honor's sensitive ears the snide whispers sounded almost deafening. Was she never to be forgiven for trying to save her family from financial ruin and her father from himself?

She was wondering at what point it would be reasonable to slip away—there were still a ton of papers to be gone through at the townhouse and nobody else was volunteering to deal with them—when she felt a hand on her shoulder.

"Hey." Devon smiled at her, and she tried not to melt. In his dark suit and black cashmere coat he looked even more hand-some and distinguished than usual, the gray flecks at his temples highlighting his dark eyes as they searched hers for a response. "How're you holding up?"

"How am I holding up?" She mimicked his formal tone, her misery making her lash out despite herself. "Why, thank you for asking, Mr. Carter. I'm just peachy. And how are you and your wife? You all looked nice and cozy together in church."

Devon grabbed her arm, lowering his voice to a whisper. "That's not fair. It killed me seeing you across the aisle, all alone, not being able to hold you. You know it's you I want to be with."

"Do I?" snapped Honor, breaking free of his grip. "You were holding her hand. I saw you."

"Christ, Honor." He shook his head. "It's a funeral. How do you want me to act?"

"I don't know," she said miserably. "I don't know and I don't care. Just leave me alone, OK?"

Alone in the safety of her blacked-out limo a few minutes later, she thought she'd want to cry, but instead she just lay back against the headrest and closed her eyes, exhausted. Forcing Devon out of her mind, she groaned at the thought of how much work still had to be done here before she could get back to Palmers. Trey's personal effects were in a hopelessly disorganized state. In some ways it was a good thing to be overloaded. It kept her from dwelling on her grief and guilt and blocked out the worst of the loneliness. And yet she felt herself teetering on an emotional precipice. Yesterday, sorting through some old files, she'd come across a black-and-white snapshot of her mother and to her horror had found herself dissolving into wracking, uncontrollable sobs.

Never much one for introspection, she found it impossible to untangle her conflicting emotions. All she knew for sure was that her father's death had crystallized something in her. Once her tears subsided, she could feel the grief hardening in her veins into something more solid: determination.

Her father had died disappointed in her, believing that she'd not only stolen Palmers from him, but that she was incapable of making the hotel a success. Now, more than ever, she had to prove him wrong. Tina and Lise could fight over the house and the trust if they wanted to. But for Honor, Palmers was all that mattered. It was, in some indefinable way, all that was left of her family. She wasn't about to let anyone take that away from her.

Anton Tisch had obviously written her off, just like her father. He wouldn't be opening his hotel next door if he didn't think Palmers was finished. But he was wrong, just as Trey had been wrong. She knew she had a mountain to climb, but she was damn well going to climb it.

She'd show them, all those vultures today who'd looked down their noses, judging her. She'd show them all.

CHAPTER NINE

CRAWLING ALONG THE LONG ISLAND EXPRESSWAY IN THE back of the Hampton Jitney, Lucas seethed quietly to himself.

As if arriving in America, a country he loathed almost as much as Britain, during a February cold snap weren't bad enough, he'd landed at La Guardia to find that not only had his suitcase been lost in transit, but the driver who was supposed to pick him up had had an accident on the Sunrise Highway, and he'd be forced to take the bus.

Ironically, from the moment Anton had offered him the managership of the Herrick, his life seemed to have become one giant stress after another. Admittedly, telling Julia she could stick her job at the Cadogan up her ass had been fun. But from then on in it had all been downhill.

Tisch had insisted that Lucas should be on-site in the Hamptons by the end of February at the latest to begin the building works, and he'd made it—just. It was a tall order, leaving him only a few weeks once he returned from Switzerland to organize his visa, move out of his London apartment, sell his bike, settle his debts, and find himself a place to live in East Hampton until the Herrick was ready. But he couldn't afford to cut corners on the time frame Anton had given him. He was expected to have the hotel built by next Christmas, including all landscaping, open in the spring, and have generated enough positive buzz to have the place heaving with celebrity guests by the following summer. That gave him only sixteen months to, as Anton put it, wipe Palmers off the map. All he had today was a bare patch of earth and a missing suitcase.

But the epic task that lay ahead of him wasn't the only depressing thought on Lucas's mind. There was also his family. Guilty because he'd barely been in touch since moving to London, he decided on a whim to fly out to Ibiza for Christmas. It was a mistake. Things at home were as bad as they'd ever been. The farmer who rented out his miserable little cottage to Lucas's mother and her waster husband had finally gotten tired of waiting for his rent and kicked them out. It wasn't until Lucas showed up at the doorstep on Christmas Eve, weighed down with gifts, that he learned they were gone. The new tenant told him they were now living in a so-called studio apartment, which turned out to be little more than a squalid, one-room bedroom in the dodgy part of Santa Eulalia.

"Your brothers had to leave," Ines told Lucas when he finally tracked her down, inhaling deeply on one of the hand-rolled cigarettes she seemed to smoke constantly these days. "No room." She looked around the tiny living quarters and shrugged hopelessly. Jose, drunk as usual, was snoring loudly on the sofa bed in the corner.

Lucas had done his best to improve things. Apart from emptying his meager savings account and giving it all to his mother in cash, he'd tried to inject some Christmas spirit into the gloomy little apartment, rigging up a garish artificial tree in the middle of the room and dashing off around the island on Christmas morning to round up his good-for-nothing brothers for an enormous, if somewhat stilted, family lunch. But in three days, there was only so much he could do. He had to be back in Geneva for a strategy meeting with Anton on the twenty-seventh.

Staring out of the grimy window of the bus now, he watched the rain pounding its steely needles onto the drab, flat landscape on either side of the freeway and tried to push thoughts of his mother from his mind. How he hated America. His loathing had begun years ago, at the Britannia, but this was the first opportunity he'd had to observe Americans on their home turf, and so far, they'd done little to reverse his prejudices.

The guy at the immigration desk was a power-hungry asshole, questioning Lucas for almost thirty minutes, though he could plainly see that all his papers were in order, before finally stamping his visa as if he were performing a personal favor. Then there was baggage claim, where the United staff first lost his luggage and then, when Lucas complained, began playing what was clearly a favorite game of theirs, entitled something along the lines of Let's See Who Could Give Less of a Shit. They were really quite competitive at it.

The last straw had been the bus driver, a man so grossly overweight he looked like he might well have eaten his previous load of passengers and who smelled like he hadn't washed this year. Having refused to help Lucas with his one remaining bag, this gem of a human being then claimed to have no idea how long the bus might take to reach its destination—despite the fact that all he'd done for the past twelve years was make the mind-numbing journey back and forth from the airport to the Hamptons fifteen times a week.

Dickhead.

But the thing that really got under Lucas's skin was the fact that so many of the lowliest positions at the airport—rubbish sweepers, toilet attendants, and the like—seemed to be filled almost exclusively by Hispanics. He'd only been in the country three hours and already he was starting to feel like a second-class citizen.

Instinctively, he lifted his hand to run it through his hair, something he always did when he felt agitated, only to be surprised yet again to find his trademark mop of curls gone, replaced with the preppy short back and sides Anton had demanded. Numerous girls back in Europe had assured him they loved the new look, but Lucas couldn't get used to it. Every time he looked in the mirror, he did a double take when he saw a clean-shaven drone staring back at him. All he needed was a college tie and some veneers and he could be a CNN newscaster.

"Thz Bridgehammon," mumbled the driver, which Lucas interpreted by means of looking at the road signs as "This is Bridgehampton." Great. He could already speak moron.

How many fucking Hamptons were there, anyway? The road had become single-lane some time ago, but it seemed to stretch on forever, through a bunch of dull clapboard towns that all looked as drearily empty and sodden as the next. He thought he saw a sign saying "East Hampton, ten miles," but that must have been a good fifteen miles ago by his reckoning.

Finally, three long hours after leaving the airport, they reached the edge of town. A few minutes later the Jitney pulled over beside what looked like the main village green, and Lucas gratefully climbed out of his cramped seat.

Outside, the rain had turned to sleet. Even so, it felt great to breathe fresh air after the muggy confines of the bus. The guy sitting next to him must have eaten enough garlic last night to sustain a small town's worth of Italians. Holding his small case over his head in lieu of an umbrella, Lucas sprinted across the green toward the nearest available shelter, a coffee shop, shaking the freezing droplets off himself like a wet dog as he staggered inside.

"You look cold."

It was hardly the most insightful of opening lines. But one look at the waitress's small but perfectly formed body, all Latin curves and breasts heaving enticingly beneath her tight cashmere sweater, helped him see past her conversational deficiencies.

"Do I?" said Lucas, grinning. "Well, you look phenomenally sexy."

The girl laughed nervously. "Er, thanks. I guess." She blushed. "You're pretty direct, aren't you?"

Lucas shrugged. "I find it saves time." Taking off his coat, he rubbed his hands together for warmth before offering one to the girl to shake.

"I'm Lucas Ruiz."

"Desiree," said the girl, shaking his hand, still somewhat warily. He was a divine-looking man. Different too—not at all like the bland, all-American Ralph Lauren–model types she was used to seeing in East Hampton. This one was more Antonio Banderas, perhaps crossed with a young Warren Beatty. And that deep, soulful Spanish accent was to die for. Even so, the way he looked at her made her feel naked and vulnerable. It was nice and disconcerting at the same time.

"Can I get you something to drink?" she asked, pulling herself together.

"Desiree," said Lucas, rolling the word over his tongue like he was tasting an exquisite wine. "Beautiful name. Very appropriate."

She blushed again, deeper this time.

"I think I will have a drink, thank you, Desiree," he said, enjoying the effect he was having on her. "Hot chocolate, please. With as much cream as you can manage on the top."

He was the only customer in the café—in fact, looking outside through the rain-splattered window, he and his fellow Jitney passengers appeared to be the only people in the entire town—and his drink wasn't long in coming.

"The place looks dead," he said, nodding toward the window and the empty village green beyond as he sipped gratefully at the creamy chocolate. "Is it always like this?"

"June, July, and August you can't move. It's a zoo," said Desiree, pulling her thick dark hair back into a ponytail and tying it with a cheap elastic band. "But off season, yeah, it's pretty quiet. I actually prefer it this way."

"Really?" Lucas looked surprised. "Why? Aren't you bored?"

"Sometimes," she shrugged. "But, you know, I read. I paint. There's more to life than party party party."

"There is?" He was so deadpan it made her laugh. She was finally beginning to relax. He'd have liked to have stayed here chatting her up and gorging himself on hot chocolate for the rest of the day, but sadly it wasn't an option. Thanks to all the delays and fuckups at La Guardia, he was already late for his meeting at the Herrick with the site manager and a bunch of potential contractors and architects, all bidding for the work. He should ask her for directions and get going.

"Tell me," he asked casually, "have you heard much about the new hotel opening up here? I gather it's going to be a big deal."

"So they say," said Desiree. "Everyone's talking about it: the Herrick, it's called. They're building just a couple of blocks away from Palmers. All the local bigwigs are up in arms."

"They are?" Lucas sipped at his drink, avoiding her eye. "But surely another big hotel means more jobs, more local business, more money. I'd have thought people would be pleased."

Desiree laughed. "You obviously don't know much about East Hampton. People here already have enough money. They like to keep things the way they are: traditional. From what I hear the Herrick's going to be anything but that. According to Honor Palmer, the building's going to be a hideous modern glass thing, designed by some trendy Manhattan architect. A real eyesore, so they say."

"Is that so?" muttered Lucas angrily. How dare Honor act like she had inside information! He hadn't even definitively picked an architect yet, although the design would be modernist. He wondered what other lies she'd been spreading, and whether the whole town was already poisoned against him.

Perhaps he was foolish to have expected anything less. With so much to do in London before he left, he'd put off reading the fat file Anton had given him on Honor until he got on the plane. It was quite an eye-opener. Born with a silver spoon in her mouth, she'd evidently decided that one wasn't enough. This girl wanted the entire cutlery set, wrenching control of her old man's assets while he was dying of Alzheimer's.

What kind of a bitch did that to her own father?

"Personally, I think this German guy, whatever his name is, is wasting his money." Oblivious of Lucas's stony face, Desiree trundled on. "Palmers may be a bit run down, but it's an institution. I can't see how some faceless newcomer can compete with it. Especially not one run by a college kid with no experience."

"A college kid?" spluttered Lucas, unable to keep up his pretense of detachment any longer. "Is that what Honor Palmer's been saying?"

"Well…yes." Desiree looked baffled.

"Who the fuck is she to talk?" roared Lucas. "This time last year she was still at Harvard fucking Business School!"

"Hey, look, what do I know?" Realizing she'd offended him in some way, Desiree was kicking herself about it. Having gotten over her initial nerves, she'd decided Lucas was fully gorgeous. "Do you want another drink?"

"No," he snapped, dropping a ten on the table and getting up to leave. "I don't." Looking up at her confused, apologetic face, he relented.

"Look, sorry," he said. "It isn't you I'm mad at, sweetheart. But I do have to get going. Do you think you could direct me to the site of this new hotel, the Herrick?"

"Sure," she said, relieved to be back in his good books and praying silently that he'd ask her for her number before he left. "Make a right into the center of town, away from the beach. You'll see Palmers about six blocks down; you can't miss it. Five hundred yards farther on and you're there. But there's nothing to see," she added. "It's just a big, muddy hole."

"Thank you," said Lucas, pulling open the café door so that a chill blast of air hit the both of them.

"Wait!" Desiree heard herself calling after him. She couldn't just let him leave. "You never said what you were doing in town. If you're staying for a while I could show you around a bit. You know. If you'd like," she finished lamely, her cheeks turning from pink to maroon with embarrassment. It had been a long time since she'd had to make the effort with a guy, and she was clearly out of practice.

Lucas smiled. "I'd like that," he said. "And as it happens, I am staying for a while."

"Oh?"

"Yeah," he grinned. "I'm the college kid with no experience who'll be managing the big glass eyesore. The one the German guy is wasting his money on."

And with a wink he disappeared into the rainstorm, leaving Desiree staring wordlessly after him.

By the time Lucas reached Palmers he was freezing once again, having trudged through the rain like a hobo for almost twenty minutes without passing another soul. But despite the cold and his intense curiosity to check out the competition he decided against going inside. Honor, he knew, was still away in Boston, dealing with her late father's affairs, but he didn't want to risk encountering any of her staff until he both looked and felt on top of his game. Right now, nothing could have been further from the truth.

From the outside, though, he was encouraged. It was hardly the all-American idyll he'd been expecting. Beneath the solid gray blanket of clouds the whitewashed wooden structure looked bleak and forbidding, and the entire upper stories were covered with an ugly latticework of scaffolding. Leaping from bar to bar like so many human squirrels, a motley crew of grumbling workers were busy stripping tiles off the roof and hurling them to the ground where they joined a growing pile of shattered debris, littering up what must once have been a heavenly formal rose garden. All that noise and mess must be driving Honor's guests crazy.

Walking around to the side of the hotel, he peered through an original sash window (very nice) into the main drawing room, and his spirits were further lifted to see that the bar and sitting areas were almost empty. The few guests that were in residence looked like the sort of permanent fixtures that all the old-name hotels relied on off-season. There was one old man with close-cropped hair and a graying moustache sitting bolt upright on one of the overstuffed sofas—ex-military, Lucas would put money on it—and two overweight matrons, conservatively dressed in tweeds and pearls, sharing a pot of tea by the roaring, baronial fire. All three were probably too old and deaf to hear the roof works. No wonder Honor had been doing her best to slag off him and the Herrick. If this was the level of occupancy she was reduced to, she must be absolutely terrified at the prospect of competition. Structurally, the place looked to be on its last legs.

On the other hand, pressing his nose to the window pane like Tiny Tim looking at the rich folks' Christmas feast, Lucas caught glimpses of what had once made Palmers the greatest hotel in the world. Yes, the furnishings were threadbare, and the antique English furniture scratched and battered around the edges. There was even a visible hole in the exquisite Persian rug. But the room gave off such a welcoming, old-world warmth and charm it seemed to draw one in anyway. It was an old truism that money and class don't always go together, but Palmers was living proof of its veracity. You could quite see how its understated ambience had been a magnet to all that old Protestant Connecticut money. Mayflower money. If he hadn't come here with the express purpose of destroying the place and its eponymous owner, he might even have felt sorry to see such a once-great giant brought so low.

But he had. And anyway, he'd never been much of one for sentimental musings. Turning away, he trudged back to the road. Honor clearly intended to play dirty with him, but Little Miss Privileged was about to meet her match. No woman was going to outsmart Lucas, not Julia Brett-Sadler, and certainly not an inexperienced trust-fund brat like Honor Palmer.

He was enjoying himself, mentally embellishing his plan to nuke his would-be rival out of the water with a few well-placed bombs in the New York press when, turning a corner, he stopped dead in his tracks, his confident defiance deflating on the spot like an old man's erection.

"Fuck…" he whispered out loud.

He knew there wouldn't be a lot to see. But somehow the quagmire in front of him, stretching across acres like an abandoned, rain-swept battlefield, was far more depressing in reality than it had been in imagination. A few beams and pieces of tape had been laid on the ground as markers, and in the far right-hand corner of the plot was a single twelve-by-twelve-foot hole, filling up with rainwater. But that was it. That was what he had ten months to transform into a five-star resort, and another six to have it heaving with celebrities. It wasn't possible, surely?

Set back a few yards from the hole, an aluminum trailer mounted on concrete breeze blocks contained a temporary office, in which one man—one! Lucas had been expecting to meet at least five contractors and architects—was sitting behind a Formica desk, tapping away in a desultory, one-fingered manner at his keyboard.

"Hey, buddy. You look cold," the guy said, looking up but not moving from his seat as Lucas squelched in. Lacking Desiree's unique advantages—this man was fat, bald, and had sweat patches under his arms the size of small dinner plates—there was nothing to mitigate the banal stupidity of the comment. Lucas exploded.

"*Cold?*" he snarled. "No shit I'm *cold*, Sherlock. It's about minus nine out there, which you'd know if you bothered to get up off your fat backside and actually do some fucking work. Where the fuck is everybody else?"

The man opened his mouth to speak, but Lucas was on a roll. "The building works are supposed to be finished by Christmas. *Finished!*"

"Well, that ain't happening," tittered the fat man, ill-advisedly.

"Where are the contractors?" Lucas was apoplectic. "Our meeting was at two."

The fat man nodded and started shuffling the papers on his desk in a distinctly nervous manner. "Ah, about that. What I understood from Tisch's office...it was never, like, a definite meeting for today. I wasn't sure exactly when you'd be arriving."

"Bullshit!" bellowed Lucas. "I faxed you my flight details myself, weeks ago. All you had to do was pull together one lousy meeting, and you haven't even done that." Grabbing a plastic chair from the back of the trailer, he dragged it noisily over to the desk and sat down. "Get them all on the phone, right now. Maybe we can salvage a conference call."

The foreman looked apologetically at the basic plastic handset in front of him. "Sorry, man," he said. "We ain't set up for conference calls and shit."

Lucas looked as though he might be about to commit murder.

"Come on, lighten up a little," said the foreman defensively. "This ain't Manhattan, you know. No one round this neck of the woods is high tech."

Slamming both fists down on the desk, Lucas leaned right across it until his face was millimeters from the man's nose. With one easy movement, he swept the computer keyboard, monitor, and several stacks of paper onto the floor.

"You're fired," he said quietly, but with such menace that the foreman shivered, his fat arms wobbling like a shaken jelly. "Get the fuck out of here, and don't come back."

Backing away from Lucas like a startled crab, clearly antici-pating imminent physical violence, the foreman made a few halfhearted protests as he gathered up the remnants of his files.

"I don't know who you think you are, b-b-buddy," he stam-mered, once safely within reach of the trailer door. "But I work for the Tischen Group, not you. I gotta contract."

Picking up a heavy brass paperweight, Lucas raised it pur-posefully above his head. The debating part of the conversation had come to an end.

Taking the hint, the fat man waddled out the door. Lucas watched his gleaming bald pate from the trailer window as he climbed into his Ford pickup and sped away, no doubt in the direction of the nearest employment lawyer or union rep-resentative. Only once he'd gone did Lucas sink back down into his chair, pick up the 1980s-throwback telephone, and call Anton.

As usual he was unavailable—"traveling" was all his uptight Swiss secretary would divulge—so Lucas left a message, briefly outlining the events of the last half hour. There was no point going into detail. Tisch would either back him or he wouldn't.

Either way, all the ebullience he'd felt earlier outside Palmers had now deserted him utterly. The next year seemed to stretch ahead of him like a life sentence, stuck in this dreary, drizzly small town trying to build a hotel from ground zero—a hotel that 90 percent of the local populace had already decided they despised, thanks to Honor fucking Palmer.

He'd felt from the beginning that landing the Herrick job was too good to be true.

Looked like he was right. It was.

———   ———

"Fuck, Caleb, what is wrong with you?"

Hopping into the bathroom, Honor turned on the shower and wrinkled her nose at the smell as she rinsed the dog shit off her bare foot.

Three weeks after Lucas's arrival in town, she had finally made it back to East Hampton herself, having handed what was left of the tangled web of Trey's affairs to Sam Brannagan, the family lawyer.

"I've done my best, Sam," she told him wearily, unloading an entire trunkload of papers from the back of her rental car. "Most of the personal stuff is filed, but I really can't give it any more time now. I have to get back to Palmers."

Sam thought how tired and stressed she looked. He hadn't seen her since that ghastly meeting in his office last summer, and she'd been tiny enough then, but now her collarbones jutted visibly through her white cotton shirt, and her sludge-gray size-zero pants hung off her hips like dirty ship's sails. Running Palmers must be taking more out of her than she'd anticipated.

In fact, her wasted appearance had more to do with grief and stress about her dead-end relationship with Devon than it did with anxiety over Palmers, although she was itching to get back, especially since word had reached her that the future manager of the new Tischen was in town and had moved into a little cottage by the beach. It was now two days since her return and, rather to her annoyance, she had yet to meet the elusive Mr. Ruiz. To be honest, she'd rather expected him to stop by Palmers and make an appointment to see her. As the new kid on the block, sent here for the express purpose of putting her out of business, she figured the responsibility of a courtesy call lay firmly with him. But maddeningly he'd made no effort to get in touch, and Honor certainly wasn't about to.

Though she forced herself to keep confident about Palmers' future, she was still hopelessly unprepared for the coming summer season. So much of her energy had been devoted to getting the structural problems under control without causing too much disruption to her few, precious off-season guests that she'd barely had time to begin her much-needed PR drive. Nervous about promoting Palmers' renaissance in case the media used it as an excuse to rehash the twisted allegations about her "betraying" her father, she'd hoped for the first few months that if she kept her head down, the bad press would eventually fizzle out. But it hadn't. Thanks to the growing media interest in Tina and Dick, and Lise's shameless attempts to add to her already whopping inheritance with interviews in glossy magazines, looking as grief-stricken as she could in Atelier Versace and vintage Tiffany emeralds, the Palmer family soap opera looked set to run and run, with Honor unfairly cast in the role of resident villainess.

After the funeral, she'd decided to adopt a different tack, pulling up the names of every guest to stay at Palmers over the last decade and placing personal calls to each of them, urging them to think about returning this summer and offering them significantly discounted rates. It was a risky strategy that could easily have smacked of desperation had she not handled each phone call with the delicate balance of confidence and humility that such a task required. It had also taken weeks to plough through the list. But it seemed to have paid off. Once people heard Honor in person, they sensed immediately that she bore no resemblance to the money-hungry monster portrayed by the gossip press. Flattered by the personal attention and tempted by the low rates, they began, slowly—painfully slowly—to call back and start booking.

The rising summer numbers were wonderful, a real shot in the arm, but they'd come at a cost. With the reduced rates they would barely cover costs, and she'd be forced to put off the major electrical work for at least another few months. In the meantime, she'd done her best to start discrediting her soon-to-be rival, emphasizing Lucas's lack of experience and Anton Tisch's penchant for Blade Runner–esque architecture, knowing how much that would piss off the arch-conservative Hamptonites. Slowly, the tide of local opinion was beginning to turn in her favor, but who knew how long that would last? Now that Lucas was here in person, he was bound to start returning fire.

"You're a rescue dog, you know," said Honor, trying to look stern at the sweetly snub-nosed boxer sticking his curious head around the door and failing miserably. "I rescued you. That means you owe me. So what's with all the crapping indoors, huh?"

Caleb responded by thumping his stumpy tail loudly against the tiles a few times before running around in an excited circle and finally launching himself at his mistress with such force he almost knocked her flying.

"Oh, all right, all right," Honor laughed, submitting happily to his enthusiastic licks as she perched on the side of the bath and began drying her foot with a fluffy hand towel. "I'll take you for another run. Just give me a minute to throw some clothes on, OK?"

It would take more than a dog-poo-stained carpet or Lucas Ruiz's pointed radio silence to dampen Honor's spirits today. Devon had called last night to tell her he was coming out early for Easter, officially so that he could deal with some local politics or other and attend a bunch of committee meetings, but actually as an excuse to spend some quality time with Honor before Karis and the kids flew out for the holiday weekend. For ten glorious days, Honor would have him all to herself, the longest they'd ever spent together. And it hadn't come a moment too soon.

She'd only seen him for one snatched, unsatisfactory night in a New Jersey motel since the day she'd let him have it with both barrels at her father's funeral. Perhaps that had been a bit unfair, she could see with hindsight. But somehow watching him play the dutiful husband to Karis had been a thousand times worse than just knowing he did it when she wasn't there. The fact she'd been burying her dad at the time probably hadn't helped her tolerance levels much either.

They spoke on the phone daily, but it wasn't the same. Despite her long years of practice at it, extended periods of celibacy weren't Honor's forte and tended to make her stress levels rocket. A few more days and she'd be able to stake her claim as the world masturbation champion. Forget "mistress of her domain." These days she was just a mistress of frustration—or a frustrated mistress. Devon wasn't gonna know what hit him when he walked through that door tonight.

Pulling on her running shorts and sneakers, she looked out the window while Caleb went demented with excitement, hurling himself at the front door to her suite like a canine battering ram. March storm clouds were gathering, but they looked high enough in the sky that there was a good chance they'd blow over. A run would do her good, warm her up for the marathon fucking session she fully intended on having later.

"Come on then, you moron," she said, ruffling Caleb's ears affectionately as she grabbed his leash from the coffee table. "Let's go."

Stuck in his trailer on the building site, Lucas was rapidly losing the will to live.

Three weeks he'd been here now—three weeks, one day, and two hours, to be precise—and he didn't think he'd had more than forty hours' sleep since his plane landed. He had bags under his eyes the size of Louis Vuitton trunks, and his voice had taken on the hoarse, gravelly Serge Gainsbourg edge it always got when he was chronically overtired, exacerbated in this instance by hours spent screaming down the phone at everyone from architects to lawyers to building suppliers.

To Lucas's amazement, Anton had been sanguine to the point of nonchalance about his depressing report from the front line and completely relaxed that he'd summarily fired the foreman.

"It's always the way," he commented blithely. "When you've been in this business as long as I have, my boy, very little that construction companies do, or don't do, will surprise you. Now that you're out there things will kick up a notch."

A *notch*? Did the man have no idea what they were up against? Naturally a workaholic, Lucas went into overdrive, spurred on by his terror of failure and his fury at the steady stream of negative campaigning that had been spewing out of the Palmers camp for months. It turned out that it wasn't only the locals that Honor had poisoned: seemingly, she'd been busy as a bee, bad-mouthing Anton and the Tischen chain generally, as well as Lucas personally, in a whole bunch of lifestyle magazines, including the influential *World Traveler*. He couldn't imagine how Anton had missed it. But then again, he'd missed it too. There simply hadn't been enough hours in the day to keep track of everything before he left Europe, and there still weren't. But from now on, he'd be all over that bitch like a rash.

By day, he spent hour after hour glued to the phone in the poky little trailer, hiring site managers, contractors, and engineers, most of whom he didn't even have time to meet before they showed up for work. It was risky, he knew, using cheap, anonymous labor like that, choosing builders purely because they were available and gave him the lowest quote. But his only hope of meeting Anton's targets was to flood the place with more workers than an episode of *Extreme Makeover: Home Edition*, and pray that they worked as fast. Already the site was crawling with men like an enormous muddy anthill, while Julian, the stressed-out architect's assistant who did most of his boss's work, yelled at them ineffectually through a bullhorn, waving his drawings in the bitter March wind like a surrender flag.

At night, Lucas spent long hours doing press searches on the Internet, perched on a packing case in the little beach cottage his moron of a relocation agent had rented for him—what did she think he was, a fucking Munchkin? The ceilings were so low he hit his head everywhere, and the place had more pink and lace than Liberace's bedroom. Though he was desperate for sleep, he knew he had to think of ways to hit back at Palmers. If Honor was to be believed, every senator, film star, and pop artist in her little black book had committed to take suites at Palmers for the summer. If he read one more puff piece about the hotel's "astonishing revival" he was going to throw up.

Then, this morning, his annoyance level had shot up still further when the expensive new multiline phone system he'd had installed in the trailer had died on him, right in the middle of a crucial conversation with Dean Roberts, his head architect and the hapless Julian's boss.

"Fucking motherfucker, son of a motherfucking bitch!" he yelled. Switching on his new state-of-the-art US cell phone to try to call Dean back, the words *no service* flashed in cheerful neon pink across the LCD screen. The guy in the T-Mobile store had warned him that reception locally was erratic and suggested that if all else failed, he could try the beach.

Sighing heavily, Lucas grabbed the keys to his rented Ford pickup, which had an extended cab. It was a fucking farce, trying to get anything done in this stinking country.

In the car he turned up the Van Halen full blast and opened all the windows to keep himself from nodding off. Not even his anger could stop the tiredness lapping at his body like a rising tide, and for once he was grateful for the light drizzle of rain blowing into the car and pricking his cheeks, keeping him awake. He had to go home and sleep tonight, no matter what.

Pulling into the almost deserted beach parking lot a few minutes later, he turned off the ignition, pulled out his phone, and looked again for the slightest flickering of a bar to indicate he had reception.

Nothing. If he lost any more time because of this, he'd sue T-fucking-Mobile…

Swearing under his breath, he grabbed an umbrella from the backseat and got out, slamming the driver's door and pulling his sweater more tightly around him against the bitter, wet wind as he set off toward the shore. It was easier to get fucking network coverage up a hill in Ibiza than it was on Long Island. Fucking ridiculous.

He must have trudged half a mile along the sand before his phone finally stuttered into life. Quickly punching in Dean's direct line, he cupped his hand against his ear to block out the roar of the ocean behind him.

"Look, darling, I don't care if he's in a meeting," he shouted into the mouthpiece at the unfortunate receptionist. "I've spent the past hour trying to get hold of him. I'm shivering my ass off on a fucking freezing beach here. I can assure you, he wants to take this call."

The next thing he heard was some tinny hold music, followed by an ominous rumble of thunder and two dramatic flashes of sheet lightning. He barely had time to open his umbrella before the heavens opened and a veritable monsoon of water began pounding down onto the beach.

"Shit, shit shit." There were some dunes about fifty feet away that would have offered him some protection beyond the feeble respite afforded by the umbrella. He contemplated making a dash for it but decided it wasn't worth the risk of losing his precious signal again.

"I'm putting you back on hold for just a moment, Mr. Ruiz," the girl's voice drifted back to him through the din of the storm. "Mr. Roberts will be with you very shortly."

"No!" Lucas shouted. "Don't put me on—" But it was too late. The whiny refrain of "Greensleeves" had already started up, and the rain, if anything, was intensifying.

"Excuse me?"

Lucas jumped a mile when someone tapped him on the back. Spinning around, his adrenaline pumping, his fear soon turned to annoyance: it was just a kid. Dressed in running shorts and a thin tank top, the tiny, androgynous figure was soaked to the bone.

"Have you seen…" it panted, "a dog? He ran into the surf ten minutes ago, and I'm worried he might have…it's so rough out there."

On closer inspection, Lucas could see that "it" was in fact a "she," and not a child but a very short young woman. Despite her tiny build, there was something unnervingly mannish about her. Her hips were thrust forward, and she squared her shoulders with subconscious aggression when she spoke to him, in a low, husky voice that also seemed quite at odds with her doll-like frame. The only touches of femininity were the brilliant green eyes, like violent slits of storm-wet grass, and the perfect smoothness of her skin.

"He's a boxer, about yay high." She held her hand up to the level of her waist, looking up at him pleadingly. "He's brown and white, with a—"

"No," said Lucas, cutting her off. "Sorry. I haven't seen anything."

He knew he was being rude. But Dean would be on the line any moment, and he needed to concentrate. If he didn't get the signed contract from this guy today and get him and his men out here by next week, he risked losing more precious months of development time. The last thing he had the time for was to go running around the beach on a wild-goose chase because some dippy girl was too stupid to control her dog.

"Look, please, he might be drowning. Would you mind helping me look for him?" The desperation in her voice was palpable.

Her arms, Lucas noticed, were thin and muscly, like a sprinter's, and her chest was so flat he could have ironed his shirt on it. Why did women do that to themselves? Exercise away all their curves like that? Didn't they realize how unsexy it looked?

"I wouldn't normally ask," the girl went on, "but there's no one else around and it's such a huge area to cover." She gazed forlornly along the sodden beach in both directions. There were tears in her eyes. "And he can't swim, you see. He thinks he can. But he's such a dumb dog…"

"Look." Lucas held up his phone bad-temperedly. "I'm on an important call here, OK? If you can't control your dog you shouldn't take him out." He turned away from her as the project manager finally picked up the line. "Ah, Dean. Sorry about that. I'm having a few technical problems I'm afraid. Where were we?"

Jogging along the sand a few minutes later, calling Caleb's name into the wind, Honor let her anger distract her from the awful worry. What a vile, rude, arrogant man! Not only had he refused to help her look for poor Caleb, but he hadn't even offered her shelter under his huge umbrella! What sort of a jerk-off stood there making phone calls when a woman was practically drowning right in front of him? And when a dog might be dying, for God's sake, struggling for breath in those huge, punishing waves?

OK, so he was a good-looking jerk-off. Why was it that handsome, rich men always figured they could get away with anything? That the rules of good manners that lesser mortals lived by didn't apply to them?

Assholes like him were ten a penny in Boston. Honor could totally picture this guy's life: probably some stinking rich investment banker, down at his beach house for a few days and pissed because of the shitty weather, used to taking out his bad moods on his wife or his secretary or whichever other of his minions happened to be around.

Bozo.

Fucking vain, spoiled…

Breaking away from her indignant thoughts, her heart suddenly soared as a very wet, very tired, and somewhat sheepish-looking Caleb came ambling across the wet sand in her direction. Thank God he was OK.

"There you are! You bad boy." She grinned.

Stopping a few feet in front of her, Caleb sat down sedately and started wagging his tail, a picture of obedience all of a sudden.

"Oh, don't you give me that," said Honor, sinking to her knees while she clipped on his leash and hugged him, pressing her face against his sodden fur. She felt quite choked with emotion. What would she have done if she'd lost him? "You are such a pain in the ass. But you can make it up to me by keeping your eyes peeled for an asshole on a cell phone, OK? If either of us sees him, I want you to kill. Got it? Kill! You think you can do that?"

Cocking his head to one side, the dog looked at her blankly.

"Never mind," said Honor, shivering as she stroked his head lovingly. Now that he was back safe, she was suddenly feeling the cold. "I'm wiped out, anyway. Let's go home."

Later that night, wrapped up in a cashmere blanket and slippers and clutching a hot water bottle to her chest, she told Devon all about her encounter with the rude man on the beach.

"I mean, he just stood there," she raged between sneezes. "It was the biggest umbrella I've ever seen in my life, and he left me standing there like a drowned rat. He'd have let Caleb drown."

"Shhh." Devon handed her the hot whiskey toddy he'd had ordered up from the Palmers bar. "Save your voice, honey. The main thing is that you found Caleb and you both got home safe." He frowned. "I don't like that you were out there half dressed in this awful weather. You need to take better care of yourself, Honor."

Honor sipped the whiskey and smiled. Sometimes it annoyed her when Devon talked down to her like a little girl. But tonight it felt comforting to be babied. Having never had that reassurance from her own father, it was a huge part of her attraction to him, and she knew it.

"Why?" she teased him. "Don't you like the idea of another man seeing me in a wet T-shirt?"

Taking off his jacket and loosening his tie, Devon climbed up onto the bed. Removing the drink from her hand, he put it down gently on the bedside table and pinned her arms back against the pillows, bringing his face right down to hers.

"No," he said gruffly. "I don't."

Kissing her, tasting the whiskey and lemon in her mouth, feeling the tiny but firm apples of her breasts rising up to meet his hands as he moved them slowly down over her body, he felt a wave of desire and possessiveness wash over him.

Being away from her for so long had been hard, stuck in Boston with Karis and her incessant demands for attention. Though he'd told Honor he no longer made love with his wife, this wasn't strictly true. Sex was infrequent and, from Devon's perspective, perfunctory. In his own mind sharing the marital bed wasn't really a betrayal of Honor, more something he kept from her out of consideration, because it would hurt her. But Karis would have smelled a rat if he'd switched their love life off completely—he daren't risk it.

It did make him feel a little weird, though. When he was at home in Boston, his life continued much the same as it always had. He loved Honor, and he missed her, missed her mind, her body, her touch, everything. And yet when he was away, there were days when his relationship with her felt almost like a dream. Karis, the kids, the office—they were reality. It was becoming easier to compartmentalize his affair, to switch it off mentally, when he needed to.

"I need you," Honor whispered. Shrugging off her blanket and sliding down the bed beneath him, she opened her legs and wrapped them tightly around his waist, like a baby monkey clinging to its parent.

"And I you," said Devon. Easing himself out of his pants, he slipped inside her, as urgent and hungry as a virgin schoolboy. "Christ, Honor, I've missed you. So much."

Arching her back, Honor gently rocked him back and forth inside her, closing her eyes the better to lose herself in his movements and the musky, masculine smell of him she'd been dreaming of for so many long weeks.

Finally, gloriously, the frustrations and annoyances of her day began to melt away like the last of the winter snow dissolving in the spring sunshine.

Caleb was OK. Palmers was improving, albeit at a snail's pace. And now her darling Devon was back in her arms, where he belonged. It would take more than one arrogant prick with a cell phone to spoil that.

CHAPTER TEN

TWO WEEKS LATER, LOLA CARTER LOOKED AT HER REFLECTION in the bathroom mirror and sighed loudly. After a sleepless night interspersed with some heavy bouts of sobbing, her face was so puffy she looked like she was having an allergic reaction.

"Fuck you, Bryan Sutton," she said, splashing freezing water onto her skin. The shock made her gasp for breath, but she had to do something to snap herself out of this funk. The bastard so wasn't worth it.

Bryan was supposed to have flown out with her from Boston to the Hamptons this weekend. He was the one thing that would have made her mom's tedious birthday cocktail party bearable. But now…now it was all ruined.

OK, so he loved himself a bit. High school quarterbacks always did. And Lola did have a worrying habit of falling for the best-looking, most popular guys around, rather than the nice, decent boys. (Being packed off to St. Mary's by her parents had done nothing to dampen her social life. Everyone knew that boys hung around all-girls schools like flies on shit.) But Bryan also had a sensitive, loving side—or at least, she'd thought he had, before she caught him red-handed with that slut Lorna Mantoni.

"No more high school jerks," she told her reflection sternly, slathering on a big dollop of moisturizer and willing herself to feel better. In an hour's time she'd have to play the dutiful daughter in front of two hundred of her parents' dullest East Hampton friends, so she had to get her shit together.

From now on, she would only date college guys. Period. Someone from Harvard College, or the law school even. That should at least make her dad happy.

Things between Lola and her father were still not good. Devon might have won the battle to enroll her in St. Mary's and steamroll her into taking a bunch of science courses that bored her to tears, but Lola still hadn't given up her dreams of becoming a designer. They fought about her future constantly. Unbeknownst to Devon, she'd already made formal applications to a bunch of fashion schools and sent them off in secret. Man, was he was going to go ape-shit when he found out. But so far she'd done a good job of hiding all the brochures and paperwork. And at least breaking up with Bryan would score her a few advance points in her dad's good books. Devon had hated him from day one.

Wrapping her green bathrobe around her shoulders, she padded back into her bedroom and opened the blinds. It was only half past five, but the sky was already getting dark. Right now it was the sort of bruise-blue color that Lola loved. She'd tried many times to capture it in a silk dye—how great would it be to have a full-length evening gown that color?—but had never quite gotten it right.

"Knock, knock?"

Karis, immaculate in a white Givenchy jacket and navy flared trousers, slipped into her room carrying a tray laden with smoked salmon and scrambled eggs on toast, Lola's all-time favorite snack.

"I thought you might be hungry," she said, smiling, setting down the tray on the end of the bed. "How're you feeling, honey?"

Both of Lola's parents had been in bizarrely good moods lately. Her dad had been practically skipping around the house since she arrived, chipper as a lottery winner—and that was before he heard about Bryan. And her mom, who could normally be counted on to get drunk and depressed on her own birthdays, seemed giddy with excitement about tonight's party. Especially since the guy who was building some big new hotel in town, this Spanish dude everyone was talking about, had agreed to come. Personally, Lola couldn't see the big deal. It wasn't like the guy was Johnny Depp or anything. But this was the first social engagement he'd accepted since coming to East Hampton, and her mom clearly viewed it as a major coup.

"I'm fine." Lola took a suspicious bite of the toast. "Do I have a terminal illness that no one's told me about?"

"What? Of course not." Karis looked shocked. "Why would you say a thing like that?"

Lola smiled. Her mother could be terribly literal sometimes.

"I was kidding." The eggs were delicious. Sitting down cross-legged on the bed, she set about demolishing them in earnest. "You're being awfully nice to me, that's all."

"Well, you've just been through a breakup. I know how tough that can be." Had she OD'd on Doctor Phil or something? All this concern was seriously out of character.

"But I do have some news that'll cheer you up," Karis beamed. "Guess who's just turned up downstairs?"

"Brad Pitt?" said Lola hopefully.

"Better," said her mother. "Nicky. He managed to get a flight out after all. Isn't that terrific?"

"Mmmm." Lola nodded through a mouthful of toast and rolled her eyes sarcastically. "Terrific."

Great. Just when she'd thought her weekend couldn't get any worse, her dipshit brother had to show up. He was bound to give her a hard time about Bryan, in between bouts of sucking up to their mom like a leech.

"Who else is coming?"

"Oh, everyone!" gushed Karis. "Well, everyone who's anyone, let's put it that way. Lucas Ruiz, as I told you…"

"Yeah, yeah, yeah," said Lola, bored. "And?"

"Oh, darling," Karis waved her hand distractedly, "I don't know. Do you really want me to list them all? The Sullivans, the Meyers, Antonia Dickinson, Reverend Jameson and his wife."

Lola took another big bite of toast.

"Anyone under the age of, like, ninety?"

"Don't be snarky," said Karis on autopilot. "Honor Palmer's coming. She's young, and fun."

"I guess," said Lola.

She'd liked Honor the few times they'd met last summer. The girl didn't take any shit from anyone.

"Hey," her eyes lit up mischievously, "d'you think Honor and this Lucas guy will have a big catfight at the table? She must hate him, right, setting up shop so close to Palmers?" Scraping up the last of the eggy crumbs, she pushed her empty plate to one side.

Karis shrugged. "I don't see why she should. Competition's a healthy thing in business. But I imagine she's as curious about him as the rest of us."

"Who's 'us'?" said Lola. "I'm not curious. At all."

She loved her mom, but she felt sorry for anyone whose life was so boring that they considered meeting a hotel manager to be a major event. The most she hoped for from this evening's party was that it would take her mind off Bryan for an hour or so. Plus it was a chance to get dressed up, and she'd had precious few of those since her incarceration at St. Mary's.

"Suit yourself," said Karis, not unkindly, smoothing down the creases in her pants as she got up to leave. "But tonight is my birthday, and it's a celebration, OK? Don't let some idiot boy ruin it for you, or the rest of us."

"Don't worry, Mom," said Lola with feeling. "I won't. I've practically forgotten all about him already."

Two hours later, Lucas was sitting in his parked truck in the Carters' driveway, tilting the rearview mirror while he adjusted the knot on his tie.

"Give me a second, OK?" he asked the impatient-looking valet hovering by the open driver's door.

He could have strangled Lucy, his assistant, for accepting tonight's invitation on his behalf. She'd only been working for him a week, and he needed the help desperately, but one more fuckup like this and she'd be out on her ear.

East Hampton was a small town, and Lucas had already heard the whispers—that the local hostesses were starting to take offense at his refusal to accept social invitations. He'd even overheard a conversation in the newsstand yesterday in which one woman had described him to her friend as a recluse.

What did these people want from him, for God's sake? Couldn't they see that he had a fucking mountain to climb at the Herrick? That in the few snatched hours he got to spend away from work, all he wanted to do was sleep? Or perhaps, if he was feeling really adventurous, crack open a beer and collapse on his couch in Liberace Cottage in front of a decent porno?

Thankfully, things had finally started speeding up on-site. The foundations were in, and three days ago Lucas had watched gleefully as the first steel load-bearing beams sprang up out of the ground like a phoenix rising from the ashes. Yesterday he'd made a rare trip into Manhattan for a presentation at Dean Roberts's office, where he saw a computer-generated mock-up of the enormous, curved, ecclesiastical arc of glass that was to form the core of the Herrick's facade. Personally Lucas thought it quite beautiful, like the bow of a ship. But if the general whispers he'd picked up from the locals so far were anything to go by, he expected most of them would disagree. Anything that wasn't eighteenth-century weatherboard counted as a hideous modern monstrosity in their book. He was sure to be dragged over the coals tonight, with every neighborhood busybody and his wife grilling him about the building works. Frankly, he could have done without it.

The only silver lining to tonight's cloud was the prospect of at last meeting Honor Palmer in the flesh. When he'd first arrived, he'd confidently expected her to turn up at the site and introduce herself, out of curiosity if nothing else. But no, Her Majesty had maintained an infuriating, regal lack of interest from the start. Well, screw her. When the interview he'd just done with American *Vogue* came out next month, she'd have to sit up and take notice. By a great stroke of luck, an old friend of Lucas's from his Ibiza days was deputy features editor there now and had been happy to do a straightforward promo piece on the Herrick as the new, hip hotel in the Hamptons. Miss High and Mighty Palmer was about to discover that the power of the press worked both ways.

"Sir." Somehow the valet managed to make the word sound like an insult. "We do have people waiting behind you. Perhaps you could take care of that inside?" He glanced disdainfully at Lucas's tie.

Climbing down from the truck's cab, Lucas towered over him like a brooding Spanish Goliath. "Listen to me, you snooty little shit." The valet swallowed nervously. "If I want to take a moment to fix my tie, then that's what I'm going to do. Would you tell those gentlemen to hurry it up?" He gestured to the pair of grumbling old buffers in the Bentley Continental behind him. "I don't think so. And you know why not? Because they're white, that's why. And I am Spanish."

"Sir, I can assure you that's not the case," the valet mumbled, backing away as Lucas drew even closer. "Your being Hispanic…"

"I am not Hispanic!" Lucas roared. "I'm Spanish. Not that I'd expect you to know the difference. Maybe you think I should be the one in that uniform. Huh? Is that it?" He grabbed at the guy's lapels but then abruptly released him. "Ah, forget it," he muttered, straightening his tie again for good measure. "You're not worth it."

Ignoring the open-mouthed stares of the other arriving guests, he walked calmly up the steps to the house—or estate, as people here pretentiously insisted on calling every decent-size property. In fairness, the Carter place was almost grand enough to warrant the title. Not that it was ostentatious or in any way flash. Quite the opposite. Everything about the house reeked of old money, from the understated white clapboard facade to the original Victorian gas lamps lining the driveway. Even the family's cars were distinctly low-key—a Jeep Cherokee and a BMW convertible that had seen better days—compared to the Ferraris, Bentleys, and Aston Martins littering the driveway. Devon Carter could clearly have afforded a fleet of Ferraris if he wanted them. But that was the point. He didn't.

As he walked through the front door, a maid relieved Lucas of his coat and led him down an apparently endless corridor toward a crescendoing buzz of voices at the rear of the house. Four years at the Ecole Hôtelière had given Lucas an expert eye for interiors, and he appraised Mrs. Carter's decor as he ambled along: simple and uncluttered with lots of white wood and enormous bunches of freesias everywhere, it was exactly what he would have expected in a wealthy Boston family's vacation home. A little too feminine for his personal taste, perhaps. But undeniably classy.

"The party's in the drawing room, through there on your left," the maid informed him, a little frostily Lucas felt, before walking off. He watched her go, an ugly girl with drooping shoulders and pimples struggling to break through her thick makeup. He wondered what had possessed Devon Carter to employ her, before the thought struck him that it was probably Mrs. Carter who made the hiring decisions at home. No doubt she didn't want some tart in a maid's uniform making her look bad.

"You must be Lucas!" Right on cue, the drawing room door swung open and a very pretty, only marginally over-the-hill blonde opened her arms wide, greeting him like an old friend and kissing him on both cheeks in the European fashion.

"Mrs. Carter." He smiled. If she weren't so uptight, he decided, she could be quite sexy. "Thank you so much for inviting me. I must say, it was unexpected."

Though hardly short of social invitations—they'd been falling from the sky like unwanted confetti since the week he arrived—the last person Lucas had expected to hear from was the wife of Devon Carter. Devon had been by far the most vocal of the Herrick's many opponents on the planning committee and was a paid-up member of the Palmers' Old Guard, Modernism-Is-Evil squad.

"Unexpected? Goodness me, what nonsense!" Karis let out a tinkling little laugh. "You're the hottest ticket in town, Mr. Ruiz, don't you know that? Our very own international man of mystery. Although," she wagged her finger at him teasingly, "I'm afraid there are quite a few people here tonight who want to have a word with you about that glass…thing you're building."

Here we go, thought Lucas. The barbed comments were starting already. On second thought, he was going to fire Lucy for putting him through this.

"I'm afraid I'm strictly off duty tonight, Mrs. Carter. No talking shop."

"Please," Karis squeezed his hand. "Call me Karis. You'll make me feel old otherwise."

"Karis." He repeated the word in his slow, knee-weakening Spanish accent, throwing in a wink for good measure that made his hostess glow with pleasure.

"Let the poor fellow catch his breath, darling, before you start haranguing him."

"Devon, there you are. This is—" Spinning around, Karis looked thoroughly put out at the interruption.

"I know who he is," said Devon.

The man who stepped forward to shake Lucas's hand was older than he'd pictured him and much more distinguished, with graying hair and the sort of deep voice and firm grip one associated with captains of industry or senior military officers. He was good-looking, if you liked the whole silver-fox roué senator thing, but stiffer than a day-old corpse. And his superior, snobbish noblesse oblige manner was instantly off-putting.

"How are you finding East Hampton?" He smiled, ostensibly in welcome, though it came off as patronizing. The Boston accent didn't help, either. It was pure JFK. Lucas found himself wondering whether it were genuine or had been deliberately acquired and decided probably the latter. Either way it made him sound like he had the mother of all sticks up his ass.

"I'm still finding my feet," said Lucas, adding jokingly, "To be honest, I feel like a bit of a circus freak tonight. People keep staring. Are they always like this?"

Devon frowned defensively. "Like what? It's natural for people to be curious," he said. "You're making dramatic changes to both the look and the spirit of their town. Or at least you will be."

"I'm building a hotel, Mr. Carter," said Lucas wearily. "Not turning East Hampton into Las Vegas."

"Hmmm." Devon sounded unconvinced. "I'd say the jury was still out on that one. But let's canvass some other opinions, shall we? Morty!"

Before Lucas could protest, his host started waving to a doddery, white-haired man with a pronounced stoop, who dutifully shuffled over.

"This is Morty Sullivan, chairman of our planning committee, among many other things," he said brightly. "I believe he's a friend of your boss. Morty, meet Lucas Ruiz."

Shit. This must be the guy Anton had blackmailed to get the Herrick project off the ground. According to the files Lucas had read, he was only fifty-two, but he looked decades older, poor bastard. As for he and Anton being friends, he presumed this was Devon's idea of a joke. A pretty cruel one, judging by the old man's terror-stricken face.

Morty shook Lucas's hand with all the enthusiasm of someone greeting the Grim Reaper. "How do you do?" he asked querulously.

"Mr. Sullivan." Lucas nodded respectfully in return. He felt genuinely bad for the guy. Devon, on the other hand, seemed to be reveling in the awkwardness of the moment. Evidently he was not only pompous, but spiteful.

Lucas spent the next half hour being thrust like a ritual sacrifice in front of the various great and good burghers of the town, smiling until his jaw ached, and defending the Herrick, or trying to, until his head throbbed. Devon stood beside him through each encounter, his smug, paternalistic smile seeming to suggest that he was doing Lucas a great favor by introducing him into "polite" Hamptons society. Which was ironic, seeing as the one thing these people were self-evidently not was polite.

"Glass is one thing, Mr. Ruiz," a withered crone dressed head to toe in black Chanel, like a crow, conceded grudgingly. "But is all the steel really necessary? That's what I'd like to know."

"Has your employer ever *been* to the Hamptons?" The crow's equally ancient friend was keen to join the conversation, closing her bony, arthritic fingers around Lucas's arm like a vise while she harangued him. "Perhaps if he actually saw the town he was defacing…"

"It wouldn't make a difference, Sheila." The crow talked through Lucas as though he were invisible. "He's *German*. None of these Europeans—no offense, Mr. Ruiz—none of them really understand the American concept of class. I may disapprove of the way Honor threw over her poor father, but there'll never be another Palmers in this town. It's as simple as that."

Lucas longed to tell the pair of them to stick their ignorant, racist opinions where the monkey stuck his nuts, but for once he restrained himself, escaping instead to the far side of the room and sinking gratefully down into an empty space on one of the couches. Some kind soul handed him a fresh martini, which he downed in a single gulp.

Beside him, a dark-haired boy was talking animatedly on his cell phone. Jumping off the call with a loud and self-important "Ciao, ciao," he turned to Lucas.

"Nick Carter," he said, pumping Lucas's hand vigorously. "And you must be Lucas. Welcome."

"Thanks," said Lucas warily. It was hard to put his finger on it, but there was something about the boy, a certain arrogance, that he instantly disliked. He reminded Lucas of every spoiled, cocky rich-kid playboy who used to prop up the bar at the Cadogan: handsome, certainly, although in quite a different way from his father. Devon might be stiffer than a porn star's cock, but he was masculine to the *n*th degree. This boy, on the other hand, was metrosexual to the point of foppishness—slicked-back hair, doused with enough Gucci Envy to stop a train, manicured nails, a mouth full of enamel veneers. He clearly hadn't done a day's real work in his life.

Just then, Lucas was distracted from his musings by the appearance of a bombshell of a redhead.

"Aren't you going to introduce me?" She addressed herself to Nick, who looked up at her disdainfully.

"Sure," he grunted. "Lucas, this is my kid sister, Lola."

"Hello*la*," drawled Lucas. At long last the evening was starting to look up.

She was wearing exactly the sort of outfit he usually hated: a long gypsy skirt that swished like a mermaid's tail when she walked and some sort of peasant smock shirt with a gilet thrown over the top. But on her, it worked. And unless he was hallucinating—unlikely after only one martini, though God knew he was tired enough—he could have sworn he saw her give him a distinctly lascivious wink.

For her part, Lola's pulse had taken off like a rocket—holy crap, was this guy *hot!*—but she made a titanic effort to play it cool, not wanting to betray any sort of weakness in front of her brother. No wonder all her mom's friends had gotten so excited over Lucas. The words "hotel manager" had conjured up an image in her mind of a balding, middle-aged bore with a paunch and a polyester suit. Who could have guessed East Hampton's public enemy number one would turn out to be such a love god?

On the other side of the room, Devon could feel the tension coiling around his arteries like a slowly squeezing fist. Honor, who'd arrived late and very obviously tipsy five minutes ago, was making a spectacle of herself flirting with one of the waiters. Itching to go over and confront her, he had to wait almost ten more minutes until Karis was safely engrossed in conversation with one of her girlfriends before he made his move.

Weaving his way through the crowd, he surprised her, grabbing her by the arm and pulling her to one side.

"What's wrong with you?" he hissed. "Are you drunk?"

"No," Honor lied, staring back at him defiantly.

She'd been dreading this evening's party for weeks and had only agreed to come because Devon insisted that everyone else would be there and it might look suspicious if she didn't. She'd been seeing him for nearly nine months now and had exchanged brief pleasantries with Karis on numerous occasions, both here and in Boston. But she'd never set foot in his family home, nor had she ever expressed the remotest desire to do so. As soon as she walked through the door, she knew it had been a mistake to come. Smiling family photographs in gilt frames littered every surface and fought for space on every wall. In panic, Honor had retreated at once to the bathroom, but in there it was even worse. Finger paintings that Nick and Lola had done in nursery school were proudly stuck up next to snapshots of Karis from her modeling days. No one could deny she looked utterly ravishing in those pictures. Nor could Honor close her eyes to the look of love, and quite genuine happiness, on Devon's face as, over the years, the camera caught the two of them together. If their marriage was a sham now, it had not always been that way. Just being in the house felt like a grave intrusion. Who was she to fantasize about marrying Devon and breaking up this once-happy home?

What made it sicker was that this was Karis's birthday party. Here she was, a mistress, attending the birthday party of her lover's wife. Now that she was actually in the house, the wrongness of it hit her like an iron bar in the face. Suddenly, she deeply regretted having opted for the blatantly raunchy, micro-short black Dolce & Gabbana dress that clung to her athlete's body now like tar. She'd thought it might boost her confidence to look sexy for once, especially in front of her rival, Karis, and had even gone to town with the makeup, buying some vampy bright-red lipstick especially for the occasion. But now she just felt foolish. Not only was she behaving like Tina, but she was dressing like her, too. Who had she become? Horribly ashamed and feeling more out of place and insecure than ever, she'd overcompensated by drinking far too much. No wonder Devon was in a foul mood with her.

"We agreed we'd keep it low-key and act natural," he hissed in a stage whisper. "And you turn up in...*that*," he looked at her dress reprovingly, "and start throwing yourself at every single man in the room. Even the goddamn serving staff."

"Bullshit," slurred Honor. "I'm not throwing myself at anyone."

But she knew he was right. She had been flirting, trying to get his attention. How pathetic was that?

"I can't help it if guys want me. Anyway, whadda you care? You've been all over your wife like a cheap suit the whole night. Everywhere I turn I see pictures of the two of you."

Devon sighed. So that's what this was all about.

"It's her birthday party, Honor. And this is our home. What do you want me to do? I'm *married*."

"I know you're *married*," she snapped back at him, downing her drink and immediately grabbing another from a passing waiter, glaring at Devon when he pulled it firmly out of her hand. "But maybe you shouldn't be, seeing as, according to you, you can't stand the sight of each other. Or maybe that's bullshit, huh, Devon? Maybe your marriage is ticking along just fine."

"It isn't," he said firmly.

"Prove it!" hissed Honor.

"What are you saying?" whispered Devon angrily. "You want me to get a divorce? Is that what you want?"

"Yes!" said Honor, loud enough for people to turn and look.

"Keep your voice down, for Christ's sake," pleaded Devon, putting on a fixed smile for their newfound audience. He waited a few minutes for the interest to die down, then dragged Honor out into the corridor.

"You want me to leave Karis?" He was surprised to find himself trembling as he asked the question. "Are you sure about that?"

"Yes. No," said Honor miserably. "I don't know. Maybe. I just…I hate this. Sharing you." She bit her lower lip, and Devon's heart softened. Suddenly she looked ridiculously young. "It was so perfect until your family came out."

There were tears in her eyes, and for a brief moment he felt a stab of guilt. He knew he loved Honor. That wasn't the issue. But divorce? Well, that was a whole other ball game, one he wasn't sure he had the stomach for. Even saying the word out loud made him nauseous.

"Honor, sweetheart. There's nothing real between me and Karis," he assured her, looking around nervously for witnesses as he stroked her hair. "Our relationship is like…"

"A business arrangement," Honor sighed, leaning into him. "I know. You told me."

"It's the truth."

"Devon? Honor?" They both jumped as Karis materialized in the hallway like a ghost, her head cocked curiously to one side. How long had she been lurking there?

"What are you two doing, skulking out here on your own?"

Honor's heart was pounding so violently she thought she might be about to black out, but thankfully Devon kept his cool.

"Honor was feeling a bit emotional. About her father," he said. "We were just having a little chat about things."

"Oh." Karis did her best to look sympathetic. But really, it was a bit much to hog the host at his wife's birthday party, especially as Trey Palmer died months ago. Couldn't Honor have found someone else to snivel on? When Karis's own father had died last year, she'd pulled off a charity ball in Boston for fifteen hundred people the very next week. Life had to go on, after all.

"Well, if she's all right now, perhaps I could borrow you for a bit, darling?" she scolded. "Lola's been monopolizing poor Lucas for ages, and I still have so many people to introduce him to. In fact, Honor," she said brightly, "you haven't met him yet, have you? Come with me."

"Oh, no, thanks." Honor blanched. She'd been hugely curious to meet Lucas for weeks, but after the gut-wrenching conversation she'd just had with Devon, not to mention the umpteen vodka and tonics she'd ill-advisedly stowed away for courage, she suddenly couldn't face it. "I'm, er...I don't feel terribly well. I think I might head home, actually."

"Don't be so silly," said Karis bossily, dragging her back into the drawing room despite her protests. "The two of you must meet. You'll have so much to talk about."

Meanwhile Lucas, annoyed because the lovely Lola had wandered off somewhere and he'd gotten stuck listening to her ridiculous, fantasist brother bang on about his Internet business— snore—was at last making his escape to the bathroom when he saw Karis Carter thundering down the corridor toward him like a heat-seeking missile.

"Speak of the devil!" she squealed. She had a girl manacled to her hand like a death-row prisoner. With a sinking feeling, Lucas realized he recognized her.

"Lucas, it's my pleasure to introduce Miss Honor Palmer," said Karis, patently thrilled to have effected the introduction that everyone in town had been waiting so long to see. "Honor, this is Lucas Ruiz. Your nemesis," she added dramatically.

"*You? You're* Honor Palmer?" For once Lucas was lost for words.

"Last time I checked," said Honor witheringly.

If it hadn't been for those distinct, slanting emerald eyes and ridiculously jutting cheekbones, he wouldn't have recognized the stunning creature in front of him as the bedraggled, flat-chested child-woman from the beach. The transformation was so dramatic he had trouble stopping himself from staring. Even without the va-va-voom dress and spiky, S and M stilettos, with her short, slicked-back hair and predatory expression, she had a violent, traffic-stopping sexual presence that he wondered how on earth he could have missed before. He must have been more distracted than he'd thought.

"Have you two already met?" Devon, appearing at Honor's other side, eyed Lucas suspiciously. He had a natural distrust of younger, more attractive men.

"Unfortunately, yes." Honor glared at Lucas, who glared back.

OK, so she was fuckable, but she was still macho as hell, exactly the sort of strident, pushy American woman he loathed. A man in woman's clothing, this time anyway. Give him Lola Carter's soft, curvaceous femininity any day of the week.

"It turns out Mr. Ruiz is the rude man from the beach. The one I told you about the other night."

Devon shot Honor a warning look, but she missed it completely. Lucas, being a much older hand at adultery, caught it at once.

Well, well, well. Mr. Up-His-Own-Ass Carter and Honor Butter-Wouldn't-Melt Palmer were sleeping together. He'd put money on it.

"You know." Honor was annoyed now, willing Devon to remember. "The asshole who wouldn't help me find Caleb? I *told* you."

"I was on a business call," Lucas shrugged, not looking remotely apologetic. "It wasn't a good time for me."

"Not a good time? My dog was drowning, and I was soaked to the bone!" Honor spluttered with drunken rage. "You didn't even offer me your umbrella, you selfish, self-important..."

"Honor, please. Don't upset yourself." Devon gave her another meaningful "for God's sake, shut up" look, but it was too late. The wheels in Karis's head had belatedly begun whirring into life. She turned to Honor.

"I'm sorry," she said. "But did you just say you told Devon about this the other night?"

"Uh-huh," said Honor. Then, finally realizing the mine-field she'd inadvertently wandered into, she blushed crimson and tried to backtrack. "Well, kind of. I...well, I er..." she stammered.

Karis looked accusingly at her husband. "But didn't you tell me this morning that you hadn't seen Honor since the funeral? I'm sure you did."

Devon went white.

Lucas, meanwhile, was starting to enjoy himself. It was fun watching the smug, self-righteous WASP Carter squirming on his wife's line like a maggot.

"I meant I hadn't seen her *properly*," blustered Devon.

He might be a raging hypocrite but he had nerve, Lucas would give him that. He looked Karis right in the eye when he spoke to her.

"We did run into one another at the coffee shop the other day, though. Very briefly."

"The other *night*." Honor corrected him hurriedly. "Remember? It was in the evening. Like I said."

"That's right," said Devon, nodding his agreement. "And you told me about what happened at the beach earlier in the day."

Nice save, thought Lucas, although it pained him to admire anything about Honor, however fleetingly. This was the woman who'd betrayed her own father, after all, not to mention all the lies she'd spread about him in the press. She was the enemy, and he couldn't afford to forget it.

"I must say," said Devon, turning on Lucas in a blatant attempt to deflect the heat away from himself. "It did sound as though you acted somewhat less than chivalrously."

"Oh?" said Karis, falling for the switcheroo and transferring her attention to Lucas like an obedient puppy. "What happened?"

Lucas despaired. The woman obviously had the attention span of a gnat and the insight to match. How could she not see what her husband was up to? He and his girlfriend had just given themselves away right in front of her!

"Nothing," he said brusquely. "Nothing happened. Miss Palmer here was unable to control her pet, that's all. Which is hardly my fault."

Devon's relief at having put Karis off the scent began to fade when he looked at Honor's face. She was clearly about to launch into a full-scale row with Lucas and was more than drunk enough to let more indiscretions slip.

"Come on, darling." Grabbing a very reluctant Karis's hand— she enjoyed a good melodrama—he dragged her away. "This is between Lucas and Honor. I think we should let the pair of them talk in private."

As soon as they'd gone, Honor jumped right back on the offensive.

"So," she glowered at Lucas. "Leaving a girl to catch hypothermia while you take care of yourself—that's considered acceptable behavior in Spain, is it? Very gentlemanly, I must say."

"Oh, on the contrary," said Lucas suavely. He wasn't going to give her the satisfaction of rising to the bait. "Spanish men consider it of great importance to show courtesy toward women. But then our women would not go out running half dressed with their nipples showing through their T-shirts, pestering men who were trying to work."

"They'd be back home in the kitchen, baking cakes, I suppose?" said Honor, coloring. Had her nipples really been showing?

"That's right," he said, smiling. It was so easy to wind her up. "Or making themselves beautiful for their husband's return. Spanish women know how to be feminine."

"You're a fucking dinosaur," said Honor contemptuously. "I'm gonna enjoy wiping the floor with you next year. How're your prebookings coming along, by the way?"

"Very well, thank you," lied Lucas. But Honor saw the way the smug smile had died on his lips.

"Really?" she said. "I'm real curious to know what big names you've managed to convince to spend their vacation under the stars on your building site."

"We'll be built by Christmas, and open for business by this time next year," said Lucas, with a confidence he wished to God he actually felt. "So please, try not to worry your pretty little head about our clientele. In any case, we won't be going after the wheelchair market—we'll leave that for you over at Palmers. Assuming your rickety old building hasn't given up the ghost before then, of course."

"Fuck you," snarled Honor.

OK, so it wasn't the most sophisticated of comebacks, but after so many cocktails it was the best she could manage. At least it came from the heart.

Lucas took a step forward, until he was so close that Honor could smell the faint lemony musk of his aftershave. For the first time she got a sense of how powerfully built he was. On the beach she'd focused on his face, then his rudeness—she'd kind of bypassed his body. But now she could see he must be twice Devon's size, at least; a real meathead. How appropriate.

"You'd like that, wouldn't you?" he whispered.

"Like what?"

"To fuck me," said Lucas, deadpan.

Honor tried to laugh in his face, but he was making her so nervous it came out as a sort of weird yelp.

Stretching out his hand, Lucas slowly traced a line down her bare forearm with his finger, making the rows of downy hair stand on end, like a swathe of ripened corn.

"Sorry to disappoint you," he smiled, "but I'm not attracted to ball breakers. You'd do better to stick with your Sugar Daddy Carter."

Honor felt her stomach lurch. Belatedly, she pushed him away.

"What do you mean?" she asked, sharply. "What do you mean by that? Devon's a family friend. Nothing more."

"Whatever you say," said Lucas.

"Listen!" fumed Honor. But before she could say another word, Lucas had turned on his heel and strode off down the corridor.

Waiting at the front door for the maid to arrive with his coat, he felt a tap on the back.

"Hey, you." It was Lola, looking even sexier than she had earlier, now that her eye makeup was smudged and her long red hair slightly tousled, presumably from dancing up a storm. "Sneaking off without saying good-bye? That's not very polite."

Lucas smiled. "Sorry. Things were getting a little heated in there between Honor and me. I figured it was best I left."

"Best for who?" pouted Lola. The next minute the maid had materialized with Lucas's coat. Seconds later the valet drew up outside with his truck.

Vaulting up into the driver's seat, he wound down the window. "I'm sure we'll see each other around," he said. It wouldn't do to sound too eager.

Wordlessly, Lola walked over and, leaning in through the window, kissed him lingeringly on the lips. Lucas felt his dick harden and his resolve soften, but she pulled away before he had a chance to do something he'd regret.

"I leave for Boston in the morning," she said, heading back toward the house. "But I'll be back in the summer. Just in case you were wondering."

Driving home along the beach, Lucas let his mind wander back over the evening. Meeting Lola had been the high point, definitely. But it was his fight with Honor that really stuck with him. There was no doubt he'd come off better than she had—and yet the encounter had left him with an oddly bitter taste in his mouth.

How could she be attracted to that pompous old fossil, Carter? He didn't know why, but the thought of Honor and Devon in bed together made his blood boil.

On the other hand, an affair was a potential Achilles' heel for Honor, one he might be able to use to his advantage in the future.

Perhaps he wouldn't fire Lucy after all.

CHAPTER ELEVEN

$\mathscr{I}$T WAS JUNE, FOURTEEN MONTHS AFTER KARIS CARTER'S birthday party, and forty-five miles away Sian Doyle was packing for her eagerly anticipated summer job at Palmers. Holding up two bikinis, one pink and tiny, the other blue and even tinier, she waved them questioningly in front of her best friend.

"So? C'mon, Taneesha. Which one?"

"I dunno." Stretching her long ebony legs out in front of her, Taneesha wiggled her newly painted toes luxuriantly. "Both?"

She should have known when she agreed to help Sian pack for the Hamptons that it would take an entire afternoon and that every single decision would have to be debated, right down to the panties and socks.

"It's not like they take up much room. Your case is practically empty. Anyway, forget about swimwear. Have you seen this guy?" Holding a copy of *Vogue* open at a double-page spread about the newly opened Herrick, she flashed a picture of Lucas, shirtless and in drawstring linen pants on the beach, staring moodily out to sea. "Marlon Brando, eat your heart out!"

"Yes, I've seen it," said Sian. "It's my magazine. But Neesh, seriously. Which one? I have a ton of reading to bring, remember?" She gestured to the wall behind her, on which a wobbly set of Ikea shelves groaned under the weight of more books than the

Bergen County Library. *Journalism Today. Media Studies in the New York Area. "Missing in Action": A war reporter's story.* "Only half the space is for clothes."

Taneesha sighed. Sian had been obsessed with becoming a reporter ever since watching *Superman* at the age of eight. In fact, the two girls had seen the movie together, having been inseparable best friends since second grade. Competitive as hell, in everything from sports to academic studies to boys, they remained closer than close. If it hadn't been for their all-too-obvious physical differences (Taneesha was black, with the body of a sprinter and beaded plaits streaming down her back like the jeweled tail of a kite, while Sian was so pale she was practically translucent) they might almost have been sisters. "You know, you're not gonna have time to read half that shit," said Taneesha, who couldn't see the point of taking a semester's worth of reading material on a working vacation to the Hamptons. "Hotel work is hard. Trust me, I know. I've been there."

Sian rolled her eyes. "Three weekends washing dishes at the W hardly makes you the world's expert."

Ignoring her, Taneesha began reading aloud from Lucas's interview.

"Listen to this: *With his movie-star good looks, Anton Tisch's achingly hip Spanish protégé is shaking up the stuffy denizens of East Hampton. As the manager of the newest and coolest Tischen hotel, the Herrick, I met him in midpreparation for the much-hyped June tenth opening party.* Hey, June tenth, that's tonight. Too bad you won't be there in time."

"Yeah," laughed Sian, deciding on the blue bikini and flinging it into her bag. "If only I were in town, I'm sure I'd be top of their guest list."

"*Lucas Ruiz has some fighting words for his local rival, Honor Palmer, owner/manager of the legendary Palmers,*" Taneesha winked at Sian, "*which has itself undergone a dramatic revival over the past year. 'I've chosen not to respond to the many false,*" malicious, and in some cases outright libelous claims that Miss Palmer has made about me personally, Mr. Tisch, and our hotel over the past few months,' Lucas tells me. 'I have the privilege to be the manager of what I truly believe to be the greatest hotel, not just in America, but in the world. That's been a tough reality for Honor Palmer to accept, especially given the murky circumstances surrounding her takeover of Palmers.' What murky circumstances?"

"Some people say she pulled a fast one on her father," said Sian, who'd followed the story vaguely but without much interest. "I'm not sure exactly."

"'A broken family is a heavy price to pay if your business then doesn't make it,'" read Taneesha, finishing Lucas's quote. "'Palmers is doing better now than in recent years, but obviously our presence here is challenging for them, and Miss Palmer has chosen to take that challenge personally. In my view, that's a reflection of her lack of experience in the industry. The market will dictate which of us succeeds. I certainly know who my money's on.'"

"Well," said Sian firmly. "I don't care if Honor strangled her old man with a clothesline. Palmers has a great guest list this summer, whatever Mr. Herrick Hot Shot says. And I'm going to be there, mingling with the stars."

As far Sian was concerned, spending a whole summer working at Palmers was the opportunity of a lifetime. For one thing, it would enable her to save enough money to prove to her dad that she was serious about going to college next year to take some media studies courses. Her parents were good people, and Sian loved them both, but they were small-town, blue-collar stock to the core. Her mom's idea of an exotic getaway was a trip to the Jersey Shore, and her dad couldn't see the point in getting educated beyond high school, especially not for a girl.

"There's plenty of jobs going right here in Lymington," he was fond of reminding his daughter whenever the subject of college came up.

"Whaddaya wanna go and land yourself with ten tons of debt for, when you could be saving right now?"

It didn't help Sian's cause that her older brother, Seamus, had left school last year and gone straight to work in a local bar.

"Making great money, I might add," as her dad liked to say. "And he's a man. You're a girl, Siany, and a beautiful one at that. You'll be married before you can say kiss-my-ass, so what's the difference with all this 'media studies,' you know?"

Sian tried not to take it personally. For her, a career as a reporter meant a passport to an exciting, adventurous life and an escape from Bergen County. But, as no one else in her family felt the slightest need or desire to escape Bergen County, this was a tough concept for them to grasp.

That was the second wonderful thing about her summer job. Working at Palmers would bring her into contact with people who *did* grasp that concept, with both hands. Successful, traveled, educated, connected people. East Hampton might be less than fifty miles away from Bergen County. But it was a different world, and one in which Sian, at least, could see a raft of possibilities.

"You know," said Taneesha at last, putting down the magazine and examining the chosen blue bikini more closely. "You ain't gonna have much time for sunbathing, girl. You do realize that?"

"Whatever. You're just jealous," said Sian, sticking her tongue out playfully as she chucked book after book into the case. Not having time to sunbathe might be a blessing anyway. Despite her father's assurances to the contrary, Sian was by no means sure she was pretty, and the idea of baring her figure on a public beach made her flesh creep. Very tall and skinny, with long, deerlike legs but no breasts to speak of and the sort of white-girl's butt that could slip into a pair of jeans without undoing them at the waist, she was extremely self-conscious about her body. Her face she grudgingly deemed OK, with its long, slender nose and huge, widely set brown eyes. But as for the rest of her, she was more than happy to keep it covered.

Deciding that her toenails were dry enough to risk a gingerly walk across the carpet, Taneesha hobbled over to the bedroom window. Outside, a warm wind was blowing, and though it was only early June, summer was already in full swing. Groups of kids eight to ten strong were loitering on the street corners, the boys wannabe gangstas with their pants hanging off them and hoodies pulled low, while the girls looked like extras from a Jay-Z video. Trainee hookers, basically.

It was good that Sian wanted something better for herself. Secretly, Taneesha wanted it too.

"I'll tell you when I will be jealous," she said, pulling her head back into the room. "When you land yourself a rich sugar daddy boyfriend from one of the stuck-up Palmers guests."

"I don't want a boyfriend, Neesh," said Sian seriously. "I want to network."

"Oh, yeah, I can picture you networking right now," Taneesha teased her. "There you are in your skimpy little maid's uniform, just happen to be bending over the bed while you're changing some billionaire music producer's sheets..."

"Taneesha!"

"...and then wham, bam, you network that sucker till he can't walk no more!"

Taneesha laughed as a barrage of missiles—bras and panties mostly—came flying at her from the bed.

"If I did get with anyone up there," said Sian, once she'd run out of ammo, "and I'm not saying I'm going to, it wouldn't be a guest at Palmers."

"Oh? Who would it be, then? Lucas, the Herrick Hunk?"

"Not my type," said Sian haughtily.

"Please," said Taneesha. "He's everybody's type."

"Not mine," said Sian, adding jokingly, "not rich enough."

Taneesha shrugged her shoulders. "You're gonna be too tired to date, anyway. Hot guys like that don't usually go for exhausted hotel maids with big bags under their eyes."

"Is that so?" said Sian, her ears pricking up as always at this hint of a challenge. "Well, a hundred dollars says by the time I get home in September I'll have at least one millionaire notch on my bedpost. How's that?"

"*Soooo* competitive." Taneesha shook her head in mock disapproval.

"You know it." Sian grinned back. "So what, do we have a bet? Or are you scared to put your money where your mouth is?"

"Oh, we have a bet, girl." Laughing, Taneesha shook her hand. "We have a bet all right."

Meanwhile, at Palmers, Honor was also sitting on her bed surrounded by a sea of clothes, as she tried to settle on an outfit for tonight's party at the Herrick.

Naturally uncomfortable in dresses and skirts, she longed to wear a pantsuit, but she didn't want to be the only person dressed for a business meeting if everyone else was in full-on party gear. Lucas's VIP guest list remained shrouded in secrecy, but if the hotel's clientele since April was anything to go by—tonight was the official launch party, but the hotel had in fact been up and running for two months—there would be enough Young Hollywood and MTV types in hot pants and tassels to make her Armani suit look ridiculous.

Not that she was contemplating the hot-pants-and-tassels look. As much as she wanted to wow the hateful Lucas and his guests, she had her own guests to think about. Lucas had once bitchily referred to Palmers' clientele as the wheelchair set, and while that might not be strictly true, they were certainly a lot older and more conservative than the racy Herrick crowd. If Palmers was to survive the onslaught from the new Tischen, their only hope was to play to their core strengths and keep sweet with the old-money families. And that meant dressing demurely, whatever P. Diddy and his entourage might be doing.

Turning away from the depressing pile of clothes, she took a moment to look at the pictures lining the wall of her bedroom suite and felt her spirits lifting. Directly above the headboard was a series of old black-and-white shots of Palmers in the twenties and thirties, at the beginning of its heyday. Her grandfather was in most of them, looking young and dapper in his dark suit and waistcoat, with the polished orb of his signature gold pocket watch hanging from a chain at his chest. The shots were almost always of groups, formally dressed men and women with daringly short hair and long strings of pearls, lounging around on the croquet lawn or ambling down the graveled paths of the rose walk. Behind them rose Palmers like a great white ship, her doors and windows flung welcomingly open in what seemed to be a permanent summer. The rocking chairs and love-seat swing on the porch were still there today—Honor had had them restored the first month she arrived—but the couples sitting in them in those old pictures came from an era so totally and utterly gone they were as alien as Martians. Occasionally, Honor spotted her grandmother in some of the shots, dark-haired and tiny, just like she was, invariably hiding toward the back of these jolly groups, content to let Tertius shine. Or perhaps she wasn't content? Perhaps she hated playing second fiddle to his larger-than-life personality and all the long nights he spent away from her, entertaining guests, throwing himself heart and soul and body into his beloved hotel? It was never easy for the partners.

To the right of the bed, another wall was devoted to before and after shots of Honor's own brief tenure. The week she arrived and fired the useless Whit Hammond, she'd taken hundreds of photographs as evidence of his negligence, and the surveyors had taken thousands more: broken windows, leaking pipes, crumbling plaster, gardens so full of mess and rust and debris they looked more like a mad old lady's backyard than the grounds of a great hotel. But lovingly, piece by piece, Honor had put the only true home she'd ever known back together. Rotten boards were replaced by new ones, but all in the same reclaimed oak of the originals, and limed in the age-old way before being white-washed. She could have saved a fortune using newer, cheaper materials, but Honor looked on restoring Palmers as akin to life-saving surgery. Better to wait and do the job right than patch it up with half measures. To Honor, the "after" pictures on her bedroom wall—of the painstakingly crafted new roof, the riot-ously flowering gardens, the restored sash windows sparkling anew in the ocean-reflected sunlight—were all the vindication she needed that her policy had been the right one, however her accountants might bitch about it.

She'd already confounded both them and her critics by pull ing Palmers back from the brink of bankruptcy against all the odds. Even *Vogue*, whose reporter was clearly in Lucas's pocket, not to mention his bed, had conceded that Honor had worked wonders with the hotel. Despite Lucas's barbed comments, most people had now forgiven her for "stealing" the place from Trey when they saw what a great job she'd done of restoring it to the jewel in East Hampton's crown. Its formerly faded, crumbling walls and weatherboarding now gleamed white like a sunbaked bone, and the tangled mess of weeds in the rose garden and lavender walk had been ruthlessly stripped away, transforming the grounds into a riot of color and scent in white and pink and deep, bruised purple. Inside, the new staff kept the hotel silently running like a well-oiled machine, as unobtrusive and low-key as civil servants, and the decor, though still a little dated, was now more chic than shabby. Staying at Palmers felt like staying at the comfortable but well-appointed home of one's very smart-est friends, which was exactly the ambience of welcoming luxury that Honor had been aiming for.

Thanks to these improvements and her dogged behind-the-scenes wooing of guests old and new, she'd achieved excellent occupancy rates. Though not as flash or media-friendly as Lucas's, her summer bookings were nevertheless very impressive and included a smattering of European royalty as well as a number of senators, Fortune 500 CEOs, and heavyweight opinion makers. As for the locals, confronted first by the vast, incongruous steel-and-glass reality of the Herrick, and then by its rowdy, vulgar rap-star guests, they had practically stampeded to align themselves with Honor and the Palmers camp, welcoming her back into the fold and vowing to help in any way they could to drive the unwanted foreign newcomer out of business.

But for all the good news—her return as East Hampton's prodigal daughter, her overbooked summer and Christmas seasons, her pride in the physical transformation she'd wrought at Palmers—Honor knew how fragile the hotel's revival really was. She'd need at least another year as good as this one if she was going to be able to afford to finish the vital electrical work and other refurbishments she hoped for. And with Lucas baying like a bloodhound at her heels, backed by apparently limitless money from Anton Tisch and beloved by all media, that was by no means a certainty. Palmers had class and charm, but the Herrick had four swimming pools, a movie theater, a helipad, a state-of-the-art gym, and a three-Michelin-starred chef for starters. Maybe that was what the new, shallow, celebrity-obsessed America really wanted? All mod cons, hold the tradition?

Turning back to the clothes littering the bed, she settled on a gray brushed-silk, high-necked midi dress and suede kitten heels. Pulling them on, she moved over to her dressing table, where her very basic makeup kit—concealer, powder, and a swipe of bronzer for the cheeks—was laid out waiting. Thank God Devon would be there tonight for moral support. For once he'd be without Karis, who'd begged off this morning with a migraine, so she might actually be able to talk to him. The early, unsettled days of their relationship were over now, and Honor felt quietly confident in his love and much more able to bear the long separations that she had been so distraught about in the beginning. She still occasionally daydreamed about marriage and children, but it had ceased to be an active topic of conversation between them, and they'd settled into the comfortable, cautious routine of long-term lovers.

She knew he wouldn't be demonstrative with her tonight at the Herrick or anywhere in public. But she'd learned to read his briefly flashed smiles or winks of encouragement and to cherish these little signals of their secret bond without pushing him for more. Just knowing he was there this evening would help make Lucas's arrogance and constant baiting more bearable.

Ugh. Lucas. Dabbing a blob of Vaseline onto her lips and eyelids, she tried to push the image of his self-satisfied, handsome face from her mind. She was used to him taking potshots at her in the press, but that last *Vogue* piece had really pissed her off. Palmers had been in business in East Hampton for the better part of a century. Who the fuck was he, two months after opening his doors, to imply that they were finished? Over the past year, the personal animosity between Honor and Lucas had grown like a particularly virulent cancer, fueled by the public PR battle and the social tensions locally. Although the official line was that everybody in the Hamptons hated Lucas and his ghastly hotel and sided with Honor, at least half of the local population (the female half) were unwilling to erase him completely from their address books. You didn't tell Brad Pitt you were washing your hair, however appallingly he may have treated poor Jennifer Aniston. Lucas was quite simply too sexy to be blackballed, which meant he and Honor still ran into each other occasionally at dinner parties and events. More often than not, such meetings resulted in fireworks.

But tonight would have to be different. However much she loathed him, this was a very public event, and Honor knew she must keep a lid on her temper. Hopefully Devon could help her with that as well.

———   ———

Over at the Herrick, Anton Tisch carefully unwrapped another Rococo Belgian chocolate and, leaning down, placed it lovingly into the open mouth of his Great Dane, Mitzi.

"Good girl," he cooed, bending his face low over the dog's like a doting parent. "Who's my precious baby girl, hmmm?" He was sprawled out on the daybed in the newly finished Daria suite (named after his mother), watching one of the homemade pornos he'd brought with him from Geneva. One of the many advantages of having one's own plane was being able to bring sensitive items of baggage—including tapes from the library that he liked to think of as a sort of virtual harem—without some underling from airport security rifling through them.

Out in the grounds, the launch party was already in full swing. Anton had flown out to the States especially to be here, and soon he'd have to put in an appearance. Not yet, though. Not until he'd come. Petting his beloved dog with his left hand, his right was thrust down his suit pants, rhythmically rubbing his throbbing erection.

God, it felt good. He was pretty close now.

An enthusiastic amateur filmmaker, over the last ten years Anton had built up an extensive video collection of himself having sex with a variety of different women. A true obsessive-compulsive, he'd cataloged the footage alphabetically by the girls' first names: the long shelf in his Geneva screening room ran all the way from Abigail to Zoe. Today he was enjoying some five-year-old footage of Heidi, the bitch who'd done so much to damage his reputation by selling her story to the *Evening Standard* a year and a half ago.

Looking back at it now, sex with Heidi had actually been pretty average. Despite being an exotic dancer back then, she'd always been disappointingly prissy in bed, reluctant even to let him do her from behind and absolutely vetoing anal. Nonetheless, watching the film now still gave him a powerful erotic thrill. As with all the other lovers he filmed, Anton had assured Heidi that he'd destroyed the tapes years ago. Knowing that, without her knowledge, he could access her naked body whenever he felt like it—rewinding and freezing the frame on her spread legs and open, inviting cunt whenever he wanted to, for his own private pleasure—felt like a sort of mental rape. Rubbing his groin faster and faster, he felt his excitement building, as much from the sensation of revenge as from the titillation of the images themselves.

"Yeaaah," he moaned, snarling at the screen as he finally came, his left hand gripping involuntarily tighter onto Mitzi's collar while his right hand cupped his twitching balls. "Fuck you, you fucking whore."

Grabbing a couple of Kleenex from the box by his side, he gave himself a perfunctory wipe and zipped up his pants. Then, turning off the flat-screen TV, he ruffled Mitzi's fur and got to his feet. "Daddy won't be long," he cooed, dropping another chocolate into the dog's slavering mouth, and heading for the door.

Once outside, he strolled around the grounds of his new hotel, watching the growing crowd with quiet satisfaction. He'd been right to hire Lucas. The boy had done a fantastic job under difficult circumstances, and today's launch party was the culmination of sixteen months of effort. It was the sort of glorious early summer's day that could make even the most lackluster of gardens look beautiful, and the Herrick's grounds were anything but lackluster. An exquisite Japanese water garden, complete with koi pond and a twenty-five-foot waterfall, dominated the landscape, adding to the overall air of tranquility and peacefulness. There were no garish flowers here, none of the riotous candy-pink blossoms so ubiquitous elsewhere in the Hamptons at this time of year. Instead, the Herrick designers had gone for a consciously muted palette of greens and whites, offset with softly winding paths of gray slate, and the occasional smooth black granite sculpture. It was a restfulness that mirrored the clean lines of the hotel itself with its curved glass frontage, which glinted and gleamed in the sunlight now like the overpolished windshield of a new car.

Yes, it was modernist. Very. But only a dyed-in-the-wool philistine could deny its serene beauty. Certainly it had exceeded Anton's own expectations. He'd seen thousands of pictures during construction, but they were nothing compared to its beauty in the flesh.

Despite his satisfaction, he felt tired. Having flown into New York yesterday afternoon, he hadn't gotten out to East Hampton until nearly ten at night but had insisted on meeting all the staff personally, then getting a two-hour rundown from Lucas on the plans for the launch party before he finally went to bed.

"More champagne, sir?" A pretty uniformed waitress offered him a flute of Cristal from a glinting silver tray.

"Thank you." Stifling a yawn, he swapped his empty glass for a full one. Across the lawn he could see Lucas, surrounded by a gaggle of journalists. Since the *Vogue* article on the Herrick's rivalry with Palmers—Five-Star Wars they'd called it, which Anton thought was rather good—media interest in both the hotel and Lucas personally had risen exponentially. This was good for business, of course, and was exactly what he had hoped for when he hired Lucas. But now that it was actually happening, ironically, he found it annoying. Lucas was getting all the press attention, not to mention his dick sucked by the prettiest girls, while he, the owner and inspiration behind the Herrick, seemed to be practically invisible. There must be more than five hundred people here, many of them genuine A-listers, yet still the hacks swarmed around Lucas as if he were the big draw.

The guest list was certainly impressive. Billy Joel had shown up with his new, very young wife, as had the Seinfelds, and even Martha Stewart, who normally turned down all invitations that were even semipublic. But the biggest coup of all had undoubtedly been getting Magnus Haakenson, the Danish action star and Hollywood's latest Next Big Thing, not just to come to the party but to book himself and his entourage into the hotel for a four-night stay. Honor Palmer must surely be crying into her cocktail over that one.

Honor, in fact, had yet to hear the bad news about Magnus. No sooner had she stepped out of her limo and wandered into the gardens than the paparazzi swooped like vultures, their flashbulbs popping.

"Miss Palmer. We weren't sure we'd see you here." A reporter Honor vaguely recognized from the *New York Times* society pages popped up at her side.

"But of course I'm here, John." She smiled serenely, hoping her gray dress wasn't washing her out too much. "It's a beautiful evening; there's free champagne. What's not to love?"

"What about the comments Lucas Ruiz made about you in last month's *Vogue*? You're not offended?"

Honor waved her hand regally, as if swatting away a fly. "I don't have time to read fashion magazines, I'm afraid," she lied. She'd read Lucas's poisonous quotes so many times now she could recite them backward in Hungarian. "I'm far too busy running the best hotel in America. Ah, Billy. How are you?"

More bulbs flashed as she strolled over to a waving Billy Joel, greeting him warmly with a kiss on both cheeks.

A few feet away, Devon was chatting to the chairman of the golf club. When he saw Honor, he shot her a furtive smile, which she returned equally cautiously. They both knew they'd have to be careful today. Lucas would be even more confident on his home turf, and he'd be watching Honor like a hawk. One slip and he'd strike at her like a rattlesnake.

Rather to Honor's surprise, since his original barbed comment at Karis Carter's birthday party last year, Lucas had made no further hints about her relationship with Devon, either to her face or, heaven forbid, in print. She was starting to think she must have misheard him that night or somehow misinterpreted what he'd said. She had been very drunk, after all, and it was deeply uncharacteristic of Lucas to let her off the hook about anything, never mind something as potentially explosive as her and Devon's affair.

But her palms still started to sweat uncomfortably when she saw Lucas cutting through the crowd and making a beeline for Devon. What was he up to? Whatever it was, it couldn't be good. If only she were close enough to overhear what they were saying.

———————   ———————

"Devon. Michael. Welcome." In his white linen suit and pale-pink shirt, Lucas looked like more of a Miami playboy than ever, his teeth shining white and predatory against his deeply tanned skin when he smiled. "I trust you're both having a good time?"

"Indeed," said Devon stiffly.

"If you'll excuse me." Mike Malone, the chairman of the golf club, gave Lucas the sort of look he normally reserved for things found stuck to the bottom of his shoe. "I'd better go and join my wife. She gets pretty antsy if I desert her for too long."

Rude son of a bitch, thought Lucas. The only thing that made Lucille Malone antsy was when the cucumber-sized vibrator she used to compensate for her husband's inadequacies ran out of batteries.

Though he feigned indifference, it really got under his skin the way the locals continued to look down on him socially. Whether it was because he was Spanish or working class or simply because his name wasn't Palmer, he didn't know. But it bugged the crap out of him.

"You must be pleased with today's turnout," said Devon.

Privately, like his friend Mike, Devon also considered Lucas to be little better than a third-rate dago waiter who'd gotten lucky. And he was livid about the vicious things he'd said about Honor in that horrible, one-sided interview. But unlike Malone, he knew how to be diplomatic.

"I *am* pleased," said Lucas. "And Anton's thrilled. I hope, now that we're up and running, we'll be seen to have answered some of our critics. She's beautiful, no?" He pointed behind him to the cathedral-like splendor of the Herrick's facade, its glass glinting in the sunlight and sending rays ricocheting off the Gucci sunglasses of the partygoers.

Devon smiled patronizingly. "If you like that sort of thing, I suppose."

"You don't?" Lucas maintained a stiff smile, but inside he was seething. Why couldn't these people give credit where it was so clearly due?

"Perhaps it's a cultural difference," said Devon, unwittingly adding insult to injury. "Our concept of beauty is rather different from yours and Mr. Tisch's, I suspect. It's a question of what one grew up with. What one was born to, if you like."

Lucas didn't like. Who did this asshole think he was, the Prince of fucking Wales?

"How's Lola doing?" he asked, delighted to see a cloud of distrust and disapproval fall immediately over Devon's face. "I was hoping she might be here today."

Lucas and Lola had enjoyed a brief fling last summer, much to Devon's fury, but it had fizzled out once she returned to Boston. The last thing Devon wanted was a rerun this year. Quite apart from his social unsuitability, Lucas was far too old for her and a well-known playboy. She should be meeting eligible boys her own age.

"She's in the city this weekend," said Devon tersely. "Staying with friends. Why?"

"Oh, no reason. She's a terrific girl, that's all," said Lucas, twisting the knife. "You must be proud."

"I am," said Devon, with a grimace worthy of someone undergoing root canal surgery without anesthetic. "I'd hate to see her get hurt or throw away her future…"

"On someone like me?" Lucas smiled sweetly.

"I was going to say, over a relationship that can't possibly go anywhere," said Devon.

"Not all relationships have to go somewhere, do they?" said Lucas. "I mean, if someone were married, say, and had a long-term mistress on the side, that arrangement might work very well for everybody, without it having to *go* anywhere. Don't you think?"

Devon's eyes narrowed. Was that a veiled reference to him and Honor?

"Lola's still only eighteen," he said gruffly. "You know very well that it's inappropriate, Lucas."

Lucas shrugged calmly. "Perhaps you're right. Perhaps I do need someone a little more worldly. Miss Palmer, perhaps? She's single."

"Honor?" Devon's teeth ground audibly. "Don't be preposterous."

Lucas laughed. "Please. I didn't mean *Honor*," he said scathingly. "I wouldn't fuck that bull dyke with somebody else's dick. No, I'm talking about the other Miss Palmer. The sexy one. Over there."

Devon spun around. Oh Christ, poor Honor. That was all she needed.

Tina, in her trademark cutoff denim hot pants and boots, her newly augmented breasts covered only by the tiniest of waistcoats—no shirt—was fawning over Anton like a groupie at a rock concert.

"Wow, Mr. Tisch, I gotta hand it to you. This place is awesome," she gushed. "How on earth d'you get it built so fast?"

Anton smiled and sucked in his paunch as the paps began snapping the two of them together.

"Please. It's Anton," he purred. "And you know, when you've built as many hotels as I have, these things become rather second nature, Miss Palmer."

"Call me Tina," said Tina, resting one red-taloned hand on his arm and leaning even farther forward, the better to show off her jaw-dropping cleavage.

She'd decided to come out to the Hamptons on a whim. Well, sort of a whim. Having finally broken up with Dick Grate, she'd been caught in bed with the CEO of Paramount a few days ago by the guy's deeply unimpressed wife, and it had all gotten a little ugly. The old battle-ax had too much to lose to expose her husband publicly, but she'd sure as hell gotten her pound of flesh in private. When Mr. Paramount suggested that Tina might like to skip town for a month or so while the marital heat died down—adding weight to his suggestion with the two hundred grand worth of Neil Lane diamonds that dangled from her wrists now—she simply hadn't the heart to refuse him.

Besides, having seen the amount of press Honor and Palmers had been getting recently (though why anyone should be interested in a tedious old hotel, Tina had no idea) she was itching to get in on the action. She was still a part owner of Palmers, after all. And the Herrick's opening party was *the* hottest ticket in New York this weekend.

Having finally managed to extricate herself from her conversation with yet another journalist, Honor seized her chance to casually wander over to Devon.

"Have you seen who's here?" he whispered, kissing her on both cheeks.

"You mean Magnus Haakenson? Yeah, I saw," she whispered back. "If Lucas got any smugger about it he'd disappear up his own asshole."

"Really, darling," Devon frowned, "your language is appalling. But I wasn't talking about Magnus. Look over there." He nodded toward Tina.

Honor went white. There was her sister, looking cheap as usual, all over Anton Tisch like shrink-wrap. "Oh. My. God," she whispered. "What the hell is she doing here?"

"Sizing up her next victim, by the look of it," said Devon.

"Don't joke." Honor shuddered.

"I'm not joking," said Devon. "Tisch has everything your sister looks for in a man, after all. Money. Money," he counted them off on his fingers, "and, oh yes, money. If he weren't such a thoroughly unpleasant piece of work, I might even feel sorry for the guy. Uh oh." Stepping back from Honor, he smiled over her head and started waving enthusiastically into the middle distance. "It's Don Hammond from the church council. I'd better go."

No sooner had he scuttled off than Honor felt a tap on her back. Expecting another journalist, she fixed on her best PR smile, but replaced it with a glare when she found herself face-to-face with Lucas.

"I must say, I'm half surprised you made it," he gloated. "It can't have been easy for you." He waved at the swarming sea of VIPs triumphantly.

"On the contrary," said Honor, "it's a welcome distraction. We've been so busy at Palmers I haven't had a second to relax. Besides, there's nothing I like better than helping your boss to waste his money. How much did all this cost, anyway?" She gestured around her at the free-flowing champagne and the hundreds of open mouths devouring Russian caviar blini, which must have cost at least twenty dollars a pop, as if they were Oreos.

"Looks like your sister's asking Anton the very same question as we speak," said Lucas. Tina was flirting so outrageously now, her back arched and her improbable chest thrust forward like an exploding airbag, that Honor couldn't help but blush for her.

"Ah. Listen." Grinning, Lucas cupped his hand to his ear as Kanye West's "Gold Digger" came thumping through the state-of-the-art outdoor Bose speakers. "They're playing her song."

Honor shot him a look of purest hatred. Lucas noticed again what incredible, Kryptonite-green eyes she had, and how they looked even more striking when lit up with anger, as they were now. Shame about the rest of her. At least she was wearing a dress, a welcome change from all those gruesomely butch pantsuits and boxy jackets, but even today's brushed gray silk number was conservative enough for an off-duty nun. Why did she go to such lengths to hide herself? He wasn't into scrawny girls, but even he had to grudgingly admit that Honor had good legs and a lovely tapered waist, so small that his fingertips could probably meet around it, in the unlikely event that he ever got to touch her. What a waste, covering it up like that.

Her sister might be soft on the outside, but you could tell at a glance that Tina was hard as nails beneath all that womanly display of flesh. Honor, Lucas imagined, was the reverse. He wouldn't be at all surprised to find that her "fuck you" exterior masked a heart of pure marshmallow. There was a woman in there somewhere, he was sure of it. She just needed a real man to bring her out—not a crusty old fart like Devon Carter.

"That *Vogue* interview you did was a crock of shit, by the way," said Honor, anxious to steer the conversation away from Tina.

Lucas shrugged. "After all the libelous things you've said about me and my hotel, you're hardly in a position to throw stones."

"Please," sneered Honor. "It's Tisch's hotel, not yours. You're just a paid employee. The way you talk about it, anyone would think you'd designed the place yourself and built it brick by brick."

Now it was Lucas's turn to look daggers. He was well aware that he was only the Herrick's manager, while Honor owned Palmers outright. He tried not to let this difference in status rattle him. After all, by any objective standard he was incredibly lucky to have climbed so far at such an early stage in his career. And yet it did rankle that his dream of owning his own hotel—his Luxe—remained years away, while Honor had had Palmers handed to her on a plate. Or rather, she'd snatched the plate out of her own father's hands while the poor bastard was too incapacitated to stop her.

"May I interrupt?"

A smiling, middle-aged woman in wide-leg sailor trousers and a blue blouse with a huge pussycat bow at the neck inserted herself between Honor and Lucas, handing each of them a business card. "Megan Grier, *Talk Today*. I'm a producer at NPR," she chirruped. "I'd really love to get the two of you on my show. That Five-Star Wars thing in *Vogue* was terrific." She smiled at Lucas. "Exactly the sort of real-life story we're looking for."

"No thanks," said Honor, tersely. These radio talk show hosts were all sweetness and light when they met you, but as soon as they got you on air, live, they ripped into you with all the balance and compassion of a great white shark in a dolphin sanctuary. "I know your show, and I don't feel it fits with Palmers' profile."

"Which is what, exactly?" said Lucas, still smarting from the "paid employee" jibe. "Stuffy, over-the-hill small-mindedness?"

Before Honor could think of a comeback, he'd turned his most flirtatious smile on Miss Grier. "I'd love to come on. It'd be great publicity for the Herrick, and I'd be happy to explain to your listeners exactly how we've eclipsed Palmers as the hotel of choice in East Hampton."

"Terrific," said Megan, returning Lucas's smile. "But we would really need a debate. I'm afraid you'd both have to be there to make it work." She looked at Honor, who was busy choking on her martini olive.

Eclipsed Palmers indeed!

"That's a shame," said Lucas to Megan, shaking his head. "It seems Miss Palmer is too frightened to put her money where her mouth is. She's used to being the biggest fish in this particular little pond, you see, and now she feels out of her depth."

Honor knew it was childish, that she shouldn't rise to his schoolboy taunting. But something about his revoltingly handsome, cocky, chauvinistic face pushed her over the edge.

"Fine," she spluttered, dislodging the offending olive at last from her esophagus. "I'm game, Miss Grier. Name the day."

A few minutes later, after Lucas had disappeared to attend to his other guests, Tina popped up beside Honor, smiling from ear to ear like a simpleton.

"Boo!" she giggled. "Why the long face?"

"Hmm," said Honor. "Well now, let me see. I'm at a party to celebrate the launch of a hotel whose sole purpose is to put our hotel out of business. I'm being harassed by the most objectionable, arrogant, sexist asshole ever to walk the face of the earth—with whom I now have to do battle on live fucking radio, by the way, with a host who clearly wants to jump his bones. And to cap it all off, my publicity whore sister shows up, without a word of warning, and starts prostituting herself to the very man who has spent the last year and a half doing his utmost to destroy what's left of our family."

"Jeez," Tina rolled her eyes, "lighten up, would you? Are you on your period or something?"

"What are you doing here, T?" Honor's voice rose in exasperation. "And what were you thinking, flirting with Anton Tisch like that? Don't you have any fucking shame?"

"Shame?" Tina looked blank. "About what? Anyway, I wasn't flirting with him. We were talking, that's all. He's a very interesting guy."

"He's trying to ruin us!"

"Oh, fiddlesticks. Stop being so melodramatic," said Tina dismissively. "He's a hotelier and he opened a hotel here. So what?" She looked around her admiringly. "I actually quite like it. I might book in myself, if Anton'll give me a decent rate."

"You will not!" said Honor furiously.

"I was joking." Tina looked at her like she had a screw loose. "You know, joke? Ha-ha? Of course I'll be staying at Palmers. It's free. Who knows, I might even hang around for a while. Things are a lot more interesting around here than they used to be."

Honor followed her gaze some thirty-odd feet away, to where Lucas and Anton stood huddled deep in conversation.

"Now that is a good-looking man," sighed Tina, whistling through her teeth.

"You are kidding me. Right?" said Honor. "Lucas? Have you read the things he's been saying about me and Dad in the press?"

"Yeah," said Tina absently, still drooling like a puppy. "He can be pretty harsh, I guess. But then so can you."

"Promise me you won't go near him." Honor grabbed her by the arm. "Near either of them, in fact."

"Are you serious?" said Tina.

Honor didn't reply, but the painful tightness of her grip spoke volumes.

"OK fine, jeez. I'll leave them alone," said Tina. "But personally I think you're missing a trick. I could be, like, a honey trap." Her eyes widened mischievously. "If I got Lucas into bed, I could pump him for insider secrets. I could be a double agent!"

"This isn't a game," snapped Honor, and stalked off.

Across the garden, Anton was listening while Lucas filled him in about the NPR talk show. Though his face gave nothing away, he was irritated. Here was yet another example of Lucas rushing to take credit and plaudits without bothering to first clear it with him. It hadn't occurred to him to suggest that Anton himself might have been a more appropriate guest for Miss Grier. Still, no matter. It was more good PR for the hotel, and there would be time enough to teach the boy a lesson in humility later. Right now another idea was crystallizing in the recesses of his mind, one for which he would need Lucas's help.

"What do you know about the sister?" he asked, interrupting Lucas midrant about Honor and how she was running scared over at Palmers.

"Tina?" Lucas smiled. "Yeah. I noticed the two of you getting cozy earlier. As far as I know, she's single. She was hooked up with some teenage kid called Big Dick or something, but that's all over, apparently."

"I'm not attracted to her, you idiot," snapped Anton, his annoyance beginning to show despite himself. "I'm wondering how we might use her to our advantage."

"Use her?" Lucas frowned. "What do you mean?"

"Well, the elder girl's obviously frigid. I doubt we're going to unearth many skeletons in her closet."

"Actually, I'm not so sure," said Lucas. "Honor's a hard-nosed bitch, but I suspect she's not as squeaky clean as she makes out." He lowered his voice to a stage whisper. "I'm pretty sure she's having an affair with Devon Carter."

"Really?" said Anton, quietly storing this golden nugget of gossip for use later, like a spider stowing away a captured fly. "Interesting. Well, be that as it may, it's Tina I'm more concerned with right now. She's a loose cannon. I want you to get close to her."

"Me?" Lucas frowned. "To be honest with you, she's not really my type."

Anton laughed mirthlessly.

"I don't give a shit if she's your type. I'm a businessman, not a fucking dating agency. I want Palmers out of business by this time next year."

"Of course," said Lucas, hurriedly. Anton seemed very touchy all of a sudden. "So do I. But how will getting close to Tina help?"

Anton, so lost in his own vitriol, didn't seem to hear him.

"I want that little cunt Honor Palmer bankrupt," he spat. "I want her penniless and scrounging at my feet, like a stray fucking bitch. Understand?"

Lucas suppressed a shiver. He was no fan of Honor's, but Anton's unbridled hatred was disturbing. It seemed to have exploded out of nowhere like a bizarre, splenetic volcano. Then again, what did he expect? Clearly Tisch hadn't gotten to the top of his game by being Mr. Nice Guy. If he was going to play in the big league himself one day, he was gonna have to learn to toughen up.

"OK," he said. "I'll work on Tina."

Anton wandered back inside, and for the first time all evening, Lucas found himself alone. Looking around, his eyes rested on Honor, who was chatting with some local bigwigs over at the oyster bar. He knew she was worried about the prospect of their radio showdown and about the Herrick's burgeoning profile in general. But watching her throw her head back and laugh, glad-handing his guests like she hadn't a care in the world, he'd never have guessed it.

She might be an heiress with no experience in the hotel business, but despite what he'd told umpteen reporters, she was also a consummate professional, and she'd fight for Palmers to the death.

Squeezing her out of business was going to be no mean feat.

CHAPTER TWELVE

EN Slater fumbled with his mouse, desperately try-ing to shut his screen down before his secretary, Tammy, could see what he was up to. But he was too late.

"I saw you stuck on that bloody stupid geography quiz again," she said, laying a stack of mail down in front of him and somehow managing to look disapproving without once glancing at either him or the computer. "If you've really got nothing else to do, why don't you piss off home and let the rest of us do the same? It's a nice day out there." She nodded toward the window, through which the July sun could indeed be seen glinting off the polished chrome and glass of the NatWest tower. "I could be down the pool with my kids having an ice cream."

"It is my company, you know." Ben defended himself sheepishly, maximizing the boring window of spreadsheets he'd been looking at before. If there was one thing Tammy excelled at it was making him feel guilty. "Anyway," he lied, "I haven't been on it that long."

The geography quiz—a borderless line drawing of Europe where you had to fill in all the countries from memory—was the latest e-mail craze sweeping the city, and it was horribly addictive. Some of the guys in the back office had got all forty-three countries in less than a minute. Ben's personal best was a less than impressive thirty-five, which, despite his protestations to the contrary, had in fact taken him most of the morning.

While Tammy tut-tutted back to her own desk, Ben gave the numbers in front of him another desultory glance. It was no good. He couldn't concentrate.

There had been a time, not so long ago, when he'd loved this business. The thrill of building up his fund from nothing, of venturing forth into the jungle of the financial markets every day and outwitting his competitors—he was sure he used to enjoy it. He couldn't pinpoint when, exactly, the excitement had faded. But faded it definitely had. Recently he'd been unable to shake the feeling that there really must be more to life than the endless accumulation of wealth. He'd tried to talk about it with his sister Karen last weekend when he'd gone down to Essex to visit her and the kids. But if he was looking for sympathy, he'd come to the wrong place.

"You're a bit young for a midlife crisis, Benny," she laughed, stirring a saucepan of SpaghettiOs with one hand and scooping dried formula milk into the baby's bottle with the other. "If you're that bored, you're welcome to stay with us and help with Darren's dirty diapers. Yesterday he did four poos in an hour. Four! *And* one of 'em went all over his new car seat. Jim was up scraping the last of it off at six this morning, before he went to work. The 'ole car smells of shit now, apparently."

Ben rolled his eyes. "What a lovely picture of domestic bliss you do paint, Karen. I think I'll pass."

"Hey, don't knock it till you've tried it," said his sister. "I'm not the one who thinks her life ain't got no purpose. It's about time you got married, Benny boy, and had a couple of kids. Then you wouldn't have time to sit around moping, staring up your own ass all day like the Dalai bleeding Lama."

God bless Karen. She certainly had a way with words. But deep down, Ben realized she also had a point. He would have loved nothing more than to find a nice girl and settle down. But for some reason, Miss Right was proving aggravatingly elusive. The last two girls he'd dated had both seemed sweet enough when he met them, but both turned out to be after more than just his personality, demanding jewelry and expensive vacations almost as soon as he'd gotten them into bed.

"What do you mean you're not going to St. Tropez this year?" Mischa, the last one, had berated him a few weeks ago, after he changed his holiday plans at the last minute. "Everyone's going. What's the point in us dating for the summer if all you want to do is stay in London and work?"

"We don't have to stay in London," said Ben reasonably. "We could go anywhere. Provence. Tuscany. Maybe even Cornwall."

"*Cornwall?*" Her face implied that this was tantamount to suggesting they vacation in a sewage treatment plant.

"What?" Ben looked baffled. "Cornwall's gorgeous in the summer. I just can't be bothered with the whole sceney bullshit in St. Tropez, you know? Or Sardinia, or any of that wank. I'd much rather go somewhere quiet. With you."

That was the last he'd seen of Mischa. Two days later she'd dropped him for a derivatives trader from Lehman. Depressed, Ben had called Lucas. Neither of them had had much time to chat since Lucas moved to America, but their bond remained as close as ever, and as soon as Lucas picked up, it was straight back to the same old banter.

"Well, of course she dumped you!" He laughed heartily when Ben explained what had happened. "Cornwall? Jesus Christ, how old are you? Sixty?"

"Not you too," said Ben. He sounded genuinely put out. "What the fuck's wrong with Cornwall? St. Tropez's a shit hole, especially in July. You know that."

"So, come out to the Hamptons," said Lucas. "Come and stay at my hotel. It is, as you would say, the bees' bollocks."

"Oh. Your hotel, is it now?" Ben teased him. "Don't let Herr Tisch hear you say that. He'll have you straight off to the Gestapo before you can say sauerkraut."

"Very funny," said Lucas drily. Honor's "paid employee" comment still rankled. He didn't need the same shit from his friends.

"Oh, come on, I'm only kidding," said Ben, sensing his shift in tone. "I've been reading all about you. There was a massive article about your launch party in *W*. It looked bloody brilliant. Cheers for the invite, by the way."

"You should have come," said Lucas.

"I wanted to. Honest," said Ben. "But work was insane last month. Your boss's fund is doing so fucking well right now, the rest of us are having to scramble to keep up."

Lucas found it hard to picture Ben "Genius" Slater scrambling to keep up with anyone, but he let it go, returning instead to the subject at hand. "I'm serious," he said. "Why don't you come out? You wouldn't even have to bring a girl. The Herrick's crawling with them."

"Yeah," said Ben. "I can just imagine the kind of birds you have propping up your bar. They're hardly likely to be wife material, are they?"

"Careful," said Lucas. "You're in danger of getting vertigo on that high horse of yours, my friend. Look, I've got to go. But think about it. You'd have fun here, I promise you. I'll save you a room, just in case." That conversation had been a week ago, and Ben hadn't thought much of it since. But now, with nothing better to do, he idly opened Outlook and clicked open Lucas's contact details again.

Fuck it. Why not take a holiday?

Tammy was right. He was only spinning his wheels in the office anyway. Every other fucker and his wife in the fund business had taken July off. Why should Ben be the only schmuck stuck at work?

"Tam," he said, buzzing the intercom next to his monitor. "Get me a flight to New York tonight, would you, darling? I'm taking a couple of weeks off."

"Great!" she said, enthusiastically. "Does that mean I get a break 'n' all?"

"No, it bloody doesn't," said Ben. "You've already taken twice your allotted vacation time this year, you cheeky cow. Someone's gotta keep this place going."

"I could 'ave you for sex discrimination, talking to me like that," said Tammy. But she was smiling broadly. Like everyone else who worked for him, she thought Ben was the best boss in the world. If anyone deserved some time away, it was him.

———

Honor looked at her brushed-steel Philippe Patek watch—a birthday present from Devon—and felt her irritation building. Where the fuck was Lucas?

She was sitting in the lobby of an NPR satellite radio station, freezing her ass off thanks to a broken fan that was belting out arctic temperatures into a room roughly big enough to house a hamster. The radio station's offices, in the attic of a grand old Victorian building on Bleecker and Broadway, were an attempt at old-world style that veered dangerously toward just plain "old." The couch Honor was sitting on had once been white, but decades of spilled coffee and clammy, newsprint-covered hands had turned it into the sort of amorphous, overboiled cabbage color of old ladies' panties. This, combined with the peeling paint on the walls, vase full of dead lilies by the door, and selection of tattered, four-year-old magazines lying forlornly on the antique coffee table gave the place a down-at-heel air that was distinctly depressing.

Shivering in her city shorts and vest—outside, temperatures were in the midnineties with the off-the-scale humidity that Manhattan summers seemed to specialize in—Honor wondered for the umpteenth time what the hell she was doing here. She'd had four weeks since the Herrick party in which to cancel today's live, on-air head-to-head with Lucas. But she remained genuinely torn about it. On the one hand, it would surely be more dignified to rise above the fray and let the interest in the Herrick burn itself out naturally. But on the other, as much as she loathed him with every breath in her body, even Honor had to admit that Lucas was proving to be a master of spin. He'd already painted Palmers very effectively as the Herrick's poorer, shabbier cousin, not to mention the damage he'd done by insinuation to her own reputation. Leaving him to run rampant in the press, unchallenged, was a very risky strategy.

"Would you like to come through, Miss Palmer?" Megan Grier's assistant popped his perfectly groomed head into the waiting room. Clearly he was more used to the air-conditioning malfunctions than Honor and was swaddled from head to toe in cashmere. "Mr. Ruiz isn't here yet," he said, plainly disappointed, "but we can go ahead and sound-check you. Save ourselves some time later."

"Sure," said Honor, hoping it would be warmer in the studio. It wasn't.

After making polite small talk with Megan, she was offered a hard plastic seat on the other side of a console covered in more switches than the Starship Enterprise and told to put on some headphones.

"Let me know if you get any feedback," said the assistant. "Just start talking in your regular voice. You can say anything you like, doesn't matter."

"Lucas Ruiz makes my flesh crawl," said Honor, smiling. "How was that?"

"Very clear." The deep, familiar male voice from behind her sounded distinctly amused. "No feedback at all, was there, Megan?"

Lucas, looking disheveled and unshaven, marched straight over to their host and kissed her on both cheeks before taking his seat next to Honor with an infuriatingly cocky grin.

With his creased shirt and baggy jeans, he looked more like an Abercrombie model after a hard night's partying than a professional hotel manager. Honor could clearly smell the stale alcohol on his breath.

"You're late," she hissed.

"I know," he whispered back. "I got held up."

In fact he'd been held up since six o'clock last night by Cassandra, an old acquaintance from his Ibiza days whose husband worked on Wall Street but was conveniently away on business for a few days. It was rare that he got an excuse to spend a night in the city, and he'd certainly taken full advantage of his chance to play hooky. Apart from a couple of one-night stands with frustrated Hamptons housewives, Lucas's sex life had been pretty barren of late. Running into Cassie again had been a chance too good to pass up, even with today's head-to-head with Honor looming. Although in hindsight, perhaps the second bottle of bourbon hadn't been the smartest idea in the world.

"My guests today are Honor Palmer and Lucas Ruiz."

Before they could exchange any further pleasantries, Megan was already into her introductory spiel and the green off-air bulb had switched to a threatening red.

"For those of you who are new to this story, they are the protagonists at the heart of what's being dubbed the Five-Star Wars, a battle for supremacy between two great Hamptons hotels: the world-famous Palmers and the new architecturally acclaimed Tischen hotel, the Herrick. Honor, Lucas. Welcome."

"Thanks, Megan," they chorused in unison.

"It's a pleasure to be here," added Lucas.

"Perhaps we could start with you, Lucas," Megan purred.

Honor noticed with rising alarm the way she dipped her head and fluttered her eyelashes coquettishly when speaking to him. She obviously still wanted him. What kind of a one-sided savaging had she let herself in for?

"What was behind the decision to open a rival hotel so close to a great name like Palmers?"

"Well, of course, that was Anton Tisch's decision, not mine," said Lucas smoothly. "I'm merely the humble manager."

He looked pointedly at Honor, who rolled her eyes. Lucas didn't even know how to spell humble.

"But without wanting to speak for Anton…"

"…you're going to." Honor couldn't resist.

"I was going to say," said Lucas, stiffly, "that while we both think Palmers has a rich and wonderful history, the hotel business has changed profoundly since its heyday. Today's guests expect more. They aren't prepared to put up with substandard service for the privilege of staying somewhere well known."

"There's nothing substandard about our service," Honor shot back testily.

"You see, this is part of the problem," said Lucas. "Miss Palmer has chosen to take personal offense where none was meant. Opening a Tischen in East Hampton was purely a rational business decision, aimed at meeting the changing needs of the luxury hotel market."

"What I take offense at," said Honor furiously, "is Mr. Ruiz's repeated implication to journalists that I cynically manipulated my father's illness for personal gain by taking over the running of Palmers. What you said in your *Vogue* interview in May was an out-and-out lie."

Lucas shrugged. "Not according to your father it wasn't. He was quoted only months before he passed as saying that you had 'robbed him blind.' I believe those were his exact words. He also went on record, saying 'my daughter is dead to me.' I'd say that was pretty clear, wouldn't you?" Leaning back in his chair, he looked Honor right in the eye and gave his knuckles an audibly satisfying crack.

Fifteen love to Lucas.

Winded with pain, Honor took a few seconds to respond. When she'd taken over at Palmers, she'd deliberately avoided reading the press reports, knowing how misinformed and poisonous they were bound to be. Having to hear Trey's confused, hurtful words for the first time now, on live radio, and from the mouth of her sworn enemy, was like taking a sucker punch to the stomach. For one hideous moment she thought she might be about to cry. But with an effort, she pulled herself together.

"He was ill," she said finally, her voice barely a whisper. "He didn't know his own mind when he said those things."

In that instant she looked so small and pale and vulnerable, even Lucas felt a stab of guilt. But Megan wasn't about to let him dwell on it.

"Lucas, you can understand, presumably, why Honor would feel emotional about her father, and a hotel that has been synonymous with her family name for over five decades?" said Megan.

"Of course," said Lucas. "But, you see, this is another difference between us. Being a woman, and naturally more emotional..."

"Oh, because all women are overemotional, I suppose?" interrupted Honor angrily.

"No," said Lucas patiently. "I'm not talking about women in general, I'm talking about you." He addressed her directly. "You were born into the sort of wealthy, privileged background most people, people like me, can only dream about. You've never had to work to get where you are. That sense of...entitlement...is that the right word in English?" he asked Megan coyly.

"It could be," said the host.

"Well, it's reflected in your attitude to business, to competition."

"How?" said Honor. "That's an outrageous accusation!"

"Well, let's take your guest list," said Lucas. "Talk about elitist. Tell me, are people without titles actually permitted to book into Palmers?"

From that point on the interview degenerated into little more than a mud-slinging match, albeit one that made for damned good radio. Honor accused Lucas of sexism, narcissism, and of cynically playing his "poor Spanish farm boy made good" card to try to glean public sympathy, when all he was really doing was buying and bribing his way into a community that didn't want him with Anton Tisch's limitless money, and doing his best to bully her out of business.

Lucas hit back that Honor was not just a snob but a racist who was terrified of competition. "Name one black guest staying at Palmers today," he challenged her. "Just one!"

By the time Megan had finished her summing up and thanks and the light had once more switched from red to green, Honor had already ripped off her headphones and was storming furiously toward the elevator lobby.

"Hey, come on." Reaching her right before the doors opened, Lucas put a restraining hand on her shoulder. "Don't be a bad sport. Admit it, you kind of had fun in there. Like a little terrier with a bone." He shook his head from side to side and made growling noises, but Honor looked far from amused.

"This may be a game to you, Lucas," she said, still shivering in her thin top. "But it's my life. My family. Although obviously family isn't a concept that means much to a guy like you."

The smile died on Lucas's lips. Wedging his body in the door, he stopped the elevator doors from closing.

"You know nothing about my family," he said, glaring at her with eyes that were suddenly quite murderous. "You know nothing about the real world at all, you spoiled little beetch." As always, when he was angry, his Spanish accent became more pronounced. "My mother has lived hand to mouth all her life."

"Spare me the sob story," said Honor coldly. "Sell that shit to one of your bimbos who's stupid enough to buy it."

"Maybe I'll try your sister," said Lucas nastily. "I don't doubt she's stupid, but at least she looks like a fucking woman."

"What's that supposed to mean?" said Honor, feeling herself blushing. She was still horribly sensitive about her physical appearance.

"It means I wouldn't be surprised to find you've got a bigger dick than your boyfriend," said Lucas, twisting the knife. "Maybe you should think about Karis Carter and her kids before you go preaching to other people about family values."

The blood drained from Honor's face. "You know what? I'm getting tired of your fucking insinuations. If you have something to say about me and Devon, why don't you come right out and say it?"

"Because I don't have to," said Lucas. "That's why. Because you know. And I know."

Stepping back, he allowed the elevator doors to creak slowly shut.

Back at Palmers, Sian Doyle was examining her reflection in the grimy, cracked mirror of the communal staff bathroom.

"Shit," she sighed. The shadows under her eyes were as deep purple as overripe plums, and her complexion, pale at the best of times, was so washed out with exhaustion that she looked as white as one of the hotel sheets that she seemed to spend her life washing.

Delving into her makeup bag for some concealer—screw Touche Éclat, she needed fucking industrial-strength whitewash to cover those eye bags—she set about trying to make herself look presentable. Tonight she was going to her first Hamptons house party with Rhiannon, another girl from work. It wouldn't work to turn up looking like something out of *Night of the Living Dead*.

Though it pained her to admit it, Taneesha had been dead right about the drudgery of hotel work. Working at Palmers had sounded glamorous on paper, but the reality was endless, mindless hours spent stripping and making beds, carrying loads of laundry so heavy that she'd developed permanent backache, and scrubbing out other people's filthy bathrooms. For such rich and supposedly upper-class people, the Palmers guests had some pretty disgusting habits.

Most nights she finished work too tired to even think about going out. On the rare evenings she forced herself to make the effort, she usually regretted it once she saw the prices in the upscale East Hampton bars. Three bucks for a Diet Coke! How could anyone afford to live here? As for networking, so far the closest she'd come to rubbing shoulders with any celebrities was glimpsing Princess Mette-Marit of Norway across a crowded breakfast room and picking up wet towels from Tina Palmer's bathroom floor. Hardly the sort of life-changing interaction she'd been hoping for. Washing her hands, she began foraging for a clean towel among the dirty heap by the shower. Man, this bathroom was a dump. Palmers itself was idyllic, its polished oak floors and candlelit corridors overflowing with vases of lilies and jasmine and dog rose, but the staff quarters, tucked away behind the garages at the rear of the hotel (right next to the garbage cans—nice) were horribly cramped. Segregated by sex, the girls slept three to a room, with two rooms sharing a single, poky bathroom. An ancient and very temperamental shower took up most of the space, leaving only one tiny wall-mounted cupboard for toiletries. Needless to say this didn't go far among six teenage girls, and the overflow of makeup, tampons, and other feminine detritus littered every available surface, including the floor.

"Borrowing" Maxine's eyeliner and mascara (her own had mysteriously gone missing days ago) Sian finished her makeup and, untying her hair from the tight bun she always wore at work, ran back into her bedroom to get changed.

Hmmm. What to wear?

The party was at some big-shot investment banker's house, one of the many ten-million-plus beach properties that Sian rode past every weekend on her bike rides. The actual owners were a couple in their sixties, but tonight's bash was being thrown by their son, a waste-of-space playboy called Alex Loeb. At least, Sian imagined him to be a waste of space. Like 90 percent of the girls going tonight, she'd never met him. But Rhiannon assured her there was an open-door policy for all passable-looking females under twenty-five. Even washed out and exhausted as she was, Sian figured she still just about fit into that category.

Rummaging through her meager options—she hadn't brought many clothes, and half of what she had was either dirty or totally inappropriate—she pulled out a short red cocktail dress and her one pair of high-heeled shoes. They were beige suede and fraying at the toe and didn't really go with the dress, but as the only alternative were flat brown open-toed sandals, it couldn't be helped. Pulling the dress up over her nonexistent hips, she slipped on the heels, spraying herself liberally with Rive Gauche and tipping her head upside down to give her long, dark hair a little more volume. Then she pulled open the wardrobe door and took a final, self appraising look in the full length mirror.

Not Angelina Jolie, perhaps. But not bad. A passable Lois Lane, anyway. And in Sian's book, that was more than good enough.

Nick Carter straightened his Hermes tie, brushed the telltale traces of powder from the tip of his nose, and headed back downstairs to rejoin the party. If you could call this tedious collection of nobodies a party.

He'd known Alex Loeb all his life, in the way that the kids of all the rich Hamptons families knew one another—that is to say, socially and superficially but with no real connection beyond a mutual desire to party at their parents' expense. Alex was the better part of a decade Nick's senior, but their paths still crossed every summer. Devon Carter's son could be relied upon to turn up at social events with at least two or three top-notch women on his arm; and Alex—in previous summers anyway—had a reputation for throwing the wildest, most extravagant parties, in a town where "thou shalt indulge thyself" was considered the eleventh commandment.

Unfortunately, though, so far tonight's effort had been distinctly lackluster.

Naomi Campbell was supposed to be here, with Puffy and the entourage of less famous (but much prettier) models that followed her everywhere. But of course, she'd failed to show, and she wasn't the only one. Alex had invited a bunch of the other big names in town—including Mariah Carey, Formula One star Luca Fattorini, and George Hambly, the hot Hollywood sci-fi director—none of whom had put in an appearance. Besides a smattering of B-list actors and the usual crowd of anorexic Manhattan model-wannabes, tonight's guests were the same tired old group of East Hampton hangers-on that Nick rubbed shoulders with every year. Even the coke that had cost him a small fortune to procure ("the hottest shit to come out of Colombia this year," according to his dealer), had been disappointing.

"There you are." His sister, Lola, accosted him at the bottom of the stairs, looking as nonchalant as he was. "Have you seen Lucas yet?"

Having gone to the effort of dolling herself up in her new A-line Marc Jacobs mini—the neon emerald green of the dress made her russet mane of hair stand out even more than usual and showed off her long, tanned legs to perfection—goddamn Lucas had decided to add his name to the long list of no-shows.

"For the last time, no," said Nick, rolling his eyes. "He's obviously not coming. He must have decided to stay in New York for another night."

Like everybody else in town, the Carter kids had tuned into this afternoon's NPR interview and heard Honor and Lucas ripping into each other like rabid dogs in the latest installment of the local soap opera. Thanks to the absence of all the promised celebrities, the radio clash was becoming the evening's number one topic of conversation.

"He wouldn't do that," said Lola. "You know how paranoid he is about spending time away from the hotel."

"Yeah, like you know him so well," said Nick snidely. "You haven't laid eyes on the guy since last summer."

Annoyingly, this was true. Lola had been staying with friends in Maine for the early part of the summer and had only gotten to East Hampton ten days ago. Having perfected her tan and lost seven pounds in preparation for seeing him again, she was itching to accidentally-on-purpose bump into Lucas and wow him with her new, more mature look. Devon, who'd been furious about their fling last year, had insisted that she break off all contact with him when she went back to Boston. Reluctantly, Lola had complied—there was no point fighting every battle, and she wanted to hold back her big guns for the inevitable fight about her going to fashion school. But her dad couldn't keep tabs on her twenty-four seven now that she was here. Sooner or later, her path and Lucas's were bound to cross, and when they did, she had every intention of reseducing him.

"Oh my God." Belatedly clocking her brother's wildly dilating pupils, she eyed him suspiciously. "Are you high?"

"No," Nick lied.

"You're supposed to be the designated driver," Lola yelled at him. "I always have to drive; it's not fucking fair."

"I am not high," he insisted, in as self-righteous a tone as he could muster. "So don't go squealing to Mom and Dad that I am, all right? I can drive."

"Hmm." Lola sounded unconvinced. "Well, let's go then, while you still can. This party blows."

Lucas clearly wasn't coming, and some nerd had just put Billy Joel on the sound system. It seemed as good a time to leave as any.

For once in his life, Nick was inclined to agree with his sister. But just at that moment, a gorgeous girl in a microscopic red dress sashayed into the room. She had the shy, coltish look of a genuine ingenue—obviously new in town—and was clinging tightly to the arm of her dumpy blonde girlfriend. "Actually," he said, grinning wolfishly, "I think I might stick around a little longer."

Lola followed his gaze toward the red-dress girl.

"Hey, don't be an asshole, OK?" she said. "Leave her alone. She seems sweet."

She knew her brother's reputation with women, and she also knew it was well deserved. One look at this girl's PayLess shoes and plastic evening purse gave her away as a blue-collar out-of-towner, no doubt here for casual work over the summer. If she was looking for a rich, handsome prince to carry her off to his tower, she'd picked the wrong guy in Nicholas.

"I'm not sure 'sweet' is the word I'd use," said Nick, ignoring Lola and making a beeline for the girl. In his eagerness to introduce himself, he pushed straight past the chunky blonde.

"Hi." Grabbing the pretty one's hand, he kissed it ostentatiously. "I'm Nick Carter. What's your name, angel?"

Sian's eyes narrowed. The boy was male-model good-looking. Everything about him, from his couture jacket and platinum cuff links to his manicured nails and immaculate dentistry, spoke of serious wealth. But she didn't appreciate the presumptuous endearment from someone she'd never met before. Nor did she approve of the way he'd just blanked Rhiannon like she didn't exist.

"My name is Sian," she said coolly, retrieving her hand. "And I'm not your angel."

"Not yet," said Nick, not missing a beat. The cheap clothes and makeup hadn't escaped his attention either. It was a safe bet a trailer-trash hottie like that would be easily dazzled by his money, if not his charm.

"But play your cards right and you could be. Ever been for a ride in a Porsche?"

Sian cringed. Oh my God. Did he really just say that out loud?

"Why, no, suh." She put on her best Black Mammy voice and widened her eyes in faux amazement. "I is just a poor, ignorant girl from the farm, suh. I ain't never been in no aut-o-mo-bile. I jus' walks ever where, in my bare feet. Ain't that right, Rhiannon?"

She turned to her friend, who dissolved into fits of giggles. Nick looked furious. He despised being made fun of, especially in public, and especially by women.

"Hey. Your loss, sweetheart," he said, turning on his heel and stalking back over to Lola. "Let's go," he said grumpily, grabbing her arm. "Uh-uh, no way," she said, wriggling free. She'd watched the whole exchange, and was cheered to see a girl standing up to her Casanova brother for once. "Just because you crashed and burned. I wanna go meet her."

"She's a bitch," snarled Nick. "I'm leaving, so if you want a ride you'd better come now."

"I'll take a taxi," said Lola firmly.

"I promised Mom I'd have you back by one," he said petulantly. Devon and Karis were up in the city for the weekend and had left Nick in charge, so he felt free to throw his weight around. "It's quarter of now."

"Breathe one word to Mom and I'll tell her you were coked out of your mind," said Lola. "I'm staying."

Nick thought about it for a moment. Their mom always took his side over Lola's. But Devon was bound to ask questions if Lola really did start squealing. It wasn't worth the aggravation.

"Fine," he pouted. "Do what you like. But I'm telling you, you're wasting your time. She's just an ignorant redneck slut."

By this time Sian had wandered out into the garden. It took Lola a minute or two to track her down, leaning against the summerhouse and looking more than a little out of place. Her friend had disappeared somewhere, and she was on her own. "I'm sorry about Nick," said Lola, proffering her hand. "That was great, the way you kicked him to the curb in there. I'm Lola, by the way."

"Sian." They shook hands. "You know that guy?"

Lola, she decided, was absolutely stunning, a pre-Botox Nicole Kidman with curves, and her green dress the most divine item of clothing she'd ever laid eyes on. Suddenly struck by an awful possibility, she blurted, "Oh, God, you're not his date, are you? Honestly, I swear to God, he came on to me."

"His date? Eeugh. No." Lola looked suitably disgusted. "He's my brother, I'm ashamed to say. For some unfathomable reason, girls normally fall at his feet. I get a kick watching his ego take a battering every once in a while."

"Oh!" Sian laughed. "Well, glad I could help." Other than their shared Hilfiger-model gorgeousness, Nick and Lola didn't seem very likely siblings. He was an Olympic-level prick, but there was something exciting and mischievous about his sister that Sian found herself instantly warming to. "So, where are you working?" asked Lola.

"Palmers," said Sian. "How did you know I was working?"

Lola blushed and hoped she hadn't just been rude. "Oh, no reason. Just a guess. I haven't seen you around before. How d'you like it? I bet Honor's fun to work for, isn't she? Have you met anyone famous yet?"

Sian shook her head. "I wish. All I do is wash sheets. I see Honor Palmer in the lobby sometimes, but that's about it. Why, d'you know her too?"

"Everyone in East Hampton knows her," said Lola matter-of-factly. "She's a friend of my parents. Sort of."

There was a general commotion as someone emerged from the house. Turning to look, Lola felt her heart skip a beat.

"Whoa," said Sian. She recognized Lucas immediately from his *Vogue* picture. "So the camera really doesn't lie. He's seriously attractive, isn't he?"

"Hands off," said Lola, only half jokingly. "I saw him first."

Catching her eye, Lucas grinned. In that green dress—if you could call it a dress, it was so wonderfully short—she looked even more voluptuously sexy than he remembered her. Ignoring the other girls who'd formed an admiring circle around him, he headed in her direction.

"Miss Carter." He gave her a look that made Lola's stomach flip over like a pancake. "Long time no see, baby. Where have you been hiding all summer?"

"*Me* hiding?" she said playfully. "Oh, that's cute, coming from you. What are you, like, half bat or something? You sleep all day and work all night?"

Lucas smiled. He liked girls to challenge him, as long as they ultimately recognized who was boss. Lola's feistiness, tempered as it was with a healthy dose of adoration, was exactly the sort he appreciated. She wasn't a rabid man-hater like Honor.

"This is Sian." Lola indicated the beanpole brunette beside her.

"Hi," said Lucas, without averting his gaze from Lola's for so much as a split second.

Rude asshole, thought Sian. I'm glad I work for Honor and not for him.

Having no desire to play third wheel, she took the hint and disappeared back inside, leaving the two of them alone. Casually resting one hand on Lola's bare shoulder, Lucas started caressing her smooth skin with the ball of his thumb.

"I've thought a lot about you, you know," he said. "Since last time."

"Is that so?" Lola raised one eyebrow archly.

She was determined to play it cool. She knew he liked her, but she also knew that deep down he considered her to be too young for him—just a kid. This time around, she was determined to prove him wrong.

"Yes," he murmured. "It is. I've missed you."

He was so close now that she could feel the warmth of his breath on her collarbone, and his voice had collapsed into a soft, husky whisper. The next thing she knew, his lips had parted as if to kiss her, and she instinctively closed her eyes and stood up on tiptoes to respond. But after two long seconds, the kiss failed to materialize. Opening her eyes, she saw to her fury that he had in fact stepped back and was waving to someone about fifty feet away.

"Sorry, sweetheart," he said, kissing her briskly on top of the head. "Hold that thought." And just like that he disappeared to join his friend, leaving her standing there like an idiot.

The arrogant bastard! How could he embarrass her like that?

In fact, Lucas was every bit as reluctant to break off their encounter as she was. As well as wanting her physically, he loved the idea of pissing off Devon Carter by rekindling his affair with Lola. That'd teach the stuffed shirt to look down his patrician American nose at him. But the guy waving at him was the head of A&R at Sony, an important guest at the Herrick. He couldn't simply ignore the man.

After the requisite five minutes of small talk, he turned to look for Lola again, but she'd gone.

"Damn it," he muttered under his breath, wandering back to the house in search of her. Moments later he felt a female arm snake around his waist.

"What's wrong, baby?" its owner purred. "Lost something?"

Tina Palmer must have only just arrived. In a full-length, tight black sequined dress and Marilyn Monroe makeup, she was overdressed enough to look borderline ridiculous. But there was still something very sexy about her, if you liked the whole brazen Anna Nicole vibe.

As a rule, Lucas didn't. But Anton had told him to get close to Tina, and this was his chance. Besides, flirting with her was bound to enrage Honor, and that alone made it worth the effort.

"No, no," he said, responding to her wandering arm with a sly squeeze of his own. "I'm a little tired, that's all."

"Worn out from making mincemeat out of my poor sister, I imagine," said Tina.

Underneath his tux, Lucas could feel her fingers already starting to slip inside the waistband of his pants. Talk about a fast mover.

"I heard the show. But don't worry." She smiled lasciviously. "I don't bear grudges. Anyway, Honor can take care of herself."

"Indeed she can," said Lucas bitterly. "Listen." Pulling a business card out of his jacket pocket, he scrawled his cell phone number on the back and handed it to her. "I have to get back to the hotel now, I'm afraid. Business."

"Business?" Tina pouted. "At this time of night?"

"I'm afraid so," said Lucas. In fact, the only business he had right now was to catch up with Lola Carter before she gave up on him completely. But he wasn't about to tell that to Tina.

"But please do give me a call, OK?" Lowering his arm, he allowed his hand to wander appreciatively over her ample buttocks. "I'd love to...you know. Sometime."

Tina slipped the card into her Versace evening bag. "Don't you worry, Mr. Ruiz," she smiled knowingly, "you'll be hearing from me again. You can bet on it."

———   ———

Five minutes later, Lucas finally caught up with Lola as she was climbing into a cab.

"Hey!" he called after her. "Where are you going?"

"Home," she said frostily. "Like you care."

"Scoot over," said Lucas. Ignoring her scowl, he opened the door and shoved her farther along the backseat, then climbed in himself, shutting the door behind him. "Woodcock Lane, please," he instructed the driver firmly.

"I don't want to talk to you," said Lola, turning her head away and staring out the window in a sulk.

Lucas responded by putting his hand on her thigh. "I think you do."

"Well, I don't," said Lola, unconvincingly. The downy hairs on her legs were already prickling upward at his touch. "I saw you giving Tina slut-bitch Palmer the come-on back there."

"Slut-bitch? Dear me." Lucas leaned in closer. Lola still wasn't looking at him, but she could hear the smile in his voice. "That's not a very nice way to talk about a family friend, is it?"

"It's not funny!" she snapped, spinning around to face him. "If it's Tina you want, why don't you go back there and fuck her? Stop wasting my time."

"If it were Tina I wanted," he said, edging his hand northward, "I would. But it isn't. It's you."

"But I saw—"

"You saw me giving her my card," said Lucas. "That was business. Believe it or not, I thought she might be able to help me build bridges with her sister."

Lola didn't believe it.

"*You* want to build bridges with *Honor*?" She laughed. "I'd say that's gonna be a tall order after today's massacre on NPR, wouldn't you?"

Lucas shrugged. He didn't want to talk about Honor. He wanted to get this gorgeous, desirable, desiring girl back into bed. Ideally her daddy's bed. Devon was away for the weekend, and Lucas couldn't think of any sweeter revenge for the condescending way he'd treated him than to take the guy's daughter between his own starched Ralph Lauren sheets.

"Lola." Murmuring softly into her hair, he finally allowed his wandering hand to slip beneath the silky fabric of her panties.

At first she jumped. But then her breathing slowed audibly and she leaned into him, her lips parting silently but tellingly at his touch.

The battle was won.

"Lovely Lola," he whispered. "I've missed you, little one. It's you that I want, I promise you. Only you."

CHAPTER THIRTEEN

"RELAX. LET GO OF YOUR ARM."

Honor's fingers were so stiff they felt fossilized as the masseur pulled at each of them in turn.

"I am relaxed," she insisted, through clenched teeth. "This is as relaxed as I get."

"If you'll forgive me for saying so, Miss Palmer, that's the problem," said the masseur, giving up on the fingers and pinning her forearm behind her back instead in a vain attempt to loosen up the latticework of knotted muscles across her shoulder blades. "You ought to be having a massage *daily*, not once a year."

"Daily, huh?" said Honor, wincing with pain as his fingers kneaded her sore flesh. "Sounds nice. Maybe next lifetime, Gerard."

This was the first time she'd taken advantage of the newly refurbished spa facilities at Palmers, complete with Moroccan plunge baths and a traditional hammam. Even now, midmassage and surrounded by burning incense sticks, with some ghastly, jangly, Zen-like Muzak wafting through the speakers, she couldn't stop herself from focusing on the cracked tiles in the floor that needed fixing (already!) and wondering whether or not it would make more economic sense to split these large treatment rooms into two and hire more staff.

That was the thing about running a hotel. You could never switch off. Or, at least, Honor couldn't.

Having said all that, this new masseur that she'd poached from the Georges V in Paris was doing a damn good job, and she could feel waves of tension leaving her body as his rough hands worked their magic.

It had been two weeks since her now-infamous radio head-to-head with Lucas, and Honor was still seething about it. She didn't know what bothered her more: his comments about her father, his implied threat to expose her affair with Devon, or the way he'd insulted her about her looks. His "bigger dick than your boyfriend" comment now played over and over in her head whenever she was alone, like a whining, insistent child, demanding to be heard. How dare he imply she was less of a woman than Tina? Stung more than she cared to admit, she'd stopped by Barneys on her way back from the studio and splurged horribly on some floaty Marc Jacob dresses and a clinging, peach-colored pencil skirt for work. As soon as she got back to Palmers, still fired up, she'd thrown open her closet, pulled out thousands of dollars worth of pin-striped suits in her trademark black and gray and flung them unceremoniously into the trash.

The next day she'd almost had a panic attack, waking up to find she had nothing to wear but dresses. Plumping for a deep maroon empire-line sundress because it was simple and long enough to wear with flats, she could feel the stares of the Palmers staff burning into her back like lasers the moment she came downstairs and bolted into her office, blushing furiously.

Desperate for male affirmation, she waited hopefully for Devon to make some positive comment on her new look. He was meeting her that morning to help her plan the next steps in her PR war with Lucas. But when he arrived, he was so enraged about Lucas's public rekindling of his relationship with Lola—after the Loeb party, the pair of them were the talk of East Hampton—he barely seemed to notice Honor's existence, never mind her wardrobe.

"I always knew he was a playboy, but even I didn't have him down as a pedophile," he ranted, pacing the office like a hungry cat. "I've put my foot down and stopped all Lola's allowance until she agrees to stop seeing him. But that child is so damned stubborn."

"Can't think where she gets it from," said Honor, raising an eyebrow. It had taken all her tact and patience to persuade him that playing the enraged Lord Capulet in all of this would only heighten the drama for Lola and fan the flames of her attraction.

"Come on, honey," she said gently. "You remember what it was like to be eighteen and in love."

"I most certainly do not," said Devon. "When I was Lola's age I was a hundred percent focused on my studies. And I respected my parents' wishes like God's law." He shook his head sadly. "I just don't know where Karis and I went wrong with those kids…"

Honor thought back to their conversation now, as Gerard worked his magic. She was fond of Devon's rebellious daughter and shared his concerns about Lola getting mixed up with Lucas. But she also knew that the heavy-handed approach would be counterproductive. She loved Devon dearly, but even she felt he overdid the whole Victorian father thing at times—especially given that he himself was hardly the saintly family man he pretended to be.

In truth, Lola's welfare wasn't her only concern. She also had a firm eye on safeguarding her own secrets. Not wanting to panic Devon—he was already skittish enough about their affair—she hadn't told him about Lucas's implied threat at the radio station. But for the last two weeks she'd been a nervous wreck, waiting for him to spill the beans, either to Lola or—even worse—the press.

So far, though, it hadn't happened. God knows why, but he had decided to keep his counsel. The last thing Honor wanted was for Devon to wade in now, raising hell about him and Lola and pissing Lucas off so much he changed his mind.

Increasing the pressure of his thumbs, Gerard started kneading Honor's glutes mercilessly. Breathing through the pain, she tried not to focus on the fact that this was probably the closest she'd come to a sexual experience all week.

Deception, like so many life skills, seemed to get better with practice, and the longer her affair with Devon continued, the more imaginative and resourceful they both became in finding ways and excuses to meet each other. The anguish of those first few months together seemed like a lifetime ago now. But the flip side was that the wild, uncontrollable passion of their early days had also gone, replaced by something calmer and steadier, something Honor told herself she much preferred but that at the same time left her with a bitter aftertaste of sexual frustration that she found increasingly hard to shake.

On the rare occasions when she voiced that frustration to Devon, he was dismissive. "I'm fifty-three, baby," he'd say with a shrug. "Even if we lived together twenty-four seven, I wouldn't want to do it all the time. I'm just not at that stage in my life anymore."

He always seemed surprised when this nugget of information failed to comfort Honor.

Few people around her knew Honor well enough to notice how bad-tempered and strung out this dwindling of her sex life was making her. Unfortunately, Tina, who'd moved into a suite at Palmers for the season, was one of the few.

The tension that had been growing between the sisters for weeks had come to a head this morning over breakfast. "You know your problem?" Tina asked loudly. "You need to get laid. *That's* your problem."

They were in the middle of the Palmers dining room, a light, oak-paneled former ballroom filled with tables dressed with white linen cloths and offset by gleaming silver jugs overflowing with white-scented stocks, lilies, and Michaelmas daisies. Around them, the great and the good were busily tucking in to their buttermilk pancakes and fresh-fruit compotes, pretending not to listen.

When they sat down, Honor had made the mistake of making a critical remark about Tina's ultralow-cut, ass-hugger jeans; that was one snide comment too far. Tina was sick to death of her big sister's assumption that her dress sense, love life, or indeed any aspect of her life, was any of her goddamned business. Honor resented the fact that while she worked her fingers to the bone trying to keep Palmers going, Tina seemed content to spend her days swanning around the pool in a series of ever-raunchier bikinis and her evenings flirting with every rich or powerful man who crossed her path. Including the hated Lucas.

"Keep your voice down," said Honor.

"No. Why should I?" Tina was on a roll. "You're so uptight right now, you could be sponsored by Midol."

"Jesus, T, *stop* it," Honor hissed, blushing despite herself. "People are staring."

"Get over yourself. If they're staring, it's at me, not you," said Tina, flipping back her perfectly coiffed blonde hair. Even at this time of the morning, she looked every inch the sex bomb in the J-Lo jeans Honor had so objected to and a skintight, hand-embroidered Fred Segal tee. Honor, by contrast, sported deep shadows under her eyes after a series of late nights and looked thoroughly washed out by the slate-gray halter-neck top and skirt that had seemed so ethereal and womanly on the rack at Barneys. She could have used a year of sleep, or at the very least an IV of coffee.

"Seriously," said Tina, pushing the point, although she did mercifully lower the volume a little. "When did you last have sex?"

"None of your business," snapped Honor, adding recklessly: "Recently, OK?"

She hated it when Tina was right. Luckily it didn't happen that often.

"Recently? Really?" Tina frowned, surprised. "With who?" Then, clapping her hand over her mouth in an exaggerated rendition of surprise, she gasped, "Oh my God!" Clearly her acting style owed a lot to the reruns of *Melrose Place* she watched endlessly on TV. "It's Lucas, isn't it?"

"What's Lucas?" said Honor, testily. "What are you talking about?"

"This whole feud between the two of you," said Tina, with the look of someone who's just solved a particularly troublesome crossword clue. "It's gotten you all fired up. Underneath all that hostility, you're hot for him, aren't you? You slept with him in New York! Admit it!"

"I will not admit any such thing," said Honor. "We did not sleep together, and I do not find him even remotely attractive. Nor would you if you knew him like I do."

"Bullshit," said Tina, warming to her theme. "OK so maybe you want him, but he's not biting, and that's what's driving you crazy. Huh?" She was laughing by this point. "C'mon. Am I getting warmer?"

"No, you are not getting warmer!" said Honor furiously. "You are fucking arctic, is what you are. How can you say that to me? Do you know…do you even have any conception of how hard I've worked to reestablish this place?"

She waved her arm around the packed breakfast room, where fifty pairs of eyes turned guiltily away and back to their breakfasts.

"I don't mind competition, as long as it's a fair fight. But that…man," she spat out the word with disgust. "The lies he's told about our family! And it's not just that. He's sexist. He's arrogant. He's common as muck. I wouldn't sleep with Lucas Ruiz if he was the last man on this earth, and if you can't see that then you're even more stupid than you look in those ridiculous pants."

"Wow." Tina shook her head slowly. It was fun to have Honor on defense for once. "Talk about protesting too much."

———————   ———————

"Miss Palmer."

The masseur's voice brought Honor back to the present with a jolt.

"If you'd like to turn over, I can begin work on your abs."

"Oh, yeah. Sure, Gerard," she groaned.

He was holding up a towel as a makeshift screen and modestly averting his eyes to allow her to flip over without having to show her breasts. A big, stocky, heavy-featured guy—the giggling gaggle of beauticians at the spa had already nicknamed him Gerard Depardieu—he was not at all Honor's usual type. But to her horror, she found herself fantasizing that he would drop the towel, climb on top of her, and fuck all the tension out of her frustrated body, right then and there.

Damn Tina.

And damn fucking Devon.

Why was he never there when she needed him?

———————   ———————

Ben Slater picked his way along the beach, trying desperately to suck in his flabby stomach and wishing he'd taken Tammy's advice and booked himself a few hours in a tanning salon before he flew out here. As far as he could tell, the average age of the blokes staying at the Herrick was about nineteen and a half, and most of them looked like professional surfers, tanned and buff and with ridiculously macho names like Chip or Chuck and a body mass index somewhere in the minus numbers.

And that was just the white guys.

Ben's skin, by contrast, hadn't seen daylight since his Easter ski trip to Val d'Isère, and then it was only his face and forearms that had caught the sun, leaving lingering tan lines at his neck and elbows that only accentuated his general pallor elsewhere. He felt like an unpleasantly overgrown larva that had crawled out from under a rock and was making all the beautiful people lose their appetites—or would be, if any of them ate anything.

Strolling by the beach volleyball nets, he smiled tentatively at a Cindy Crawford lookalike in a red bikini. She was limbering up on the sand before her match, like her girlfriends, arching her body in a sort of yoga-meets-porn way that seemed to Ben to be positively begging for attention. Yet she returned his smile with a "fuck off" look so frosty he almost felt like he'd molested her.

He'd mentioned this phenomenon to Lucas last night.

"American girls are weird," he said, taking a philosophical sip of his third beer at the Herrick's Japanese-themed bar. "Every time you try to start a normal conversation with them, they shoot you down. But five minutes later and there they are hanging off every word of some bragging wanker in a Ferrari telling them how much his last year's bonus was in every bloody currency. What's that about?"

Lucas laughed. "You have to be forceful here," he said. "The girls don't understand the whole reticent, understated British thing. If you're successful, they expect you to shout it from the rooftops."

"I'm not reticent," said Ben indignantly. "I'm completely bloody up for it! I just don't like talking about money, that's all. It's tacky. Aren't these birds interested in anything else?"

"Sure," said Lucas, waving to a pair of *Playboy*-perfect blonde twins giggling at the other end of the bar. "Fame. And enormous dicks."

Ben stared down at his beer morosely. "Great. Well, I'm fucked then, aren't I?"

"Or not," said Lucas drily, "as the case may be."

"It's all right for you," Ben grumbled. "You've got the lovely Lola. You don't need to flirt around."

When Lucas had told him over the phone that he was dating a teenager, Ben's disapproval was palpable. But now that he'd met Lola, he felt confident she was mature enough to hold her own. She was feisty and funny, a good match for Lucas. He liked her a lot.

"I've told you," said Lucas, downing the remnants of his own drink and ordering another, "Lola and I aren't serious. It's just a casual summer thing."

Ben frowned. "I hope she sees it that way, mate."

Lucas hoped so too, especially as Anton was on his case again about getting intimate with Tina Palmer. The Herrick was going great guns, but Anton clearly considered Palmers' continued survival as some sort of personal affront—a chink in the formerly foolproof Tischen business plan. He wouldn't be happy until the great old hotel was on its knees, and he remained weirdly convinced that Tina held the key to its downfall.

Privately, Lucas wasn't sure what bagging Tina was going to achieve, besides winding up Honor and appeasing his boss. Still, he could think of worse assignments. And Lola had been getting a bit clingy recently. It was probably time he rocked the boat a little.

Continuing his walk along the beach, Ben's thoughts turned back to Lola. It was obvious she worshipped the ground Lucas walked on, just like every other woman he'd dated. But beneath all the teenage rebellious bravado, she was actually a sweet kid. He hoped she wasn't going to get too badly burned.

The farther he got along the public beach, the more the crowds began to thin. It was another gloriously hot day, with the sun bouncing off the ocean like so many fireflies and a cloudless, kingfisher-blue sky. But despite the undeniable natural beauty of the place, there was something about the Hamptons that Ben didn't really like. It was all a bit too precious and dollhousey for his taste.

The Herrick itself was an impressive building, and with an objective eye he could see that the architects and interior designers had fulfilled their brief thoughtfully and with flair. All that glass gave it incredible light on every level, and the myriad fountains and water features, simple bamboo and teak furniture, and pervasive Oriental scent of lotus flowers were undeniably calming. But, though he wouldn't dream of saying as much to Lucas, he still felt the hotel lacked soul.

Palmers, on the other hand, was much more his cup of tea. Classy, welcoming, but not over-the-top cutesy, he could quite see why it had such a unique reputation, and the building itself was gorgeous, as stately as any Southern gentleman's estate with its wood porches, stone fireplaces, and wisteria-clad white walls. He was approaching its private beach club now, with its striking blue-and-white-striped sun umbrellas and the waiters all dressed in white, except for the dark blue piping on their blazers. They looked like they'd just come from Henley Regatta. More English than the English, but then New Yorkers all seemed to love that.

Ben knew about Lucas's feud with Honor, of course. The whole world seemed to know about it by now. Lucas would eat him for breakfast if he caught him now, sticking his head over the fence to get a better look at his archrival's grounds. But his curiosity got the better of him, and a few moments later, he was very glad it had.

There, standing by the poolside among the snoozing, elderly guests, picking up dirty towels, was a girl with the most incredible legs Ben had ever seen. Without thinking, he started looking for a gap in the rickety wooden fence and, finally finding an appropriately weak-looking spot, set about clambering over it toward her.

"Er, excuse me. Can I help you?"

The skinny, obviously gay head waiter who accosted Ben looked as though he could happily have replaced the word "help" with "castrate."

"This is private property."

"I know," said Ben, blushing. He had one leg inside the Palmers compound and the other stuck awkwardly through the slats of the fence—not the most dignified of positions for one of the wealthiest, most successful financiers of his generation. "Sorry. I, er…I'm meeting someone here actually," he blushed. "For lunch."

"Oh?" The waiter looked unimpressed. His right eyebrow had taken on a life of its own, disappearing up somewhere dangerously near the line of his toupee, and his thin, neatly groomed moustache twitched with irritation. "And who might that be? Sir."

"It's, erm…" For some reason Ben's mind had gone completely blank. Shaking his back foot as hard as he could, trying to pull it free, he willed himself to conjure up a name—any name. But it wasn't happening. "It's, er…it's her!"

He pointed at the long-legged pool attendant. Just then, his foot suddenly burst free from the fencing, sending him flying, face-first, into the sand.

"Sian?" The waiter was fast approaching the end of his tether. "Sian is working at the moment, sir, as you can see. She doesn't have a lunch date with anyone. Now, who are you? And why are you trying to break into this hotel?"

Sian, who'd spent a thoroughly dull morning carrying piles of towels back and forth from the beach to the laundry room, was watching the commotion by the fence with amusement. Rico, her boss, was a total bitch. He was obviously letting the poor blond guy have it. Now that he stood up she could see the intruder was enormous, twice Rico's size at least. It was a bit like watching Pooh getting a dressing-down from Piglet.

"Miss Doyle. Come over here, please. Hurry up."

Rico clicked his fingers imperiously, a favorite habit, and began hopping from foot to foot like an impatient hobbit.

Sian dropped her pile of towels and did as she was told.

"Do you know this gentleman?" he asked. A vein on his forehead was throbbing visibly. He looked seriously ticked off.

Sian looked up at the blond guy. He had freckles and kind of a bashed-up face, but there was definitely something attractive about him. She'd never seen him before in her life. But something about his urgent, pleading, wide-eyed stare made her decide to play along.

"Sure," she said, scanning his face again for clues. "He's my, er...he's my..."

"Doctor," blurted Ben.

"Yes." Sian grinned at him. "Exactly. Thank you. He's my doctor. How are you doing, Doctor...?"

"Slater." Ben grinned back, dusting the sand off himself and offering his hand to his still-skeptical inquisitor. "I'm Doctor Benjamin Slater. Sian...Miss Doyle, is a patient of mine."

"I see," said Rico witheringly. "Well perhaps next time—Doctor," he looked Ben's garish surf-shorts-and-tank-top combo up and down, allowing his eyes to linger on Ben's paunch with ill-concealed disgust, "you'd do us the courtesy of using the front entrance like everybody else. And of picking a more convenient time for your...consultations. Sian is on the clock now, as I said. She has a lot to do."

Reluctantly taking this as her cue, Sian turned to go.

"No!" said Ben, grabbing her arm. He'd gotten this far after all. He may as well see it through. "You don't understand. I'm afraid it's very important. An emergency, in fact. I have to speak with her...with Miss Doyle...right away."

"You're saying this is a medical emergency?" said Rico. He couldn't have looked more scathing if he'd tried.

"Exactly," said Ben, turning from pink to scarlet at this second lie. "An emergency."

Sian smiled. Cute. Definitely cute. And the Lock Stock cockney accent was to die for.

Rico wasn't convinced for a moment, but decided he was tired of his part in this charade. He'd have words with Sian about it later. In the meantime, one of them needed to get back to work.

"Make it quick," he snapped. "Very quick." And with a meaningful glare at Ben, he turned on his perfectly polished heel and stormed off.

"So." Sian cocked her head to one side, curiously. "What's wrong with me, Doctor Slater? I must confess I'm dying to know."

Close up she was even more stunning than she had been from forty meters away. With her pale skin and straight, silky brown hair she looked so...strokeable. And the white shirt-dress uniform she was wearing made her legs look even more endless than they had from the other side of the fence. "There is nothing at all wrong with you," said Ben dreamily. "You're perfect. That's the problem."

Now it was Sian's turn to blush.

"Who are you?"

"Oh, fuck, shit, sorry. I'm Ben. Ben Slater," he babbled nervously. "That is my actual name. I'm not a doctor. Obviously. That was a bit of a fib. I just wanted to think of something to get rid of Elton John," he nodded toward Rico, who was still eyeing the two of them suspiciously from the outdoor bar, "and it was the first thing that popped into my head."

"Genius," Sian teased him. "He *totally* bought it." For a long, awkward moment, silence fell between them.

Oh, bollocks bollocks bollocks, thought Ben. Why was he such a lame-o with women? Why couldn't the right words just flow for him, like they did for Lucas?

"Look," he said eventually, screwing up the courage from somewhere. "I'm crap at chatting up girls. Especially American ones."

"How many have you tried to chat up?" Sian looked amused.

"Oh, God, loads," said Ben, unthinking. Then, noticing her grin broaden, he tried to undo the damage. "I mean, not literally *loads*. Some. You know, one or two. Shit."

Sian laughed. "And are we really that different than British girls?"

"Fuck, yeah. You're all bananas," said Ben. "I mean, not you personally. You're not bananas. You're gorgeous. When I saw you from the beach just now, I sort of…found myself coming over here, and yeah, sure, then I made a bit of a tit of myself, but the thing is, what I was wondering was, if you're not busy, you know, which you probably are, obviously…"

"I'd love to go out with you," said Sian.

Ben did a double take. "Really? 'Cause American girls never fancy me."

"Is that so?" She laughed again. He was such a dork, but it worked for him. "And you so suave and smooth and all? Incredible."

Rico was advancing toward them again, and this time he'd brought reinforcements. Ben decided to quit while he was ahead.

"What time d'you get off tonight?" he whispered.

"Six," said Sian.

"Great. I'll pick you up outside the front of Palmers at seven." After watching Ben vault back over the fence, cleanly this time, and run off down the public beach, Rico turned to Sian.

"You seem to have made a miraculous recovery, Miss Doyle," he said archly.

"You know what, Rico?" she beamed. "I think I have."

After the long, boring summer she'd had, a date with a handsome stranger was just what the doctor ordered.

————   ————

Standing outside Palmers a few hours later in the one good suit he'd brought with him from London, clutching a wilting bunch of roses, Ben was sweating buckets.

What if she thought better of it and didn't show up? He could hardly blame her. She was stupidly far out of his league anyway, plus he'd behaved like a complete fucking fruit loop this afternoon. If she had any sense, she was probably on the phone to her lawyer right now, sorting out a restraining order.

Then again, sometimes it paid to aim high and have a crack at a woman out of your league. Look at Billy Joel and Christie Brinkley. They used to live in the Hamptons when they were married, before Christie jacked him in for a bloke that didn't need to wear stilts to kiss her. But then that bloke ran off with a teenage intern. Or something. Come to think of it, maybe Billy and Christie weren't such a great example...

"Hi."

His internal ramblings were interrupted by Sian, who emerged from the front door of the hotel in jeans and a cute yellow daisy-print sweater. Ben didn't think he'd ever been so pleased to see anyone.

"Are those for me?" She nodded toward the flowers.

"No, actually," said Ben, deadpan. "They're for Sir Elton. I thought we ought to kiss and make up, you know. After this afternoon. Is he around?"

Sian giggled, and Ben felt his confidence rising. If he couldn't be Brad Pitt, he could at least be funny.

"You look amazing," he said truthfully, kissing her on both cheeks.

"Thanks," she smiled. "I'm absolutely starving. Should we eat?"

He took her to a tiny out-of-town place, where there was no menu to choose from, just a different set meal every night. The concierge at the Herrick, a local boy, had told him about it this afternoon after he'd vetoed all of Lucas's suggestions—the Almond, Tierra Mar, and the like—as being far too flashy for a first date. It was more like a farmhouse kitchen than a restaurant, with mismatched tables covered with ancient, threadbare squares of gingham cotton trimmed with red ribbon, and the only lighting coming from cheap church candles wedged willy-nilly into old wine bottles. Sian loved it.

Afterward they drove back into town, where Lucas had invited Ben to join him at the launch party of a new club.

"We don't have to go if you don't want to," said Ben, struggling to keep his eyes on the road rather than Sian's tiny but perfect daisy-covered chest. "My friend Lucas has put us on the guest list, but it'll probably be a bit of a scene."

"Lucas?" Sian's ears pricked up. "You don't mean Lucas Ruiz, by any chance?"

"Yeeees," said Ben warily. "Why? Do you know him?"

Please God let her not have already fallen for Lucas. Oh fuck. Maybe she'd even slept with him? That'd be just his luck.

"Not really." Sian sounded reassuringly unimpressed. "He's dating a really nice girl…"

"Lola, I know," said Ben. "She's lovely. Not as gorgeous as you, mind you."

"Yeah, right," Sian laughed. "Anyway, the one time I met your friend he looked right through me like I didn't exist. Which I guess to a guy in his position, I don't," she added philosophically. "I don't know. To be honest, I didn't think much of him. Are the two of you very close?"

Ben thought about it for a moment. "We are, actually," he said. "I've known him a long time. But we're very different. I won't deny Lucas can be a wanker when he puts his mind to it. He does love himself a bit."

"A bit?" said Sian.

"But there's a good bloke lurking under all the bullshit," Ben qualified. "Honestly. He's a seriously loyal friend. And he sees through a lot more of the pretentiousness around him than he lets on. I guess in the hotel business you have to make nice with everyone."

"Maybe," said Sian. "Then again, he hasn't been too shy in making enemies around here. Anyway, let's not talk about

Lucas." Reaching over, she rested her hand on Ben's thigh and smiled at him encouragingly. "It's boring."

"Fine by me," Ben grinned. "I don't even know a Lucas. Lucas who?"

***

Inside Omega, Lucas sat at the bar, rubbing his throbbing temples. How could people come to these places for fun? The music was merciless, pounding techno crap, the sort of violent, tuneless rant beloved only of neo-Nazi teenagers and the clinically deaf, and the cramped subterranean bar was heaving with more hot, sweaty, overexcited people than a Baptist church on Easter Sunday.

To make matters worse, Lola had been stuck to his side all night like fucking Teflon. At least, she had been until a few moments ago, when he'd finally snapped at her to give him some space, and she'd disappeared off to the ladies' all upset. It was funny: when she wasn't being insecure and needy, he was genuinely fond of her. But the cocky, devil-may-care party girl he'd had so much fun with last year seemed to have gone for good this time around. It was only a couple of weeks since Alex Loeb's party, but she'd already started referring to him as her boyfriend—a warning sign if ever there was one—and quizzing him boringly about his movements whenever they weren't together. Sooner or later, he thought gloomily, something was gonna have to give.

Catching sight of Ben hovering tentatively in the doorway, his eyes lit up.

"Slater! Over here!" he shouted through the din, waving wildly like someone bringing in a plane to land.

"Blimey," said Ben, once he'd finally battled his way through the crowds to Lucas's side. "I think my eardrum might have just shattered. Is it legal to play music this loud?"

"I wouldn't call it music," grumbled Lucas. "Drink?"

"Er, no, I'm all right. I'm driving," said Ben. "I daresay Sian would like one, though. Angel?"

He stepped aside to reveal his date.

"Just a white wine spritzer, please," said Sian, turning to Lucas. "We've met, actually. At that awful party out at the Loeb place. I was chatting with Lola. I think it was the night you guys got together. Remember?"

"Sure," said Lucas, who plainly didn't. "Hi."

Sian felt her mood darken. God, he was rude, too self-obsessed even to follow this monosyllabic response with a "good to see you again" or "how are you?" What did Ben see in him?

"Sian and I just had the most incredible dinner," said Ben, oblivious of the tension between them. "That place your concierge recommended was the bollocks, wasn't it, babe?"

"Hmm," said Sian moodily, still pissed about Lucas.

Lucas glanced at Ben and, clocking the puppy-dog eyes he was giving Sian, immediately found himself feeling protective. Who was this girl, anyway? Now he came to think of it he did dimly remember her from Alex's party: skinny, no tits, those cheap Bridge and Tunnel clothes—a real Polyester Polly. She was in another shocking outfit tonight. What was that flowery sweater all about? No doubt about it, a girl that poor was bound to be after Ben for his money.

"Sian? Is that you?" Lola, back from the bathroom at last, was still looking a little red-eyed. But it didn't detract from her overall gorgeousness in a tight, chocolate-brown Roland Mouret dress and vertiginous calfskin boots. "Oh my God. *You're* Ben's big hot date! That's so funny."

Sian looked teasingly at Ben. "Your 'big hot date'?"

"I didn't say you were big," he mumbled.

"This is *soooo* great," said Lola excitedly, grabbing Sian's hand. "You should have heard him waxing lyrical about you this afternoon. Lucas and I were practically at barf-point, weren't we, sweetie?"

Lucas gave a bored grunt that could have meant anything, and Sian noticed how Lola's face fell. Boy, did this man think he was the shit.

"Well, anyway," said Lola, making an effort to hold it together in public, "it's great to see you again. We should make sure we swap numbers this time. We should get together."

"Sure," said Sian, pulling out her cell phone. "Let's do it now. In case we're too drunk later."

While the two girls punched digits into their cell phones and caught up on the past two weeks' worth of East Hampton gossip, Lucas pulled Ben quietly aside.

"You can do a lot better, you know, mate," he said.

Ben just laughed. "As if!"

"I'm serious," said Lucas. "Are you sure you trust this girl?"

"Yes, of course," Ben frowned. "Why shouldn't I trust her?"

Lucas shrugged. "It's just a feeling I get with her."

Part of him, he realized uncomfortably, didn't like Sian because she reminded him too much of himself in his younger days. Despite the cheap clothes, you could smell the ambition on her, and she wasn't stupid either. For a hotel maid, she'd already done well getting herself invited to the local rich kids' parties and had obviously come to the Hamptons on the make.

"Well, Lola obviously likes her," said Ben, nodding toward the two girls, who were huddled together in a corner, chatting like old friends.

"Lola's a terrible judge of character," said Lucas.

"Which explains why she's dating you, I suppose?" Ben didn't miss a beat.

Lucas grinned. "Touché. Look, I'm only trying to watch your back, that's all. You'd do the same for me."

"Thanks," said Ben. "But I'm a big boy now. I can cope. Anyway," his chest swelled as he looked over at Sian, "I think she's bloody gorgeous."

Just then Esther Cañadas, the Spanish supermodel, sauntered into the VIP section of the club. With the briefest of *excuse mes* to Ben and not a word to Lola, Lucas took off like a rocket in her direction. "You shouldn't take it personally," said Ben, watching Lola's face crumple. "It's just work to him. I'm sure he'd much rather be at home, tucked up in bed with you."

"Well, why isn't he then?" said Lola bitterly.

"I agree," said Sian firmly. Why was Ben making excuses for him? "It's totally disrespectful. Look at him."

Ben had to admit that Lucas wasn't doing his own case much good, with one arm around Cañadas and the other coiled around the rather ampler waist of a newly arrived Tina Palmer. The pirate grin, unbuttoned shirt, and cigar clamped between his teeth completed the picture. If this was work, it was hard to imagine what he must look like at play.

"Fuck this. I'm leaving," said Lola, kissing first Ben and then Sian on the cheeks. She was doing her best to look angry and brave, but it was pretty obvious she was suffering. "Call me, OK?"

Once she'd gone, Sian turned accusingly to Ben. "And you still figure he's a good guy?"

"He can be," said Ben awkwardly. "Not always. Look, I thought we agreed not to talk about him. You wanna get out of here too?"

Standing up on tiptoes, Sian kissed him softly on the lips. Being so tall, she usually had to stoop to kiss guys, so the whole tiptoes thing made a nice change.

"Yes, please," she said. "I thought you'd never ask."

Later that night, Honor sat slumped over the coffee table in the living room of her private suite at Palmers, catching up on paperwork. Why was it that no matter how many bills she paid or letters she answered, her to-do pile seemed to grow by the hour, like an out-of-control weed?

Rubbing her eyes sleepily, she looked at the grandfather clock against the wall, a relic from Tertius's days. Shit. It was almost two a.m., and she had a breakfast meeting with the new head chef at seven. She'd better turn in.

On top of the pile of ripped and discarded envelopes lay one addressed to Tina that she'd opened by mistake. It was a note from one of the trustees, upbraiding her for overspending her July allowance to the tune of almost twenty grand. Twenty grand! On what, for fuck's sake? The girl slept till four and barely set foot outside of Palmers (where everything went on her never-paid tab) from one week to the next. Pulling on her old, coffee-stained robe over her sweatpants and T-shirt, Honor grabbed the letter and slipped out into the hall. Tina's rooms were at the other end of the corridor. It was too late for a confrontation tonight, and after such a long day she didn't have the stomach for it anyway. But if she slipped it under the door, they could at least talk about it first thing—whatever Tina's idea of "first thing" turned out to be.

As she drew nearer, she was surprised to see the door to the suite ajar and music—loud, thumping rock music—coming from inside.

"Tina?" she called through the din. No answer. Pushing the door open, she marched over to the stereo and ripped the plug out of the socket. Typical Tina. They'd be inundated with complaints tomorrow. People didn't pay a thousand bucks a night to have their sleep shattered by Van Halen at two in the morning.

Wearily, she opened the door to the bedroom. Though how anyone could be sleeping through that racket, unless they were drunk out of their mind, of course, which was always a possibility with Tina...

But the bed was empty. Judging by the wildly disheveled sheets, it didn't look as if it had been that way for long.

"Tina? Are you in there?" Peering into the en suite bathroom, still clasping the trustee's letter, the question died on her lips. For there, lying back in the bubble-filled Jacuzzi, with his arms spread wide and a look of rapture on his face, was Lucas.

"You?" Honor exploded. "What the hell are you doing here?"

Lucas's only response was a beatific smile. Two seconds later, Tina popped up from under the water, sleek and glistening as an otter.

"Hey, baby." Lucas pulled her naked, bubble-smeared body toward him as she opened her eyes. "I think your sister would like a word."

"My sister?" Turning around, Tina at least had the decency to look a smidgen shamefaced. Unlike Lucas, who had stood up, naked as the day he was born and apparently completely unperturbed by Honor's presence, and was making no effort whatsoever to find himself a towel.

"Made you look," he laughed, catching Honor's involuntarily glance at his dick.

"Oh, grow up!" she snapped.

Lucas walked past her into the bedroom, and she slammed the door shut behind him before turning her fury on Tina.

"How could you?" she hissed, keeping her voice down so as not to give Lucas the satisfaction of eavesdropping. "*Lucas?*"

"Look, I'm sorry, OK?" Tina climbed out of the tub, still dripping, and wrapped herself in a toweling robe. "We were both at this new club tonight. I guess we both had a bit to drink," she giggled. "What can I say? One thing led to another. Does it have to be a big deal?"

"Yes, it has to be a big deal," said Honor, tearing at her hair in frustration. Catching sight of herself in the mirror, she noticed for the first time how awful she looked: tired, with greasy hair and the sort of sallow, waxy complexion commonly associated with heroin addicts. It was typical that the first time she'd seen Lucas since New York should be the one day she'd chosen to wear a shapeless pair of sweatpants rather than the feminine clothes she'd been wafting around in like an idiot for weeks, hoping to bump into him. "Did you tell him anything?"

"About what?" Tina looked baffled.

"About Palmers, of course," said Honor. "Did he ask you anything? I don't know, about our bookings rate or…or the electrical problems?"

"Are you for real?" Tina's nanosecond of remorse was apparently over. "He was fucking me, Honor," she said witheringly. "You know, that thing you don't do anymore, where the man puts his penis inside the woman's vagina?"

"Oh, Jesus, enough." Honor put her hands over her ears. "I don't wanna know."

"You are so fucking obsessed with this stupid hotel!" yelled Tina. "You really think that's what we were doing? Talking about Palmers?"

"So he wasn't pumping you for information?" Honor looked skeptical. "Well, I guess maybe he wouldn't, not the first time…"

"He was pumping me all right," said Tina, tipping her head upside down and shaking out her wet hair like a dog. "But it wasn't information he was after. Hey. Where are you going?"

Honor had stormed into the bedroom, but it seemed Lucas had already made a swift exit.

"I'm going to catch up with him," she yelled. "Give the bastard a piece of my mind."

"You'll only make a fool of yourself," Tina called after her. "It was a one-night stand, Honor, for God's sake. We're both adults. Get over it!"

But Honor was already gone.

After sprinting down three flights of stairs, she finally caught up with Lucas in the deserted lobby, fumbling in his jeans pocket for his car keys. "Ah," he said sarcastically, seeing her enraged, diminutive figure heading in his direction. "If it isn't Aurora, Goddess of the Dawn. You know, if you can't afford laundry detergent," he glanced disdainfully at the coffee stains on her dressing gown, "you're more than welcome to pop by the Herrick anytime and use our laundry facilities. Really. Anytime. *Mi casa, su casa.*"

"Ha-ha," said Honor, pulling the filthy robe more tightly around her and wishing that she'd bothered to wash her hair this morning. But Devon never noticed, so there hadn't seemed much point. Lucas, of course, was looking godlike despite the lateness of the hour, his enormous, bronzed biceps clearly visible in a short-sleeved Abercrombie T-shirt and his preppy haircut offset by a dark shadow of distinctly rock 'n' roll stubble. It was tough getting the upper hand over a living slab of testosterone while looking like something the cat sicked up oneself, but Honor was determined to give it her best shot.

"My sister might not be the sharpest tool in the box," she said, "but you shouldn't think I can't see right through you."

"I'm not sure we should be talking about tools and boxes where your sister's concerned," quipped Lucas. "But I'm happy to hear you have me figured out, Miss Palmer. In that case, you have nothing to worry about, do you?"

"And you can quit with the 'Miss Palmer' bullshit," said Honor. "I don't need your fake respect. And I'm not worried. I'm disgusted. Apart from anything else, how could you do this to poor Lola?"

For the first time, Lucas's fixed face of arrogant amusement slipped. He looked annoyed. "You are a piece of work, you know that?" he told her. "Lecturing me on fidelity? And on hurting Lola's feelings?"

"She's crazy about you," said Honor. "Fuck knows why, but she is. Of all the women you could have picked to screw around with in this town…why'd you have to pick her? She's just a child."

"She's not a child," said Lucas hotly. "Besides, if you're so fucking concerned about her welfare, maybe you should think twice about sleeping with her father and screwing up her parents' marriage."

"I…I…" Honor spluttered. There was no point denying the affair with Devon, but at the same time she didn't want to have to defend it to Lucas. "I'm not screwing up their marriage. It's already screwed up. It has been for years."

"Please!" He laughed in her face. "Is that what he told you? Talk about a cliché."

"It's the truth," said Honor furiously. "You know nothing about it."

"Are you sure about that?" asked Lucas. "Don't you think Lola ever talks to me about her parents, her home life?"

Honor could feel her blood pressure rising. She didn't like the turn the conversation was taking.

"Karis and Devon tolerate each other for the kids' sake," she said firmly. "That's it."

"They still share a bed," said Lucas.

"Crap," said Honor. But inside she could feel her stomach lurching, like someone had just cut the elevator cable. Devon had sworn to her that he and Karis had slept apart for years. "Anyway, we're not talking about my relationship." She jumped back on the offensive. "We're talking about you and Lola."

Lucas gave her a pitying look.

It was weird. He hated Honor. Despised everything she stood for. But at the same time it drove him nuts to think of her being pawed by that arthritic hypocrite Devon Carter. Couldn't she see what a lying douchebag the man was?

"Listen, sweetheart," he said, opening the night door leading out into the parking lot and striding toward his car, so Honor was forced to follow him outside barefoot. "I like Lola a lot. She's a sweet kid. Why else do you think I've kept your sordid little liaison with her daddy a secret? It certainly wasn't to protect you."

Honor hadn't thought about it that way before, but she supposed it did make sense. Still, if he expected her to be grateful just because he'd kept his mouth shut, he could forget it.

"Well if you care about her so much," she snapped, "what were you doing upstairs in my hot tub with my sister?"

"I was getting a blow job," said Lucas, matter-of-factly.

Honor was grateful he couldn't see her rising color in the darkness.

"And as long as you don't go spilling your guts to lover-boy, Lola will never know about it, and never get hurt. Deal?"

Honor glared at him. "You're a bastard, Lucas Ruiz," she hissed. "A selfish, manipulative bastard."

"Yeah? Well you're a bitch," said Lucas, climbing into his car and slamming the driver's door firmly behind him. "Lola's not my wife, OK? It's a summer fling, nothing more and nothing less." Revving the engine loudly, he jerked the car forward. Honor had to jump out of the way to avoid being run over.

Lolling his handsome head out the window, Lucas delivered his parting shot.

"Seriously, sweetheart," he said, "you should look at your own messed-up love life before you start throwing stones at mine. Karis Carter still loves her husband. And she still sleeps with him. Whatever bullshit he's been feeding you."

Only once he'd driven off, leaving Honor standing alone in the gravel driveway, did she realize she was shivering. Not from the cold night air. But from hideous, crawling, paralyzing doubt.

Devon was her rock, her anchor of truth and goodness. He was her safety net.

She told herself that Lucas was just being spiteful. But if she really believed that, why did she feel like the ground had just opened up beneath her feet? Like she was falling, falling so far and so fast and so hard that she knew, once she hit the ground, she'd never be able to get up again?

CHAPTER FOURTEEN

EN SLIPPED BOTH HANDS UNDER THE SMALL OF SIAN'S naked back and slowly dragged them down the bed until he was cupping the two firm, warm globes of her bottom.

"Don't worry, Miss Doyle. This won't hurt a bit," he whispered, bringing his mouth so close to her ear that his breath tickled as he eased himself back inside her. "You can trust me. I'm a doctor."

It was the morning of his last full day in the Hamptons, and he and Sian were in his bed at the Herrick, savoring each precious minute they had left in each other's company. Tonight Lucas was throwing him a farewell party on the beach. But right now all he cared about was Sian.

Letting out a noise that was half laugh, half moan, she arched her hips against him. She loved the size and scale and weight of him, the way his back and shoulders seemed to go on for miles when she ran her fingertips across them. Being so tall, she rarely got to feel fragile or feminine. But Ben made her feel tiny, like a precious china doll. It was liberating.

Their lovemaking had been intense from the beginning. It was only two weeks since Ben had stumbled, quite literally, into her life. But already Sian found it hard to imagine being without him, or to remember clearly how independent and complete and happy she'd felt before they met.

The irony was, he was the absolute antithesis of her type. She'd always been drawn to sophisticated, educated, urbane guys—Clark Kents. Admittedly, Ben had vaguely hinted that he had a financial job back in England, so he must have been to college, but she found his life back home impossible to picture. To her, the boy she had come—in a frighteningly short time—to love seemed to be a classic model of the beach-bum genre, complete with scruffy hair, a worrying penchant for loud, vulgar Hawaiian-print shorts, and a wickedly irreverent sense of humor. Best of all, he loved her. She could feel his passion in the tightening of each muscle across his back as he made love to her, as though his body were one giant engine designed for the sole purpose of pleasing her. And please her he did, more than she could have believed possible.

"Mmmmm," she moaned, feeling her climax build as he brought one hand back across her hip and stomach and allowed his thumb to explore downward into the welcoming softness of her pubic hair. Finding her clitoris, he began stroking it gently, the lightness of his touch in sharp, delicious contrast to the quickening rhythm of his thrusts. "That is *sooooo* good."

"I love you," he murmured, half into her ear and half into the pillow as he came, and Sian's own orgasm immediately followed. "God, I fucking love you!"

He rolled over onto his side, propping himself up on his elbow. To his amazement, he saw she was crying.

"Hey. What's wrong?" Gently, he stroked the damp tendrils of hair back from her face.

"What's wrong?" asked Sian, her watery eyes widening and her bottom lip wobbling with emotion. "How can you ask me that? You know what's wrong. You're leaving."

Ben sat up and ran his hands through his hair. "Please understand," he said. "I don't want to go. I have to. I have a business to run. If I don't get back to London, that bloody Kraut Tisch is gonna swipe this deal right out from under me."

In all honesty, he should have flown back to the office a week ago, as soon as he heard that Excelsior, Anton's fund, was moving in on one of his biggest institutional investors. Sian was the only reason he'd stayed. But he couldn't put things off indefinitely.

Sian looked at him blankly. She didn't understand, not really. "Hedge fund," "fund of funds," "fixed income," "return performance": they were all just meaningless words to her. Meaningless and boring.

"It doesn't mean things have to end between us," said Ben, resting a comforting hand on the flat expanse of her belly. "That's why God invented airplanes. And it definitely doesn't mean I don't love you."

"I know that," she said, sounding utterly unconvinced.

Pulling her to him, Ben wrapped his arms around her and squeezed her so tightly Sian worried about breaking a rib. But it was a good feeling, to be straitjacketed against the comforting warmth of his chest. She felt safe, the way she had as a little girl when her father held her in his arms.

And yet, at the same time, she knew the security was an illusion. Soon Ben would be gone, back to his real life, and the fantasy of their summer romance together would fade into a milky, nostalgic haze.

He'd forget her. She knew he would.

"I promise you," he said solemnly. "I won't be gone forever. But for now, let's just try to enjoy today, OK? I want tonight's party to be fun. For both of us."

"Me too," said Sian, doing her best to sound positive and brave. If this was to be the last night they spent together, she didn't want to waste it crying. There'd be time enough for that later.

Over at Lucas's beach cottage, he and Lola were also in bed.

"What do you mean you can't?" Kneeling over her with an erection the size of a baguette, Lucas playfully tried to prize her legs apart. "You're a woman. Women can always do it. We're the ones that have to come up with the goods."

"I know," Lola smiled, idly stroking his dick with her fingertips but keeping her thighs firmly clamped together. "And I can see you've come up with the goods fabulously, sweetie, as always. But if I don't get home before my mom realizes I'm gone, I'm dead meat. So are you, I might add. My dad'll come over here with a rusty pair of garden shears before you can say coitus interruptus."

The thought of Devon advancing toward his genitals with a sharp implement was enough to dampen even Lucas's ardor. Feeling himself wilting, he reluctantly climbed off Lola and slumped back against the pillows.

"I guess twice will have to do," he said grumpily, staring at the ceiling. Actually, what he really needed was not more sex but an extra hour of sleep. But there was no chance of that. His mind was racing.

His hot-tub shenanigans with Tina Palmer and the run-in with Honor had left a bitter taste in his mouth that still lingered now, weeks later. At the time, he'd gone on the offensive with Honor, turning the heat onto her and Devon. But the truth was he did feel guilty about sleeping with Tina. Lola was part of that guilt, although he stood by his belief that what she didn't know wouldn't hurt her. In any case she'd be back at school in Boston within a week, and would no doubt soon forget all about him, like she did last year. What bothered him the most was a general sense of unease that he had somehow let himself down, and in the process allowed himself to become Anton Tisch's puppet.

At first he'd been as keen as Anton to play dirty with Honor if it meant wiping Palmers off the map. But as time went on, he found himself navigating increasingly murky moral waters.

He still wasn't sure what seducing Tina Palmer had achieved other than forming an illicit pseudofriendship between the two of them—what Anton called a bond. During the last two weeks he'd encouraged Lucas to use this bond to arrange introductions for Tina with some of his business associates, including a guest at the Herrick by the name of Toby Candelle. All Lucas knew about Candelle was that he was a personal friend of Anton's, was unusually obsessive about privacy and anonymity, and was well connected in the movie business. In any case, Tina had seemed perfectly happy to entertain the guy, and a few days later Anton had shown his pleasure by offering Lucas an unsolicited pay rise.

Taking advantage of his upbeat mood, Lucas had decided to risk asking him for a favor. For months now, he'd felt guilty about spilling the beans to his boss over Honor and Devon's affair at the Herrick's launch party. Now he wanted an assurance that Tisch wouldn't go public with the information, so he could keep his side of the deal he'd struck with Honor.

Anton seemed taken aback by the request but agreed to do as Lucas asked. "If it's really that important to you, of course I'll keep schtum," he said. "Consider it forgotten."

And Lucas had. But still the miasma of guilt hanging over him failed to lift. He heartily wished he'd never gotten tangled up with either of the Palmer sisters.

"Have you seen my cell?"

Lola, washed and dressed and with her damp, bracken-red hair tied back in a loose bun, emerged from the bathroom looking harassed. Even in yesterday's old T-shirt and jeans after a sleepless night and without so much as a scrap of makeup on, she was edible. Still, Lucas reflected with a pang, she did look terribly young. With that smattering of sun freckles across the bridge of her nose and the pink fluffy shoulder bag she took everywhere that wouldn't have been out of place in an elementary school cubby, she combined her sexiness with an innocence that could be quite disconcerting at times.

Maybe Honor was right.

Maybe he shouldn't be fucking with her?

"On the couch, in the living room," he said. "Right there, beside the white cushion." Shoving the phone into her purse, Lola pulled out her car keys and skipped over to the bed to give him a good-bye kiss. To her surprise, he grabbed her and pulled her face down to his, kissing her back with much more tenderness than usual.

"What was that for?" she smiled.

"Nothing," he said, smiling back.

He was relieved she was going back to Boston. But at the same time, he knew he'd miss her. Since his one-night stand with Tina, guilt had made him start treating Lola more kindly. As a result, the clinginess that had so irritated him earlier in the summer had disappeared. Their last two weeks together had been almost as much fun as the old days.

"Don't forget it's Ben's party tonight," he said, dragging himself out of bed too.

"As if I could forget," said Lola. "I feel so bad for poor Sian. She's really upset about him leaving."

"Hmm," said Lucas grumpily. "So she says."

It niggled him that Lola had become so tight with the scrawny little maid from Palmers. Quite apart from suspecting Sian of being a gold digger, he was pretty sure that she was one of the loudest voices warning Lola off him. The sooner she pissed off back to nowheresville, the better.

"What's that supposed to mean?" said Lola.

"Nothing. Just that she'll get over it," said Lucas, who didn't want a fight. "She'll be leaving herself soon enough."

"Yeah, I guess." Lola ran her fingers absently through his short, preppy hair as he sat on the edge of the bed. "At least she won her bet."

Lucas yawned. "What bet?"

"Her girlfriend from home bet her a hundred bucks she couldn't land herself a millionaire in the Hamptons," said Lola, getting up to go.

"Hey, it was just a joke," she added hastily, seeing Lucas's face darken and his forehead knot into a disapproving frown. "Sian adores Ben. You know that. She couldn't care less whether he's loaded or not."

Like so many people born into money, Lucas reflected, Lola underestimated its importance to those born without it. Her loyalty to her new best friend was endearing, but it was also naive.

"I gotta run." She kissed him. "Say a prayer that Mom and Dad are still in bed when I get back."

"I'm praying, I'm praying," said Lucas, as she shot out the front door, slamming it behind her. The mental picture of Devon and Karis entwined in one another's arms made him turn his thoughts once again to Honor.

Lola wasn't alone in her naiveté. Even a tough cookie like Honor could be blind where love was concerned. She seemed to have swallowed Devon Carter's lies whole, like a credulous bait-hungry fish.

Feeling inexplicably irritated all of a sudden, he rolled over, pulled the duvet up over his head, and tried once again to fall back to sleep. What did he care about Honor's love life anyway? Or Ben's, for that matter?

Right now he had more than enough problems managing his own.

——————— ———————

It was already nearly noon in London when the courier arrived at Anton's Mayfair mansion.

"Package for Mr. Tisch," he grunted through his motorcycle helmet visor, thrusting a clipboard under the butler's nose. "Sign 'ere."

William, Anton's long-suffering butler and head of all the domestic staff in London, scrawled something across the paper and took the parcel. The boss had been hopping up and down like a cat on hot coals all morning waiting for it. He'd better take it straight in.

"Ah, at last. There you are." Anton, still in his silk Turnbull & Asser dressing gown, was pacing around his study. "Give that to me."

He'd been up since six, trying to woo a US pension fund's finance director into investing in Excelsior, and between that and looking over the third-quarter figures for the Tischens, he hadn't had a second to dress. His hair, usually meticulously smoothed down, was sticking up on one side at an oddly jaunty angle, quite at odds with his humorless face and making his dodgy dye job look even more obvious.

William handed over the package with a polite little bow, although inside he was seething. Tisch thought he was so proper English, but he still hadn't mastered the use of "please" or "thank you." One of these days someone'd strangle him with that damned tasseled dressing gown cord.

"You may go now."

Fumbling in the desk drawer for a letter opener, Anton didn't even bother to look up.

Once the butler was gone and he'd found the little silver Asprey's dagger, he ripped open the package and triumphantly pulled out a VHS tape. With one press of a button on his universal remote, the door to the study locked, the lights dimmed, and metal blackout blinds began closing automatically over all the windows. A second button made the two faux-Chipperfield bookcases swoosh to one side, and an enormous flat-screen plasma TV emerged from the recess in the wall behind them. Anton took a childish delight in these James Bond touches, although on this occasion the effect was rather spoiled when he realized he would have to walk across the room and load the tape manually into the VCR.

Just as he was doing so, the phone rang.

"Tisch," he answered, brusquely.

"Anton, I'm sorry to disturb you," came the whining voice on the other end. "It's Jordy here."

Jordy McKenzie was the new editor of the *New York Post*. A former gossip columnist, he'd first crossed paths with Anton years ago when, desperate to make rent, he'd accepted a bribe not to run a negative story about one of his political friends. It was a mistake Anton had never let him forget.

When he decided to leak the story of Honor Palmer's affair with Devon Carter, it was Jordy Anton he turned to. Partly because he knew he'd be too scared to refuse, and partly because a New York paper was the natural place for a piece about Hamptons gossip. Having the *Post* lead the story would also add credibility to the idea that Lucas was behind the leak, as they'd covered a number of Herrick-related tidbits in the past, so he would be assumed to have a relationship with Jordy.

Anton had been casting around for a while for a way to get rid of Lucas—ever since the boy had started taking sole credit for the Herrick's success and mouthing off in interviews as if he owned the place. He could simply have sacked him, of course, but that would have been too easy, not to mention lacking in all the elements of revenge that Anton found fun. Teaching Lucas a real lesson required something more…imaginative. Ironically it was Lucas himself who'd finally drawn Anton's attention to his Achilles' heel, by pleading with him not to spill the beans about Honor and Devon. He had in fact forgotten all about their suspected affair, but now set about gathering hard evidence of Lucas's suspicions with a firm of top-notch New Jersey PIs. Now he was at last ready to break the story that would not only shatter Honor's reputation at a crucial point in the year— by making her and her family synonymous with Palmers and its revival, she'd ensured that any negative personal publicity would have a huge effect on the hotel's image—but would also create the perfect excuse to fire Lucas by outing him publicly as the mole behind it.

"Listen, Anton," said Jordy, doing his best to sound firm. "I've been having second thoughts about this. Tina Palmer's a well-known name, but her sister? Outside the Hamptons, Honor Palmer's nobody very much. Who cares if she's banging some married guy?"

"I do," said Anton coldly. "So will Palmers' clients, and the entire US hotel industry."

"So run it in an industry paper," said Jordy. "This isn't news."

"I've told you," said Anton, his voice rising. "That's not good enough. I don't want her compromised, I want her ruined. It has to be the *Post*."

While he spoke, the plasma screen in front of him flickered into life as the video at last began to play. Glancing up, his eyes widened. The quality and clarity of the images was extraordinary. It took a lot to shock Anton, but this tape had almost done it.

"Look, Jordy," he said soothingly. He must be careful not to be all stick and no carrot. It wouldn't do to alienate a now powerful editor completely. "Something else is about to break that will make this story very newsworthy indeed."

The editor sighed. "I suppose it's too much to hope that you might tell me what that something is?"

"I can't—yet," said Anton. "You're going to have to trust me and run with what you've got for now. But you won't regret it."

The flip side of this promise—the threat that if he didn't run the story, he would regret it—hung on the line between them like a cloud. In the end, with no realistic choice, Jordy reluctantly agreed.

"I can't run it for at least a week," he said petulantly. "And if something really big comes up in the meantime, I may have to push it back further." He had no idea what this poor Palmer girl had done to upset Anton Tisch so badly. But she was soon going to regret it, whatever it was.

"Of course," said Anton, happy to be conciliatory now that he'd gotten his way. "I leave that up to you."

Settling himself down on his antique Chesterfield couch, he lay back to enjoy the rest of the show, confident in the knowledge that, in a matter of days, millions of eager Internet users would be doing exactly the same thing.

"I thought you said it was gonna be a quiet barbecue. Just a few friends, remember?"

Ben stared in dismay at the champagne-swilling hordes, crowded onto the Herrick's private beach like sardines. He barely recognized any of them.

"I lied." Lucas grinned. "You didn't seriously think I'd send you back to rainy old London without a proper send-off?"

As usual, Lucas had put together a spectacular party in record time. Admittedly, nature had provided an ideal setting. The sun, which was just beginning to set, glowed the rich red of theater curtains, its light just soft enough to allow the outdoor candles and shimmering crystal champagne flutes to dance and sparkle like so many fireflies. But the music (six barefoot flautists dressed as nymphs), food (mouthwatering sashimi and miniature, individually garnished blueberry cream pies), and dancers (a Hawaiian fire-eating troupe) were all courtesy of Lucas.

Ben was touched that he'd gone to so much effort. But nothing Lucas had laid on could distract him from Sian. She was luminous tonight, paddling in the surf with Lola, her long gypsy skirt wet at the bottom and her dark hair flying around in the wind like gossamer. He still hadn't figured out the practicalities of how to keep the relationship going after tomorrow. Long-distance romance was a killer, he knew that, but he was determined to make it work. The alternative—walking away and letting her go—was as impossible to him now as stopping breathing.

"I tell you what, mate," he said to Lucas, unable to tear his eyes off the girls as they splashed each other and giggled in the water like the teenagers they were. "We are both seriously lucky."

"Hmm." Lucas sounded bored.

"What's the score with you and Lola, then?" asked Ben. "Are you gonna keep seeing her after she goes back to Boston?"

Lucas gave him a questioning look. "Of course not," he said bluntly. "How could I? She's going back to school, and I'm going back to work. It was only a summer romance, you know. I don't know why everyone's so keen to marry us off."

Ben shrugged. "Fair enough. I suppose I'm so happy with Sian, I want everyone else to have what we have. You know what I mean?"

Lucas cleared his throat. "About that," he said. "Are you quite sure…how can I put this? Are you sure you have what you think you have?"

Ben sighed. He was starting to get seriously tired of Lucas's negativity on this subject. "Don't you ever stop? I love her, all right? And she loves me. Be happy for me."

Lucas looked pained. "I would," he said. "If I really believed that, I would be happy for you. But I heard something else today…"

"What?" said Ben, biting back his anger. He didn't want to fall out with Lucas tonight, after all the trouble he'd gone to. "What did you hear?"

"Lola told me that Sian had a bet. With a girlfriend from back home."

"So?"

"Apparently," Lucas took a deep breath, "she bet this friend a hundred bucks that she'd land herself a rich man out here before the end of the season."

"That's bullshit," said Ben, his face draining of color. "Sian would never do a thing like that. She doesn't have a materialistic bone in her body."

"OK." Lucas held out his hands in innocence. "If you say so."

"I do say so," said Ben crossly. "You don't know her."

"Do you?" asked Lucas. "You only met the girl two weeks ago. What do you really know about her? Look, I'm sorry," he added, sensing he'd already ruined his friend's evening. "I don't want to see you get hurt."

"Crap," said Ben bitterly. "You just can't stand it that for once I'm the guy who's happy with a terrific woman, while you're still…"

"What?" Lucas's eyes narrowed. "I'm still what?"

"Lost," snapped Ben. "Lost, lonely, and fucking insecure, all right?"

To be honest he didn't really know what he was saying. He simply wanted to lash out at Lucas. To pay him back for what he'd said, for trying to make him doubt the best thing that had happened to him since…well, ever, really.

"If you don't believe me," said Lucas angrily, "ask her yourself." And with that he stalked off, but not before adding under his breath: "Of course, she'll probably lie to you." He knew he was being spiteful and childish. But Ben's last comment had really ticked him off. Lost, indeed! He wasn't *lost*. He knew exactly where he was going. Unlike some people he could mention.

Sian, meanwhile, was happily oblivious to the unfolding drama. Chasing Lola up and down the surf, she was hampered by her now completely drenched skirt, which clung to her legs like shrink wrap as she tried to splash water over her friend's way-too-perfectly blow-dried hair. She'd promised Ben to try to enjoy tonight, and it was a promise she meant to stick by.

"You look like a news anchor!" she yelled into the waves. "Come back here! You look like Diane freakin' Sawyer! I'm trying to help you!"

Lola squealed and started running back toward the beach. Sian made an ill-timed lunge as she came past and lost her footing, collapsing into the water in fits of giggles.

Wiping the salt water from her eyes and pushing back her dripping hair, she looked up to find Ben standing over her. "Hey, babe. What's going on?" she spluttered. "Are you having fun?"

His body loomed in front of the fading sun, so his features were mostly in shadow. It wasn't until he spoke that she realized something was wrong.

"Not really," he said. His voice sounded strangled.

Struggling unsteadily to her feet—her clothes weighed a ton and the sand beneath her was uneven in the current—Sian put one hand on his arm to steady herself.

"Ben? What is it? What's wrong?"

"Am I a bet?" he asked.

"What?" She looked genuinely baffled. "A bet? What are you talking about?"

"Did you make a bet with your friend before you came out here? About getting a rich guy to sleep with you?"

Sian felt her stomach drop to the floor and her heart start pounding. She'd murder Lola. "Who told you that?" she asked warily.

"Never mind who told me it!" Ben exploded.

Sian shrank back. She'd never seen him this mad. Never seen him mad at all, come to think of it.

"Jesus Christ." Shaking his head angrily, he pushed away her hand. "It's bloody true, isn't it?"

"No!" said Sian, "Well, yes, *technically* it is true. But it's not what you think. You seriously believe that's what you and me have been about? That bet was a joke. It was nothing. Anyway, you're not that rich, are you?" She tried to make a joke of it. "You've got holes in your socks and your business is something to do with hedges. That hardly makes you Bill Gates."

But Ben wasn't listening. He'd already turned away and started storming through the shallows back toward the beach and the rest of the party. Sian tried to run after him, but her skirt dragged her down into the water like concrete with every step.

"This is crazy!" she yelled after him. "For God's sake, Ben. You asked *me* out, remember? It's not like I made a play for you. Ben!"

Having made dry land, Ben ran up the beach, brushing past bewildered partygoers, staring into space and muttering like a crazy man.

"Hey." Lucas grabbed his arm as he shot past. "Wanna talk about it?" He nodded toward Sian, who was scrambling inelegantly out of the water now, dripping and screaming like something out of a badly made horror film. "I was right, wasn't I?"

"Fuck you," said Ben. He looked so desolate in that moment, Lucas almost felt guilty. But it was better he find out now, before his heart got really trampled on. "Fuck you and fuck your stupid party."

By the time Sian reached the spot where they'd been standing, Ben was gone.

"Where is he?" she panted, turning on Lucas. "What did you say to him?"

Lola, who'd just caught sight of the commotion, came over to join them. Sian spun around to face her, shaking her head in disbelief.

"You told Lucas about my bet with Taneesha," she panted. "It was a *joke*, for God's sake."

"I know it was," said Lola vehemently. Now both girls were glaring at Lucas. "I totally told him that. Why? What's happened?"

"Your shit-stirring boyfriend here told Ben I was a gold digger," said Sian. "That's what happened." For the first time, she began to feel the cold. Her whole body had started to shudder.

"Lucas?" Lola looked at him furiously. "Tell me you didn't."

"I'm sorry." He shrugged, not looking anything of the sort. "Ben's a friend of mine. I don't like seeing him being taken advantage of."

"For God's sake. Sian's not taking advantage of him," said Lola indignantly. But Sian waved for her to stop.

"Forget it," she said. In the last two minutes she'd gone from shock to fear to nausea. But right now all she felt was anger. "If that's what Ben chooses to think of me, he can shove this relationship up his ass."

"But, sweetie, you can explain to him," said Lola. "Tell him it's all a big misunderstanding."

"No," said Sian firmly. "Why should I have to explain anything to him?"

She might not be as beautiful, or as smart or as rich as all the rest of them. But she had her pride. If Ben Slater was going to take the word of an asshole like Lucas over hers, he could take a running jump.

Peeling off her sodden skirt and T-shirt so she was down to her chocolate-brown string bikini, she bundled the wet clothes under her arm and stormed into the hotel in search of a towel. Lola was about to follow her, but Lucas held her back.

"Leave it," he said. "It's for the best."

"The best?" she scowled at him. "How'd you figure that?"

Catching the flash of anger in her eyes, Lucas felt his dick start to harden. He wished she'd pluck up the courage to challenge him more often. It was no fun dominating someone who never fought back.

"Let's go to bed," he said, pulling her tightly against his chest.

"What? No!" Lola squealed indignantly. "I don't want to go to bed with you. You're a horrible man. How could you do that to poor Sian?"

But a few seconds later she was melting into his kiss, just as Lucas knew she would—sisterhood was no match for raw desire.

"Come on," he said, leading her by the hand. "If it's meant to be, they'll sort it out between them. Let's not let it ruin our night."

"Well," said Lola, weakening as she followed him inside, "OK, but I'm not staying long. I have to go and find Sian and apologize. If I'd known you were gonna do something this dumb, I'd never have told you."

"Yeah, yeah," said Lucas, not listening. "Whatever."

CHAPTER FIFTEEN

$\mathcal{A}$ WEEK LATER, STROLLING DOWN MAIN STREET WITH A spring in her step, Honor was lost in her own contented thoughts.

It was a Sunday morning, bright and clear but markedly cooler than the days preceding it. September seemed to have crept up on East Hampton and dealt a guillotine blow to summer. All at once, the most stressful and yet in many ways most rewarding summer of Honor's life was over, blown away on the first of the cool fall winds. Tourists had begun oozing out of town like pus from a lanced boil, taking with them their frenetic New York energy, and once again the calmer daily rhythms of the full-time locals reasserted themselves, reclaiming the town along with a smattering of older, wiser vacationers who'd sensibly put off their holidays until after the high-season crush.

Palmers was still at 95 percent occupancy, a very respectable rate for the time of year, particularly given the effort certain people had gone to to drum them out of town altogether. Honor knew she couldn't afford to rest on her laurels, but she did allow herself to savor the sensation of relief, and not a little pride, that she'd successfully sailed her tired, rickety ship through such stormy waters. It was a good feeling.

She hoped her dad was up there somewhere, watching. And that maybe, at long last, he was proud of her too.

The pressure was lifting in other parts of her life as well. Though she felt guilty admitting it, she was actually relieved to have an enforced break from Devon, who'd flown back to Boston with his family four days ago. They'd had an almighty fight a few weeks ago, after Honor had challenged him about whether or not he still slept with Karis.

"Of course not," he'd replied, heartbeat-quick. "Why on earth would you think that?"

"Oh, I don't know," said Honor bitterly, her fear and insecurity morphing into anger. "Because your daughter says you do? Because she's been telling Lucas all about your fucking healthy marital sex life?"

Devon, who was also fearful—although in his case, it was a fear of being caught out—had fought fire with fire, yelling himself hoarse at Honor for being so "fucking naive" as to listen to Lucas's poison. "You trust that little Spanish shit's word over mine?" he roared. "How stupid are you?"

They'd made up, and afterward made love with more passion than they had in months. But an indefinable tension still hung in the air between them, and for once Honor had been glad to see him go. She still loved him, and of course she trusted him above Lucas; why wouldn't she? But even so, the prospect of a couple of weeks of peace to sort out her own feelings was a welcome one.

Speaking of peace, the icing on the cake for Honor's new-found sense of Zen had been Tina's departure last night. Officially, she'd dragged her perfectly rounded ass back to LA for work, although in reality it was more a case of swapping one round of parties for another. The Hamptons was, to quote Tina, "dull as shit" in the fall. Having Palmers to herself again was nothing short of joyous for Honor. All she had to do now was steer clear of Lucas and finally get around to fixing those fucking electrics—thankfully, the surveyors' dread prophecies had failed to come to pass, and they'd gotten through the summer season without incident—and then life could settle back to something approaching normal.

"Morning, Nate!" Jogging past the pharmacy, she waved cheerily at the owner, whom she'd known since she was a kid. Oddly, he didn't wave back but scurried inside his store without even acknowledging her.

Oh well. He must not have seen her. He was getting older, after all.

But as she made her way farther along Main Street, her sense of unease grew. At first she thought she was being paranoid. But no. People were definitely looking at her funny. When she stopped into the bakery to pick up her walnut loaf, a regular Sunday morning treat, she could actually hear the conversations shut down, replaced by a silence so thick you could eat it with a spoon.

Her last stop was the newsstand. Scooping up her usual Sunday paper from the pile on the floor, she smiled at the normally friendly woman at the counter. "Hey, Nancy," she began. "I don't mean to sound weird, but do I smell funny to you? Or have I got spinach stuck in my teeth? People keep staring at me like I just climbed out of a UFO or something." The newsagent, a kind, motherly woman in her fifties with round cheeks like a chipmunk, blushed scarlet.

"You haven't seen it, then?" she whispered.

"Seen what?" Honor looked blank.

"Oh, dear." Looking dreadfully flustered, Nancy handed her a copy of *US Weekly*. "It's pages six and seven."

Honor flipped open the tabloid.

"Oh, God," she said, feeling suddenly dizzy. "Dear God, no."

The only fractional mercy was that the editor had deemed it inappropriate to show Tina fully naked and had strategically blacked out the most sexually graphic parts of each of the four pictures. Nevertheless, it was pretty clear what was happening from the visuals alone—although anyone in any doubt could also refer to the text.

"Socialite Starlet in Coke-fueled Orgy," proclaimed the headline.

Tina Palmer, aspiring actress and daughter of one of America's most privileged families, was this morning revealed as a class-A drug abuser, willing to sell her depraved sexual services for money. Along with two other high-class prostitutes, our shocking pictures show the heiress:

- *Engaging in intimate lesbian acts as part of her "performance"*
- *Videoing herself and others during a series of graphic sexual encounters*
- *Snorting cocaine herself, then offering it to ANOTHER woman.*

Honor felt the bile rising up in her throat. The sex shots, weirdly, she could deal with. It was the pictures of her sister crouched over another girl's naked body, snorting a long white line of coke off her back, that made her want to vomit. She knew that Tina liked to party and had seen her smoke the odd joint. But that was enough cocaine to stop a train. She'd truly had no idea her sister had a drug problem.

"I'm afraid there's more," said Nancy, not unkindly, bringing a chair around for Honor and helping her to sit down into it. "It's in the *Post*." Honor took the paper with her heart in her mouth. At first glance she couldn't even tell what the piece was about. But then she noticed a small picture of herself and Devon standing together, raising champagne glasses. It could have been taken at any number of this summer's parties and in and of itself was hardly very incriminating. Unfortunately, the article that ran with it most certainly was.

Tina Palmer's publicity-shy older sister, Honor, owner-manager of Palmers hotel, has been carrying on an illicit affair with a MARRIED *multimillionaire for the past* TWO YEARS! the writer drooled salaciously. *Devon Carter, a respected Boston lawyer and father of two, who had been happily married to former model Karis Carter for over two decades…*

"Could I get a glass of water?" asked Honor, unable to read on. Her eyes were blurring, as though she had a migraine coming on. But it was going to take a lot more than a couple of ibuprofen to erase this particular pain.

"Sure, honey," said Nancy, bustling off to get one. A couple more customers wandered in, but much to Honor's relief Nancy shooed them out of the store and locked the front door behind them.

"There you go." She handed a glass to Honor, who was still staring into space looking shell-shocked. "I thought it was very unfair, that second article," she said kindly. "It's always the poor woman that gets the blame in these things. I expect he strung you along, did he, my dear?"

"Hmm?" said Honor absently. Her mind was racing, but she was not yet fully capable of speech.

How had the press gotten wind of her and Devon? As for Tina…those pictures. Who'd taken them? And where? Surely it couldn't be a coincidence that the two stories should break on the very same weekend? It was a coup, a carefully orchestrated coup, that's what it was, designed to finish her and Palmers for good. And it had blindsided her completely.

"Did you know?" Nancy was talking again. "About Tina taking drugs?"

"No," said Honor vehemently, finding her voice at last. "No, I didn't. I had no idea that she was…no."

And that was another thing. If the *US Weekly* shots were genuine, this was more than simply a PR disaster. Tina was in serious trouble. She needed help.

"Look, I'm sorry," she mumbled, getting to her feet. "Thank you, and everything. You've been really kind. But I have to go."

She staggered out of the store in a daze, like a survivor emerging from the wreckage after a plane crash. Come to think of it, that was exactly what it felt like: she'd been flying high, cruising at forty thousand feet without a care in the world, and then—BAM!—someone had fired a rocket launcher and blown both her wings off.

Except it wasn't just someone. It was someone in particular. And it didn't take Einstein to figure out who. She had no idea how she made it back to Palmers. But somehow she found herself there, having battled her way through the first few reporters who'd begun to gather outside. Finally reaching the safety of her office, she bolted the door, only to turn and see some joker with a camera trying to open the window.

"Fuck off!" she yelled at him, but not before he'd gotten a good three shots of her advancing toward him, screaming and openmouthed—not her best angle. "Get off this property before I call the cops!" Closing the heavy wooden shutters with a thud, she sank down into the chair at her desk, put her head in her hands, and tried to will her muddled, panicked thoughts into some sort of order. She'd already instructed the hotel staff on her way in to keep the press out at all costs and to try to make life as normal as possible for the guests. Anyone who said so much as "boo" to a reporter could consider themselves fired. She'd also had the receptionist call the local chief of police, who'd promised to get some men there within twenty minutes.

So far so good. But what now?

She longed to talk to Devon. Just hearing his strong, capable voice would reassure her. He always seemed to know what to do and was far calmer in a crisis than she was. But punching in his cell number for a second time, she found it was still switched off.

Where the hell was he? And why hadn't he called her? Surely he'd heard the news by now. God knows everybody else had.

Right on cue, her phone let out the annoying series of beeps that meant she had a new text. It was from him.

Sit tight, it read. *I'm denying and so should you. If they had proof they'd have printed it. Delete this. Don't call me. D.*

Despite herself, Honor felt her heart sinking. It was hardly the warmest of notes. Not so much as a *love* or an *xxx*, never mind a "how are you doing?" But maybe that was too much to ask under the circumstances? He was probably having a nightmare at his end too, besieged by these bloodhounds just like she was, dying to talk his way out of trouble with Karis at the same time.

His advice to deny the story made her feel distinctly uneasy. What if he was wrong and the paper did have proof? Then again, she could hardly admit to the affair if he denied it. That would land him right in the shit. If his marriage to Karis ended, it had to be his doing, not hers.

Pushing thoughts of Devon aside for a moment, she turned her attention to Tina. Clearly, the two of them badly needed to talk. But when she dialed her sister's number, she was greeted by a recorded message of Tina's voice, chirpily informing her that she'd be "back real soon!" and inviting Honor to leave her number.

Hanging up, Honor banged her fist on the desk in frustration. What was she supposed to do now? Go outside and make a statement? But saying what? Sit here and do nothing until all the reporters gave up and went home?

She was tempted to call Lucas. Obviously he was the one behind this whole nightmare, the fucking Judas. He'd sworn to her on his honor that he wouldn't tell a soul about her and Devon. So much for his word. She strongly suspected the pictures of Tina had also been taken at the Herrick—she recognized the minimalist decor in the background. What had he done, she wondered? Rigged up cameras and lured her in there somehow? Was it possible for a person to sink that low, just to promote their hotel? A hotel that they didn't even own?

But before she had a chance to try Lucas's number, her direct landline started ringing. Without thinking, she jumped on it.

"Hello?"

"Why did you pick that up?"

It was Sam Brannagan, her attorney from Boston. Not even Devon's voice whispering sweet nothings could have sounded more reassuring to her at that moment.

"From now on do not pick up any calls unless you can see the caller ID flashing. And turn off your cell. Got it?"

"Sam! Oh my God, thank God it's you." The relief in her voice was palpable. Words started tumbling out of her mouth in one long, continuous exhale. "Have you seen all this shit? What am I going to do? Can I sue the paper? I know who leaked the stories, if that helps."

"You can only sue if it isn't true," said Sam. "I'm afraid Tina's pictures rather speak for themselves, although there is a question of invasion of privacy. But what about you and Mr. Carter? Is what was printed accurate?"

There was a pause while Honor considered her answer. "Sort of. I mean, it's sensationalized."

"But you have been having an affair?"

The lawyer's tone was matter-of-fact. He was her lawyer, not her priest, after all. But somehow he still managed to make her feel guilty, like a kid caught with her fingers in her mom's purse. She wondered if Devon's instructions to deny everything applied to attorneys too?

"Look," she mumbled, deciding on balance that Sam could be trusted to keep a secret. "We do…have something together. But I don't think the papers have proof."

"Hmm," Sam sounded skeptical. "I wouldn't bank on that if I were you. But let's not worry about it now. The main thing is not to panic or say anything you might regret later. I'm already at the airport, so I should be with you by early afternoon, tops."

"Thank you," said Honor weakly.

"Do you think you can stay inside and away from the press until then?"

"Sure," she shrugged. "Where am I gonna go?"

"Good." Sam sounded satisfied with this response. "Oh, and there is one other thing you need to be aware of. Have you checked your e-mail in the last twenty minutes?"

"No." Honor shuddered, her heart racing. The nausea that had subsided when she first heard his voice on the line was suddenly back with a vengeance.

"I sent you a link," said Sam calmly. "It appears that the *US Weekly* pictures aren't actually photos at all, they're stills from a video. Someone has released the rest of it anonymously on the web."

Honor groaned.

"Yeah," said Sam. "It's not pretty."

"Please tell me *that's* not legal," said Honor. "Taping a person without their consent, invading privacy, profiting from illegal footage, I don't know."

"It's a gray area," admitted Sam. "But we can talk about that when I get there. Have you spoken to Tina yet? Do you know how this happened, exactly?"

Honor shook her head but said nothing. While he was speaking she'd opened her inbox and downloaded the video clip.

"Honor?" His voice sounded miles away. "Honor, are you still there?"

"Barely," she replied, at last.

The tape was horrific. In made *One Night In Paris* look like *The Sound of Music*.

"Have you and Tina spoken?" Sam asked again.

"No, not yet," said Honor. "But I'm a hundred percent certain how this tape happened. Lucas Ruiz set her up."

"All right. Well, just sit tight," said Sam, kindly.

He'd always liked Honor. Having an affair with a married moralizer like Devon Carter might not have been her smartest move ever, but she didn't deserve this shit storm. Especially not after she'd worked so hard to turn the family business around. He suspected these twin scandals, but particularly Tina's tape, would be a deathblow for Palmers. But he tried to keep his tone optimistic, for Honor's sake.

"I'll be there as soon as I can," he told her. "And remember: you don't talk to anyone until I get there. That's my job."

While Honor was holed up at Palmers, a steady trickle of reporters had been gathering at Lucas's beach cottage. When he hadn't shown up by eleven thirty, most gave up and dragged their equipment up the hill to set up camp outside the Herrick. This was lucky for Lucas, who, by the time he finally arrived home at noon, had the sort of hangover that could stop a train.

"Can I help you?" The small group of stragglers who'd decided to wait it out at the cottage looked up excitedly when he rolled up, unshaven and looking distinctly the worse for wear. "Are you guys waiting for me?"

He'd spent last night with Becca, a barmaid from Bridgehampton, and thoroughly enjoyed himself. But boy, had she put him through his paces! Not since Carla Leon had he been with such a voraciously sexually demanding woman. Becca also had the alcohol tolerance of a hippo. Fuck knew how many vodka shots they'd got through at the bar, and that was before they moved on to the tequila at her place. Lucas had barely managed to crawl out of her bed an hour ago, still feeling like a rat's ass. But when he left, she was already out on the terrace, doing yoga and drinking some hideous green sludge, looking fresh as a fucking daisy. It was actually kinda depressing. He must be getting old.

"Is it true you set the whole thing up?"

"Who's the guy in the video, Lucas? Is he a friend of yours?"

Before he could even unlatch the gate, Lucas found himself surrounded by people and beset by a barrage of questions that made his head spin.

"How well do you know Tina Palmer?"

"What about her sister's affair? Any comment on that?"

"I have no idea what you're talking about," he said truthfully, elbowing his way to the front door. "Now, if you'll all please excuse me, I have an urgent date with my espresso machine."

"It's a bit late to plead ignorance, buddy!" one of the hacks shouted after him, prompting snorts of laughter from his colleagues. Lucas firmly closed the door in their faces, doing his best to look confident. But inside, he could feel the anxiety building in his veins like a pulmonary embolism. What the hell were these people doing here?

The first thing he noticed was his answering machine light flashing furiously on the desk.

"You have NINE messages," it announced, with its usual automated lack of concern.

The first, from Lola, was terse, tearful, and to the point.

"Fuck you!" she sobbed. "You're a fucking asshole and I hope you fucking die!"

Nice.

The second and third were both from newspapers, asking for comments and indicating they'd be prepared to pay handsomely for an exclusive interview about Tina Palmer—what the fuck did they think he knew about Tina?—but neither spelled out what all this was actually about. He was on the point of checking the fourth message when the phone rang and, like an idiot, he picked it up.

"Lucas? Thank God. Where have you been? Your cell's been switched off."

It was Guy Harrington, the PR guy who'd been helping him orchestrate the media war with Palmers over the summer.

"Sorry," said Lucas wearily. "I was kinda tied up last night. But look, what the hell is going on? There are reporters at my house. My ex-girlfriend wants to kill me. Has this got something to do with Tina Palmer?"

Guy laughed mirthlessly. "Do you have cable?"

"Sure," said Lucas.

"Turn on E! Entertainment. Right now."

After a brief hunt for the remote, Lucas did as he was asked. Silently, he listened to the breaking news report on the Tina Palmer sex-and-drugs tape scandal.

"And this tape was shot at the Herrick?" he asked Guy, once he'd gotten the gist. "That's why they want to talk to me? As the manager?"

"Lucas, this is me you're talking to." Guy sounded weary. "Don't bullshit me, OK? You set this up." For a second, Lucas was too flabbergasted even to defend himself.

"Jesus." The PR guy seemed irritated by his silence. "There's not much point being coy about it. Anton Tisch admitted the whole thing in his statement a half hour ago."

"What do you mean *admitted*?" said Lucas, angrily. "Admitted what? I'm telling you, Guy, this is complete fucking news to me. How can Anton admit something on my behalf? Something that I haven't even done? My God. I would never—"

"Oh come on," said Guy. "You hate the Palmer sisters. Everybody knows that. How could hidden cameras have been rigged up in your hotel without you knowing about it?"

"I have no idea," said Lucas truthfully.

"You introduced Tina to this guy Candelle, right?"

"Toby Candelle? *He's* the guy in the video?"

"Lucas." Guy's exasperation was building. "You introduced them!"

"Only because Anton asked me to!" said Lucas vehemently. "I don't even know the man. I've met him twice, and that's the God's honest truth."

"Uh-huh. And Honor's affair with Devon Carter? Devon Carter, whose kid you're dating?"

"Was dating," said Lucas.

"I suppose you're gonna tell me you knew nothing about that either?"

Lucas ran his hands through his hair. He could see it must look bad.

"I knew they were having an affair," he admitted. "But I never told any—"

The words died on his lips as he remembered the one person he had told. And how that person had sworn to him, sworn on his honor, that the story would never see daylight. "That must be why Lola left that message," he muttered to himself. "She thinks it was me." Slowly, horribly slowly, the pieces of the puzzle were starting to fall into place. Tisch had set him up.

"Who ran the Honor/Devon story? Which paper?" he asked. Guy didn't reply.

"Look, humor me, OK?" said Lucas. He knew Guy didn't believe him, but he didn't care. All he wanted right now was the information.

"The *Post*. A paper whose entire features desk claims to be on first-name terms with you," said Guy. "The networks only picked up the story this morning, after Tina Palmer's home vid got released on the web. Or at least parts of it did. The rest's gonna be Pay-Per-View starting Monday, apparently. Not that you know anything about that either, right?"

Lucas hung up at this point. If his own PR guy didn't believe him, the conversation was pointless.

What if no one else believed him either?

The Tina story was still running on E! but he switched the TV off. He needed to think. Picking up the phone again, he dialed Anton's number in Geneva.

"I'm sorry, but Mr. Tisch is unavailable at present," barked his rottweiler Swiss assistant.

If it were Monday, Lucas could have called dear old Rita in London, but the business office would be shut up like a clam today.

"Ask him to call me back," he snapped. "It's urgent."

But he was already starting to get the sinking feeling that Anton had no intention of calling him back. Now or ever. He'd made a preemptive strike against the Palmer sisters. And he'd deliberately set Lucas up to take the fall.

His next call was to the Herrick.

"Ah, Debs, thank God it's you," he said, relieved that the competent head receptionist had picked up the phone and not one of the useless temps. "I need you to keep calm and keep the press out until I get there. I'm in a bit of a jam here right now, but I hope to be with you soon."

"Lucas—" She tried to interrupt him, but he ignored her.

"These fucking hacks are everywhere. But once I figure out a way to get past them, I'll come straight to the hotel—"

"Lucas!" She spoke louder this time. "Look, I'm really sorry. I hate to be the one to tell you this. But we've had instructions from Mr. Tisch himself this morning not to allow you back into the building." Her voice dropped to a whisper. "I shouldn't even be talking to you now. If anyone heard me, I could lose my job."

"Debs, that's ridiculous," he laughed. "You must have misunderstood. I had nothing to do with these stories. Mr. Tisch knows that better than anyone," he added, bitterly. "Now listen, I'm still your manager, OK? And I'm telling you, as your manager—"

"I'm sorry, Lucas." The poor girl sounded near to tears. "But I don't think you are my manager anymore. I have to go." And to his utter amazement, she hung up on him. His heart was beating at a mile a minute and his brain, still foggy from alcohol, sex, and an almost complete lack of sleep, struggled to keep pace. He'd have liked to call a lawyer, but he didn't have one. Weirdly, he found his thoughts turning to Ibiza and his mother, eking out her pitiful existence in that squalid one-room flat. He'd promised to come back one day and rescue her. Promised to build his own hotels, his Luxes, and make enough money that she would never need to work or worry or go hungry ever again.

How was he going to keep that promise now?

If he really had been fired from the Herrick—and it was starting to look that way—what then? People would think he was some kind of Rick Salomon–type asshole. He'd be branded a pervert and a blackmailer. No one in the luxury hotel world would touch him. Not if Anton made this stick.

But why? It didn't make sense. Whichever way he flipped it, he couldn't figure out why Tisch would want to do this to him. What had he ever done to deserve it?

——— ———

Meanwhile, in London, Ben was lying in bed in his London apartment, morosely chomping his way through a family-sized tub of rum-and-raisin ice cream and idly flipping through the channels on cable, when he stumbled upon *E! News* and caught the tail end of the Tina Palmer story.

Since he'd gotten back to England he'd sunk into something close to real depression. Sian hadn't called since his going-away party, and neither had he called her. He was still furious with her about the bet. But it didn't stop him from missing her so badly it felt like a physical pain in his gut. He didn't think he'd ever been so miserable in his life.

He still dragged himself into the office every day, plowing through his workload on autopilot. With Tisch's Excelsior fund snapping at his heels like a tiger shark, he really didn't have any choice. But as soon as he got home he unplugged every phone in the apartment and crawled straight into bed, then proceeded to spend the rest of his evening watching trash TV and drinking beer until he eventually passed out in a sea of potato chip crumbs and used Twinkie wrappers.

But the footage of Tina was enough to rouse him from his stupor. When the presenter mentioned Lucas's name he leaped off the bed, plugged his bedside phone back into its socket, and immediately called Lucas at home. The answering machine picked up: "Hi," said the recording, in Lucas's distinct Spanish accent. "You have reached Lucas Ruiz. Leave a message."

"Mate, it's me," said Ben. "If you're there, pick up."

"Ben?" There was a click as he came on the line. Even in that one short syllable of greeting, Ben could hear the strain in his voice.

"Yeah. You all right?"

"Not really," said Lucas. "You've seen it?"

"I'm watching it now," said Ben. "Shit." He almost dropped the phone. "Anton just came on. D'you want me to turn it up so you can hear what he's saying?"

"Yes," said Lucas shakily. "They're on a commercial break here." Retrieving the remote from beneath an empty Doritos packet, Ben turned the volume up to high.

Tisch was being interviewed on the lawn of his Geneva mansion. Lake Geneva shimmered in front of him, and behind him stood the gothic splendor of his palatial pile, bordered on either side with perfectly symmetrical formal gardens.

Neat freak, thought Ben. But it was an impressive display of wealth. And it looked every bit as old-money and conservative as Anton could have hoped.

"Bloody hell," he said, genuinely shocked. "What's he done to his face? He looks like one of the Thunderbirds. His lips are the only things that move."

"Shhhh," said Lucas. "I want to hear."

"All I can do is apologize to both the Misses Palmer for this grave intrusion into their privacy," Anton was saying smoothly, with barely a hint of his native German accent lacing his clipped, proper vowels. "The individual responsible for leaking these stories is no longer in the employ of the Tischen Group, and I am looking into what legal measures, if any, are open to us at this time."

"Legal measures!" spluttered Lucas. "This is insane. He wants to fire me *and* sue me? I haven't done anything!"

"Quiet," said Ben. "Listen first, fight back later."

"I can only imagine the anguish of both the Palmer and Carter families," Anton went on, glancing at his manicured nails while he spoke, like a cat examining its bloody claws after a kill. "And I would like to extend my sympathies to all concerned. That's all I have to say at this point."

The camera panned out as he strolled back into the chateau, affording an even more glorious view of the estate. Then they cut back to the studio, where a presenter was trawling through archive footage of Tina Palmer with various former boyfriends in the absence of any further actual news.

"Is that it? Is that all he said?" On the other end of the line Lucas's voice sounded hollow, as if he'd been winded.

"That's it," said Ben.

A long silence followed, broken in the end by Ben.

"You didn't really set her up, did you?"

"Of course I didn't!" Lucas was practically shouting. "I would never do a thing like that."

"All right, all right," said Ben. "I didn't think so. But I had to ask. 'Cause, you know, you did sleep with her."

"So did half of East Hampton," said Lucas reasonably.

"Yeah. But they didn't do it 'cause their bosses told them to," said Ben. "And they're not trying to put her sister out of business."

"Maybe not," said Lucas. "But it wasn't me. It was Anton, obviously. He's setting me up."

"Why would he do that?" asked Ben.

"I don't know!" Lucas sounded close to tears. "I should never have told him about Honor's affair with Carter."

"Whoa, whoa, whoa," said Ben. "Did you say Carter? Honor's been sleeping with Lola's wanker brother?"

"Try father," said Lucas.

"*Devon?*" Ben laughed. "No! Are you serious?"

"It's been going on for years," said Lucas, "since before I moved out here. I mentioned it to Anton in passing, ages ago, mind you. I know I shouldn't have, but it was before me and Lola got together, and he promised me he wouldn't say anything. But now it's all over the papers, and Lola thinks it was me who blabbed, of course, because I'm being blamed for this stupid sex tape…Christ, it's a mess. Doesn't she know me better? I mean, I would never betray her like that. Not deliberately."

Ben couldn't help but think that screwing Tina Palmer rated pretty high on the betrayal scale, but he didn't say anything. Lucas was already being punished enough for what he'd done, as well as for quite a few things that he hadn't, apparently.

"What am I going to do?" he wailed. "I'm innocent, but I can't prove it. Anton's crucifying me."

"Come here," said Ben. "Come to London."

He hadn't spoken to Lucas since telling him to go fuck himself at his going-away party last month. But their friendship ran far too deep to let one silly spat come between them now. If Lucas was in trouble, Ben wanted to help. Besides, maybe focusing on Lucas's problems might help take his mind off Sian for a nanosecond.

"There's nothing left for you in East Hampton," he said bluntly. "You need to lie low for a bit and let the dust settle. You can stay with me."

"Thanks," said Lucas. He was so touched by the offer, he felt quite choked. "But you don't need me getting under your feet."

"Bollocks," said Ben. "If you really wanna know, I could use the company. I'm turning into a right lard ass, sat here on my own moping about Sian. Pretty soon they'll be winching me out of the window with a crane."

Lucas laughed. "I'm sorry about Sian," he said sincerely. "Maybe I shouldn't have gotten involved."

"Forget it," said Ben. "This business with Anton is much more important. I doubt he'll sue you, though, whatever he says. If you're right and he did set you up—"

"Of course I'm right," said Lucas indignantly. "There's no 'if' about it."

"Well, *if* he did, the last thing he'll want to do is go to court. Besides, he's a typical Kraut, isn't he? All mouth and trousers."

Lucas laughed. He'd missed Ben's pearls of cockney wisdom.

"Of course, your job's fucked."

"Thanks for that," said Lucas drily.

"If you want my advice, tell anyone who asks that you had nothing to do with it. Then get yourself to JFK pronto and disappear. I can book you on a flight right now if you like."

Listening to Ben start up his laptop thousands of miles away, Lucas was shocked to find himself blinking away tears. He hadn't cried since the day he'd left home at fourteen. But with his world crashing around his ears, Ben's stalwart friendship moved him more than he could put into words.

"Thanks," he said, reining in his emotions with an enormous effort.

"I owe you one."

"Don't mention it, mate," said Ben cheerfully. "That's what friends are for."

By four o'clock Honor was back in her office at Palmers, having made a brief statement to the press. Sam Brannagan's flight got delayed, and she couldn't keep them waiting indefinitely. At least, not without looking like she'd gone into hiding, which was the last thing she wanted people to think.

Even so, a large group of reporters was still hanging around outside the gates, hoping for something juicier than the terse two-liner Honor had given them, blaming Lucas for orchestrating a smear campaign against her family and denying the affair, as Devon had asked her to.

Ideally, she'd have liked to have made a joint statement with Tina and presented a united family front. But typically, her sister, having not deigned to return any of Honor's calls, had gone ahead with her own press conference in the Beverly Hills Hotel, which Honor had watched on TV along with everybody else.

It was quite a performance. Dressed in a demure cream pencil skirt and chocolate-brown jacket, her hair swept up under a silk Louis Vuitton headscarf, Tina had channeled Grace Kelly for all she was worth. Putting on a faltering, little-girlish voice while her nervous fingers fiddled constantly with a boulder-sized Tiffany solitaire on her ring finger (was she engaged?), she had evidently mastered the Princess Diana gaze (half-shy, half-coquettish, guaranteed to reduce grown men to dribbling idiots from twenty paces). Peppering her public apology with charged words like "betrayal" and "entrapment," she somehow managed to turn the tables and shift her own role from vixen to victim. By the end of it even Honor was starting to feel sorry for her.

Unfortunately, not all of the guests at Palmers felt the same way. Four families had already cut their stays short and checked out, disgruntled to find their relaxing vacation hijacked and themselves thrust into the eye of a breaking media storm. When not fielding calls from the press, Honor spent most of the hours waiting for Sam desperately trying to convince her fall and winter bookings not to cancel.

"C'mon Danny, you can't do this to me," she pleaded, squeezing a rubber stress ball with her left hand while trying to type a begging e-mail with her right.

"I'm sorry, sweetheart. No choice." Danny McGee, an old family friend and Republican senator, was explaining that he would no longer be able to spend Christmas at Palmers. "I just can't be seen to be endorsing drug taking, in any way. This is purely about Tina and that awful tape, you understand. It's not about you and Devon."

"There is no me and Devon," said Honor, grateful that he couldn't see her blushes over the phone. Unlike Tina, she was a terrible liar. But it hadn't made any difference.

"What you do in your private life is your own business," said Danny. "But it's different for me. I'm a public figure, and Palmers is indelibly linked in the public mind with you and Tina. I'm sorry, angel, really I am, but I can't swing it."

When the knock finally came on her office door, Honor jumped, dropping the phone with a clatter as Betty ushered in a harassed-looking Sam Brannagan.

"Why did you make a statement?" were his first, accusatory words. "I told you not to talk to anyone. And certainly not to lie to anyone. Can't you see that's gonna make things worse?"

"Worse?" Honor let out a hollow laugh. "How could they be worse? Anyway, relax. People are far more interested in Tina's bedroom antics than mine. Devon and I agreed to stick to our story and let it all blow over."

"Yeah, well," said Sam, "it looks like your story got a little unstuck."

"What do you mean?" Honor's eyes narrowed.

"I mean, lover-boy admitted the whole thing." Sam threw his arms wide in a dramatic I-told-you-so. "I heard him myself on the radio on the way from the airport."

Honor shook her head in disbelief. "That's not possible. He wouldn't do that. Not without warning me."

"Well, he did," said Sam bluntly. "Half an hour ago."

Poor girl. Underneath her whole tough, feminist facade, she was still terribly young. Devon Carter had pulled the oldest

Indian rope trick in the book, and she'd fallen for it, hook, line, and sinker.

The guy was a walking cliché. All that drivel he spouted about family values; it was only a matter of time before he got caught with his pants down. Sam only wished that it hadn't been with Honor. She could have done so much better.

"Like I say, I only heard it," he said, more gently. "I haven't seen the footage yet. But apparently he went the whole nine yards, standing outside the family home with his wife, looking suitably contrite. He said some bullshit about how much he regretted what happened, blah, blah, blah."

"He said he regretted it?"

Bent forward, clutching her stomach as though she'd just been punched, Honor's body language gave away her anguish more clearly than any words. Sam's heart went out to her.

"He asked for privacy for him and Karis, so they could rebuild their marriage," he went on. "Basically, he painted you as Monica to his Bill. The decent man led astray. I'm sorry, Honor. I did warn you."

Walking across the room to the window, Honor cracked the blinds open a fraction and peered outside. The rhododendrons were in full bloom, heavy with blossoms that looked ready to drop into the gathering carpet of russet-red leaves already littering the lawn. Between the blanket of fall leaves and the copper-yellow light of the early autumn sun, the whole garden glowed as peacefully golden as a sepia photograph. Only the noisy gaggle of cameramen shattered the idyll. Forced by the local cops into a compact group in front of the hedge, their long lenses jutted out viciously like weapons, and their ugly, furry boom mikes protruded into the still afternoon air like giant mechanical bulrushes.

Honor closed the blinds. She felt sick.

She didn't want to believe what Sam had just told her. That Devon would cynically and deliberately sell her down the river, saving his own reputation without a shred of concern for hers. But she did believe it. Most bizarrely of all, it didn't even surprise her, not really. On some deeper level, it all rang horribly true.

"He said he was going to deny it," she said, turning back around.

Sam shrugged. "He lied."

They both jumped when Honor's cell phone started jumping up and down on the desk, buzzing like a demented insect. Picking it up, her eyes widened.

"Oh my God. It's him." She held the flashing screen aloft. "Should I answer it?"

"No!" said Sam. But she couldn't help herself.

"You've got a nerve, you lying son of a bitch," she began furiously. "How dare you call me? How *dare you*? You're not talking your way out of this one, asshole."

But when she heard the faltering female voice on the other end of the line, her bravado deserted her.

"I didn't have your number. But I figured my dad would," said Lola, "so I'm using his phone."

"Listen, Lola…" Honor began. She had no idea what to say, but felt that she had to say something. "I…your dad and I…"

"Save it," said Lola, cutting her dead. "I'm not interested in anything you have to say. I'm only calling because I thought you ought to know what you've done. We're in the hospital."

"What? What hospital? Why?" She hated herself for caring, but she couldn't help it. "Is Devon…your dad…is he OK?"

"Dad?" said Lola witheringly. "Oh, he's fine. He's just peachy. It's my mom who's fucked up. You remember my mom? The woman whose life you just ran over with a bulldozer?"

Honor winced.

"After that sick charade Dad put her through for the TV cameras, she totally flipped out. She locked herself in the bathroom and took an overdose."

"No!" It was more of a gasp than a word, and it was out of Honor's mouth before she had time to think.

"Yeah," said Lola. Even through her anger, Honor could hear she was fighting back the tears. "She emptied a fucking bottle of painkillers down her throat, and Dad had to break the door down. So if anything happens to her, it's on your conscience, you heartless bitch. I hope you're happy."

And she hung up, leaving Honor shaking, phone in hand, and looking about as far from happy as it was humanly possible to be.

PART TWO

CHAPTER SIXTEEN

*L*OLA CARTER PULLED HER TRENCH COAT MORE TIGHTLY around her and struggled vainly with her crappy drugstore umbrella as the rain started to pour in earnest.

She loved London, even though it had rained pretty much ceaselessly since she'd moved here in January. The same week that her father's affair had hit the press and her home life had come crumbling down around her ears, she'd discovered she'd been offered a place at the prestigious St. Martin's School of Fashion. At the time she'd been too distraught to give the idea much thought. It felt like years since she'd filled in the application, along with a slew of others, behind her father's disapproving back, and her long-cherished dreams of becoming a designer seemed frivolous and stupid when she thought about what her poor mom was going through. But as the weeks rolled by and the tension at home went from bad to utterly unbearable, escaping Boston began to look like a more and more attractive possibility.

It was now March and officially spring, but the monsoon season seemed far from over. If anything it was getting colder. Lola could feel the wet tips of her toes growing numb through her loafers as she splashed along King's Road, jumping in and out of puddles like a naughty five-year-old.

So much had happened in the last six months, good and bad, that in a way it felt appropriate to be in this strange, sodden city, starting again. Already the events of last summer felt so distant they might as well have been someone else's life.

Devon's affair with Honor had changed everything. Initially, one of the worst things was knowing it was Lucas who'd exposed it. Despite the way he'd blown hot and cold with her over the summer, Lola had left East Hampton still nursing a serious soft spot for him. She knew he didn't love her. But she had thought he at least liked and respected her. The idea that a man she'd willingly shared her dreams and fears and body with could throw a nail bomb of pain into her family like that…it shook her. For one thing, it meant she must be a pretty terrible judge of character. She'd honestly thought Lucas was a good guy at heart, but he'd turned out to be a snake of the lowest order. As for Honor, whom she'd come to look up to almost as an elder sister, she was even worse: a lying, calculating bitch. And her father? Even now Lola couldn't really get her head around it. Sure, she and her dad had never gotten along, even before this bombshell. But deep down she'd always believed that he, too, was a decent, honorable, upstanding man. That he practiced the strict morality he preached, not just to her and her brother, but to the world at large. Underneath all the teenage tantrums, she'd respected him. But now that respect was shredded.

It was harrowing, having to stand by uselessly while her mom crumbled like a stale piece of wedding cake. Her parents might never have been the Waltons, but they'd depended on and trusted each other for the better part of thirty years. The affair blew her mother's world apart.

Lola could still remember feeling sick to her stomach in the hospital, watching her dad hold her mom's hand as they waited for her to come around after the overdose, playing the concerned husband when he was the one who put her there in the first place. It was gross. All he seemed to care about was how things looked.

Even so, both he and Nick, who wasn't normally known for dramatic displays of emotion, burst into tears of relief when Karis finally came to. But not Lola. She couldn't. She just felt numb inside.

On the drive home, she wouldn't even look at her father. For the next month, while Karis recuperated in the hospital, the only time Lola agreed to be anywhere near him was during visiting hours, and that was purely for her mother's sake. At home the two of them rattled around like strangers, Lola having refused point-blank to contemplate retaking her SATs at St. Mary's.

"The doctor says Mom can come home next weekend," said Devon one gloomy Sunday night, forcing the cheeriness into his voice. "I thought maybe you and I could throw her a welcome-home party, now that Nick's gone back to LA."

He was sitting on a red damask couch at one end of their enormous Boston living room while his daughter, coiled like a snake into a rattan armchair at the other end, refused to look up from *Harper's Bazaar*.

"Do what you want," she snapped, still not looking up. "I won't be here."

"Oh?" said Devon, trying hard to mask his annoyance. "And why's that?"

"I've been offered a place at fashion school. In London," said Lola nonchalantly. "I've decided to take it."

"I see," said Devon.

"My course doesn't start until the new year, but I've booked a flight out on Friday to start looking at apartments and get the lay of the land."

He looked across at her determined, defiant face. A month ago he'd have slapped her down for talking back to him like that and sent her back to St. Mary's with a flea in her ear. But everything was different now. The contempt in her eyes burned so brightly it frightened him. If he tried to lay the law down now, she'd bolt. Then he'd have lost her for good.

"What's the name of the college?" he asked, playing for time.

"St. Martin's," said Lola truculently, flipping the page of her magazine with unnecessary violence and keeping her eyes down. "Like you care."

"Well," said Devon, projecting a calm that he was far from feeling, "you're not moving to England on your own. I'm sorry, but you're far too young for that."

"I'm eighteen," Lola shot back at him, looking him in the eye at last. "Plenty of kids younger than me leave home. Besides, I'm not asking you, I'm telling you. I'm going, whether you like it or not."

Wisely, Devon had decided to let the conversation lie at this point. For all her fighting talk, she would of course need him to fund her studies, not to mention her accommodation, if she wanted to go. But keeping her in Boston as an economic prisoner would be the surest way to drive a permanent wedge between them. Morally, she had him over a barrel, and they both knew it. The affair had robbed him utterly of his authority as a father. As much as he disliked it, he realized that if he was to have a chance at winning Lola's forgiveness and earning back her love, he'd have to let her go.

In the end, he'd agreed to rent her an apartment in Chelsea, on the condition that she room with a friend. Both he and Karis had hoped she'd pick one of the daughters of the many respectable old Boston families that they knew socially. But Lola had other ideas.

"But darling," Devon had tried to reason with her, watching her bent over the sewing machine in the kitchen one November evening, lost in concentration as she restitched one of Karis's skirts. Despite Devon's best efforts to encourage her to eat, Karis had been losing weight at an alarming rate since she came home, and most of her clothes hung off her now like rags on a skeleton. "A girl like Sian would be so far out of her depth in a cosmopolitan city like London. How do you think she'd afford the rent?"

Lola shrugged, biting off a stray thread with her front teeth. "We can subsidize her. Until she finds a job."

We? thought Devon. *Who the hell was* "we"? He was on the point of demurring but thought better of it. The daughter of some blue-collar New Jersey bum might not be ideal company for Lola, but at least the two girls would be safe together. And if agreeing to fund Sian meant Lola moved even an inch toward a reconciliation with him, he figured it was a price worth paying.

Ever since Karis had come back home, he'd begun to feel like a stranger in his own house. His wife drifted aimlessly from room to room like a zombie; his son had hightailed it back to LA as fast as his legs could carry him; and his daughter looked at him like something that had crawled out from under a rock every time he walked through a door.

He did regret the affair. Part of him still missed Honor and the thrill of youthfulness and excitement that being with her had given him. But for the first time the enormity of what he'd done to Karis really hit home. Underneath all the bickering and social climbing, he now realized, she still loved him. The damage to his reputation, much as it pained him, wasn't half as bad as the crushing guilt he felt watching her struggling to rebuild her life and carry on as normal while inside she was clearly still in a million shattered pieces. The other day he'd watched her from their bedroom window, chatting happily to one of the gardeners as she planted out bulbs for the spring. But as soon as the man left, she'd dropped her head into her hands, and he'd watched helplessly as her frail shoulders began to shake with sobs. Tears had come to his own eyes then. He wanted desperately to make things right. But the affair and all the ensuing publicity had left him so far adrift, he had no idea where to start.

Part of him hoped that with Lola abroad and Nick back in LA, things might get easier at home. But whether they did or didn't, he knew he had little choice but to let his headstrong daughter go.

Turning onto Tite Street now, Lola closed down her umbrella—the stupid thing was practically useless against such a pounding torrent anyway—and fumbled in her purse for the front door keys. The flat Devon had rented was comprised of the ground and first floors of a white stucco-fronted Victorian house, overlooking pretty, communal square gardens. Through the bay window at the front, Lola could see Sian slumped over her PC at the kitchen table, and banged on the glass to get her attention.

"Can't find my keys!" she yelled, lifting up her purse and rattling it to illustrate the point. "Can you let me in?"

A few seconds later Sian was at the door. Barefoot and in sweatpants, she had a long, chunky-knit cardigan pulled tightly around her and her hair scraped back in an elastic band. She looked tired.

"Have you been to sleep yet?" asked Lola.

After months of interviews Sian had finally landed herself a job at the *News of the World*, but it was mostly night shifts copyediting, which didn't pay her enough to cover the rent. Lola was always telling her not to worry—"my guilty asshole father can pay"—but Sian had no intention of freeloading and was still trying to write and pitch freelance articles during the day to supplement her meager salary. Unfortunately, this didn't leave her a lot of time for sleep. In the last week she'd started sporting full-on panda eyes, which didn't do much for her already pasty, sun-deprived complexion.

"Not yet." She shook her head. "Nice swim?"

"It's unbelievable!" Lola laughed, shaking out her wet hair and peeling off her coat and shoes. Her socks were so wet she had to wring them out on the porch like used washcloths before she could come in.

"Well, maybe the rain agrees with you," said Sian. "You certainly look a lot more cheerful." Padding back into the kitchen, she flipped on the kettle to make them some tea. Both the girls had taken to drinking Earl Grey and eating chocolate digestive biscuits when they got home from work, a ritual that made them feel marvelously English and Mary Poppins–ish, especially when the storms set in. "Did Ego call?"

"Ego" was the nickname Sian had given Lola's latest boyfriend, Igor, a revoltingly chiseled Russian in the year above her at school. A part-time model, he was also a full-time jerk, although it had taken Lola until yesterday, when he dumped her by text message, to see it.

"No." Lola shoved the last biscuit from the open packet into her mouth before greedily ripping open a new one. It never ceased to amaze Sian how a girl who ate like a sumo wrestler and whose idea of exercise was stretching for the TV remote kept such a sickeningly perfect body. Not to mention her flawless, alabaster complexion. "He didn't call, and I don't give a shit," she said, spraying biscuit crumbs across the table with happy abandon. "Asshole. His designs were all lame Vivienne Westwood rip-offs anyway. He can fuck-right-off-ski."

Sian bustled around making the tea, opening and closing cupboards and hunting for the quaint flowery teapot they'd picked up at Portobello Market. Man, she was exhausted. Even getting out the china and tea bags felt like a monumental effort today.

She was pleased Lola was over Ego and tried not to envy her friend's uncanny ability to bounce back from heartbreak like a human Tigger. Since they'd come to London Lola had gone through boyfriends like other people went through toilet paper. She never mentioned Lucas, not once, and seemed to have succeeded in blocking out the painful events of last summer completely by diving headfirst into her new life at fashion school.

How Sian wished she could do the same. She was fed up with being the Eeyore in their partnership, moping and brooding and worn out all the time. But she wasn't like Lola. She didn't have the supreme confidence, born of lifelong wealth and serious, super-model beauty, that protected Lola like a magic cloak from whatever stones life might throw at her.

Not that life was treating Sian too shabbily at the moment. Being offered the chance to come to London was a miracle for a girl like her. She still remembered getting Lola's phone call, back home in Lymington. Looking back, it was like the opening scene from a movie: her mom in the kitchen, making dinner; her dad and brother sprawled on the couch in the living room, Budweisers in hand, engrossed in the final minutes of the game; and Sian herself, running down the stairs screaming with excitement, holding the phone in front of her like a talisman, begging her parents to let her go.

"I can pay my own way," she pleaded. "I've got almost three thousand dollars saved up now. And I'll find work as soon as I get there, I swear."

"I thought that money was for college?" said her mom. "How long have you been telling us about wanting to get more education?"

"This is *London*, Mom," Sian explained patiently. "It is an education. Anyway, you and Dad always wanted me to start work right after high school. So now I will."

"We meant work here," said her father. "In Lymington. Not halfway across the world with some heiress kid we've never even met."

They'd taken some persuading. To her parents, moving to London was equivalent to saying you wanted to spend a year on the international space station or join the submarine corps. It was something they couldn't picture and consequently feared.

"Soon as you get homesick, you get right on the next plane," her mom said tearfully at the departure gate. "There won't be no 'I told you so's.' You just come on home, all right, honey?"

"Sure, Mom," said Sian. "Of course I will."

But inside she was rolling her eyes. Like she was gonna be homesick! For what? Burgers at Dino's on a Friday night? Hanging out at the mall?

Yet to her surprise, she found she did miss home, almost from the moment she landed in England. Two solid months of waitressing at a greasy spoon café in Earl's Court probably hadn't helped. But even now that she'd finally landed a job on a Sunday tabloid, her dream for as long as she could remember, there was still a feeling of restless unhappiness she couldn't seem to shake.

She hesitated to attribute this to Ben, who she soon discovered was some kind of microcelebrity in England, a sort of Donald Trump mini-me. Like most eighteen-year-old girls, she found the financial pages deathly boring, useful only as cat litter, or possibly to start a fire. But Ben's name cropped up in the *FT* with such regularity it was impossible not to take a morbid interest. Seeing his name in print was like picking at an emotional scab—disgusting, painful, and yet weirdly addictive. It wasn't long before she found herself actively scanning the hedge fund articles, looking for a mention or a picture.

He'd told her when they met that he worked in finance, so she'd assumed he was reasonably well off. To stay at the Herrick he'd have had to be. But despite Lucas's assumptions to the contrary, she'd actually had no idea Ben was a fully paid up member of the superrich. In some ways she supposed it explained his sensitivity over the whole bet thing. Explained it, but didn't excuse it. Even after six months the pain of their parting was still raw, and the wound to her pride still stung like acid every time she thought of him. Which, these days, was pathetically often.

"You know," said Lola, pouring herself a second cup of tea, into which she heaped three towering teaspoons of sugar. "Breaking up with Igor does leave me with one problem."

"It does?" Sian looked disbelieving.

"Kind of. It means I'm gonna be dateless for the Burnstein wedding."

Araminta "Minty" Burnstein was the daughter of family friends from Boston. Her wedding to some random shipping heir or other promised to be one of the grandest seen in New York since Liza Minnelli's. Lola had had mixed feelings about going. She hadn't been back to the States or seen her parents since Christmas, but she knew from Nick, who'd spent the holiday at home, that things at home were still walking-on-eggshells tense. Minty's wedding would be the first big social event her mom had attended since her dad's affair with Honor became public. Lola wasn't sure she could bear to watch the forced, brittle smiles of people trying to pretend nothing had happened. And what if her mom broke down?

On the other hand it looked set to be an *awesome* party. And Lola Carter had always been an awesome party kind of a girl.

"Wanna be my date?"

Sian choked on her tea, spraying hot liquid and biscuit crumbs all over her copy.

"Me?" she said, cleaning up the mess as best she could with a tea towel. "You don't want me cramping your style. Anyway, it's not for another ten days. You'll have guys lining up by then."

"Probably," said Lola, not bothering to deny it. "But I really don't wanna bring some guy I barely know. Not to this. And I don't want to go alone, either. I need someone to carry the bucket for me if my dad starts playing the devoted husband and I have to puke halfway through the vows."

"As glamorous as that sounds," said Sian, "I really can't."

"Why not?" Lola looked crushed.

"I can't afford the plane ticket, never mind a hotel," said Sian simply. "Anyway, I ought to be working."

"You're always working, sweetie," said Lola. "It's only one weekend. You could see your mom and dad afterward," she added, by way of further incentive.

Sian rubbed her tired eyes, and to her horror found she was on the verge of tears. She tried not to dwell on it too much, but she missed home and Taneesha like crazy.

"I can't afford it, Lo," she said again. "And please, don't tell me your dad will pay, OK? We've been through all that a million times."

Leaning across the table, Lola grabbed her hand. "I know you don't believe in taking handouts," she said. "That's cool. But I already paid for Igor's ticket. It's transferable but it's not refundable. If you don't come, I'm literally gonna have to throw it in the trash."

"Really?" Sian looked skeptical.

"Yes, really," said Lola, sensing her resolve weakening. "Absolutely. And I have a double room at the Four Seasons, also bought and paid for. We can share the bed, have our own girlie slumber party. Oh come on! It'll be so much fun."

Sian wavered. *Oh, what the hell.*

"All right," she said, grinning. It really would be wonderful to see her folks. "Count me in."

"Yay!" Leaping to her feet, Lola clapped her hands and whooped around the table in an impromptu victory dance. "Fuck you, Igor. New York, here we come!"

CHAPTER SEVENTEEN

I'M SORRY, SIR, BUT THE CAPTAIN HAS SWITCHED ON THE FAS-ten seat belts sign. I'm going to have to ask you to buckle up."

Lucas opened one eye lazily and looked up at the stewardess. She was young and pretty, but her looks were ruined by the drag-queen makeup that airlines seemed to insist upon nowadays—thick brown lip-liner filled in with pink shimmer gloss, too-dark foundation that stopped with an abrupt tidemark at the jaw line, and mascara so thickly caked it was a wonder the poor girl could open her eyelids at all. Combined with her severely pulled-back hair and starched orange-and-white uniform, the overall look was more dental hygienist than sex siren.

Pity. He could have done with the distraction.

"How long till we land?" he asked, running a hand through his thick curls. One of the few good things about his ignominious firing from the Herrick was that he no longer had to keep the hated Matt Lauer buzz cut and could revert to his favored disheveled look. For the flight back to Ibiza he was wearing battered jeans and a faded blue open shirt with a string of worry beads underneath. No one would have recognized him as the preppy East Hampton playboy of six months ago.

"Not long now, sir," said the girl. "You on 'oliday?"

She was eager to engage this gorgeous man in conversation for as long as she could and hoped fervently that he might ask her for her number before they landed. Sadly for her, Lucas was in no mood for chitchat.

"No," he said grumpily, clicking his belt buckle closed and gazing stonily out the grimy plastic window. "I'm going home."

He'd tried to tell himself that coming back to Ibiza was nothing to be ashamed of. That he was here to visit his mother and brothers, to help out, to do the right thing. But it wasn't working. The truth was he was coming back with his tail between his legs because he'd failed. And because he'd reached a point where he honestly felt he had nowhere else to go. Since leaving the Herrick under such a massive cloud last September, his mood had swung violently between deep troughs of self-pity and murderous, obsessive hatred of Anton, whose weirdly impassive, Botoxed face had begun to haunt his dreams. Sometimes it would appear, unbidden, during his waking hours too: after every failed job interview, when door after door was slammed in his face at hotels from Rome to Paris to London. Overnight, Lucas had gone from being the industry's wunderkind to persona non grata. Even the family-run boutiques seemed to have banded together against him. It was as though they were all part of an exclusive private members' club, from which Anton had had Lucas blackballed.

His name was now synonymous with Tina Palmer's infamous sex tape. He could protest his innocence until he was blue in the face, or pay a fortune to have lawyers do it for him, but his reputation was already shot. By October, the clip of Tina snorting coke at the Herrick was the single most downloaded item on the web. By Christmas *Palmer-Gate* had outsold *One Night In Paris* by almost three to one. The fact that Lucas could prove that he had never received a cent of its proceeds was apparently immaterial. As manager, he was technically responsible for everything that went on at his hotel. His dismissal from the Herrick was quite legal.

Meanwhile, Anton had been careful to ensure that he emerged from the whole sordid affair looking whiter than white. No money from the Pay-Per-View could be traced to his accounts either, and his "friend" Toby Candelle, now a minor celebrity in his own right as Tina's costar, flat-out denied ever having met or spoken to him, which meant it was their word against Lucas's. Two against one. How much had Anton had to fork out to secure that little shit's loyalty? Lucas wondered bitterly. A lot more than thirty pieces of silver, that was for sure.

Ironically, the only person who had ended up doing well out of the tape was Tina herself, Anton's intended victim. She was cautioned over the drug taking but never charged. And as no one else was stepping forward to take responsibility for the footage, she ended up winning retrospective ownership to the rights herself. When she announced she'd be donating all the proceeds to Guatemalan orphans, Angelina Jolie–style, her media rehabilitation was complete. All of a sudden America couldn't get enough of Tina Palmer.

Lucas, on the other hand, was very far from being forgiven. After over five months of job hunting, he had yet to get so much as a sniff of interest from any of the top-tier hotels in Europe. (He'd already given up on the US, where the press had shit on him so hard employers could smell him before he walked in the door.) Unless he found something soon, he'd be forced to slide right back down the ladder and take a junior management position in some anonymous chain somewhere. How the mighty had fallen. Then two days ago, to add insult to injury, he'd been skimming through *Hotel World* on the way home to Ben's apartment—financial necessity had turned his two-week stay into a semipermanent arrangement, and the boys were now roommates—when he saw a double-page spread on the Herrick's new manager.

He recognized her instantly. Her once-black hair was now supershort and dyed platinum, and her snow-white skin had gained some artificial color over the years. But the cruel, ice-blue eyes were just the same, as was the permanent man-hating sneer that hung over her angular, Slavic beauty like a shroud.

Petra Kamalski.

Surely it couldn't be a coincidence that Anton had hired his old enemy and rival from his Lausanne days to be his replacement? It must be his idea of a sick last laugh—a metaphorical kick in Lucas's ribs when he was down. If so, it worked. When he saw Petra's picture, he felt sick to his stomach.

According to the article, a sycophantic wank-fest obviously written by one of Anton's pet journos, Petra had returned to Moscow after graduating from EHL. Lucas had always assumed she'd shove her MBA in a drawer, marry some other ludicrously wealthy trust-fund bratski and go off to make Damian babies in a palace somewhere. She didn't need to work, after all. But it seemed he'd misjudged her ambition. After working her way up at the notoriously political Ritz-Carlton Group, she'd gone on to become number two at the Palace, the grandest hotel in St. Petersburg. That in itself was impressive less than four years out of college. But to go from there to the Herrick was almost as big a quantum career leap as it had been for him, leaving the Cadogan two years ago. She must have made quite an impression on Anton. Or maybe he just recognized a kindred spirit. Lucas couldn't think of anyone who'd make a more perfect bride to Tisch's Frankenstein.

The plane finally landed in Ibiza, and Lucas followed his sheep-like fellow passengers down to baggage claim. He made no effort to hide his disdain for the Easter holiday tourists huddled around the lone rickety conveyor belt. Fat women, squeezed into Bermuda shorts designed to make their ample backsides look even more bovine, stood beside their already drunk husbands—most of them had their noses stuck in their pints since before they'd left Gatwick—while their unruly kids jumped on and off other people's luggage, swarming around arrivals in their Manchester United soccer jerseys like so many red ants.

His own bag, as usual, was practically the last to arrive, which did little to alleviate his foul mood. And when he finally struggled out to the taxi line, a pixie-like American woman barged past him and shamelessly stole his cab.

"Sorry," she said, not looking anything of the sort as she flashed him a mouthful of porcelain veneers and chucked her Louis Vuitton tote onto the backseat. "I'm in a real rush."

Lucas yelled obscenities after her as the cab sped away. With her scrawny little body, spiky hair, and outrageous sense of entitlement, she reminded him of Honor Palmer.

He'd thought about Honor a lot since he'd left America.

"Why don't you call her and apologize?" Ben suggested innocently at Christmas, after Lucas had brought her name up yet again in conversation. "Put the past behind you."

"Apologize?" Lucas looked amazed. "Why the fuck should *I* apologize to *her*?"

"Because you feel bad?" offered Ben. "Because if you hadn't slept with Tina and set her up with that guy and spilled the beans to Anton about Honor and Devon's affair, none of this shit would have happened?"

"That's crap," said Lucas hotly. "Firstly, I didn't know the Tina thing was a setup."

Ben raised an eyebrow. "Oh, come on. You must have had your suspicions. Why did you think Anton frog-marched you into bed with her? And why would he go to so much trouble to arrange introductions for a woman he barely knew?"

Lucas scowled. Ben's perceptiveness could be quite annoying at times.

It was true, of course. He had smelled a rat. He simply hadn't cared enough to dig any deeper. Nor had it crossed his mind that he might be the one at risk. But he wasn't sure he was ready to admit that to himself yet, never mind Ben.

"Honor has no one to blame but herself," he said firmly. "She shouldn't have been screwing around with someone else's husband. Especially not one old enough to be her father," he added with disgust. "She deserved to get caught."

Ben laughed. "Talk about the pot calling the kettle black! What are you now? The patron saint of fidelity? How many older, married women have you banged in your time?"

Lucas looked sulkily at his shoes and said nothing.

"For fuck's sake, call the woman and straighten things out," said Ben. "You know you want to."

But Lucas was adamant he did not want to. Honor was a hostile, self-important cow. *His* life was the one in ruins. Why should he call her?

Despite his loudly proclaimed indifference, he found himself keeping an eye out for references to Honor and Palmers in the press. In the same *Hotel World* article where he'd read about Petra's appointment, the journalist claimed that Palmers had been losing market share to the Herrick at a consistent rate since last summer and that its bookings for the coming season were at an all-time low. Of course, it might not be true. The writer was clearly a Tisch stooge, and Honor, as usual, had been "unavailable for comment" and so couldn't confirm or deny the rumors. Since the scandal had broken, she'd become a virtual recluse, leaving it to Tina to bask in notoriety in the pages of the gossip magazines.

Staring out the window at the scrubby palm trees battered by the recent gales and the squat, low-rise apartment buildings that had sprung up like toadstools along the main road from the airport, Lucas felt sad. Every time he came back, this part of the island seemed to have gotten uglier. Soon he'd be in his mother's dingy apartment, doling out what little money he had left like Santa Claus, all the while knowing it would almost certainly be wasted on booze by his stepfather or sucked into the black hole of the family's debts.

He closed his eyes and let his head flop back against the soft plastic of the headrest. He felt bone weary but was too wound up to sleep. Instead, as usual, he allowed a picture of Anton's smug, smiling face to float into his consciousness. It wasn't long before he felt his simmering rage bubble up to boiling point.

———————   ———————

Some twelve hours later, at just after midnight, he staggered blindly out of a dive bar onto the filthy sidewalk.

"And don't come back, asshole!" the owner shouted after him in Spanish. "You're lucky my bouncer had the night off. Next time, he'll break both your arms, tough guy." Lucas didn't bother to shout back, partly because he wasn't at all sure he could string a sentence together, but mostly because he knew the guy was right. He had been an asshole, picking a fight with two of the patrons over some bullshit politics or other, purely because they were American.

In his defense, it had been one hell of a rough day. He'd arrived at the apartment to find that his mother, at the age of forty-one, was pregnant again—heavily pregnant—a fact she'd omitted to mention in any of their phone conversations of the past six months. Quite apart from the head-fuck of being about to have a baby brother or sister he was old enough to have fathered himself, Ines's pregnancy was yet another financial and emotional pressure thrust onto his already overloaded shoulders. He couldn't deal with it.

In the end they'd had a titanic row about it, with an incoherently drunk Jose and Tito, the only one of Lucas's waster brothers not in prison, both throwing in their two cents' worth, adding fuel to the fire.

"Take it!" he finally snapped, emptying his wallet and pockets of every last note and coin and flinging them hopelessly onto the floor at his mother's feet. "It doesn't matter what I make; it'll never be enough, will it, Mama? There's always another mouth to feed, another fucking bill collector at the door. You're your own worst enemy."

He stormed out with the sound of Ines's sobs and his stepfather's slurred abuse still ringing in his ears. Heading straight for San Antonio, he walked into the cheapest bar he could find and set about the important task of drinking himself into oblivion.

On the street, the cool night air hit him with sobering force. Ibiza in March could be quite cold, and Lucas found himself shivering in just a shirt and jeans. Slinging his one small bag over his shoulder, he set off in the direction of Plaza della Playa, where he hoped one of the cheaper, off-season B and Bs might give him a room, even at this time of night. It was far too cold to sleep on the beach, even warmed from within with whiskey as he was.

Without thinking, he turned a corner and found himself standing at the foot of the front steps to the Britannia, the ghastly dive where he'd worked as a teenage no-hoper all those years ago. Looking at the place, it might have been yesterday. Nothing had changed, from the dingy facade with its depressing, peeling paint to the stench of pine disinfectant that wafted out of the lobby and into the street like chemical warfare. The smell made him retch. And yet some strange impulse seemed to draw him up the steps. Putting one blind foot in front of the other, he soon found himself standing, swaying like a reed in the breeze, in the middle of the deserted reception area.

"Well, well, well."

The taunting, malevolent voice was accompanied by a slow hand clap. Lucas turned unsteadily around.

"If it isn't the prodigal son returned."

Miguel, the manager, emerged from the shadows like a fat, bald genie of the lamp. His face was markedly more lined than when Lucas had last seen him, and his grotesque, wobbling beer belly now protruded a farther inch or two from beneath his straining, food-splattered T-shirt. But otherwise he was the same sneering bully he'd always been. Lucas had assumed that even a deadbeat like Miguel would have moved on to new pastures by now. But apparently not.

He looked his old boss up and down as if he had scabies. "Miguel. What an unpleasant surprise."

"So tell me." The manager eased his spreading thighs down into the one threadbare sofa shoved against the wall in reception and threw his arms wide with exaggerated bonhomie. "Just how exactly do you move from managing a famous Tischen Hotel to flogging homemade porn on the Internet? Is that the sort of savvy career move they teach you at EHL?"

But Lucas wasn't playing along.

"You know," he said, wrinkling his nose in distaste. "Something smells rotten in here. You'd have thought disinfectant this strong would wipe out all the vermin." Sniffing pointedly, he looked Miguel right in the eye. "But I guess not. Will you excuse me? I'm afraid I have to go outside and vomit."

The poisonous smile melted from Miguel's face.

"Sticks and stones, Ruiz!" he shouted, waddling after Lucas's retreating back like a venomous toad. "Say what you like about me, but at least I have a hotel to run. You were so full of it when you left, swanning off to Lausanne. Remember your Luxe?" he jeered. "You were going to blow the hotel world wide open. Show us all how it was done. Ha!"

With an effort, Lucas kept walking. What on earth had possessed him to come back to this shit hole?

"But of course, you've come crawling back. Just like I said you would." Miguel called after him, struggling up from the sofa to follow Lucas out. "Staying with that junkie slut mother of yours, are you? No wonder you got tangled up with Tina Palmer." He laughed, a horrible, wet, gurgling sound, like someone drowning in phlegm. "They say boys are always attracted to girls that remind them of their mamas."

Lucas had reached the bottom of the steps now and was standing in the Plaza. Only one desultory pizza place was still open, its few patrons glued to the big screen above the bar, which was showing a welterweight boxing match. Miguel was a couple of steps above Lucas but was short enough to still be at his eye level. Which meant that when Lucas turned around and launched his first punch, a wild swing directed straight at his opponent's nose, Miguel had plenty of time to see it coming. Luckily for him, after so much booze, Lucas's reflexes were not what they otherwise might have been.

Ducking to avoid the blow, Miguel swiftly hit back, landing one of his own right hooks in the pit of Lucas's stomach—this was no time for gentlemen's rules of combat—winding him just long enough to land a second blow across the top of his jaw. Jolted, Lucas staggered backward. Having grown up taking beatings from a powerhouse like Jose, Miguel's feeble efforts were little more than bee stings. But, like bee stings, they were irritating. And the more irritated Lucas got, the less he seemed able to make his tired, drunken body do what he asked it to.

The patrons in the pizzeria had turned their attention from the dull televised fight to the much more exciting live action. But it was a bit like watching a small child baiting a bear: Lucas had all the strength but apparently no idea what to do with it.

Letting out a great, bloodcurdling roar of frustration and rage, he ran headfirst at the steps like a charging bull. For a split second, Miguel panicked—jammed between solid stone stairs and two hundred pounds of lean, angry muscle, there was nowhere to go. But to his great relief, Lucas lost his footing just at the crucial moment. With a collective, audible gasp, the pizzeria diners watched as his head slammed down onto the bottom step with a sickening crunch.

"Not so high and mighty now, are we?" snarled Miguel, swinging his fat leg back and launching a kick at Lucas's head as if it were a football.

A semiconscious Lucas merely groaned. Then he lay back as slowly, pixel by pixel, the world faded to black.

When he next opened his eyes, the first thing he was aware of was the drill that seemed to be soaring through his skull and into the soft tissue of his brain. He'd never known a headache like it.

"Where am I?" he groaned, trying to sit up but instantly regretting it as a wave of nausea slammed into him, and he sank back down onto the bed.

"You're in the Euro Clinic Eivissa," said the middle-aged woman who seemed to have materialized out of the ether.

"The German hospital?" said Lucas, weakly.

"Yes. You were lucky. A German lady at the Plaza Pizzeria called an ambulance for you. The rest of them would have left you there to bleed to death or freeze."

Typical. Just his luck to be rescued by a bloody German.

"What happened?" asked the woman.

Fractured memories of Miguel's malevolent face came floating back to him, interspersed with images of his pregnant mother, Anton, and, bizarrely, Honor. What was she doing right now? he wondered. This very second?

He still kept a mental picture of her from that first day on the beach, before he knew who she was, when he'd been so unforgivably rude and refused to help her. What was it about Honor that always seemed to bring out the absolute worst in him?

"Lucas?" The woman's voice was back.

How did she know his name? He must have had his driver's license on him when they brought him in. He couldn't imagine any of his credit cards were left.

"Do you know who did this to you? The German lady said it seemed as though you knew the other man. The two of you were talking…"

"No," Lucas shook his head. "She must be mistaken. I can't remember anything. Sorry."

He didn't want to go after Miguel. What was the point? At the end of the day, everything he'd taunted him with was true. Maybe, in a twisted way, he'd done him a favor. Maybe it had to come to this—waking up alone, broke, and bloodied in a strange hospital—for him to finally see the light.

He'd left Ibiza with a dream—to build his Luxe. But somewhere along the way he'd lost sight of it.

Being made manager of the Herrick so young had gone to his head. He'd gotten sucked into this stupid war with Honor Palmer, jumping whenever Anton said jump, like a performing monkey, desperate to hold on to his status as the US hotel world's next big thing. And he'd sacrificed his morals and his judgment in the process.

His vanity, he now realized, had hurt a lot of people. Some of them, like Devon Carter, might have deserved to suffer. But others—Karis, Lola, even to a lesser extent the Palmer sisters—they'd all been collateral damage. The person he'd hurt the most though, ultimately, was himself. It was his dreams that had come to nothing. His future that had folded before his eyes, like a house of cards.

He still hated Anton for double-crossing him. And he was still determined to get his revenge. But he would no longer let his hatred consume him. From now on he would focus his energies on something positive.

Tomorrow, Lucas would sit down and rewrite his business plan. Screw finding a job.

The next time he saw Miguel Munoz, he'd be the owner—not the manager; not, as Honor had once goaded him, "a paid employee," but the *owner*—of the best boutique hotel in the world.

"Luxe," he whispered, under his breath. Even saying the word out loud revived him.

"What was that?" The nurse pricked up her ears. "Have you remembered something?"

"Yes," said Lucas, with a smile. "Yes. As a matter of fact, I have."

CHAPTER EIGHTEEN

ONOR CHECKED HER HAIR IN THE ELEVATOR MIRROR and fiddled nervously with her silver-and-topaz cuff links. Officially you weren't supposed to wear white to a wedding other than your own, but she hoped her wide-cut Marni pantsuit would count as oatmeal. Maybe the white rule didn't apply to pants anyway? Or maybe pants were just a total no-no at a wedding? Oh shit, what if they were? If only she weren't so damned nervous.

The Burnstein wedding was the first big social event she'd agreed to attend since last year's scandals. Her first instinct when the stiff white invitation had landed in her in-tray at Palmers was to decline, the same way she'd declined everything else she'd been invited to since her affair and Tina's tape were made public. But a series of things had made her change her mind. Firstly, the Burnsteins and the Palmers had been friends for generations. Honor had been friends with Arabella, Minty's elder sister, since elementary school in Boston and had known the bride since the day she was born. Secondly, Billy Malone, her ex-professor, ex-lover, and dear friend had been staying with her at Palmers the week the invitation arrived and had read her the riot act about chickening out.

"Listen, Howard Hughes," he told her sternly. "This whole recluse shtick has gotta stop. If you're not careful you'll wind up sleeping in an oxygen chamber and telling people that your cats are like your children. Go to the damn wedding, OK?"

But the deciding factor was when yet another old friend from Boston had called to assure her that Devon and Karis Carter, who also knew the Burnsteins, would be in Asia that weekend and would categorically *not* be going.

Even so, she thought, wondering if the flash of aquamarine Manolo heel visible beneath the hem of her flared pants was too much, today was gonna be an ordeal. All the questions, the curiosity veiled as sympathy, the stares…she was dreading it.

Since the very public end of her love affair with Devon, Honor's self-confidence had been at an all-time low. She could understand him wanting to protect his family. After all, she'd devoted all her energies to trying to protect Palmers from the fallout (for all the good it did her). Even she could see that saving a hotel was hardly on par with saving a marriage.

But nothing had prepared her for the brutal way he had simply exorcised her from his life, overnight. Once the worst of the storm had died down, she'd waited for him to make contact. She wasn't expecting hearts and flowers. A simple "how are you coping?" would have sufficed. "Sorry" would have been even better. But what she got was deafening silence.

Because of all the furor about Tina, the story of their affair wasn't allowed to die a natural death in the media. Every time Tina did another interview (which was every other week—the girl knew how to milk a story), Honor's and Devon's names would get dragged up again. Honor felt helpless. Her life, her private heartbreak, was being served up as the glacé cherry on the top of Tina's self-made soap-opera sundae, for people to pick over at their leisure.

To make matters worse, article after article started appearing painting Honor as the scarlet woman, the manipulative home wrecker. Anyone would have thought she'd drugged Devon, clubbed him over the head, and dragged him into bed to rape him.

Not once did he defend her or lift a finger to contradict this impression in the press. Not once did he call. When the chips were down, he'd abandoned her and their relationship without a backward glance. And Honor didn't see him for dust.

Now, six months later, she was over the heartbreak. Mostly. But she was still left with the nagging doubt that comes from having trusted, deeply, and been so terribly let down. She'd always considered herself to be a good judge of character. But clearly she'd been kidding herself. When it mattered the most, none of her so-called instincts had been worth a dime.

Which was a shame, because right now she needed those instincts more than ever. Things at Palmers were going from bad to worse, and she had no idea how to turn the tide. When the Herrick had first opened, she'd gambled on survival by differentiation and played the old-money conservative card for all it was worth. Up until the scandals broke, it had worked. But now her strategy had turned around to bite her. Palmers' guests were the last people on earth to be attracted by notoriety. These were the sort of people who packed their kids off to rehab after one puff of a joint. As for sexual liberalism, most of them viewed even marital relations with distaste, never mind four-in-a-bed lesbian orgies and S and M shows caught on film. With her core client base leaving in droves, Honor had no choice but to change her tactics and go after the younger, hipper crowd more typically drawn to the Herrick. But to those people, Palmers was the last word in stuffy. It was a classic lose-lose situation.

The elevator came to a stop with a worryingly sudden jolt. But after a few nerve-racking seconds the doors glided open and Honor stepped out into the hallway.

On the sixty-fifth floor of Number Thirty Rockefeller Plaza, the Rainbow Room restaurant with its incredible views, sky-high ceilings, and revolving dance floor was the epitome of classic New York chic. It was unashamedly old-fashioned—more Rat

Pack than *Sex and the City*—but then Honor would happily take Sinatra over Carrie Bradshaw any day. Clearly the Burnsteins felt the same way.

On a good day you could see every square inch of Manhattan from up here. But today the March clouds hung low and heavy over the city, and what would have been the view was smothered in mist.

Honor sighed. What a shame.

"I'd offer you a glass of champagne, ma'am." An elderly waiter in white tie appeared at her side. "But I'm afraid the service is about to start. Perhaps you'd like to slip in quietly at the back?"

He was a kind man, with that part-of-the-furniture air about him common to staff in grand old restaurants. Honor suspected he'd worked here his whole life.

"Oh, no! I thought I was early," she said. Glancing at her watch, she realized belatedly that it had stopped. Damned antiques. "I can't believe I'm late for a wedding! Maybe I should just wait it out. I'd hate to cause a scene."

"Wait it out? You mean, miss the ceremony?" The old man looked horrified. "Nonsense, my dear, we can't have that. Come with me. I'll slip you in there without a fuss."

Inside the anteroom-cum-makeshift-chapel, Lola was suffering from a serious attack of the giggles.

"Kick me!" she hissed at Sian, her mouth twitching at the corners. "Pinch me. Do something. I'm gonna lose it in a minute, I swear." But Sian wasn't faring much better herself. She was too busy biting back her own mirth to help Lola. The service was so unutterably corny, it could have been made by Orville Redenbacher. She wasn't sure what she'd expected from a high-society New York wedding. But it definitely wasn't this.

First, the bride had arrived in a dress so over-the-top wide it couldn't fit through the specially built rose archway. After much red-faced pushing and tugging, she was forced to reverse while the arch was dismantled, with the organist gallantly playing "Here Comes the Bride" throughout the entire five-minute charade.

"Whoever designed that dress should be shot," Lola whispered in Sian's ear, as poor Minty, flushed as red as the roses in her bouquet, finally made it to the altar. "She looks like a poodle that swallowed a hand grenade."

That comment marked the start of the girls' giggling fit. But it was the vows that really finished them off. Both bride and groom had written their own.

"I love you like the stars love the moon," intoned Stavros, the groom, who at least had the decency to look embarrassed as he said it. Minty, by contrast, gushed so enthusiastically through her own efforts she had the entire chapel wincing: "I am you. You are me. We are one," she bleated.

"She sounds like a frikkin' perfume commercial," giggled Sian.

"Smells like one too," said Lola. "The poor rabbi must be about to pass out. Death by Eternity asphyxiation. I bet that's a medical first."

Quite apart from the hilarity value, Lola was glad she'd decided to come, and even gladder that she was here with Sian and not Igor the Ego. Nick had bailed at the last minute, an added bonus—apparently the world of global e-commerce would grind to a shuddering halt if he took one weekend off—but her parents had braved the gossips and made it. Sitting two rows ahead of her and Sian, Lola could see that they were actually holding hands, which made her feel strangely but deeply happy. Having said that, her dad looked anxious. He'd lost weight, and hair. The last six months had clearly taken their toll on him, not that he didn't deserve it. But her mom seemed much, much better than she had the last time Lola was home. She was no longer skeletal, but attractively slender, and her cheeks had finally regained some of their former color and glow. It was good to see. "Hey." Sian leaned over and whispered in her ear. "Check it out. Two o'clock. Superman can't keep his eyes off you."

Lola glanced across the aisle to her right. A tall guy, she guessed in his early twenties, with a shock of jet-black hair and glasses that were indeed *fully* Christopher Reeve, flashed her a fifty-megawatt smile, which she returned.

"He's cute," said Sian, nudging her in the ribs.

"He is, isn't he?" said Lola, grinning from ear to ear. This wedding kept getting better and better. "Sold to the girl who hasn't got laid in a week."

"A *week*?" said Sian, more loudly than she'd intended to, so she had to try to turn it into a cough when people turned around and glared at her. "Jesus. I haven't had it since last summer. Oh my God. Speaking of last summer…"

"What?" said Lola.

"All right, now don't freak out." Sian laid a restraining hand on her arm in anticipation. "But Honor just walked in."

"No!" Lola went white, and her lips pursed in fury. "She wouldn't dare!"

For the second time, scores of people spun around to look as Lola raised her voice in indignation. One of them was Devon, who began by scowling at his daughter, but whose frown rapidly morphed into a look of purest panic as he caught sight of Honor, hovering at the back of the room like a ghost.

Lola looked around too and gave Honor a murderous stare. But she needn't have bothered. Honor could see nothing but Devon.

This couldn't be happening.

How could he be here? *How?* He was supposed to be in Asia. Regaining his composure, Devon looked away, leaving her staring at his broad, tuxedo-clad back. He seemed to have developed a sudden intense fascination with the ceremony, which had reached the stage of exchanging rings. Only his stiffened shoulders and the tightness of his arm muscles as he gripped Karis's hand gave away his inner emotional maelstrom.

Meanwhile, Honor's own stomach was flipping cartwheels. If only she could sneak away! But the double doors had been firmly closed behind her, and opening them now would only cause more of a scene. There was nothing she could do but wait it out.

After what felt like an eternity, Stavros was finally invited to kiss his bride, and the vast, lacy meringue that was the new Mrs. Minty Pavlos swayed back down the aisle and out into the lobby. Bolting out of her seat, Honor tried to dash after her. But to her dismay, she found herself being collared by Arabella, the matron of honor, before she could make her escape.

"Oh, Hon, I'm so glad you made it. But my gosh, haven't you gotten thin," she said, hugging Honor tightly.

"I know." Honor tried to smile. "It's been a stressful year."

"Well, sure," said Arabella understandingly. "I was so sorry to hear about your dad. And, you know…that other business."

"Thanks." Honor looked longingly toward the exit, but now it was clogged with departing guests. Thankfully, Devon and Karis seemed to have already made their own escape.

"You bitch!"

Honor jumped as Lola, a vision of red-headed righteous indignation, stormed over and physically shoved her back against the wall.

"What on earth…? How dare you!" said Arabella, stepping between them. "What do you think you're doing? This is my sister's wedding, not a bar brawl."

"I'm not talking to you," hissed Lola rudely, lunging at Honor again. Her russet curls, which moments ago had been pinned into an intricately formal updo, now broke free of their restraints and started tumbling down over her shoulders like lava. In a short green taffeta dress and no jewelry other than an exquisite pair of emerald-and-diamond drop earrings that swung wildly now as she flung herself forward, she looked scary but stunning. Somehow she also seemed much older than Honor remembered her. The innocent little girl of last summer, the kid that Honor had worried about Lucas Ruiz corrupting, had morphed into a fully fledged young woman.

"Lola, listen to me. I didn't know your parents were coming," she explained. "I was assured they were in Asia. Otherwise I would never have accepted the invitation."

"Yeah, right!" spat Lola. "You fucking liar."

Arabella Burnstein was a strong woman, but even she was having trouble containing the wildcat Lola as she scratched and clawed to get at Honor. She was very grateful when Sian arrived to help.

"Look, I'm sorry." A visibly shaken Honor was close to tears. "I'll go, OK? I'll just go."

"You'll do nothing of the sort," said Arabella firmly. "You're a guest here—*my* guest—and I'll be mortally offended if you don't stay for the reception. You haven't done anything wrong, Honor." She glared defiantly at Lola.

"Like hell she hasn't!" Lola yelled back. "She's done nothing but wrong. Bitch!"

Sian finally managed to pull her away, steering her out into the lobby and on toward the bar before things got really out of hand.

"Honestly, Bels," said Honor, once they'd gone. She was still shaking with shock. "I don't feel comfortable. I'd rather go."

"Listen," said Arabella kindly, "if you leave now, it'd be tantamount to admitting that you *are* the marriage wrecker he's made you out to be. Devon was the one who broke his vows, honey, not you. Let him leave if he wants to."

"But…I'll have to see him. At dinner. And Lola won't let it go. I don't want to ruin Minty's big day."

"Don't worry about Lola. I'll straighten her out. I'll even throw her out if I have to. And you won't have to see Devon at all if you don't want to. There's over a thousand people in that reception, and I happen to know for a fact that your table is about as far from his as it could be."

Honor looked doubtful.

"Come on," said Arabella, taking her hand. Apart from a couple of stragglers, they were the last ones left in the chapel. "You have to come out of hiding sometime. It may as well be now. I'm going to have Johnny fix you a big fuck-off martini, and then we're walking into that ballroom with our heads held high. OK?"

Honor nodded miserably.

"Good," said Arabella. She'd make a great White House Chief of Staff. Or head coach at a fat camp. "Follow me."

The service itself may have been more farce than fabulous, but the reception was quite another matter. Having safely deposited Lola at the bar in the care of two ushers (unsurprisingly, they were more than happy to devote the rest of their evening to keeping an eye on a showstopping redhead while she got busy with the hard liquor), Sian set off into the throng to star-spot.

Not even at Palmers had she seen so many famous, wealthy people gathered in one room. Socialites, actresses, politicians, fashion designers: everyone was there. Sofia Coppola was loitering glamorously in one corner while in the other the Clintons were chatting with old friends. And not ten feet away stood Lola's longtime role model, Donna Karan, outshining beauties half her age in a simple midnight-blue column dress that clung to her curves like a mud wrap.

By the time dinner was served, Sian's brain was groaning with names and snippets of overheard conversation. If only she had her notebook with her! Still, with any luck she'd be able to remember enough to put together a witty diary piece that she could pitch to the *Daily Mail* when she got back to London. The Brits pretended to be uninterested in the New York social scene. But beneath the veneer of disapproval, editors still fell over themselves for insider pieces like this. Especially if they had a decent celebrity angle.

Taking her seat, Sian looked around in vain for Lola at the bar, but she appeared to have vanished.

"Hello."

She looked up to find Superman had taken the seat next to her.

"Is your friend not staying for dinner?" He gestured forlornly to the empty place opposite Lola's name tag.

"She's supposed to be," Sian shrugged. "She's having a microcrisis tonight. Family trouble. I left her at the bar earlier, but she seems to have gone AWOL."

His face fell. It was so cute, Sian had to laugh. He looked about two.

"I wouldn't worry too much," she said kindly. "She'll turn up eventually. If it makes you feel any better, she already told me she thinks you're cute."

"She did?" The pout evaporated and his face lit up again like a firework.

Obviously, he wasn't much of a liar. Which would make a refreshing change from the two-faced dickheads Lola usually went out with. Sian liked him at once.

"Scout's honor," she assured him. "She likes you. But for now you're gonna have to settle for me, I'm afraid. Sian Doyle." She thrust out her hand.

"I'm so sorry," he stammered. "That was so rude not to introduce myself." His accent was educated but deep enough to save it from sounding effeminate. "I'm Marti. Gluckman. Really, I feel awful. I don't normally behave like a—"

"Goofy teenager?" offered Sian.

"Was I really that bad?" Marti blushed even deeper.

"Fraid so."

"It's just that your friend is so...mesmerizing," he said dreamily.

"So I'm regularly told," said Sian.

"I couldn't find her after the service, but a guy told me her name. So I ran around every table in here trying to find where she was sitting. Which is more exercise than I've gotten in years, by the way. Have you seen how many people there are? Goddamn freeloaders."

Sian laughed.

"Anyway, I finally found her, and I had to beg this weird Armenian guy to switch places with me—I don't know, his English wasn't the best. I think he thought I wanted to sleep with him later or something, but anyway, he moved. But now," he sighed heavily, finally drawing a breath, "she's not here. Although, obviously," he added hastily, "it's terrific to have met you. Sian Doyle."

Despite this less than auspicious start to the conversation, the two of them were soon chatting away like old friends. Only when Marti left for the bathroom did Sian realize she'd been completely ignoring the girl sitting on her other side.

"Hi," she said, turning around and realizing for the first time that the girl was actually supermodel stunning. Her thick black hair glugged like molasses down her bare back, the only flesh visible in the floor-length fire-hydrant-red dress she was wearing, and her skin was that gorgeous, smooth milk-chocolate color unique to South American women. Combined with her voluptuous figure, wide-set, nut-brown eyes, and perfect, naturally full lips, she looked every bit the storybook Inca princess.

Sian was all set to start hating her, but infuriatingly, she turned out to be perfectly charming.

"I would have introduced myself earlier," she said, smiling shyly, "but you and your boyfriend seemed a bit, you know... engrossed. I didn't want to interrupt."

"Oh," Sian laughed, "he's not my boyfriend. We just met, actually. He wants to put the moves on my friend, but she's already hooked up with a Mr. Jack Daniel, so the poor guy got stuck with me."

"Really?" said the girl. "Well he looked like he was having a great time to me. My name's Bianca, by the way."

"And I'm Sian," said Sian. "So. Are you a friend of the bride or the groom?"

"Neither," said Bianca, lighting up a Marlboro red and inhaling deeply, then blowing the smoke out through her rounded lips in a perfect O. Whoever said smoking was a dirty, unsexy habit had obviously never seen Bianca do it. "My boyfriend's a friend of Stavros's. An acquaintance, really. We were supposed to come together, but he had some work crisis as usual, so here I am, alone. Again. I know nobody."

"Me either," said Sian, recrossing her legs and moving her chair closer to her new friend. "Lola, the girl I mentioned to you—her family knows the Burnsteins. I'm just tagging along for the ride."

"Well in that case, we should stick together." Bianca beamed. For such a beautiful girl, she really was disarmingly nice.

Marti's trip to the bathroom seemed to have taken a turn for the permanent. For the rest of dinner the two girls chatted away happily, making fun of the more outrageous fashion victims swanning around the room like overdressed matchsticks. After that, they told each other their own potted histories. Bianca, surprise surprise, was a model and split her time between New York and London. Sian's life felt so dull by comparison, she skipped most of it and instead told her new friend about her friendship with Lola and the background to the earlier drama in the chapel with Honor Palmer.

"So," she finished finally, wolfing down the last crumb of her meltingly delicious pecan dessert, "when Lola saw Honor here today, you can imagine. She totally flipped."

"I'm not surprised," said Bianca with feeling. "What nerve, turning up like that! I've never met the girl, but I've heard a lot about her—most of it bad. But she is very beautiful," she added, looking across the room to the top table, where Honor was throwing her head back and laughing at some joke of the bride's.

She's not half as beautiful as you, thought Sian.

In her simple pantsuit, Honor was underdressed for the occasion, but somehow the plainness of her outfit only served to emphasize her unique face with its beautiful, hawk-like features.

"I can see why your friend's father fell for her," said Bianca. Honor seemed to have taken Arabella's advice to heart and decided to enjoy herself despite Lola's histrionics. Unlike Devon, who, Sian noticed, was sitting next to Karis at the opposite end of the dance floor, looking about as cheerful as a prisoner awaiting the firing squad.

"My boyfriend actually knows her a little bit," said Bianca.

"Honor?" Sian, still looking at Lola's parents, was only half tuned in.

"Yeah. He ran into her in the Hamptons last summer. A few times, I think."

"Really?" said Sian. "How funny. I was working out there myself last summer. At Palmers. Small world, huh?"

Bianca nodded. "My boyfriend stayed at the other hotel, not Palmers. You know, the new one."

"The Herrick," said Sian.

"That's it. His best friend used to run it." Bianca took a long sip of champagne. "He doesn't anymore, but that's a whole other story."

Sian felt her blood run cold. "You mean Lucas? Lucas Ruiz is your boyfriend's best friend?"

"Uh-huh," said Bianca. "A lot of people didn't want to know Lucas after he got fired. But Ben's never had a bad word to say about him. He's really loyal like that."

"Oh yeah," said Sian bitterly, as a creeping nausea rose up from her belly. "Ben Slater's loyal all right. As long as you're a guy."

Bianca's eyes widened. "You know Ben?"

Sian kicked herself. Why couldn't she have kept her mouth shut?

"Er, yes," she admitted. "I used to know him. We dated actually."

"You *did*?" Bianca looked suitably surprised. "Ben never mentioned he was seeing someone out there."

"Well, it wasn't serious," said Sian hastily. "Honestly. It was, like, five minutes. It was nothing."

She had no desire to open up a conversation about Ben. Bianca was lovely. But it still hurt to think that she'd been traded in for someone so incomparably stunning—and that Ben hadn't even deemed their relationship important enough to mention to his new girlfriend. All at once she felt her confidence oozing away, like air from a slow punctured balloon.

Gluing on a fake smile for Bianca's benefit, she gave herself a stern talking to. So Ben had moved on. Well of course he had. Big deal. That was hardly news. It had been six months, after all, and they'd dated for only a couple of weeks. Besides, what did she care what he did or who he was with? He'd accused her of being a gold digger, let's not forget, and taken the word of a try-hard like Lucas Ruiz over hers. According to Bianca, he and Lucas were still thick as thieves. Who needed him?

"Look, let's not talk about Ben, OK?" she said. "I'd much rather hear more about modeling. Are the agents really as sleazy as people say they are?"

Bianca smiled. She was evidently as keen to drop the subject as Sian was.

"Honey," she said conspiratorially, "you have no idea."

Meanwhile, in a janitor's closet hidden away next to the ladies' room, Lola Carter was straddling Marti, arching her back and squeezing her muscles tightly around his dick as she came.

"Shhhhh," he laughed, cupping one hand over her mouth to stifle her full-volume moans. "Someone'll hear us."

Marti had been feeling marginally guilty about taking advantage of a girl he'd only just met, and who was clearly very, very drunk. But after Lola had torn his clothes off and leaped on him like a starving animal, his concerns had alleviated considerably. Gazing rapturously at her flushed, happy, postorgasmic face, he decided she was clearly a young lady who knew exactly what she wanted.

Pushing aside a pile of stacked chairs, sending them flying to the ground with an almighty clatter, she sprawled out on her back and spread her legs wider, grabbing hold of his butt and pulling him hungrily inside her.

"Your turn now," she grinned.

With her red hair spreading around her like a halo and her green dress pulled down to the waist to reveal the two large orbs of her breasts, as plump and ripe as grapefruits, she was a vision of desirability. Marti was justly proud of himself for having held on this long, but he didn't have an ounce more restraint in him. Closing his eyes, he gave himself up to the slippery, needy warmth of her body and came, driving himself so hard into her that she slipped along the linoleum floor and clunked her skull against the back wall of the closet.

"Ow," she giggled, rubbing her head as she finally, reluctantly squirmed out from underneath him.

"Sorry," said Marti. Leaning down, he tenderly kissed the bump on her forehead.

Lola smiled. Watching him putting his pants back on, pulling up his zipper and trying to straighten out his disheveled hair, she felt bizarrely affectionate toward him. She didn't make a habit of one-night stands, never mind dragging guys she bumped into outside the ladies' room into dark corners and ravishing them. But the combination of the Jack Daniel's, being blindsided by Honor, and Marti's deadly attractiveness seemed to have brought on a bout of temporary insanity. "You probably think I'm a real slut now, right?" she said, straightening her own dress and scrabbling around in the semidarkness for her shoes.

"What do you mean 'think'?" said Marti. "I know you are. I have firsthand evidence."

Lola gasped. He wasn't serious, was he? But she relaxed as she felt his arm snake around her waist. The next thing she knew he was kissing her passionately on the mouth.

"It's a compliment," he whispered, coming up for air. "I'm a big fan of sluts. The biggest. You have no idea."

Lola laughed, a deep, full-bodied cackle. Life was so freaky. Only an hour ago she'd been sobbing into her drink, swearing off men forevermore. And now here she was, half-naked in a broom closet with a total stranger, so happy she felt like she was walking on air.

Stavros's ushers had finally abandoned her at the bar at eleven. Even pretty girls got boring when they wouldn't quit crying. Meanwhile, her parents seemed to have forgotten she was even here—neither of them had come over to say hello, Sian was off mingling and having a good time, and fucking Honor Palmer was so deeply embedded with the bride's family, Lola couldn't have gotten near her, even if she'd been sober enough to try it. Which she wasn't. If she hadn't been so desperate for a pee, she'd probably be slumped over the bar where the ushers had left her. But Cupid, fate, and a weak bladder had conspired to bring her and Marti together. And now he'd rescued her from her misery, just like the real Superman.

"Listen," he said, opening the closet door a crack to check that the coast was clear. They could hear the Hora, the traditional Jewish wedding dance, in full swing next door. "I don't know about you, but I'm kind of weddinged out. I don't suppose you want to sneak back to my place?"

"Definitely not," said Lola teasingly. "My mom told me never to go with strangers. You could be an ax murderer, for all I know."

"Me? No way," said Marti, squeezing her hand. "I'm a terrible coward. Faint at the first sight of blood. I'm more of the poisoning, smother-you-with-a-pillow type."

Lola giggled.

"So're you coming or not?"

"Yes, please," she said, kissing him again.

He wasn't as good-looking as Lucas, or even Igor. But he was fifty times funnier, and nicer. Suddenly she longed to be waking up with him tomorrow, eating bagels in bed like an old married couple. Sian would be OK to find her own way back to the hotel.

Marti took her hand and was just about to slip out into the lobby when raised voices made them both slink back. Lola felt her heart jump into her mouth and squeezed his hand even tighter. She recognized the voices. It was her father and Honor Palmer.

"Because I miss you," Devon was saying. "That's why. Hell, Honor, can't we even talk to each other anymore?"

"No." Honor sounded furious. "We can't. You have some fucking nerve, Devon Carter. Just leave me the fuck alone, OK?"

Grabbing her by the hand, Devon dragged her down the side corridor directly toward the closet where Lola was hiding.

"Get back!" Lola hissed at Marti. He did as he was told, pulling the door almost completely closed, but leaving a crack so Lola could still see what was happening.

Honor, jacketless now, looked so tiny in her aqua shirt and pants she could almost have been a child. She'd always been skinny, but Lola could see now that she'd lost even more weight. Her collarbones visibly jutted out, like a human rack of lamb.

"I know you're angry." Devon's voice was smooth and conciliatory. "You have every right to be."

"Don't tell me about my rights," Honor snapped, freeing herself from his grip and backing away. "Or my feelings. You threw me to the fucking wolves!"

"That's not fair," said Devon. "I couldn't control what the press were writing. You think it didn't hurt me too, seeing them lay into you like that?"

"I'm sure you were devastated," said Honor, witheringly.

"I was, sweetheart. Truly I was."

Lola winced at the endearment. *Sweetheart?* But painful as it was to listen to, wild horses couldn't have torn her away from that door.

"So devastated you forgot my number?" Clearly Honor was in no mood to let him off the hook. "Not one call from you, Devon, in all this time. Not one shred of concern. You let those bastards paint me as the marriage wrecker, while you sailed off into the sunset with Karis on your little boat of so-called regret. You make me sick."

"I hardly sailed off into the sunset." Devon laughed bitterly. "Life at home has been hell, complete hell. Karis has me under surveillance night and day. I'm trapped. But I don't love her, Honor. I love you." Lola gripped Marti's hand so tightly her nails were in danger of drawing blood. He could feel her breathing stop dead.

"After the overdose, I couldn't risk pushing her any further. For me to defend you in the press, contact you, even mention your name—don't you see? It might have pushed her over the edge. She had me by the balls, sweetheart."

"What balls?" said Honor.

"Damn right," Lola whispered indignantly from the closet. Up until now it had been easy to believe what she read in the papers and blame Honor for everything. But suddenly, for the first time, she wondered if maybe her father wasn't the true villain of the piece. A few hours ago, he'd been holding her mom's hand in the chapel, playing the contrite husband. But now here he was, telling his mistress it was her he really loved. He was so two-faced it made Lola's blood curdle.

"Darling, listen to me." Stepping forward, Devon laid a hand on Honor's shoulder. "I think we're over the worst. Tonight, when Karis realized you were here, she was OK about it."

Honor's eyebrows shot up. "*What?*"

"I mean, she wasn't thrilled, obviously," Devon conceded. "But, you know, she didn't insist we go home. She didn't try and confront you."

"She didn't have to," Honor shivered. "Lola did that for her. Not that I blame her, poor kid. After everything we've put her through…"

"You're not listening." Devon grabbed her hands.

Despite herself, Honor let him. She hated the fact that the warmth of his palms wrapped around her own still felt so comforting.

"A few months ago Karis would have been in pieces," he said. "But today, she didn't even cry. I think this whole mental instability of hers—this depression or whatever it is—I think it's gonna pass. And when it does…"

"When it does, what?" said Honor.

Bending down, Devon kissed her softly on the neck. "Well," he whispered, "we can carry on where we left off."

For a second, Honor stood there, stock-still, while he nuzzled into her. Then, like someone snapping out of hypnosis, her head whiplashed up and she pushed him away.

"Karis isn't mentally unstable," she said, ignoring his frantic hand signals and making no effort to keep her voice down. "I am. Or at least I was. For ever trusting you in the first place. *My marriage is a sham. We haven't slept together in years.* Jesus. How could I have fallen for that old cliché?"

She was a brilliant mimic and had his hectoring tone down to a T. It gave Lola goose pimples to hear her. Was that really what her dad had told her to get her into bed? Suddenly, Lola could believe it. Had all his protestations of love and regret to her mother been a crock of shit too?

"It might be a cliché," said Devon, doing his best to sound wounded. "But it happens to be true. Karis and I haven't shared a bed in years."

"Bullshit!" said Honor and Lola simultaneously. Luckily, Honor's roar of rage drowned out Lola's furiously hissed whisper.

"Lola told Lucas she had to put earplugs in at home to block out the sound of you guys making love through her bedroom wall," said Honor. "Lucas told me all about it."

"And you believe Lucas Ruiz over me?" said Devon, indignantly.

"I didn't at the time," said Honor. "I loved you, God help me. But now? Now I'd believe Osama bin Laden over you, Devon."

"But Lucas was the one who exposed us! If it weren't for that little shit, we'd still be together."

"Well, in that case, he did me a favor," said Honor. "I'll have to write and thank him."

And turning on her heel, she stormed off.

Only once Devon had gone too and he was sure they were alone again did Marti speak.

"You OK?" he asked Lola, pushing open the closet door and stepping out into the light. But one look at her tear-streaked face told him the answer.

"Not really." She shook her head miserably. "Let's just get out of here."

——————— ———————

Honor was already downstairs, scanning the deserted streets in vain for a cab. Above her, the night sky, its natural blackness stained by the dim orange glow of the city's light pollution, rumbled ominously. At first the rain fell in slow, heavy drips that burst like water balloons on the sidewalk. But it wasn't long before the ponderous early splashes had turned into a full-scale torrent that left her soaked to the bone.

The rain was so cold it made her gasp. But at the same time, it was exactly the physical shock she needed. Soon she was laughing out loud as she skipped about in the puddles. Maybe she really was losing it. She'd expected to feel pain after her conversation with Devon. Or shock, or disillusionment, or regret. Something bad, anyway.

But in fact, the overwhelming sensation was relief. It was as if some terrible, heavy weight had been lifted from her shoulders. But when it was set down in front of her, she could see that it wasn't a boulder at all. It had been nothing but a tiny, insignificant pebble all along.

Falling in love was incredible. But falling *out* of love, she now realized, could be even better.

At last the scales had fallen from her eyes completely. She had her self back. And for the first time in years—probably since before her mother died—she felt truly, deeply content.

CHAPTER NINETEEN

$\mathcal{A}$ YEAR TO THE DAY AFTER THE BURNSTEIN WEDDING, Lucas stood in the newly finished lobby of his new hotel, Luxe Ibiza, feeling like Lazarus risen from the ashes. All the new-building smells still lingered: varnish mingled with sawdust and drying paint, overlaid by the scent of freshly laid turf, which wafted in through the open French windows. Lucas inhaled joyously.

In a few weeks, all these smells would be gone, replaced by the ubiquitous aroma of calming lavender. Lucas had already received the first shipment of scented Dyptique candles from Paris—expensive but worth it—and the midnight-blue gas lamps that would burn essential oils of lavender and cedarwood in each suite should arrive in the morning. A local artisan glassblower had made the lamps for next to nothing, with his brother throwing in the hand-pressed oils at an even more outrageously knocked-down price. They should have asked for more. Lucas would happily have paid them. Local, natural products were at the core of the Luxe ethos, and he was quite prepared to pay a premium to get the ambience of his new hotel pitch-perfect.

Connor Armstrong, his Irish partner and financial backer, was a pompous, preening prick of a man and a pain in Lucas's ass on many levels. But at least he knew better than to try to tinker with Lucas's artistic vision. The twelve bedroom suites and two guest studios were all furnished with low, unfussy teak beds, decked out in old-fashioned starched white linen. Lucas was allergic to those stupid little decorative cushions so beloved of other luxury hotels, and to beds piled high with enough pillows to give people neck ache. At Luxe, nothing was extraneous. Flower arrangements were simple and fresh, with lots of greenery. Artwork was minimal and calming, mostly local landscapes, mixed up with the odd interesting antique map or illustrated page from an old book. Every room had an open fire, the pine logs carefully chosen for their scent and crackle, and was well stocked with books to suit every taste and inclination. There were no televisions, no ghastly piped Muzak, nothing to remind his guests that only a few miles below them, at the bottom of a hill scattered with olive trees, was the neon, drug-fueled buzz of Europe's most infamous party island.

Stepping through the open windows into a central courtyard garden overhung with faded pink roses, Lucas offered up a little prayer of thanks. Sometimes he still found it hard to believe that he'd actually made it this far, that his fantasy had at last taken solid, physical shape. Two weeks from now they'd be open for business.

He could still remember the phone call he'd made to Ben last June, the day that Connor had agreed to back him.

"I've done it!" he panted breathlessly, leaning against the plastic wall of a phone booth in Santa Eulalia.

"You have? That's great!" said Ben, who had no idea what he was talking about but didn't want to burst his bubble by asking "what?" He'd only heard from Lucas twice since he'd gone back to Ibiza. The first time he'd been drunk out of his mind, rambling incoherently about Anton and Petra and the great injustices of the world. The second time he was sober as a judge, but also deeply depressed. He'd insisted that he was going to turn his life around and that he wouldn't call Ben again until he had. That was six weeks ago, and he'd been as good as his word, not even leaving a number or address where a worried Ben could get in touch with him.

"I've got a backer for Luxe," said Lucas excitedly.

It took Ben a moment to remember what Luxe was: the fantasy hotel that Lucas had been banging on about ever since they first met in Murren, all those years ago.

"Wow," said Ben. "Who?"

"A guy called Connor Armstrong," said Lucas. "You remember him, right? He used to drink at the Cadogan sometimes. Irish. Bit of a twat."

More than a bit, thought Ben, but all he said was, "Sure, I remember."

Connor was exactly the sort of smug, self-important prick that gave bankers a bad name; a man who considered it a great joke to harass his secretaries or tell the minimum-wage Pakistani janitor in his office how much he'd spent on dinner the night before. He wore too much aftershave, spoke too loudly on his cell phone, and affected a nauseating mid-Atlantic accent that made him sound like a local radio DJ trying to be cool.

"I didn't know he was in the hotel business."

"He isn't," said Lucas. "Well, he is now, but he wasn't. He's in property. He made some canny deals in Marbella: villas, condos, tourist apartments, that sort of thing. He's done well."

"I don't doubt it," said Ben truthfully. The assholes always did.

"Anyway, now he wants something in Ibiza. I told him about my ideas for Luxe, and he was sold."

"That's terrific," said Ben. "How'd you convince him?"

Lucas made a grunt that seemed to imply he didn't understand the question. "I didn't have to convince him," he said. "He knows any hotel of mine will be the coolest thing to happen on this island since manumission. Why wouldn't he want in?"

Ben smiled but said nothing. It was a relief to hear some of the old Ruiz arrogance making a comeback. Without it, Lucas just wasn't Lucas.

As it turned out, it wasn't just idle boasting. From the beginning, there was a buzz of excitement on the island about the Luxe project that gave Lucas an incredible frisson and fueled his already rampant ambition. The name alone seemed to have a sort of magic to it, generating hype and anticipation even before the first brick had been laid. Leveraging off that magic for all he was worth, Lucas worked inhuman hours to get the thing off the ground, whirling like a dervish from supplier to supplier and breathing down the necks of his builders like a jealous lover.

Knowing that Petra Kamalski had replaced him at the Herrick only added to his sense of inner urgency. It wasn't enough to build a great hotel. Luxe had to be the greatest, the boutique David that would one day bring down the Goliath Tischen brand, and with it both Petra and her scheming, two-faced bastard of a boss. As far as Lucas was concerned, Ibiza was just the beginning. Once he'd achieved success here, he could tweak the concept, ironing out any early glitches or issues, then roll his Luxes out across Europe and, eventually, America and Asia too.

Unfortunately, Connor turned out to be rather less of a big thinker. From the beginning he'd moaned on like an old woman about risk. And that was just on the Ibiza project.

"It's too remote," he whined, the first time Lucas drove him up to the site he'd found, high up in the hills close to where he was born. He'd chosen it because land was still relatively cheap up here, and the views were nothing short of spectacular. "No one's gonna want to hike all the way up here," said Connor gloomily. "They'll need a chopper just to get to the clubs at night."

"Fine," said Lucas stubbornly. "We'll build a helipad."

A screaming match ensued, but Lucas eventually got his way. His raw energy and natural flair, combined with Connor's cash and contacts, acted like rocket fuel, propelling the building work forward at a frightening speed despite Connor's cup-half-empty attitude and almost ceaseless naysaying. Lucas acted as architect, project manager, and PR chief rolled into one. Having had every detail of the plans in his head since he was a teenager, he was damned if he was going to pay some outsider to come and tinker with them, wasting money and time on sketches and pie charts.

He'd also learned a number of lessons from building the Herrick. All the construction workers on the Luxe site, down to the lowliest plumber's assistant, had their pay tied firmly to deadlines. The result was that now, a mere ten months after construction began, the hotel was finished. And a fucking work of art she was too.

"Fuck you, Anton Tisch!" Yelling at the top of his lungs, Lucas listened as his voice ricocheted off the walls and steep hillside in a volley of echoes. With the contractors finished, paid, and sent home, he had the place entirely to himself—king, at long last, of his castle.

"Fuck you, Petra!" he roared, sending a second ripple of sound off in pursuit of the first. "I'm back! Lucas Ruiz is fucking back!"

Annoyingly, he was interrupted midshout by a buzz from his inside jacket pocket.

"Yes?" he barked grumpily into his battered old Motorola. But seconds later the annoyance was gone and his face suffused by a broad grin.

"That's wonderful! How long are you here?" he asked, picking up a stray pebble and hurling it high into the air, then watching it fall out of sight into the depths of the valley below.

"Tonight then. At seven." He laughed, shaking his head as he hung up the phone.

Well that was one for the books. It looked as though his already glorious day was about to get even better.

Bounding up the gravel path a few hours later, clutching a chilled bottle of Moët and a fistful of wild daisies he'd picked on the way, Lucas rapped loudly on the front door with his fist.

God it felt strange to be here! The last time he'd been in this garden—three years ago now, although it felt like thirty—he'd been running the other way, taking off down the hill like a bat out of hell before old man Leon could get his hands on him. He remembered his feelings so clearly: the panic and adrenaline mingled with the joyous rush of the great sex he'd just had and an overwhelming urge to burst into laughter. Nothing had seemed very serious to him then. Now, he thought with a pang, everything did.

But his gloomy thoughts were banished the next moment as the door swung open and he found himself face-to-face with a gloriously naked Carla.

"*Querido*," she breathed huskily. "Flowers, for me? You shouldn't have."

Gazing in unashamed admiration at her body, he wondered if she'd had any work done since he last saw her. If she had, then her surgeon deserved a medal of honor. She must be, what, forty-seven now? But her skin showed no signs of sagging, and her breasts, as brown and full as coconuts, the tiny pale-pink nipples standing to attention to greet him, were as firm and high as ever. Her dark hair had been cut shorter and dyed a striking, deep red, but it suited her. And her bush, he noticed with delight and amazement, had been trimmed and shaped by some extortionate pubic topiarist into the shape of a heart and dyed to match the hair on her head. In nothing but a pair of red Louboutin stilettos and a diamond choker, she looked like every schoolboy's fantasy, with only a few faint fans of lines around her eyes and lips to indicate middle age.

Dumping the bottle and flowers unceremoniously on the floor, Lucas gathered her up in his arms without a word and carried her straight up the stairs.

"That way," she giggled, pointing to a door at the end of the corridor as he burst into bathrooms and offices, looking for a bed. Following her directions, he carried her to what he assumed must be the marital bedroom and laid her gently down on the black satin counterpane.

"Very Ozzy Osbourne," he said, clocking the deep-red velvet curtains and vast, black onyx sculpture of a panther at the foot of the bed. "I wouldn't have thought old Pepe had it in him."

"That's Rex," said Carla, nodding at the panther as she fumbled with the buttons on Lucas's fly. "He's supposed to protect me from intruders when Pepe's away. Symbolically, obviously."

"Well, he's doing a pretty lousy job," said Lucas, freeing his rock-hard erection at last and boring into her like a freight train.

Carla gasped at the force of him. He hadn't even taken his shoes off, so desperate was he to get inside her. Though it was over quickly, she was gratified that he hadn't lost any of his skill or generosity as a lover, going down on her afterward for a languorous twenty minutes until she had come twice herself. Pepe went down on her occasionally, usually on Valentine's Day or their anniversary, but he always made her feel as though he were bestowing some hugely irksome favor. With Lucas, she felt like an ice cream that he was taking his sweet time to enjoy. It was pure heaven.

Afterward they showered together, dressed, and went downstairs to the kitchen, where Carla put together a simple supper of cold meats, salad, and a perfect Spanish omelet, washed down with plenty of chilled Chablis. As it was still so warm they ate out on the terrace, drinking in each other's company, the heady scent of bougainvillea, and the beauty of the view, which looked even more lovely in the milky moonlight than it did by day.

"You have to come up and see her before you leave." Lucas, who'd talked about nothing but Luxe since they'd rolled out of bed, was still waxing lyrical. "You were the one who made her possible, after all. If it hadn't been for you, for your inspiration and help and support—"

"You'd have made it anyway," said Carla, pouring herself a third glass of wine. "No, don't shake your head at me, Lucas. You were the most ambitious man I'd ever met back then. I suppose you still are now," she added dreamily.

Lucas's face darkened. "My ambitions have changed," he said grimly. "It's not only about personal success anymore."

"Oh?" Carla looked at him questioningly. His features had set hard, and the veins on the back of his hand, she noticed, stood up like swollen tree roots as he clenched the stem of his wine-glass. "What is it about, then?"

A muscle in Lucas's temple twitched involuntarily. "Revenge," he said quietly. "It's about revenge."

He told her the whole story, of how Anton had set him up and blackened his name throughout the industry.

"It wasn't enough to get rid of me at the Herrick," he said bitterly, stabbing at the remnants of the omelet on his plate with a fork. "He wanted me bankrupt, ruined. He tried to take away everything I've ever worked for."

"Why would he do that?" asked Carla rationally.

"How the fuck do I know?" said Lucas, getting increasingly irate. "Because he's a fucking psychopath. He even tracked down Petra fucking Kamalski and hired her as my replacement."

"The girl from EHL?" Carla remembered Lucas's passionate rages about Petra from years ago. Privately, she'd always thought his hatred of Petra was at least partly fueled by sexism. Much as she adored him, Lucas had always been pretty old-fashioned when it came to women in the workplace, particularly women who threatened to outperform him. But she wisely kept her thoughts to herself.

"Yeah, can you believe it?" said Lucas furiously. "He pulled her out of the Ritz in Moscow, *hugely* overpromoted her."

"Look who's talking," teased Carla gently.

"That was different," snapped Lucas. Clearly, he wasn't in the mood for banter. "Look, I'm sorry," he said. "I don't mean to take it out on you. But you don't understand. Anton's evil, and so is that bitch."

Getting to his feet, he wandered over to the edge of the terrace. Below him, the olive groves glowed an eerie white gray in the moonlight, and beyond them the calm waters of the Mediterranean stretched out like a giant sheet of silver foil. Coming up behind him, Carla slipped her arms around his waist and pressed her lithe, soft body against his. She could feel the tension coiled inside him like a mattress spring about to snap.

"Be careful," she whispered softly. "Tisch is a very powerful man, and not just in the hotel world. From what I've read he has a lot of contacts in Russia still, and those guys don't mess around. You might end up with polonium slipped into your tea."

Turning around, Lucas kissed her tenderly on the forehead.

"Don't worry," he smiled. "I don't drink tea."

But Carla did worry. It was wonderful to see him bouncing back after all he'd been through, and she didn't doubt he would make a roaring success of his new hotel. But he was still so headstrong and stubborn, and now he was determined to make an enemy of one of the most powerful men in the world. She only hoped he'd come to his senses before Tisch decided to finish the job he'd started and wipe Lucas off the map once and for all.

CHAPTER TWENTY

$\mathcal{E}$ SSEX IN THE AUTUMN COULD REALLY BE QUITE BEAUTIFUL, thought Ben, putting his foot down and pushing his trusty Mini Cooper to a chassis-rattling sixty miles per hour. As soon as you turned off the M it was all wooded lanes and half-timbered thatched cottages, their chimneys smoking a welcome amid the chill wind and the swirling, golden tumble of autumn leaves. Everyone associated the county with dumb blondes and blank, faceless suburban towns. Both of which existed, of course—his own parents lived in probably the blankest, most faceless of them all. But there was a lot more to Essex than bimbos and charmless apartment blocks.

Maybe one day he'd move down here with a young family of his own. Buy somewhere rural. Have…pigs. Or something.

Or maybe not.

A lot had changed in Ben's life in a few short years. His fund, Stellar, had had its third rough quarter in a row, which was bizarre, given their investment performance had held steady in a very dicey market. But for some mysterious reason, his investors kept redeeming their shares and jumping ship to Excelsior, Anton Tisch's fund. Three years ago, Ben had been almost neck and neck with Anton at around the five billion mark, but now Excelsior was the clear market leader, hoovering up the Russian money flooding into London at a rate that none of its rival funds could compete with. It was depressing.

Today, though, business woes were the last thing on Ben's mind. He was driving home for the weekend, which ought to have been relaxing, if it weren't for the fact that he knew he'd get a grilling about his love life. The moment he walked through the door, his mum and sisters were bound to strike up their familiar refrain—the one that sounded like a train gaining momentum and was about as difficult to stop: Marry Bianca, Marry Bianca, Marry Bianca.

Grinding the gear stick belatedly up into fifth—no wonder his poor car sounded so wheezy—he wondered again how he might try to change the subject. Last time his dad had taken pity on him and dragged him down the pub to watch football, but Ben doubted he'd be so lucky again today. Apparently Dad got a right ear-bashing about it afterward. Ben could just picture his poor father, trying in vain to defend himself from three screaming Slater women, all intent on frog-marching their precious boy to the altar.

The problem was, he really didn't have an answer for their biggest question: Why didn't he propose? Bianca was wonderful, a real gem. Beautiful, smart, devoted, funny—he couldn't think of a single thing about her that he'd change. She'd moved into his Kensington apartment a year ago after a year and a half of dating, and to this day had yet to get on his nerves, which was quite a feat. Even more amazingly, she seemed to be suffering from some sort of rare glaucoma that blinded her to his own all-too-obvious faults: the midnight chip eating, the hopeless fashion sense, the complete inability to put the toilet seat down after having a pee. All this on top of the fact that he was no Brad Pitt, whereas Bianca could give Angelina a run for her money any day of the week.

She loved him. And in his own way, Ben loved her back. But the idea of marriage still made his blood run cold, which was something he couldn't explain to himself, never mind his matrimony-crazed mother.

Passing Thorney Bay, he felt a wave of nostalgia wash over him. He used to come here sometimes as a kid, looking at the lights from the trailer park across the water and dreaming of making it big amid the even brighter lights of London.

By all objective standards, Canvey Island was a dump: rampant unemployment, blocks of apartment buildings, and cheap housing that must have looked awful even before the decades of neglect, sea wind, and graffiti had worn them down. Nothing to do but hang out at the waterfront drinking miniature bottles of Baileys and trying to get off with girls. But Ben had happy memories of the place. It would always be special to him.

"Blimey. At last. What time d'you call this?" Nikki, the younger of his two sisters, came running out as he pulled the Mini into the driveway of his parents' house. "Mum's going nuts. She 'ad dinner ready quarter of an hour ago."

With her short-cropped peroxided hair and uncompromisingly tight stonewashed jeans, Nikki had never fully grown out of her Roxette phase. But she was very pretty in an eighties-throwback, Essex sort of a way. And she took good care of her body, which was more than Ben could say for himself right now. "You've put on weight," she said cheerfully as he climbed out of the car. "Lard ass."

"Fuck off," he responded, kissing her and linking arms as they walked up to the house.

"Where's Bianca?"

Ben sighed wearily. "I told you. She's in New York, on a job. She does work, you know."

Like all successful models, Bianca traveled a lot. Though he didn't like to admit it, Ben suspected that her long absences might be part of the reason that they got along so well when they were together. Any relationship comprised of a series of joyous reunions strung together was going to seem fresher and more passionate than one based on the predictability of daily routine. More passionate than marriage, in other words.

"What if she meets another bloke out there?" Nikki raised an eyebrow in warning. "Someone who ain't afraid to make an honest woman out of her?"

They hadn't even gotten indoors yet, and already she was off on one.

"She meets loads of blokes, all the time," said Ben, "and most of them look like David bloody Beckham. What can I say?" he shrugged. "I guess she must have a thing for lard-assed commitmentphobes. Hello, Mum."

He bent down to kiss his mother, who looked adorably furious in her apron with a wooden spoon in hand. Dear old Mum, she did love her props. They all knew that dinner, whatever it was, would have come straight out of a Stouffer's box and that the only kitchen implement she'd actually have used was a fork for piercing the film lid several times. But Eileen Slater was not a woman to let insignificant details like that spoil her sense of occasion.

"You're late, Benny. No Bianca?" She made a great theatrical show of hunting for his missing girlfriend, as if he might have hidden her in a pocket. But her son was so big, and she was so small, it was like watching a penguin trying to see around an iceberg.

Ben rolled his eyes to heaven.

This was going to be a long afternoon.

Lunch passed predictably enough. Ben fielded the questions and accusations as best he could, in between mouthfuls of Birds Eye Sunday Special: incinerated strips of roast beef smothered with gravy so thick it almost certainly qualified as a solid, which he soaked up with floury roast potatoes and three servings of Yorkshire pudding, earning himself a reproachful "steady on, Hagrid," from Nikki.

By the time the Iceland trifle arrived in all its quivering, gelatinous, artificially colored glory, conversation had mercifully turned to other matters.

"'Ere, look at this." Ben's dad shuffled over to the sofa to retrieve the travel section from one of the Sunday papers. "That's your mate, isn't it? El Spic-o."

Like everyone of his generation from Canvey Island, Rog Slater peppered his speech with racist, sexist, and generally politically incorrect references. But you wouldn't find a kinder man in England, and Ben had long ago ceased to be offended.

"His name's Lucas, Dad," he said, patiently. "And yeah, that's his new hotel. Looks brilliant, doesn't it?"

It was only a little over a year since Luxe Ibiza had opened her doors to rave reviews in travel periodicals all across Europe. Never one to let the grass grow under his feet, Lucas had already capitalized on his early success and launched the second hotel in his franchise, a chichi urban boutique in Paris.

The article was a double-page spread of the sumptuous new Luxe, a tiny townhouse off the Boulevard St. Germain. So discreet it was practically invisible from the outside, inside it was an oasis of luxurious tranquility, with the sort of minimalist, less-is-more glamour that only Lucas could pull off. In contrast to the white walls of his Ibiza flagship, he'd opted for a warmer decor of claret-red velvets and deep-green baize, though it was still lit exclusively by candlelight. To Ben's untrained eye it looked part spa, part bordello, and part eighteenth-century salon. The pictures were out of this world.

"Let me see." Karen, his other sister, snatched the paper off him and spread it open on the dining table so her husband could look too.

"Oooh," she cooed. "Very nice. D'you think you could get us the friend rate, Benny?"

Ben laughed. None of his family could resist a bargain.

"Dunno," he said. "I can certainly try."

Although back in semiregular touch, he hadn't actually seen Lucas since the launch party for the Ibiza hotel last summer. It was a great night, not least because Lucas and Bianca had hit it off famously.

Wrapped around Ben like a wood nymph in a pale-green chiffon wisp of a dress, she'd proclaimed herself to be a fully paid-up fan of the Luxe aura, complimenting Lucas on everything from the canapés to the candlelit rock pools.

"They look so natural, like the garden of Eden. Hey, maybe Ben and I should go skinny-dipping later? This is Ibiza, after all."

Ben blushed and mumbled something suitably English about not wanting to frighten the horses. After she'd gone, Lucas drew him aside.

"Stunning girl," he said approvingly. "Congratulations. You see? I told you you could do better than that anemic little maid from Palmers, didn't I?"

Ben could recall that comment now as if it were yesterday, could still feel the way it had sent his stomach lurching like a free-falling elevator. Even now, thoughts of Sian still bothered him. It bothered him that they bothered him.

"You finished, darling?"

His mum's voice brought him back to the present with a jolt.

"Yes, thanks," he said, handing her his empty trifle bowl. "It was really delicious."

Eileen blushed, as happy with the compliment as if she'd made the dessert herself from scratch, and handed him a mug of his favorite PG Tips tea, with two bourbon biscuits for dunking. "Take those through to the lounge if you like," she said.

The family decamped en masse to the enormous living room, sinking themselves into the various supersized World of Leather sofas and continuing to ooh and aah over Lucas's new Paris hotel. The rest of the Sunday papers were still on the dinner table, and Ben hung back, having caught sight of the lurid red print of the *News of the World* at the top of the pile. Flipping the pages idly, he wondered if Sian would have a byline in this week.

Ever since she'd graduated to the features desk at the infamous Sunday gossip rag, Ben had become a regular reader.

Bianca couldn't understand it.

"But it's such a horrible paper," she pointed out each week, when he guiltily handed over his change to the newsagent. "All they do is prey on people, trying to break up marriages and wreck families. Why on earth do you buy it?"

"Good football coverage," was his stock, lame excuse. He felt bad lying, but there was no point in rocking the boat with B by telling her Sian was a columnist. Since Bianca had actually met Sian two years ago, at that New York wedding—what sort of sick celestial sadist had sat his girlfriend next to his ex, for God's sake?—she'd had a face to put with the name, and as a result had always maintained a slightly anxious curiosity about her and Ben's relationship.

There was no way he could excuse his interest in Sian's writing without sounding suspect. And he couldn't very well tell the truth: that reading her pieces gave him a strange sensation—part pride, part nostalgia, part something else he couldn't quite put his finger on—that had become weirdly addictive. Putting his personal feelings aside, she was a terrific writer. He loved her unique brand of acerbic wit and often found himself laughing out loud at things she'd written, taking the piss out of some fat-cat politician in the withering, deadpan voice he remembered so well from their brief summer together.

He still regretted the way things had ended between them. With hindsight, he could see he'd overreacted. What the hell had he been thinking, taking love life advice from Lucas of all people? Lucas, who wouldn't know true love if it bit him in the ass and whistled Dixie? It was like asking Donald Trump for a lesson in humility. He'd have liked to have had the chance to say sorry, at least. But the moment for apologies had long since passed. Sian probably wouldn't even remember him. And anyway, he had Bianca now.

Even so, he'd lost count of the times he'd sat in front of his screen at work, struggling to compose a suitably casual e-mail, congratulating her on her writing and just saying hello. But he always lost his nerve before he pressed send.

"Ben!" Nikki crept up behind him and made him jump. Why were all the women in his family cursed with voices that sounded like pneumatic drills boring into bedrock? "What are you doing hiding in here? We all want to talk to you about Bianca. You needn't think you're off the hook."

"Heaven forbid," muttered Ben, shutting the paper like a guilty teenager caught fingering a porno mag, as he walked into the other room to face the inevitable music.

CHAPTER TWENTY-ONE

$\mathcal{A}$ FEW DAYS LATER, IN A RESTAURANT OVERLOOKING THE Seine, Lucas leaned back in the comfort of his padded Louis XIV chair and inhaled deeply and luxuriantly on a Gitane. His temporary move to Paris had provided a perfect excuse to take up smoking again. In fact, without his pack a day of lethally strong French cigarettes, he doubted he would have made it through the stress of the last two months.

Hotel construction was always hell, but French contractors were a unique breed of nightmare. The union regulations here made Ibiza look like a walk in the park, and the local officials took more bribes in a week than your average banana republic dictator saw in a year. But somehow, after untold sleepless nights and near misses, they'd pulled the thing off. Luxe Paris was open for business.

Come to think of it, "they" was probably pushing it. In Ibiza, Connor had shown a token interest in proceedings, but he'd been against the Paris hotel from the start, leaving Lucas to carry the can completely solo. Not that he minded. He preferred to work alone and was finding Armstrong's worrywart tendencies increasingly annoying. The business was taking off faster than either of them had imagined, and global interest in the Luxe brand was already building at a satisfyingly robust pace. But while Lucas sprinted to meet these challenges, full of optimism and energy, Connor hung back in the shadows like a nervous old woman, muttering about the dangers of overextending and the importance of sticking to the business plan.

If it carried on much longer, Lucas would have to start scouting around for a new backer, although buying Connor out wouldn't be easy. But for now, sadly, they were still in this together, and he struggled to hide his irritation over lunch, as Connor regaled him with one self-aggrandizing anecdote after another.

"Do you enjoy your meal, *messieurs*?"

The shy, very young waitress serving them blushed as she presented their bill. Lucas, for one, welcomed the interruption to Connor's interminable monologue and smiled at her warmly. But Connor was annoyed.

"I've had better," he said gracelessly. "But don't worry, love. I always tip pretty waitresses, no matter how crap the chef." He winked and, pulling out a wad of large bills, allowed one to flutter down onto the table like a falling leaf, as if to indicate how little it meant to a man as rich as himself.

"Oh, *non, non, monsieur*." The girl shook her head. "*C'est trop*. Is far too much. I bring you change."

"It's nothing," leered Connor. Reaching around, he groped her ass so blatantly the poor creature jumped a mile. "Now take it and skedaddle, all right, gorgeous? Before I get carried away."

Lucas felt his fists twitching. Jerk. It was all he could do not to lean over the table and slam Connor's boorish features down on the wood so hard his nose would break. But he managed to restrain himself. Until he had another partner lined up, he needed Connor.

"So," Connor smiled, unaware anything was wrong. "The Herrick's been nominated in the Relais Chateaux rankings. D'you see that? Apparently it's a two-horse race between them and the Post Ranch for the number one spot. I bet your mate Anton's pleased."

Lucas inhaled even more deeply on his cigarette and struggled to keep his temper. To Connor, his rivalry with Anton and Petra had always been a big joke. But this was one subject about which Lucas would never see the funny side.

"When are *we* gonna get that kind of recognition, eh?" Connor delighted in pushing his buttons.

"When you toss me enough money to buy off the judging panel, you clueless fuckwit," was what he wanted to say. But he settled for a more straightforward lie.

"I'm not interested in the Herrick," he said, stubbing out his cigarette so violently that it snapped in two. "They're welcome to their five minutes of fame. Relais Chateaux don't know their ass from their elbow, anyway."

In fact, ever since the nominations were published last week, Lucas had been consumed by a rage so violent he could barely sleep. Not that he wasn't enjoying his own fair share of recognition: if Anton was the industry's god and Petra its queen bee, then Lucas was without doubt its favorite prodigal son. Word was spreading that Luxe Ibiza and now Luxe Paris were *the* hot new vacation destinations in Europe, and with only fifteen rooms apiece, competition for prime-season bookings was fierce. The Ibiza hotel's waiting list already read like a Who's Who of the European A-list, and Lucas had no doubts that even the notoriously sleepy Relais Chateaux would catch on to their success eventually.

But with the Herrick up for the number one spot, his own success suddenly lost all its sweetness. Nor had it escaped his notice that all but one of the names in the top five were American hotels. Conquering Europe was no longer enough. He had to claw his way back into the US market and blow Anton Tisch out of the water for good.

As much as it preoccupied him, returning to the States remained a frightening prospect. Anton had seen to it that his name remained mud in the US industry. Going back would be tough, no question. He couldn't afford to fail a second time.

"I tell you what," said Connor, still determined to get a rise out of Lucas before their meal was done. "That Russki bint's no slouch in the looks department. I'd do her over Honor Palmer any day. Here, take a look."

Reaching into his briefcase, he handed Lucas a copy of the latest *Robb Report*, open at a three-page feature on the Tischen Group. In the section devoted to the Herrick was a small sidebar mentioning Palmers, with an accompanying head shot of Honor. Set beside it was a much bigger picture of Petra, Rosa Klebb–like as ever in a severe black suit, standing in front of the Herrick. She had her arms spread wide in a "Look at me! This is all mine!" pose, and her thin, Slavic lips were wrenched up at the corners in a stiff attempt at a smile. If she was trying to look welcoming, she failed miserably. She looked like Jack Nicholson's Joker, only creepier, and with Carol Brady hair. How Connor, or indeed anyone, could fancy her was quite beyond Lucas.

To the right of her picture, she'd given a quote about Anton ("my mentor") that was so grovelingly sycophantic Lucas had to look away. His eyes were drawn instead to the small picture of Honor.

What a change! Although it was only a head shot, she looked unrecognizable from the boyish, spiky-haired virago he remembered. In a pale-lemon silk blouse, with her dark hair now grown out almost to her shoulders and cut in soft, feathery layers around her face, she was suddenly all woman. The razor-sharp cheekbones were as unforgivingly beautiful as ever, but the light tan and smattering of freckles she'd acquired over the summer made them somehow less regal and forbidding. And was that a pearl necklace she was wearing? The last time Lucas had seen Honor, she might just about have stretched to a signet ring but otherwise had an allergy to jewelry almost as strong as her aversion to makeup and feminine clothes. Had it not been for those narrowed, emerald-green cat's eyes, battle-ready as ever, he wouldn't have believed it was the same girl.

Her new look wasn't the only thing that drew his attention. He'd always suspected there was a vulnerability lurking behind Honor's bravado. Now, in this picture, he could actually see it for the first time. There was something bravely tragic about her, like the Polish cavalrymen charging hopelessly on horseback against the incoming German tanks; or the brave Southern soldiers making their doomed stand against the Yankees at Gettysburg. It was a miracle Palmers hadn't folded by now, battered by scandals, then drowned by the tidal wave of the Herrick's success. But it hadn't—not yet, anyway. Somehow, like a lone, desperate shipwreck survivor, Honor had managed to keep the place alive. He found himself wanting to reach into the page and rescue her and wished more than anything that she didn't still believe that he was the one who'd betrayed her and Tina.

Staring at the tiny picture of her face, thousands of miles away, he suddenly had a revelation. It wasn't only Palmers Honor was fighting for. It was the whole way of life that the hotel represented. A quieter, gentler, more decent way of life. A way of life that the likes of Anton and Petra and Connor Armstrong didn't understand. He hadn't understood it either, back in his own Herrick days. But he did now. The irony was that in a way, it was the same magic that he was trying to create with his Luxes, albeit in a different vein. A magic that the global chains like Ritz-Carlton and Tischen were intent on destroying, no matter what the cost.

"You all right?" Connor's Americanized drawl broke his concentration. "You've gone all comatose on me."

"I'm fine," snapped Lucas. "I'm reading."

Against his better judgment, he turned back to Petra's interview.

I really can't claim much credit for our success this year, she told the reporter. *Anton Tisch is a genius. His hotels sell themselves.*

Jesus. She had her forked tongue so far up Anton's anus you could probably see it when he opened his mouth.

My only real challenge was to rebuild our reputation and rela-tionships locally, she went on. *I don't want to remind people of the way my predecessor behaved,* she said, reminding people. *That's not what the Tischen Family is all about. But I think the trust is slowly coming back. I know Honor Palmer. We get on well.*

Lucas choked on his espresso at that. Everybody in the busi-ness knew that Honor and Petra loathed each other.

"Oh, I nearly forgot," said Connor, retrieving his magazine before Lucas sprayed coffee all over it. "Before I go, I want to talk to you about that interview in the *Times*."

"What about it?" said Lucas.

"I've changed my mind. I don't think you should do it."

Lucas pulled out another Gitane and lit it. "Sorry," he said. "Too late. I spoke to the journalist this morning."

After the flurry of interest in Luxe Paris, a writer for the *London Times* had asked for a no-holds-barred interview with Lucas. They were going for the rags-to-riches angle, focusing on his impoverished childhood. But Lucas had dropped heavy, enticing hints that he also wanted to discuss his "feud" with Anton Tisch, and it was this aspect that worried Connor.

"For fuck's sake," he growled. "Why didn't you discuss it with me first? You know how litigious Tisch is. Please tell me you didn't bang on about your ridiculous conspiracy theory and Anton being out to get you."

"It's not a conspiracy theory," snapped Lucas, losing his cool. "It's a fact. That bastard set me up, and he's been out to destroy me ever since. Why do you think he hired Petra as my replace-ment?"

"Because she's good?" said Connor. "Because he wanted to get his leg over? I don't fucking know. So what did you say?"

Lucas took another long drag on his cigarette.

"I may have mentioned my intention to open another Luxe in America. And I may possibly have said that it would piss all over the Herrick when we do open."

"What! *Why?*" spluttered Connor, his florid face turning an even deeper shade of puce. "We've discussed this, Lucas. I am not going to be bullied into overextending our franchise just because you've got a bee in your bonnet about Anton bloody Tisch. The US was never in the business plan. We are not opening there, and that's final. You'll have to call the journalist and retract it."

Lucas shrugged. "Fine. I'll call him."

He had no intention of doing any such thing, but he didn't have the energy to debate the issue with Connor. In any case, there was no point. Today's lunch had crystallized his decision once and for all: he needed a new partner. Connor Armstrong had served his purpose, but he didn't have the vision to carry the Luxe brand to the next glorious stage in its future. And he was a dickhead.

There was a global conference coming up in the new year, in Vegas. He'd scout around for a suitable new backer there. In the meantime, he had enough work on his plate in Europe to last him a lifetime, not to mention the small matter of finding a suitable site for Luxe America.

As he'd told the *Times* journalist only a few hours ago, East Hampton had a good ring to it. After all, the town was crying out for at least one *really* world-class hotel...

A few days after Lucas's lunch in Paris, Honor ducked into the East Hampton market, grateful for the blast of warm air that enveloped her as she slipped through the automatic doors.

"Good grief, it's cold out there!" She smiled at the checkout girl, who smiled back. "Can you believe it's still only October?"

"Gonna be below freezing tonight, they said on the radio," said the girl. "Better bundle up."

Honor shivered at the thought. With the electrics at Palmers now on their very last legs—"borrowed time" was how the last engineer to inspect the system had described it—she'd been trying to use the central heating as little as possible in the public areas, relying instead on open fires. Happily, the guests all much preferred this arrangement, but if this cold snap continued she'd need more than pine logs to keep out the chill.

Unfortunately, time wasn't the only thing that Honor had borrowed recently, in her increasingly desperate attempts to shore up the hotel. The scandals of three years ago had hit the business hard, and she was now remortgaged up to the hilt. New hotels like the Herrick could get away with a high guest turnover and expected to see different faces around the poolside every season. But Palmers relied on her regulars, families who returned to the hotel like clockwork every summer and Christmas. When they started defecting, as they did in droves after Tina's sex tape, Palmers' profits went into free fall. Thanks to a relentless and bravely fought rearguard action, Honor had managed gradually to claw some of these deserters back. But it was a long and arduous process, and in the meantime Anton was pouring money into the Herrick like Croesus, funding ever more indulgent facilities— an Olympic-size mud bath was his latest folly—making it harder and harder for her or anyone to compete. How could Palmers not look tired and shabby when up the hill Petra was offering diamond-dust facials and eight-handed massage in his-and-hers Polynesian love-pools, whatever the hell they were.

Things had been tough for Honor on the personal front too. Her affair with Devon, not to mention Tina's sex-and-drugs shame, had shaken sleepy East Hampton to its judgmental, Republican core. Only now, three years later, was Honor finally beginning to be accepted again.

A number of circumstances had conspired to help ease her back into the social fold. Firstly, Devon had rented out his Hamptons summer home and decamped to Boston for good, so he and Karis weren't around to remind people of what had happened. Last Honor heard, they were still together and (outwardly, at least) happy. They'd even bought a new place on Martha's Vineyard, where Devon was apparently already busy reinventing himself as a local politician and general all-around good guy. Good luck to him. Thankfully, his wannabe-Kennedy fantasies weren't Honor's problem anymore.

Secondly, Palmers was visibly struggling, and everybody loved an underdog, particularly a homegrown one. Thirdly, and perhaps most importantly from Honor's point of view, there was the Petra factor.

Whatever she might have told the *Robb Report*, the Herrick's new manager was in fact universally loathed by the locals. Many of the older generation were simply anti-Russian: the "poor Ron Reagan would be spinning in his grave," "once a commie, always a commie" brigade. But even the younger, more broad-minded Hamptonites rapidly took against Petra's frosty, regal bearing, not to mention her complete disregard for the local community and its wishes.

She'd made things worse at one of the few local events she'd deigned to attend—a charity auction on behalf of the Make-A-Wish foundation—by refusing to join Honor in auctioning herself off to local businessmen as a double date.

"Come on, Ms. Kamalski." Walt Cannon, the rotund, sweet-natured former mayor who was organizing the event tried to egg her on. "It's just for fun. And remember, it's all for the kids in the end."

"I've already made a donation," said Petra haughtily. "A generous one, I might add. I'm afraid prostituting myself to men I don't know is not my idea of fun, Mr. Cannon. I'll leave that sort of thing to Miss Palmer."

From that remark on, it was open war between Honor and Petra, and the town knew whose side it was on. With the Wicked Witch of the West installed up the street, it was inevitable that Honor would eventually be reinstated as Dorothy, albeit a morally tainted one. Her new, more feminine style helped too. It was so much easier to feel protective toward a woman who looked like a woman and not a K.D. Lang–alike who might pull a jack-knife on you at any moment.

Unfortunately, it would take a lot more than local goodwill to save Palmers. Honor could no longer afford to keep topping up the hotel's coffers from the family trust, especially not now that she had interest to pay on the whopping new mortgage. Lise, her wicked stepmonster, had successfully sued Trey's estate last year for a bigger payout, swanning off to the Bahamas with her new tennis instructor boyfriend and a chunk of Honor and Tina's inheritance. The judge must have fallen for her sob story. Either that or her gravity-defying new boob job, which Lise had displayed in court to great effect in a low-cut Roland Mouret dress. (Black, of course. She was mourning, after all.)

Anyway, the point was that the black widow had won. Meanwhile Tina was still spending what was left of the family money like water, despite the fact that she was now earning millions in her own right. The dubious celebrity she'd earned from the sex tape had translated into modeling and endorsement deals up the wazoo. Only in America, right? But none of that money made its way to Palmers.

To make matters worse, no sooner had the money started rolling in than Tina got herself hooked up with a pseudoreligious group called The Path. A bunch of former hippies and con artists, they were happy to relieve her of the burden of her wealth in return for "speerchal" enlightenment, LA style. So while Tina continued to pay extortionate rent on a Holmby Hills penthouse she never used, she now spent most of her time at one of The Path's "wellness centers" in Santa Fe.

The last time Honor had called her there, she'd been stoned out of her mind.

"You know," she mumbled drowsily down the phone, "you really need to reconnect to your well."

"My *well*?" Honor sighed.

"Sure. Your energy well. We all have a pool of positive energy deep within us that we draw on, that we need to grow. Like flowers," Tina added helpfully. "I'm sensing a lot of negativity from you right now, Honor. Your well is drying up."

"Listen, Tomasina Cruise," said Honor. "The only well drying up around here is the Bank of America well. That's looking pretty fucking parched right now. We have to talk about your spending, T. How much money are you giving these wackos, exactly?"

"Spiritual growth can't be measured in dollars and cents," said Tina, in the new, serene voice she'd affected recently, which she thought projected inner peace and Honor thought made her sound retarded.

"I couldn't agree more," she said robustly. "So go ask your guru for your money back. What does he need it for? More incense sticks?"

But she may as well have been speaking Martian. Tina wouldn't give an inch. Nor did she give a rat's ass about Honor's problems bailing out Palmers.

Turning into the organic produce aisle, Honor threw a few essentials into her shopping cart—milk, whole wheat bread, recycled toilet paper. Suddenly seized by a very nonorganic craving for Oreo cookies, she was about to make a U-turn to the junk food section when she overheard something that made her stop in her tracks.

"If he does open here, I'm definitely applying."

Honor recognized the voice of the Herrick's maître d'.

"Careful," said his friend. "Walls have ears. I wouldn't put it past Petra to have bugs in the supermarket. KG Bitch."

They both laughed.

"But I wouldn't bank on Lucas being any easier a boss. All the old staff say he could be a real hard-ass when he ran the Herrick."

"He was never as bad as Kamalski," said the maître d'. "He only yelled at you when you'd fucked up. I can handle that.

Besides, it'd be worth a few ear bashings to work at Luxe. Those hotels are gonna be the new Tischens, you mark my words."

Honor, who was marking his words, edged closer to the shelf, moving aside some packets of lentils so she could hear them more clearly without being seen.

Surely Lucas couldn't be planning to open a Luxe here?

No, no. It was a European brand. And East Hampton would be the last place Lucas would want to return to. Wouldn't it? They must be mistaken.

"Well if you go, I'm going," said the maître d's friend. "I can't take much more of that snake pit. I've even thought about moving to Palmers."

The maître d' laughed. "Forget it. They'll be bust in six months." Honor flushed red. Was that what everyone thought? That they were finished already?

"We'll just have to hope Ruiz doesn't lose his nerve," the maître d' went on. "I don't mind admitting, I wouldn't wanna take Petra on head-to-head. The woman scares the living shit out of me."

They moved on toward the cash register at that point, out of Honor's earshot. She was itching to follow them, but there was no way to do it without being spotted. And as soon as they saw her, they'd clam up, so there was no point.

Grabbing a packet of Oreos on autopilot, her mind raced as she ran over the significance of what she'd just heard.

Of course, it was only gossip. But she knew from experience that hotel gossip was usually accurate. And they'd both sounded horribly specific about the details.

Lucas was planning to open another Luxe here, in the Hamptons. She tried to imagine worse news. But short of nuclear war, a direct meteorite hit on Palmers, or Devon Carter being elected president, she couldn't think of anything.

How could he? After what he'd done to her, betraying her in the worst way possible, how could he have the balls to even contemplate showing his face in this town, never mind setting up shop here with one of his damn stupid, overhyped Luxes? God, how she hated that name. It sounded like a fricking soap.

Like everyone else in the business, Honor had read reams of copy about Lucas's famed comeback. Unlike everybody else, however, her heart wasn't remotely warmed by his rags-to-riches story. What kind of karma was it that allowed assholes like him to bounce back from ruin like a pinball, while decent, hardworking people like her got to sit in a shower of shit that never seemed to end?

If there was a God, she decided, he was definitely a man.

As for the whole Luxe phenomenon, she couldn't see what all the fuss was about. A bunch of candles and lavender oil and a few velvet cushions. That was the big concept, as far as she could tell. Big hairy wow. Like no one had ever done boudoir chic before.

"Are you OK?" The girl at the checkout looked concerned, and Honor realized with embarrassment that she'd been mumbling out loud. "Sorry," she said. "I'm fine. Just tired."

The two Herrick workers had gone, and she was once again the only customer in the store. Listening to the lonely *beep, beep* of the scanner as her items passed through it one by one, she thought about Lucas. In her mind, his handsome, arrogant face was laughing at her.

"*You* couldn't beat Anton Tisch," he seemed to be saying. "But I'm gonna show you how it's done."

Outside, weighed down with groceries, she drew her chunky-knit cardigan more tightly around her against the bitter wind.

She couldn't let him have the last laugh. Not this time. She'd have to come up with some sort of plan.

A week later, Anton arrived back in London in excellent spirits.

He'd spent the last week at St. Hubert's, an exclusive private clinic in Switzerland, having his Botox secretly touched up and was highly satisfied with the results. St. Hubert's no TV, Internet, or phones policy was a pain in the ass, but the cosmetic surgeons there were such artists, it was worth the inconvenience once a year.

Marching through terminal three at Heathrow while his chauffeur struggled on ahead with the luggage, he allowed himself a small smile of satisfaction. Life was pretty damn good right now. Excelsior had had a fantastic write-up in last week's *Wall Street Journal*—the European Superfund, they were calling it now, much to his delight. Ben Slater's Stellar Fund had barely rated a two-line name check.

It particularly amused him how no one in the city could fathom how he'd managed to poach quite so many of Stellar's clients over the past eighteen months. As if it weren't patently obvious. He might have gone out of his way to distance himself socially from the Azerbaijani oligarchs to whom he owed most of his vast fortune, but that didn't mean he was above accepting their money. They were all the same, these Slavs and Russians and Central Asians: sheep. Born followers. Not like the Germans or the British, or even the Americans. Now that a select few of them had come into such phenomenal personal wealth, they were still following one another blindly, investing in the same funds, the same cities, the same yachts, the same property deals. All Anton had to do was to massage a few of his old contacts and land one or two big fish for Excelsior, and the rest of them had jumped on the gravy train like lambs to the slaughter.

But the fund's performance wasn't the only reason Anton had to celebrate. The share price of his Tischen Hotel Group had gone up sixteen points on the news that the Herrick had been nominated for the coveted number one spot in the Relais Chateaux rankings. And he had the incomparable Ms. Kamalski to thank for that.

When Petra had first contacted him after he'd fired Lucas, suggesting herself for the Herrick managership, he'd thrown her

CV in the trash along with all the others. But a few days later she had the good sense to e-mail a second version—this time with a photograph—and at once his interest was piqued. Something about her stark cheekbones and cold, predatory eyes spoke to him. She looked simultaneously sexual and frigid; controlled, but with the promise of raging passions bubbling beneath the skin. His original intention was to fly her to Geneva, string her along until he got her into bed, then get rid of her. But from the moment he saw her in the flesh and their eyes locked, everything changed. He recognized a kindred spirit.

For one thing, she hadn't needed the slightest encouragement to sleep with him. She agreed immediately to his request that they have the interview at his home, then showed up for it wearing nothing but a trench coat and patent black stilettos. Thinking about that afternoon now, as his limo surged smoothly out of the airport onto the M, he felt his cock start to harden. After almost three years, he still wanted her constantly.

From that very first time, sex with Petra had been a revelation. Insatiable, athletic, submissive, yet strong, she was like the missing piece of the jigsaw that Anton had been searching for his whole life. In the past he'd had to pay girls to do the depraved things he wanted. With Petra, he was begged for more. He only had to look at her wildly dilating pupils, or her nipples, hard as frozen berries, arched longingly toward him, to realize her excitement was every bit as real and intense as his own.

Not only was she a world-class fuck, she was an astonishingly gifted hotelier. Lucas had gotten the Herrick off to a flying start, but Petra took those early seeds of success and multiplied them a hundredfold. She'd broadened their guest list, from the New York–centric music-business types that Lucas had exclusively gone for to the new superrich from across the globe, and she was also a genius at schmoozing stuffy industry types like the buffoons at Relais Chateaux. The locals might not like her, but who cared? The time when Anton had needed their support was long since past. When Petra had confided to him one night in bed that her main motivation in applying for the job had been to put one over on Lucas—the two of them were lifelong enemies, apparently—Anton's admiration for her became complete. He admired people who pursued their vendettas to the end, who didn't get distracted or allow the passage of time to smother their righteous indignation. Petra was a woman after his own heart.

"Your tea, sir."

Gavin, the butler Anton always brought with him when traveling, handed him a bone china cup brimming with piping hot Earl Grey. Anton had had his entire fleet of cars fitted with tea-making facilities, along with the standard plasma screens and state-of-the art phone systems. He took the cup wordlessly and settled down to peruse the last week's papers. See what he'd missed while he'd been stuck at St. Hubert's.

Two minutes later, he let out a roar so loud it sent his driver skidding all over the road and promptly spilled scalding tea down his Turnbull & Asser silk shirt.

"*Sheisse!*" he roared, pulling the wet cloth away from his skin, but not before a spreading red burn had formed across his chest and stomach like a birthmark. "The little shit."

Lucas, it appeared, had taken advantage of his absence to give an interview to the *London Times*. And it wasn't pretty.

The Tischens have become a victim of their own success, he was quoted as saying, in response to a question about whether he saw himself as being in competition with Anton. *When a brand explodes to that degree, it soon becomes corporate and faceless, like every other global five-star chain. Mr. Tisch doesn't like the word "chain," but that's what his hotels have become. And I should know. I ran one of them.*

White-lipped with rage, Anton read on.

Luxe offers something very different. Personal. Unique. So in that sense, no, I don't see us as competing, not directly anyway.

Once we open in the Hamptons, I guess some people might choose to see it that way. But that's not my view.

"Get Petra on the phone," Anton barked at Gavin.

"She won't be up, sir," he stammered timidly, shrinking back in his seat like a mouse before a rattlesnake. "It's not even six on the East Coast yet."

"Don't tell me what fucking time it is, you stupid fuck," bellowed Anton. "Just get her on the line." Already his buoyant mood of a few minutes ago had evaporated completely. Fuck Lucas. Who the hell did he think he was dealing with?

When Anton killed off an enemy, he expected them to stay dead, and he saw Lucas's revival of fortunes as a personal affront. He'd been too busy with the fund in recent months to take any further concrete action against him. But he saw now that that had been a mistake. He'd given Lucas an inch and he'd taken a mile, threatening to open a new Luxe in the Hamptons, of all the outrageous...

"About time." Petra's sleepy voice ricocheted around the limo in surround sound. "Where the hell have you been all week?"

"Never mind that," snapped Anton. He wasn't about to admit his surgical sabbatical to anyone, least of all the woman he was sleeping with. "I just read Lucas's interview. He claims he's setting up shop in East Hampton. Why didn't you tell me about this before?"

"How was I supposed to tell you?" Petra snapped back. "By carrier pigeon? I've left you about a hundred messages; you never returned a single one. I haven't even been able to make a statement to the press. Where *were* you?"

"Don't challenge me," said Anton.

He sounded angry, but Petra could sense the lust simmering underneath. Their role-play was always the same: she was the petulant schoolgirl, he the disciplinarian teacher. But Anton never seemed to tire of it.

"Speak to me like that again and I'll spank you," he said.

Gavin the butler blushed scarlet and stared firmly out the window.

"Apologize."

"Sorry," purred Petra meekly.

In the back of the car, Anton's hard-on was now clearly visible through the twill of his suit pants. How he wished Petra were here in the quivering, pliant flesh, and not on the other end of a phone line. But she wasn't. And they had business to discuss.

"So," he said. "Our friend Mr. Ruiz has crawled out from under his stone while I've been gone, has he?"

"It's pathetic," said Petra, her voice dripping with vitriol. "He opens two paltry hotels in Europe—Luxe Paris is so small it's practically a guesthouse—and already he thinks he's Rande Gerber. He's a joke."

Anton didn't find the prospect of a Hamptons Luxe remotely amusing. But neither was he intimidated. Being forced to crush Lucas a second time was an unwanted irritation—like finding a cockroach you thought you'd killed still wriggling on the bottom of your shoe. But it was hardly a serious concern.

"Lucas is all talk," said Petra. "He always has been. He clearly hasn't found a site for this mythical new Luxe yet, or he'd have been boasting about that too."

"And he's not going to find one," growled Anton menacingly.

"To be honest," said Petra, "That stuck-up bitch Honor Palmer worries me far more than Lucas does."

Honor's dislike of Petra was nothing compared to the boiling hatred that Petra harbored for her local rival. Not since Lucas had tried to eclipse her in college had she felt so threatened and, at the same time, so irrationally resentful of another human being. She despised everything about Honor, from her deep, growling voice with its faint Bostonian twang, to her tiny, doll-like body, to the easy way with which she seemed to wrap all the local snobs around her little finger. People treated her like aristocracy, and Petra like some low-life immigrant, when in reality Petra's family was far older, grander, and richer than the Palmers. Honor was also routinely described in the press as "cute" and even "beautiful," which incensed Petra, who thought her own physical charms outshone Honor's like the sun outshone a candle.

"Honor?" Anton sounded amazed. "Don't be ridiculous. She's no threat to us. I've seen Holiday Inns in Des Moines with better occupancy rates than Palmers."

"Hmm," said Petra skeptically. "Maybe."

Now that Palmers was clearly on its way out, Anton was perfectly content to watch the old hotel die a slow, lingering death. Cancer, as long as it was terminal, was as good a way to finish off a rival as the firing squad. But Petra remained much more antsy. As long as Palmers was standing and open for business, and as long as that poisonous dwarf Honor Palmer hung around like a bad smell, playing the town sweetheart, she would never feel completely secure, no matter how many Relais Chateaux accolades they won.

"You mustn't fret so much, darling," said Anton, reading her mind. "The locals can huff and puff for Honor as much as they like. They won't blow our house down. And nor will Lucas. We'll see to that." The limo eased to a halt outside his Mayfair mansion, and Anton hung up and hurried inside, leaving Gavin and the driver to manage his cases.

His week away had been rejuvenating. But now there was work to be done. This time around, he'd make damn sure he finished off Lucas Ruiz for good.

CHAPTER TWENTY-TWO

$\mathscr{A}$ FEW MILES NORTH OF MAYFAIR, IN THE GROUNDS OF AN-other mansion in St. John's Wood, Sian Doyle crouched uncomfortably in the bushes, trying to calculate exactly how many minutes she had left before her bladder gave out and she was forced to pee right here in the rhododendrons.

She wouldn't have minded so much if it weren't for Keith, the lecherous photographer crouched beside her. Watching her take her pants down would be the closest thing he'd come to a sexual experience (with something that didn't take batteries or need blowing up with a foot pump) since high school.

There were days when Sian loved working at the *News of the World*. Like this Monday, after one of her pieces ran, and Simon Davis, the features editor, told her it was "only slightly crap"— praise indeed from a man known affectionately to the rest of the desk as Satan. His wife had once berated a man for calling Simon a cunt on the grounds that it was an insult to women's genitalia.

But Monday's praise already felt like a distant memory. Today was Thursday, and Sian was on the worst of all possible assignments—a stakeout. After the crappy pay (she was pretty sure trash collectors made more than she did per week) and even crappier hours (whoever scheduled her shifts had clearly been raised in a cave, by bats), stakeouts were the worst part of her job.

This was the third day running she'd spent with Keith, knee-deep in foliage at the house of Sir Jago Wells, a Tory grandee that the paper suspected of having an affair with a stewardess. In thirty-six hours of mind-numbing surveillance they'd only seen the man twice, for a total of about sixteen seconds. Both times he'd been alone, hurrying to and from his Jaguar with a sheaf of papers under his arm. Given that Sir Jago must weigh about the same as a smallish hippo but with a markedly less attractive face, the absence of a girlfriend failed to surprise Sian as much as it did her editor.

"It's incredible he convinced one woman to do him, never mind two," she'd told a seriously unimpressed Simon an hour ago. "He makes Jabba the Hutt look like George Clooney."

But Satan wasn't in the mood for jokes. If she and Keith didn't have the goods on his desk by the end of their shift tomorrow, they could both "sling their 'ook," as he so poetically put it.

Sian was under no illusions. He meant it. No pictures, no tearful interview with the wife, no job.

"At this rate you're gonna 'ave to sleep wiv 'im yourself, love," said Keith, licking his lips.

Sian looked at him witheringly.

"What?" He tried to look innocent. "It'd make a lovely picture."

He had so many pimples on his face they outnumbered the patches of clear skin, and his round, owlish glasses were so grimy it was a wonder he could see anything at all. Sian's mind wandered bitterly to Paddy, her boyfriend, who was on assignment in Dubai for the *Telegraph*. He was probably yukking it up with some billionaire sheikh and his harem right now, having a fabulous time. Paddy was an Irish racing journalist whose assignments always seemed to involve being sent to hot countries and/ or luxury hospitality tents at race courses, swilling Guinness and eating strawberries until his stomach exploded, while Sian's were all about bushes, perverts, and outdoor urinating. It wasn't fair.

"Why don't you quit the Screws and get yourself a proper job?" he'd asked her in bed the other morning, after another of her hour-long moan-a-thons. "Show most editors a pretty face and a bit of leg and you're in like Flynn. My boss'd snap you up in a heartbeat. I can see the interview now." He fluttered his eyelashes coquettishly and put on his best Renée Zellweger voice: "You had me at hello."

"Oh, shut up," said Sian, laughing and hitting him with a pillow. Paddy had an uncanny ability to see the funny side in almost any situation and to get others to do the same. Skinny as anything, with merry, dancing gray eyes and the same classically Irish coloring as she had—pale skin made even paler by his shock of black hair—he habitually looked as though he'd spent the previous night sleeping under a hedge. Not handsome, but definitely attractive in a roguish, new-romantic kind of way, he was as much her best friend as her lover. People often commented that they looked like brother and sister, which annoyed Paddy so much that Sian had never dared to tell him she sometimes felt that way, too.

Given that they were in the same profession, it was ironic that they hadn't in fact met through work, but through Lola's boyfriend, Marti. He and Paddy had been friends for years, since Paddy's days as an intern at the *New York Post*. Marti brought him over to the girls' flat one night for dinner, and the rest, as they say, was history.

Sian liked being part of a couple, if only to give her something to talk about with Lola, who'd been blissfully loved-up with Marti ever since the Burnstein wedding. The two of them had been clocking up the air miles flitting back and forth from New York to London to see each other, and they were still revoltingly besotted.

Last year, against Sian's advice, they'd decided to go into business together, with the newly graduated Lola designing evening gowns and Marti selling them online, through one of his many successful Internet shopping sites.

Happily, Sian's fears about the wisdom of mixing business with pleasure had proved groundless. Their love remained as strong as ever, and Marti was now in London almost full-time. Trading under the name of Marla Fashions (as in Marti and Lola—sick-making, right?), the fledgling venture was already having remarkable early success. Only last month a famous British soap actress had worn one of Lola's designs to the National Television Awards, and since then orders had been up a staggering 300 percent.

Sian was happy for her. She deserved her success. But there were times when her own life—job, relationship, bank balance, you name it—looked pretty pathetic by comparison.

Today, squatting on her aching haunches next to the most irritating sex pest on Fleet Street, was definitely one of those times. Swatting away a mosquito, she shifted uncomfortably from foot to foot. Her right leg was starting to get pins and needles from all the crouching.

"Pass me one of your boxes, would you?" she whispered to Keith. "If I don't sit down soon I'm gonna fall down." Silence.

"Keith?"

Looking over her shoulder, Sian saw to her horror that her so-called partner was sprinting away through the trees as fast as his pudgy little legs could carry him. Moments later she realized why. Two burly men in overalls materialized out of thin air, grabbed hold of her roughly, and pinned her arms behind her back.

"Let go of me!" she screamed, kicking her legs uselessly like a captured cartoon character as they frog-marched her to the front of the house.

"Get off! This is assault!"

"No it's not, love," said the larger of the men. "It's a citizen's arrest. You're trespassing. And you're caught. So be a good girl and sit quietly until the old bill gets here. All right?"

Two hours later, stuck in a cell in Swiss Cottage police station, Sian racked her brains trying to think whom else she could call.

Simon, her editor, who only hours ago had been plaguing her nonstop with phone calls, had mysteriously disappeared in her hour of need. Probably holed up with the paper's lawyers somewhere figuring out how best to throw her to the wolves without getting his own hands dirty. Lola would have been her next call. She was a grand master at talking herself out of trouble. But unfortunately she was on vacation in Hawaii with Marti and totally incommunicado. Paddy was in Dubai.

She was rapidly running out of options.

"No one's given me a lawyer, you know," she shouted through the door to the duty sergeant. "I'm entitled to a lawyer. And a phone call. I know my rights. I'm an American citizen!" she added, more than a touch desperately.

"This is a north London nick, love, not *NYPD Blue*," said the sergeant, brilliantly managing to roll his eyes without looking up from his *Sun* crossword. "The DI'll get round to you as soon as he can. In the meantime, there's a pay phone in the corner there, and a paper if you're bored. You can ring whoever you like."

Feeling slightly deflated—partly because she had no one to call, and partly because being arrested was a lot more dramatic on TV—Sian picked up the copy of the *Daily Express* lying on the Formica table in her cell and gave it a desultory glance. Murphy's law decreed that the first thing she saw, slapped across the society pages, was a picture of Ben and Bianca.

It wasn't the first time she'd seen them pictured together, of course. Being so showstoppingly stunning, Bianca was a natural favorite with the picture editors, and since becoming the new face of Marks & Spencer her profile in the UK had shot up even further. She and Ben were rapidly becoming an It-couple to rival Posh and Becks.

Sian wished she could just ignore them, but working for a tabloid made it doubly hard. It had been three years since she'd last seen Ben in person. But she'd never forgotten the humiliation of that day, at his going-away party, when he'd walked out on her in front of all those people. Even now, thinking back to it made her flush with embarrassment.

Why did she even care anymore? All that stuff had happened eons ago, back in another life when she was a lowly maid from Butt-Fuck-Nowhere, New Jersey. Now she was a reporter for a national newspaper, living abroad, with a nice boyfriend and an awesome apartment. She'd moved on, hadn't she? Who gave a shit what Ben self-righteous Slater did, or who he did it with?

"Know 'im, do you?"

The duty sergeant, who was actually a kind man, came in with a cup of tea he'd made for her. They certainly didn't do *that* on *NYPD Blue*.

"Not really," said Sian. "I used to. He's a jerk," she added, taking the tea gratefully.

"He's a rich jerk though, isn't he?" said the sergeant. Sian shrugged.

"Listen, love. A word to the wise," he said. "If *I* had a rich mate like that, I'd get him on the blower, sharpish."

"You want me to call Ben?" Sian translated. She was getting quite adroit at deciphering cockneyisms these days. "Why would I do that? I told you, he's a jerk."

They were alone in the cell, but the sergeant still looked around him and lowered his voice before he spoke again.

"The DI hasn't been in to see you yet because he's still interviewing Sir Jago," he whispered. "If the shouting's anything to go by, I'd say the old git wants to make an example of you and your paper. You 'eard from your editor yet?"

Sian shook her head nervously.

"No. I thought not," said the sergeant. "They're hanging you out to dry, love. You need a decent brief and you need him right now. The bloke they're sending you from legal aid is a muppet. Couldn't argue 'is way out of a paper bag."

"But…but…you don't understand," stammered Sian. "I can't call Ben. Certainly not to ask him for a favor. Uh-uh, no way. I'd rather die."

The sergeant shrugged. "Up to you, love. Of course, I don't know the bloke. But if it were me, I'd swallow my pride. I'd say you need all the help you can get."

He returned to his desk, leaving Sian pacing the room, willing herself to think of someone, anyone else she knew in England who could help her. Surely somebody here owed her one? Or simply cared enough to get involved?

But try as she might, she couldn't dredge up a name, and panic was starting to get the better of her. Sir Jago Wells was an important man. What if he pulled enough strings to have her sent to prison? Or deported? That would be even worse. The thought of going back to her old life in New Jersey filled her with dread. She couldn't do it.

Her hand shook as she punched out the number for directory inquiries.

"London, please," she told the operator. "It's a company called Stellar, in the City, EC I think. Yeah. You can put me straight through."

Honor watched as the last few passengers from the United LA flight straggled into the arrivals hall at JFK. Still no sign of Tina. Please, please let her not have missed the fucking plane. Not today.

But no. Miraculously, there she was, floating through the double doors in a flouncy gypsy skirt and waist-length beads like a top-heavy Joni Mitchell, flashing a two-fingered peace sign to the ubiquitous paparazzi.

"Hey." Drifting over to Honor, she enveloped her in a photo-friendly hug. "Sorry it took so long. I had some trouble with one of the customs guys."

"I'm not surprised," said Honor, reeling from the overpowering smell of marijuana on her sister's clothes and hair. "How'd you talk your way out of that one?"

Tina flashed her a wicked smile. "I didn't need to talk."

Honor felt almost relieved. Evidently her Mother Teresa of Topanga makeover didn't run *that* deep.

"Thanks for coming," she said, pulling out of the airport onto the expressway twenty minutes later, once the paps had finally let them leave, and swerving into the fast lane as soon as she got a chance. "I appreciate it."

They were on their way back to Palmers. Honor had arranged a dinner with a possible investor tonight, an Australian hotelier called Baz Murray, who was looking to link his small chain with a high-visibility brand in the US. He'd specifically asked to meet both sisters together. Evidently the Australian public was a lot more relaxed about sex scandals than their American counterparts, and it was the Palmer family connection that really interested him. Honor had put a call in to Tina with low hopes, but to her simultaneous amazement, relief, and terror, Tina had agreed to fly in for the meeting.

Petra had done her best to sabotage things by throwing an impromptu celebrity birthday party at the Herrick tonight and inviting Murray along. How she knew he was in town was anybody's guess, but as the woman had more spies in the hospitality industry than the CIA, it was more of an annoyance than a surprise. In any case, to Honor's great delight, Baz had turned her down, earning himself untold brownie points in Honor's book. As long as Tina didn't say or do anything too outrageous over drinks, things were looking good. God knew they needed a cash injection, and fast.

"You are, er...you are gonna change before dinner, right?" Honor asked, glancing at Tina's gaping peasant blouse disapprovingly.

"You should talk," said Tina, shooting her a look that was more pissed than peace.

It was a fair point. Honor had been in such a rush this morning, she was still in her workout clothes: a pair of juicy velour sweatpants and a blue Nike tank top that clung to her small, sweaty frame so tightly that her nipples were clearly visible. Shit. What if they showed up in the pictures those photographers had just snapped at the airport? They were bound to, weren't they, circled in the goddamn *National Enquirer*? That was all she needed.

"So," said Tina, changing the subject. "I heard about Lucas coming back to East Hampton. What do you think? Is he serious?"

Honor bit her lip. How could Tina talk about Lucas's plans as if they were nothing more than an interesting tidbit of local gossip? Had she forgotten that it was Lucas who'd tried to ruin them in the first place? And who'd damn near succeeded?

But she had to try to stay on her sister's good side, at least until tomorrow. Of course, if it weren't for Tina's feckless spending, they wouldn't need to suck up to an outside investor. But that was beside the point now.

"I doubt it," she said, with admirable calm. "He's probably just shooting his mouth off as usual. Trying to gain some publicity for Luxe Paris. But we'll see."

For the rest of the journey, she steered the conversation toward safer topics, where they were bound to agree, like Lise and what a bitch she was and their dreadful, money-grubbing cousin Jacob Foster. "Did you see that interview he did with *US Weekly* about me discovering Jesus?" ranted Tina indignantly. "As if my spirituality could be confined by one religion. And as if that freak show even knows me!"

By the time they reached the windswept outskirts of East Hampton, they were back on amicable terms.

"That's funny," said Tina idly, watching a fire truck thunder through the dreary landscape of marshland and empty holiday homes, and saying a tiny prayer of thanks that this place was

Honor's life and not hers. "That's the second fire engine to pass us in the last five minutes."

"Probably got a call to come deal with the smoke blowing out of Petra Kamalski's ass," muttered Honor.

They both laughed.

But a few minutes later, their smiles disappeared. As they neared Palmers, a huge, gray mushroom cloud of smoke loomed in front of them. Soon it had all but filled the windshield, plunging the road ahead into darkness like a solar eclipse. Honor slowed the car. Moments later a cop emerged out of the gloom, waving at her to stop.

Winding down the window, she was immediately hit in the face by a gust of acrid smoke so strong it made her eyes water. This must be quite some fire.

"I'm sorry, ma'am, I'm gonna have to ask you to turn around," said the cop. Honor didn't recognize him. He was young and obviously new in town, and he had the intent, nervous look of someone seriously out of his depth.

"No, no," she said, nodding at the road in front of her. "You don't understand. We have to get through. My hotel's down there."

"You mean Palmers?" said the young man. He'd obviously mistaken her for a guest. "I'm afraid that's where the fire is coming from, ma'am. There's no need to panic," he added, seeing Honor's face drain of color and her hands start to shake. "Everyone's been evacuated safely. We're only talking property damage."

Honor shot out of the car. Pushing past the cop, she ran blindly through the makeshift roadblock and into the smoke.

"Miss. Miss!" he yelled ineffectually after her. "You can't go down there!"

"Leave her." Tina got out of the car more slowly and stared toward the beach in disbelief. She'd never seen smoke like it. "Trust me, officer. My sister can take care of herself."

A couple of the young cop's colleagues, alerted by the shouting, ran after Honor. But years of training meant she was fitter than all of them and was easily able to shake them off in the maze of sandy alleyways that led to the rear of the Palmers complex.

Down on the beach, a gathering crowd stared in horrified silence at the inferno, held back by more police as well as the natural barrier of smoke and heat. Like a zombie, Honor joined them, unable to speak or move as a third fire truck pulled up and its occupants began pumping yet more water at the blaze.

She didn't know why they bothered. It was clearly too late. Rushing around like red-suited termites, the firemen reminded her of desperate parents, trying to give mouth-to-mouth to an already-dead baby. *Her* baby. Next to the thirty-foot flames, which roared and leaped and licked the sky like the forked tongues of some giant lizard, their puny jets of water and foam were as ineffectual as water pistols in a volcano. Palmers was already a charred skeleton. The fire had consumed her alive, like a flesh-eating virus.

"Hey. Hey, you! What are you doing?"

One of the spectators, a middle-aged man watching the drama with his family, shouted out as Honor slipped through the police lines and ran kamikaze-like toward the hotel.

She couldn't hear the man, or anything other than the wild beating of her own heart. All she knew was that some force outside herself was pulling her forward, oblivious of the searing heat and choking fumes that poured down her throat and into her lungs like poison. Closing her eyes, she stumbled blindly on.

"Over there!" The man grabbed hold of one of the firefighters and pointed. "Some crazy girl just ran into the building. Look!"

"Where?" yelled the fireman.

"Over there!"

Within seconds, he and two of his buddies were inside. Thankfully, Honor hadn't made it more than a few feet into what used to be the kitchens, so they spotted her almost at once.

Dragging her outside, disoriented and barely conscious, they handed her over to the waiting paramedics.

"Shit. It's Honor Palmer," Honor could hear one of them saying.

"Miss Palmer?" asked a second voice. "Honor, can you hear us?"

But before she could tell them that she could, the voices, and everything else, had gone.

CHAPTER TWENTY-THREE

$\mathcal{T}$HE NEXT SIX WEEKS WERE THE WORST OF HONOR'S LIFE.
Confined against her will to a recuperation ward
in Southampton Hospital ("I assure you, Miss Palmer," said Dr.
Reeves, her consultant, firmly, "if I catch you trying to discharge
yourself one more time, I'll have you committed. Do you understand the damage you've done to your lungs?") she spent the bulk
of her days having increasingly circular, frustrating conversations with the insurance agents, who were determined to link
what happened to the hotel's substandard wiring, despite hard
forensic evidence that it had not been an electrical fire.

"Why do you keep asking me these questions?" she complained, for the hundredth time. "The police report was clear; it
was arson."

"Our investigators have yet to determine that," said the
charmless girl sent to interview her. She couldn't have been much
over twenty-one but had already developed the hardened, cyni-
cal manner common among her profession. She was dressed all
in black, like a particularly unsympathetic funeral director. "And
even if they do, the fact that you failed to bring your electrical
wiring up to code, despite repeated warnings, may well prejudice
your claim even if it was arson. Which we dispute," she added

with a smile that made Honor want to rip the clipboard out of her hands and ram it down her scrawny, heartless throat.

Thankfully, the police were more sympathetic, although their sympathy had yet to translate into progress.

A few days after the fire, an earnest cop had shown up by her bedside, armed with a long printout of questions.

"Do you have any enemies, Miss Palmer?" he began gently. "I know it's difficult. But can you think of anyone who might want to cause you or your family harm?"

Honor laughed bitterly. "How long have you got, detective?"

The cops seemed quite certain that the fire had been set deliberately, and it wasn't a case of some careless guest forgetting to stub out their cigarette. But despite a list of possible suspects as long as the East Hampton telephone directory—disgruntled former employees, business rivals, embittered lovers—there were actually very few people that Honor could imagine going to such extreme, criminal lengths to hurt her. She thought briefly of Karis Carter, but quickly dismissed the idea as ridiculous. If Karis were the crazed, vengeful type, she'd have acted long before now. Who else? Her greedy cousins, the Fosters, were too stupid, not to mention gutless. Lise wouldn't have had the energy or the foresight to start a fire. Besides, she was so plastic she'd probably be terrified of melting, like the wicked witch that she was.

There was a suggestion that Tina's former Mafia connections might have had something to do with it, but as far as Honor could tell, this was a theory based more on a lack of any other leads than on anything more concrete. Not even the policeman who'd suggested it seemed particularly convinced.

Honor had had to be physically restrained by two nurses when the cop informed her that her insurance company had hinted to the police that she herself should not be considered above suspicion.

"They simply asked us not to formally close any avenue of inquiry at this stage," explained the hapless officer. "To be fair to them, it's no secret that your business was in some trouble financially at the time the fire occurred."

"So what?" Honor was practically foaming at the mouth. "You think I torched my own hotel? Palmers was my life! There were people in there, for Christ's sake. Guests, staff. Friends of mine. It's a miracle nobody lost their life."

As with previous tragedies in her life—her mother's death, the feud with Trey, being abandoned by Devon—the worst part for Honor was the feeling of utter helplessness. It wasn't just Palmers that had burned to the ground that day. All her hopes for the future had perished with it.

Tina finally stopped by the hospital for a visit a week after Honor was admitted. She'd been too busy partying up a storm in Manhattan to come any sooner.

"So what'll you do?" she asked, devouring the bunch of seedless grapes she'd brought for Honor while flicking through a gossip magazine. "Go back to Boston?"

Secretly, Tina was rather enjoying all the drama. The Palmers fire was the most fun she'd had since the sex tape came out. Talk show producers were once again beating down her door for interviews, and photographers tailed her whenever she went out for coffee. It was fabulous! Plus, with Honor incapacitated in hospital, it fell to her to show the world just how the devastated (but plucky) Palmer sisters were coping with the tragedy. No one could turn a sob story into TV gold better than Tina.

"I guess I will go back to Boston. For now," said Honor, wincing as the nurse changed one of the dressings on her arm. As well as serious smoke inhalation, she'd suffered extensive burning to her arms and hands and had already undergone one skin graft. She'd never known pain like it. "But as soon as I've screwed my goddamn money out of these insurance leeches, I'm coming back. I'm gonna rebuild Palmers just as she was. Brick by brick."

"Really?" Tina put down the magazine and looked at her skeptically. "You don't think maybe the fire was a sign? You know, like, time to move on? Open a new chapter in your life? Just think of all the things you could do with that insurance money."

"Like what?"

"I don't know," shrugged Tina. "Whatever you want. Move to Paris. Buy a fuck-off yacht. Give it to charity. Who cares?"

Honor looked horrified.

"The only thing it's a sign of," she said grimly, "is that someone's determined to run us out of town. But they picked the wrong family to mess with. Palmers will be back, and it'll be bigger and better than ever."

Tina wasn't the only one who felt her sister's obsession with rebuilding the hotel might be a sign of mental instability.

"She won't let it go," she told Dr. Reeves. "I'm actually worried about her. She's turning into a fucking fruit loop."

"I wouldn't quite put it that way," said the doctor. But he was also concerned about his patient's state of mind. So far Honor had been unable to give the psychiatric team any explanation for why she'd run into a blazing building on the brink of collapse when she already knew there was nobody left inside. She denied being suicidal and claimed her mind had simply gone blank. But combined with her frequent outbursts of temper and repeated attempts to check herself out of the hospital long before she'd made a full recovery, these delusional fantasies about reopening Palmers as early as next year were a real cause for concern. Anyone could see it wasn't going to happen.

At long last, one crisp, late-November morning, Honor's release day dawned. She still wore bandages on her arms, and it would be two more weeks before she could risk taking a proper shower. But otherwise, save for a lack of exercise, she was in good health, and Dr. Reeves had run out of excuses to force more rest on her.

"I suppose there's nothing I can do to get you to go somewhere peaceful and continue your recuperation?" he asked.

He'd stopped by her room to formally discharge her and was dismayed to find Honor hopping about impatiently, rechecking her long-completed packing. She was itching to get on the phone to her lawyer and see what could be done to pressurize the insurers, but she didn't dare turn on her cell phone in front of Dr. Reeves in case he ordered her back to bed again. Secretly she was terrified that the horrible girl agent was right and she *had* voided her insurance by putting off that electrical work. Then she'd be ruined, and it would all be her own fault.

"Nope," she said, trying to sound cheerful. "There's nothing you can say. So don't even try."

Watching his patient fidgeting, the doctor smiled. She'd gained a little weight during her stay, but it suited her. In a coral-pink cashmere dress that clung to her like a second skin, you couldn't miss the fact that her small apple breasts had swelled into grapefruits, and the cheeks that had looked so sunken and hollow when she was first admitted were now fuller and rounded with health. When she'd first arrived in her scorched sweatpants, she had looked so skinny and angular, making love to her would have been like sticking your dick into a fistful of thistles. This new, softer, smiling Honor was really much more alluring.

"Your friend's here to pick you up, by the way," he said, signing the requisite papers and dragging his thoughts back to the professional matters at hand. "And please let him carry your suitcase. None of your feminist nonsense today, all right? Don't even think of overexerting yourself."

"Friend?" Honor looked puzzled. "What friend?"

She hadn't asked anybody to pick her up, other than the car service that was coming to take her to the airport for her three o'clock flight to Boston.

"Hello, Honor."

She spun around. For a moment she thought the good doctor must have slipped something into her water and she was hallucinating. For there, leaning against the doorway looking lean and tanned in a blue open-necked shirt, with his raven curls so long they were almost at his shoulders, stood Lucas.

"We're good now, thanks Doc," he said, shaking the doctor's hand as he ushered him out. Honor could see that in his other hand he held a small bouquet of peonies, her favorite flowers, although Lucas couldn't have known that.

"I'll take care of her from here."

"Make sure you do," said the doctor, jovially. "She's a handful, this one." And with a last smile at Honor, he was gone.

Annoyingly, for the crucial first few seconds, Honor was too flabbergasted to get a single word out. But inside her mind was racing.

What the hell was Lucas doing here, looking like a rock star just back from a relaxing break in the Maldives, while she looked pale and pasty and...in fact, screw all that, what the hell was he doing here, period?

"I'm calling security," she spluttered.

"Now that's not very welcoming, is it?" said Lucas, his upper lip curling in amusement. "Aren't you at least going to put these in some water first?"

"No." Snatching the peonies, Honor flung them on the bed. "Thank you," she added, automatically. "In case you hadn't noticed, I'm leaving. Right now. I have a plane to catch."

Ignoring Dr. Reeves's express instructions, she picked up her heavy case and began struggling toward the door. But Lucas was too quick for her. Placing a firm but gentle hand on her shoulder, he prized the suitcase easily from her grip.

"You heard the doctor," he said bossily. "You're not to lift anything. I'll do it. Nice dress, by the way. And the long hair's a big improvement."

Honor erupted. "What the fuck do you think you're playing at?" she demanded. "If you came to gloat, consider it done already, OK? Get the hell out of my face."

"Why would I come to gloat?"

He cocked his head to one side like a confused puppy. If Honor didn't know what a scheming, self-obsessed bastard he was, she might almost have found it endearing. As it was, his feigned innocence only fanned the flames of her fury.

"Because my hotel is gone," she said, her eyes welling up with tears despite herself. "Because you've got what you wanted at last."

Lucas put down the suitcase. "This is not what I wanted," he said quietly.

"Yeah. Right. Whatever," said Honor.

"Maybe it was once, years ago. But not anymore." He looked up, willing her to believe him, but she glared implacably back. "I was in town anyway, scouting out possible sites for my new Luxe—"

"That's great for you," said Honor bitterly.

"I knew about the fire, obviously, but it wasn't until I got here that I realized you'd been hurt. As soon as I heard, I came straight to the hospital. I wanted to say how sorry I was, and to see if there was anything I could do. You know, to help."

"There is," said Honor, deadpan. "Drop dead."

Lucas sighed. Her feminine makeover clearly didn't extend to her personality, or her language.

"Do you really think I could ever forgive you, after what you did to me? Not to mention Tina?"

"Oh, come on." Lucas's voice was rising with exasperation. "Haven't you figured it out yet? Your sister's tape had nothing to do with me. It was Anton. He set her up. He set us both up, can't you see that?"

"No," said Honor stubbornly. "I can't."

Lucas had been the enemy for so long, the idea of casting him in any other role was almost frightening. She must hold on to her anger or she'd be lost.

"So what about leaking that story about me and Devon?" she challenged him. "You're gonna tell me that was Anton too, I suppose?"

"Yes," said Lucas calmly. "It was. Jesus. You'll be accusing me of starting that fucking fire next."

Honor narrowed her eyes. "Did you?"

"No!"

Not sure what to think anymore, she sank down onto the bed. All this arguing was beginning to tire her out.

"You know, for a smart woman you can be incredibly stupid at times," said Lucas. "Granted, I may have said some unpleasant things about you in the press when the Herrick first launched—"

"May have?" Honor looked at him, incredulous.

"Hey, you weren't whiter than white either, you know," Lucas reminded her. "So up yourself, so fucking self-righteous. My God! Anyone would think you had a divine right to the East Hampton market. You said some terrible things about me back then, too."

Honor simmered furiously but didn't say anything. She supposed he might be very, very slightly right on that one.

"I told you I'd keep my mouth shut about you and Carter, and I did. I wouldn't have put Lola through all that crap on purpose."

"Right. Because you cared so much about Lola," Honor shot back. "I could tell that the night I caught you in my hot tub with my sister's head between your legs. That guy, I thought, is *all* about his girlfriend. Talk about loyalty. You were quite the gentleman."

"You know what?" Lucas sprang angrily to his feet. "Believe what you want."

He was through trying to convince her. He'd actually come here to bury the hatchet. Because he'd thought about her almost every day since he'd left. Because when he heard she might be seriously hurt, he felt like someone had kicked him hard in the stomach and wouldn't stop. But there was no point offering an olive branch to Honor. All she wanted to do was beat him over the head with it.

"I have a hotel to build," he said, storming out.

"Oh yeah?" Honor yelled after his retreating back as he disappeared down the corridor. "Well, guess what? So do I! Asshole. You haven't heard the last of Palmers yet, you hear me?"

But Lucas was already gone.

Three thousand miles away in London, Sian sat at the table at Nobu, a fixed grin glued to her face, conjuring up mental images of the various tortures she would inflict on Lola later for suggest ing tonight's dinner

What in heaven's name had possessed her to come?

There were six of them at the table: herself and Paddy, who seemed to be having a grand old time swapping football stories with the boys and getting drunk on sake; Lola and Marti, who, as usual, spent most of dinner gazing gooily into one another's eyes like a couple of half-wits; and Ben and Bianca.

The dinner was intended as a thank-you to Ben for saving her ass after the whole Sir Jago Wells disaster. Once she'd finally plucked up the courage to call him, he'd gone to bat for her brilliantly, organizing a hotshot lawyer within an hour and calling her editor himself, threatening to take private legal action if the paper so much as thought about making Sian a scapegoat and denying responsibility.

Thanks to his strong-arm tactics, she'd gotten away with just a warning from the police. But Simon, her editor, didn't take kindly to being threatened. After three weeks of being given dead-end stories about Thames water or runaway guinea pigs,

Sian took the hint and resigned from the *News of the World*. She was now back to freelancing again and absolutely hating it.

"In a way, it must be liberating, though, isn't it?" asked Bianca, taking another sip of her vodka lime and soda, the models' drink of choice. "Being able to write what you want. Set your own agenda."

She had no makeup on, her hair in a ponytail, and was wearing a simple white tank top and jeans. But despite this every man and most of the women in the room were mesmerized by her, craning their necks to catch every word that fell from her goddess-like lips.

Sian tried hard not to be jealous, but she was only human.

"Kind of," she said. "But you never really set your own agenda. Editors always get to call the tune, whether you're freelance or in-house. That's the nature of the business."

"What are you on about, now?" said Paddy, wrapping a long, skinny arm around her shoulders and kissing her tenderly on the top of the head. "Not work, I hope. We're supposed to be having fun, babes. Remember?"

Ben, who couldn't help but notice the kiss and the affectionately proprietorial arm, felt a knot forming in his stomach. He really must pull himself together and grow up.

When Sian had called him from the police station that day, his elation was hard to describe. He'd thought about her so often since they'd parted and wanted to make amends for so long for his idiotic behavior in America. But, of course, he'd been too chicken-shit to make the first move. Then out of the blue came her lovely singsong voice on his direct line, not only calling him, but actually needing his help. It was the perfect chance to put things right. And he had. At least, he thought he had.

So why was it still so awkward between them? If she really had forgiven and forgotten, why did she still avoid his gaze whenever he looked at her? And why, despite immediately taking to Paddy, did Ben find himself suffering repeated, strong urges to strangle the guy with his own shoelaces every time he touched her?

"What you need is one really good story, to make your name," said Bianca to Sian. "Something all the papers'll be lining up to buy."

"Yeah," said Lola, picking up a sliver of raw scallop with her chopsticks and dropping it adoringly into Marti's mouth. "A scoop."

What I need is a boob job, thought Sian, looking miserably from Lola's ample cleavage to Bianca's, then down at her own flat-as-a-pancake chest. She'd made an effort tonight too, in a flowing red dress from Top Shop and the patent black leather boots that Paddy called her Fuck-Me Specials. She had been feeling quite pleased with her look until first Lola and then Bianca rocked up looking like Lindsay Lohan and Angelina Jolie, respectively. No wonder Ben kept giving her that weird look. He must be thanking his lucky stars he'd traded her in when he did. Talk about an upgrade.

"Speaking of good stories," said Marti, tearing himself away from Lola for a nanosecond, "did any of you guys read about the fire at Palmers hotel? I heard a rumor that Honor Palmer might have done it herself, for the insurance."

"No way," Lola shook her head vehemently. Though still not Honor's biggest fan, ever since she'd eavesdropped on the conversation with her father at Minty Burnstein's wedding, she'd stopped viewing her as the scarlet woman. Instead, she'd redirected her anger equally between her old man, for his rank hypocrisy, and Lucas, for his vindictiveness in going to the press about the affair. "Honor may be many things, but she's not an arsonist. That hotel was her life. There's no way she'd torch it. Not in a million years."

"Well, someone doesn't like her," said Marti. "It was almost certainly arson."

"Maybe it was Lucas," said Lola, only half joking, raising an eyebrow at Ben. "He hates her guts. And he's certainly vicious enough."

"I don't think so," said Ben mildly. He understood Lola's hostility—after the shoddy way Lucas had treated her, he could hardly blame her—but she was wrong about this. "He doesn't hate Honor. Not deep down. And he's got better things to do with his time than run around starting fires."

"Oh, of course it wasn't Lucas!" laughed Bianca, who didn't know his history with either Lola or Sian and had always gotten along well with him. "He's a sweetheart, isn't he, Ben? He wouldn't hurt a fly." The two other girls caught each other's eyes and giggled.

"If Lucas has a vendetta against anyone, it's Anton Tisch," said Ben, chasing a sliver of tuna around his plate with a chopstick he had no idea how to use. He hated Japanese food anyway. Bloody rip-off. "And may the force be with him, I say. That man has single-handedly blown a hole in my business the size of the Grand fucking Canyon."

"Aww," said Sian archly. "Down to your last five hundred mill, are you? Poor thing."

Ben blushed, and she instantly regretted being so flippant.

"Well I think Tisch is dreadful," said Bianca loyally. If she'd picked up on the awkwardness between Sian and Ben, she didn't show it. "He makes himself out to be this charitable, caring guy, but he treats women like shit. And what he did to poor Lucas was unforgivable."

This was a bridge too far for Lola.

"Poor Lucas? Are you kidding me? The guy entrapped a woman into making a porno in his hotel, then released the video on the Internet! Not to mention what he did to me and my family. I'm sorry, Bianca, but he deserved to get fired, and then some."

Realizing belatedly that she'd stepped on a land mine, Bianca shut up.

"Lucas has always said Anton was behind that tape," said Ben bravely. He knew that both Sian and Lola would happily order

Lucas's head on a plate if it were on the menu, but felt an obligation to try to stick up for a mate.

"Yeah, well. He would, wouldn't he?" said Lola. "Anyway, can we not talk about that asshole? I'm trying to enjoy my meal."

"Hear, hear," said Marti.

For a few minutes the conversation drifted on to other matters, chiefly fashion and whether Bianca could be prevailed upon to consider wearing one of Lola's designs to a big fashion-week party. But Sian's mind was still stuck on the previous topic.

"It is interesting about Tisch, though," she piped up after a while.

"What is?" said Paddy, not really listening. "Does anybody else think this black cod tastes like shit?"

"Well, he's this mystery figure, isn't he?" said Sian, ignoring him. "He has a public image, like Bianca said, and it's all good, even though people actually know a lot of the bad stuff."

"Like him not paying child support," said Bianca angrily.

"Exactly," said Sian. "Why hasn't that damaged him?"

"It has, to a point," said Ben. "But he's rich as Croesus and famously litigious. The media are afraid of him, I reckon. Plus he's so bloody secretive, I doubt his own mother really knows him. But I agree, there are plenty of things about him that don't add up."

"Like?" asked Sian.

"Well, like how the hell he keeps persuading my clients to leave Stellar, for a start. And why he went after Lucas the way he did. I mean, without opening up the whole Lucas debate again, what significance is a little guy like him to a global player like Anton? It's like a blue whale hunting down a lone pilot fish. It don't make sense."

"*Doesn't* make sense, darling, not don't," Bianca corrected him.

Sian tried not to feel pleased when Ben shot her a dirty look in return.

"Maybe that's your scoop, babes?" said Paddy to Sian. "Dig up some proper dirt on Anton Tisch and every paper in the land will want to hire you."

"I'll write you a check myself if you nail his slippery German arse," added Ben with feeling, "but it won't be easy."

"Thanks," said Sian sarcastically, "but I don't want your money."

Ben bit his lip. Note to self: must remember to rip out tongue when you get home.

"Shhhh now, Siany, don't upset him or he might not pay for dinner," said Paddy, in a stage whisper that made everyone laugh. "Heaven knows none of the rest of us can afford this place."

After dinner Ben and Bianca drove straight home, while Marti and Paddy decided to walk into Soho together and find a late-night bar, leaving Sian and Lola to share a cab.

"This feels just like the old days," said Lola, kicking off her Jimmy Choos and putting her bare feet up on the fold-out seat in front of her. "You and me, cabbing it home together. Before the boys came on the scene."

Sian smiled.

"You know, Ben really is such a nice guy," Lola went on blithely. "He hasn't changed a bit. Fuck knows what he sees in Lucas, but I guess he's entitled to one fatal flaw. Bianca's sweet too, don't you think?"

It hadn't occurred to her that, after three years, Sian might still be harboring any romantic feelings toward Ben, especially now that she seemed so settled and happy with Paddy.

"I guess," said Sian, without a shred of enthusiasm. "Yeah, she's OK."

In fact she wasn't thinking about Bianca, or even Ben. (Though later, in bed, she'd spend several hours torturing herself by picturing the two of them making love.) Right now, her head was full of Anton Tisch. There were too many things about him that didn't smell right. For the first time in months, she felt her journalistic curiosity stirring groggily back to life.

Tomorrow, she'd do a little digging. She wouldn't spend too long on it; maybe a couple of hours on Google. There was probably nothing in it, after all. But she didn't have much else going on. And who knew? Maybe it'd be worth a look.

CHAPTER TWENTY-FOUR

HE 2.7-BILLION-DOLLAR WYNN LAS VEGAS WAS THE MOST expensive hotel and casino ever built, anywhere in the world. Nine-foot floor-to-ceiling windows in each of its 2,700 bedrooms looked down over a spectacular view of the strip. Guests could choose between twenty different in-house restaurants, shop in the hotel's full-scale designer mall, or indulge themselves at the spa or on the world-famous golf course. They could even buy themselves a Ferrari to tour around town at the dealership downstairs.

Like all the big Vegas hotels—the monsters, as Trey Palmer used to call them—the Wynn aimed to provide a world so complete that once you stepped inside its glass doors, you'd never want to leave.

But Honor did want to leave. The hotel, the city, the conference. If only she'd remembered to pack her ruby slippers.

This January's conference at the Wynn was the IHA's biggest ever. Some sixteen hundred hoteliers from all over the globe were attending, as well as academics, journalists, investors, chefs, construction companies—anybody who was anybody in the hospitality industry.

Right now, as Honor was all too acutely aware, she was officially nobody in the hospitality industry. With the police still no nearer to solving the Palmers arson riddle—they'd interviewed

Danny Carlucci and his cronies numerous times but hadn't been able to pin so much as a parking ticket on any of them—her insurance money remained stuck in offshore permafrost. Realizing that it might be years, if ever, before she saw a penny of her claim, she'd decided to throw all her energies into plan B: finding a private investor to fund the rebuilding.

The first thing she did was recontact Baz Murray, the Australian magnate who'd been so keen on an alliance with Palmers a few months ago, before disaster struck. But having been a guest there when it caught fire and narrowly avoiding being burned to a crisp himself, he'd understandably lost his enthusiasm for the place.

Which was what brought her to Vegas, armed with high hopes and the PowerPoint presentation she'd spent her entire Christmas vacation putting together, which included a fabulous set of computer-generated architect's images of what the new Palmers might look like.

At first she'd wanted to recreate the place exactly as it had been, down to the last bent nail and crooked door frame. But she soon realized that idea owed more to nostalgia than good business sense. Tina was right about one thing. The fire had provided her with an opportunity. An opportunity to start again, without any of the structural problems that had had her eating through money like a Biblical plague of locusts, and without the ghosts of her father and grandfather watching her every move disapprovingly from the rafters.

The new Palmers would be Honor's creation—a chance to make her own unique mark on her family history. She would maintain the period charm, of course. The sense of history and tradition that had become synonymous with her family name. But shabby chic would make way for real chic; down-at-heel, faded gentility would be replaced by a more confident, assured, quietly monied ambience. There would be none of the vulgarity and bling of the Herrick. And none of the spa-like hippyishness of Luxe. Palmers would once again become a bastion of understated American wealth and privilege. No one knew how to create that better than Honor.

On the plane ride up to Vegas, she must have looked at her own presentation twenty times, awash with confidence and excitement. How could investors *not* buy in to her vision, backed as it was by a brand name far too enduring to be destroyed by any fire? Soon, everyone would be talking about the new Palmers and how it had risen like a phoenix from the ashes of the old.

But the minute she checked in at the Wynn, her chutzpah deserted her. The sheer scale of the place made Palmers seem like a dollhouse, one of a million little white clapboard nothings viewed from a passing plane, a mere dot on the landscape. And the first few days of the conference had done nothing to lessen her sense of insignificance. Almost all the seminars were big-picture stuff, with titles like Globalization, Branding, and Expansion or Debt Restructuring in the High-Interest Era. There was no opportunity for the sort of face-to-face schmoozing that Honor needed to do if she was going to bag herself a suitable backer. Even if there had been, she seemed to be the only person here with business on the brain. Everyone else, from the grandest CEOs to the lowliest MBA students, seemed to want to spend their free time at the roulette tables and/or checking out the local strip joints. Even the women. Star-spotting was the other leisure activity of choice, and the Wynn was like a physical incarnation of the pages of *People* magazine. Honor had no interest in celebrities and avoided casino floors much as she would the gates of hell, but even she had already clocked Ben Affleck and Nick Lachey wandering around in the lobby. She'd even shared an elevator with Lisa Marie Presley, much good it did her.

She couldn't remember feeling so out of place anywhere since the age of twelve, when her father had forcibly enrolled her in ballet school in Boston, hoping to knock the tomboy out of her. She'd spent every class sulking in the corner in jeans and

Doc Martens boots, while the other girls pirouetted around her in their fluffy pink tulle and organza.

Unfortunately, sulking wasn't an option now. Not if she wanted to rebuild Palmers. As much as she hated Vegas, she had to get involved.

Today was day four, and so far the only approach she'd had was from the odious Bruce Austin, a big cheese over at Hilton. He'd sidled up to her during the lunch break, wrapped an unwanted arm tightly around her waist, and suggested with a wink that she might like to give him her presentation "in private...if you know what I mean."

"Thanks, Bruce," she'd replied stiffly, trying not to stare at the way his beer belly was bursting through the buttons of his shirt at the bottom or the sweat patches the size of dinner plates under his arms. "But if it's all the same to you, I'd rather choke to death on my own vomit."

She was desperate, but she wasn't that desperate.

It was evening now, and all the seminars were over. Honor headed for the largest of the Wynn's numerous cocktail bars, sorely in need of a drink. Plonking herself down on an empty stool, she tried to blot out memories of the day. As if Bruce's clumsy come-on hadn't been bad enough, the afternoon lecture turned out to be a two-hour drone-a-thon from the owner of a Swiss group of motels. It was so boring she'd actually nodded off in the middle of it and slipped ignominiously from her seat onto the floor. She was woken not by the fall, but by the deafening laughter of the delegates around her. Not her finest hour.

"Scotch on the rocks, please. Better make it a double."

"You got it."

The barman, a wannabe actor with the same perfect features and toothpaste smile as all the other staff at the Wynn, jumped to her request. She had to admit, the service here was excellent. When the drink arrived she took a big, thirsty gulp, but regretted it when she felt the alcohol scorch her throat. Soon she was coughing and spluttering like a TB victim. At the very moment she expelled a mouthful of amber liquid through both nose and mouth across the polished top of the bar, like a whiskey sneeze, Petra Kamalski sauntered into the bar with a bunch of Tischen Group acolytes, all of them male.

Great. That was all she needed.

"Honor." Smiling evilly, Petra walked toward her. In a bright-red Chanel suit and matching ruby heels and lipstick, with her peroxide hair gleaming on the top of her head like a tight, white helmet, she reminded Honor of a toy soldier, so much so that she half expected her to click her heels together and salute at any moment, possibly shouting "*Sieg Heil!*"

"What a surprise to see you here. Reliving old times, are we?"

"Get lost, Petra," said Honor, wishing that her eyes and nose weren't still running like faucets from the burning liquor.

"Now, now," chided Petra. "There's no need to snap. You seem stressed, my dear." She was clearly enjoying herself. "Perhaps you'd like a cigarette? Although I'm sure Mr. Wynn would appreciate it if you remembered to put it out in an ashtray when you're done."

With an effort, Honor smiled thinly and let this not-so-veiled reference to the Palmers fire pass.

"Hey, boys," Petra called over her shoulder to her gaggle of groupies. "Can anyone offer Honor Palmer a light?"

Much sniggering broke out. One crony tossed Petra a lighter, which she made a great show of flicking open, waving the naked flame under Honor's nose.

"No? Not a smoker?"

Honor ignored her and turned back to what was left of her drink. But Petra wasn't done yet. Her hatred of Honor ran so deep she couldn't rest until she'd gotten her to rise to the bait.

"Come on," she said. "I was only kidding. You shouldn't be sitting here, drinking alone. Why don't you come and join us?"

"I'll pass," said Honor, coolly.

"Are you sure?" said Petra. "We're all headed back to my room. Apparently they have one of your sister's movies available upstairs, on the X channel. I've heard it's very good. Can't I tempt you?"

Her posse watched Honor for her reaction like a drooling pack of hyenas. But they were disappointed. Tightening her grip around her glass, she took a moment to compose herself. Much as she'd love to leap on Petra like a wildcat and scratch her malicious, ice-blue eyes out, she knew she was outnumbered and that a scene was exactly what the vicious cow was hoping for. Why give her the satisfaction?

"Sorry," she said, draining the rest of her drink and leaving a twenty-dollar bill on the bar. "Not for me. But hey, you kids have fun. Every dollar that movie makes goes to UNICEF. I'm sure they'll be grateful for your contribution."

Only once she had reached the sixteenth floor and the safe privacy of her own room did she allow herself to react. Shutting the door behind her, she turned the TV up and screamed at the top of her lungs for a full minute:

"Bitch!" she yelled. "Fucking Russian slut, whore, BIIIIITCH!"

Then, peeling off her sweater, white pants, and underwear, she jumped naked onto the oversize bed   and began pummeling her fists into the pillows in frustration.

Finally, exhausted but feeling a whole lot better, she slipped into the nude Calvin Klein camisole and panties that served as her nightwear, opened the minibar, and pulled out four miniature bottles of Jack Daniel's. It wasn't malt, but it'd have to do.

Stretching her legs and wiggling her toes luxuriantly in the thick pile of the carpet, she turned down the volume on the TV, flipped channels to *Seinfeld*, and began the long process of drinking herself into a stress-free oblivion.

Across town at McCarran International Airport, Lucas's evening was proving to be anything but stress free.

Thanks to a French air traffic controllers' strike that had brought Charles de Gaulle to a grinding halt, he was already three days late for the conference. But now it transpired that the stupid fuckers at Air France had sent his bags, including his laptop, to Milwaukee or Mogadishu, or some other place beginning with M that sure as hell wasn't Las Vegas. Between this and the thundering headache that had gripped his skull forty thousand feet over Colorado and clung on like an asylum-seeker to an undercarriage ever since, it was safe to say he was not in the warmest of moods.

He'd had a shit Christmas, working constantly and battling ever more bitterly with Connor, his so-called partner. The crux came when Lucas had drawn down on a bank loan to pay for an expensive plot of land in the Hamptons, about a mile farther along the beach from the Herrick, on which he intended to build his new hotel, tentatively—and more than a little grandly— entitled Luxe America.

Connor had hit the roof, showering Lucas with more expletives than Ozzy Osbourne with a stubbed toe: "Fucking Spic!" "No fucking restraint!" "Greedy, ignorant, paella-eating peasant!" It amused Lucas when people's racism and prejudices emerged in anger or drink, like so much scum floating up to the surface. In Connor's case, the tirade had provided him with the excuse he needed to break away and look for a new, better-capitalized partner. For all Connor's protestations about not wanting out of the business, they both knew they couldn't go on as they were.

His biggest problem was finding the time to hunt for such a person. Rushing around like a blue-assed fly between the East Hampton building site and his two existing hotels, he barely had time to sleep, never mind network.

Standing in the arrivals hall, searching in vain for a sign with his name on it among the many placards being waved around, he wished fervently he were back in Paris. He much preferred it there to Ibiza, where he'd installed a very competent local guy called Alessandro as interim manager. The city itself was astonishingly beautiful, of course. Lucas had never been much of a culture vulture, but Notre Dame blew him away, and the Louvre was a labyrinthine world of its own that he never seemed to tire of. But it was the women who really had him hooked. French girls had a natural sexual confidence that was so much more attractive than the brash sluttishness of their Ibizan counterparts, all tits, tan, and tassles. It was something like the difference between Honor and Tina Palmer. To this day, he regretted having had sex with the Ibiza Palmer sister and not the Parisienne. But he wasn't about to lose sleep over it. It was Honor's loss.

After fruitlessly scanning every single sign and finally running out of people to scream at, he filed a complaint with the airline and made his way, bagless, to the taxi line.

"The Wynn," he snapped bad-temperedly at the driver, then felt guilty when he saw a crucifix and rosary beads hanging from the rearview mirror, along with pictures of the man's kids. The poor guy was only trying to make a living, after all. He didn't deserve to have his head bitten off

He spent most of the forty-five-minute journey checking his BlackBerry for e-mails—thank God he'd kept *that* in his pocket and not in his bag, or he really would have been screwed. Only in the last few minutes of the ride did he put it away and focus his attention on the insane display of lights that signaled the approaching city.

Despite his exhaustion, he was horny. Sandrine, an exotic dancer from the Crazy Horse who he'd been dating on and off back in Paris, had sent him a couple of X-rated texts that had helped to push the whole lost-baggage drama to the back of his mind. One of the perks of his insanely hectic travel schedule was being able to have three totally separate, concurrent sex lives—in Ibiza, Paris, and the States—without fear of discovery, jealousy, or tedious female tantrums of the kind that Lucas previously had an uncanny knack of attracting. Emotional women bored him to tears. Happily, Sandrine wasn't remotely given to that sort of nonsense. He had no doubt she'd be screwing half the fourteenth district while he was away, a mental picture that, combined with her graphic texts and the prospect of the many libidinous pleasures awaiting him in Vegas, made his dick begin to harden in his pants.

He wondered how complicated it would be to get ahold of a hooker once he got to his room. Not very, he imagined. Although it wouldn't do his reputation much good if anyone at the IHA conference saw him paying for sex. To many people in the US, he remained indelibly connected to Tina Palmer, sex, drugs, and videotapes, an image he needed to change if he was going to make Luxe America a success. Being caught calling dial-a-vagina would be a major PR disaster.

When they got to the Wynn, he headed straight for check-in.

"You're in room sixteen O six, Mr. Ruiz," the blonde at the desk told him brightly, "on the sixteenth floor. Is there anything else I can help you with at this time?"

"Actually, yes," quipped Lucas. "You could you find my fucking bag for me. I think it might be in Maryland. Or Munich. One of the two."

The girl looked at him blankly. Like most Vegas girls, she had the body of a goddess and the face of an angel but the eyes of a retarded rabbit. Lucas suspected her IQ was somewhere around the level of a floret of broccoli. A small floret.

"Never mind," he said wearily. "I'll see myself up."

On his way to the elevators—there were banks of them; the place was so huge it felt like the Pentagon—he stuck his head into the cocktail bar off the lobby, but withdrew it again instantly when he caught sight of Petra. It was the first glimpse he'd had of her in the flesh since his Lausanne days, although he'd seen her picture countless times in the trade press. Somehow photographs failed to capture her aura of chilly, brittle malevolence that Lucas remembered so well. Her hairstyle and dress sense might have changed, but she hadn't.

Having said that, from the brief glimpse he'd caught of her, she seemed to be the worse for drink, which was distinctly out of character. Or perhaps in Petra's case, he should say the better for drink. The alcohol had evidently loosened her up a bit. Her red stilettos had been kicked off and at least one button of her crisply severe white blouse had popped open at the top. No doubt Connor would have found this sexy, thought Lucas with a shudder. He was welcome to her.

Desperate to get away, he slipped into the waiting elevator. All he wanted right now was some room service, his bed, and possibly a decent porno—if he could keep his eyes open long enough.

"Oooh! Turn *off*, you stupid thing!"

Honor, blind drunk, stabbed away at the TV remote with rising annoyance before realizing that it was actually her cell phone she was jabbing.

"Crap. Where is it?" she mumbled, staggering around the room looking under cushions and sweeping aside the minibar detritus that lay strewn across the floor: empty bottles, beer cans, and boxes of peanuts were everywhere. She'd even eaten the cheese-and-onion Pringles, which she hated, on the assumption that the more food she ingested to mop up the booze, the better.

Giving up, she ripped the TV cord out of the wall, sending sparks flying and a sharp, stabbing pain shooting up her arm before the entire room plunged into darkness.

"Fuuuuck," she whispered. "Goddamnit."

At least the TV was off. Ty from *Extreme Makeover* had really been starting to get on her nerves. Why did he have to shout the whole time? Opening the minibar fridge provided a sliver of light, enough to see that she'd somehow managed to get through an entire tray full of ice and consequently had none left for the two remaining miniature bottles of vodka. Remembering vaguely that she'd seen a sign saying "ice" near the elevators, she got unsteadily to her feet and padded out into the corridor.

The lights were off out here too. She must have shorted the entire floor—oops! Only the dim glow from the emergency floor lighting enabled her to get her bearings. On the plus side this meant she could run to the ice machine under cover of semidarkness, fill up her glass, and get back to her room without anybody noticing she'd forgotten to put a robe on over her underwear. Double oops!

Finding the ice machine was the easy part. Making her way back to her room—what number was it again?—without spilling the precious contents of her crystal tumbler proved to be a lot tougher.

Finally swaying to a halt outside her door, she reached for the key-card in her pocket. Except there wasn't any pocket. Or any key-card.

"Shit." She stared blankly at the impassive wooden door, its key slot blinking red as if taunting her. Seconds later, she let out a wail of horror as the lights came back on. All of a sudden, the full force of her predicament was brought home to her: she was locked out of her room, as good as naked, standing in a public corridor in glaringly unflattering platinum-bright light.

Where the fuck did she go from here?

"Can I help you?"

Honor froze. The voice came from behind her, but she didn't dare to look.

It couldn't be him. Could it?

"Forgot our key, did we?"

Lucas tried not to laugh, but it was impossible. She was just standing there, stock-still, like a two-year-old playing hide-and-seek who thinks that by not moving and covering her own eyes, she can somehow make herself invisible. It was awfully cute.

The last time he'd seen her was in the hospital, when he'd brought her flowers to try to make peace and she'd thrown them back in his face. Then, the weeks of bed rest and starchy food had given her body a certain softness at the edges. But it was all gone now. Her figure was leaner than ever—too lean, actually. She couldn't weigh more than a hundred pounds, and five pounds of that was her newly long hair. Even so, in that truly minuscule underwear, her tiny, boyish body was displayed to highly alluring effect.

And what a treat to have caught her in such a humiliating, compromising position! For once in her life, Little Miss Prim and Proper was going to have to be polite to him. In fact, if she wanted his help, she was going to have to do more than that. She was going to have to grovel.

Apparently, however, she didn't want his help.

"Go away." Turning around reluctantly, she glared at him as if he were somehow responsible for her predicament. "I'm fine."

Her nude camisole was sheer enough for him to make out the dark berries of her nipples beneath the fabric. It stopped about an inch above her G-string panties, allowing the faintest of glimpses of flat, toned belly, which was almost more tantalizing than the barely covered triangle of pubic hair below. But it was the brazen aggression in her eyes that really did it for him. How he longed to screw all that poor-little-rich-girl rage right out of her.

"Oh, well, if you're fine," he shrugged, feigning a nonchalance he knew would drive her crazy. "I'll go then. I was going to suggest you come to my room to borrow a robe. But if you'd rather go down to the front desk on your own...like that..."

He gave her the sort of look a hungry lion gives a gazelle. Honor blushed, and belatedly tried to cover her breasts with her hands.

"Be my guest."

He started to walk away.

Honor was torn. Damn him! Why couldn't it have been someone else, anyone else, who came to her aid?

The way he'd looked at her just now had sent her pulse racing—something she put down to shock, possibly combined with extreme drunkenness. It may have felt like desire. But it definitely wasn't. It couldn't be, because she was absolutely, categorically not attracted to Lucas. God no. She'd rather sleep with George Bush.

On the other hand, a robe would seriously come in handy right now. The alternative—going down to the lobby in her underwear—would mean public humiliation on a scale that would dwarf today's earlier litany of indignities. She couldn't do it.

"Wait!" she shouted after Lucas's retreating back. Slowly, infinitely slowly, he turned around.

"Yes?"

You bastard, thought Honor. You're loving every minute of this.

"I will borrow your robe," she mumbled, gracelessly.

"Oh, you will, will you?" said Lucas. "Well I'm not so sure anymore. I mean, you haven't asked very nicely. What's the magic word?"

Honor gritted her teeth. "I hate you," she muttered murderously.

"Sorry?" said Lucas. "I didn't quite catch that."

"*Please*," said Honor. "OK? *Please. Please* may I borrow your robe?"

"Of course you may." Lucas's grin broadened. "See? That wasn't so hard, was it?"

The corridors at the Wynn were longer than most East Hampton streets, and it seemed to take an age before they reached Lucas's room, especially as he insisted on ambling along deliberately slowly, prolonging her agony. But at last they got there. As soon as he slipped his card in the door, Honor darted inside like a fish, making straight for the bathroom. She emerged moments later wrapped in an enormous toweling robe, her hands lost somewhere inside the cavernous sleeves so that only her feet and tiny, doll-like head were visible.

Lucas burst out laughing. "Help me, Obi-Wan Kenobi! You're my only hope!"

"Ha-ha," said Honor mirthlessly. She started for the door, but he stepped in front of her, barring her way.

"What do you think you're doing?" She was angry, but for some reason her voice emerged all high-pitched and strangled. Reaching over her head, Lucas pulled the bathroom door shut behind her, pinning her between it and his body.

"I'm doing exactly what you want me to," he said. And before she could respond, he'd slipped a hand inside her robe and started caressing the bare skin on her shoulder.

For a split second Honor closed her eyes as an erotic charge shot through her body. Then she stiffened.

"Fuck off!" she said, pushing him away. "You make me sick. You think you can...you can..." Fuck. Why had she drunk so much? She longed to come out with some witheringly acerbic put-down, but all she could do was babble like a cretin. "Oh, just fuck off, all right?"

"No," he said, pulling her close again. "It's not all right. Not until you listen."

"And why should I listen to you?" said Honor, not bothering to try to push him off again, as it clearly wasn't going to work and the effort was making her feel dizzy. "Give me one good reason."

"Because," said Lucas, "you're wrong about me. You always have been, since that first day on the beach."

"You reckon?" Honor's cat's eyes narrowed distrustfully. She wished the smell of his aftershave weren't quite so distracting.

"I had nothing to do with your sister's tape," said Lucas, looking her right in the eye. "And it wasn't me who leaked your affair to the papers. I swear to you, Honor, on my mother's life. I didn't do it."

Once again she felt torn. She didn't know what to believe. He looked like he was telling the truth; he really did. But then, consummate liars knew how to pull off that trick, right?

"It was Anton," said Lucas, his voice dropping to the low, husky whisper that seemed to make every woman but Honor melt. "Why can't you believe that? What are you so scared of? Admitting you were wrong?"

"Scared?" Honor bridled defensively. "I'm not scared."

But in that moment, she realized that she was. Horribly scared. Scared of forgiving him. Scared that if she stopped hating him, even for a moment, she might feel something else. Something beyond her control.

"Let's just say for a minute that you're right—that it was Anton," she said. The fear seemed to be helping sober her up. "That still doesn't let you off the hook. You introduced Tina to that guy."

"I did," said Lucas. "But only because Anton told me to. Look, he told me to do a lot of stuff that I regret now, OK? But, you know, he was my boss. I didn't realize he had this whole hidden agenda."

"Hmm." Honor looked up at him, willing her anger not to desert her. "So do you always jump like a monkey when the organ grinder says jump?"

"I don't know," said Lucas. Pushing his knee forward between Honor's legs, he brought his face so close to hers she could feel the heat of his breath on her cheeks. "Do you always lash out at men when you want them?"

"I don't want you…" she stammered. But he stopped her with a kiss so passionate she could barely breathe, let alone speak. Closing her eyes, she gave in to the sensation, allowing her senses at last to overwhelm her. Before she knew it she was kissing him back, tentatively at first but then hungrily, her desire escalating in response to his.

Staggering toward the bed, kissing and grabbing and scratching at each other like two wild animals, they finally collapsed on top of it. Honor's robe was already on the floor, and Lucas had somehow managed to scramble out of his jeans as he wrestled her beneath him.

"I meant what I said," Honor panted, gasping as he ripped off her camisole, tearing the thin silk as his hands grasped hungrily for her breasts. "I still hate you. You're arrogant...you're..." It was hard to get the words out while being manhandled by someone with a body weight roughly three times your own. "You're sexist. And boorish. And...rude."

"Yeah, well, I hate you too," growled Lucas, struggling out of his boxer shorts and nudging her legs wider with his knees. "You're a snob. You're horribly spoiled..." He kissed her again, delighted and amazed by the strength of her response and the way her tongue darted into his mouth like a slippery bullet.

"Pushy American bitch," he said, pinning her arms down on the mattress with all his weight so she was spread like a butterfly on a pin-board. "Stop trying to take the lead."

Looking down, Honor saw his ramrod-straight erection jutting up toward her belly like a fence post and felt a curious mixture of excitement and dread. Devon had been big, but not that big, and obviously Lucas was far more sexually experienced than she was. He had her arms pinned, so she had to draw one leg up in order to touch his dick with her foot, gently rubbing up and down the shaft with the smooth skin of her instep. Lucas closed his eyes and moaned, moving one hand down to guide himself inside her. But Honor was too quick for him. With a boldness that surprised her as much as it did him, she seized her chance, wriggling free and flipping herself around like a gymnast so that she was on top of him, and their positions were reversed. At least this way she would have some control over how deep he went.

Lucas groaned as she slipped his cock inside her. Part of him wanted to pull away and teach her who was boss. But the other part felt so fucking fantastic, as her tight muscles clenched and released him in a perfect, slowly accelerating rhythm, wild horses couldn't have made him move. Closing his eyes, he reached up and ran his hands down her bare back, letting his fingers curl around the nape of her neck and run over each of her ribs in turn.

"You're too thin," he said.

Honor opened her eyes for a moment and looked at him. She was about to tell him she didn't need his approval of her weight, or anything, but to her surprise she saw that there was genuine concern in his eyes. So she decided to be honest instead.

"I know. It's stress," she said, shrugging. "When it's bad, I can't eat." For the next two hours, they fucked like a pair of hormonally crazed weasels. Now that he'd finally gotten her into bed, Lucas realized just how much he'd been wanting her, and for how long. Sexually, she was a revelation, wilder than even he had imagined, and far more skillful in bed than her blow-up-doll sister. Her physical fitness and stamina were quite awesome. Honor's body might look fragile, but making love to her, Lucas discovered it was anything but. She was pure muscle. And as for her flexibility...not even the rhythmic gymnast he'd dated in Ibiza last summer could compare. The woman had rubber bones.

For Honor, the experience was equally powerful, but in different ways. Lucas had broken her defenses and allowed years of sexual and emotional frustration to come tumbling out. Yes, he was a good lover—he ought to be, after all the practice he'd had—but it wasn't just that. Tonight was the first time Honor had had sex since Devon. It had reached the point where she'd gone without it for so long she'd convinced herself that she didn't need it. That she was happy to let Palmers be her life, lover, family, everything. But Lucas's touch had changed all that. Like an H-bomb exploding through her body, blasting away all the fear and the pain and the loneliness, he'd reduced her to her most primitive, animal self. The delight she felt with him inside her was indescribable.

At last they collapsed side by side on the sheets like two sweat-soaked marathon runners.

"If I ask you something," said Honor, staring at the ceiling, once she'd regained enough breath to speak, "do you promise to give me a truthful answer?"

Turning onto his side, Lucas propped himself up on an elbow and looked at her. She looked like she'd been swimming. Her hair glistened with sweat like dewy grass, and all her makeup was smudged off. Above anything else, she looked incredibly young. He didn't think he'd ever wanted another human being so much.

"Of course," he whispered seriously. "I'll never lie to you."

"Am I better in bed than Tina?"

The question was so unexpected, Lucas burst out laughing.

"Sorry," he said, seeing Honor looking crestfallen. "I'm sorry. I've just never heard you sound so insecure before." Her face fell further, and he quickly added: "Of course. Of course you're better. Jesus, Honor, your sister...she was...it was nothing."

"Nothing, sexually? Or nothing..."

"Nothing, nothing. Nothing sexually, nothing emotionally. Nothing to me," he said fervently. "Nothing like you."

Apparently satisfied, Honor fell silent.

"So, can I ask *you* something?" said Lucas eventually.

"Oh, yeah, you were great too," Honor murmured, half asleep already. "Much better than Devon and everything."

Lucas laughed. "I know *that*," he said, without a hint of irony.

"Oh, you do, do you?" said Honor, sitting up. She'd forgotten just how infuriatingly arrogant he could be. "So what's your question, then?"

"Do you believe me? About Anton, and all the shit that happened that summer?"

Honor nodded slowly. "I think I believed you at the hospital," she admitted. "I thought about what you said a lot, afterward, and it all made sense. I just couldn't process it then. It was too soon, after the fire, losing Palmers." She shook her head, fighting back tears. "It was like I was at emotional ground zero. I didn't want to have to think about anything else. I didn't have the energy."

"I understand," said Lucas softly. "Believe me. I do."

Nestling against each other in the silk sheets like two sleepy, satisfied cats in the sun, they reveled in each other's warmth and the luxury of their surroundings.

"Isn't it great, being in someone else's hotel for a change?" said Lucas, dialing room service and ordering up a bottle of vintage champagne and a large bowl of french fries for Honor. "If I owned this place I'd be stressing about every crack in the ceiling right now."

"Me too!" laughed Honor. "I thought I was the only person neurotic enough to do that sort of thing."

"God, no. I don't think anyone in this business can switch off," said Lucas. "Not if they're any good at it anyway."

The fries arrived, as hot and salty and greasy as Lucas could have wished for, and he was encouraged to see Honor tucking into them with undisguised relish, in between gulps of ice-cold champagne.

"Sorry," she mumbled, her mouth full, blushing as she wiped away a trickle of vegetable oil with the back of her hand. "I guess I worked up an appetite."

"Good." Grinning, Lucas slid beneath the covers like a torpedo and began kissing her between her thighs, gently parting her pubic hair with his fingers. "Let's get you a bit hungrier, and then we can order more."

Honor gasped and giggled, her legs spontaneously opening wider as his tongue darted across her clitoris. She came embarrassingly quickly.

"Hey. What's wrong?" Emerging from beneath the sheets, Lucas was horrified to see she was crying.

"Nothing," she sobbed. "That was just…so nice."

Pulling her against him, Lucas stroked her long, tangled mane of hair as she lay on his chest. "It was nice for me too," he said, gruffly. "Better than nice. Christ, I've wanted you for so long." Slowly, as the long hours of the night rolled by, he told her about everything he'd been through since leaving the Herrick: his long, desperate job search in London; the street brawl with his old boss in Ibiza that marked the low point for his battered self-esteem; the chance meeting with Connor Armstrong that changed his fortunes.

"Every day, when I walk into my hotel in Paris, or onto the new site in East Hampton, I pinch myself. I still can't believe this is my life."

"Lucky you," said Honor bitterly. "Every time I walk onto that charred patch of earth that used to be Palmers, I pinch myself too. I can't believe this is my life. But it is."

Lucas kissed the top of her head tenderly. "I'm so sorry."

"Hey, I don't want your pity, OK?" said Honor, suddenly tense again. He could feel the latticework of muscles in her back and shoulders tightening up, one after the other, like a subcutaneous Mexican wave.

"Palmers isn't done yet, whatever people might think. I'm gonna rebuild."

Lucas didn't say anything, scared of putting his foot in it again. Privately he thought she hadn't a snowball's chance in hell of convincing anyone to fund her little pipe dream. Not with the Herrick riding high less than two blocks away and now his new Luxe hot on its heels. Being a boutique, and modest in scale, he hoped to have the place built and open within a year, assuming he found a new, supportive partner.

"How are things with you and Petra?" he said, steering the conversation back to their mutual enemies.

Honor rolled her eyes. "Dreadful. That bitch has been out to get me from day one," she said, wriggling around in an effort to get comfortable in the heat of Lucas's arms. "She's even worse than you were."

"Thanks a lot," said Lucas.

He told her about his own long-running feud with Petra and his theory that Anton hired her as a deliberate, final slap in the face to him.

"If I were you, I'd have fought back," said Honor. "Set the record straight in the media about all this stuff. Or, failing that, gone over to the bastard's house with a baseball bat."

"I've thought about it," said Lucas, "believe me. In the early days I thought of little else. But then I realized: there's no better revenge than success. Anton wanted to crush me, and he failed. Now I'm an owner, just like him. And I'm setting up shop right in his backyard. If I know the man at all, that's causing him more pain right now than a baseball bat ever could. I'll bet Petra's choking on her vodka too." He chuckled quietly. "Come to think of it, maybe she only drinks blood?"

He looked across at Honor to check whether she was laughing and was annoyed to see that she'd fallen asleep. But he couldn't stay angry for long. Curled up in the fetal position with her back toward him, her truculent, hawk-like features softened in repose, hair falling across her apple breasts like Eve, she was already murmuring in her dreams. She looked so innocent and childlike, he wished he had a camera handy to capture the image so he could tease her with it in the morning.

Watching her sleep beside him, her breathing becoming deeper and slower with each passing second, he felt stupidly, deliriously happy. For a moment, he let himself indulge in a little White Knight fantasy. He imagined himself somehow finding her the backer she needed and helping her to rebuild her beloved Palmers. He pictured her slavishly grateful to him for saving her ass, offering to do "anything, anything at all" to thank him, while Petra struggled on foot down the Long Island Expressway's breakdown lane, dragging her suitcases behind her like a hobo.

Laughing at his own hubris, he pulled the sheet up over Honor and himself and flicked off the bedside lamp. Life, unfortunately, rarely turned out like one's fantasies. But one thing he intended to make sure of: this time next year, Luxe America would be a reality.

As for helping Honor, he'd just have to see what came up.

——————— ———————

The first thing Honor was aware of when she woke was the glaring, blinding sunlight pouring in through the floor-to-ceiling windows. The second was the fact that she was not in her own bed. And the third was that someone seemed to be busy sawing through her skull with a hacksaw.

Groaning, she sat up, shielding her eyes from the light and trying to get her bearings. The next thing she knew, Lucas, fresh from the shower and wearing only a blue towel wrapped toga-style around his snake hips, was looming over her like a gladiator.

"Good morning," he said brightly, chuckling at her all-too-evident hangover. "Feeling a little the worse for wear, are we, darling?"

Immediately, Honor felt her hackles rising. One night together did not make her his darling. Her brain was still foggy with sleep, but she knew she must have let her guard down horribly, a thought that left her gripped by a stomach-churning fear. But before she could say anything, Lucas had kissed her on the top of her head (patronizing!) and launched into a monologue about his own plans for the day.

"As soon as I've called the lost baggage morons at the airport, I need to get going," he said, dropping his towel without a hint of embarrassment while he rummaged around in his bag from a clothing store for underwear and a shirt. "I have a meeting with a possible new partner at one over at the Venetian. Oh, that reminds me. Be an angel and call down to housekeeping, would you? Ask them to bring my blue suit up. They must have pressed it by now."

Honor's mouth opened and closed furiously, but no words came out. Who did he think she was? His little Geisha?

Slowly, through the molasses-thick fog of her brain, the events of last night began falling into place. She felt sick. The sex had been amazing, no doubt about that. She still felt sore between her legs, and every muscle in her body ached after her energetic performance. Even now, with her head throbbing and stomach churning like a washing machine on spin, the memory of his touch excited her to her a ridiculous degree.

But that was the problem. OK, so he fucked like Mick Jagger. And OK, so he hadn't betrayed her and Tina, like she thought. But he was still Lucas. Still one of the most arrogant, chauvinist pigs to walk the planet. If not the most arrogant. Still the guy who, after one fuck, expected her to run wifely errands for him. Who assumed automatically that his stupid meetings were more important than hers.

Watching him pull his Calvins on over his perfect tennis-player's ass, she began to justify her anger in her own mind: he'd taken advantage of her in a vulnerable moment. She'd been drunk out of her head. She didn't know what she was doing.

But the real truth was, she was frightened. She'd opened up to Lucas last night, both literally and metaphorically, in a way she'd never done before with any man, not even Devon. She'd allowed him to see her vulnerability, her weakness, her need. That gave him power over her. Power she was now desperate to claw back.

"Get your own suit," she snapped, wrapping the sheet around her body and heading for the shower. "I'm busy too, you know."

Still giddy with the rapture of last night, Lucas misjudged her mood completely. Running after her, he grabbed the corner of the sheet and whipped it off.

"Call housekeeping," he grinned. "Now. Before I put you over my knee." Somehow she looked even more gorgeous this morning, all crumpled and grumpy and still warm from bed. He made a clumsy lunge for her breasts and was taken aback when she first ducked, then lashed out at him like a rattlesnake, only narrowly missing landing a karate chop right on his balls.

"Whoa!" Backing away, he frowned, confused. "What's the matter?"

"What's the matter?" said Honor. "Are you kidding me? Get your own fucking suit! I have meetings of my own today which, thanks to you, I'm now late for. I was supposed to be having breakfast with Fred Gillespie at nine."

Gillespie had been a big name in hotels in San Francisco and Seattle back in the sixties, around the time Trey took over at Palmers, and was still respected. He was something of an unofficial godfather to Honor. She hoped he might be interested in funding her rebuild, or at least loaning her some seed capital until the insurance money came through, so she could make a start.

"What time is it, anyway?" she snapped.

"Eleven," said Lucas sulkily.

"Why didn't you wake me?"

"Because I didn't know you had a meeting, did I?" he yelled. "Jesus, Honor. I'm not psychic."

This was just great. Fucking American women and their fucking career bullshit. You never knew where you stood from one day to the next. Last night Honor had practically begged him to be the big, strong, macho man, and if her orgasms were anything to go by, she'd loved every minute of it. But this morning he seemed to have woken up with Germaine fucking Greer.

Well if she wanted to pick a fight, he knew how to play that game.

"I can't believe you're seriously comparing sitting around drinking tea with some old Harvard club friend of your father's with my investor meeting," he said.

"Fred's a serious investor," Honor insisted.

"In what?" snapped Lucas. "Scorched earth? You don't have a hotel for him to invest in, Honor. Wake up! Palmers is gone."

For a moment she looked so wounded he regretted losing his temper.

"Look, I didn't mean that, OK?" He took a step toward her.

"Oh, sure you did," said Honor, storming into the bathroom and slamming and locking the door behind her.

"Honor." He banged on the door, gently at first, but when she didn't respond his knocks became louder and more irritated. "Stop being such a spoiled child. I'm sorry if I hurt your feelings. I shouldn't have. But you have to face reality. Palmers is gone. I wish that weren't the case, but getting angry about it doesn't change the facts. And I do have a global business to run. Now, if that makes you jealous—"

"Jealous?" She took the bait. The door flew open. "You think I'm jealous? Of you?"

Pushing past him, she grabbed her torn underwear from the bed and yanked it back on. Then, picking up the robe from the floor, she pulled it tightly around her tiny frame. Fuck the shower. She'd have one in her own room.

"Not in this lifetime, sweetheart," she snarled. "*Global business* indeed! You have two hotels, Lucas. Two. And neither one of them can hold a candle to mine."

Lucas snorted derisively. "Rather an unfortunate turn of phrase, don't you think? Seeing as someone *did* hold a candle to yours?"

Honor walked to the door. "Last night was a mistake."

"At last," said Lucas. "Something we agree on."

Down at reception, the desk clerk was very understanding about Honor's lost key, producing a new one in seconds and insisting on sending a bellboy up with her to make sure it worked properly. At last, alone in her room, she sat down on the bed and tried to banish the barrage of negative thoughts bombarding her brain.

It was odd. She'd done everything in her power this morning to push Lucas away. And yet part of her was crushed when he'd agreed so readily that their sleeping together was a mistake.

Down the hall, lying on his bed, Lucas wondered how it was possible to want to strangle someone and make love to them at the same time.

But neither of them put their thoughts into words. Instead, true to form, they got ready for their respective days ahead and pretended that they didn't care.

CHAPTER TWENTY-FIVE

SIAN WALKED ALONG THE STRAND, CLAPPING HER GLOVED hands together against the bitter, late-January cold.

"Why are you doing this?" she asked herself out loud, her breath shooting out in little warm clouds with each word. "You've lost your mind, girl. You've totally lost your mind."

Anyone watching her mumble as she weaved through the choking traffic would probably have agreed with this assessment of her mental health, although perhaps for different reasons. Sian's concern stemmed not from the fact that she was talking to herself, but from the fact that she was on her way to Ben's office. And that she was going there to ask for money.

He didn't know she was coming, which sort of made it both better and worse. Better, because it had spared her the impossible task of trying to explain everything on the phone beforehand (tricky, when every time she started dialing his number she had to rush to the bathroom to throw up with nerves). But worse, because it opened up the shameful possibility of him being too busy to see her.

She tried to encourage herself that he was the one who'd suggested she look into Anton Tisch in the first place. At least, she thought it was his suggestion—she'd drunk so much at that excruciating triple-date dinner she could barely remember her own name the next morning, so she couldn't be sure—and she hadn't seen or heard from Ben since.

But what if it was just a throwaway remark about Tisch? Something he'd said to be polite and show an interest in what she did for a living? Sian still tended to think of him as the tall, awkward, British beach bum who had fallen through Palmers' fence to ask her out—they used to joke that he'd literally fallen at her feet. But in reality, he had never been that guy. He was a seriously rich, successful businessman. An important man. Naturally he had better things to do than run around the globe helping his summer romances follow up leads for some dumb story they were working on.

Except, she told herself, tilting her head down as the wind changed direction and began slicing into her cheeks like a razor, it wasn't a dumb story. It had the makings of a great story. The kind of story that really *could* make her a big name in investigative journalism, if she wasn't forced to let the trail go cold now through lack of funds and support.

She did have other options. She could go to one of the papers with what she had so far. But that would mean handing over control—and credit—to some megalomaniac news desk editor, and she'd rather stick pins in her eyes than do that. Besides, she thought, clutching the worryingly thin manila envelope that represented her "evidence" more tightly, she really didn't have that much on paper—yet.

Anton Tisch, she was rapidly discovering, was a master at subterfuge. No matter which avenue of inquiry she tried to pursue: his love life, business life, even his childhood, she was met with roadblock after roadblock. And all along the way were littered the dead careers of reporters who'd trodden the path before her, whose editors had been either bribed or threatened into squashing their stories.

Whatever his secret—or secrets—Anton Tisch had gone to inordinate lengths to hide them. Which of course only piqued Sian's interest all the more.

Passing John Adam Street, she could see the top two floors of the impressive Adelphi building, where Tisch had his offices, jutting proudly into the skyline. She wondered if he was inside right now. The thought made her shiver even more violently than the cold, with the same mixture of excitement and fear that had propelled her through the last few weeks of late nights and dead ends on nothing but adrenaline and caffeine.

Ben's offices were another mile's walk at least, along the river toward the City, London's ancient financial district. Looking around in vain for a taxi with its light on, Sian stepped up her pace and began to jog. The sooner she got there, the sooner she'd get it over with. And at least the exercise would warm her up.

———————   ———————

Up in his third-floor office on King William Street, Ben flipped through the pink pages of the *FT* without much interest. The FTSE and Nasdaq were both up. But the dollar was having its third bad month in a row against the Euro, which would certainly mean more redemptions from Stellar investors.

Bollocks to the lot of them.

Outside the sky was a dull silver, and the few trees in the City's green spaces looked spartan and spindly, waving their leafless limbs in the biting winter wind, as though sending a distress signal. Everyone's spirits seemed to fall on a day like today, and Ben was no exception. Christmas and New Year's were over. All that stretched ahead were endless dreary weeks of work and cold, dark, miserable afternoons. Oh, and wedding planning. Even bloody worse.

"For God's sake, cheer up. You could curdle milk with that face." Tammy, who'd returned from a winter break in Barbados with a bright-orange tan and her blonde hair streaked platinum, brought him his mail. "You've only been engaged five minutes," she added helpfully. "Aren't you supposed to still be in your honeymoon phase?"

"I am," said Ben, moodily. "Can't you tell?"

Tammy frowned but said nothing.

"I know you women think weddings are the answer to everything. But just 'cause I'm getting married doesn't mean I have to like the sodding weather. Or the fact the dollar's going down the shitter."

He'd finally given in to the inevitable and proposed to Bianca on Christmas Day, having run out of reasons not to. For a couple of days, he actually felt quite good about it. She was so happy when the ring fell out of her brightly wrapped Christmas cracker—a favorite tradition of Ben's—at lunch, she burst into tears on the spot and didn't stop crying until dinner. It made him realize how much she really did love him, and he thought what an idiot he'd been to have prevaricated for so long.

But soon his doubts came creeping back, invading his peace of mind like a guilty lover stealing back into the marriage bed after dark. Bianca was already going on about having a glitzy engagement bash and getting *Tatler* to cover the wedding. It so wasn't his thing. But when he'd tried to explain that to her it all came out pear-shaped and she got furious with him, accusing him of having second thoughts.

It didn't help that his mum and sisters were totally on Bianca's side about everything. Within days of the engagement, they'd filled the Canvey Island house with wedding magazines and started banging on endlessly about dresses and flowers and Chantilly fucking lace. Bianca was in seventh heaven. But the happier everyone else got, the more Ben felt the pressure piling onto his shoulders. He wished he could feel like they did, all giddy and excited. But he couldn't. He just couldn't.

Tam left him leafing through his mail. Half an hour later he was deep in the legal language of an offering memorandum when she barged into his office again, looking even more orange and furious than before. "You need to come to reception," she announced.

"Not now, Tam, all right?" he said. "I'm busy. Can't you deal with it?"

"If I could deal with it," said Tammy, in a martyred, God-give-me-strength voice, "I wouldn't be standing here, would I?"

Wearily, Ben put the memo down. "What's the matter then?"

"A mad cow has chained herself to the settee in the lobby," said Tammy.

"I'm sorry. A *what*?"

"A girl. A very rude girl turned up without an appointment demanding to see you," Tam explained. "She wouldn't tell me what it was about, so I told her to sling her hook. She then padlocked herself to the settee."

"Are you serious?" Ben laughed.

"Do I look like I'm joking?" asked Tammy, who didn't. "I've called security, but every time one of them comes near her she starts screaming the bloody place down, saying she'll only talk to you. She's a complete nutcase. She'll be singing 'We Shall Overcome' in a minute I 'spect. It can't be good for business."

"I see," said Ben, still smiling. And here he'd been thinking today was going to be dull as ditchwater. "Well I'd better come and have a look then, hadn't I?"

Coming down the grand, sweeping staircase into reception, he could see a small crowd of staff and visitors, who effectively obscured his view of the girl.

Stellar's back offices were dull and functional, but the public areas were lavish, designed to scream wealth and permanence to potential investors. With this in mind, the lobby boasted a polished marble floor, overhung by a glittering antique chandelier, and the artfully placed furnishings were all of the ornate, eighteenth-century French variety. One of these, a walnut sofa with intricately coiled arms, was the focus of the current drama.

"Excuse me." Ben cut a swath through his gawking staff and walked up to the girl. She was bent double, apparently securing the chain, so all he could see was the top of her dark head and a pair of white fluffy snow boots.

"I'm Ben Slater," he said. "Can I help you?"

Sian looked up and smiled at him ruefully. "Yeah," she said, blushing. "You can help me undo this padlock. The key just snapped in half."

Twenty minutes later, once Jimmy the handyman had arrived with a hacksaw and a mutinously grumbling Tammy had been dispatched to make some tea, the two of them were alone in Ben's office.

"I'm sorry for the dramatic entrance," said Sian, gnawing nervously at her fingernails.

"Yeeeees," said Ben. "I did wonder what that was all about."

"The chain was a last resort. But that bizarrely colored woman wasn't going to let me see you."

"You carry a chain around with you?"

"Only for emergencies," said Sian, as if that explained everything.

"What is that woman anyway? Half human, half citrus fruit?"

"Tammy's all right," he said. "She was trying to protect me. I think she thought you were nuts."

Sian blushed. "I guess I can see why."

She started to peel off layer after layer of coats and scarves and sweaters, dumping them all unceremoniously on the floor at her feet. When she finally got down to her pink skinny-rib sweater and jeans, her cheeks were flushed from heat and embarrassment, and her hair made her look as if she'd just been electrocuted. But to him she looked absolutely perfect.

"So, what's this all about?" he asked, genuinely curious. "I'm assuming it's something pretty important for you to go all suffragette on me. Rather than try something more traditional. Like, ooh, I don't know, picking up the phone."

"It is," said Sian. "Important, I mean. And maybe I should have called you first. But it's kind of hard to explain. I wanted to do it in person."

Handing him her manila folder, she waited for him to leaf through its contents.

"I don't understand," he said eventually, pulling out one of many similar photographs of seminaked teenage girls. "Who are these kids?"

"They're hookers," said Sian. "But you're right, they *are* kids. Every one of these girls is underage. And look what else they have in common."

She pointed out a piece of paper with a bunch of names on it, six of which had been highlighted in bright-green pen. The letterhead at the top of the page said *Children of Hope Care Home, Southwark.*

"They were all in care?" said Ben, shrugging. "Is that really so surprising? Most British prostitutes started out that way, I imagine."

"Yes, but they're all from the *same* home. And they've all posted their pictures on the same website, www.hothookups. com." She handed him a second piece of paper. "Guess who's on the board of Children of Hope? And guess who *also* holds a majority stake in Delta Media, the company that owns Hot Hookups?"

"Who?" Ben looked blank.

"Look!" Reaching over, Sian pointed to one of the names in the small print at the bottom of both documents. "Anton Tisch, that's who. And that's just the beginning."

She walked him through more pictures, and testimonials from past lovers who'd accused him of everything from indecent assault to rape, until they were paid—or threatened—into retracting their claims.

"This is all very well," said Ben, trying not to sound too discouraging, as he could see the passion and expectation written across Sian's face. "I can see he doesn't exactly come across as Santa Claus. But then, don't people know that already? That he's, you know, a bit dodgy with women?"

"*A bit dodgy?*" Sian looked at him, incredulous. "He's pushing vulnerable children into prostitution! Children he has a legal duty to protect. He's probably fucking them himself, for Christ's sake."

"You don't know that," said Ben reasonably. "None of what you've shown me here proves it."

"Sorry to interrupt." Tammy appeared at the door and gave Sian a look of purest contempt. "But your *fiancée's* on line two." She gave the word as much emphasis as possible. "She wants to know if you've remembered you're interviewing the wedding planner at lunch."

"Oh," Ben looked awkward. "Yeah. I forgot, but that's cool. Tell her I'll see her at home at one."

"You don't want to tell her yourself?" Tam held the portable phone out to him.

"No," said Ben, getting irritated. "I don't. And please don't put any more calls through to me, all right? I'm busy."

He turned back to Sian, who had a fixed smile glued to her face, not unlike a corpse in the early stages of rigor mortis.

"You're engaged?" she said, still smiling. "I didn't know. Congratulations."

"Thanks," said Ben, wishing he didn't feel so empty when he said it.

"Bianca's incredibly beautiful," said Sian. She had no idea why she said it. The words just seemed to fall out of her mouth, like lines in a play.

"Er, yes," said Ben absently. "Yes, I suppose she is. Thank you."

A horrible, awkward silence fell between them. They looked at each other, each willing the other to say something. In the end, Ben spoke first.

"You and Paddy must come to the wedding."

"Of course!" said Sian. Right after I've finished pulling the shreds of my heart out of the blender. "We'd love to. We'll probably be next down the aisle ourselves. You can give us some pointers."

More silence.

Oh God. What had possessed her to say that? If she'd happened to have a cyanide tablet on hand, she'd happily have swallowed it in that moment. She was no more planning to marry Paddy than fly to the moon.

"Good," said Ben, his tone brusque and businesslike all of a sudden. "Fine. Now look, about this Anton business."

"I know what I've got so far is shaky," said Sian, grateful that he'd changed the subject. "I do know that. But I really feel like I'm on to something here, Ben. First there are all the stories already in the public domain, about that lap dancer and him not paying child support. Then, according to you, he set up that whole Tina Palmer thing."

"So Lucas tells me."

"And that tape, by the way, also first came out on the web via another Delta Media site—what a coincidence." She was barely pausing to draw breath now, so convinced was she of her own argument. "And now these girls from his care home mysteriously find their way onto his website...come on. You don't find any of this even the least bit suspicious?"

Ben was silent for a moment. He found it all highly suspicious. But suspicion and proof were very different things. His dislike of Anton might be prejudicing his judgment.

"What are you looking for?" he asked. "From me, I mean?"

Sian started mumbling incoherently. She hadn't got as far as thinking up a specific figure and didn't want to be the first to suggest one.

"I assume you need money to fund your research?"

Sian nodded, blushing as red as a double-decker bus.

"Is a hundred grand enough?" said Ben.

Her jaw dropped. "A hundred...oh, no, goodness, that's way too much. I couldn't possibly ask for that much."

"You didn't ask for it," said Ben. "I'm offering. Look." Reaching forward, he took her hand in his. "I have to be very careful. I don't want to be seen to be supporting some kind of witch hunt against my biggest business rival."

"Of course not," said Sian, horrified. "And it isn't a witch hunt. I'm only interested in the truth."

"Nevertheless, my name has to stay out of it," said Ben firmly. "Understood?"

"Absolutely." She nodded vehemently. "On pain of death, I swear."

"The truth is, if Tisch goes out of business, that'll be worth a lot more than a hundred grand to me," admitted Ben, instinctively reaching for her hand and squeezing it. "But more importantly, if he is trafficking kids, he deserves everything you can throw at him. Besides, after all the shit he pulled on Lucas, I'd like to see him get a taste of his own medicine. I'm happy to help."

Sian, whose heart had practically stopped beating when he took her hand, immediately pulled it away at the mention of Lucas.

"Why do you even still care about that guy?" she said, shaking her head. "He's such a jerk."

"He's changed," said Ben. "People do, you know. You should give him another chance."

"Hmm," said Sian, skeptically. "Maybe next lifetime."

Gathering up her ridiculous pile of outerwear, she thanked Ben again profusely and promised to call with regular updates on her progress.

"E-mail me your account details and I'll have Coutts wire the money first thing in the morning," said Ben, as she made for the door. "Oh, and don't forget this." He handed her her broken padlock and chain. "You never know whose sofa you may need to lay claim to next, right?"

"Right." Sian blushed, kissing him briefly on the cheek. "Sorry again. About that."

When Tammy bustled into his office five minutes later, Ben was still standing in the exact same spot where Sian had left him, staring into space.

"Good," she said briskly. "She's gone. Right, then. D'you want me to book you a car at twelve forty-five, or are you driving?"

"Hmm?" said Ben.

"The wedding planner," said Tammy, with a lot more patience than she felt. "Remember?"

"Oh. Yeah. Book the car," said Ben. But wedding planners were the last thing on his mind. He now had a legitimate reason to talk to Sian, and even to see her regularly. Bianca was so wrapped up in bridesmaids' dresses and placements, she wouldn't bat an eyelid. And who knew, maybe he'd even get a bonus out of it and knock Anton Tisch and the unstoppable Excelsior off their market-dominating pedestal?

Today was starting to look up after all.

Anton grabbed Petra's breasts with both hands and squeezed tightly, sucking in his paunch as he thrust inside her.

Not bad for fifty-two, he thought smugly, feeling his glutes contract and his lower back muscles give a satisfying ripple as he moved. Fucking Petra was like driving a Bentley Continental: smooth, easy, and immensely satisfying. She was always wet for him, but he made sure to slather her between the legs with a generous dollop of Astroglide anyway. It made it easier for him to shift gears from drive into reverse, as he liked to think of it. And although it didn't take her pain away completely, listening to the woman's muffled, high-pitched squeals was all part of the thrill of anal sex—yet another activity that Petra excelled at.

"Ah," she hollered now, right on cue. "Not so hard, Anton, please. It hurts."

But the arching of her back and stiffening of her nipples beneath his palms told a different story.

"Be quiet," he said, smiling as he felt her tighten the muscles gripping his cock in an involuntary little spasm of excitement.

Her body, displayed in front of him on all fours and to spectacular effect in the mirrored walls of the hotel bedroom, was a work of art. Her skin was white and smooth, her breasts and buttocks full but firm (he despised scrawny women), and her legs long and infinitely spreadable. Between them was a neatly trimmed landing strip of pubic hair, dyed the same white-blonde as the hair on her head, around which everything else had been waxed into oblivion: perfect.

Better in bed than a prostitute, more discreet than a KGB agent, well bred and smart to boot, she was the best lover he'd ever had, as well as one of the finest managers he'd ever employed. Thanks to her daddy, Oleg, a Russian press baron, she was also independently wealthy—for Petra, her career was purely about ambition, never money—and had as little interest in marrying him as he did in marrying her.

In short, he thought, grabbing hold of her hair as he felt his orgasm building, she was his ideal woman. He must be careful not to attach himself emotionally, or he'd be sunk.

"Turn around," he grunted, pulling his twitching dick out of her body and holding it in his hands. She complied, positioning herself the way she knew he wanted—kneeling, but very low, so that he could kneel over her. Grabbing her skull, he yanked her head backward, then came, showering her alabaster cheeks with warm spurts of semen, one after another.

When he was finished, he sank back against the fluffy white pillows and gazed contentedly at the ceiling. He liked the Hotel Pennsylvania. There was something so very New York about it that appealed to him. Not the minimalist, modern, self-conscious Schrager New York. This was the old-school version: classy, luxurious, stylish in its own understated, confident way. He adored the fact that Duke Ellington and Glenn Miller had once been guests. Miller had even written a song incorporating the Pen's telephone number. Best of all, they let him bring Mitzi here, a concession Anton considered highly civilized.

In normal circumstances he'd have stayed at the Herrick. But East Hampton was so desolate and dreary in winter, and he couldn't face the trek out there. Besides, he was only in New York for two days, on fund business, so it didn't make sense to stay out of town.

"Tell me more about Vegas," he called after Petra, who'd disappeared into the bathroom to clean up.

"Oh, it was hilarious," she said, reemerging still damp from the shower and crawling under the sheet beside him. "I wish you'd been there. You'd have laughed."

That was another thing he loved about her. No matter how much he degraded or controlled her in bed, as soon as sex was over it was back to conversation as usual. Sitting up naked in bed, she looked as clean and flushed as if she'd just finished an energetic game of tennis. Certainly she wasn't remotely ashamed.

"Would I?" he said, kissing her indulgently.

"Lucas was strutting around like Mick Jagger, talking up his new hotel."

Anton had tried his damnedest to stop Lucas from acquiring any land in the Hamptons, but he'd underestimated the strength of local hostility toward the ever-brasher Herrick. All his bribes to the planning committee were rejected, and his threats—perhaps foolishly—ignored. As a last resort he'd promised the owner of the plot that Lucas had eventually bought three times Lucas's offer not to sell to him. But the seller was rich enough not to need Anton's money and stubborn enough not to appreciate being bullied. The deal had gone ahead.

"You know he's calling it Luxe America now?" Petra gave a short, derisive snort. "Talk about megalomania! Why not Luxe Planet Earth? Luxe Cosmos? He's so ridiculous, with his pathetic little postage stamp of land. It's not even on the good side of town."

"Has he started building yet?" asked Anton casually. Though irritated Lucas had found a site, Anton didn't feel threatened by him. The tiny scale of what he was proposing in the Hamptons would barely impact the Herrick, like a flea on the back of a camel.

Petra shook her head. "No. I drove by the site yesterday morning, and it was deserted. He's cleared planning though. Fuck knows how he managed that."

"Indeed," growled Anton.

"And he's hired a site manager, a Frenchman, who's been running around town telling everyone they'll be open by Christmas."

"Has he indeed?" said Anton. "Well, we'll see about that. Who's funding him, do you know? He's only just opened in Paris, so he must be stretched pretty thin."

"If he is, you'd never know it, the way he was strutting around like cock of the walk," said Petra sharply. "Word is, he's had a serious falling out with his partner and is scouting about for someone new."

Anton raised an eyebrow. That was interesting. He made a mental note to find out the name of Lucas's partner and get in touch.

"The funniest thing of all wasn't Lucas, though," said Petra, her eyes lighting up with cruelty like a cat before a kill. "It was Honor Palmer, running around the Wynn with her little bag of architects' plans, trying to find someone to cough up for a complete rebuild. If I didn't hate her so much, I might actually have felt sorry for her. Talk about the mighty fallen."

Anton smiled. He didn't share Petra's passionate loathing for Honor, but he could still relish the image of East Hampton's one-time princess wandering Las Vegas cap in hand like a pauper.

"No takers?" he asked.

"Of course not!" Petra sneered. "Well, unless you count Fred Gillespie, who agreed to lend her a couple of hundred out of pity.

She needs ten million for that project, at least; the insurers aren't budging and all the Palmer family money's gone up Tina's nose. She'll probably end up laying the bricks herself. I can just picture her in a pair of overalls and a hard hat, can't you? Or perhaps she and her humanitarian sister can shoot a new home movie. That should raise a few bucks."

"Not to mention a few dicks," said Anton, and they both laughed.

It was a novel sensation for him to feel so companionable with a woman. But Petra really did feel like a partner. An equal, even. He was also flattered that she found him funny. In England people continually made jokes about Germans being humorless, and though he pretended to laugh along, inside these jibes needled him more than he liked to admit. He'd always considered himself to be really quite witty. It was a pleasure to have finally found a woman who thought so too.

"Let's have a party," he said, out of the blue. Petra looked perplexed. "A party? What for?"

"To celebrate our being voted Relais Chateaux's number one." Throwing back the covers with a sigh, Petra got out of bed and started pulling on her clothes. "You're jumping the gun a bit, aren't you?" she said, doing up the fly on her white Calvin Klein jeans with an audibly brusque zip. "The results aren't out until next month."

"Actually," said Anton smugly, "I got a call from Matthieu Fremeau in Geneva yesterday. Strictly off the record, of course, but he says we've got it."

Shrieking like a banshee, Petra dropped her bra and sweater on the ground and made a flying leap, topless, back onto the bed and into his arms.

"Really?" she beamed, her face flushed with triumph and excitement. "He's quite sure?"

"Quite," said Anton, laughing and cupping her soft, milky-white breasts in his hands. "We'll do the party in the summer.

Make sure it's so fabulous that the press lose interest in Lucas and his pathetic efforts to compete with us."

"Oh, don't worry," said Petra. "It'll be fabulous all right."

Flipping onto her knees, she lowered her head and wrapped her lips lovingly around his cock, her tongue caressing him expertly until he hardened like cooling lava.

Closing his eyes, Anton relished the sensation. Did life get any better than this?

He had the number one fund, the number one hotel, and now the number one woman in the world.

He deserved a fucking party.

CHAPTER TWENTY-SIX

ONOR LEANED HEAVILY ON THE HANDLE OF THE WEED-whacker and peeled off the blue cotton shirt that was glued to her back with sweat. Tying it around her waist, she took a moment to get her breath back.

In front of her was a thing of rare beauty, at least in her eyes: a wooden skeleton of a building, half finished on the west side but still open to the elements everywhere else, its slate-tiled roof just beginning to take shape beneath a blindingly bright April sun.

The great Palmers rebuild had been underway for ten weeks now. Sometimes, waking up in the little cottage she'd rented in town, her muscles aching from the previous day's labor, she still found it hard to believe that it was really happening. That the dream that had seemed so utterly hopeless in Vegas was actually coming to fruition.

After her disastrous one-night stand with Lucas—an error of judgment that still haunted her daily—Honor's luck had finally changed. First Fred Gillespie, bless his triply bypassed heart, had agreed to an interest-free loan of two hundred and fifty thousand to get the ball rolling, as he put it.

"Of course I'll help you, kiddo," he said, taking her hand between his own great bear paws over lunch at the Venetian.

"Your father was like a brother to me. And I know he may not always have shown it too well, but Trey loved you. If he'd still been in his right mind at the end, he'd never have behaved the way he did, leaving your trust so vulnerable."

Honor was so choked, she burst into tears. The fiasco of her night with Lucas, on top of the stress of the last few months, had left her seriously tired and emotional. Fred's kindness was just too much.

The quarter of a million he was offering was barely a drop in the ocean of what she needed, but his faith in her marked a turning point in her own thinking. How could she expect an outsider to invest, with no security beyond an insurance payout that now looked ever more unlikely, if she wasn't prepared to lose the shirt from her own back?

As soon as she got back from the conference, she met with a bunch of contractors, hired one, and set them to work at once, blowing almost all of Fred's money on their first retainer and initial materials. Knowing that if she didn't raise more cash immediately she would lose everything, her next step was to meet with the mortgage company and come to an agreement for paying off her debts slowly that stopped just short of declaring herself bankrupt. After that, she put her old Boston bachelorette pad on the market and began systematically selling off every last asset, from stocks and premium bonds to valuable family paintings. With gut-wrenching regret, she even sold the jewelry her mother had left her as a keepsake—two valuable ruby bracelets and a topaz-and-diamond choker, so precious to her that she'd never even worn them once for risk of losing them.

"Are you quite certain, Miss Palmer?" the kind man at Christie's in New York had asked her, watching her lovingly finger the stones as she handed them over. "I'm sure we can fetch a good price for them, but sentimental items like this…you may live to regret parting with them."

I'm already regretting parting with them, thought Honor with a pang. All she had left of her mother now were some dog-eared photographs and few letters she'd gleaned from the chaos of Trey's home office after he died. She tried not to think about Tina, lounging around getting stoned in Santa Fe while that blood-sucking cult bled her bank accounts dry. She must stay focused on Palmers—keep her eyes on the prize, as Trey always used to say. Besides, she reasoned with herself firmly, it was only jewelry, and no more part of her mother than Palmers had once been.

Depressingly, even after turning her entire life into one big yard sale, she was still a long way short of what she needed to finish the building project. Day to day, week to week, she lived on a knife-edge, watching her funds deplete, sucked into the black hole of construction far faster than she could replace them. Desperate, she swallowed her pride and allowed gossip and life-style magazines to write features on her. They all wanted to know about her relationship with Tina, who by now had achieved iconic pinup status similar to Pam Anderson's as America's favorite slut-turned-saint. Honor quickly learned the art of providing them with exclusive "new" information without actually revealing anything significant, and soon became a regular on the pages of *US Weekly*, *In Style*, and even European magazines like *Hello!* and *OK!* She tried to tell herself that it would all be good publicity for Palmers when it opened next year (please God let it open next year!) and that in any case she needed the money and had no other choice. But she still felt like a prostitute every time she saw airbrushed pictures of herself lounging on a couch looking pampered and privileged. They normally had her in floaty John Galliano dresses, holding a flute of champagne. What a joke! She seemed to spend most of her time these days in overalls or sweat-pants, schlepping bricks and tiles around like a cart horse.

Not that she was complaining. Despite the back-breaking work and constant financial worry, coming on-site every morning was a joy, and she wouldn't have sacrificed her hands-on involvement for anything, however much Petra Kamalski might scoff. Whether looking at spreadsheets, arguing with suppliers, or getting down onto her hands and knees to inspect the damp proofing, this was Honor's dream made real. She needed to be a part of it, to live it and breathe it like the oxygen that, for her, it was. All the old magic from her childhood—the Palmers magic—was still there. She could feel it in the air. But this time, Honor controlled it. She was the sorcerer, conjuring the building and the gardens to her will. Even now, in its half-built state, it was so fucking beautiful it made her want to cry.

The toughest times came at the end of the day, when she was forced to leave the magic behind and go home. It would be many months yet until she could move into the hotel. Until then, "home" was a quaint but impractical cottage smack dab in the middle of town—impractical because there was nowhere near enough space for the mountainous piles of paperwork that the building project seemed to generate on an hourly basis and because there was no privacy. Many a morning Honor had woken to the sound of clattering downstairs and charged into the kitchen with the nearest blunt instrument only to find it was Mrs. Miggins from next door returning the cup of sugar she'd borrowed, or Joe, the site manager, letting himself in to look for some plans, or just in search of a cup of coffee. While it was nice to feel part of a community, and to feel that local people—Petra aside, of course—were rooting for her and for Palmers, Honor was discovering that you could definitely have too much of a good thing.

Last week, to her passionate relief, she'd received a phone call from her old bank manager and former family friend, Randy Malone.

"You've come a long way with your rebuild I see," he told her warmly. "In the light of what you've achieved, and the investment already made, the bank might be prepared to reconsider that loan you asked for a few months back. Why don't you pop in for a chat?"

On cloud nine, Honor skipped into town to meet him, but her euphoria soon vanished when she heard the rate of interest they were offering.

"That's daylight robbery!" she gasped indignantly, the figures swimming before her eyes. "You've known me since I was born, Randy. How can you even think of ripping me off like that?"

"It's a competitive rate, Honor," the old man insisted sanctimoniously. "If you'd prefer an equity partner, by all means go and look for one. But I think you may find it harder than you anticipate. Hotels are always a high-risk proposition, especially when you've got one as successful as the Herrick already established up the road. All commercial real estate's looking very soft right now."

Not as soft as your backbone, thought Honor, mutinously. But she desperately needed the money. With a loan this size she could guarantee finishing the construction on time. She couldn't afford to refuse, and they both knew it.

At least she could enjoy the small comfort of knowing that Luxe America, the grand project Lucas had been so insufferably arrogant about in Vegas, had yet to get off the starting blocks. Bogged down in a complicated, multinational lawsuit with Connor Armstrong (funded, or so it was rumored, by Anton Tisch), he and his new American partner were forbidden to start work until the case was settled. Crushed under a pile of injunctions fatter than the Koran, they had no choice but to sit on their hands for the foreseeable future.

Lucas's enforced absence from East Hampton was a bonus for Honor, but it didn't mean he wasn't on her mind. Ever since Vegas she'd been plagued by flashbacks of their night together. She tried hard to focus on the negative: his arrogance the morning after, how dismissive he'd been of her plans to rebuild Palmers. But the physical memory of his touch still haunted her.

More than once she'd woken in the middle of the night, after a particularly erotic dream, feeling so frustrated that she'd had to throw on her gym shorts and go for a run just to get it out of her system.

Reaching the end of the strip of turf, she switched off the rickety old weed-whacker and turned around to admire her handiwork. Not bad, especially considering that the closest she'd come to manual labor growing up was handing her dirty laundry to the maid. Petra and her cronies could make fun of her all they liked. Honor didn't care. When this place was finished, they'd all be eating their words. Trendy, flash-in-the-pan hotels like the Herrick always burned themselves out in the end. That was the nature of the beast—no one place could remain the It-spot forever. However high-end they were, and however hard they tried to differentiate themselves, the Tischens were a chain. So were the Luxes, whatever Lucas might claim. Only Palmers was a one-off. Unique. Only Palmers had the magic.

It was hard to define what made a hotel a classic. Even Honor wasn't sure she could put it into words. All she knew was that whatever alchemy it took, the Palmers of her grandfather's day had had it in bucketloads.

And she vowed that, by this time next year, her version was going to have it too.

Walking back to her hotel room in the sweltering, ninety-degree heat, Sian felt the weight of the world on her bony, sunburned shoulders.

She was in Grand Cayman, on the last leg of an exhausting paper trail that might or might not throw more light on Anton Tisch's links with the corrupt Azerbaijani government. Right now, unfortunately, her money was on the latter option. Or rather, Ben's money, seeing as that was what she was spending.

The last three months had been the most exciting, hard-working, and frustrating of her life. Tisch was a uniquely compelling subject, and unraveling the murky depths of his past had rapidly morphed from a professional interest into a deeply personal obsession. Regularly putting in eighteen-hour days, which often involved skipped meals, she'd now reached the point where she even dreamed about Anton at night, his pale, waxy, emotionless face competing with Ben's freckled, broken-nosed loveliness for her unconscious's attention.

But as driven as she was, she constantly seemed to be moving one step forward and two steps back. An unexpected source would suddenly pop up from nowhere, providing her with the name and address of one of Anton's underage playthings, then she'd travel halfway across Europe to discover that the girl was too drugged out of her mind to make a statement. Unsolicited letters, hinting darkly at possible involvement with the Russian Mafia and ex-KGB underworld, had Sian buying a plane ticket to St. Petersburg, only to find that her British Press Association accreditation wasn't recognized and she was denied access to even the most basic documentary evidence. Other letters, threatening letters, had also started hitting her and Lola's doormat with depressing regularity. Sian told Ben about the first one, from some illiterate Eastern bloc hood with an overactive imagination and a well-developed knife fetish. But Ben had overreacted so massively, threatening to pull the plug on the whole story if she put her personal safety at risk, that she'd kept mum about the rest of them.

The frustrations of the investigation were nothing, however, compared to the torture of working with Ben. As the weeks rolled by and the case against Anton built, Sian spent more and more long evenings over at his apartment, poring over documents and planning the next prong of attack. At the beginning, Bianca had taken off and left them to it. But lately, perhaps sensing the longing that poured out of Sian like water through a sieve and wanting to guard her territory, she'd taken to hanging around, even taking a nominal interest in the story herself. Never anything less than physically perfect, she lolled on the couch next to Ben in her skinny-rib sweaters and spray-on fucking jeans, resting a flawless manicured hand on his thigh in a gesture of casual possessiveness that made Sian want to leap up and bite her, like a snake. Of course, she felt desperately ashamed of her hostility. Bianca was so self-evidently a good and loving person, and much more deserving of Ben than she was. But she couldn't help it.

Like a horror movie she couldn't switch off, she played every glance, touch, and gesture over and over in her mind, analyzing Ben's responses to Bianca and to her with the obsessive precision of a microbiologist poring over a single cell. Often she thought she noticed him distancing himself from Bianca, withdrawing eye contact or shifting positions when she came and sat next to him. Occasionally, he even seemed to look lingeringly at Sian herself, or to jump with the same high-voltage shock that she did when their hands accidentally brushed against each other. But perhaps this was just wishful thinking, in both instances? His wedding to Bianca, scheduled for this August, was still very much on. And despite numerous opportunities, he hadn't made the slightest pass at Sian in the twelve long weeks they'd been working together.

She would have loved to confide in Lola about her feelings and her fears. But ever since the story had hijacked her life, a growing distance had been developing between the two girls. It got worse about a month ago, when Sian had finally bitten the bullet and broken up with Paddy. "But you can't," said Lola incredulously, and not a little tactlessly, when Sian told her the news. "You two are so perfect together."

"Believe me," said Sian sadly, "we're not."

"But he's such a wonderful guy. And he really loves you."

"I know," snapped Sian, guilt and lack of sleep making her more than usually irritable. "OK? I know. Why d'you think I dated him for so long? We just ran out of steam, that's all. I can't explain it."

She couldn't admit that Ben coming back into her life had so completely poleaxed her, sexually and emotionally, that she felt physically sick every time Paddy touched her. That seeing his loving, unsuspecting face come home in the evenings, clouded with doubt and rejection that he didn't understand, made her want to sob out loud with guilt. Paddy was a lovely guy; the best. He deserved to be with someone who could love him back, who didn't have to pretend.

Knowing that Lola thought she was simply being selfish, and that it was her obsession with work that had come between her and Paddy, made the whole awful episode even more painful. Unable to deal with the criticism, or to bear watching Lola and Marti so happy and cocooned in love for each other, she started working even longer hours, coming home later and later and sneaking out of the apartment at the crack of dawn. Inevitably, the distance between the two girls grew, at the very time when Sian most longed to be able to bridge it.

Boarding the plane for Cayman had been a relief, a welcome escape from Ben and Bianca, and Lola's ever-present resentment about Sian's work. But as soon as she landed in the famously secretive tax haven, and official home of most of Anton's businesses, she'd felt her positive spirits fading.

Less than five hundred miles south of Miami, the so-called Caribbean paradise of the Cayman Islands was Sian's idea of hell: luxuriously soulless hotels, like the Hyatt Regency where she was staying, loomed up out of the surrounding poverty like insensitive giants, their gazes focused firmly on the sunny blue sky and still waters of the ocean beyond, and not the slums at their feet. Like Miami, extreme wealth and extreme poverty walked hand in hand here. But somehow, lacking Miami's vibrancy and the hope and energy of its ethnic melting pot, the division of wealth seemed starker and more brutal in Cayman. To Sian, it felt like a Swiss version of an island paradise: Jamaica, run by civil servants. She could quite imagine Anton feeling at home here, even without the tax breaks, and was unsurprised to learn that, unlike most of the internationally wealthy with accounts and trusts on the islands, he'd actually bought a villa on Grand Cayman and used it regularly for a number of years.

She'd hoped he might have had some neighbors from that time who remembered him and could fill in some of the many blanks in her narrative so far. Perhaps he'd joined the local golf or yacht club? Become buddy-buddy with the Ferrari dealership in the harbor? But no. If he'd made any social contacts on Cayman, he'd taken pains to keep them as discreet as his business dealings. After three exhausting days here, Sian had still not found the lead she'd hoped for. There had been one interesting development today, a bank account number that hadn't cropped up before on any of her searches, which she'd traced to a personal account at Uneximbank in Moscow.

When she finally got back to the Hyatt, she slid her key-card into the door of her room and sighed with relief as she walked into a cooling air-conditioned breeze. Peeling off the linen jacket that had stuck to her skin like a cheesecloth, she kicked off her shoes and flung herself back on the bed, luxuriating in the soft welcome of the mattress.

She only intended to take the weight off her feet for a minute, but the next thing she knew she was woken by the insistent ringing of the phone by her bedside. Groggily lifting the receiver, she noticed it was dark outside. How long had she been asleep?

"Hello?" she mumbled.

"It's me." Ben's booming cockney voice sounded crackly, diminished by distance. But Sian's innards turned to liquid just the same. "Just wondering how you got on today?"

"Fine," said Sian. Still half asleep, she stifled a yawn.

"Shit, I didn't wake you, did I?"

"No, no, not at all. Of course not." Desperate to prolong the conversation, she forced herself to pep up and launched into a garrulous monologue about the day's progress, or lack of it. "I did come up with one new lead though," she said, and told him about the Russian bank account. "I'm thinking of leaving here early and flying out to Moscow in the morning to do some digging."

"I don't think that's such a good idea," said Ben, who suddenly had visions of her being pursued down a dark alleyway by a bunch of murderous Kremlin hoods. "If Tisch is involved with anything dodgy out there and you show up sniffing about, things could get very nasty very quickly. Those Russkies don't just put the frighteners on people. They mean business, and they don't give a shit if you're a woman or what country you're from."

"Come on," said Sian teasingly. "Don't you think you're being just a teeny bit melodramatic? What are they gonna do, slip strychnine into my tea?"

"They might," said Ben, trying not to sound as desperately anxious as he felt. Sian was so obsessed with getting her scoop, she might easily do something reckless. And the former Soviet underworld was no joke. "Or they might just shoot you in the head, like poor old Anna Pollywhat's-her-face."

"Politkovskaya," said Sian. "And they won't. She was after Putin. I'm after a German financier the Kremlin probably hasn't even heard of. Don't worry."

But Ben did worry.

Sitting alone in his empty office—it was half past nine in London, and apart from the poor drones in M and A, the rest of the City had long since gone home to bed—he launched the Google home page. Typing in "Russia, Journalist, Murder," he was horrified to read that almost three hundred members of the press, many of them foreign nationals, had been killed since the fall of communism in Russia. Sian was incapable of being discreet. She was bound to go barging in there like Ruby Wax on speed, demanding "airn-sers," as she would put it. You could hear her American accent from a hundred paces, he thought lovingly.

Why the fuck had he written her that stupid check up front? Now he had no control over where she went or what she did.

Switching off his PC, angry at himself, he grabbed his jacket from the back of the chair and flipped off the light, wishing that the thought of going home to Bianca didn't make him feel so irrationally depressed. Tam was right. For a soon-to-be-married multimillionaire, he really was turning into a miserable old git. He had to get a grip.

CHAPTER TWENTY-SEVEN

$\mathcal{S}$IX WEEKS LATER, LUCAS WAS SITTING IN THE SPECTACULAR vaulted Gothic waiting room of the Palais de Justice in Paris, waiting for the latest round in his case with Connor Armstrong to be called. He'd begun the morning angry. After months of legal wrangling that had seen him flying back and forth from Paris to Madrid to the European courts in Strasbourg like a fricking shuttlecock, they were still no nearer a resolution. But now, after three hours numbing his ass on a hard wooden bench, he was simply bored.

There weren't even any good-looking women to distract him. He shared the waiting room with a shaven-headed French-Arabic boy in a light polyester suit three sizes too big for him, who had the word "defendant" written all over him (although it was his tailor who deserved the life sentence), two lawyers, and a middle-aged matron with tightly curled red hair, whose bottom seemed to spread across the bench like dough, threatening to engulf Lucas at any moment.

"Would you like to have a look?" Smiling warmly, the matron offered him the copy of *Hello!* magazine she'd just finished reading. "It's a good one."

"Thank you," said Lucas, who wouldn't normally have wiped his ass with *Hello!* but who was so bored he welcomed any distraction. Flipping through the glossy, picture-filled pages, he sneered inwardly at the ludicrous pretensions of the "celebrity" subjects. Horse-faced minor aristocrats blabbed on shamelessly about their relationships with royalty while posing outside their crumbling estates. Trained for nothing and having never done an honest day's work in their lives, this was probably one of the few ways they knew to make money, money they so clearly needed to prop up their oversize houses. Lucas pictured them once the cameras had stopped rolling, sending the ball gowns and jewelry back to the pawn shop and retiring to the two rooms of the stately home they could still afford to heat, to rustle up some canned baked beans on toast. Everything these magazines pedaled was a sham. But a few pages later, his internal diatribe came to an abrupt halt when he found himself face-to-face with a quite stunning photograph of Honor. In a wood-nymph-green silk dress, sprayed onto her tiny body like gold leaf, five-inch Jimmy Choo heels, and with a simple but exquisitely cut amethyst pendant resting on her bronzed chest, she looked sexier than he'd ever seen her. Her hair, which had been mermaid-long in Vegas, was now cut into shoulder-length layers that had been streaked alternately in honey and chocolate, a perfect shade for her darker, sun-kissed skin. She was lying on a stone bench in the rose garden at Palmers, propped up on one elbow with her haunting, angular face cupped in one long-fingered hand, and her green cat's eyes burned out of the page like two nuggets of kryptonite. Lucas, for one, felt his superpowers waning when he looked at her, so regally, coolly beautiful and yet at the same time so vulnerable and slight, like a leaf that might blow away on the wind at any moment.

The piece was about Palmers, a three-page spread combining archive shots of the old hotel with bigger, sunlit pictures of the rebuild that Honor had famously commissioned now. Tucked away in the corner was a small shot of the charred remnants of the old building, taken the day after the fire. Looking at it, Lucas felt sick, thinking how close Honor must have come to being killed that day.

The insurers are still refusing to pay our claim, even though the police have said they're forensically certain the fire was a deliberate act of arson, she was quoted as saying to the reporter.

"Disgusting," said Lucas out loud, surprising his fellow waitees with this burst of indignation on Honor's behalf. "Fucking bloodsuckers."

Without an arrest and a conviction, they say, the causes are still open to question. He read on. *It's been a tough slog to raise the money to rebuild her. But I'm really proud of what we've achieved.*

I bet you are, thought Lucas, looking at the pictures of the new hotel rising up from the earth, as white and pure as a spring snowdrop. He was still angry at Honor for the hot and cold signals she'd given him in Vegas, and for being too stubborn to call him and apologize afterward. Why was it that women could never admit when they were wrong? But he had to admit she'd had more balls than he'd given her credit for when it came to rebuilding Palmers. They weren't finished yet, but Honor had already pulled off what he and most others in the business had considered an impossible feat. She deserved serious kudos for that. Still, she must be absolutely desperate for money to have agreed to a cheesy *Hello!* feature like this one. Gossip mags were complete anathema to Honor—she considered them very much Tina territory—and Lucas could only imagine the frantic prideswallowing that must have gone on before she poured herself into that deliciously revealing dress.

It was ironic that, even with her money problems, Honor was storming ahead at Palmers while he (who thanks to his new investor, the oil heir Winston Davies, had money coming out of his ears) was stuck not passing Go at Luxe America. Perhaps he'd been naive. But Connor had complained so vociferously about the business before Vegas it hadn't occurred to Lucas that he would object to being bought out. And indeed, he'd already accepted the more-than-generous offer for his shares both verbally and by e-mail by the time Anton had gotten involved in February, stirring the pot as only he could do.

Everybody knew what had happened. But unfortunately, none of them could prove it. Tisch had gotten in touch with Connor and started throwing money around like a newly signed footballer in a brothel, promising him the earth and all its riches if he refused to sign the contract and stayed on at Luxe as a "spoiler" partner, preventing further expansion, including Luxe America. Lucas and Winston countered, citing their verbal agreement and the e-mails, not to mention the fact that Connor had already taken receipt of the first installment of Winston's funds by the time of his sudden change of heart. In the end, it was highly likely that the courts would rule against Connor, but that wasn't the point. With Anton's legion of international lawyers behind him, Connor was quite capable of dragging out the case for months or even years, flitting from one jurisdiction to the next each time a decision went against him, and lodging appeals every time Lucas's attorney opened his mouth.

So far, Winston had been very patient. He had the sort of wealth that made it easy to shrug off a million-dollar-plus lawsuit. Besides, he believed in Lucas and the Luxe brand and didn't take kindly to people trying to bully him out of his business decisions. But as grateful as Lucas was for his support, it still left him nowhere in terms of getting his new hotel off the ground. And in the meantime, not only had the Herrick been voted the number one luxury hotel, with Petra planning the mother of all victory parties to celebrate this summer, but now Honor looked set to revive the Palmers franchise for a second time.

Time, in this instance, was not only money. Time was everything, and Lucas was fast running out of it. "Monsieur Ruiz?" The sour-faced woman clerk, a Gallic Barbara Walters who reeked of Jolie Madame and Elnett, emerged through the wooden double doors and nodded curtly in his direction. "*Suivez moi, s'il vous plait.*"

"At last," said Lucas, handing the magazine back to his dough-bottomed neighbor, who blushed and smiled as she took it. Getting wearily to his feet, he followed the clerk into the almost-empty courtroom with a heavy heart. Despite all the waiting, he knew today's hearing would be just like all the others: a monumental waste of fucking time.

"Yes, yes, I can see a lot of work goes into them," said Ben, trying to keep his temper.

"It's more than just work, duckie," Maxwell, the flamingly gay wedding coordinator pouted furiously. "It's artistic genius. Ice sculptures of this sort of scale and complexity are…well," he dabbed his brow with a monogrammed linen handkerchief, "they're the stuff dreams are made of."

"Not my dreams," said Ben bluntly. "Twenty grand and by the end of the night it's a dirty fucking puddle. Come on, B, don't you think this is just a bit extravagant?"

Bianca bit her lip and fought back tears. It wasn't that she cared about the ice sculpture so much, although she did think that the scale model of Notre Dame, complete with miniature frozen gargoyles, was exquisite. But would it really have killed Ben to show just a smidgen of enthusiasm for any of her and Maxwell's proposals?

The three of them were in Wedding World's offices, which took up the entire top floor of a trendy converted warehouse in Clerkenwell. The place was a cross between a New York loft and a giant padded cell. Every surface was soft, even the walls, which were covered in some sort of foam-filled white fabric that looked like stuck-on clouds, and the rounded, rubbery desks scattered around the room like so many colorful children's toys. Ben and

Bianca were at one end, ensconced in a white sofa so ridiculously soft it kept threatening to swallow them whole, opposite Maxwell in a pink sixties bubble chair that had an annoying habit of swiveling and creaking whenever he moved. Between them was a white rubber coffee table, on which were spread out various books and magazines, all depicting the gruesomely vulgar weddings of Maxwell's former clients.

Ben was there on sufferance. He'd said from the beginning that he didn't want a big, flashy wedding, just a traditional ceremony in a pretty country church somewhere with a meal and dancing afterward. But Bianca had had her heart set on a fairy tale from the beginning and, encouraged by his mother and sisters, had pressed ahead regardless, concocting ever more extravagant and, to Ben's mind, ridiculous plans with bloody Nathan Lane over there. He'd already been steamrollered into having the wedding at some damn stupid castle in Ireland and signed off on jugglers and fire-eaters and God knows what else. Next they'd be flying in Siegfried and Roy or riding up the aisle on fucking unicorns.

"The sculpture was only an idea," said Bianca coldly. "If you don't like it, perhaps you'd like to suggest another centerpiece? You haven't exactly been awash with contributions so far."

She knew she sounded snappish and nagging, and she hated herself for it, but her nerves were frayed to ribbons. Things had been so horribly strained between them lately, ever since Ben got involved with Sian and that stupid story. Not a naturally mean person, Bianca made valiant efforts not to hate Sian or to blame her for Ben's distancing and patent lack of interest in the wedding. But it was hard. This morning he'd been going on about her again, even trying to wriggle out of their appointment with Maxwell to go and meet her at the airport.

"She's coming back from Azerbaijan this afternoon," he said plaintively. "She says she really needs to talk to me."

"Well, can she join the fucking line?" Bianca snapped. "I need to talk to you, Ben. About our wedding. It's less than two months away now, you know."

"How could I not know?" he snapped back. "You remind me often enough."

"And why do I have to remind you?" she yelled hysterically. "Because you're always holed up with bloody Sian in your little club of two, that's why! Obsessing over Anton Tisch. Anyone would have thought it was her you were planning to spend the rest of your life with, not me."

"Well, it isn't," said Ben guiltily. "It's you." He knew he'd been neglecting Bianca, but it was hard when all she wanted to talk about was a wedding he was increasingly coming to dread.

"Look, all right," he said now, flicking through one of Maxwell's magazines with about as much enthusiasm as a mother superior with a copy of *Playboy*. "What about something like that? That'd make a good centerpiece, wouldn't it?" Maxwell wrinkled his nose in a "did I just tread in dog shit?" way and looked at Ben pityingly. "A cake?" he said.

"What's wrong with it?" asked Ben.

"It's hardly very original," said Bianca, gently.

"So? Do we have to be original about everything? Does it always have to be skydiving angels leaping off chandeliers?"

"Oh, no, of course not," said Maxwell snidely. "Tell you what, why don't we just have a nice bunch of flowers on the top table and be done with it? Perhaps you could pick them up from the Shell garage on your way to the service, Ben?"

"I've had enough of this," said Ben, getting angrily to his feet. He'd given Bianca a blank check for this wedding and resented the implication that he was being a cheapskate. Why couldn't people see that the reason he didn't want a big to-do was that it a) was tacky as shit and b) was turning the whole thing into a performance? Couldn't Bianca tell he was nervous enough already?

"Where are you going?" she asked, getting up after him. She looked anguished, and he felt awful leaving her, but the whole thing was doing his head in.

"Back to work," he said, picking up his briefcase by the door. "Look, I'm sorry, B, but I'm no good at this stuff. You and Maxwell pick what you want. I'll pay for it."

I don't want your money, thought Bianca bitterly. *I want your interest. I want your heart.*

As if reading her mind, Maxwell plonked his ample backside down in Ben's vacated seat and wrapped a comforting arm around her.

"There, there, duckie," he said. "He'll come around. The grooms are all like this in the last few weeks. It's only nerves."

"Really?" Her eyes welled up with tears, and her beautiful, full lower lip began to tremble.

"Definitely," said Maxwell, who couldn't understand why such a showstoppingly gorgeous girl was throwing herself away on a philistine like Ben Slater anyway. "Trust Uncle Maxwell. I've seen it all before."

CHAPTER TWENTY-EIGHT

"RULY, MR. TISCH, WE CAN'T THANK YOU ENOUGH."
The painfully earnest charity worker pumped Anton's hand with her clammy palm and stared at him with her bulging bug-eyes. She must have some sort of thyroid problem. The woman looked like a blowfish with earrings.

"The difference you've made to these children is incalculable. Incalculable!"

"Not at all," said Anton magnanimously, retrieving his hand and wiping it with distaste on his starched white handkerchief. Honestly, wasn't it enough to give money to these people, without having them paw at you afterward with their sweaty hands, like vermin?

He was in Vauxhall, an area of London he would typically go out of his way to avoid. But tonight was the grand opening of an arts center for troubled inner-city teens, a spin-off from the Children of Hope charity of which he was patron.

Personally, he found the whole place deeply depressing. All the garish primary colors and walls covered with the dreadful, talentless paintings that the kids had produced. To call it art was an affront to common sense and probably a blatant breach of the Trade Descriptions Act. But then what could you expect from a bunch of dead-eyed crackheads brought up on welfare? The only children with any "hope" were the girls pretty enough to make a living off their nubile young bodies, a few of whom he'd been happy to help out personally. As for the rest, they had no future. The mindless optimism of charity workers like the blowfish woman never ceased to amaze him. Did she honestly believe a few afternoons a week throwing paint around was going to change the lives of these pond scum?

Noticing that a *London Tonight* TV crew was hovering just behind her, Anton gave her a second, ingratiating smile. "I'm thrilled to be able to help in my own small way," he said. "What the children have achieved here is truly magical. You must be very proud."

"Oh, I am, I am." She beamed. "God bless you."

He was pleasantly surprised by the good press turnout. Most journalists expected more from a charity do than carrots and a few plates of jelly sandwiches, but all the major papers and news channels were here. He supposed he had Saskia to thank for that.

Saskia Kennilworth, the PR girl he'd hired last year to oversee his charity work and personal branding, was already proving herself to be quite an asset. Her privileged bubbly blonde persona hid a steely business acumen that was rare in public relations, an industry largely staffed by the inbred daughters of British aristocrats whose combined IQ would be unlikely to impress a self-respecting earthworm.

But Saskia was a pearl among swine. She was the one who'd steered him toward teen charities and away from the more elitist opera and polo events he used to be associated with. It had turned out to be an inspired move. He'd read more positive articles about his philanthropy in the last six months than ever before. And his star definitely appeared to be rising in those all-important establishment circles.

Saskia was attractive too, albeit in a completely opposite way from Petra. She had tits the size of balloons, wore far too much makeup, and had a raspy, filthy smoker's laugh that was as infectious as it was sexy. She'd come on to him like a train in their initial meeting, but he hadn't slept with her yet, as much from a lack of opportunity as anything else. He'd been traveling an awful lot lately. But Saskia was definitely on his to-do list. He needed to break the unhealthy cycle of monogamy he'd gotten into with Petra, and Ms. Kennilworth should provide the perfect antidote to the Slavic hauteur he'd grown to find so addictive.

"...don't you think, Mr. Tisch?"

Damn it. The blowfish was speaking to him again, and he'd been miles away. Now the cameras were trained on him hopefully, waiting for a response.

"Absolutely," he said, smiling broadly.

Saskia was big on smiles. They made him more approachable, apparently.

It was a further twenty minutes before he was finally able to extricate himself from the glad-handers and escape to the safety of his waiting Daimler.

"Thank God," he sighed, as the driver glided across Vauxhall Bridge back toward civilization. The MI building loomed above them, illuminated an ethereal green at night, like a comic-book Gotham City. Below them, the Thames oozed as shiny black and sinister as an oil slick. Anton flipped open his laptop in the backseat and went straight to his e-mails.

The top four were all from Petra. Two were about the arrangements for next month's "number one" party at the Herrick. As always, she'd done a stellar job organizing things and had already put together a guest list and entertainment program to rival the Oscars. Scrolling down the attached list of confirmed attendees, Anton felt a warm rush of contentment: Hollywood royalty, rock royalty, fashion royalty. There wasn't a C-lister among them. Only real royalty had failed to succumb to Petra's charms—they'd had a no from Lady Helen Taylor. Uptight bitch. But looking at the last page, he brightened considerably and let out a half-stifled squeal of delight: the Duchess of York was listed as a maybe, along with both her daughters. Put that in your pipe and smoke it, Lady Helen!

He wondered how Petra would react if he brought Saskia in to help corral the press coverage. Not well, he imagined, chuckling quietly. Petra responded to other attractive women the way that the majority of her sex responded to spiders. You could visibly see her flesh crawl in their presence. A brassy, British ballbreaker like Saskia would be Petra's equivalent of a fat, hairy tarantula. Throwing the two of them together was bound to result in some serious fireworks.

But he'd save that particular bombshell for later. For now, he kept his responses to Petra's messages as neutral and businesslike as usual.

By the time he clicked open her third e-mail, with its multiple JPEG attachments, he was almost home. But the title "Palmers Pics" piqued his interest, and he instructed his driver to make a detour through Shepherds Market and around Berkeley Square so he could finish downloading it in the car.

"Thought you might like to see these," Petra had written. "From this month's *Hello!*"

Opening the first image, Anton gave a little snort of surprise, bordering on admiration. Honor had made startlingly rapid progress.

The building wasn't finished, but it couldn't be more than a couple of months from completion, and what he saw here was impressive. The facade was strongly reminiscent of the old hotel but fell short of the sentimental replica he'd been expecting. It was grander, for one thing—the portico was taller by a good three feet, he reckoned, and it was rendered in stone rather than the cutesy Huck Finn whitewashed wood of its predecessor. The landscaping was also done on an altogether bigger scale, although to his mind it was still drearily conservative: rose gardens, topiary, lavender-lined gravel paths. No vision. No daring. It reminded him of a slightly grander version of Southampton's 1708 House.

"Did you know she was this far down the line?" he instant-messaged Petra, before moving on to the interior shots: simple, classic bedrooms with heavy mahogany four-posters and lots of white linen and ceiling fans; bathrooms with freestanding copper tubs and big enough proportions to accommodate the comfy antique armchairs and paintings that gave them the feel of living rooms.

Petra IM'd him back.

"I've been trying to tell you for months. You didn't want to know."

Anton scowled. He didn't appreciate being upbraided by his staff, or his lovers. He'd always felt that Petra overestimated Honor's significance as a threat, her judgment clouded by her own personal hostility. But perhaps he should have heeded her warnings after all?

Clicking open more of the pictures, he saw that Honor had given more than a nod to her family's colonial heritage. There was bound to be a pretentious, walnut-lined library in there somewhere, crammed with first editions of Hemingway. And she'd eschewed all the modern touches normally considered to be *de rigueur* in a top-flight hotel these days. There wasn't a plasma screen in sight, and the doors all had traditional locks and keys. Still, for a woman who most of the industry had written off as a crackpot, she'd done well. He wondered how on earth she'd raised the money.

"Interesting, but not important," he wrote back to Petra. "She can't touch us now."

Ninety-five percent of him believed this—that with the Herrick so firmly established, and now at world number one, Palmers stood no chance of regaining its old supremacy. But the five percent of doubt irritated him almost as much as the pictures of Honor looking so effortlessly beautiful in that green dress, a perfect match for her defiant eyes, as she lounged on the hard stone bench.

He cheered up when he read the next e-mail, a gloating note from Connor Armstrong about yesterday's hearing in Paris. Lucas, apparently, had first shot himself in the foot by turning up to court without a tie—Madame Justice Dubois, the lesbian battle-ax judge, was not remotely impressed—and then damned himself further by losing his temper when she'd quizzed him about employing illegal immigrants in the Luxe kitchen.

"Show me a hotel chef in Paris with a kitchen full of legal workers, and I'll show you a liar," he'd apparently roared at her. "What does any of this have to do with Mr. Armstrong deliberately sabotaging my business?"

Needless to say, she'd ruled against him.

Anton was no admirer of Connor's. He found him pompous and his pretensions at being a big hitter in property nothing short of pathetic. But he'd really outdone himself with this court case, devoting an energy and effort to destroying Lucas that was almost a match for Anton's own. As well as the endless legal wrangles, Connor had had a hand in most of the other blows that had rained down on the nascent Luxe chain in recent months: drug raids in Ibiza, strikes in Paris, a lurid kiss-and-tell with a girl from the Crazy Horse in last month's *Paris Match*. He'd been worth every penny of the blood money Anton had paid him.

So much for Lucas's boasts about opening Luxe America by the end of the year. At this rate he'd be lucky to open at all. As irritating as Honor's progress at Palmers was for Anton, he knew it would be a thousand times more galling for Lucas to see his old rival storming ahead while his shitty little business foundered in the muddy shallows like the dying fish that it was.

"D'you want me to keep circling, sir?" The driver had already gone past Annabel's four times and was starting to think about his bed.

"No, Michaels," said Anton imperiously, switching off his computer. "I've seen all I need to see. We can go home now."

Bianca stared at the pile of dirty mugs and overflowing ashtrays in the kitchen sink and pursed her lips with annoyance.

"There are three fucking adults in this house," she muttered furiously under her breath, scraping used cigarette butts and congealed takeout remnants into the trash before filling up a second sink with hot water and detergent. "How come I'm the only one capable of cleaning up after themselves?"

It was the evening after Ben had stormed out of the meeting with the wedding planner, and she'd hoped he might have shown a little sensitivity to her feelings. But no, he'd been on the phone to Sian first thing this morning, unable even to wait until he got into the office, and promptly invited her over for an evening progress meeting. Progress my ass, thought Bianca bitterly, peering through into the living room to see the two of them laughing together over yet another dumb piece of paper. They'd been working on Sian's scoop for five months now, but she'd yet to mention a publication date for the piece and seemed as far away from finishing the damn thing as ever. Bianca tried not to believe that both of them might have an ulterior motive for dragging the thing out indefinitely. But she couldn't be sure of anything anymore.

Mindlessly dropping dirty plates and silverware into the sink, she thought back to how much she'd liked Sian when they'd first met at that wedding in New York, and how long ago that seemed now. Back then she'd seemed spunky and fun, a real girls' girl. But Bianca had evidently misjudged her spirit of sisterhood. Sian was over at the apartment all the time now, whenever she was in England anyway, shamelessly monopolizing Ben without a thought for Bianca's feelings and pointedly excluding her from their discussions. The pair of them would smoke up a storm (Ben knew Bianca now loathed smoking), emerging from their stinking den only to order huge, revolting-smelling

Domino's pizzas and leaving the empty boxes and grease stains for Bianca to deal with.

She'd never been one of those up-herself, high-maintenance models that expected minions to clean up after her. Nor was she afraid of a little housework. But she wasn't a doormat, and she was tired of being treated like one.

Feeling left out and taken for granted wasn't even the worst of it. It was the horrid, creeping realization, a sort of slow-growing panic, that Ben preferred Sian's company to hers. She'd tried to talk herself out of this a thousand times—to tell herself that his interest in the story was purely business, about exposing Anton as a crook so that he could win Stellar's investors back. But each time she watched him giggling with Sian over a shared joke, or even fighting with her about which angle to pursue, she felt the fear start to crawl back over her body, like lice.

Last night in bed, she'd finally plucked up the courage to voice her anxieties to Ben.

"You're being ridiculous," he assured her. "Sian and I were over years ago."

But Bianca couldn't help but notice that he turned away from her when he spoke, as if his face might give him away.

"Well if you do love me," she said, stroking the bare curve of his back, "why don't you make love to me?" She hated herself for sounding so weak and jealous, for having to ask. But she needed the reassurance. "You haven't touched me for weeks."

Turning around with a sigh, Ben pulled her into his chest and kissed her on the forehead.

"I'm sorry," he said gently. "I'm just tired, that's all. It's got nothing to do with Sian. Honestly. Work's hellish, and this story's taking up a crazy amount of my time."

"So leave it to Sian, then," said Bianca, pulling back and kissing him on the mouth, desperately hunting for some sort of a response that went beyond brotherly affection. "You're paying for the stupid thing. Let her do the bloody detective work."

"She is doing most of it," he said. "She sometimes needs a sounding board, that's all."

Bianca raised a skeptical eyebrow.

"I'm the one who stands to gain the most financially if we do nail him, so I want her to succeed," said Ben. "If Excelsior goes down, that would be a huge coup for me. For us."

Reaching for her breasts, he started to stroke them, something he hadn't done in ages. Bianca closed her eyes and tried to feel comforted. They made love afterward, and though the sex was clumsy and brief, it felt so good to be connected again, she barely noticed. Then, this morning, they'd slept in an extra hour. He'd been so sweet to her, promising they'd spend more time alone and even setting aside a whole evening next week to go through wedding plans properly with Maxwell.

But just as she was starting to relax, he'd picked up the phone to Sian, and the whole downward spiral began again. Stacking the dripping plates to dry, Bianca was horrified to find herself fantasizing that Sian might be hit by a bus on the way home.

"Hey, chica."

She jumped out of her skin as two strong, deeply tanned arms coiled themselves around her waist. Spinning around, she squealed with delight to see Lucas.

"I can't believe he's got you barefoot in the kitchen already," he joked, standing back to admire her flat, toned belly, exposed between a midriff-baring tie-dye T-shirt and sexy low-cut jeans. She was Ben's girl, but he could still look. "You're not even married yet."

Bianca smiled. Lucas had always had an uncanny ability to make her laugh in even the blackest of circumstances. Standing in front of her, a lit Gitane in one hand and a bottle of beer in the other, he looked mightily pleased with himself. His grin was almost as broad as his shoulders.

"At this rate, I'm starting to wonder if we ever will be," she said ruefully. "Married, I mean."

Lucas frowned. "What on earth makes you say that?"

"Oh, nothing." She turned back to the dishes so he wouldn't see the tears welling her eyes, but it was obvious she was upset. Stubbing out his cigarette on one of the takeout boxes, Lucas gently spun her back around to face him.

"Come on, angel," he said gently. "You can tell Uncle Lucas."

Bianca gave a sob. Desperate to confide suddenly, it all came flooding out: Sian's investigation into Anton and Ben spending more and more time with her, the growing distance between herself and Ben, the fights over the wedding. When she'd finished, Lucas looked stone-faced.

"That bitch," he said viciously. "No wonder Ben's been so bloody evasive with me recently. He didn't want to admit he's let that little gold digger back into his life."

"I wouldn't say she's a gold digger, exactly," said Bianca, shocked by the strength of his reaction. "It's just that she's incredibly...intrusive. Getting Ben to focus on the wedding when she's around is like trying to teach astrophysics to a goldfish."

"Where is he?" Lucas still looked far from pleased.

"He's next door in the living room. With her."

"With Sian?" his eyes widened. "She's here now?"

Bianca nodded. "But listen, darling, please don't say anything. Ben already thinks I'm overreacting and—"

"Don't worry," Lucas said firmly. "You leave this to me."

The fight that erupted over the next five minutes was so loud it could be heard on the street below.

"I can't believe you lied to me about this!" Lucas could be heard yelling at Ben. "All this time Anton's been crucifying me in court, and you never even mention you've been spending the last five fucking months investigating him? I could have used some of that information. I thought we were friends."

"No one lied to you," said Sian furiously. "This is my story, and it's none of your damn business."

"You keep out of this, you poisonous little shit-stirrer," Lucas roared at her. "What the fuck are you doing here anyway? Still trying to get your grubby little hands on Ben's money?"

"That's enough," said Ben, who was still recovering from the shock of Lucas's presence, never mind his tirade. "Don't speak to Sian like that."

"Why the hell not?" Lucas was incandescent with rage. "And you ought to spend less time worrying about this tramp and more time worrying about poor Bianca. I just found her in the kitchen in floods of tears, cleaning up your mess." He glared in disgust at the half-eaten pizzas and empty beer cans littering the room.

"I would have done it myself later," mumbled Ben guiltily. "Is she all right now?"

"No," said Lucas. "She's not. She's miserable as hell and she thinks you don't love her. You should get in there and sort it out."

Ben headed for the kitchen, then looked at Sian and hesitated. "You all right?"

"Hey, don't worry about me," said Sian, looking daggers at Lucas. "I can handle this prick. Go do what you've got to do."

Ben left the room, and for a few seconds the pair of them stared silently at each other, basking in mutual loathing. Then the fighting began in earnest.

"I'll give you this, you're a tenacious little cow," said Lucas. "Just when did you get your claws back into him exactly?"

"No one got their claws into anyone," she shot back indignantly. "Ben's a friend. The only money he's given me has been to fund my research into Anton, a guy who, believe it or not, turns out to be an even nastier piece of work than you are."

"At last, something we agree on," said Lucas sarcastically. "So Ben was the only person in the world you could have gone to for help, was he? It had nothing to do with you still holding a torch for him or wanting to come between him and the only woman he's ever really loved?"

Sian tried to hide how stung she was. Had Ben said that to Lucas? That Bianca was the only woman he'd ever loved?

"He wasn't the only person, but he was the person with the most to gain from seeing Anton brought down. Apart from you, of course. But frankly I'd rather have taken money off Ted Bundy than let you back into my life, on any level."

"Something else we agree on," said Lucas bitterly, though inside he was impressed by her poise and thinking how much she'd matured since her days as a summer maid at Palmers. He still didn't trust her an inch, especially not where Ben was concerned. But it took a tough cookie to take on the likes of Anton. She must have known that digging into his affairs would be dangerous and difficult, but if the thick slab of a file spilling its contents all over Ben's coffee table was anything to go by, she'd already gotten a lot to show for the risks she'd taken.

"So," he said, idly flicking open the file and pulling out a couple of documents, "what sort of a return have you shown him on his investment? Other than a weeping fiancée."

"Oh no you don't." Sian was across the room in a flash. Whipping the papers out of his hand, she shoved them back into the file and, not knowing quite what else to do, sat on it. "You think I'd trust you with my story? You can read it when it's finished like everyone else."

"Right," said Lucas, languorously stretching out his long legs as he sat down on Ben's leather Chesterfield sofa. "And when will that be? The twelfth of never, evening edition?"

"Actually, I hope to be ready to run with it next month." Despite his needling, Sian couldn't entirely hide her excitement. "That's why I came to see Ben tonight, before we were so rudely interrupted. I just got back from Azerbaijan. Let's just say that in the last forty-eight hours things have taken a quantum leap forward."

Ben came back in looking tired and shut the door behind him. Lucas noticed for the first time how gray and drawn his complexion had become and how much weight he'd lost. Bianca obviously wasn't the only one with prewedding nerves.

"How is she?" asked Sian, earning herself a withering look from Lucas.

"She's upset," said Ben. "It's my fault. I was being a bit of a dick to her yesterday about this wedding planner she's hired. And then tonight, spending so much time in here with you, I think I might have added insult to injury."

"But didn't you tell her what's happened? What we've found?" said Sian, who still found it hard at times to remember that not everyone was as obsessed with bringing Anton Tisch to justice as she was.

"No." A soft voice came from behind Ben as Bianca opened the door. "He didn't tell me anything. He never does."

Having washed off her tears in the bathroom and changed into a clean sleeveless T-shirt and hot-pink cut-off Bermuda shorts, she looked like a darker, more mysterious version of Gisele Bündchen on a really, really good day. Sian, who by contrast looked tired and washed out in a sludge-brown shift dress the same color as her ancient, overwashed panties, felt a stab of envy so violent she actually clutched her chest. Pointedly ignoring Ben, Bianca made a beeline for Lucas, her protector, curling herself up next to him on the sofa. The message was clear: it wasn't two against one anymore; Lucas had arrived to even the odds. Sian got it in a heartbeat.

"We didn't think you'd be interested," said Sian, trying not to sound as hostile as she felt. She knew she had no right to be. "You're always complaining about how much time we spend working on it."

"I complain about how much time *Ben* spends on it," interrupted Bianca. "Frankly, Sian, I couldn't care less what you do with your time."

This sudden boldness was completely out of character and took Sian by surprise. Meekly, she shut up.

"But seeing as you're here, again, monopolizing my home and my boyfriend, again," Bianca smiled at her rival thinly, "I think I would quite like to know what all the fuss has been about. And I'd like Lucas to know too."

Sian gave a splutter that was half laugh, half naked outrage. "Yeah, well, sorry, but it'll be a cold day in hell before we tell that scheming bastard anything. Lucas's secret-keeping record is right up there with Judas Iscariot's."

"OK, OK." Ben held up his hands like an overwhelmed referee trying to separate rival teams at a football match brawl. "I don't think any of this is particularly helpful. Bianca does have a right to know what's been going on."

"But—" Sian tried to interrupt him, but Ben wouldn't have it.

"No, come on Siany, she does. She's put up with a lot." He looked sorrowfully across at Bianca, whose eyes immediately started welling up again as she tried to smile back. Sian felt winded with jealousy, but said nothing.

"And I also think we should tell Lucas," Ben went on, "on the understanding that whatever gets said tonight remains between these four walls, and none of us breathes a word of it outside this room."

"No way!" Leaping back to her feet, Sian sounded properly panicked. "Ben, no, you promised. You promised not to tell anyone. That was our deal!"

"I know," said Ben. "But that was before we knew what we know now. Before Azerbaijan." Walking over, he put a reassuring hand on her shoulder, unconsciously increasing the "them and us" atmosphere of two opposing teams, himself and Sian versus Lucas and Bianca. "I honestly think Lucas can help. He wants to see Anton finished as much as any of us."

"That's the second time someone's mentioned Azerbaijan," said Lucas, who had calmed down now and whose curiosity was well and truly piqued. "What's the connection? I mean, I know Tisch made his fortune from Russian oil."

"It goes a lot deeper than that," said Ben.

"First you have to swear," said Sian. "Swear on…" she tried to think of anything that was important to Lucas other than himself but drew a complete blank. "Swear on your honor," she finished sarcastically, "that you will keep what we're about to tell you to yourself, until I tell you you can do otherwise."

"Fuck off," snarled Lucas. "I don't take orders from you."

"You do on this," said Ben firmly. "This is Sian's story, and she's sweated blood to pull it together. You can either respect her authority or get out."

It was hard to tell who was more pissed off by this show of support for Sian, Lucas or Bianca. Both of them looked as if he'd just offered them a bite of a dog-shit sandwich. But in the end, Lucas's curiosity got the better of him.

"Fine," he said grudgingly. "I swear. Now come on, what's all this about?"

———

Ten minutes later, in a break from the usual, Lucas was lost for words.

"Pretty incredible, isn't it?" said Sian, with more than a touch of pride. "Up until this point, most of the shit I had on him was sexual. And a lot of that was pretty fucking creepy: underage girls, prostitution, the odd sexual assault allegation here and there, although the girls always changed their tune before things got to court. But this shit?" She shook her head, still astonished by the revelations herself. "This puts us in a whole new ball game."

"I don't understand," said Bianca eventually. "He's committed a serious crime. Surely it's your absolute duty to go to the police?"

"And lose my exclusive? Are you out of your mind?" snapped Sian. "I haven't worked my tits off for half a year to lose my scoop at the last hurdle. We finish the story. We print it. Then we get dickhead locked up."

"Darling?" Bianca turned to Ben, who'd suddenly developed an intense interest in his cuticles. "Surely you don't agree with that?"

Ben shrugged awkwardly. His instinct was to defend Sian—this was her story, after all—but it was hard to stick up for her when she got so strident and hostile. "It's not really up to me," he mumbled lamely.

"Bullshit," said Lucas. "You're implicated up to your eyeballs, and so are Bianca and I, now that we know too. Suppressing evidence is a crime."

"Please," Sian snarled, fear making her even more aggressive. Lucas and Bianca were threatening to flush her entire story down the toilet, and Ben wasn't lifting a finger to help her. "Like you're such a fricking Boy Scout all of a sudden. Tell it to someone who doesn't know what a scheming little player you are, Ruiz."

Lucas started hurling abuse back at her, but Sian ignored him.

"In any case, we still don't have all the bank account numbers we need, for the police or the papers," she said defiantly. "The worst thing we could do is make a move before this thing is watertight. The slightest weakness and Tisch will pounce on us like that." She snapped her fingers for emphasis. Not even Lucas could argue with her about that.

"I'm going back to Azerbaijan the day after tomorrow for some more meetings."

"What? You never mentioned another trip." Ben, all animation suddenly, looked pained. "What meetings? With whom?"

Sian, who'd sat back down again, now shifted uncomfortably in her seat, tugging at the hem of her shapeless dress like a schoolgirl hauled before the principal.

"With some rebels, OK?" she said, then seeing Ben's face, added: "I know what I'm doing. I trust these guys."

"Then you're a bloody moron," shouted Ben, so loudly that Bianca and Lucas both turned to stare. "How can you possibly know who to trust? It's the Wild fucking West out there. They're terrorists, for God's sake."

"That's ridiculous," said Sian sulkily. "They're freedom fighters."

"I don't care," said Ben. "Call them what you like, but you are not going back out there. It's too dangerous. I'm not having you risk your life over this. It's insanity." Watching him, Bianca felt her heart lurch. His face was a study in anguish. Obviously the idea of Sian coming to any harm was tearing him up inside, so much so that his usual diplomacy seemed to have deserted him, and he hadn't even made an effort to hide it.

For her, it was the last straw. Turning on Sian, she sprang across the room in two long-legged bounds and physically yanked her up out of her seat.

"Get out!" she whispered, shaking with rage. "Get the fuck out of our house and don't come back."

Sian, who before tonight had never known Bianca to be anything other than painfully polite and accommodating, was too shocked to react. Ben had no such qualms.

"Jesus, B," he said, pulling the two of them apart. "What the hell are you doing?"

But Bianca was not about to let up "I'm doing what I should have done months ago," she sobbed, tears of anger and hurt and frustration rolling down her perfectly chiseled cheeks. "I'm getting this bitch out of our lives before she poisons everything. She's all you fucking care about these days, Ben. She's all you see!" Wriggling free from his grip, she lashed out at Sian again wildly, landing a painful kick to her shin before covering her face with her hands and fleeing the room in tears.

"I'm so sorry," stammered a shell-shocked Ben as Sian bent double, rubbing her bruised leg. "She's never normally…I have no idea what's gotten into her."

Lucas, who'd sat back and watched in silent horror as this little drama unfolded, now shot Ben a "who are you kidding?" look.

"It's OK," said Sian, who was actually deeply shaken. "I'm fine. I should go."

"You don't have to." The mark on her leg was already spreading, he noticed, and would no doubt soon morph into the deep plum shade she so often wore as eye shadow, which gave her pale face an even more ethereal, otherworldly beauty. Life would be so much simpler if only he didn't want her so dreadfully much.

"I do," said Sian, forcing a smile for his sake. "Really. I can see myself out."

The front door slammed shut behind her, followed by a second slam from the bedroom door at the far end of the corridor. For a few seconds Ben just stood there, forlorn, like a little boy dumped on a station platform. "I'm going after her," he said eventually, patting his various pockets frantically, looking for his car keys and only stopping when Lucas laid a hand on his shoulder.

"No you're not," he said firmly. "Bianca's the one who needs you. You stay here and sort things out with her."

Ben looked torn. "But Sian…what if she?…she mustn't take that flight back to Russia. I'm serious, Lucas. What if she got killed? I'd never forgive myself."

"Give me her address," said Lucas. Ben looked dubious.

"For fuck's sake, give me the girl's address, all right? I promise to go easy, and I promise to keep her on the ground, at least for the time being."

Grabbing a piece of paper from the desk, Ben scrawled something down and pressed it into Lucas's hand.

"She lives with Lola Carter, you know," he said. "You might want to take a bulletproof vest."

"Thanks," said Lucas grimly, nodding down the corridor in the direction of Bianca's still-audible sobs. "So might you."

———————   ———————

Back at the apartment on Tite Street, Sian was relieved to find that Lola was out, no doubt staring doe-eyed across a candlelit table somewhere at Marti, who'd been staying with them again for the last few weeks. She truly couldn't have faced Mr. and Mrs. Love's Young Dream tonight, nor was she in the mood for talking things through, which was always Lola's answer for everything.

Flinging herself down on her bed, still unmade from this morning, she pummeled her fists into the pillows and howled for a few minutes until she felt marginally better. Then she walked into the bathroom, splashed her face with a sink full of ice-cold water, half of which splattered down the front of her dress, and tried to marshal her muddled and depressing thoughts into some sort of order.

How the fuck had it all gone wrong tonight? She'd been so happy on the way over to Ben's, armed at last with the breakthrough they'd both been hoping for. OK, so he might not love her, and he might be about to marry officially the most beautiful woman on the planet. But their work together, this story, had built a bond between them that was uniquely theirs. Anton Tisch, of all unlikely people, had brought her and Ben together. It was a closeness that she knew couldn't last, but she'd cherished it all the more for that. And now it was gone. Just like that.

For all she knew Bianca might be at the police station right now, ruining everything. Spurred on, no doubt, by that shit-stirring motherfucker Lucas, her own personal bad penny.

"Open up!"

She was disturbed from her moping by a loud and very insistent knocking at the front door. Christ, it couldn't be the cops already, could it? She hadn't even begun to get her story straight.

"Just a minute." Frantically scraping her unruly hair back into a bun and slipping her bare feet into slippers, she hobbled to the door. Her shin was still throbbing from where Bianca had clocked her one. Naturally Miss Fucking Accomplished at Everything turned out to be a black belt in friggin' karate too. "I'm coming."

Pulling open the door, she was equally shocked and enraged to see Lucas, who pushed past her and swaggered into the sitting room as though he owned the place.

"Lola here?" he asked, looking around.

"No," said Sian furiously. "What the fuck—"

"Good," Lucas cut her off. "We need to talk in private."

"We sure as hell do not." Sian looked murderous. "You have no business being here, and you know it. Why don't you fuck off and leave me alone?"

"I knocked. You let me in," said Lucas, with maddening nonchalance, picking up a glass paperweight from one of the side tables and examining it idly before setting it back down.

"I didn't know who it was," said Sian. "Obviously."

"You shouldn't have opened the door then, should you? Those the kind of survival skills you're going to use in Azerbaijan, are they? With a bunch of lawless, crackhead rebels with Uzis stuffed under their trench coats? You won't last a day."

Suddenly too tired to argue, Sian retreated to her bedroom, climbed under the covers, and pulled the rumpled sheet up to her chin. Maybe if she simply ignored him, he'd give up and bugger off. But apparently not. Following her, Lucas closed the door behind him, calmly removed a pile of dirty clothes and underwear from the chair by her dressing table, and sat down, crossing his legs and looking at her with his head cocked to one side, in the manner of a psychiatrist assessing a new patient. Irrationally, Sian found herself wishing that she'd bothered to put makeup on earlier, or at least had the foresight to tidy up her pigpen of a room. Lucas looked ludicrously out of place in his Savile Row suit and silk sunflower-yellow tie surrounded by her journalist-on-a-deadline squalor (complete with used tissues on the floor and old mug of tea growing mold on the windowsill), like a Hugo Boss model posing on a Baghdad bomb site.

"I have a suggestion for you," he said coolly.

"Does it involve you dying? Or having your testicles surgically removed and bequeathed to the women of the nation in a pickle jar?" asked Sian, deadpan.

"Sweet, but no," said Lucas. "It involves you making a much bigger splash with your story than you would do by simply selling it to one newspaper."

"Oh, so now you want to help me with my story?" Sian gave a hollow laugh. "What happened to rushing off to the police with your pal Bianca? Over our law-abiding citizen phase now, are we? That was quick, even for you."

"Look," said Lucas. "You can bitch or you can listen. It's your choice." Sian was silent for a few seconds.

"Go on," she said skeptically.

"Petra's throwing a party next month to celebrate the Herrick being voted number one luxury hotel."

"I know," said Sian, with an unimpressed shrug. "So?"

"So she and Anton have invited half the world's media to be there. I'm not just talking print press either, but TV, news crews, all the LA gossip shows like *Entertainment Tonight* and *Extra!* None of them give a shit about the hotel, obviously; they're there for the celebrity guests. But it's turning into one big circus. Now, if you could hijack that event," he raised an eyebrow temptingly, "you'd have coverage beyond your wildest dreams. Here, the US, Asia…"

Sian allowed herself to imagine this for a moment. It was certainly an appealing fantasy. But it wasn't long before reality and reason reasserted themselves.

"There's no way," she said. "Anton'll have major security at that party, and that's aside from all the personal heavies the stars'll bring with them. It'll be like Fort Knox."

"I agree," said Lucas. "I'm not saying it'd be easy. We'd need a lot of inside help, and someone on the ground out there to coordinate things. Someone with access." Sian looked at him quizzically.

"I don't get it," she said. "You don't give a shit about me."

"Correct," said Lucas.

"So what do you care what happens with my story? What's in it for you?"

Lucas stood up and walked over to the window. Outside, the Victorian streetlamps glowed orange, illuminating kissing couples as they strolled home after dinner on the King's Road. When it wasn't raining, London could really be quite charming, especially on warm summer nights like this one.

"Anton set me up," he said quietly. "He's spent the last three years systematically trying to ruin me. He's even backing Connor in this damn court case. I want revenge. I want to see his reputation shredded, the way he shredded mine. And I wouldn't mind seeing Petra Kamalski brought down a peg or two either. We go back a long way."

Sian could see the muscles of his back and shoulders tighten visibly beneath his suit jacket, and his left hand coiled itself unconsciously into a fist. She'd heard Lucas's version of this sob story from Ben many times and wasn't sure how much of it she believed. But there could be no doubting his anger. That was palpably genuine.

"So what are you saying?" she asked. "Do you have insiders at the Herrick who could help us?"

Lucas turned around. "I can probably call in a few favors, yeah. Petra pays her staff well, but she treats them like shit. I don't imagine it'll be too tough to find some bitter, disaffected soul to help us."

"I don't know," said Sian. "I don't like the idea of sharing information with some random bellboy we barely know. What's to stop them from selling whatever we tell them to the highest bidder?"

"We don't have to tell them anything material," argued Lucas. "Come on, you're the investigative journalist here. Surely you're not above a little spin?"

But Sian wasn't budging. "It won't work," she said. "It's too complicated; there are too many wild cards. Besides, I can't be in the Hamptons to pull it all together. I have to go back to Azerbaijan."

"Forget that," said Lucas, walking over to the bed and sitting down next to her, to Sian's unspoken alarm. God, the man was pushy. "Ben's right, it's far too dangerous."

"No, Ben's wrong," said Sian, starting to lose patience. Why was she even having this conversation with Lucas? "I need that information."

"Then get it," said Lucas. "There are other ways. You can stay in London and work on that from here. I'll take care of things in the Hamptons."

Sian wavered. He was so forceful, so sure of himself, it was hard not to get swept along. And though she'd die rather than admit it to him or Ben, she was in fact scared shitless about the thought of going back to meet the rebels on her own.

"What about your court case? Won't that keep you in Europe?"

"Yeeeees," Lucas admitted, acknowledging a snag in his argument for the first time. But the doubt was gone as soon as it had appeared, and with a eureka snap of his fingers he suddenly said: "Honor!"

"Excuse me?" said Sian.

"Honor Palmer. We should bring her in on this. She'd be the perfect person to manage things on the ground. She and I can work together when I'm there, and when I need to go to Europe—"

"Whoa, whoa there," said Sian. "Have I missed something? Doesn't Honor, like, *loathe* you?"

Lucas shook his head. "That's just a front, because she wants me so badly. Women always get aggressive when they can't handle their own desire."

The arrogance was breathtaking. Sian opened and closed her mouth in wordless fury before finally managing a disbelieving, "My God, you are such an asshole."

"One thing I would like you to do, if you have time," said Lucas, ignoring the insult, "is to do a little digging into the Palmers fire."

"I don't have time," said Sian, truthfully.

"Those bastards at the insurance company really did a number on Honor, and they won't pay out until someone's actually charged with arson," Lucas went on, once again ignoring her objections. "The Hamptons police are a lazy bunch of doughnut eaters; they're never going to find anything. But you're obviously...good at this."

She could see how much it pained him to bestow this compliment, and smiled. "Thanks."

"Maybe you could, I don't know...come up with something? Once you've got what you need on Anton."

Again, Sian looked puzzled. "You want me to help Honor Palmer. Why?"

"Look, it's not a big deal, OK?" snapped Lucas, defensive all of a sudden. "If you have time, that's all. So what do you think?"

"About?"

"About holding off going to the papers? Ambushing this party?"

Sian was silent for a moment. The ridiculousness of her current situation had not escaped her. Here she was, lying in bed, casually chatting to the man she loathed most in the world about a plan so audacious and fraught with difficulties it would almost certainly see her ending up with egg on her face. But the combination of Lucas's boundless confidence, his unexpected faith in her abilities, and the tantalizing possibility of worldwide coverage for her story proved too much to resist.

"I think," she said, grinning, "it's a crazy idea. But what the hell. I'm in."

Watching her face light up with excitement, Lucas realized for the first time what it was Ben saw in her. She'd always be too pale and scrawny for his taste. But there was a charisma about her, a combination of intelligence and courage, that could floodlight a stadium if she put her mind to it.

"Listen," he said, fishing a Gitane out of his pocket and lighting it without asking her whether she minded. "There's one other thing we need to talk about."

"Oh? And what's that?" she said, humoring him.

"Ben," said Lucas. Inhaling deeply, he blew out a long stream of smoke through his nostrils.

Sian's eyes narrowed. "There's nothing to talk about."

"You're in love with him, aren't you?" Lucas cut right to the chase.

She thought about denying it. But after everything that had happened this evening, it seemed a little late for secrets.

"I always was in love with him," she said, throwing caution to the wind. "But you could never accept that, could you? You always knew better. I was a chambermaid; he was a millionaire. So you decided it must have been all about the money. But it never was. Not for me. Not then, and not now."

The tears in her eyes were obviously genuine. Lucas felt a pang of guilt. Maybe the real reason he'd been against her from the start was not that she was a gold digger, but that she reminded him so much of his younger self, a poor, desperate self he wanted to forget, a self with ambition oozing out of every pore like sweat. Or maybe he'd simply been afraid that she was going to take Ben away from him? How pathetic if that were true.

"I'm sorry if I misjudged you," he said, lighting a second cigarette from his first and offering it to her. Warily, Sian took it. "I made a lot of mistakes back then. Perhaps that was one of them."

"Jeez," said Sian, relaxing slightly as the nicotine flooded her system. "Lucas Ruiz, apologizing? Stop the press."

Lucas looked awkward.

"What happened? First you want to help Honor Palmer, now you're apologizing to me. You're not in therapy, are you?"

"Don't be ridiculous," said Lucas.

"AA?"

"Hardly." He forced a smile. "My doctor says I should think about donating my liver to science, and he's a Frenchman."

"NA?"

"Stop avoiding the issue," he said gently. "I'm not in any kind of A. I admit I was wrong for the things I said about you back then."

"You said them tonight, too," Sian reminded him.

"Fine, so I'm a dickhead, OK? Maybe I should never have come between you and Ben in the first place. But the point is, it doesn't matter now." He looked her square in the eye. "He's getting married. Bianca's made him happy, happier than I've ever seen him. He loves her, and she loves him."

"I know," said Sian miserably, twisting a loose strand of hair around and around her fingers.

"Bianca's a good person," said Lucas. "I mean really good. Not like you and me."

"I know that too," whispered Sian.

"So don't ruin it for them," said Lucas. Stubbing out his cigarette on a dirty plate on the bedside table, he did the same with hers, then took her hand in his. "If you really loved him—I mean really—you'd let him go."

"You sound like a Hallmark greeting card," said Sian. But she was only bitching at him out of force of habit. She knew he was right. What could she possibly offer Ben that Bianca couldn't? She couldn't even say her heart, because Bianca's feelings were obviously every bit as deep as her own.

The next thing she knew, Lucas had pressed her hand to his lips.

"You're a beautiful girl," he said, softly. "You'll find someone else."

"I don't want someone else," said Sian, the tears in her eyes at last brimming over.

"You and Ben would never work. He needs a calming influence. Someone steady. A homemaker. That's not you."

"It could be," she said desperately.

"Not in this lifetime, sweetheart." Lucas laughed. Leaning forward, he kissed her full on the lips. Shocked for a second, Sian found her mouth tentatively opening in response. Before she knew it, she was kissing him back, with more passion and longing than she could remember feeling since Ben.

"Oh my *God*!"

Lola's screech was car-alarm loud. Lucas jumped out of his skin and off Sian's bed, turning around midleap to see Lola standing in the bedroom doorway like a redheaded angel of retribution.

"What...what the hell is he doing here?" she screamed at Sian.

"OK, calm down," said Sian, "I can explain. It's not what you think."

"No?" Lola gave her a look so laden with bitterness and disappointment it made Sian blush scarlet. "Well what is it, then? Because it sure looks a lot like Lucas Ruiz is in my fucking apartment, making out in bed with my so-called best friend! How could you let that freak in here?"

"It's business. He's here about the story," said Sian, realizing at once how ludicrous an excuse it must sound, given that she'd just had her tongue halfway down the man's throat.

"You can talk to me directly, you know," said Lucas, regaining some of his usual sangfroid. "I am here."

"Shut up!" yelled Lola and Sian in unison.

"What's going on?" Marti, a little unsteady on his feet after two very good bottles of Chilean cabernet at dinner, washed down with a couple of grappas, appeared behind Lola, resting his chin on the top of her head as much for his own support as for hers. "Why all the shouting?"

Lola gave a hollow laugh. "This is Lucas," she said, pointing at Lucas like she was picking the killer out of a lineup. "You know, Lucas, the guy who ruined my family's life? But it's OK," she added bitterly. "He's here on business. As long as it's for the good of the story, right Sian? What's a little thing like friendship and loyalty, if he helps you get your precious scoop?"

She was more than a little drunk herself. In a microshort gold dress from French Connection that clashed gloriously with her wild, titian hair, she looked like a space-age cavewoman who'd just been ravished by a group of marauding Martians and was pretty goddamn furious about it. Lucas, already aroused from his kiss with Sian, felt his budding erection start to strengthen and edged behind a chair in an effort to hide it.

"My mom tried to kill herself because of this guy," said Lola, getting increasingly hysterical.

"I know, I know," said Marti gently, trying to calm her down. He hated seeing Lola upset, but he especially hated seeing her upset with Sian. The two of them used to be such good friends. "He went to the press about your dad's affair."

"Actually, he didn't," said Sian, unthinking. "Anton was behind that story, not Lucas."

"Again, I am here," muttered Lucas, to no one in particular.

"Oh, what, so you're *defending* him now?" said Lola. "Unbelievable. So what else don't I know about him, huh? Please, enlighten me! Has he brokered peace in the Middle East since we were dating? No? Won a Nobel Prize for physics? No, really, I'm serious. I'm dying to hear what a great guy he really is and how none of the shit he did to me, or my family, was actually his fault at all. Please, go on. I've got time."

"Well, it's been lovely, but I should go," said Lucas, emerging from behind the chair now that his ardor had died down, replaced by a splitting headache. "Nice to almost meet you." He nodded at Marti, who nodded back. "Sian, call me in the morning to discuss where we go from here."

"No." Darting back into the doorway, Lola barred his way. "You stay and have your discussion now. I can't stay in this building one more minute. Not until it's been fumigated." She looked at him with such hatred, Lucas shivered. It was hard to believe that they had once been lovers.

"But Lola, you live here," said Sian, stating the obvious.

"That's right," Lola hissed. "I do. And as of tomorrow, you don't. Marti and I'll spend tonight in a hotel. I want you gone by the time I get back in the morning."

"Honey, come on," said Marti, following his furious girlfriend as she ran into her own bedroom to grab some underwear and a toothbrush. "Don't you think you're overreacting just a tad?"

Clearly Lola didn't think so. Cramming her stuff into an overnight bag, she grabbed his hand and physically dragged him to the door. On the way out she turned for one last parting shot at Sian, who'd now made it as far as the sitting room. "You know what? I'm glad you broke it off with Paddy. I figure he had a lucky escape. You and Lucas deserve each other." And with a slam that echoed around the building like a lone gunshot, she was gone, the hapless Marti following in her wake.

"She'll come around," said Lucas, putting a comforting hand on Sian's shoulder. "Her boyfriend seems like a decent guy. He'll talk some sense into her."

With no one else to rage at, Sian turned on him like a pet cat gone feral.

"What is it with you?" she yelled. "Every relationship I have, you have to destroy it. Now, because of you, I'm fucking homeless!"

"Because of *me*?" Lucas looked astonished. "What the hell did I do?" But Sian was done arguing.

"Get out!" she roared, manhandling him toward the front door with surprising strength for one so slight. "Get the hell out of my life, Lucas. And don't come back!"

CHAPTER TWENTY-NINE

WO WEEKS LATER, AT THE CARTERS' SUMMER HOME IN East Hampton, Lola helped Marti into his tuxedo.

"You know what?" he said, as she fiddled with his tie. "This whole dressing for dinner thing is starting to make me real nervous. I feel like I'm in a bad episode of *Falcon Crest*."

Lola laughed. "Don't let my mom hear you say that. My parents think soap operas are the root of all America's problems. Them and MTV. And women being allowed membership into the Bridge Hampton Polo Club."

"Yeah, that was a big one," said Marti, deadpan. "Didn't that knock the Iraq invasion off the top spot on CNN?"

He always made jokes when he was nervous. It was a defense mechanism he'd learned in childhood, when kids at school in Queens used to tease him for being so skinny and wearing such thick, nerdy glasses. He hadn't grown into his looks until his early twenties, but a childhood marred by acne and bullying had had some positive side effects on his character. Wit was one of them. A ferocious drive and determination to succeed was another. Sadly, he doubted very much whether either of these attributes would mean as much to Lola's family as the right surname. And that was the one thing he didn't have.

When Lola first floated the idea of a few weeks in the Hamptons, the morning after her titanic fight with Sian, he'd been all for it. Though she put on a tough front, he could tell that Lola was deeply upset by what had happened and that she needed to get away. Returning to Tite Street to find Sian and all her things gone with not so much as a note or a forwarding address must have been like a bullet to the chest. Though he hadn't dared ask her whether she regretted being so harsh to her friend, Marti was pretty sure that she did and that the trip to the Hamptons was her way of running away from that guilt and sadness. Not that she'd presented it like that, of course.

"I just need a break from the business. We both do," she said, forcing the cheerfulness into her voice. It might have been an excuse, but it also happened to be true. Marla had been consuming both of them for months, and Marti also had his other online businesses to run. Physically, he was spent.

"Besides," Lola added, "it's time you really met my folks." This was also true. The last and only time Marti had seen Devon, he'd been hiding inside a broom closet with his pants around his ankles, which didn't really count as a meeting. So they'd made plans for the trip, with Marti spending the next week imagining long, lazy days on the beach with Lola, just the two of them exploring her childhood haunts together.

Unfortunately, as so often with vacations, the reality turned out to be rather different.

His first misgivings came on the drive from the airport, when their little Volkswagen rental car was overtaken by an eye-popping series of Porsches, Lamborghinis, and Bentleys, all heading for Walter Mill, the Hamptons' hippest and most exclusive beach.

"I thought you said it would be low-key?" He looked at Lola nervously.

He could easily have afforded to hire a flashy set of wheels—since his Internet company had taken off four years ago, money was no longer an issue—but cars had always bored him. Now, though, he wished he *had* gone for something a bit further up the food chain. He wouldn't want Devon to think he was a cheapskate who couldn't take care of his daughter.

"It is low-key," said Lola. "I mean, you know," she added breezily, as a gleaming silver Vanquish roared past, burying them in a cloud of dust. "It's all relative."

Their arrival at the Carter house had done nothing to calm his nerves.

Karis greeted them at the front door in a daze, looking like a younger Miss Haversham, all white-blonde hair and jutting bones.

"Holy crap, she's gotten skinny again," whispered Lola, squeezing his hand for moral support.

"No shit," he whispered back, a terrified grin of welcome fixed across his features. "She looks like Mary-Kate Olsen on Valium."

Lola had conveniently forgotten to mention that this was the first time any of her family had been back to East Hampton since her dad's affair had been made public. Karis, highly strung at the best of times, had insisted she could face it, but since arriving had spent most of her time wandering around the house like a shell-shock victim, permanently on the brink of tears. She point-blank refused to venture into town, even for groceries, in case she ran into Honor, which meant that Devon and Nick, strapped for cash and visiting on sufferance from LA, were under virtual house arrest too. By the time Marti and Lola showed up, the strain on everybody was already starting to show.

At least Karis had made a token effort to be welcoming. Devon, on the other hand, made a great show of bear-hugging Lola before stiffly offering Marti his hand as if he were greeting the guy sent to unblock the drains. After that he'd disappeared off to his study for the rest of the evening, not to be seen again until the following morning.

After four days spent climbing the walls in the house, the last thing Marti felt like was tonight's ludicrously formal at-home dinner.

"Did you happen to see tonight's menu?" he asked, as Lola finished with his tie and smoothed down the lapels of his gleaming new tux. "It wasn't Grilled Jew, by any chance?"

"Don't be silly," she said firmly. "You'll be fine."

"Can I please not sit next to Nick?" asked Marti, feebly. Lola's brother had turned out to be even more obnoxiously arrogant and dull than she'd described him, which was quite a feat. The way he talked about his business, anyone would have thought he was Warren Buffett, yet it was painfully obvious that the only reason he was here was to screw some more money out of his poor, tapped-out parents.

"Not my call," said Lola. "Mom'll seat us." Flinging her arms around his neck, she gave him a long, lingering kiss.

"What was that for?" he asked, smiling. She looked more beautiful than ever tonight in an empire-line blue chiffon dress, with her glorious red hair flowing long and loose over her shoulders. Like a Pre-Raphaelite goddess.

"For being here," she said. "I know they're difficult. But they're my family. And so are you now."

Incredibly touched, he pulled her closer. "I love you," he said. "But if they sit me next to your brother, I can't promise not to strangle him."

"Oh, please," laughed Lola. "Don't hold back on my account. I'll bring the rope if you like."

Dinner was predictably horrible.

"So," said Devon, swirling the burgundy around his glass and sniffing appreciatively at the deep-purple whirlpool he'd created, "tell us a little more about yourself, Martin."

"It's Marti, Dad," said Lola, through clenched teeth. "No one calls him Martin. And you know all about him. He's an Internet entrepreneur, and he's brilliant." She beamed across the table loyally.

Marti smiled sheepishly back. "I wouldn't say brilliant exactly," he mumbled. "Well, maybe I would."

Devon didn't laugh.

Miserable douchebag. He was a classic closet anti-Semite, Marti had decided. Loads of Jewish clients, even Jewish friends, staunchly pro-Israel. But to have his daughter marry a Jew? Forget it. He'd rather die.

"Online business, it's a tough game," piped up Nick self-importantly from across the table. "Of course, I was lucky. I got in in ninety-eight. First-mover advantage. But guys like you, coming late to the party?" He shook his head knowingly. "Not easy. Not easy."

"You got in in ninety-eight?" Marti looked baffled. "Weren't you in, like, ninth grade in ninety-eight?"

Nick's model-perfect features clouded over with irritation. "I was young," he admitted. "But then I've never been a time-server." He waved his hand airily to indicate his devil-may-care entrepreneurial credentials. "Very few of the big guys are. Trump. Branson. Gates. None of them went to college. It's all about starting young."

"Did you compare yourself to Donald Trump?" Lola sniggered, choking on her wine.

"Yeah," said Nick aggressively. "So?"

"I'm pretty sure Bill Gates went to college," said Marti.

"Did not too," said Nick.

Nice comeback. Maybe he was still in ninth grade?

"Well," said Marti, deciding to be the bigger man and take the high road. It'd be too easy to shoot Nick down, and it was unlikely to win him many points with the parents. If the looks on their faces were anything to go by, Mr. and Mrs. Frosty McFreeze didn't need another reason to hate him right now. "I've nothing against people not going to university, or starting work young. Your sister's business has been incredibly successful already." Lola smiled at him gratefully. "But I guess I am what you would call a time-server. I had a wonderful time in college."

"Where did you attend?" asked Karis.

"Wharton," said Marti. "My grandfather came from Pennsylvania. He worked the mills in Pittsburgh. His side of the family always had this big thing about Wharton."

"Pittsburgh?" said Karis. "Did your people know the Mellons?"

"Er, no," laughed Marti. "I don't believe their paths ever crossed."

"His grandfather worked in the mills, Mom," said Lola, crossly. "Didn't you hear that part?"

"And what do your *own* parents do?" asked Devon. "Are they educated?"

"*Dad!*" Lola looked suitably horrified. "You can't ask people questions like that!"

"It's all right," said Marti, determined to keep his temper. Devon was a petty-minded snob, but he was here for Lola, not anyone else. "No, they aren't educated, not beyond high school, anyway. My mom's a part-time nurse at the old people's home down the street. And my dad runs a kosher deli. We're not kosher ourselves," he added, "but it's a good business. He used to run a hardware store, but then they opened a Home Depot four blocks away and wiped us out."

"A *Home Depot*?" said Karis, turning the words over as she spoke, as if examining a rare stone. "How fascinating."

Clearly, ordinary people with ordinary jobs were completely outside her frame of reference. With two such out-of-touch parents and a megalomaniacal fantasist for a brother, it was a miracle Lola had turned out so normal.

Somehow Marti made it to dessert—a sinfully creamy tiramisu—without losing his cool, and at last the general conversation changed tack.

"This party at the Herrick should be fun," said Nick, helping himself to a second slab of dessert and greedily cramming a spoonful into his mouth. "From what I hear, that Russki chick's really pulled out all the stops. Alex Loeb said the Clintons are gonna be there."

The Herrick party, less than three weeks away now, was the talk of the town.

"Good for them," said Devon, without looking up. "However, we won't be going."

"Speak for yourself," said Nick. "I'm going. Gisele Bündchen's on the guest list, along with half the Brazilian Elite girls. I'm not missing that for anyone."

"Yeah, right. Like you have a chance with them," muttered Lola.

"Enough!" roared Devon, losing his temper and banging his fist down on the table so hard the crystalware shuddered. "None of us is going and that's final. We're here to enjoy a quiet family summer together, not go running around town chasing after floozies."

"You'd know all about that," muttered Nick under his breath. Unfortunately he wasn't quite quiet enough.

"What did you just say?" Devon's voice had dropped to its normal level again, but his lips had gone white with rage.

"Darling, leave it," whispered Karis. "Please."

Marti shifted uncomfortably in his seat. This was going to get ugly. Nick pushed back his chair and got defiantly to his feet. "I'm sick of being stuck in this house, creeping around like a criminal because you two are running scared of Honor stupid Palmer."

"Nicky!" hissed Karis, on the verge of hysterics. "Do not say that name in this house. Ever."

Lola reached across the table and squeezed her mother's hand, but Karis seemed not to notice. Meanwhile Devon's face had gone from white through every shade to purple and was now, Marti noticed, roughly the color of a baboon's backside.

"Get out!" he yelled at Nick. "I mean it, Nicholas. Get out of this house, before I throw you out."

"Fine," said Nick, kicking his chair to the floor as he stormed off, slamming the dining room door behind him.

For a few precious moments silence fell. Then Devon looked up and smiled around the table as if nothing had happened.

"Would you like some coffee, my dear?" he asked Karis.

"Yes," she said, a little nervously. "I think so. Why not? As long as it's decaf. Lola darling? Will you and Martin be having any?"

Half an hour later, up in their bedroom, Marti undid his tie with relief.

"Was it just me? Or was that like something out of *The Stepford Wives*? Your mom was smiling so hard she looked like her jaw might go into spasm."

"I know," said Lola, unzipping her dress and kicking off her gold stiletto shoes.

"How can they live like that, in such a constant state of denial? I've never seen two people more repressed."

"I did warn you we weren't exactly the Waltons," said Lola ruefully. "Look on the bright side. At least Nick's taken off."

"Not for long, I bet," said Marti. "Your dad hasn't written him a check yet, and isn't likely to if he doesn't stick around to eat some humble pie. Something tells me he won't be going to that party at the Herrick either."

"Poor Gisele'll be sooo disappointed," giggled Lola.

Crawling under the covers together, they soon fell asleep, content as always just to lie in each other's arms.

At eleven the next morning, Honor sat at a table in the newly finished Palmers' dining room, sampling some mouthwateringly delicious roast monkfish.

"What do you think?"

"Fantastic," said Don Bradford, her saintly accountant whose own mouth was still full of the succulent, juicy fish. "Fucking amazing, if you want the truth."

Don had been brilliant this year, guiding her gently through the minefield of IRS demands and escalating interest payments that had become her life since the rebuild, never complaining when his bills were settled months after they were due. It was so rare to find someone kind and decent in the financial world. Honor had been hugely touched by his generosity and was always looking for ways to repay it. Knowing he was a paid-up foodie, she'd invited him along this morning to help her choose one of three Michelin-starred chefs to run the new Palmers' restaurant. He was clearly having a whale of a time.

"You know, the food is great," he said, dispatching the last of the monkfish parcels. "Truly, outstanding. But don't you think it might be a little rich for some people, with all the cream and garlic and drizzled balsamic jus?"

Honor laughed. The menus were a little pretentious.

"Have you considered trying something simpler? I know an awesome Mexican chef in the city who might consider a move." Honor laughed. He was joking, wasn't he?

"No offense, Don. But when people pay a thousand bucks a night for a room they expect a little bit more than enchiladas, guacamole, and a bucket of refried beans for dinner."

"They wouldn't if they'd tried Tito's food," said Don, affably. Looking around the dining room, with its dramatic floor-to-ceiling windows and limed oak floor, Honor felt her chest swell with pride. Her financial worries were far from over, but after so many months of hard work and sleepless nights, she was finally getting to the fun part: finalizing the soft furnishings, arranging contracts with florists, hunting around local antique markets for the perfect grand piano for the cocktail bar. She remembered, the Christmas before her mom died, Santa had brought her a beautiful handcrafted dollhouse in the style of a French chateau. For years afterward, she'd spent every cent of her pocket money buying furniture for it. Her favorite piece was a tiny working replica of a chandelier, which attached with red wires to a switch on the back of the house. At night she would turn off all the lights in her bedroom in Boston and switch it on, watching with delight as the dollhouse and its residents were bathed in a magical red glow that seemed to imbue them with a life of their own.

Decorating Palmers gave her the same thrill. She'd even found a similar light fixture for the dining room. By any rational standards it was far too ornate and completely at odds with the rest of the decor. But she couldn't resist. Hanging above their table now, she thought it looked absolutely magnificent. And Don adored it.

He also approved of her hiring decisions—which was a good thing, as she didn't know what she'd have done if he'd told her the money couldn't stretch to more than a skeleton staff. The chef they were choosing today would be one of only a handful of new appointments, since almost all the old Palmers staff were coming back, a testament to the excellent working relationship Honor had built with them over the years. After the ruthless cull she'd initiated when she first took over, it had taken a while for the remaining workers to feel secure again. But they soon came to realize that their new boss was as quick with her praise as her censure, and scrupulously fair.

When Petra took over at the Herrick, she'd given all the workers there a blanket pay raise and made sure that everyone at Palmers knew they could make more if they jumped ship. But Honor hadn't lost so much as a single waiter. There was a camaraderie at Palmers that simply didn't exist anywhere else. Certainly not at the Herrick, where staff turned over almost as frequently as the bed linen.

Of course, after the fire, Honor's workforce had been forced to move elsewhere, and some had gone to the Herrick then, out of necessity. But almost all were taking pay cuts to return to the new hotel in the fall. There was a palpable sense of excitement about getting the old gang back together, and for the first time in years Honor felt that perhaps, this time, the gods were with her.

She'd promoted Enrique, her old head barman, to overall head of hospitality. He and a handful of core staff were already living on-site, as was Honor herself. They shared the unfinished space with a legion of workmen, painters, plumbers, and gardeners who still showed up daily, and who Honor was still scrambling to pay on a week-by-week basis.

Even with the constant hammering and disruptions, it was bliss to be out of her poky little cottage at last. Her new rooms were considerably smaller than the old ones: a modest, wood-paneled bedroom that opened out onto a secluded terrace just big enough for a wrought-iron table and two chairs. She also had a simple sitting room with a pair of matching white denim couches, an antique standard lamp, and her grandfather's old writing desk tucked into the corner; and a bathroom, as yet unfinished, although the shower worked and the toilet flushed, which was all she needed right now.

Her old suite had had a kitchen, but she'd never used it—more wasted square footage that could have been used for another paying guest. The new Palmers was all about economy. If Tina turned up next summer demanding a free room, she could forget it.

"Excuse me, Miss Palmer?" Betty, the faithful receptionist Honor had so terrified when she first arrived at Palmers, but who adored her boss now, appeared at the table looking uncharacteristically anxious.

"There's a visitor…someone…here to see you."

"Oh?" said Honor, springing automatically to her feet and dabbing the corners of her mouth with her napkin. "Is it that guy from the tiling company? Because I told him already, a quote is a quote. I'm not about to renegotiate now just because he lost a ship somewhere. I need those bathrooms finished this week or he doesn't see a red cent from us, right, Don?"

"No. No, it's not him," Betty stammered. "It's…I did tell him you were in a lunch meeting, Miss Palmer. But he wouldn't go away."

"Who wouldn't?" said Honor.

For one awful moment, it crossed her mind that it might be Devon, come to try to wheedle his way around her yet again. That would explain Betty's embarrassment. The last she'd heard from him was after the fire, when he'd had the brass balls to send a get-well card to the hospital, in which he'd scrawled the sort of self-pitying half apology she'd come to expect from him. She'd heard he was in town—bad news traveled like wildfire in East Hampton—and had resigned herself to the fact that she would almost certainly run into him at some point. But she could have done without it right now, in front of Don.

But it wasn't Devon. "I see they set three places. Were you expecting me?"

Lucas strolled casually over to the table, extending his hand to Don, who'd stood up.

"I don't believe we've met." He smiled. "Lucas Ruiz. I'm a friend of Miss Palmer's."

"Don Bradford, her accountant," said Don, shaking his hand with the same warmth with which he greeted everyone. "You're just in time. I'd have wolfed that last bit of fish myself in a minute."

Lucas had already helped himself to the last plate of monk-fish and was halfway through it by the time Honor had time to blink, never mind tell him to take a running jump. Grinning at her all the while, wearing a loud pair of Bermuda shorts, an open Hawaiian shirt, and flip-flops, he looked disgustingly relaxed for someone in the midst of a major court battle and whose business was supposedly in crisis.

"Great job you've done here, sweetheart," he said, nodding appreciatively at the decor while cheerfully shoveling food into his mouth. "Don't you agree, Mr. Bradford?"

"Absolutely," said Don, who seemed not a bit put out to be joined by an unexpected guest.

"Food's good, too," said Lucas between mouthfuls. "Could do with a leetle more coriander. But not at all bad."

"OK, that's enough," said Honor, looking daggers at Lucas. Belatedly, Don realized that perhaps something was amiss. "Is everything all right, my dear?" he asked.

"Everything's fine," said Honor. "Mr. Ruiz was just leaving. Weren't you?"

"Was I?" said Lucas, holding her eye contact. "I don't think I was, actually."

An awkward silence fell.

"Perhaps I should go," said Don, getting to his feet. "Let you two talk."

"No, no, no," said Honor. "Please, you really don't—"

"Thanks," said Lucas, shaking his hand again with friendly finality. "Under the circumstances I think that might be best. Honor and I have some very important business to discuss, you see. It's a little…delicate."

"He's kidding," said Honor, laying a restraining hand on Don's arm. "Lucas and I have absolutely nothing to say to one another."

In a short, fitted red dress, with her hair slicked back into a ponytail and her emerald eyes flashing fury, she looked like a fire hydrant about to explode.

"I think I know you well enough, my dear, to see that that is quite patently untrue," said Don with a chuckle. He lived a life so free of dramatic passions that he had always found other people's amusing. "Thank you for a wonderful meal, but don't get up. I can see myself out."

"Nice guy," said Lucas, once he'd gone. A second course of rack of lamb had arrived while Don was saying his good-byes, and Lucas was liberally grinding pepper onto his helping now, looking for all the world like a paying guest. He'd be ordering a cold beer and a doggie bag in a minute.

"You know what?" said Honor, pulling her hair out of its elastic band and letting it fall loose, a gesture that made Lucas automatically look up. "I'm actually too tired to do this."

"To do what?" he said, taking a bite of lamb. It was so soft it melted on his tongue like a truffle.

"To fight with you," said Honor calmly. "To play whatever dumb-ass game it is you're playing this time. So why don't you tell me what it is that you want. And then go away and leave me in peace."

Dropping his knife and fork with a clatter, he gave her a look so intense and serious it made her momentarily nervous.

"Do you remember that night in Vegas?"

"Barely," she lied, taking a leisurely bite of her own food. "I was very drunk. And the sex really wasn't that memorable."

"I'm not talking about the sex," said Lucas. "Although I'm flattered that was the first thing *you* thought about."

Honor blushed beet red. Bastard. How did he always manage to do this to her? To twist things around? He was the one who brought up Vegas, not her.

"You'll be flatt*ened* in a minute," she shot back furiously. "So what are you talking about?"

"Anton," said Lucas. "You remember I told you how he set us both up that summer?"

"Of course I remember," snapped Honor. "You think I'd forget a thing like that?"

"And you told me we ought to fight back? Get revenge?"

"I said *you* should get revenge," said Honor, looking proudly around her. "I've already gotten mine. I've built this place back up from nothing."

"Yeah, yeah, yeah," said Lucas, waving his arm impatiently. He hugely admired what she'd done with Palmers, but he wasn't here to massage her ego. "I'm talking about real revenge."

"It's a lot more than you've done!" said Honor indignantly.

"Something that would destroy him," said Lucas, ignoring her. "The way he tried to destroy us."

Honor was silent. She didn't like him using the word *us*. It scared her.

"I've come to see you because I have a plan," he said. "And it's a pretty damn good one. It involves some other people, people you know. But we won't be able to pull it off without your help."

Honor sighed a deep, heartfelt sigh and closed her eyes. "I know I'm gonna regret this," she said. "But go ahead. I'm listening."

CHAPTER THIRTY

WHAT THE HELL DO YOU CALL THAT?"
The gardener froze halfway across the polished marble floor. He was carrying a cripplingly heavy potted bamboo through the Herrick's lobby and had rivers of sweat streaming down between his shoulder blades, not to mention a steady stream of lactic acid coursing through his aching biceps. But when Petra Kamalski yelled at you, you stopped.

"These are the plants you ordered," he panted, staggering from foot to foot under the weight. "For the party?"

"I know what they're for," said Petra scathingly. "But they most certainly are not what was ordered. I said black bamboo, and I said a minimum of eight feet. That's practically a pot plant."

"A pot plant?" he muttered under his breath. "You try lifting it, lady."

"Don't talk back to me," hissed Petra. Her bat-like hearing was legendary among the Herrick staff. "And don't even think of putting that filthy tub down on my floor. Get it out of here. Out, out, out!"

"But, ma'am," wheezed the gardener, "we have a truckload of plants outside. I have the order sheet right here. You can check it yourself."

"I don't have time to waste on your mistakes," said Petra, "and nor do my staff. Fix it. Today."

Even by her own autocratic standards, she was unusually short-tempered this morning. The "number one" party was in forty-eight hours, and there was still so much to do. The downside of having A-list guests was that they came with A-list requirements, some of them frankly ludicrous. One particular pop diva, for example, had refused to book a room for the night unless she could bring her own bed—not bedding, *bed*—and have twenty Figuera Dyptique candles lit in the bathroom exactly two hours prior to her arrival. Another guest, an actress, demanded that *her* arrival be carefully choreographed to upstage that of a younger Hollywood rival who'd also been invited. There were people who had to run into one another and others who must *under no circumstances* run into one another. And overshadowing it all was Anton, who was treating the whole thing like his private birthday party and who was delighted by the celebrity attendance just so long as it didn't eclipse his own shining star.

Retreating to her office, she barely had time to sit down before she was rudely interrupted.

"Ah, Petra, there you are. Jolly good." Anton's pet PR girl, Saskia, the one person whose presence in the hotel, in fact whose very existence, caused Petra more stress than all the other bullshit put together, had barged in without so much as a "pardon the intrusion."

"We've got an awful lot to do today, duckie," she trilled efficiently, "so it's all hands to the mill. I've just had the producer from E! on the line asking about the outdoor lighting. Now where are we with that?"

Petra's top lip began to curl upward, like a sliver of dried orange peel.

There were so many things she hated about Saskia it was hard to focus on any particular one. She was vulgar, overweight, and overbearing. She wore enough cheap perfume to qualify as a biological weapon. Her laugh, forced, loud and braying, was a cross between a witch's cackle and a particularly insidious car alarm. At this moment, she was wearing a tight, luminous orange T-shirt in a material so shinily synthetic it would melt rather than burn if you put a match to it (which somebody really ought to) and a pair of white shorts that left nothing to the imagination, beneath which she was plainly pantyless. The woman had all the class and style of a mongrel puppy, and yet she projected an innately British air of superiority that gave Petra fantasies about tying her to the back of a pickup truck and driving off at speed. Not since Honor Palmer had she met a woman so sickeningly full of herself, with so little reason to be so.

But worse than any of this was the way that Saskia had muscled her way in on tomorrow night's party. Ever since Anton had brought her on board, she'd been acting like the proverbial queen bee, throwing her considerable weight around with Petra's staff and generally making a royal nuisance of herself.

Anton denied it, but it was perfectly obvious to Petra that he and Saskia were sleeping together. This in itself didn't bother her. She'd never been the jealous type. If Anton had so little taste as to find a blowsy little tart like Saskia attractive, more fool him. But the vile creature clearly felt that, as the boss's lover, she had carte blanche to behave as she pleased and flout Petra's authority as manager. And that was a problem. A big one. She'd already grabbed a chair and parked herself on the other side of the desk and was reaching over to grab the phone when Petra snapped.

"Get out of my office!" she commanded, snatching back her telephone. "I've told you before, if you need to make calls, you may do so from the business center like everybody else. This is my private office, not some sort of common room. And I am not your duckie."

"Anton's made it very clear he wants us to work together," pouted Saskia. "We can't very well do that from separate offices. There's only thirty-six hours to go now, you know."

Petra's antipathy was heartily reciprocated by Saskia, who considered her rival to be about as sexy as a deep-frozen stick insect and considerably less pleasant company. She couldn't fathom what Anton saw in her. It must be like sticking your dick into one of those automatic pencil sharpeners.

"I'm well aware of the time pressure, thank you, Saskia," said Petra tartly. "I've spent the last three months putting this party together. You've been here three minutes."

She glanced out the window at the hive of activity going on in the grounds. The marquee company had arrived and were busy unloading scaffolding and canvas. The entire Japanese garden was going to be covered by a series of Moroccan tents, turning it into a sort of impromptu souk, although Saskia had put a cat among the pigeons at the last moment by insisting everything be opened up on one side to allow easier access for the TV crews. She'd also demanded glaring spotlights be hung from every conceivable tree, but so far Petra had vetoed this idea on the grounds that it would ruin her carefully planned candlelit effect. It was this battle over lighting that the E! channel had been complaining about again this morning.

"You're ridiculous!" snapped Saskia. "If it weren't for me you'd have had one man and his dog covering your precious party. As it is, our TV coverage is under threat because of your ludicrous candle obsession. Anton gets here tomorrow, and he wants this resolved. Petra! Are you listening to me?"

But Petra wasn't. She'd just noticed a familiar figure milling around among the workmen outside.

"I don't believe it," she muttered under her breath. "What the hell is he doing here?"

"Who?" asked Saskia.

Ignoring her, Petra prized open the window and stuck her head outside. "You're trespassing!" she yelled.

Lucas cupped his hand to his ear and shook his head, pretending not to be able to hear her, before turning back to his conversation with the marquee guys.

"Call security," Petra barked at Saskia, slamming the window shut and sweeping out the door in a whirlwind of righteous indignation. "I may need help getting rid of him."

"Oh, may you," said Saskia, once she'd gone. "Well that's tough titties, isn't it, duckie? Rude bitch. You can whistle for your help."

Whoever it was that had gotten the Ice Queen's knickers in a twist, Saskia felt more inclined to give him a medal than have him thrown off the property. Sinking her ample backside down into Petra's vacated chair—it was so much more comfortable than her own—she returned to her phone call. Someone had to sweet-talk the E! producers or they'd pull out altogether.

Outside, Lucas saw Petra goose-stepping furiously across the lawn toward him. Knowing it would infuriate her, he flashed her his most winning smile. In a black wool pencil skirt and matching jacket, she must have been roasting, but she didn't have so much as a bead of sweat on her forehead to show for it.

Maybe she didn't sweat. She probably just leaked antifreeze every now and then.

"You're spying." She looked at him accusingly. Then, turning to the workmen he'd been talking to, demanded: "What did he ask you? If any of you has breathed so much as one word about tomorrow night's arrangements—"

"Relax, Pet," said Lucas, remembering the nickname she'd so despised in college. Judging by the angrily throbbing vein at her temple, she was none too keen on it now, either. "We were only making chitchat. I was about to offer these poor guys something to drink. They tell me they haven't had a sip of water all day."

"That's because they're working," said Petra. "Do any of you have any complaints you'd like to make to me?"

She glared at them each in turn, daring them to challenge her further. But no one was brave enough, and one by one they all slunk off back to work, leaving Petra and Lucas alone.

"The next time I catch you spying on this property," she told him curtly, "I'll have you arrested. Today I'll make do with having security throw you out." She looked over her shoulder for the expected reinforcements, but no one appeared to be coming. Bloody Saskia obviously hadn't bothered to call.

"Don't panic," said Lucas amiably, sussing out her predicament. "I'll go quietly. You don't need your heavies."

"So tell me, what brings you to town, Lucas?" asked Petra, trying to regain the upper hand. "Nostalgia? A longing to relive your glory days? How touching."

"Hardly," said Lucas. "I'm here for some meetings about my new Luxe."

"Ah, yes, the late, great Luxe America. How's it going over there? You were going to open by Christmas, weren't you?" She laughed—a horrible, empty, tinkling sound with nothing but spite behind it. "Can't see that happening now."

Lucas bit his tongue. He'd already gotten what he came for and wasn't about to indulge her by losing his temper.

"I won't keep you." He smiled. "Shall we say au revoir, then? Until tomorrow night?"

"What do you mean?" Unusually for her, Petra let her guard down. "You're not invited tomorrow night."

"Oh, but I am," said Lucas brightly. "Got my invitation three weeks ago. A charming lady by the name of Saskia was kind enough to call me in person." He clapped his hand over his mouth in mock surprise and gasped. "Didn't Anton tell you?"

Petra's lips pursed into a puckered anus of fury. "It must have slipped his mind."

"Dear oh dear." Lucas was starting to enjoy himself. "And to think, you two used to be so close."

As soon as he'd gone—for all his bravado, Lucas didn't relish being manhandled off the grounds by Petra's security heavies, who were bound to show up eventually—Petra stormed back into her office. Saskia was on the phone, but she reached down and ripped the socket out of the wall, cutting her off midsentence.

"What the hell are you playing at?" she roared. "Inviting Lucas Ruiz to the party behind my back? And what happened to the fucking security I asked for?"

"You didn't say please," said Saskia, who wasn't easily intimidated. "And you aren't my boss, duckie. As for Lucas, it was Anton's decision to invite him, not mine. He's invited the Palmer sisters too."

"*Whaaaaaaaaat?*" Petra was apoplectic.

"I assumed he'd told you," said Saskia. "But if you and he don't talk anymore..." She gave a winsome little shrug. "It's hardly my fault if you've grown apart, is it?"

"Wipe that smug look off your face," said Petra. "Let's get one thing straight. I know you're fucking him, and I really don't give a shit."

Caught off guard, Saskia blushed, her cheeks clashing horribly with her revolting T-shirt.

"Men like a cheap thrill every once in a while." Petra looked at her witheringly. "And let's face it, thrills don't come any cheaper than you."

"You bitch!" gasped Saskia.

"Go on," Petra called after her as she gathered up her things and ran out of the office. "Call him. See how much sympathy you get."

She wasn't worried about Anton. Whining women bored him. It wouldn't be long before he tired of a sniveling lump of lard like Saskia.

But Lucas was another matter entirely. What was he doing here this morning? He was up to no good, she was sure of it.

She was also sure that inviting him and Honor tomorrow was a mistake, and not just because Anton had done it behind her back. He wanted to gloat, to rub their noses in his success. Petra, of all people, could understand the impulse. But her gut told her that this time it was a wrong move.

Keeping one's enemies close was all very well. But Lucas was getting too close for comfort. Why wasn't he in Europe, holed up with his lawyers? Something didn't add up.

Meanwhile, in London, Sian tried hard to be patient with the moron at the Virgin check-in desk.

"Look," she said, willing herself to keep calm as the girl took out a nail file and started ostentatiously fiddling with her cuticles. "Perhaps I haven't explained the situation properly. I'm a journalist. I have a crucial interview in New York, and I have to make that flight. I'll pay first class. I'll pay cash." Reaching into her bag, she pulled out a wad of notes and laid them on the counter to emphasize the point. "Can't you ask anyone if they'd be willing to give up their seat for cash?"

"Sorr-ay," said the girl, who clearly wasn't. "We can't do that I'm afride." She had striped blonde hair extensions, a fake tan that made Donatella Versace's look real, and the sort of whiny, nasal voice that could double as a garage door opener.

"Why not?" asked Sian. If she didn't stop filing in the next ten seconds, Sian would be forced to reach over the desk and snap off her hideous French-polished talons one by one.

The girl gave her a look of infinite boredom.

"Policy, innit."

"I'd like to speak to a manager," said Sian, ignoring the loud groans and mutterings of "bloody Americans" from the lengthening line of passengers behind her.

"Fine," said the moron. "You'll 'ave to wite. Over there."

She pointed to a firmly closed check-in desk with a couple of plastic seats in front of it. Hopelessly, Sian shuffled over and took one of them.

What a day.

She'd been up at five this morning putting the final touches to her case against Anton, knowing that the slightest flaw in her evidence could bring the whole story crashing down around her ears. And it wasn't just her ears anymore. Ben, Lucas, and now Honor Palmer as well were all deeply implicated in what they were about to do. The stakes couldn't be higher.

Having caved in to pressure from Ben and Lucas to ditch her trip to Azerbaijan, she'd spent the last three weeks in London trying to pull together information by phone and through face-to-face meetings with the large, disaffected community of Russian émigrés scattered all across the city. In all that time, she'd barely slept, rushing from interview to interview, tracking down ex-girlfriends, classmates, business associates—anyone who might be able to shed more light on the murky depths of Anton's pre-London life. At night, bone tired, she'd returned to the dingy hotel in Marylebone where she'd been camping out since her fight with Lola and begun the arduous process of editing the new information she'd gleaned. But it had been worth it, worth every grueling, frustrating minute. At least, it would be worth it, if she made this flight. If she didn't...no, she couldn't bear to think about it. They had to let her on.

Pulling out her cell phone, she scrolled down her address book, stopping at Ben's name and allowing her finger to hover over the "call" button for a few seconds. She'd never have a better reason to call him—he was a personal friend of Richard Branson's and would undoubtedly be able to pull the necessary strings—but she didn't make the call. Ever since that night at his apartment, the night Lucas had kissed her and Lola had thrown her out of the apartment, she'd tried to keep her distance. At the time she'd lashed out at Lucas, blaming him for her falling out with Lola as well as for coming between her and Ben. But beneath her veneer of anger, his words kept coming back to her, haunting her far more than his unexpected (and unexpectedly pleasurable) kiss had done. If she really loved Ben, he told her, she wouldn't ruin things for him and Bianca. She and Ben had never really been right for each other.

All this time she'd been keeping alive a tiny flame of hope that, even if he *did* marry Bianca, he would wake up one day and realize that she, Sian, was the one. But Lucas was right. She'd been kidding herself all along. Ben didn't need her. He needed someone calm and maternal and...all those other things Lucas said.

She hated him for it, but Lucas had done her a favor and finally woken her up to reality. Ben had been with Bianca for years. He was going to marry her, and soon. Working with him on the story had been wonderful, magical. But it wasn't reality. She'd been allowing herself to exist in a dream, and now she was going to have to pay the price.

She was still staring at her cell when it rang, and jumped when she saw the word "Lucas" flash across the screen.

"That's serious ESP," she said. "I was just about to call you."

"Is everything OK?" He sounded jumpy. Evidently she wasn't the only one shitting herself about tomorrow.

"I have everything we need," she said. "It's looking good. But I'm having a *teeny* little problem getting on the plane."

"What sort of problem?" said Lucas. "Can't you speak to the manager or something?"

"D'oh!" said Sian sarcastically. "Why didn't I think of that? I'm at the airport, waiting for her right now, but there's no sign. And the bimbo airhead at check-in won't let me on the fucking flight for love nor money."

Sian could hear Lucas's brain ticking into life on the other end of the line. As infuriating as she found him personally, she had to admit he'd been great to work with these last few weeks, pulling the various strands of their plan together with all the authority and cool-headedness of a field marshal.

"Which airline?" he asked.

"Virgin."

"Have you spoken to Ben?"

"No," she said softly.

"Well why not?" shouted Lucas.

"Jeez, because I haven't, OK?" Sian shouted back. She didn't need shit on that subject, especially not from him.

"OK, OK," said Lucas more gently. "Put me on the line with the check-in girl."

"She won't talk to you," said Sian. "She's a bitch and a half."

Just at that moment a dour-faced woman in a red Virgin jacket that did her florid complexion no favors at all, and whom Sian took to be the manager, waddled over.

"Is there a problem, madam?"

"Yes," said Sian, thrusting the phone at her. "This gentleman will explain."

Lucas couldn't have any worse luck than she'd been having.

Thirty minutes later, she was kicking off her shoes in an Upper Class seat, sipping at a much-needed glass of champagne. Lucas's magic touch with women was apparently just as effective over the phone as it was in person: he'd managed to sweet-talk the battle-ax Virgin supervisor in about ten seconds flat. Not that Sian was complaining. It was nice to have his legendary charm working in her favor for once.

"Do I have time to make a quick call?" she asked the passing stewardess.

"Of course," the girl smiled helpfully. Evidently they reserved their moronic nail filers for the cattle-class check-in desk. "We won't take off for fifteen minutes."

Simon Davis was passing a dull afternoon at his desk at the *News of the World*, alternately playing solitaire on his computer, picking his nose, and thinking up imaginary offenses for which he could bawl out his reporters, when his direct line rang.

"What?" he barked, Rottweiler-friendly as ever. Belatedly recognizing Sian's voice, he added, "Oh, it's you. Haven't you been deported yet?"

But within a minute, his dismissiveness had gone, replaced with rapt attention. Sitting bolt upright, he leaned forward over his paper-strewn desk with the receiver superglued to his ear, waving at everyone around him to be quiet. One thing you could say for Simon: he might be a miserable bastard, but he knew a good scoop when he heard one.

"Absolutely," he said, once Sian had finished. "We can run it this Sunday. How much did you say you wanted again?"

Sian repeated the figure.

"Fine."

He didn't hesitate, and she instantly regretted not having asked for more.

"But if you shop it around to the *Mail on Sunday* behind my back, I'll tear you limb from limb."

"I won't," said Sian, hanging up.

Taking another sip of her champagne, she closed her eyes and finally allowed herself to relax. There was no need to tell Lucas or the others about her little backup deal. But now, whatever happened tomorrow night—whether Lucas and Honor pulled off their ambush of the Herrick party or not—Sian would have her story. While most of America was still asleep and the party was drawing to a close, the first copies of the *News of the World* would be hitting newsagents and corner shops all across England.

She might not ever be Mrs. Ben Slater. But she was damn well going to be the next Lois Lane.

CHAPTER THIRTY-ONE

$\mathcal{A}$NTON SAT CONTENTEDLY IN THE BACK OF HIS LIMOUSINE the next morning with Mitzi drooling loyally by his side, watching the flat Long Island scenery roll by. Tonight was going to be one of the greatest nights of his life, public affirmation of the success he'd worked so long and hard to achieve.

All he needed for his happiness to be complete was for his knighthood to finally come through. But his man in the ministry had assured him he needn't worry on that score. He was a shoo-in for the next honors list, after the obscenely large loan check he'd written to the government last month. The first time he heard himself addressed as Sir Anton would truly be a day to remember. But tonight's party at the Herrick would be a good start—a taste of the recognition to come.

He was also excited about seeing Petra again. Saskia had served a useful purpose. She'd kept Petra on her toes and done an A job whipping up press coverage for the party. But sexually he was already tiring of her, like a little boy gorged on too-rich birthday cake. He longed for Petra's skinny, unforgiving body and the icy, imperious way she looked at him when they made love. Knowing that she was furious about the way he'd foisted Saskia on her made the prospect of their reunion all the sweeter.

Few things in life gave him more pleasure than fucking an angry, resentful Petra into submission, bending her to his will. Making love to Saskia was like diving into a sea of marshmallow. With Petra, it was more like taming a wildcat.

He was also relishing the prospect of the *This Is Your Life*–style presentation that Saskia had planned for this evening. It was being billed as a surprise, so he'd have to look suitably humble in front of the press and VIPs and feign embarrassment.

But in reality he'd overseen every detail of the footage, and even gone so far as to run the twelve-minute film past his civil servant friend to make sure it was on message from a knighthood point of view. He'd been assured he came across as powerful but compassionate—"a magnanimous magnate," as the ministry man had put it, a turn of phrase Anton liked so much that he'd suggested it to Saskia as a title for the film.

He wondered what Lucas would make of it.

He'd extended invitations to both Lucas and Honor, largely so that none of the press could accuse him of grudge bearing, but was amazed when Saskia told him that Lucas had accepted. Surely the boy must have deduced by now that he and Connor were in cahoots and that he was both the brains and the bank behind the court case? Of course, it was possible his intention was to cause a scene, to try to upstage the event by airing his grievances among Anton's famous guests. But if he did, it would be his funeral. No one would be interested in the drunken ramblings of a washed-up conspiracy theorist like Ruiz. Not when they had the party of the century waiting to be enjoyed.

Honor, more predictably, had declined to attend, citing pressure of work. The new Palmers was opening later this year, and she was busy putting the final touches to it—much good may it do her. Anyone with even the most rudimentary business sense would have seen it was ludicrous to try to open a niche boutique next door to the most successful hotel in the world. Anton had built up his Tischen empire by building close to big-name hotels, but they were always fading giants, never rising stars like the Palmers. Plus, he had unlimited funds with which to force his rivals out of the market. By all accounts, these days Honor Palmer could barely afford to buy a sandwich and, according to Petra, had last week been spotted varnishing Palmers' fences herself, by hand. Talk about David and Goliath!

Ruffling the fur on Mitzi's head, Anton closed his eyes contentedly and turned his thoughts back to Petra. Why waste precious thinking time on Honor, or Lucas? As far as he was concerned, they were both yesterday's news.

While Anton savored his impending hour of glory, Lucas was in Honor's old cottage, frantically delving under cushions and piles of paper for his car keys.

He was supposed to be picking Sian up from the airport this morning, but after a late night with Honor working on the master plan for tonight, he'd overslept and was now hopelessly late.

"Shit." He sent another two groaning accordion files flying across the room. "Honor!" Sticking his head into the narrow stairwell that led up to the cottage's lone bedroom, he shouted into the void. "Have you seen my keys? I can't find them anywhere and I have to go. Now!"

A few moments later, a sleep-addled Honor appeared at the top of the stairs, rubbing her eyes. In a pair of oversize men's pajamas—*whose were those?* Lucas wondered jealously—and with her cheeks still creased from the bedsheets, she looked adorable. All she needed was a teddy clasped to her chest and a Linus blanket trailing on the floor to complete the picture.

"What time is it?" she murmured.

"Ten," said Lucas testily. He was tense as hell about this evening, and his brief night spent on the cottage's hard sofa had done little to improve his mood. "I'm seriously fucking late, and this place is a pigsty. No wonder I can't find anything."

"Hey," said Honor, getting annoyed herself, "if you lost your keys, that's *your* fault, not mine. As for the pigsty, I didn't see you in a rush to clean up after yourself last night."

It had been a long night and they were both strung out. With another two months to run on her lease, Honor had held on to the cottage as a sort of overspill office, a place to store the mountains of as-yet-unfiled paperwork relating to the new Palmers building works.

Since Lucas's unscheduled arrival, it had morphed into the nerve center for Operation Anton and served as his temporary base while he was in town. Normally he would have slept in the bed, and Honor would have gone home to her suite at Palmers. But it was so late when they'd finished last night, there was no point in her going home. In an uncharacteristic display of chivalry, Lucas had offered to take the tiny couch.

He regretted it now. He hadn't slept a wink. Quite apart from the logistics of trying to get comfortable on a piece of furniture designed by a sadist for a midget, just knowing that Honor was upstairs, probably naked, in his bed, kept him tossing and turning through the small hours like a prisoner on the rack. The combination of sleep deprivation, sexual frustration, and stress about what lay ahead of them—what if they blew it and got thrown out, or worse, arrested?—conspired to make him moodier than a teenage girl in the throes of PMS.

"Your keys are on the counter," said Honor, coming wearily down the stairs. "I can see them from here."

Snatching them up with an irritated frown, Lucas thrust them into the back pocket of his jeans.

Grabbing a bagel from the bread bin on his way out, he left, slamming the cottage door behind him so hard that the sea of papers fluttered up into the air like windblown leaves.

Honor surveyed the mess he'd left behind.

"A simple *thanks* would have been nice," she mumbled, crossly. But she still hoped he'd drive safely on his way to Kennedy. He could be awfully reckless when he was stressed out, and on two hours' sleep those one-lane roads out of town could be lethal.

When Lucas saw Sian struggling through customs with two battered suitcases and a groaning briefcase, she looked distinctly travel-worn. Notwithstanding their kiss in London, he'd never been the biggest fan of her looks, but he didn't think he'd ever seen her looking quite so preternaturally pale as she did now. Her dark hair was greasy and hung long and lank to her shoulders. As for the clothes she was wearing—combat shorts, tatty sneakers, and a faded orange T-shirt covered in coffee stains—they were only a small step above bag lady.

"You look tired," was all he said, relieving her of both suitcases. Uncharacteristically, she let him take them without a fuss. Her shoulders were killing her, and she was too drained to take a feminist stand about it today.

"You've been pushing yourself too hard."

"Yeah, well, I had to, didn't I?" said Sian grudgingly. "You made it pretty clear you wouldn't wait around for me to get the rest of the evidence together. It had to be this weekend or never. I haven't slept in two weeks."

"Me neither," said Lucas. "Jesus." He frowned at the heavy bags in each hand. "What the hell did you pack in here? Lead?"

They'd reached the elevator, and he put down both cases while he pressed the call button.

"No." Sian grinned triumphantly. "Tapes."

"Tapes? What tapes?" The lift arrived and they stepped inside.

Sian looked at him witheringly. "Anton's high school reunion. Jeez, what do you mean *what* tapes? It's the sexual stuff, you idiot. Your hors d'oeuvres for the party tonight, before we pull out our big guns."

"You do have the big guns, though?" said Lucas nervously.

"Relax," said Sian. "I got it all. This stuff is just interviews with some of the girls from his homes who went on the game. All on the record, mind you. Sixteen hours of audio, five and half of visuals. You would not *believe* some of the stories. It goes way beyond what we thought."

"We're gonna have ten minutes up on that podium tonight, total," grumbled Lucas. "Maybe less. Honor and I have it timed to the last second. What are we supposed to do with five hours of footage?"

"Hey, you wanted pictures, remember?" said Sian. "Don't fucking whine when I bring them to you."

Why was he being so negative? He ought to be ripping her arm off. This stuff was white-hot. It would certainly focus people's attention, so by the time they got to tonight's real shock they'd have a captive audience.

The elevator doors swooshed open at the fourth floor. Lucas walked over to the car and began loading the bags silently into the trunk.

He knew he was being churlish. If Sian had brought another nail to hammer into Anton's coffin, that was great news, and the American press were bound to salivate more over a sex scandal than any other sort of wrongdoing. This was a nation that had impeached their own president over a blow job, for God's sake. But part of him resented the fact that it was Sian's work, her research, that was ultimately going to bring Anton down. In his mind, tonight was the culmination of his revenge, his private, personal battle against the man who'd set out to ruin him.

"We've got the whole afternoon," said Sian, climbing into the passenger seat beside him. "We can edit it."

"I suppose," he grunted. "We're cutting it a bit close, though, don't you think?"

Sian struggled to keep a lid on her anger. She'd flown halfway across the world to get these tapes and the rest of her evidence here on time. A little pat on the back might have been nice.

"You don't have to worry," she said bitterly. "I'll do all the editing. I already know where the money shots are."

"As it were," said Lucas, raising an eyebrow.

Despite himself, a smile had started to creep across his features. Despite herself, Sian returned it.

"I spoke to Ben earlier, by the way," said Lucas, changing the subject. "He wished us all luck."

"I wish he was here," said Sian, her tiredness making her drop her guard of indifference.

To her amazement, Lucas stretched out an arm and wrapped it around her shoulder in sympathy.

"I know you do, sweetheart," he said. "So do I."

It wasn't until they'd pulled out of the airport and onto the expressway that Sian remembered the other thing she had meant to tell him.

"Oh!" she said suddenly. "There's something else. I can't believe I didn't tell you before."

"What's that?" asked Lucas, keeping his eyes fixed on the road ahead.

"The Palmers fire," said Sian. "You know, you asked me to check it out?"

Lucas looked up. She had his attention now.

"Well I did," she said. "And I'm pretty sure I know who started it."

CHAPTER THIRTY-TWO

ETRA ADJUSTED THE VINTAGE DIOR BROOCH AT HER décolletage and admired her reflection for one final time in the mirror. The gown she had chosen for tonight, a black Narciso Rodriguez column dress, was elegant rather than sexy, a deliberate statement designed to contrast with Saskia's vulgar, neon-pink Dolce & Gabbana minidress. Honestly, if that woman got any tackier you could use her as human flypaper.

Anyway, it worked. Petra's white-blonde bob and flawless milky skin looked even more striking against the severe black taffeta. The overall effect was positively regal, appropriate given that tonight she intended to show Saskia up in front of Anton and their many illustrious guests as the cheap pretender to her throne she really was.

Outside, the party was beginning to warm up. Twisting her office blinds a fraction, she could see the swelling crowd, and in the midst of them, Anton, glad-handing the media and more important corporate guests. Only two hours ago, he'd been in her office, arguing furiously with her about Saskia. She was still livid that he'd had that fat slug issue invitations to Lucas and Honor behind her back, and had let him know her views on the subject in no uncertain terms.

Anton always got turned on by confrontation. But after this afternoon's fight he'd been positively foaming at the mouth, so desperate was he to fuck her. For once, Petra had resisted and decided to make him wait. Submission in the bedroom was all very well, but after all the shit he'd pulled with Saskia, he needed to be taught a lesson. By the time he'd stormed out of her office, with a hard-on the size of Canada bulging visibly in his suit pants, he was angrier than she'd ever seen him. But she wasn't worried. Later tonight, once the party was over, he could have what he wanted. And by then he'd want it so badly he'd be prepared to make ample recompense. Saskia's remaining hours in his employ were now officially numbered.

She opened the blinds a little farther. Only a few big-ticket names had turned up so far: Teri Hatcher was here with her new boy-toy, and Oprah and Stedman were deep in conversation with the head of Random House at the entrance to the Moroccan marquee, sipping the Dom Perignon that Petra had insisted on. (Saskia had wanted the irredeemably tacky Cristal, of course.)

Petra was quite relaxed about the paucity of celebrities. Stars always liked to make an entrance, and that meant turning up late. But she could tell Anton was fretting. In yet another of her craven bids for his affection, Saskia had put together a cringe-making mini biopic, *A Magnanimous Magnate*, which was scheduled to run at ten thirty. In his typical German way, Anton was obsessed about the thing starting on time, but he also wanted as many VIPs as possible to be there to see it.

Gliding back outside to join him—if she left his side for too long, Saskia would swoop in to try to play hostess, and she wasn't having any of that—Petra drew him to one side for a pep talk.

"You must try to relax," she whispered in his ear. "The film is for the media, not the guests. If you run around looking antsy and like you're not having a good time, believe me, so will everyone else."

"I'd be a lot more relaxed if you'd opened your fucking legs two hours ago," he hissed back.

Surreptitiously she allowed the back of her hand to brush against his crotch. "Temper, temper," she said. "Good things come to those who wait. Didn't your mother ever tell you that?"

——————— ———————

Meanwhile, back in the kitchens, Sian was battling with her own nerves. Honor had done a meticulous job stage-managing the plan for tonight. With the help of some of the disaffected Herrick staff, she'd managed to wangle a job for Sian as a temporary waitress and get access to the detailed timing of the night's festivities. All Sian had to do was follow instructions. But as everything was based around the timings Honor had been given, they could only pray that Petra hadn't had a last-minute change of mind and reshuffled something. This was the part that worried Sian.

"We'll be OK," Lucas had tried to reassure her this afternoon, while simultaneously mocking the hell out of her French maid's outfit. "Petra's a compulsive organizer, and Anton's even worse. Trust me, they don't do spontaneous. They'll stick to the schedule."

Sian prayed he was right. Yanking down her much-too-short skirt—she was sure Lucas had had a hand in ordering her uniform, which had clearly been intended for a child or one of those miniature Filipino women, not a strapping Irish Jersey girl like her— she picked up a tray of canapés and ventured out into the grounds.

But as soon as she turned into the Japanese garden, she caught her breath and dived for cover behind the nearest shrub. There, right in front of her, was Lola's brother, Nick. He had his arm around the waist of a vacuous brunette, a twig-like giantess who could only have been a model, and his whiny, insistent, arrogant voice cut through the general buzz of conversation around him like a chainsaw.

"So you see, I'm all on my lonesome," he was saying. "My folks have officially become East Hampton's first agoraphobics. And my sister's too caught up with Super-yid to care about anything else. They're probably at home making matzo balls together."

The twig laughed dutifully. Crouched behind the bush, Sian's heart was pounding. Nick being here was bad enough. If he saw her, he'd blow her cover in an instant. But since when was Lola in town? Lucas hadn't mentioned anything, and the last Sian had heard, the whole Carter family was avoiding East Hampton like the plague.

"Come on." Nick led the girl by the belt of her dress toward the marquee, much as one might a recalcitrant puppy. "Let's check out the Russki's attempt at La Mamounia. I bet it's lame."

Once she was sure he'd gone, Sian reemerged, brushing the dirt and leaves off her apron and legs. Please God, don't let Lola and Marti show up tonight. Any more stress and she was going to go completely bat-shit.

On the other side of the gardens, at one of the myriad outdoor bars, Petra shimmered beside Anton like a towering black shadow. Saskia, she noticed happily, was still stuck behind the newly built podium, sorting out technical difficulties with the sound system. Petra watched her scurrying around among the technicians like a fuchsia-pink mother hen—the tiny dress she was wearing made the absolute worst of her chunky, shot-putters' thighs, and even from here you could see her breasts spilling over the top of it like cookie dough. Better still, she appeared to be having a perfectly miserable time.

Much as she would have liked to spend the entire evening watching Saskia squirm, Petra was distracted moments later by another voluptuous blonde. Along with her sister, she was making quite an entrance, preening and pouting in front of a vast bank of cameras, whose flashes were going off one after another like sheet lightning. "I don't believe it," she muttered furiously to Anton, under her breath. "Tina Palmer's here. With Honor. I thought you said they weren't coming?"

Excusing himself from the Viacom CEO, Anton pulled her to one side.

"They weren't," he said. "Honor declined, and as far as I know Tina was never even on the list. But I don't see that it matters much. Do you?"

"Hmm. I suppose not," said Petra, grudgingly. But inside she couldn't shake the feeling that it probably did matter. That the Palmer sisters' unexpected presence was a danger signal they ought not to ignore.

"Don't you find it odd, though? I'd have thought this was the last place Tina would want to show her face, wouldn't you? And look how pally she is with her sister. I thought they hated each other."

Anton shrugged. "So they kissed and made up. Who cares?"

"Apparently they're not the only ones," said Petra, her concern mounting. "Take a look at that."

Lucas had just arrived, looking dapper in a Paul Smith suit and Hermes tie. Marching straight up to Honor, he kissed her warmly on both cheeks, then proceeded to offer the same friendly greeting to her sister. Once again, Anton didn't seem bothered.

"You knew we'd invited Lucas," he purred, running one finger languorously up the length of Petra's spine and massaging the nape of her neck. "Now who's getting too tense?"

"I knew he was coming," she said testily. "But look at the three of them, thick as thieves. Not so long ago those girls had a death warrant out for Lucas. What's changed?"

"I don't know," said Anton. "Luxe is going down the toilet faster than a lead turd, and Tina Palmer seems to have money to spare again these days. He's probably trying to butter her up for a loan."

"And Honor?"

Anton shrugged. "Maybe she's doing the same."

Petra looked skeptical. "I don't like it."

"You're being paranoid," said Anton. "Besides, what do you want me to do about it? Have security throw them out?"

"Don't be facile," snapped Petra. Grabbing a flute of champagne from a passing waiter, she drained it in one long gulp and put the empty glass back on the tray. "You invited them. I just think we should keep an eye on them, that's all. A close eye."

Finding himself enveloped in a bear hug by Tina, Lucas tried to breathe through his mouth and wondered how long it would be before he passed out from the fumes of her cloyingly sweet scent.

"Shalom," she whispered breathily in his ear. "It's been too long, my friend."

With typically appalling timing, Tina had turned up at Palmers six hours ago, although Lucas hadn't actually seen her in person until now.

As usual, her arrival had been unscheduled. Wafting into the hotel lobby barefoot, wearing some sort of Hari Krishna kaftan (but incongruously followed by two minions weighed down with six massive Louis Vuitton trunks), she noisily demanded to see her sister.

"I'm afraid Miss Palmer isn't here," the receptionist told her meekly. "She's over at the cottage on Main Street."

"Fine," said Tina serenely. "Give me the address. And find rooms for my staff, would you please? They all need feeding and watering." She waved airily at her entourage like Marie Antoinette to the peasantry.

"But...we aren't open for business yet," stammered Betty. "We don't have rooms. Or a kitchen staff. Miss Palmer?"

But Tina wasn't listening. She'd already set off into the village in search of Honor.

When she eventually found her, she was sitting cross-legged on the living room floor with a dark-haired girl Tina didn't recognize, surrounded by a jungle of editing equipment, CD burners, and wires, and staring intently at the TV screen.

"Peace!"

Standing in the doorway, Tina threw her arms out wide. But Honor and her friend were so engrossed, neither of them looked up.

"I said, peace!" said Tina again, more sharply. When no one looked up, she resorted to shouting: "Is anyone going to tell me what's going on?"

In the end, Honor had decided it would be easier to let her in on the plan than to try to come up with a cover story at this late stage.

"She's got as much of a reason to hate Anton as any of us," she reasoned with a deeply skeptical Lucas over the phone. "And as nothing I say or do will keep her away from that party tonight, we may as well have her help us. She's actually not as stupid as she looks, you know."

"No one's as stupid as your sister looks," said Lucas moodily. "Can't you send her back to LA?"

"Oh, sure, like she does what I tell her!" Honor laughed. "Look, she's here now, like it or not."

Lucas definitely didn't like it. But as he couldn't come up with a viable alternative, other than have Tina motormouthing her way through the party, asking awkward questions and drawing unwanted attention to all of them, he'd reluctantly agreed to clue her in.

Looking at her now, though, dressed about as discreetly as a transvestite at Mardi Gras, his misgivings returned with a vengeance. Feeling increasingly like a rodent in the grip of a Chanel 19–soaked boa constrictor, he gently prized himself free from her embrace.

"It's good to see you too," he lied, wondering not for the first time what had ever possessed him to sleep with her. She was an attractive girl underneath, if you liked that sort of thing, but with all the makeup, and the diamonds and the hairspray, she looked much older. She actually reminded him of Zsa Zsa Gabor, and not in her young starlet days either.

By contrast, Honor's simple, white empire-line dress and face almost completely bare of makeup was so much more alluring. She'd changed beyond recognition from the spiky tomboy of old. When he'd kissed her earlier, she'd smelled of some faint lemony cologne, like the stuff they used to put on babies back home in Ibiza—fresh and natural. He loved it.

"You know, we shouldn't spend too much time together," he warned Tina. "Not here. Petra's already looking over. I think she can smell a rat."

"Takes one to smell one," said Honor. "Honestly, just look at her, glued to Anton like the Grim Reaper." But she took Lucas's advice and, dragging Tina by the hand, disappeared across the lawn and into the crowd to mingle.

Seconds later, Lucas felt a tap on his shoulder.

"Well, well, well." The familiar, put-on British accent with just the faintest undercurrent of German menace made Lucas's blood run cold. "Look who it isn't."

It was the first time he'd seen Anton in the flesh in almost five years. If you could call it flesh—the man had so much botulism and fillers running through his veins these days he looked more like a Madame Tussauds waxwork than a human being. Despite himself, Lucas felt his pulse start to race with nerves.

"Anton." He held out his hand. After a brief moment's hesitation, Anton shook it. "Congratulations. Great party."

"I'm thrilled you're enjoying it." Anton smiled. "Although I must say, Petra and I were surprised you could spare the time away from your own...empire." He injected the last word with enough sarcasm to sink a ship. "Some might say you were fiddling while Rome burns. Or in your case, while Paris burns. How's the court case going?"

"Oh, you know what the EU contract laws are like," said Lucas breezily, determined not to betray any hint of weakness. "These things take an age, but there's no doubt we'll win in the end. Luckily my partner is a patient man. We'll get through it."

"That remains to be seen," said Anton frostily. Not even the powerful freezing agents in his face could completely suppress the spite suffusing his features as he spoke. Lucas felt his own hatred bubble inside him like lava, but he kept his cool and smiled affably.

"True," he said. "None of us can predict the future, can we? Even a great hotel like this one can fall from grace."

Sure that he was being provoked but unsure how to respond, Anton let out an impotent mewl of annoyance.

"If I were you," he said curtly, once he'd rediscovered his voice, "I'd focus on what was left of my own pitiful business before throwing stones at others."

"Again," said Lucas, draining his glass. "Good advice. I'll do that. Now, if you'll excuse me…"

And handing his empty flute to a speechless Anton, he walked off.

By ten thirty-five, Saskia decided she could wait no longer. Anton was positively twitching with impatience, chatting distractedly with a radiant Christie Brinkley twenty feet away, and shooting her looks that got more and more agitated by the second. With any other client, she'd have held off. Madonna and Guy Ritchie were still not here, nor were Donald and Melania or the Hilton sisters. But if she didn't start soon, she ran the risk that some of the A-listers who had shown up might start leaving. And wouldn't that bitch Petra just love that? She'd already contrived somehow to turn Anton against her, quite how Saskia had no idea, but she wasn't about to hand her any further ammunition.

"Ladies and gentlemen."

Up on the podium, microphone in hand, she made a brave bid for the now-massive crowd's attention.

"People!" She shouted louder, signaling to the sound guys to up the output on her mic. "If I could ask you all to look this way for just a moment."

Slowly but surely, the noise levels began to dim as an enormous, multiplex-sized screen loomed up behind her on the stage, apparently out of nowhere.

"As you know," she went on, her braying British accent strangely at odds with her mutton-dressed-as-lamb-crotch-skimmer dress, "we're here today to celebrate the Herrick being voted world number one." A polite ripple of applause punctuated by a few drunken whoops and cheers echoed around the grounds, bouncing off the hotel's glass walls.

"But some of us also wanted to take this opportunity to pay tribute to a remarkable man," Saskia simpered.

On cue, a lone spotlight made a great show of sweeping searchingly across the crowd before alighting on an apparently unsuspecting Anton.

"A man whose vision, hard work, and above all, generosity of spirit, have made not just the Herrick, but the entire Tischen family, such an outstanding global success story," said Saskia.

Lucas laughed out loud at Anton's blatantly fake surprise, complete with hand on chest, possum-wide eyes, and "surely you don't mean li'l old me?" expression. He'd have liked to catch Honor's eye, but couldn't find her in the crowd. Instead he saw Sian, slipping unnoticed through the guests and looking whiter than her starched apron with nerves. He prayed she wasn't going to bottle it.

"The following short film, *A Magnanimous Magnate*, from award-winning director Bowen Langford," Saskia went on, "is a tribute to your host, and my friend," she beamed at Anton adoringly, "Mr. Anton Tisch."

"Who is that creature?" a woman close to Petra could be heard asking her friend as the footage began to roll, earning herself untold brownie points by adding in a sotto voce whisper, "She looks like a billiard ball with legs."

Clearly, no expense had been spared on production values. *A Magnanimous Magnate* opened with some rousing John Williams–esque music, accompanying a number of stills from Anton's childhood: Anton as a baby in an old-fashioned stroller, wearing a frilly sun-hat; Anton aged about eight, standing at the foot of a ski slope, clutching a medal with an oddly endearing gap-toothed grin; Anton looking groomed and preppy at sixteen in an official high school photograph. But it wasn't long before the stills gave way to a series of high profile talking heads, each giving suitably glowing testimonials about the great man himself.

"Tisch is a fighter." A smiling, casually dressed Richard Branson spoke straight to camera, his legs dangling from a swing seat on the veranda of his Necker mansion. "I've known the guy fifteen years, and I still wouldn't want to meet him in a dark alley."

More polite laughter from the crowd.

Testimonials followed from a slew of British politicians and business leaders. From where she was standing Petra could see the eyes of a number of the Hollywood contingent glazing over.

"What's ICI?" one starlet could be heard asking her friend.

"I think it's a studio," the friend replied earnestly.

But just when it seemed she was about to lose her audience's interest altogether, Saskia suddenly began pulling out the big guns. Arnold Schwarzenegger told a genuinely funny joke about Anton's golfing prowess, or rather lack of it, then praised him for his charity work on both sides of the Atlantic. He was followed by a glowing Brangelina, neither of whom said anything particularly interesting but whose impossibly beautiful features were enough to ensure the rapt attention of every sexually active person there, male or female. Finally, warm words from Kofi Annan and the chairman of the international Red Cross were interspersed with shots of smiling children, mostly cancer or liver transplant patients, thanking Anton for his generous contributions to their various hospitals/research foundations.

"Mr. Tisch doesn't have children of his own," an adorable, wispily blonde girl of six lisped in finale. "But he's been like a father to me. Thank you, Mr. Tisch. I hope you enjoy your party."

The screen went blank, to wild applause. Anton, still hamming up his surprised and embarrassed shtick, was beckoned up to the podium by Saskia. At yet another prerehearsed cue, the press were ushered farther forward, and space was miraculously created for the TV crews with their bulky boom mics and camera equipment. Only once the media were all in place did Anton start to speak.

"I won't bore you with a long speech," he said, taking the microphone, "not least because I had no idea they were going to spring this on me." He wagged an admonishing finger at Saskia. From their various posts, Lucas, Honor, and Sian all cringed. "So I have nothing prepared. But I would like to say a few words of thanks, off the cuff, as it were. To all of you," he held his hands out magnanimously, "for being here tonight to help celebrate the Herrick's remarkable achievement." More cheers. "To my loyal staff, especially Ms. Petra Kamalski, my outstanding manager here, whose hard work is in large part responsible for this happy occasion."

Despite herself, Petra flushed with happiness. He'd singled her out publicly, without giving Saskia even a passing mention. Knowing how crushed her rival would be filled her with a warm inner glow.

"But most of all, I'd like to thank the children, like little Leila whom you saw there, with whom it has been my honor and privilege to work over the last twenty years. I can truly say that they have given me more, far more, than I have ever given them."

"Ain't that the truth," muttered Sian.

Reaching for the perfectly pressed white handkerchief in his breast pocket, he dabbed at his eyes with one swift gesture: manly but compassionate. It was a bravura performance. Even Lucas, at the back of the audience, was impressed.

The applause for his speech, respectable at first, swelled to an almost deafening crescendo. Standing on the podium, basking in the adulation, it took some seconds before Anton realized that it wasn't, in fact, he who was the focus of this rapturous reception, but Tina Palmer, who had somehow appeared behind him onstage. Wearing a (for her) conservative creation in blue-gray bias-cut silk, she nevertheless looked every inch the star, with Elizabeth Taylor–size diamonds at her throat, ears, and wrists and her blonde hair piled on top of her head in a solid hair-sprayed mountain. The drag queen look that Lucas found so off-putting up close seemed to evaporate with distance, as well as on camera. To the partygoers below, and all the viewers at E! and beyond, Tina looked Screen Siren perfect.

She was holding up an enormous bouquet of lilies, freesias, and roses, a vulgar but impressive riot of color finished off with a red silk bow the size of a small child's head. Leaning forward, she presented it to a bewildered Anton. More than a little annoyed to have his limelight so shamelessly usurped, but with the spotlights trained firmly on him, he had little option but to smile and take the flowers, which obscured him from view almost completely. As he reached for the bouquet, Tina deftly relieved him of his mic.

"What the hell is going on?" hissed Saskia, stepping forward and looking officious. "You shouldn't be up here." But Tina held her ground, shooing her away with all the languid unconcern of a cow flicking its tail at a fly. Saskia reviewed her options silently for a moment, then withdrew into the shadows. Tina Palmer was bona fide A-list these days. She could hardly have her manhandled from the stage.

Watching proceedings from the audience with a rigid-jawed stare, Petra shared Saskia's sense of impotence. Tina was clearly up to no good, but there wasn't a lot they could do about it, not unless she really overstepped the mark.

"I apologize for this unscheduled diversion," breathed Tina huskily, channeling her best Marilyn Monroe. "But given my own work with UNICEF, I felt it was appropriate. I believe many of you here tonight are familiar with my work."

Suddenly a still from her infamous porn movie flashed up on the screen behind her. The crowd gasped as one, then erupted with laughter.

"Thank you; you're too kind," giggled Tina, camping it up.

Honor, who'd worked her way to the front of the crowd, blushed scarlet. The naked image had been her idea—a surefire attention grabber—and she was relieved Sian had managed to commandeer the projector as planned. But looking at her sister like that, all creamy, udder-sized breasts and candy-pink nipples, still floored her with embarrassment.

"Anyway, given my own charity work—and Mr. Tisch's involvement with it, of which more later," Tina smiled mysteriously, "I felt I couldn't let this evening pass without a small, personal tribute. So if you'll bear with me…Sian?"

Inside the summerhouse, converted by Saskia into a make-shift projection room for her tribute film, Sian's hands were shaking like someone in the final stages of Parkinson's. Thanks to Honor's careful planning, everything had gone seamlessly. As soon as the credits rolled on Anton's biopic, she'd been able to slip unnoticed into the building and lock it from the inside. But now that she was actually here, with her finger on the button both metaphorically and literally, she felt sick as a dog. Media from across the globe were lined up outside, their cameras trained on the screen behind Tina: *her* film, *her* story. Back in London, Simon would have already gone to print. The first copies of the

News of the World would be on the newsstands within hours, with her exclusive exposé plastered all over the front three pages. It wasn't just Anton Tisch's life that was about to be changed forever. It was hers, too. Christ, she hoped she hadn't fucked up the editing. Weaving her extra footage into the film they already had had been painstaking work, and everything had been so rushed this afternoon at Honor's cottage. What if she'd somehow cut out something crucial? Or what if they had technical problems? Basic editing she could just about do, but Sian was no technician.

Seconds later, she had the surreal experience of seeing her own face pop up in front of her, on-screen.

"Good evening, ladies and gentlemen." Sitting in a black leather chair in a nondescript white room, she spoke directly to camera. "My name is Sian Doyle. I'm a journalist. And I'd like to show you all another side to Anton Tisch."

The camera panned outward to show a very young girl sitting opposite her in a second, identical black leather chair. Bug-eyed and visibly shaking with nerves, she was hauntingly beautiful but didn't look a day over fourteen.

Up onstage, Anton's hands tightened involuntarily around his bouquet. He didn't even notice when the thorns from the roses skewered his palms and blood began to trickle over the flowers' plastic wrapping.

"Find Petra," he mouthed urgently over his shoulder to Saskia. "I want this stopped. Now!"

"At first, I thought Mr. Tisch was just being friendly. I was very grateful to 'im for trying to help me," said the girl, in a childish whisper littered with cockney cadences. "The first pictures I done was all right. Tasteful and that. But then there was this other man, Bill or Billy I think 'is name was, who worked for Mr. Tisch on his website. He wanted me to do...other things." She looked away. "He showed me pictures what some of the other girls from the home had done."

Three stills filled the screen in quick succession, all of nude underage girls in sickeningly graphic sexual poses. A collective gasp of disgust erupted from the crowd.

"These images were posted on a website that's a wholly owned subsidiary of the Tischen Group." Sian was talking directly to camera again. "All three of these girls spent time in care homes paid for by Anton Tisch. All three were known personally to him."

"This is preposterous!" spluttered Anton. Dropping the flowers on the ground, he made a lunge for Tina's microphone, but she stepped back, whipping it away like a matador taunting a bull. She had no idea what any of this was really about—Honor's explanations earlier about some sort of movie exposé sounded boringly convoluted to Tina. But she was definitely starting to enjoy being a part of it now.

Those of the guests who weren't still reeling with shock began giggling as they watched Tina Palmer evading Anton's grasp. Aware that he was starting to look like a laughingstock, as well as a pedophile, Anton cut his losses and stormed offstage.

"Where's Petra?" he roared at the hovering staff behind the podium steps. "Can none of you switch off this fucking thing?"

"Whoever's in the summerhouse has locked it from the inside, sir," piped up one brave soul. "They're trying to break in there now. Saskia's got a bunch of guys down there."

Back in the summerhouse, Sian could no longer hear her own projected voice over the frenzied rattling of the door behind her. As well as locking it, she'd managed to wedge it shut with various bulky items of furniture, but the guys outside weren't giving up in a hurry. Aware that she was running out of time, she made an executive decision to skip the next section of footage altogether and cut straight to the finale. Activating her wire for the first time that evening, she sent a warning message to Lucas.

At the back of the garden, he clutched his ear, trying to make out what she was saying through the heavy crackle. "Need a minute. I'm g...second tape. Can you get Tina...cover?"

Getting the gist, he stood up on an empty champagne crate and waved a prearranged signal to Tina. *Please God let her have remembered...*

In fact, he needn't have worried. With Sian reloading the tape decks, the screen faded to black, but Tina stepped forward quite unfazed and kept everyone occupied with a little show of her own.

"The story doesn't end there, folks," she said huskily, her diamond choker dazzling in the spotlight. "In a moment, our lovely hostess, Sian, will be back with some even more shocking revelations." The crowd oohed and aahed. Their earlier disgust apparently forgotten, Tina had suddenly transformed them into gullible participants in a cheap reality show. "But in the meantime, I'd like to share my own personal experience of Mr. Tisch," she went on. "Unfortunately for me, his interest in the sex-tape industry wasn't entirely restricted to teenagers. I now know that Anton Tisch himself was personally responsible for my own debut in the adult movie world. That's right." She gave a wounded pout, preening for the TV cameras all the while and making sure she kept her chin firmly down. "He was the one who entrapped me, not poor Lucas Ruiz," she wagged her finger playfully at the press, "whom you awful swine were so quick to blame at the time."

A shocked murmur rose up from the hotel industry people scattered among the crowd. No one in the US would forget in a hurry how Lucas had been pilloried over that tape, and the self-righteous fever of condemnation that had swept the business at the time.

"But the good news," said Tina archly, "is that we've raised over two million dollars to date, ladies and gentlemen. Well, I guess it's primarily the gentlemen I have to thank." Another loud burst of laughter. "So please, keep watching!"

She might be best known as a porn star, but there was no doubt Tina Palmer was East Hampton's sweetheart tonight.

"And on behalf of UNICEF and the poor children of Africa, I'd like to propose a toast of my own: to Anton Tisch. A *true* humanitarian!"

Just as the roars of applause were dying down again, the screen behind Tina lit up once more.

"Atta girl," whispered Lucas under his breath. He'd lost radio contact with Sian again, but she'd obviously come through.

"We now come to the final, and most disturbing aspect of tonight's short film." Still in her black chair, talking straight to camera, Sian's clear, steely voice filled the night air. "Most of you probably don't know much about Azerbaijan, so let me fill you in on the headlines. It used to be part of the Soviet Union. It's got a lot of oil—expected oil revenues over the next twenty years of around a hundred and twenty billion dollars. And it's run by one of the most corrupt regimes on the planet. Oh," she added, breaking into a rare smile, "and it's where Anton Tisch first made his fortune."

A couple of stills followed of rugged, mountainous scenery, some enchanting coastline, and vast pipelines built to ship the country's oil to the West. But just as people were starting to wonder quite where Sian was going with this geography lesson, another, horrifying image filled the screen. It was the body of a young boy, no more than eleven or twelve, his torso riddled with bullets, still clutching an ancient Kalashnikov rifle to his chest.

"We don't know his name." Sian's voice, somber again now, drifted out of the speakers as they cut to more shots of dead children, some burned and tortured beyond recognition. "Or his. Or his." Relentlessly the pictures kept coming. A number of people in the audience looked away.

"I think I'm gonna be sick," said the starlet to her friend.

"What we do know, and what I can prove, is that Anton Tisch supplied arms to boys like these, children forced to become armed warriors against President Aliyev's ruthless regime. And this is what he bought with the profits."

A shot of Anton's stunning Geneva mansion loomed into view, followed by one of another child soldier, this one still alive but malnourished, his eyes wide with terror and confusion. More of the same followed: Anton's yacht, and a pile of rebel bodies;

Anton smiling as he shook hands with President Bush, and an Aliyev labor camp, complete with emaciated faces pressed up against the barbed wire. Then the screen abruptly went black.

"They must have got into the projection room," mumbled Lucas to himself, trying in vain to raise either Sian or Honor on their wires. So much for state-of-the-art communications technology. But it didn't seem to matter. They'd been on air long enough to get the point across. Within seconds, pandemonium broke loose. Everybody wanted a piece of Anton, but he seemed to have melted into the melee. Happily, Tina was still up onstage and more than willing to step into the breach in his absence, sacrificing herself to the media feeding frenzy.

"Tina, can you prove any of this?" yelled reporters, thrusting microphones and cameras at her from all angles. "Who is this Sian Doyle? How do you know her?"

"Please." Holding up her hand, Tina did her best to look harassed and perhaps just a touch little-girl-lost. "One at a time, OK? Don't crowd me."

"Why didn't you go straight to the police?" A pretty Asian TV reporter from one of the local news shows forced her way to the front. "If you had proof of criminal activity, why'd you wait?"

"To be honest with you, I'm just the front woman here," said Tina. "You'll have to ask my sister about that sort of stuff."

"Honor's behind this?" The Asian girl swooped on this new information like a hawk diving for a shrew.

"Well, no, I wouldn't say behind it exactly." Tina sounded uncertain.

"Where is she right now? Is she here tonight?"

At that moment Saskia came careening through the lines of press like a furious pink cannonball and hurled herself at Tina, knocking her to the ground.

"You bitch!" Climbing on top of her, she clawed at her face and neck like a savage, much to the delight of the TV crews. Her heavy mascara was running in thick black rivulets down her face, and her fuchsia lipstick was smudged everywhere, making her look like a psychotic clown. For a moment Tina was genuinely frightened.

"Do you know how much effort went into this party?" Saskia shrieked. "Do you know how hard I worked?"

As she raised her arm for another blow, Tina closed her eyes and flinched. But instead of the expected sting of talons ripping into her cheek, she felt a weight being lifted off her.

"Take her inside." Petra's voice sounded as ice-cool and imperious as ever. "She's hysterical." The only hint that the crisis was affecting her at all was that her Russian accent had become slightly more pronounced. "And help Miss Palmer to a chair, please."

Opening her eyes to see two burly and by no means unattractive security guards looming over her, Tina decided not to put up a struggle. Though it pained her to yield the limelight, she was feeling a little shaken. Honor never mentioned anything this afternoon about the risk of being assaulted by fat British lunatics.

With Tina temporarily out of action, the reporters lost no time in cornering Petra instead.

"Ms. Kamalski, I take it tonight's allegations against your employer have come as a complete surprise to you?"

"I'll be making a full statement later, once I've had a chance to speak with Mr. Tisch," said Petra calmly. "Right now, you'll understand, I have over a thousand guests I need to deal with. I really don't have the time for questions."

"But you must have been shocked by these revelations, the abuse of young girls, the terrible lives and deaths of those poor children..."

Petra gave a magnificently dismissive wave of the hand. "None of which has anything to do with Mr. Tisch. To be honest with you, I'm not surprised to hear that Honor Palmer orchestrated this entire debacle. Clearly she and Lucas Ruiz dreamed this up together as some twisted form of industrial sabotage."

"A little extreme, don't you think?" A paunchy print journalist from the *LA Times* looked at Petra skeptically. "To make up a pack of lies that elaborate? Why would they do that?"

"Because the Herrick is number one, of course," said Petra scathingly. "We're the best in the world, while their respective hotels are foundering."

"But according to Ms. Doyle..." the reporter pressed on bravely.

"Miss *Doyle*?" said Petra sharply, her paper-thin facade of politeness beginning to crack. "Sian Doyle is a money-grubbing former waitress, nothing more. The police are on their way here as we speak, and when they arrive, they will arrest her. She is not to be taken seriously."

"What about the girls' evidence?" the Asian girl piped up again. "Or Tina Palmer's accusations? You can't dismiss all of them out of hand, surely?"

"A few teenage hookers and a porn star with an ax to grind?" Petra snorted in derision. "I most certainly can dismiss them. This is nonsense. What Mr. Tisch decides to do about these libelous and, quite frankly, ridiculous accusations is a matter for him. My priority right now is to ensure that the people responsible for destroying tonight's celebrations are brought to justice. Aha!" She looked up gleefully. "Here come the police now."

A troop of uniformed officers, eight or nine of them, pulled up in front of the hotel and began spreading out in various directions. Two made straight for Petra, who greeted them with a brusque, professional smile.

"Thank goodness you're here," she began. "The girl, Doyle, is in our summerhouse in the care of my security. If you follow me, I'll take you there. But it's clear she wasn't acting alone. Lucas Ruiz and Honor Palmer were both here earlier, although I suspect they may have taken off by now. I—"

"Actually, Ms. Kamalski, it's you we need to talk to." The older, more senior officer laid a hand on her shoulder. "I need to bring you downtown for questioning. If it's not too much trouble."

"Don't be ridiculous. I can't possibly leave the hotel," said Petra, with a look that left the word "moron" hanging in the air. "Whatever you need to ask me, you can do it while we walk. But I want these people off hotel property."

The senior cop gave a nod to his colleague. Before she even had time to register what was happening, Petra found herself being handcuffed and escorted toward the podium steps.

"We could have done this the easy way, you know," said the officer, shielding his eyes from a sudden barrage of camera flashes. "This is your choice, lady. Petra Kamalski, I'm arresting you on suspicion of instigating an arson attack on Palmers hotel. You have the right to remain silent. Anything you say—"

"This is ridiculous." Petra's voice was shaking. "I had nothing to do with that fire. You can't possibly link me to it."

"On the contrary, ma'am, we have some very strong links, courtesy of your friend Miss Doyle, and two solid witnesses who say they saw you entering the hotel kitchens that morning."

"Anton!" Catching sight of him across the garden as she was dragged down the steps, Petra called out in panic. It had been so long since the fire, and the police had drawn such a total and consistent blank, she'd long ago started thinking she was home free. How on earth had Sian found witnesses? But she'd done it for Anton, for both of them. He'd see that, surely? He'd help her.

Having gone AWOL for the last twenty minutes, Anton had suddenly popped up arm in arm with a scowling, obese man in a suit, whom Petra recognized instantly as his lawyer, Bob Singer. Swarms of people were pressed around them on all sides, but they, too, were flanked by cops and being ushered politely but firmly in the direction of the waiting squad cars.

"Anton!" As they got closer, she shouted again. "Darling!"

Glancing up, he caught her eye. He had never seen fear on her face before—never seen any kind of weakness, in fact. It unnerved him so much, he dropped his gaze. Moments later he was bundled into the back of a squad car with Bob.

On his attorney's advice, Anton hadn't uttered a single syllable to either reporters or the police. To be honest, he hadn't needed the advice. He had no idea what to say and was still in a state of stupefied shock, wondering if this was some sort of nightmare from which he would imminently wake. He also knew that in the long run, the US police were likely to be the least of his worries. Even if, by some miracle, Bob could talk him out of these charges, Aliyev was not a man known for his mercy toward his enemies. Anton had taken what he could from his government in the early years, and for a while had been happy to take his money and run. But seeing so many of his former Russian buddies surge past him in the wealth stakes these past few years, greed had gotten the better of him and he'd decided to get back in, switching allegiance to the rebels, who for a while had looked set to seize control of the pipelines in Azerbaijan's east. Supplying arms was the easiest and cheapest way to buy himself a slice of that pie. What did he care if a few young boys took a bullet along the way? They were born into lives of such unutterable misery anyway, it hardly seemed to matter.

Through the windshield, he saw Sian being ushered into the car in front of them. She wasn't handcuffed, as Petra had been—and what was that about? Petra had nothing to do with any of this—but she did appear to be under arrest. Nevertheless, Sian looked not just relaxed but happy. When her sixth sense kicked in and she caught him staring, she flashed him a grin that he could only interpret as one of triumph.

Whatever happened to him now, that girl would have made her name in the tawdry world of investigative journalism and, he imagined, her fortune too. He didn't think he'd ever hated another human being quite so much. Why hadn't she come to him with what she knew? He'd have paid her fifty times whatever she'd been offered for her story. They could both have been rich, safe, and free.

"Do you know her?" asked Bob, catching the exchange of looks. Anton shook his head. "No. I never laid eyes on her before tonight. Although she sure as hell seems to know me."

"Quiet," ordered Bob, nodding at the cops in the front seat. "No she doesn't. She's a fantasist, got it? Let me do the talking."

Hidden in the shadows of one of the Herrick's perfectly clipped yew hedges, Honor watched as the cars containing Anton and Sian sped away, followed by a clamoring press pack. With Tina there to work the crowds and the media, she had been able to hang back and focus on making sure the plan ran smoothly behind the scenes. Which it had, until Sian had been arrested. That was most definitely not supposed to happen.

"Hey."

Honor jumped like she'd just been jabbed with a cattle prod. Lucas had crept up behind her and, wrapping both arms around her waist, begun dragging her farther back into the shadow.

"Let go of me!" she said crossly, wriggling free.

"Shhhh," he whispered in her ear, clapping a hand across her mouth. "Someone will hear you. You don't want the press on your case, do you?"

Honor shivered. It was late and getting cold, and all this standing still was making it worse. Plus Lucas's warm breath on her neck tickled.

"You've got goose bumps," he said, staring at the upright hairs on her forearms. "Am I making you nervous?"

Honor looked at him witheringly. "No," she said. "I'm cold. And I'm worried about Sian. Did you see the cops take her away just now?"

He nodded.

"I think they arrested her," said Honor. "Why would they do that? We have to get down to the station, right now. We have to straighten this out."

She made a move to go, but Lucas grabbed her arm.

"No," he said firmly. "Trust me. Whatever it is, Sian can take care of herself. She knew what she was getting into."

"What's that supposed to mean?" said Honor indignantly. What a classically selfish, Lucas response. "We can't just abandon the poor girl!"

Just then, the gaggle of media parted like the Red Sea and an ashen, handcuffed Petra was shoved unceremoniously into a third waiting police car.

"Oh my God." Honor turned back to Lucas. "Petra too? This is ridiculous. What's going on?"

Lucas shrugged and gave her an innocent "beats me" look. But Honor wasn't buying it.

"What don't I know?" she asked, her eyes narrowing suspiciously. "What haven't you told me?"

Lucas took a deep breath. Now was probably as good a time as any. "Come with me," he whispered. "We need to talk."

CHAPTER THIRTY-THREE

"Y OU CAN'T DO THIS TO ME!" YELLED SIAN AT THE TOP OF her lungs. "I'm a reporter! Whatever happened to freedom of the press? And where the hell is *he* going?"

Anton, still glued to his attorney like a barnacle to a rock, was being escorted across the lobby and out the back door of the East Hampton station. His brows were corrugated in concentration, and he seemed not to notice the racket coming from the holding cell behind him, or Sian's furious little face glaring at him through the wooden porthole.

"He's going to New York," said the duty sergeant patiently. "Thanks to you he has a date with the FBI. That's what you wanted, right?"

"What I *want*," said Sian, "is the key to this door. Or failing that, an attorney, a phone, and something to eat. A Big Mac'd be nice." It was hard to be taken seriously while wearing a semipornographical French maid's outfit, but she did her best to sound like she meant business. "And I'd like a copy of the early edition of the *News of the World*."

"News of the *what*?" The sergeant looked blank. "Listen, kiddo, you'll be outta here just as soon as one of your rich buddies shows up with your bail money."

The East Hampton police station had a retro *Leave It to Beaver* ambience that, under other circumstances, Sian might have found endearingly quaint. The lobby looked like it hadn't been touched since the fifties, all heavy wooden fixtures and fittings, with a polished brass handbell on the desk for attracting the duty officer's attention. But appearances could be deceptive. It might look like the kind of place where the worst that ever happened was some old lady's cat getting stuck up a tree or a bunch of kids getting a little overenthusiastic with the trick or treating at Halloween. In fact, in the last two years alone, three local murders had made the national news, not to mention a Mafia money-laundering operation that had seen two brothers from Bridgehampton arrested and sent down for consecutive life sentences. Anton Tisch was hardly the first big fish to pass through these musty old halls, nor, she imagined, would he be the last. The sergeant returned to his Sudoku puzzle, and Sian skulked over to the chair at the back of her cell. This was so annoying!

The cop who'd dragged her out of the projection room muttered something about trespassing and impersonation, false pretenses, or some other bullshit. Didn't these guys realize what undercover reporting *was*? What was she supposed to do, wander up to Petra Kamalski bold as brass and say: "Excuse me, my name's Sian. Do you mind awfully if I ruin your party, expose your boyfriend as a gun-running pedophile, then have you arrested for getting kerosene-happy at Palmers last year? You don't? Great! Thanks!"

If the police had done their job right and smelled Anton and Petra for the rats they were, she wouldn't have had to trespass and take matters into her own hands. But for some reason, the arresting officer hadn't been swayed by the obvious logic of this argument and had gone ahead and booked her anyway. Worse, the bastard had only allowed her two phone calls before shutting her in the lockup. She'd tried Honor's cell, then Lucas's, but both were switched off. How the hell was she supposed to make bail if she couldn't call anyone to come get her?

Half an hour passed, and soon her stomach was rumbling so loudly you could have measured it on the Richter scale. Too nervous to eat all day, she found she was suddenly famished. Given the option of burger or phone, at this point she'd have gone for the Mac and fries, hands down.

Outside, she could hear the low hum of the chattering TV crews, no doubt pitching camp in the hope of getting a decent shot of Anton being led away.

"I should be out there," she moaned to no one in particular. "This is my story that's breaking. It's not fair."

A few minutes later, she was distracted from her pity party by the arrival of Petra. Looking like a death's-head in her funereal black dress and staring straight ahead, she was whisked away immediately to an interview room at the rear of the building, followed moments later by another black-suited woman, presumably a lawyer.

"Spoilsports," said Sian, as the detectives closed the door behind them. "You might at least let me watch. Haven't you got one of those see-through glass thingies you could put me in? Oh, come on. I won't tell."

The duty sergeant laughed and shook his head. "You know, the time'll pass a lot quicker if you just go to sleep. There are blankets in there and a pillow. It is almost midnight."

"Yeah, right," grumbled Sian. "As if I could sleep. I'm too fucking hungry to sleep."

―――――――   ―――――――

The next thing she knew, she was being jolted roughly awake by somebody shaking her shoulder.

"Hey, sleeping beauty."

It was a different cop, a weasel-faced little man with a nose so long and thin and protruding it could have been designed to search out termites. His friend must have finished his shift and gone home. How long had she been out?

"Wake up. Looks like your prince has come."

For one fleeting, mad, sleep-confused moment, Sian thought he meant Ben. But she was almost as pleased when she opened her eyes and saw who it actually was.

"Don't say anything, OK?" said Lola. "I know I look like shit."

In a pair of green sweatpants-cum-pajamas, with one of Marti's thick fisherman's sweaters over the top and with her feet thrust into a pair of frankly filthy Ugg boots, she had clearly just been dragged out of bed. But even without makeup and with her long red hair matted and tangled, she somehow managed to project an aura of sexiness that had weasel-face and his buddies staring at her like dogs slavering over a steak.

"Yeah, well, check out my outfit," quipped Sian, throwing off the blanket to reveal her ridiculous frilly apron. "Talk about fashion forward, right?"

But Lola was way too overemotional for banter. Stepping forward with tears in her eyes, she opened her arms, and Sian ran headlong into them, hugging her back like a long-lost sister.

"I'm sorry," they both said simultaneously, then giggled.

"How did you know I was here?" asked Sian.

"Nick told me," said Lola. "Marti and I were sound asleep when he got back to the house and…oh, hi!" She smiled at the weasel-faced cop, whipping out her platinum credit card along with a killer Carter smile. "I need to pay her bond. Do you guys take Amex?"

"That'll do nicely, thank you," said the cop with a leering smile, then turning to Sian, added, "Looks like you got yourself some friends in high places."

The girls spent the first ten minutes of the car ride shaking off reporters. Thankfully, Lola knew the local back roads like the back of her hand, and only the most dogged of the press pack dared follow her once she started weaving in and out of the maze of lanes and bumpy beach tracks at rally driver speed.

"You know, I could just get out and talk to them? Give them a quote or whatever," said Sian queasily, as the jeep made another lurching left-right-left combination of turns and almost veered into a ditch. "Holy crap, Lola, please slow down. I know I told Simon that I wouldn't talk to any other papers, but it's not worth dying for, you know?"

"We aren't gonna die," said Lola, in the same breath switching off her headlights and plunging them, the road, and everything into total, abject darkness. "Try and catch me now, asshole," she grinned in her rearview mirror.

Sure enough, within minutes they'd shaken off the last of the stragglers and Lola pulled over into the deserted parking lot of a diner so that they could finally have a chance to talk.

"Thanks," said Sian, a little nervously, once Lola had killed the engine. "For coming to get me. And for paying that bail money."

"No problem." Lola smiled. "Now that you're a world-famous investigative reporter, you can pay me back, right? So you sold Satan the exclusive, huh? How much d'you manage to screw out of him for that?"

"More than he wanted to pay," said Sian. "But less than it's worth, I reckon. I knew it was gonna be a big story as soon as I got the girls from Children of Hope to talk. But the arms dealing was more than even I expected. Those poor little boys." She shook her head sadly.

"Well, those assholes chasing us certainly seemed to think it was big news," said Lola.

An awkward silence fell, which Sian was the first to break.

"About Lucas," she said, staring straight ahead, tracing patterns in the stars through the windshield. "What you saw. Believe me, I didn't want him in the apartment that night any more than you did. And that kiss…it totally took me by surprise. There's nothing going on between us, truly."

Lola raised a hand for her to stop. "Forget about it," she said.

"No, really," said Sian, "it's important to me that you know. I don't have any feelings for Lucas. But I do have to admit he's been phenomenal in getting everything together for tonight. And, please don't yell, but he actually does have a nicer side to him. I wouldn't have believed it myself until now."

"It's OK," said Lola. "I'm sure he does. I needed someone to blame for Dad's affair, that's all. For what it did to my mom."

"Oh, don't, please don't cry," said Sian, watching the tears welling up in her eyes.

"It's OK." Lola sniffed, wiping at her face with the back of her hand. "The point is that Lucas was a handy scapegoat. But it was never his fault. My dad was the only person to blame."

"Well," said Sian reasonably, "I don't know if I'd go that far. Honor was there too, remember? It takes two to tango. And Anton was the one who leaked it to the press."

"Yes, but it's not just the affair." Lola shook her head angrily. "All my life, my father's set himself up as this big moral example. He used to criticize Mom for being shallow—and maybe she is—but at least she's honest, you know? Dad's such a fake. In his eyes Mom was shallow, I was spoiled, and my brother was a lazy jerk."

"Your brother *is* a lazy jerk," said Sian, reasonably.

"I know." Lola smiled. "Dad always acted so *baffled* by that. Like 'How could such a great guy like me wind up with such a selfish kid?' And yet underneath all the bullshit, he and Nick aren't so different. Marti was the one who made me see it."

"Really?"

"Yeah. I always knew my parents were conservative. I even knew they were snobs. But bringing Marti home really opened my eyes. My dad is so racist, so self-righteous, so full of…"

"Shit?" offered Sian.

"I was gonna say hate," said Lola, shivering despite the warmth of the car with the heaters turned up full blast. For a moment the word hung in the air between them, like a stale smell. "*He* actually looks down on *Marti*," Lola went on. "He looks down on Marti. Where does he get off? Anyway." She smiled, abruptly shifting gears. "The point is, it was never really about Lucas, or you. I'm glad he helped you get your story."

"Honestly?" Sian's face lit up.

"Absolutely," said Lola. "Are you kidding me? Anton Tisch is clearly, like, the world's biggest asshole. You totally nailed him."

They hugged again, all traces of awkwardness gone.

"So what now?" Sian asked warily, as Lola turned on the ignition again. "I can't go back to Palmers, or the cottage. The press'll be everywhere."

"You can sleep in our guest house," said Lola. "It's private, alarmed, and we have dogs."

"Sounds perfect," said Sian. Suddenly she longed for a bed, any bed. There'd be time enough to savor her triumph and catch up with Lucas and Honor in the morning. After five minutes with her head lolling exhausted against the window, she suddenly sat up. "Hold on. Isn't your house in the other direction?"

Lola smiled. "Er, yeah. We're making a quick detour."

"A detour, really? Now?" said Sian. "I don't wanna sound ungrateful, Lo, but couldn't it wait till tomorrow? I'm wiped out."

"Not really," said Lola. "You'll see."

They'd reached the bottom of an unlit dirt road. Winding down her window, Sian could hear the lapping of waves. Somewhere in the near distance, she could also make out a dying buzz of chattering voices and revving engines—the remnants of the Herrick party heading home.

"Lola! You moron," she said good-naturedly, climbing out of the car onto the deserted beach. "You took us in a circle; we're right outside Palmers, aren't we? I thought you wanted to avoid the press. This place'll be crawling with them soon, if it isn't already."

"Actually," the voice came from behind her, close to the shore, "most of them sloped off once they realized Honor and Tina weren't here."

Sian froze, unable to bring herself to look around. She looked for Lola, but she seemed to have mysteriously vanished.

"And you, of course," the deep cockney rumble went on. "They all wanted to talk to you. But some bright spark convinced them you'd been whisked off to New York for interviews. Don't know his name, but I heard he was English, charismatic, and looked a bit like Brad Pitt. Only fitter."

Sian felt her stomach crunch itself into a fist, then flip over like one of those jumping frog bath toys she used to have as a kid.

"Shouldn't you be in London?" Turning around at last, she put on her best platonic smile.

"Oh, well, that's nice," said Ben, walking slowly across the sand toward her. "Would you rather I was in London? That's just charming, that is, after I've flown halfway across the world to see you."

He was wearing the same tattered pair of shorts he'd had on the day she first met him, and a Rolling Stones T-shirt that had seen better days. He looked tired and pale, and his hair, as usual, was all over the place, sticking up at all angles in the night breeze. But his smile was like a sunburst, so big and broad and joyful that it dominated not only his face, but all of him, from his scruffy bed-head to his threadbare tennis shoes. If she'd wanted him any more, she would have burst into flames.

"I didn't see you at the party," she stammered. "Were you there?"

It seemed easier to focus on facts and logistics than feelings, and she hadn't the courage to ask him why he'd come.

"No."

As he moved closer, Sian could hear the rumble of Lola's engine fade into the distance. So much for sisterhood!

"It all went great," she babbled, "better than I could have expected, actually. Although they did book me for trespassing."

"So I heard." Slowly extending one arm, Ben laid his hand on her hip and drew her toward him.

"They took Anton straight into the city." She couldn't seem to stop talking. It was as if she hoped her words could form a physical barrier between them. "The FBI want to interview him—I bet you know about that already—and I'm sure Interpol won't be far behind. They're gonna want to talk to me too, I'm sure, but the local cops are so hopeless they let me leave with Lola, so at least I'll get one full night's sleep before I face the music. Anyway, I saw Anton leave with his lawyer, the fat guy, but I don't think he saw me. Maybe he did, though. And then they brought Petra in—"

"Sian." Ben put his index finger to her lips. "I don't care."

Ba boom. Ba boom. Someone seemed to have turned up the volume on her heartbeat to full. She finally stopped talking.

"I don't care what happens to Anton, or Petra. I don't care about Interpol. I don't even care about the fund anymore. Not if I can't have you with me."

"But…" Somehow Sian forced the sound from her lips. "What about Bianca?"

"Bianca's lovely," said Ben, tenderly stroking a stray tendril of hair back from her face. "And I've tried to love her. Really tried. But I don't."

"Oh," said Sian, who knew it was wrong to grin but couldn't seem to help herself. "I see. Probably not the greatest idea to marry her, then. Is it?"

Ben burst out laughing, sweeping her up into his arms and spinning around on the sand. "No, you cheeky cow," he said. "It probably isn't. Then again, I'm not so sure I should risk it with a gold-digging slapper like you, either."

"*Slapper?*" she laughed, hitting him on the head. "How dare you! Anyway, I'll have you know I don't need your money. I'm a woman of independent means now, thanks to the dear old *News of the World*. I have a big career ahead of me, traveling the world, exposing injustice."

Ben's face fell. He set her down on the ground again. "You can't," he said. "You can't travel the world."

Sian looked up at him quizzically. She couldn't tell if he was serious or not. "Why not?"

"Because," he said, frowning. "Because it's dangerous. There's...terrorism. And stuff."

"Oh, for heaven's sake!"

"I'm serious," said Ben. "And anyway you'll be too busy in London to go gallivanting around the globe."

"Busy with what?" said Sian.

Ben grinned. "Having my babies."

Sian's eyebrows shot up. "Oh, is that so?"

"Yes," said Ben firmly. "You bloody well will." And leaning down, he kissed her, so hard and for so long that she started to feel dizzy.

"By the way," he said, finally coming up for air. "Whose idea was the maid's outfit?"

"Anton's," said Sian, blushing. "All the party staff had to be in full uniform. Fucking pervert."

"You know, maybe we've been a bit too harsh on old Anton," Ben whispered, his fingers creeping slowly up beneath her ludicrously short skirt. "I'm starting to think he wasn't *all* bad."

Closing her eyes, ensconced in Ben's arms at last, Sian was almost inclined to agree.

———————   ———————

About ten miles away, in the passenger seat of Lucas's rental car, Honor was starting to get concerned.

"Are you sure you know where we're going?" she asked, again. "Because I've been coming here my whole life, and I have no idea where the hell we are."

When they'd left the party, Lucas had sped off in the direction of the city, then forked right into remote farmland where a dizzying latticework of lanes seemed to be leading them farther and farther into the boonies before jackknifing back in the direction of the coast.

The drive had been eventful. As soon as they were out of sight of the Herrick, Lucas dropped the bombshell that Petra was the one responsible for the Palmers fire. Honor's first inevitable question—"How do you know?"—was more shell-shocked than accusatory.

"Sian told me this morning, on the way back from Kennedy," said Lucas, "and we tipped off the police just as Tina got up onstage. I asked her to look into it back in London, but to be frank with you, I never thought she'd come up with anything, and certainly not with this."

"But Petra…she could have killed me," Honor murmured to herself, after a long initial silence. "She could have killed a lot of people. And she was already so far ahead of us at the Herrick. Why would she take that risk when there was no need?"

Lucas shrugged, keeping his eyes on the road. "Why did Nixon bug Watergate when he was about to win a landslide? For some people, getting to the top is the easy part. It's staying there that panics them. Petra's always been obsessively ambitious. And she hates your guts. Maybe she wanted to impress Anton? Maybe she just wanted you gone."

Honor shuddered. Did he mean "gone" as in not a commercial threat, or "gone" as in dead and gone? It was a scary thought.

"Sian thinks Tisch didn't know what she was up to," said Lucas. "If she's right, that's just about the only dirty pie he didn't have his finger in."

But Honor was barely listening. "Did you say you asked Sian to look into the fire?" she asked, suspiciously. "Why would you do that?"

"We're here," said Lucas, not answering the question as he brought the car to a screeching, dust-spraying halt. "Come on. Out you get."

"We're here?" Honor stepped gingerly out of the car, lifting up her long dress with her hands to stop it from trailing in the sand. "Oh my goodness, we're *here*. How did we get back to town so fast?" They were at the entrance to one of the many winding paths leading to Water Mill, the beach where the two of them had first met so inauspiciously all those years ago.

It was pitch-dark. The stars were out in force, but the moon was only the merest sliver of a crescent, and with the car's head-lamps off it was hard at first to make out anything in the black ness. But once her eyes adjusted, Honor could see the familiar slope of the ground and the tufts of spiky, windblown grass bursting through the sand at intervals, like an old woman's beauty spot sprouting unwanted hair.

"Follow me," said Lucas, taking her hand to help her over the uneven ground.

"Would you slow down?" she pleaded, stooping to remove her stilettos as she felt the white chiffon of her dress catch and tear on some brambles. "I almost broke my ankle on that last slope."

"You shouldn't wear such ridiculous shoes then, should you?" said Lucas, scooping her up into his arms without break-ing stride.

"They're party shoes." Honor looked at him indignantly. "I didn't know I'd be going moonlight hiking, did I?"

But she allowed him to carry her the final few yards down to the beach, closing her eyes and taking instinctive comfort in the warmth of his body. Her own body rocked in sync with his big, loping strides, like a child swinging in a hammock, a motion that stirred dim memories of being picked up and carried across the lawn at Palmers by her father. She must have been very young then. It would have been before her mom died. Afterward Trey could barely bring himself to touch her, never mind hold her close, as Lucas was doing now.

"Here we are."

Setting her down on the sand, he stood back and watched for her reaction. Laid out in front of them was a midnight-blue cashmere blanket, weighted down by heavy onyx candleholders that glowed orange from the tea lights within. It was simple—nothing over-the-top or cheesy—but it was an undeniably romantic gesture.

"What else did you bring down here, Casanova?" she teased him, trying to hide her own nervousness by going on the offensive. "Barry White CDs and a cocktail shaker?"

"Of course not," said Lucas defensively.

"What is this, your lovers' lair? Bring all the girls here, do you?"

"Don't be ridiculous," he snapped, sitting down grumpily on one side of the blanket and leaving her no option but to do the same. "It's just somewhere off the beaten track where I figured we could talk in peace."

"OK." Honor sounded less than convinced. "So, now that you've lured me here, what do you want to talk about?"

Lucas stared awkwardly at his hands, as if the answer to her question might be revealed by the calluses on his palms. He had so much to say to her, but in that moment, watching her provoking, elfin, defiant little face flickering in the candlelight, his carefully prepared speech tumbled out of his head like so many rice grains through a colander. He felt his mouth go dry and swallowed hard.

"You asked me a question earlier," he began awkwardly, "about why I had Sian do some digging into the arson attack at Palmers."

"Oh yes," said Honor, feigning unconcern. She was regretting having shown him her vulnerable side yet again by letting him carry her down here, and thought some aloofness might help her regain the upper hand. "I just wondered, that's all. It's not important."

"I did it because I knew you were struggling financially," said Lucas.

"What do you mean?" said Honor, immediately defensive. "I'm doing great, thanks. I'd worry more about your own business if I were you."

Lucas laughed. "After tonight, our worries are over," he said confidently. "Connor won't want anything more to do with Anton after this, just you watch. The court case'll go away, he'll pay my costs without a murmur, and we'll be back to business as usual."

"Whatever you say," said Honor, who was feeling more and more rattled.

"Look," said Lucas, exasperated that once again things were not going according to plan. Why was it that whenever he tried to do something to impress Honor, she ended up throwing it back in his face? "If you'd stop ranting for a moment and listen—"

"I am not ranting!" Honor ranted.

"I'm trying to tell you that I did this because I wanted to help you. I wanted to help you get your money. The insurers will have to pay out now, right?"

"Oh, come on," said Honor robustly. "You don't do anything unless there's an upside. There must have been something in it for you. So what was it? Getting your own back on Petra for taking the Herrick job? Or do you get a cut of Sian's money?"

"Neither," said Lucas.

"Well, what then?" said Honor.

"Why is it so hard for you to believe I'd do something good and decent and right without an ulterior motive?"

"Erm…because I know you?" said Honor, only half-jokingly.

"OK," said Lucas defiantly. "OK, fine. It was you. You were what was in it for me."

"Me?"

"Yes, you stupid bitch. You!" he shouted, so loudly that Honor jumped. Standing up, he began prowling around the blanket like a lion guarding his territory, or perhaps sizing up a possible kill. "Does that really surprise you so much? That I might want to help you, because I care? Because I care about you?"

The last sentence came out with all the reluctance of a pulled tooth.

"You care? About me?" Honor repeated, aware she must sound like a parrot, or a lunatic, or both, but not sure what else to say. "But you're Lucas. You don't care. You don't care about anyone."

"Thanks," he laughed bitterly.

"Oh, you know what I mean," said Honor. "You're so ambitious."

He looked at her, incredulous. "I'm ambitious? And you're not?"

"Well, yes," she admitted. "Maybe a little bit. But that's different. I have a responsibility for Palmers. My family...anyway, this is beside the point!" she added crossly, back on the offensive. "If you care about me so much, why were you such an asshole in Vegas?"

"An asshole?" Lucas looked genuinely hurt. "How was I an asshole?"

"You took advantage of me," said Honor.

She did at least have the decency to look shamefaced when she said it.

"Oh, please," said Lucas. "Bull-sheet!" His Spanish accent was always strongest when he was angry. Grabbing her by the wrists, he pulled her to her feet and, without thinking, kissed her. "You wanted me so badly in Vegas you were practically begging."

Honor opened her mouth to protest, but he kissed her again, with such force that she staggered backward, tripping over one of the onyx candleholders and landing ass-first on the sand. The next thing she knew Lucas was lying above her, propped up on his elbows, while she tried ineffectually to writhe out from beneath him.

"Admit it," he said, smiling for the first time since they'd gotten there. "You wanted me from the beginning. From the first day I met you, right here on this beach, when you were still doing your best to convince the world you had a dick between your legs."

Honor shook her head violently. "You are so fucking delusional. If anyone wanted anyone, it was you who wanted me."

"All right, yes," he admitted, rather throwing her off stride. "I did want you, despite how awful you looked."

"I did *not* look awful!"

"But you were too busy making a fool of yourself with that middle-aged jerk-off Devon Carter to notice."

Honor blushed scarlet. "Well *you* were too busy screwing my sister, along with every other female that moved."

"Fine," said Lucas, sensing the mood deteriorating. "Let's say we were both fools, shall we? Can't we make up for it now?"

For a split second, Honor thought about keeping up the fight. About telling him to fuck off and berating him for meddling in Palmers and her life. But then he bent his head, brushing his lips along her collarbone and down, tantalizingly slowly, toward her breasts. And she changed her mind.

"I'm too tired to argue with you," she murmured, closing her eyes and sighing as he slipped a hand between her thighs. "I don't have the energy."

Lucas grinned. "Really? I'm not so sure. Let's see how much energy you have, shall we?"

Three hours later, lying naked in his arms with the blanket curled around them as the waves lapped softly against the deserted dawn shoreline, Honor extended her limbs in a long, luxuriant stretch.

"It's gonna be tough, you know," she whispered, her lips brushing the top of Lucas's ear. "Making this work. The whole long-distance thing."

"What long-distance thing?" Flipping over onto his side, he turned to face her, pressing his broad nose against her cheek.

"Well, you'll be in Paris, won't you? Or Ibiza."

"What makes you think that?" asked Lucas.

"Well…" she stammered. "Luxe America is kind of…dead, right? There's no reason for you to stay here."

"On the contrary." Lucas smiled. "Now that Anton and Petra have rather bigger problems on their plate, I'm anticipating a miraculous easing in our legal and planning problems. As long as I'm on-site to push it, I can't see why we wouldn't be up and running by this time next year."

"I do admire your tenacity, darling," said Honor, kissing him chastely on the lips. "But you must realize you're wasting your time."

"Oh, am I indeed?" Cupping his hand around her right breast, he squeezed it tightly. "And why's that?"

"Because," she said, without a hint of irony, "Palmers is the greatest hotel in the world, and we'll be up and running by Christmas. I'm sure your Luxes are lovely in their own way. But you can't seriously hope to compete with me."

Lucas laughed. "Actually, my darling," he said, "I'm looking forward to spending the rest of my life doing exactly that."

ABOUT THE AUTHOR

TILLY BAGSHAWE WAS BORN IN London and raised in a large family in the English countryside. She enrolled at Cambridge University and later launched a successful career as a headhunter in London. At twenty-six, she became the youngest-ever partner in the number-one global search firm, before changing course to pursue a writing career. After a brief stint at *The Sunday Times*, she followed her novelist sister's example and wrote her first book. Today she is a happily married mother of four and author of ten novels, including *Adored*, *Showdown*, and *Sidney Sheldon's Mistress of the Game*. In addition to her bestselling novels, Tilly has contributed to numerous British newspapers and magazines including *Cosmopolitan*, *Glamour*, *Elle*, *The Sunday Times*, *The Times*, and *The Daily Mail*. She divides her time between Los Angeles, London, and Nantucket.